EMBER'S KISS

"The Dragonfire series continues to delight its fans with the dragon shifters finding their destined mates and the danger they face as they complete their trials. If you love dragons, this series is sure to please."

—Romance Reader's Connection

"*Ember's Kiss* is another well-written, fascinating and amazing storyline in Deborah Cooke's Dragonfire series. Deborah creates a world of beautiful dragons and timeless love. I have loved Deborah's dragons since the very beginning and I was immensely pleased that she brought together the *Pyr* in this amazing tale."

—The Reading Cafe

FLASHFIRE

"Deborah Cooke is a dragonmaster of a storyteller...Lorenzo fills the pages with enigmatic glory only rivaled by his mate, Cassie, and I did not stop turning pages until the firestorm was ended."

—The Reading Frenzy

"Cooke's long-running series continues to be a sexy and thrilling winner!"

—Romantic Times

"Thrilling and unpredictable...*Flashfire* is another great addition on one of my favorite paranormal romance series."

—Paranormal Haven

to Deborah Cooke's Dragonfire series—it is marvelous!"

—Romance Junkies

Winter Kiss

"A beautiful and emotionally gripping fourth novel, *Winter Kiss* is compelling and will keep readers riveted in their seats and breathing a happy sigh at the love shared between Delaney and Ginger...Sizzling-hot love scenes and explosive emotions make *Winter Kiss* a must read!"

—Romance Junkies

"A terrific novel!"

—Romance Reviews Today

"All the *Pyr* and their mates from the previous three books in this exciting series are included in this final confrontation with Magnus and his evil Dragon's Blood Elixir. It's another stellar addition to this dynamic paranormal saga with the promise of more to come."

—Fresh Fiction

Kiss of Fate

"Second chances are a key theme in this latest Dragonfire adventure. Cooke keeps the pace intense and the emotions raging in this powerful new read. She's top-notch, as always!"

—Romantic Times

"An intense ride. Ms. Cooke has a great talent...If you love paranormal romance in any way, this is a series you should be following."

—Night Owl Reviews (reviewer top pick)

"Those sexy dragons are back in the second chapter of Cooke's exciting paranormal series...The intriguing characters continue to grow and offer terrific opportunities for story expansion. Balancing a hormone-drive romance with high-stakes action can be difficult, but Cooke manages with ease. Visiting this world is a pleasure."

—Romantic Times

"The second book in Deborah Cooke's phenomenal Dragonfire series expertly sets the stage for the next thrilling episode."

—Fresh Fiction

"Entertaining and imaginative...a must-read for paranormal fans."

—BookLoons

"Riveting...Deborah Cooke delivers a fiery tale of love and passion...She manages to leave us with just enough new questions to have us awaiting book three with bated breath!"

—Wild on Books

"Epic battles, suspense, ecological concerns, humor, and romance are highlights that readers can expect in this tale. Excellent writing, a smart story, and exceptional characters earn this novel the RRT Perfect 10 Rating. Don't miss the very highly recommended *Kiss of Fury*."

—Romance Reviews Today

"Deborah Cooke has only touched the surface about these wonderful men called the *Pyr* and their battle with the evil dragons...I am dying for more."

—Romance Junkies

"Cooke, a.k.a. bestseller Claire Delacroix, dips into the paranormal realm with her sizzling new Dragonfire series...Efficient plotting moves the story at a brisk pace and paves the way for more exciting battles to come."

—Romantic Times

"Paranormal fans with a soft spot for shape-shifting dragons will definitely enjoy *Kiss of Fire*, a story brimming with sexy heroes, evil villains threatening mayhem, death and world domination, ancient prophesies, and an engaging love story...An intriguing mythology and various unanswered plot threads set the stage for plenty more adventure to come in future Dragonfire stories."

—BookLoons

"Deborah Cooke has definitely made me a fan. I am now lying in wait for the second book in this extremely exciting series."

—Romance Junkies

"Wow, what an innovative and dazzling world Ms. Cooke has built with this new Dragonfire series. Her smooth and precise writing quickly draws the reader in and has you believing it could almost be real...I can't wait for the next two books."

—Fresh Fiction

LOOK FOR THE ENTIRE SERIES OF DRAGONFIRE NOVELS IN NEW EDITIONS IN 2018!

THE DRAGON DIARIES

BLAZING THE TRAIL

"There are so many twists in this book, I loved it. I could not put it down, and read it in a day. If you have read Deborah's adult books, with the adult dragons, then you will love this series with the kids!"

—Books Complete Me

"I have been a huge fan of Deborah Cooke for many years. When a new release comes across my path, I truly do a happy dance. Cooke has lived up to her previous work with *Blazing the Trail*. I loved how Zoë deals with the everyday issues in front of her while trying to save the world with the *Pyr* and fellow shifters."

—Fresh Fiction

WINGING IT

"[Cooke's] clever ability to convey what it means to be going on sixteen while being faced with dark, world-altering dilemmas has created a unique and compelling young-adult series bursting with magic, mayhem, and danger."

–Fresh Fiction

"Zoë is as kick-butt as ever...another fast-paced, well-thought-out novel in [Cooke's] Dragonfire universe. Teen readers will love that Zoë and her friends get to be the stars."

—Romantic Times

"Whether you're young or just young at heart, you will equally enjoy this brand-new series by Ms. Cooke...It's entertaining, it's exciting and it's adventurous...a wonderful new series."

—The Reading Frenzy

"The first of a new dragon series sure to become a classic...Cooke has written a fantastic offshoot of her *Pyr* universe...After turning the final page, I sat for a moment with a sense of excitement I haven't felt since I finished my first of Anne McCaffrey's Pern books."

—Fresh Fiction

"This story crosses the boundaries. It will appeal to both teens and adults across the board. The story is engaging and fun. It's bringing to life a world of dragons and magic that appeals to all."

—Night Owl Reviews (5 stars, top pick)

"The writing is swift and fun, just like I'd imagine flying on the back of a dragon...If you're looking for a break from vampires and werewolves or you're a fan of Cooke's adult Dragonfire series, you won't be disappointed."

—All Things Urban Fantasy

"This. Book. Rocks."

—One a Day YA

"Zoë is a wonderful heroine—smart, strong and sympathetic. Bring on book two!"

—#1 New York Times Bestselling Author
Kelley Armstrong

FIRESTORM FOREVER

A
DRAGONFIRE
NOVEL

Firestorm Forever
By Deborah Cooke

Cover by Frauke Spanuth of CrocoDesigns
Title page by Kim Killion

Dear Reader;

And so we come to the final book in the *Dragonfire* cycle of paranormal romances. Sloane's story has been a gleam in my eye from the very inception of this series: I always knew his firestorm would be the last one of the Dragon's Tail Wars, because it had to be the Apothecary of the *Pyr* who healed the earth. This book is longer than other titles in the series, as there were more details to resolve. Conveniently for me, the end of the Dragon's Tail node of the moon is marked by three lunar eclipses in relatively quick succession, so there are three firestorms in **Firestorm Forever** and a slightly different structure to the book to accommodate that. Many of you have written to me to express your wish that the series continue, but all wars must come to an end.

All species, however, do not.

Dragonfire was always intended to be a finite cycle of books, with somewhere between ten and twelve titles in all (**Firestorm Forever** brings us to eleven books, a short story, and three novellas, as well as the spin-off YA trilogy, the *Dragon Diaries*) but it was never intended to be the sum of my writing about dragon shape shifter heroes. I have another series in progress called the *Dragons of Incendium*, which features dragon shifter princesses from space, which I've been writing while awaiting the reversion of rights for the Dragonfire books. Now that the reversion is complete, more *Pyr* can have their stories told, too.

In 2018, the entire *Dragonfire* series is being republished in new editions. You can tell the new print editions from the older ones because they have dragons on the page. **Here Be Dragons: The Dragonfire Companion** will also be published in 2018.

I had always planned to step back in time next, to witness the extermination that left Erik so distrustful of humans, the evolution of *Slayers* and the discovery of the Dragon's Egg. This will be a trilogy of paranormal historical romances—but in writing **Firestorm Forever**, more *Pyr* caught my imagination and their stories jumped the queue. You'll meet a new villain in this book, as well as learn more about Theo, the current leader of the Dragon Legion, who is the reason I've been distracted. There's an excerpt at the end of this book for **Hot Blooded**, the first book in my upcoming contemporary paranormal series *DragonFate*.

And now, I'll let you dig into Sloane's story and the culmination of the

Dragon's Tail Wars. I hope you enjoy reading the finale of Dragonfire as much as I enjoyed writing it.

Until next time, I hope you have lots of good books to read.

All my best—
Deborah

Books by Deborah Cooke

ONE MORE TIME
ALL OR NOTHING

Flatiron Five
SIMPLY IRRESISTIBLE
ADDICTED TO LOVE
IN THE MIDNIGHT HOUR
SOME GUYS HAVE ALL THE LUCK (2018)

For Claire Delacroix books,
please visit
http://delacroix.net

Firestorm Forever

PROLOGUE

April 2014 — Chen's lair in the mountains of Tibet

he *Slayer* Jorge was determined to consume every drop of the best source of the Elixir he'd found in years. Chen had finally fallen, and the lacquer red and gold *Slayer* was sprawled before Jorge, dead. Chen promised to be a generous feast, and Jorge was glad that Chen had expired in his dragon form.

It would prolong the pleasure of the meal.

Unfortunately, Lorenzo and Thorolf had damaged the cavern beneath the mountains that was Chen's lair and summoned an earthquake. The ceiling was cracking overhead and rocks were falling all around Jorge. The other pair disappeared in a flash of light, and Jorge knew it was time to move his meal elsewhere.

He was currently without a lair himself, but there wasn't a lot of time to think about it. He seized his prize and willed himself to manifest elsewhere. He gripped Chen's body tightly as that familiar wind swirled around him and wished to be somewhere safe.

He was flung down hard, as was so often the case, and opened his eyes to find that he still had hold of his trophy.

But Jorge had no idea where he was. The tranquility was a startling contrast to the collapse of Chen's lair and it took Jorge a moment to realize that he was safe.

The chamber appeared to be a library. The walls were covered with bookcases, all of which had locked glass doors, and the shelves rose to the very tall ceiling. The decor was ornate, with no expense spared, which suited Jorge well even if it was a bit old-fashioned. There was a massive stone fireplace on one wall and he breathed dragonfire to light a blaze there, since the room was damp enough to make him shiver. Carpets were piled underfoot and there appeared to be no electricity—the chandelier contained candles.

That made him wonder *when* he was as well as where.

Jorge lit the candles easily, and the room filled with a golden glow. It was warming up and was much cozier.

That was when he realized that the room had no door.

Was he imprisoned? Or was the door hidden?

There was a rumble and a distant clatter, the walls vibrating ever so slightly until the sound faded.

It could have been a train, which only encouraged his curiosity. He listened intently and heard the murmur of distant conversation, discernible only because of his keen senses. People. Jorge's eyes widened. Speaking Russian. Could he be close to home again?

He prowled the perimeter of the room, his excitement rising when he realized that one wall contained books in Russian, at least according to the gilded letters on their leather spines. The other books were in a variety of languages—Hebrew, Latin, and some he didn't recognize. One glass-doored case held curiosities instead of books, all of them lovingly displayed.

A collection. How quaint. Jorge peered through the glass, wiping the dust from its surface to see better. The glass was rippled and contained bubbles, and he knew it was float glass. In the middle of the case, in the position of pride, was what looked like a stone egg. No, it was closer to an olive in size, green with red veins across its surface. Jorge forced open the locked door and sniffed the stone, knowing immediately what it was. He replaced it with care.

He looked around then and guessed his location. There was no better or safer lair than a place that had been lost for centuries, yet was still rumored to exist, like the library of Ivan the Terrible. There was no better item to have at his disposal than a legendary cure for all ills, such as the Dracontias.

And there was no better feast than the corpse of his most deadly opponent, Chen. The Elixir in Chen's body would only fortify the Elixir that coursed through Jorge's own veins.

It might be prophesied that only *Pyr* or *Slayers* would survive the Dragon's Tail Wars, and he might be the last surviving *Slayer* of note, but Jorge had a definite sense that the tide had just turned in his favor.

Perhaps he would be the *only* survivor.

He loved the sound of that.

Jorge crossed the floor, chose his first bite, and bent to devour his prey. He had plenty of time to enjoy the meal—and to plot the destruction of the *Pyr*.

CHAPTER ONE

Wednesday, October 8, 2014—California

loane Forbes, the Apothecary of the *Pyr*, was frustrated.

He was exhausted by his efforts to find a cure for the plague ravaging the Pacific Northwest and knew he'd spent more hours in his lab than were healthy. He was discouraged, though, because he'd made so little progress. Every time he thought he had a good lead, it came to a dead end, and he had to start over again.

Yet another one was in the petri dish in front of him. This vaccine had showed promise, killing the virus as he watched through the microscope. Within minutes, though, the tables had turned and the ridiculously efficient virus was encircling and destroying the antidote that should have finished it. He supposed he shouldn't have been surprised. There had to be dozens of scientists working on this, with better equipment and better training.

They didn't have his sense of responsibility, though, or his conviction that a plague begun by dragon shifters should be halted by dragon shifters.

By the Apothecary of the *Pyr*.

Sloane grimaced and shut down the lights. He sealed up the lab, ensuring that the virus was contained. He had a smaller version of a lab designed for working with Level 4 biohazards, buried into the hill under and behind his house. He followed all the protocols in locking up and cleansing himself, then wearily climbed the stairs to his house. He was nude, but it didn't matter.

The house was sealed from human eyes, and the dragonsmoke barriers were piled thick against curious dragon shifters.

The fact was that while Sloane searched for a cure, people were dying. That knowledge burned. It was the responsibility of the *Pyr* to defend the treasures of the earth, which included humans, so he felt like a failure. That this malady had been brought from the ancient world by one of his own—well, by Jorge, a *Slayer* but still a dragon shifter—only multiplied his sense of duty.

Tempted by the sparkle of water in his pool and the option of a way to work off his frustration, Sloane strode into the yard. He dove into the pool and began to swim laps, working his body furiously.

If nothing else, he'd make sure he slept.

The worst of the worst was that there would be another full moon on this night, and another lunar eclipse. That meant there probably would be another firestorm, and another *Pyr* would feel the spark light that identified his destined mate. Sloane had always been patient about the firestorm, trusting that his time would come, but his patience was disappearing fast. He realized that he'd always assumed he'd have his firestorm before the end of the Dragon's Tail cycle of eclipses.

Once it had seemed as if the Great Wyvern were steadily working her way through the ranks of the remaining *Pyr*, and that his own firestorm had to be soon. Now, there were dozens of new *Pyr*, thanks to the darkfire crystal and Drake's adventures in the past. The odds were skewed decidedly against any of them having a firestorm next.

Thorolf had had his firestorm in April. There would be an eclipse tonight, another in April 2015 and the final eclipse of the cycle next September. Only three left, before the fate of the *Pyr* was decided forever.

Sloane was beginning to feel as if he were being punished for his failure to solve the riddle of the plague.

In addition to that, the presence of his new neighbor made him resent the fact that he couldn't choose his own mate. He turned underwater and roared through another pair of laps. Samantha was exactly the kind of woman he'd have chosen for himself. She was blond and delicately built, but clever and sensitive. He suspected that she was stronger than even she knew. She was feminine but pragmatic, too, which had to be the most enticing combination.

He'd met her when she'd moved in and talked to her again when she'd come to buy herbs from his greenhouse. She was a tarot card reader who said she sometimes cast spells with herbs for her clients. She had a secret, though — Sloane could smell it on her — and a vulnerability that got him right where he lived. Something had hurt her badly and she'd made a big change in order to deal with that injury. Sloane wanted to help more than he knew was sensible.

The thing was that until he had his firestorm, he couldn't promise anything more than a short fling to any woman. He sensed that Sam needed more than that and plowed through another half dozen laps disliking that he didn't have more to offer.

The moon moved, the first shadow of the eclipse touching its radiant glow.

Sloane swam harder.

He closed his eyes as a firestorm sparked, his heart sinking with the realization that it wasn't his. He reached the end of the pool with a growl, pulled himself out of the water, then caught a whiff of jasmine and musk.

Sam's perfume.

She was standing at the gate, watching him in silence.

Sloane froze, braced on the side of the pool, and stared, transfixed. It was as if he had conjured her out of nothing, willing her to appear. He halfway thought she was a vision, but he could sense her uncertainty. He saw her swallow and wanted to reassure her.

No, he wanted to protect her forever from whatever she feared.

And he wanted to spend the night making love to her first.

Sam evidently took his silence as an invitation, because she opened the gate and stepped into the paved yard. She slipped out of her flip-flops and eased the linen shirt from her shoulders. She was wearing a bikini so small that Sloane's mouth went dry. She flicked a glance at him, then smiled as she unfastened the clasp in the middle of the top. She bared her breasts to the moonlight, then slipped out of the bikini bottom. Sloane could have been turned to stone.

She walked toward him, and he told himself he had to be

dreaming. The moonlight made her skin look silver and her eyes luminous. She sat down on the lip of the pool beside him and put her feet into the water. She smiled, licked her lips, then touched his shoulder.

"I was so hot," she whispered, her gaze clinging to his. He didn't dare survey her again, because he didn't want to spook her, but he could see the patina of perspiration on her upper lip. He wanted to kiss it off. "It made me think of you," she admitted, and her words astonished him.

She wasn't lying.

So, he wasn't going to.

"I was just thinking of you," Sloane admitted, and she smiled with pleasure.

"But you're too much of a gentleman to have done anything about it," she charged, then shook her head.

Sloane might have defended himself, but she was right. He wouldn't have gone knocking at her door on a moonlit night, no matter how much he wanted to do so.

"Is that why you were swimming laps so hard?"

Sloane dipped his head and grinned that she'd guessed at least part of the reason for his frustration. "Caught," he murmured, daring to look into her eyes once more.

She was pleased by that and her eyes started to sparkle. She looked good enough to eat, but whatever happened had to be her choice. Sloane was keenly aware of her vulnerability, an indication of an emotional wound, and instinctively wanted to help her to heal. He sensed she was trying to make a change, to move past something, and it was in his nature to facilitate that.

Which meant he had to wait.

He wasn't sure how long they stared into each other's eyes before Sam reached out and touched his mouth with her fingertip. "I'm hoping you're not too much of a gentleman to do something about this," she whispered, then bent closer and replaced her fingertip with her mouth.

Her lips were soft and sweet, her kiss gentle, her scent beguiling him as little else could have done. Her mix of boldness and vulnerability kicked all of Sloane's desires into overdrive. Before he could think twice—much less be cautious and responsible—she was in his arms and he was slanting his mouth over hers, deepening his kiss.

That distant firestorm burned hotter, sending fire through Sloane's veins.

It wasn't his firestorm.

It might have been a thousand miles away.

But the funny thing was, Sloane no longer cared.

Virginia

She'd always known that he'd come.

Yet when she turned and saw Drake watching her, Veronica Maitland couldn't believe her eyes.

It had been more than four years since she'd last seen Drake, more than four years since he'd brought her the news she'd dreaded but had needed to hear. A thousand times, she'd remembered the flicker of compassion in the depths of Drake's dark eyes, felt the crinkle of the photograph he'd brought to her from Mark's corpse, remembered the firmness of his cheek beneath her lips as she impulsively granted him a kiss of thanks.

Drake had been both strong and gentle, tough and kind. He was a warrior, just as Mark had been, and she'd recognized that on sight. He had a family, she'd guessed that immediately, because he'd known just how to talk to Timmy. Drake had been a rock for her, when she'd most needed something to cling to.

He had delivered the most devastating news with respect and understanding. Ronnie would never forget him, or that.

Those first years without Mark had been challenging. She'd had to adjust to raising her son alone, which had never been part of her plan and was a change she deeply resented. It had been lonely, as well as difficult. She'd had to go back to school and finish the degree she'd abandoned when Timmy had been conceived, but do it when she was older and had more responsibilities. She'd started a new job and a new career, beginning at the bottom with more bills than her co-workers. She'd had to find a place for them to live and get Timmy settled in a new school, as well as figure out how to be a working mom on her own.

She'd had to stop crying herself to sleep at night.

There was something about triumphing against adversity that had made Ronnie feel strong again. She had built them a new life and Timmy was thriving. At eleven, he looked more like his father every day. He was hardworking and a good kid, the kind of son who would make any mother proud. She'd stopped worrying about him quite so obsessively and dared to think that there might be a future for her, as well.

That had led her thoughts back to Drake. She'd known that she'd never be able to find him on her own, though she had asked both the embassy and Mark's commanding officer about him four years before. It seemed that no one knew anything about him, but Ronnie was sure that was just proof that he was also in covert operations. She hoped that Drake's fate was better than Mark's and began to include him in her nightly prayers.

It probably shouldn't have been a surprise when Drake showed up in her dreams.

It should have been less of one when he started to star in her fantasies. He was a ruggedly handsome man, unabashedly masculine, but it had been the gentleness that tempered his strength that captivated Ronnie.

She'd added Drake's family to her prayers, remembering her conviction that he was also a father, but also recalling the shadow that had touched his eyes when she'd asked him about it. Had he lost them? Was that why he'd understood her grief so well?

It seemed Ronnie would never know.

Until the evening she hefted a bag of groceries out of the trunk of her car, turned around, and Drake was there.

She nearly dropped the bag in her shock.

Yet, it felt absolutely right to see him again.

There had been a lunar eclipse earlier and Ronnie had felt shivery all day. Timmy was staying at a friend's before they departed on a school trip to the capital the next morning, and she'd assumed she was on edge because she always worried about him when they were apart.

But that unsettled feeling intensified as Ronnie stared back at Drake, and she realized it was rooted in a much more earthy response than fear for her son.

She wanted to be touched.

By this very man.

Joy had teased her about having a hot date tonight, and Ronnie had rolled her eyes, unable to even imagine herself having sex again. That part of her life had died along with Mark. She hadn't been able to even think of bringing another man home when Timmy might discover them, and in all honesty, she hadn't been sure she'd be able to survive falling in love again.

In this moment, though, many things seemed possible again.

Drake stood, eyes narrowed slightly, watching her from the shadows surrounding the entrance to her townhouse. He studied her so closely that Ronnie wondered whether he could read her thoughts. He was completely motionless, still dressed in olive drab, though these were casual clothes instead of a uniform. She surveyed him, hungry for details of how his life had changed these past four years.

He was still muscled and stern, still tanned and resolute. His hair had a little bit more salt than pepper now and was still cut short. His gaze was just as unwavering, his attention absolute. He still looked coiled to strike and ready for anything, and she again had no doubt that he could kill with his bare hands.

Ronnie's heart was pounding and her mouth was dry. She told herself it was just that she'd had a start, but she knew better.

Drake was back.

And she was glad.

Ronnie tried to act as if she weren't surprised and probably failed completely. This man missed nothing.

It would have been part of his training.

"Hello, Drake," she managed to say. She took a step closer and felt the dampness on her hands. "How are you?" It was a lame question, but she couldn't think of what else to say.

"Well enough," Drake said, his gaze sweeping over her. A glint of appreciation lit his dark eyes, and she felt both flustered and pleased. "You look well, Veronica."

She liked how he said her name, how deep his voice was and how slowly he spoke. Had he ever called her by name before? She was sure she would have remembered it if he had. There was that foreign inflection to his words that she remembered, and he still spoke with a formality that made her think English wasn't his native tongue.

That glimmer of admiration in his eyes was unmistakable as

she stepped closer. "How is Timmy?"

Of course, he would think of her son. He had seemed to have such an intuitive connection with him.

Ronnie smiled, unable to hide her pride. "Taller! He looks so much like his father now." She faltered and licked her lips, wondering whether she'd said the wrong thing, but Drake simply waited. He didn't look offended. "This week, he wants to be an astronaut."

A ghost of a smile touched Drake's mouth, lifting one corner an increment before disappearing from view again. "Good. A boy needs confidence to have dreams. You've given him that."

"I've tried."

They stared at each other for a moment that seemed too long to Ronnie. She felt flustered and warm and knew she was blushing. Maybe that was because of her fantasies, and her fear that Drake knew what she was thinking.

Well, if he knew that and was like most men, he'd push his advantage.

But Drake didn't move.

Ronnie knew he wasn't like most men. He was waiting for her to decide what would happen. The fact that he was standing in front of her probably said it all, as far as he was concerned. Nothing like a man of few words.

Ronnie was aware that they were standing fifteen feet apart in the parking lot and that it was only a matter of time before one of her neighbors came home.

She should invite him in for dinner.

Yes. She should.

Ronnie took a deep breath and strode toward Drake with purpose. "Look, you never let me really thank you for what you did..."

He raised his fingertips to touch his cheek, and Ronnie could have sworn that was the exact place she'd kissed him. "Your expression of gratitude was more than sufficient." He swallowed and his voice dropped low. "Indeed, I owe you my thanks."

"Really?"

"You gave me new purpose, Veronica," he said solemnly, his gaze clinging to hers with such intensity that she couldn't look away. "That has no price and leaves me forever in your debt."

It was impossible to believe that she had given this man any more resolve than he already possessed, but Ronnie wanted to believe it was true. "How can that be? What do you mean?"

"I had lost faith in the battle," Drake confessed quietly. "I was no longer certain that there was a reason to fight."

Ronnie had a lump in her throat. "Finding Mark can't have helped with that."

"Giving you the answer you needed did help." His eyes glittered. "I understood then that the battle was about the people who don't fight, about defending them, that you, and others like you, were the reason to fight for good."

His focus upon her made Ronnie shiver. It was remarkably warm for this time in the early evening, and there seemed to be a golden radiance in the parking lot, one that hovered between her and Drake. She hugged her groceries, forgetting the carton of eggs. "But you're here. After all this time. Why?"

"To give you a choice," Drake said with soft heat. "I can stay or I can leave."

She knew exactly what he meant, and the prospect made her mouth go dry. "But..."

Drake lifted a hand either to silence her or reach for her. Ronnie wasn't sure which because a brilliant orange spark leapt from his fingertip. She stared at it, not believing her eyes, but the spark flew directly toward her. She flinched when it exploded against her shoulder and gasped at the wave of heat that rolled through her body from that point. She rubbed her shoulder reflexively but there wasn't a burn mark on the fabric.

Just a simmering heat beneath her skin.

No, the heat was simmering lower than that, making Ronnie keenly aware of how long she'd been alone.

And wanting to do something about it.

Had she imagined the spark? There was no question that she felt she'd been touched by fire. She was hot, and she was shivery.

She was also more aroused than she'd been in years.

She stared at Drake, recalling all those fantasies and adding another few. She caught her breath and took a step closer, knowing with complete clarity what she wanted from him. His gaze sharpened and it seemed that there was a halo of flame around his body. She reached for him and he caught her hand in his, his touch sending a jolt of heat surging through her veins. There was brilliant orange light around their joined hands, so bright that she couldn't see their fingers but she could feel the strength of his hand holding hers.

Ronnie sensed that Drake was tempering his strength, that he was being gentle with her by choice.

She looked up at him, mystified by the light, and was awed to see him smile again.

"You decide," he whispered, and she heard the tremor in his voice.

He wanted her.

He'd returned to her.

Which meant there was no choice to be made. Ronnie didn't understand the sparks and she didn't care. The man she'd been waiting for, the man she'd been dreaming about, the man she'd yearned to see again was standing right in front of her.

Ronnie had learned that you could never count on having a second chance.

"Come and have dinner with me," she invited, feeling both bold and shy. "I'd like to cook for you."

"Are you sure?"

She stretched up to kiss Drake for the second time in her life, but this time, Ronnie touched her lips to his, answering him with her touch. His arm locked around her immediately, lifting her to her toes and drawing her against his chest, surrounding them both in a blaze of brilliant yellow light. Ronnie opened her mouth to his kiss, hungry for all he had to give, letting him taste her deeply.

He felt so good.

Her bag of groceries was crushed between them, but Ronnie wasn't worried about the eggs any more.

In fact, this hunger would only be satisfied by Drake's touch.

Seattle

Jacelyn settled deeper into the couch to watch the video for the millionth time. Her throat was tight with unshed tears, but she'd cried enough. This time, she watched the video with a hardened heart, greedy for details about those bastard dragons called the *Pyr*.

It was their fault that she'd been cheated.

Now Jac was going to make them pay.

The video showed a golden dragon suddenly appearing in the middle of a throng of people in downtown Seattle. There was blood on the dragon's scales and a severed human arm in its mouth. People screamed and started to run, but not fast enough. The dragon shook the arm and blood flew through the air.

The virus was transmitted by the exchange of body fluids. Sam had told her that.

The person whose arm was in the dragon's mouth clearly had been infected.

The dragon gnawed on the arm with savage glee, making it bleed more profusely. Then he took flight, dripping the infected blood over as many people as possible. There was a lot of screaming and panic in the streets, and even though it was just a video, when the golden dragon turned his glare upon the camera, Jac shivered to the bottom of her feet.

She'd better get used to that look, if she was going to hunt these vermin.

Jac stopped the video before the worst part. She played the beginning again, fighting her instinctive response. She had to learn about her opponent. This *Pyr* was huge, easily twice the height of every person in his vicinity. He was all muscled power, raw strength and agility. He was a fighting machine, or a weapon of war in his own right. He breathed fire and slashed at people with his powerful tail, snatched and tore with his claws. He looked invincible but that couldn't be the case.

Every creature had a weakness. Clearly, these dragons weren't susceptible to this disease, because the gold dragon had the infectious blood all over it. But they had to have another vulnerability.

Even if this dragon looked as if he were armored in gold.

He had to sleep sometime.

Didn't he?

There were more of them. Maybe there was one he cared about. Maybe he had an emotional vulnerability.

Although he didn't look like he cared about much other than slaughtering humans. He shimmered blue and disappeared in the blink of an eye at the end of the video, which made Jac play it again. What exactly were his powers? How could he appear and disappear so quickly?

Or had he shifted shape, becoming human, then blended into the crowd, like the other one had done? Jac navigated to Maeve O'Neill's website, the one called *Dragons Bite*, and went through the list of other amateur videos. Maeve's broadcasts, calling for people to exterminate the *Pyr*, were all there, too. Jac chose the older video that showed a big blond guy changing into a moonstone and silver dragon in Washington. He'd changed into a human, proof of his shifter nature. The other reporter who had a fascination with the *Pyr*, Melissa Smith, said they were dragon shape shifters. As skeptical as Jac had been, this video made it look so real.

She had her doubts about the photographs taken by Cassie Redmond, the ones that supposedly showed a man becoming a dragon in the desert. It defied belief that they could be real, but she couldn't find a flaw.

They did say that truth was stranger than fiction.

Jac went back to the first video and slowed it down, trying to see whether the gold dragon had changed into a human. He didn't. He just shimmered and disappeared. She sat back and drummed her fingers on the arm of the couch. She couldn't exactly learn every detail of her opponents from YouTube videos, even such a long list of them as on Maeve's site. They were glimpses of the fiends, no more than that, and Melissa Smith's broadcasts were clearly just pro-*Pyr* propaganda.

But where else would she find more information?

She wrote an email to Maeve, using the contact link on the reporter's website. That woman might know more, but Jac was skeptical she'd get a reply.

If she documented what she did know, some patterns might appear. She took a new notebook and printed out the best shot of each dragon from each video. She gave each one a page of his own and noted every detail she could—where the video had been filmed and when, the color of his scales, his human appearance if it had been visible. She even guessed at their alliances and antagonisms, since they sometimes were filmed fighting.

There wasn't nearly enough information to make a plan, but

Jac had moved to Seattle to hunt dragons, and she had to find a way.

She was going to succeed at *something* before she died.

Even if she died doing it, it would be a noble way to go.

At least embarking on this quest made her feel less numb and less alone.

The light was weird on this day, and Jac had heard there was supposed to be a blood moon. She shivered and reviewed her notes, seeing that she'd included everything she knew. It wasn't nearly enough. She grabbed her jacket, deciding to go to the gym again and work out some of her frustration. There was a kickboxing class at ten and she could use every bit of exercise and fighting experience she could get.

She opened the door to find a dark-haired guy standing there with a package in his hand, his other hand lifted to knock at her door. He was the hunk who had moved into the apartment above her the month before. That in itself was interesting—people were moving out of Seattle to get away from the plague, and the apartment building had been getting progressively more empty. Jac thought there were only three or four apartments rented now.

But this guy had moved *to* Seattle.

She had also moved to Seattle, and it was intriguing to have that in common.

It didn't hurt that he was gorgeous. Jac had seen him at the gym a couple of times—they evidently had a membership there in common, too—but didn't know his name.

He smiled slowly at her, as if he liked what he saw, and offered her the package. "I think this is yours." His voice was low and husky enough to give her shivers.

Good shivers.

Jac looked down, seeing that the parcel had her name but his apartment number. There was no return address, and it was wrapped in brown paper and tied up with string.

Maybe it was somebody's favorite thing.

"I'm not expecting anything," she said, then took it from him.

"Maybe it's a gift from a secret admirer," he said, obviously having also noticed that there was no return address.

Jac smiled. "I should be so lucky," she said, then tucked the parcel under her elbow. "You'd think with so few people left in the building, the delivery guy could get it right."

"The odds would seem to be on his side."

"I'm Jacelyn," she said, offering her hand. "But people call me Jac."

His smile started in his eyes and they were twinkling long before his lips curved. "I'm Marcus," he said, his hand closing resolutely around hers. "But people call me Marco."

Jac smiled because she couldn't do anything else, not when the hottest guy she'd met in years was holding her hand, smiling at her, and looking as if he felt the same powerful attraction she did. Was her luck turning? Or was he another good-looking loser who would use her, break her heart and disappear forever? She had a gift for finding them.

Jac couldn't quell her optimism. That was a gift, too. "We go to the same gym, don't we?" she said. "I was just going down for the kickboxing class."

"Sounds good, but I've got a commitment this morning." Marco's gaze dropped to the parcel. "Maybe you should open it, in case it's important." Then he released her hand and stepped back. "Nice to meet you, Jac. Maybe I'll see you at the gym one day."

Maybe?

She'd make sure of it.

Jac took a good look at Marco's tight butt as he strolled down the hall and admired it mightily. Then she shut the apartment door and considered the parcel. Maybe it *was* important. It couldn't hurt to find out and she did have a few minutes.

She tore open the corner to find a plain box inside. She got the scissors from the kitchen to cut the string and opened the package, surprised by the weight of it.

There was an old book inside, but no note or message of any kind. She looked through the paper, but she hadn't missed anything.

She turned the book over. *Habits and Habitats of Dragons: A Compleat Guide for Slayers* by Sigmund Guthrie.

A shiver slipped down Jac's spine.

Seriously?

She flipped open the book to discover that it was about the *Pyr*.

Even better, it specified how best to hunt and kill them.

How had anyone known to send her exactly what she needed? She fanned the pages, amazed by the age of the volume, and started to read. In no time at all, she'd forgotten all about kickboxing class.

But not about her new neighbor.

It was only when her hunger compelled her to put the book aside that she wondered. Did Marco know more about this parcel than he'd let on?

Chicago

Erik Sorensson, leader of the *Pyr*, awakened suddenly. The shards of his dream were fading quickly, but he remembered that he had seen his lost son, Sigmund, in his dream. He had dreamed that Sigmund had come to him with a message, and that his son had been agitated.

It had been the second time he'd had the same dream.

This time, though, he could remember Sigmund's words.

The blood moon will ripen the eggs.

He could still hear Sigmund repeating the words, his anxiety increasing each time. That was probably because Erik hadn't understood his meaning and Sigmund had known it.

The blood moon will ripen the eggs.

Erik frowned and rolled out of bed, striding to the living room for a pen and paper. He wrote the words down, but could make little sense of them.

What eggs?

He knew that the Dragon's Tail of the moon's node would culminate with three blood moons in succession, three lunar eclipses in which the eclipsed moon would appear to turn a russet red color. He knew the first one had occurred earlier today, on the morning of October 8, 2014. Actually—he checked his watch—it had occurred the day before. It was after midnight. The next would be on April 4, 2015 and the third on September 28, 2015. The moon's node would turn to the Dragon's Head on October 1, 2015, ending the prophesied cycle of rebalance and retribution.

That would also mark the end of the Dragon's Tail Wars. Erik didn't want to jinx the result by speculating on whether it would be the *Slayers* or the *Pyr* who survived. One kind of dragon shifter would be eliminated from the earth by that final eclipse, and Erik knew which kind he wanted it to be.

There were few *Slayers* left, and he knocked his knuckles on the wood desk for luck even as he thought as much.

Erik also expected the three lunar eclipses to spark three important firestorms for the *Pyr*. Did Sigmund refer to the eggs of the women who would be the mates of those three *Pyr*? It seemed an unnecessary detail to confide in Erik, and somewhat more intimate than he preferred.

But what other eggs could Sigmund have meant?

He spun in his chair, then booted up his laptop, verifying that there were three full moons in a row. There were photographs online of the one that had just occurred, including some dramatic shots from Hawaii.

Erik looked up "blood moon," because he knew that humans had a number of superstitions about them. In fact, there were four blood moons in a row, the one the previous April that had sparked Thorolf's firestorm being the first of the sequence. He found a Blood Moon Prophecy, which declared this sequence of eclipses to be a mark of the end times, based on a line in the Book of Joel, a minor prophet. Erik supposed that wasn't overly different from the *Pyr*'s view that karma must be rebalanced before the end of this cycle of the moon's node. He knew that the first full moon after the equinox was called the Harvest Moon and the subsequent one, the Hunter's Moon, but wasn't sure it mattered which this one was.

He pushed back the laptop with disgust, just as Eileen came into the living room. She yawned when she saw him, then smiled. "Oh good, you're still here. I thought maybe there was some drama over the firestorm."

"Not so far."

"Excellent. I do love a world with fewer *Slayers*." Eileen frowned then. "Unless there isn't a firestorm?"

Erik closed his eyes and smiled as he attuned himself to the spark. He could feel the firestorm, even at a distance, and the heat of its burn. "Yes. In Virginia."

"Are you staying up? Do you want coffee?"

"No and no." Erik went toward the couch, extending a hand to his partner, mate, and lover. "Come sit with me for a minute."

"Whose firestorm is it?" Eileen asked, curling up beside him on one of the black leather couches.

"Drake's."

"Really!" Eileen twisted around to smile at him, as if she didn't believe him. "I thought he'd had one before. He had a son he left behind, right?"

Erik tightened his arm around her. "He wouldn't be the first to get a second chance."

"True." Eileen nestled against him with satisfaction. "Maybe a new life means a new firestorm."

"Maybe."

"Well, either way, I'm pleased to hear that. I like Drake."

"I didn't realize you'd talked to him much."

"I haven't, but I have a weakness for strong, silent types," Eileen confessed with a smile, then kissed Erik's cheek when he snorted. She studied him for a moment. "Why are you up if there's no trouble?"

"A dream."

Eileen sobered. "The same one?"

Erik winced. He got up and retrieved the pad of paper, then gave it to Eileen.

"What eggs?" she asked immediately.

"I don't know."

There was a shuffling then and their daughter Zoë appeared at the end of the corridor that led to her room and Eileen's office. She'd be six in November, but already resembled Erik so strongly that Eileen joked that she'd been just a womb for rent. Erik saw his partner in his daughter, though, in her creativity and her intelligence, as well as the warmth of her smile. Zoë was carrying her favorite stuffed toy of the moment and looked like she was sleepwalking.

"The blood moon will ripen the eggs," she said, her words devoid of inflection.

The hair on the back of Erik's neck stood up. Had Sigmund appeared to Zoë in a dream, as well? Or was this some mustering of her prophetic abilities as Wyvern? He would have gone to their daughter but Eileen moved first and more quickly, and he settled back against the couch with reluctance.

His desire for Zoë to show her abilities sooner rather than later was a sore point between himself and his mate, so he tried to temper it.

Erik didn't feel any more successful than he usually did.

"Shhh," Eileen counseled, then went to Zoë and picked her up. "You'll get cold," she whispered. "Let's get you back to bed." She kissed her daughter's temple as she picked her up, grimacing at the weight. Erik bit back a smile when Eileen glanced his way. Zoë curled instinctively around her mother, settling against her shoulder to doze contentedly.

Erik beckoned, wanting his family close for the moment, although he couldn't have said why.

"She's growing up so fast," Eileen whispered, guessing the wrong reason for his invitation.

Not quickly enough for Erik, although he tried to savor every day. The fact that he and Eileen had had a daughter indicated that Zoë would be the Wyvern of the *Pyr*, the only female of their kind and the one *Pyr* with the powers of prophecy. Zoë, though, seemed to have no such powers, and Erik suspected she would develop them at puberty—if at all—which was when male *Pyr* came into their powers.

Eileen carried Zoë back to the couch, settling beside Erik, and he pulled a blanket over the two of them. Zoë looked like any other child then, nestled against her mother and spared any dark dreams. Erik had a moment to hope that the *Pyr* would triumph in this war with the *Slayers,* even without the assistance of a Wyvern and her abilities, before the glass in the living room window shattered.

Zoë awakened immediately. Eileen gasped and clutched their daughter close.

Erik was on his feet, already shifting shape to defend his family.

Because there was a large ruby red and brass dragon on the other side of the cracked window, and he was swinging his tail to finish what he had started. He was the spitting image of Boris Vassily, the *Slayer* Erik had killed, dismembered and incinerated seven years before.

But Boris didn't look as if he were dead anymore.

CHAPTER TWO

onnie hadn't realized her kitchen was so small, not until Drake was in it. He leaned against the counter at one end of the room and watched her, his presence so powerful that Ronnie almost forgot her own name. She was keenly aware of him, and hotter than she could have believed possible.

She was aroused, too, all of her fantasies about Drake at the fore of her thoughts. That bright yellow light she'd noticed in the parking lot seemed to be even brighter inside, and it might have been the middle of summer. She felt flushed and self-conscious, aware now that they were alone in her kitchen that it had been decades since she'd had a first date.

If that's what this was.

"It's so warm in here! That thermostat must be off again," she said, hurrying to the living room to adjust it. It looked fine and was set low, but there was no doubt that the kitchen was hotter than a July day in Texas. She closed the drapes over the windows and was amazed by how cozy her home felt.

She'd already hung up her jacket and now removed her cardigan, casting it across the back of a chair on her way to the kitchen. She felt that her skin was a bit pale for a sleeveless top, but Drake didn't seem to have any issues with her appearance.

In fact, his eyes glowed when she came back into the kitchen and her pulse raced when he surveyed her with obvious approval. She felt competent and composed most of the time, had felt feminine a few times since Mark's death, but hadn't felt sexy in a very long time. It was good to be with a man who was obviously attracted to her, especially as the feeling was reciprocal. Ronnie knew that Drake wasn't always easy to read, and she appreciated that he was letting her see his reaction so clearly.

Maybe he'd noticed her nervousness. Ronnie stepped past him to retrieve her groceries and felt the heat emanating from his body. The light in the kitchen seemed brilliant but it wasn't a harsh light—it seemed to gild everything, making Drake look delicious. She had to hope it did the same trick for her. Ronnie opened the fridge and piled the groceries in, a part of her mind concluding that it would be a miracle if any of those eggs survived. She felt a trickle of perspiration slide down her spine, yet her nipples were as tight as pebbles.

She was glad she'd worn this flattering skirt and heels to work on this particular day. She felt more like a woman and less like a mom in this outfit, even though it had been more expensive than what she usually bought for herself.

She pivoted to find that tiny smile on Drake's lips and her heart skipped. Had there ever been a man so still, so patient, as this one?

It would take forever to make love to him—or for him to make love to her. Ronnie felt dizzy in anticipation.

"Would you like a cup of coffee?" she asked, losing her nerve for a moment.

She reached for a mug from the cupboard and her hand shook so much that she dropped it. She didn't see Drake move, just found his solid strength suddenly beside her. He caught the mug, then his hand closed over hers as he gave it back to her. His other hand landed on the back of her waist. It wasn't an embrace, exactly, but she felt surrounded by him.

Protected.

Safe.

Ronnie let out a long breath, knowing she could get used to this sensation. It wasn't easy to parent alone, but she was getting way ahead of things to assume that Drake wanted that much of a part in her life.

She licked her lips. "It's been a long time," she whispered, hearing how husky her voice was. "There's been no one since Mark."

Ronnie wasn't sure what she expected from Drake, but when he bent, his lips touching her ear, she shivered with need. "No one since Cassandra," he murmured.

She looked up at him at this confirmation of her earlier guess that they had both known grief. "Your wife?"

Drake nodded, and she saw again that shadow touch his features.

"How long?"

"Too long."

There was a weariness in his tone that touched Ronnie deeply. They had this in common, this loss of a beloved, and she lifted a hand to his chest. "I thought once that you had a son, too."

Drake frowned and his throat worked. "Theo is also lost to me."

It was an odd way to express it, but Drake often spoke formally and there was no mistaking his pain. Ronnie didn't know how she would have survived if she'd lost both Mark and Timmy: many of those early days, she'd dragged herself out of bed to keep up appearances for her son. She flattened her hand against Drake's chest and felt the steady pulse of his heart beneath her fingers. To her surprise, their hearts seemed to be beating at the same rhythm, and she glanced up to find Drake gritting his teeth.

When he opened his eyes to look down at her, his eyes glittered with a thousand lights. "Veronica," he whispered, as if he were powerless to do anything else.

There were so many similarities in their experiences. That was why this felt right. He'd said she'd given him purpose before and on this night, Ronnie knew she could give him solace.

Perhaps they also understood each other's unspoken needs. He'd certainly gone into danger to get the answer she'd needed, four years before. He'd filled her dreams, but had given her time to heal. He was trustworthy. He was honorable. He was precisely the kind of man she found most appealing.

And even though there was a lot Ronnie didn't know about Drake, she realized she knew more than enough.

"I don't want coffee," Drake whispered, his voice hoarse.

"Neither do I," Ronnie admitted and put the mug down on the counter. She turned to face him. Her heart was racing and she couldn't take a full breath, but she knew what she wanted and she wasn't going to chicken out now. "I want *you*, Drake," she said, amazed by her own audacity. Once she wouldn't have been able to say such a thing aloud, but Ronnie had changed.

She hoped Drake would still want her.

Drake's smile was so satisfied that Ronnie could have no doubt. He moved slowly but with purpose, his hands locking around her waist. His grip almost encircled her, and he made a little growl in his throat, as if that pleased him. He pulled her closer, so that her breasts collided with his chest, and backed her into the counter. It felt good to have his erection press against her and the radiance of the light between them—never mind the heat it generated—made Ronnie gasp in awe.

She might have asked after it, but Drake's mouth closed over hers in a possessive kiss. Ronnie surrendered completely. His was a kiss that turned her blood to fire and destroyed any vestige of doubt, a kiss that melted her bones and branded her with his touch. It was a kiss that claimed her, a proprietary kiss of such passion that she knew she'd remember it forever.

She was Drake's, at least for this night, and Ronnie Maitland was glad.

In fact, she couldn't imagine anything better.

The firestorm was a gift unexpected.

That it should spark for Drake again was good fortune beyond any he had ever known.

That it should burn between himself and this woman, this woman who had haunted him for four years, was a marvel he refused to question.

He could have found Veronica even without the spark of the firestorm, for the scent of her was seared into his very being. It had been her blend of resilience and vulnerability that had snared him four years before, her fragility matched with a conviction that she could change her own circumstance. She wore her heart on her sleeve, and her thoughts were clearly read in her eyes, but she had a resolve that would surprise most people.

Veronica fascinated Drake. Contrast seemed to characterize her, not just in her nature but in her choices. He had to think it would have been simpler for her to have married again than to have raised her son alone. He hoped she was a person guided by principle and that they had that trait in common. He liked that though her life was modern, the necklace she wore was of pearls old enough that they'd been perfectly matched. Her home showed the same contrast, being simply decorated but elegant, with a few well-chosen pieces. It felt like a sanctuary.

He'd known four years before that he could love this woman, that he likely would idolize her, given half the chance, but when they had met, she had just lost her husband. He'd known she had to grieve her loss.

He'd checked on her at intervals, without her knowing of his presence, because he felt protective of her. He liked to think that someone had taken an interest in his lost wife Cassandra after he had failed to return from battle. Drake had noticed that on occasion, Veronica seemed to sense his presence, but he was sure she had never seen him.

He'd never dared to hope that she might remember him with more than kindness.

Never mind that she would melt into his arms so readily, a desire in her eyes that fueled his own. He was amazed that she had no questions, that she made no demands, that she needed no explanation of the firestorm and its sparks.

She must be one of those humans who now knew about the *Pyr* and must understand the import of the firestorm. Relief surged through him that there were no questions to answer and no explanations to make. It was all so simple between them that he could believe in destiny again.

That he had come to her appeared to be enough for Veronica.

That she wanted him was certainly sufficient for Drake.

He wanted to make love to her slowly, but the firestorm combined with Veronica's enthusiasm to undermine his intention. When he'd seen her in that short skirt, the hem of it fluttering around her knees, he'd been sure that no woman had such perfect legs. When she'd turned in the parking lot to find him waiting for her and smiled, her eyes lighting with such obvious pleasure, his heart had started to thunder.

The firestorm's heat had doubled and redoubled with every step she'd taken toward him, the inferno of its demand obliterating everything from his world other than Veronica. That she'd kissed him of her own volition had been enough to take his desire to a fever pitch. Snared in the brilliant yellow heat of the firestorm, he'd felt her every breath, her every shiver, and her touch had filled him with a burning need to possess her. When his heart had matched its pace to hers, he'd felt disoriented with desire.

Drake backed her into the counter, holding her captive there with his hips, gripping her waist as he lifted her to his kiss. She wrapped her arms around his neck, stretched to her toes and returned his kiss with more fervor than he could have hoped. Her breasts were pressed against his chest, so full and soft that he wanted to cup them in his hands. Her hair was shorter than it had been, falling just to her shoulders like chestnut silk. He found his hands tangled in it, his fingers bracketing her face, his kiss deepening as she pulled him ever closer.

"Too many clothes," she whispered when he broke their kiss. Her impish smile made her look younger and less careworn. He liked that she was forthright, as it would make it easier to ensure that she was pleased.

Veronica seemed to feel the same need for haste, and the same desire to feel skin against skin. Her hands were on his jacket, unzipping the front and pushing it over his shoulders, tugging his shirt free of his pants. The first touch of her hands on his bare back was electrifying and he caught his breath, which made her laugh.

Drake had never heard such a wondrous sound.

It made him playful.

He spun her around and found the zipper on her top, then the one on her skirt. He peeled her out of those clothes, casting them aside with impatience, then cupped her breasts from behind. He closed his eyes and leaned his head against hers, fingering her nipples through the soft fabric of her bra. He kissed her neck and her ear and her nape, loving the way she squirmed against him. She was so responsive, and the smell of her arousal gave him a primal pleasure.

Veronica gasped and arched her back, leaning against him with an abandon that made his heart clench. He unfastened her bra and cupped her breasts in his hands, awed by the softness of her skin. She was as perfect as a goddess. He rolled each nipple between finger and thumb, and she moaned.

"Don't tease me," she whispered and spun in his embrace. Her eyes sparkled as she held his gaze, and she stripped off the rest of her undergarments. He could only stare, and made no effort to hide his admiration.

She reached to unclasp the pearls but he stopped her with a fingertip. "They suit you," he murmured. "And I like how they glow against your skin."

"Naked except for my pearls?"

"A beautiful woman needs no other adornment."

Veronica laughed with pleasure and tugged at his T-shirt. "It's no fair that I'm the only one naked," she said. He peeled off his shirt and her fingers fell on his belt buckle, shaking a little in her haste to strip him bare. In moments, his khakis were on the kitchen floor and he was as naked as she.

She took a breath, her lashes sweeping her cheeks as she eyed the size of him, then her fingertips landed on the tattoo on his upper arm. It was a dragon rampant, the mark of the Dragon Legion, and the sparks that flew between her fingertips and the tattoo made it burn as if it were new again. "Your company," she whispered, her eyes aglow. "Mark had a tattoo for his, too."

If she found similarities between him and her dead husband, Drake could have no issues with that. He knew her husband had been a man of merit and honor, and he was glad that she found him of the same ilk. Indeed, he saw much of what he had admired in Cassandra echoed in Veronica, and the similarities made him think well of the future. The differences made this all seem new.

He reached for her, sliding his fingers along the softness of her jaw, and she pressed a kiss into his palm that electrified him. Their gazes clung for a potent moment, then she was in his arms again and his mouth was locked over hers. She slipped her tongue between his teeth and closed her hand around him, making a few demands of her own. Drake was only too glad to provide whatever Veronica wanted of him.

How could Boris be back?

Erik shifted shape at first glimpse of his old adversary, roaring with rage that the *Slayer* was back again. Boris breathed a plume of dragonfire, the orange flames brilliant against the night. As he turned, his ruby and brass scales glittered in the light. He looked fit and fighting trim, and his eyes shone with that familiar malice.

It was impossible. Boris was dead!

But the *Slayer* swung his tail hard and broke the massive window, the force sufficient that shards of glass flew into the apartment. Eileen bent over Zoë, protecting her from the flying splinters, and Erik leaped through the gap to fight his foe.

They locked talons in the ancient fighting pose and flew high above the city.

"Back from the dead again?" Erik taunted in old-speak. *"You need a new trick, Boris."*

"This is *a new trick,"* Boris said, then laughed. *"I'm reborn as myself!"*

Erik failed to see the humor in that. *"Too bad you didn't trouble with any improvements."*

"You're more observant than that, Erik Sorensson." Boris laughed as his tail entwined with Erik's. *"You have to have noticed that each time, you get older and weaker, while I keep getting younger and stronger."* His eyes narrowed and his old-speak dropped to a threat that resonated in Erik's thoughts. *"Maybe this is the time that the balance will be tipped."*

Erik had a definite sense that Boris had some advantage that he wasn't in a hurry to reveal, but he didn't care. He'd finish the old *Slayer* as many times as was necessary.

"Let's find out!" Erik breathed fire, scorching the red plumes that trailed from Boris's wings and tail. Boris bellowed in outrage as they pushed away from each other. They retreated, eyed each other, then the battle began in earnest.

The two dragons collided with enough force to make the windows rattle in the darkened towers of the city. They snatched and bit and grappled for supremacy, each as slippery as an eel and a hundred times more strong.

Erik realized with dismay that they were more evenly matched than they had been before. Maybe Boris *was* stronger. The *Slayer* was savage and forceful, striking Erik with a power that left the leader of the *Pyr* reeling.

Boris couldn't be right about winning this time! Erik had only to think of what Boris would do to Eileen and Zoë to roar with rage and attack again. He slashed at Boris's wings and ripped a claw through one of the tendons. Boris bellowed and spun, a line of black blood flowing from the wound. He pounced on Erik and bit in the middle of his chest, sinking his teeth into Erik with savage force. The pain was excruciating, and Erik saw his own red blood flow over his scales.

Erik ripped himself free by kicking Boris in the gut, then used his tail to smack his adversary in the head, sending the *Slayer* flying. He seized Boris's tail and flung him through the sky. Boris growled and spun, leaping at Erik with talons extended on all four claws. He slashed and bit, while Erik raged dragonfire. The last of Boris's red plumes were fried to cinders and his scales were scorched.

When Boris tore open Erik's chest again, Erik saw the *Slayer* take a deep breath. The wound was deep and dragonsmoke would cheat Erik of strength too quickly, maybe even doom him.

Erik pretended the injury was worse than it was. He closed his eyes and fell back, apparently in anguish, keeping his wings from flapping. He let himself tumble through the sky and summoned his will to breathe dragonsmoke as he fell. He felt Boris following him closely, the *Slayer*'s dragonfire singing the tips of Erik's wings. Erik filled his lungs with dragonsmoke and focused his mind on his scheme for it, then pivoted sharply and exhaled it at Boris.

Surprise was on his side. Boris flew backward, but not quickly enough to evade the dragonsmoke. It followed Erik's will and sank into the wound on Boris's wings like a well-aimed dart. Boris tipped back his head and screamed with pain. The line of dragonsmoke tightened into a conduit and Erik felt a surge of power as the dragonsmoke cheated Boris of his strength.

"So you have *learned a new trick,"* Boris taunted, a satisfying anguish in his voice. He then broke the line of dragonsmoke with his claws and tail, even though it had to burn. Erik smelled the smoke emanating from Boris's claws and saw the *Slayer* grimace in pain.

The injury didn't stop him, though, or even seem to slow him down. Erik feared that Boris was still filled with the Dragon's Blood Elixir. The color was already returning to his scorched scales, after all.

Where could Boris have gotten more? Was there another hidden stash of it somewhere in the world? Had Jorge made more? Erik couldn't imagine that Jorge would share any Elixir he made or found.

But how could Boris even be alive?

The *Slayer* laughed and lunged at Erik again. He ripped that wound in Erik's chest so that it gaped wider, and Erik's red blood flowed. He was feeling faint, but couldn't surrender. Boris seemed intent on making that one injury as bad as possible.

Again, Erik let himself fall, caught his breath and breathed dragonsmoke at his foe. This time, Boris anticipated the trick and was already raging dragonfire when Erik turned. The flames caught Erik across the face, singing his scales and feeding his fury.

As they grappled, Erik managed to tear off Boris's wing fully and cast it to the ground. Boris howled in pain, but simply beat the other wing harder to stay aloft. Erik felt his strength fading and knew that if he didn't triumph in the next few minutes, he might lose.

Boris seemed to understand the same thing. His eyes glittered as he charged at Erik once more, but Erik flew suddenly sideways so that the *Slayer* raced past him. Erik spun neatly and landed on Boris's back, sinking his talons in deeply. He thought of Eileen and Zoë and buried his claws even more deeply into the *Slayer*'s hide.

Then Erik bent and bit at the root of Boris's other wing. Boris tasted of *Slayer* blood, of old rot and mold, and the wound emitted a vile stench. It was a disgusting smell and taste but Erik had to finish his foe.

They had exchanged challenge coins, after all, and though that had been long ago, the tradition still stood: only one of them could survive a blood duel.

No matter how many times Boris returned from the dead to fight it again.

Boris thrashed and spun, but was unable to dislodge Erik. He kicked and squirmed, but couldn't free himself, and no matter how he raged dragonfire, he couldn't do more than singe the end of Erik's tail. He must have been too agitated to breathe dragonsmoke. Boris spun through the air, but Erik held fast. He slammed his back into the brick wall of a tall building, but Erik didn't let go. Boris swore then, as thoroughly as only a *Slayer* who speaks four languages can swear, and Erik had to laugh.

Then he tore deeply into the *Slayer* with his teeth, even as the black blood burned his mouth. He shredded the second wing as Boris struggled, ripping it free of the *Slayer*'s back as Boris screamed in frustration. Erik flung it away and spat after it, wanting only to remove the taste.

Boris howled, flailing as he bled.

Erik gripped his burden and flew toward the gleaming darkness of Lake Michigan, flying far from shore were the water was cold and deep. He felt Boris breathing slowly and knew the *Slayer* was summoning his dragonsmoke. Erik flew more quickly and dropped low over the water. Boris exhaled and the first tendril of his dragonsmoke locked around Erik's tail.

Erik caught his breath at the burning pain and felt his strength being sapped. Boris was draining him quickly, but he flew on with determination.

To his shock, a second stream of dragonsmoke locked around his other ankle. Erik spun to look, only to find a second uninjured Boris Vassily flying leisurely beside him, breathing a long thick stream of dragonsmoke.

How could this be?

The wounded Boris in his grip began to laugh, and Erik felt his own strength fading. He realized with horror that they meant to suck him dry, and that with two of them, they might well succeed. He spun and swung the wounded Boris at the second one, breaking the dragonsmoke conduit with the *Slayer*'s body. His move sent a spray of black blood flinging into the air, and it fell into the lake with a hiss.

"And you thought there were no new tricks," the two *Slayers* said in unison, their words echoing in Erik's mind. Erik used the momentum of the swing to fling the wounded Boris through the air. He then flew in the opposite direction, racing back toward Chicago, hoping the healthy *Slayer* would save the injured one.

It was impossible to know for certain whether a *Slayer* would help anyone, even a fellow *Slayer*. He heard the splash of the wounded Boris landing in the lake, then a cry of frustration. Could he swim? Erik didn't care.

True to the selfish nature of *Slayers*, the second version of Boris abandoned his drowning fellow. He flew in pursuit of Erik, breathing fire that scorched Erik's tail. This one was fresh and strong, as well as gaining fast. His own wound was deep. Erik eyed the distance to the shore, wondering whether he would make it.

Then he felt a hail of ice pellets, conjured out of a clear sky and smiled.

The *Slayer* faltered in his surprise and glanced up, just as Donovan, the Warrior of the *Pyr*, descended out of the sky in lapis lazuli and gold glory. Donovan roared and flung open his claws, revealing the sharp steel talons that the Smith had forged for him. He fell on the surprised *Slayer*, who snarled and breathed fire in his own defense, but Donovan slashed him in a dozen places with those knife-like claws. Black blood flowed over the *Slayer*'s ruby and brass scales, and Erik felt the battle turn back in favor of the *Pyr* again.

Erik left Donovan to finish off the *Slayer* and concentrated on getting to shore. He'd lost a lot of blood from that chest wound, plus he was burned on his tail and his face. He felt his vision dimming as his strength faded.

He smelled *Pyr* as another dragon swooped low over him and seized him from above. Delaney! The emerald and copper *Pyr* escorted Erik to shore, supporting the older *Pyr*'s weight.

"Hit me with some dragonsmoke," Delaney invited. "I can take the drain and you need the power."

In gratitude, Erik closed his eyes and did as instructed, knowing the energy from the dragonsmoke would help him to recover more quickly. He breathed slowly and deeply, creating a conduit between himself and Delaney. He began to feel restored as Delaney's vigor flowed through the dragonsmoke, and he understood how tempting it might be to drink so deeply that the other dragon shifter died. The incoming flux of power felt so good that a *Slayer* wouldn't want to stop.

But Erik wouldn't be a parasite. He took what he needed to survive and no more, then snapped the dragonsmoke with his own claw. He could already feel that the blood was flowing less easily from his wound, and knew he would heal in time. He also could make it to the shore. He and Delaney flew the last increment together. The pair of them shifted shape as they landed on the docks, then turned back in unison to look over the lake.

Donovan was flying toward them, but there was no sign of either Boris.

"They disappeared," Donovan said in old-speak. He landed

beside them and shifted shape smoothly, shoving a hand through his hair as he frowned into the darkness. "One minute, I had him," he said aloud. "And the next, he was gone."

"The other one?" Delaney asked.

Donovan snapped his fingers. "Vanished, as if he'd never been there."

"Spontaneous manifestation elsewhere," Delaney said, no less grim than his brother. "I guess we shouldn't be surprised that the Elixir doesn't really fade."

There was more than that in the wind. The Elixir didn't fully explain Boris's return from the dead, or his appearance in duplicate. Erik sensed a new peril but didn't have nearly enough answers. Did this incident have anything to do with his dream? He held his clawed chest and acknowledged that he was shaken by the strength of Boris's attack. He lifted a glance to the buildings around them and the few lights that were on. "We need to beguile any human witnesses," he said, not truly knowing whether he had the strength to do it.

"We'll take care of it," Donovan said. "Then we'll meet you at your place."

Erik extended his hand to first one brother, then the other. "Thank you. I don't know why you're here, but I'm very glad you are."

"I had a feeling," Donovan said with a grin. "Even though you're supposed to be the one with foresight."

Erik frowned at that. Was he losing his abilities?

How much change would the end of the Dragon's Tail Wars bring to the *Pyr*, even if they survived? Erik couldn't see that future and felt a new concern that his kind might *not* survive.

Who would defend the earth and its treasures then?

Marco was playing with fire, and he knew it.

Worse, he believed it was the best possible choice. He was convinced that the *Pyr* could only survive by walking through the flames, so to speak, and confronting their worst nightmare. Erik Sorensson was concerned about the past repeating itself, about the prospect of *Pyr* being hunted by humans as they had been once before. It was already happening. Marco could see it all around him. He heard it in the tone of news reports about the outbreak of the Seattle virus and its insidious spread through the population. Marco heard the fear and he heard the blame. That video of Jorge, willfully scattering infected blood over the crowd, had been shown so many times that it was burned in his memory.

As well as that of everyone else. Just two minutes of any broadcast by Maeve O'Neill made it clear that she not only hated the *Pyr*, but that she had an enthusiastic following. Who knew what those people would do to rid the world of dragon shape shifters, whom they saw as responsible for the Seattle virus?

It would only get worse, unless the *Pyr* revealed themselves and fought fire with fire.

Seattle's population had dropped to a quarter of its former total, some of the loss by deaths to the illness, but more to people choosing to move. Of course, in relocating to other parts of the country, people had unwittingly spread the virus. It remained untreatable and fatal, but it was now clear that it had a tendency to lurk in the blood of a victim for an unspecified amount of time. Symptoms could appear days after exposure or years. There appeared to be no rhyme or reason to it. There had to be another contributing factor, but no researcher had yet identified it. Worse, there was no test to identify carriers before they began to show symptoms. Isolation wards had been set up in every hospital, but the virus kept spreading.

And killing.

Sloane had explained it all to Marco, when Marco had last visited him.

Marco had listened, then left the Apothecary to his hunt for a cure.

As ever, Marco followed his own intuition and the spark of the darkfire. He'd gone from Sloane to Erik the previous summer and listened to the concerns of the leader of the *Pyr*. He found himself in vehement disagreement with Erik, but didn't argue with him aloud. Marco couldn't, after all, articulate why he thought Erik was wrong, and he doubted that Erik's mind could be changed with discussion anyway.

Marco knew Erik certainly wouldn't trust the darkfire with the intuitive conviction that he did. The darkfire was in Marco's blood.

It was attuned to his very nature. He felt a stronger link to the darkfire than to any other creature alive, or even to any substance. It was a part of him and he liked to believe that he was a part of it.

Marco wasn't sure he could survive without the sight—and the feel—of its blue-green spark in his proximity. To deny the impulses it gave him would have been a violation of everything he believed to be true.

Instead of arguing with Erik, he stole Sigmund's book from that *Pyr*'s hoard, the darkfire urging him on. While in Erik's hoard, Marco had seen the last of the darkfire crystals, its spark extinguished. He knew that Drake had returned this stone to Erik after the adventures of the Dragon's Tooth Warriors, and that both Erik and Drake believed the stone's task to be done. Marco wasn't so certain. He took the extinguished crystal, as well.

Then he moved to Seattle, drawn by a leyline sparked with darkfire, drawn to this particular apartment. His direction was nothing he could have explained clearly, but Marco knew that this was where he should be, that the one apartment—of all the ones shown to him—was the one he must occupy. He wasn't sure why he was there or what he was waiting for, but he waited.

When, one night, the darkfire had sparked in that darkened crystal, Marco had believed himself to be on the right track.

To wherever he was going.

That was the night Marco had heard one of Maeve's broadcasts emanating from the apartment below him. He'd recognized the sound of the video with Jorge and heard Maeve's call to humans to rise up and destroy the *Pyr*. He knew that the darkfire was right. He'd sauntered down the corridor of the floor beneath his own and passed his neighbor coming out of her apartment. Marco knew that she looked familiar but couldn't place her.

The darkfire urged him to find out more.

A day of research made everything clear. The woman who lived below him was actually in that video of Jorge. She was part of the crowd spattered by the blood. She was holding the hand of a young boy, who looked up at Jorge in his dragon form with awe and then fear. She ducked and pulled her hood over her head, trying to tuck the boy protectively beneath her. He was fascinated by Jorge, though, staring open-mouthed at the *Slayer*. Marco saw the infectious blood flick from that severed arm into the boy's mouth and shuddered as the boy cried in pain.

The boy, too, looked familiar. It didn't take much more research to reveal that he had been the first victim of the Seattle virus. The boy's picture had been inescapable after his death, and the fury for hunting dragons had grown louder.

The tragedy was that this Nathaniel had been the only child of a biologist who hunted viruses and isolated them to create antidotes and vaccines. She'd failed to isolate this one in time to save her son.

She wasn't the woman downstairs, though.

Marco didn't know his neighbor's relationship to the boy. She'd known him, that was clear, and she'd loved him. Her expression in that video had revealed all of that.

There were other signs of her affection, too. She'd lost weight since the video had been made and she seemed both focused and grim. Marco noted the purpose in her stride when she came and went from the building. He noticed how determinedly she worked out at the gym. He was aware that she alone in all of Seattle seemed driven by a fierce goal, one that demanded she train to the utmost of her ability, even to the detriment of everything else in her life.

She was listening to Maeve O'Neill.

The darkfire twinkled in the crystal and he guessed her plan. Vengeance, as they said, was a dish best served cold, and humans had a touching conviction in their own abilities to defeat evil. She didn't have a chance against Jorge, if she could find that *Slayer*, but humans could accomplish more than was reasonable to expect when they were as driven as this one was.

She might, at least, surprise Jorge.

Marco realized that he'd like to see that.

He wouldn't, however, like to see Jorge's reaction to that surprise, or his retaliation against Jac.

So, Marco gave her the book.

Then he waited for her to act, as still and observant as only the Sleeper could be.

In fact, Marco dozed in his empty apartment in his dragon form, fairly daring his neighbor to discover his truth. He breathed dragonsmoke, weaving the boundary mark high and deep around his temporary lair, as much for the meditative value of the exercise as for his own defense. He knew humans wouldn't be able to discern it.

Possibilities floated through his mind as he dozed. He wondered whether the crystalline ping of the completed barrier would be heard by *Slayers*, whether it might draw one or more to seek him out. Would his dragonsmoke lure Jorge? Would Jorge's presence draw Jac to him? Marco didn't know and he had no desire to hide. The darkfire in the crystal crackled and burned, telling him to trust that Jac would come.

Marco was content to let her choose the time.

When the eclipse was done and the firestorm had sparked, a prophecy unfurled in his mind, as leisurely as a dream. Marco opened his eyes. The words clung to his thoughts with a persistence he knew better than to ignore. He shifted back to his human form, then took a Sharpie marker and began to write the words on the living room wall.

Maybe this was why Jac would come.

Liz Barrett, marine biologist, wife of a *Pyr* and a Firedaughter, looked up from her sample as an involuntary shiver rolled over her body. She wasn't cold, but she'd had the sense of someone walking over her grave. The boat bobbed slightly where it was anchored near the Great Barrier Reef. She looked east, certain the ripple had come from that direction, but there was nothing but water discernible as far as the horizon.

"What is it?" Brandon asked, obviously having noticed her reaction. He was playing with the boys and resting in preparation for his next surfing competition in December, as well as helping a little now and then with Liz's research. She was part of a team determined to observe the influence of the eclipse upon the fall spawning of the coral in the reef.

Being a working mom with two young sons and a professional surfer husband who traveled to competitions for a good part of the year made their lives hectic enough, without Brandon's obligations to his kind. She knew that Brandon would likely be summoned by the *Pyr* during this key year, and hoped they could juggle it all.

She doubted she'd be involved in this project all the way through to the fourth eclipse in this sequence, but she'd ditch any project if she could help to ensure the survival of the *Pyr*.

There would be more eclipses.

"Something. Like a spark, but not." Liz bit her lip, trying to feel it again. "It was there, then gone. It burned really hot, then cold, then died." She shivered once more. "I've never felt anything like it before."

"The eclipse is in progress," Brandon said, scanning the cloudy sky. Although the eclipse might have been visible from this point, the skies were overcast. Liz knew that Brandon could feel its progress because of his *Pyr* nature. "Do you think you felt the firestorm it sparked?"

Liz shook her head. "I never do. Did you?"

He nodded. "It's Drake's. In Virginia."

"It can't have been that. This was closer."

"Darkfire?"

Liz narrowed her eyes as she considered the horizon. "No. Something new. A kind of quickening." She looked at Brandon. "Does that make any sense to you?"

"No, but it might make sense to someone else. Let me ask the other *Pyr*." He smiled and indicated the ocean sample she'd just gathered. "Carry on with your tests and I'll see what I can find out."

CHAPTER THREE

he first time was fast and hot, just the way Ronnie needed it. Drake's urgency was a perfect echo of her own, and the sparks overwhelmed her with desire. She'd never been so impulsive about sex, but it felt absolutely right.

Ronnie was going with it.

Drake lifted her in his arms, balancing her on the counter in his embrace. She knew he would have caressed her, but she wanted him inside her when she climaxed. She turned to straddle him, felt his surprise, then wrapped her legs around his waist. He shuddered when his hardness touched her soft heat, then there was no holding back.

He felt so good, so strong and so resolute. That light brightened even more, becoming almost blindingly white in its brilliance. Ronnie closed her eyes and surrendered to the moment. She felt as if there was a fire burning beneath her skin.

Had she ever wanted a man this much? Ronnie couldn't recall, couldn't think beyond the pleasure of Drake's body entwined with hers.

She kissed his shoulder when he was within her and felt him shaking with self-control. He was so protective of her, so determined to do what was right. It was enough to make her heart burst. Ronnie ran her hands over him, loving the muscled power of his body, and felt his reaction to her caress. She deliberately drove him on, touching him more boldly, and locked her legs around his waist to draw him deeper inside.

He caught his breath so that his nostrils pinched shut, then his hands cupped her buttocks. She felt his fingers flex and liked it. He started to move rhythmically and Ronnie smiled at him.

Then she pulled Drake's head down for a demanding kiss. The way he rubbed against her was perfect and she felt the tumult rise within her immediately. She gripped his shoulders and he kissed her as if he'd devour her whole. She dug her nails into his shoulders, letting herself follow her every impulse. She kissed him and nibbled at him, licked him and nipped at him. She scratched him and moaned, then whispered to him of what she wanted him to do to her. She watched his eyes blaze as she confided a fantasy.

In fact, Drake swore softly under his breath. Ronnie didn't know the word, but the inflection made its meaning obvious. He whispered her name, as if to apologize, but his body wouldn't be commanded any longer. He drove into her with a vigor that she loved and she felt a patina of perspiration on his skin. She caught his head in her hands and felt the thunder of his pulse under her palm as she kissed him hungrily. Again, it was beating the same rhythm as her own, and she liked the sensation.

She felt the tremor begin within Drake as he lost control and was proud of her ability to affect him. His eyes opened and his gaze locked with hers, his eyes glittering with that intensity she associated with him. The light became so brilliant between them that there was nothing but Drake in Ronnie's world. She gripped him more tightly and rode him hard, needing all he could give her. In a trio of heartbeats, the passion overwhelmed everything except the feel of Drake, and Ronnie cried out in her release. Drake buried himself deep within her and growled, his grip tightening convulsively around her as he came and came and came.

Ronnie smiled into his skin, then pressed a kiss to him. "Wow," she whispered.

Drake leaned his forehead on her shoulder and held her close as he took a shuddering breath. "Indeed," he murmured, then looked at her, his eyes gleaming. That enticing smile curved his lips again, but he studied her, clearly seeking evidence that she had been pleased as well.

Ronnie smiled at him. "Coffee?" she asked and was gifted with a chuckle. She'd never seen Drake smile fully, and the expression made him look younger. Less burdened.

"I am not done with you yet," he said, sending a thrill through her, then lifted her from the counter. Ronnie wrapped her arms around his neck, content to be compliant with whatever he wanted. "We have barely begun on the fantasies you confided."

"I have more."

"We shall make a list," Drake vowed and Ronnie laughed.

The weird thing was that the light was gone, and so was the heat.

Had she imagined it?

It was hard to care when she was so drowsy and sated. Drake surveyed her living room, then walked up the stairs of the townhouse to the master bedroom suite. He nodded satisfaction when he carried her into the ensuite bathroom and plucked her robe from the back of the door. He disentangled them and wrapped her protectively in her robe, then set her gently on her feet. He kissed her again, his fingers in her hair, and it was a tender, sweet kiss.

A perfect kiss in this moment.

He turned away all too soon and began to fill the Jacuzzi tub that filled one corner. Ronnie seldom used it, because it was a lot of trouble to clean, plus she didn't often have time to luxuriate in a bath. "The shower is big enough for two," she suggested but Drake gave her a serious glance.

"But less satisfying than a bath," he said firmly. "On this night, all will be satisfied."

Ronnie could hardly argue with that. She leaned back against the wall, content to watch him arrange details the way he wanted. He had the water running and the room filling with steam in moments. He went through her lotions and found the shower gel that she favored, nodding with approval when he sniffed it, then added a liberal amount to the running water.

"Don't you intend to share the bath with me?"

"Of course."

"You'll smell like a woman."

Drake flicked a look at her that made her blood simmer again. "I will smell like *my* woman," he corrected, and clearly the prospect didn't concern him.

In fact, it looked as if he liked the idea as much as Ronnie did.

When the tub was almost full and the room was wonderfully warm, Drake reached for the lights, frowning as if dissatisfied with the ambiance. There wasn't a dimmer, so they were either on or off.

"There are candles," Ronnie said, guessing what he wanted. She gathered half a dozen fat candles from the cupboard and set them around the tub. She'd bought them one day at a sale, briefly entertaining the fantasy of having a romantic bath. Of course, she'd never had time — or she'd never made the time to so pamper herself. It was incredible to be savoring that bath with Drake, and she found her desire rising again as he lit the candles. He turned off the lights then, and nodded with pleasure, then glanced her way.

Ronnie dropped her robe. Drake's eyes glowed and she saw that he was ready for more. So was she. She took a step toward him and he met her halfway, sweeping her into his arms again.

"You don't have to carry me everywhere," she chided, hearing the pleasure in her tone.

"I like to hold you like this," he said, suddenly solemn. "But if you dislike it, I will cease." He was so serious, so concerned with her pleasure, that Ronnie's heart squeezed tightly. Drake really had been worth waiting for — and was every one of her dreams come true.

"I love it," she admitted, once again wrapping her arms around his neck. Again, that seductive smile touched his lips. She resolved to make him smile as often as possible.

Drake stepped over the lip and into the tub, surveying her as the water swished a bit. The candlelight was golden, much as it had been when she had seen him in the parking lot, and it made him look as if he were made of a precious metal. He held her gaze and smiled as he sank into the water, lowering them both into first the tickle of the bubbles, then the caress of hot water. Ronnie's mouth was dry and she was tingling with anticipation of his kiss.

When she was cradled in his lap, pressed against his erection, he kissed her with possessive ease. He held her against his chest with one arm, while the other hand slipped between her thighs to pleasure her.

Ronnie was glad she'd waited for this bath to be the first.

Eileen was so keyed up after Boris's unexpected assault that she couldn't even sit down. She was pacing the loft, not having been particularly reassured by Erik calling her on Donovan's phone.

She'd heard the strain in his voice and wished he'd come home, rather than supervising the beguiling of witnesses.

Ginger and Alex were similarly concerned, the three of them creating enough nervous energy that they could have fueled a power plant. The other two mates had arrived shortly after Erik's departure, along with their sons, Nick, Darcy, Liam, and Sean. Eileen had been relieved to know that the other *Pyr* had come to assist Erik.

The three women had swept up the broken glass together and nailed some plywood over the broken window. That made the loft unusually dark and Eileen felt as if she hunkered in a cave, waiting to be attacked. She missed the view of the sky the window had afforded, especially since there were dragons on the hunt.

She wished that she had some ability to sense the integrity of Erik's dragonsmoke barrier. The broken window, the surprise attack and the presence of the children made her feel unusually vulnerable.

Never mind that a *Slayer* had come back from the dead.

Eileen made coffee and the women cupped hot mugs in their hands, sipping without real interest. The boys had fallen asleep, and Eileen knew that had only been possible because they hadn't come into their *Pyr* natures as yet.

If they'd been able to smell *Slayer*, the loft would have been full of dragons.

"We saw him from the street. He looked just like Boris Vassily," Alex said, giving voice to Eileen's thoughts. "But I thought Boris was dead."

"He *was* dead," Eileen agreed. "I saw him die. It's been years now."

"February 2008," Alex affirmed, and Eileen recalled that she hadn't been the only one glad to see Boris breathe his last. Boris had hunted Alex during her firestorm with Donovan, and the fact that Alex seldom talked about it implied it had been terrifying. "It's been almost seven years."

"Where the hell could he have been?" Ginger demanded, but the women had no answers. "Do you think they've made more of the Elixir?"

Eileen shuddered at the prospect. "I hope not."

"Me, too," Ginger agreed worriedly. Delaney, Ginger's partner, had been force-fed the Elixir by Boris and his fellow *Slayers*, but had been saved from its effects because of his firestorm with Ginger. "I'll never forget how Delaney suffered."

Alex put her hand over Ginger's and squeezed her fingers. "But he beat it and healed, because of you and the firestorm."

"I think sometimes of what would have happened to him if we hadn't had the firestorm," Ginger murmured.

"The *Pyr* would say that the Great Wyvern was defending him, as one of her own," Eileen said and the women nodded agreement.

The three *Pyr* returned to the loft then, interrupting the women's conversation. Eileen immediately saw that all of them were worn out, and she was glad that the kids had been tired enough to go to sleep for a few hours. Eileen watched Erik inhale slowly then nod with satisfaction on their return.

So the dragonsmoke barrier was intact. Good.

He glanced at her, his eyes bright, and she knew he was worried about Zoë. She tilted her head in the direction of their daughter's room. "The kids have all fallen asleep, in Zoë's room and my office. They're worn out." The *Pyr* relaxed visibly at the confirmation that their families were okay.

That was the moment Eileen realized how badly Erik was injured. He had wrapped Delaney's jacket around himself and she hadn't immediately seen the blood on his chest. When he opened the jacket and winced at his injury, she hurried to his side. Erik waved off her concern, retreating to their suite.

"He'll be fine," Delaney said reassuringly, and Eileen saw how tired he looked. "I let him fuel up with dragonsmoke."

That Erik had even needed to do that wasn't the most reassuring thing Eileen could have heard. She knew he hated her to fuss over him, though, and guessed that he would prefer she tend to their guests.

She'd express her opinion on that when they were alone together.

"We beguiled everyone we could find," Donovan said, lifting Alex's mug out of her hands to take a sip. "Fortunately, it was early enough in the morning that everyone was pretty much asleep."

"Another few hours and we could have had thousands of commuters to deal with," Delaney agreed.

"What does it mean, though?" Erik said, his voice carrying from the master suite.

"Your dream," Eileen said, seeing that the others were confused. "Erik dreamed that Sigmund warned him."

"The blood moon will ripen the eggs," Erik repeated, his voice slightly muffled. If anything, the sound of his frustration reassured Eileen. "That's all he said. Over and over again."

"And Zoë dreamed it, too," Eileen added.

The other four exchanged glances of confusion. "What eggs?" Donovan asked, but no one had any answers.

Eileen sat down in front of Erik's laptop. "If the light of the blood moon is important, we should find out exactly where it was cast."

"That's a good start," Alex said. She topped up her coffee, surrendered it to Donovan, and came to look over Eileen's shoulder.

Eileen followed Erik's bookmark to the NASA website showing lunar eclipses. "'At the instant of greatest eclipse (10:54:36 UT) the moon lies near the zenith from a location in the Pacific Ocean about 2000 km southwest of Hawaii,'" she read. "'The entire October 8 eclipse is visible from the Pacific Ocean and regions immediately bordering it.'"

"Not very much turf to cover there," Donovan said, a thread of humor in his tone.

"Actually, there isn't," Alex said, gesturing to the map on the screen. "That's pretty much all ocean. Wouldn't any eggs have to be on land to be exposed to the light?"

"Or floating on the ocean, if these eggs do," Ginger added.

"What happens when they ripen?" Delaney asked. "Do they hatch?"

"Into what?" Alex asked, her tone skeptical. "*Slayers?*"

"We don't hatch like chickens," Donovan said with disdain. "It makes no sense!"

"Maybe Sigmund was messing with Erik," Delaney suggested quietly.

Eileen winced. It wasn't as though Erik and his son had always been on good terms. They had reconciled before Sigmund's death, thanks to her intervention, but still, their history was long and complicated.

Erik returned to the main room then. He had changed but he was paler than Eileen would have liked. He was limping slightly and there was a burn on the side of his face. She'd thought that was a trick of the light earlier, but it wasn't. He came to her side and she abandoned the chair, noting how stiffly he moved as he sat down.

And the way he sighed with relief. Eileen's lips tightened that he was hurt but pretending otherwise. She put her hand on his shoulder and he brushed his lips across her fingertips. Duty. It was always duty first with Erik, and she knew she shouldn't expect otherwise from him.

Not so long as he was leader of the *Pyr*.

"I'll ask Brandon if he's felt or seen anything unusual," Erik said, but Eileen could tell he wasn't very happy with such a vague query. "He and Liz are at the Great Barrier Reef for her research."

"Is Brandt in Australia with Kay?" Donovan asked and Erik nodded, even as he typed.

"And Thorolf's in Bangkok with Chandra still," Delaney said.

"They must not have run out of pie yet," Ginger murmured and the group chuckled at the reminder of Thorolf's appetite. "Can she bake?"

"I don't think Chandra spends a lot of time in the kitchen," Delaney said.

"I would have thought that the only way to Thorolf's heart was through his stomach," Ginger said with a smile.

"He has other appetites, too," Delaney joked. "And I think Chandra has those covered."

Eileen put on another pot of fresh coffee and was glad to have something to do with her hands. She thought about the Elixir being formulated again and shuddered. She didn't even want to speculate on what other *Slayers* might return to life, much less how they'd get even with the *Pyr* who had slain them.

Mates and children were the weak link, after all.

"Neither of you said anything about coming to Chicago for the eclipse," Erik said to the other *Pyr*. "Although I'm glad you did."

"It's been too quiet," Donovan said, pacing the loft with

frustration. "I knew *something* had to happen. This is it, the big finish, but the *Slayers* are down to just Jorge. I knew he wouldn't just sit back and let us win."

"Where *is* Jorge?" Eileen asked as she returned to the main room. The three *Pyr* shook their heads as one.

"We never know, not since he drank the Elixir and learned to disguise his scent," Erik said. "Never mind his ability to spontaneously manifest elsewhere. He could be anywhere."

"Especially as he got another infusion of the Elixir when he devoured Chen's corpse," Delaney said with a grimace.

"It's disgusting," Ginger said.

"He's addicted to it," Delaney explained, closing his hand over hers. "He'll do anything to get more at this point, and there aren't many options left." He shuddered visibly and concern lit Ginger's eyes.

"You said it was Sigmund who spoke in your dream," Delaney said, and Erik nodded agreement. "Whatever happened to the book he wrote. What was it called?"

"*Habits and Habitats of Dragons: The Compleat Guide for Slayers*." Eileen smiled at their surprise. "I never forget a title or an attribution."

"It's in the hoard," Erik said. "Maybe there's an explanation for those eggs in there." He left them, purpose in his stride as he went to retrieve the book. Eileen knew better than to ask if she could get the book for him.

The hoard was a *Pyr*'s most private sanctuary.

Eileen was amused by the way Donovan and Delaney strove to appear disinterested. They cleared their throats and made small talk about the battle. It was beyond rude for a *Pyr* to eavesdrop on any details of another *Pyr*'s hoard, but their hearing was so keen that they had to know exactly where Erik's was secured.

They probably could hear every sound of him moving an item aside, and identify the item in question, without even trying.

"It could be that Jorge has formulated the Elixir again," Delaney said with obvious distaste. "That second *Slayer* did appear out of nowhere."

"And they disappeared right before my eyes," Donovan said.

"The Elixir does allow any *Slayer* who's consumed it to heal very quickly, even from the worst injuries," Ginger contributed.

"But Jorge wouldn't share, would he?"

"Not unless he wanted to enslave the others, just the way Magnus did, and end up with some new version of shadow dragons," Delaney said.

"But where did these dragons come from?" Alex asked. "Are there any *Pyr* missing, who could have switched sides?"

"Wait a minute." Donovan frowned in sudden thought. "Did you get a good look at the second one?" he asked Delaney.

"He was garnet and gold," Delaney said. "With long streaming red feathers."

"Exactly." Donovan's manner was intent. "What if he was ruby and brass?"

Delaney inhaled sharply, but Eileen didn't follow.

"*Boris* was ruby and brass," she said, confused.

"Exactly!" Donovan said. "The second *Slayer* looked so much like Boris that he could have been his twin brother."

"They could have been long-lost siblings taking vengeance for their brother's death," Alex suggested.

"But how could we not have known anything about them until now?" Delaney demanded. "Where were they hidden?"

The possibility of hidden *Slayers* wasn't a good one, in Eileen's view, especially if they were going to reveal themselves now and be fueled by the Elixir.

Eileen heard Erik's footsteps as he returned. "Did Boris have a brother?" she demanded of him.

"Boris?" Erik frowned. "No. he was an only son, just like me."

"Well, that's really weird," Donovan said. "How could there have been two *Slayers* here at the same time who look exactly like Boris?"

"When Boris is dead," Alex added. "Two *Slayers* we knew nothing about."

"The Elixir," Ginger said, with obvious discouragement.

"I'm healed," Delaney murmured to her and caught her in a tight hug.

"But the book is gone," Erik said, propping his hands on his hips. Before any of them could ask, he lifted a hand. "I haven't checked on it in a while. I thought it secure in my hoard. But it's gone, and so is that darkfire crystal."

"I thought the one in your hoard had gone dark after Drake's journeys with the Dragon Legion," Donovan said.

"It had," Erik agreed. "But now it's gone, and the *Pyr*'s scent that lingers where the book was is that of Marco."

"Marco!" they all echoed in unison.

"Marco," Erik said grimly. "Marcus Maximus, the Sleeper."

"He had a connection with the darkfire. Maybe he believed the crystal should be his," Delaney suggested.

Erik scowled. "Then he should have asked me for it. I probably would have given it to him. That he stole it and the book only reminds me that he's the nephew of the *Slayer*, Magnus Montmorency."

"The *Slayer* who formulated the Dragon's Blood Elixir," Ginger whispered.

"Exactly," Erik said, his displeasure clear.

"Marco couldn't have turned *Slayer*," Donovan said, but there was no real conviction in his voice.

"We don't really know him," Delaney said.

"He likes it that way," Donovan said. "A lot of us are private."

There was silence in the loft then, excerpt for the sputtering of the coffee maker as it finished its cycle and steam rose from the filter. Eileen could hear their doubts, but there was no old-speak.

Just the tinge of uncertainty.

Eileen poured freshly brewed coffee. Could there be a traitor in the *Pyr*'s own ranks? She didn't want to even think about it.

Instead she gave Erik a mug of coffee, then looked him in the eye. "So, are you going to call Sloane about these injuries of yours or am I?"

Erik gave her a smile, then reached for his cell phone. She was glad that even a dragon as stubborn as hers recognized a battle he couldn't win.

Sloane drowsed, liking how Sam curled against his side. Her breathing was slow and relaxed, but he knew she wasn't asleep. They'd loved silently and slowly the second time on the patio, only the stars overhead to witness them. He didn't know how much time had passed and he didn't care.

Sam was beautiful and sweet and responsive. It had been

awesome, which made Sloane wonder how great lovemaking would be if and when they knew more about each other. He couldn't help feeling there was an intuitive connection between them, although he couldn't explain it.

She wasn't his destined mate, after all. He frowned at that, disliking that his romantic future wasn't his own to choose.

Not that his nature hadn't influenced their lovemaking. The spark of that distant firestorm had fed Sloane's passion and his determination to ensure that Sam was pleased. He'd felt as if the dragon side of him had been hovering in his thoughts, and he'd even caught himself on the cusp of change more than once. Everything seemed more potent to him, the feel of Sam's silken skin, the sense of unity with her, the power of his release. Sloane felt different afterward, momentarily sated yet still tingling with need.

He wondered whether it was Sam, or whether it was the firestorm.

She turned to face him, her eyes open only a little bit. Her eyes were a clear blue. He liked how her lashes were dark like chocolate. Her hair fell over her shoulders in waves when she let it hang loose as she had on this night. He found it sexy that she tied it up in the daytime and one stray tendril curled against the back of her neck, capturing the sunlight, inviting his caress. He caught a fistful of it now, savoring the silken feel of it around his fingers. Her hand landed on his chest, her fingertip tracing circles over his heartbeat. Sloane didn't want to move, didn't want this intimacy to end.

In fact, he wanted more.

"I hardly know anything about you," he murmured, pressing a kiss to her temple.

Sam smiled and braced her chin on her hand, regarding him with twinkling eyes. "Isn't that my line?"

"What do you mean?"

"It's supposed to be women who want to talk all the time, and who want to know everything about their lovers." She rolled her eyes at the very notion, but he sensed that she was hiding a truth beneath her playful manner. "I should warn you that I'm different."

"Meaning?"

"Meaning maybe you and I know all we need to know about each other." Her hand slid lower, undoubtedly in an effort to distract him, but Sloane wasn't ready for another round.

And he wanted to know what she was hiding.

What had wounded her.

He caught her hand in his. "But I'm curious."

Although her expression didn't change, Sloane felt that Sam had raised a barrier against him—and his questions. "You know what they say about curiosity and the cat," she said lightly, and he saw the new wariness in her eyes.

"I doubt that asking a question or two would lead to that dire a fate," he said with a smile, well aware that she was agitated.

"Okay," she ceded with obvious reluctance. "One question."

"Are you really a tarot card reader?" Sloane saw her eyes widen and knew she wasn't.

"What makes you ask?"

He shrugged, keeping his tone easy. "You just seem pretty direct for someone who casts spells and reads tarot cards."

Sam arched a brow. "Instead of floating around in dreamy clothes and being incapable of managing real life?"

"I didn't mean to offend you. You just have a pragmatism about you." Sloane mused. "More like a scientist than a mystic. And that made me curious about you."

He saw alarm flash in Sam's eyes before she averted her face.

"Maybe the stereotypes aren't true," she said, her voice a bit breathless. "How many tarot card readers and mystics do you know, anyway?" She was hiding something from him, and her evasiveness only made Sloane more determined to unravel the truth.

They had, after all, shared an incredible physical intimacy. He sensed that she needed to heal, and that this refusal to confide in him—or anyone, likely—was an obstacle to her recovery.

Healing, after all, was Sloane's business.

He chuckled at her question, watching her all the while. He didn't want to miss a nuance of her reaction. "I've met plenty here in California. You're definitely unique."

"Maybe that's my niche," she said stiffly.

"Maybe. I'm skeptical, though, that tarot card readings paid for that house."

The property adjacent to Sloane's had been for sale for a year or so, since the previous owner's death, because the heirs had wanted a high price for it. They had to split the profit six ways, and Sloane thought that desire had informed their choice of price more than the assets of the property itself. It was a nice house on a large lot, but in need of updates. Real estate wasn't cheap in the area, by any means, but their price had been too high for most buyers — even Sloane. He'd been surprised to learn that the house finally and suddenly sold, no less that the sellers had gotten their asking price. That deal had changed perceived values throughout the area.

Sam was visibly discomfited, which told Sloane he was getting close. "Maybe I don't own it."

"But you do." He kept his voice low and even, speaking slowly but with conviction. "It says Samantha Wilcox on the title and doesn't list the liability of a mortgage."

She glared him. "You *checked* on me."

Sloane tried to reassure her. "I check *all* of my new neighbors. I'm kind of private that way." He smiled in an attempt to ease her concerns. "Call it a weakness."

Sam dropped her gaze and he guessed she'd lie. "I used my divorce settlement," she said, her tone hard. "I married well and divorced better. There. Mystery solved."

There was bitterness in her voice and Sloane knew better than to press her any more, at least for the moment. He wondered how recently the divorce had happened.

"I'm sorry," he said, and meant it.

"Don't be. It's better this way." Sam sat straight now, as invincible as a warrior princess, and Sloane wished he hadn't said anything. She was so distant than he doubted he'd get close to her again.

But then Sam surprised him. She took a deep breath and eased closer to him again. She smiled and slid her hand over his skin in a slow caress. Her fingertips felt good, her light caress making him think about how things should go from here. The tension that had arisen between them was dispelled, as easily as that, pleasure pushing complications aside.

He was ready for another round and she knew it. Sam's gaze swept over him, and she smiled with satisfaction. "Let's keep things simple," she suggested in a low murmur. "This was good —

very good—and I wouldn't mind doing it again."

"Tonight?"

"Even after tonight." She held his gaze with resolve, and Sloane recognized that they were negotiating. "But no questions. No emotions. No confidences."

"No commitment for the future?"

She shook her head.

"Just sex?" Sloane said, not believing that was even possible.

"Just sex," Sam said firmly. "Plain, simple, wonderful sex. It's good for the immune system, you know."

Sloane laughed despite himself. "I thought you'd say it was good for the soul."

She wrinkled her nose. "Got to keep the element of surprise on my side." Sloane wondered but she eased her hand down his stomach and over the tops of his thighs, teasing him with her fleeting caress. "*If* you're as interested as I am."

"Can you doubt it?"

The stars glinted overhead and the heat of the other firestorm was fading steadily. Sloane felt powerful but in control of his dragon. That would have been worth celebrating, even if he hadn't been naked beside the pool with a beautiful and mysterious woman.

"Are you cautious because of your divorce?" he dared to ask, hoping she could admit it.

"In a way," she acknowledged with a shrug. "I'm never going to marry again, so there's no point pretending that possibility is in my future. What's the point to surviving anything if we don't learn from our mistakes?"

"The next time you marry might not be a mistake," Sloane suggested.

"There won't be a next time," Sam said with resolve. "I'm alone now and staying alone."

"You sound very sure."

"I'm positive. And I don't want you to have expectations I can't fulfill."

"Can't or won't?" Even though she was offering a solution that was perfect for Sloane, who had to be able to commit to his destined mate whenever his firestorm sparked, he understood intuitively that 'just sex' wasn't the right answer for Sam.

He wanted to be part of the solution for her, not create another issue.

"Does it matter?" Sam leaned over him, her hair spilling on his chest, and brushed her lips over his. Her eyes were sparkling again as she surveyed him and he was pleased to see her lips start to curve in a smile. "What kind of man are you to turn down sex with no commitment?"

"One who might surprise you."

There was a glint of hope in her eyes, one that she dismissed quickly but Sloane still noted. She wasn't as invulnerable as she wanted him to believe. "I don't think so."

Sloane slid his hand down her back, his admiration for more than Sam's slender curves. "Maybe I'll take that as a challenge."

Her brow quirked. "Maybe I'll check the cards on your prospect of success."

Sloane shook his head, pretending to be dismayed. "There you go again, making me curious." He locked his hands around her waist and pulled her closer.

Sam's eyes narrowed a little and she braced her hands on his chest. "Curious about what?"

"Why a mystic wouldn't check her tarot cards *before* seducing her neighbor."

"Maybe I was just too hot to take the time."

"Maybe." Sloane grinned up at her. "Maybe you like talking more than you insist you do."

Her smile flashed, then she bent to kiss him with a passion that fed his own.

Could he heal Sam's scar? Sloane was amazed by how much he wanted to do just that. A divorce could be a deep wound, but most people moved past it. It took time, and maybe someone to listen.

He could be that person. Even if he couldn't commit to Sam for the duration, he could help her to move forward with her life. It was an appealing prospect. Sloane rolled onto his side as he kissed Sam, feeling his desire burn brighter. He deepened his kiss when she wrapped her arms around his neck with a contented sigh.

He wouldn't trust Sam until he knew all of her truth, but he supposed she didn't know all of his, either.

Maybe simple pleasure was just the beginning of what they

could offer each other.

Maybe it would be the way to win her trust.

When Sloane broke that kiss, they were both breathing hard again. Her eyes were sparkling and Sloane bent to kiss her throat, then between her breasts. Both of her hands trailed over his shoulders, then suddenly she froze.

He lifted his head to find that she was staring at the tattoo on his upper arm. "A caduceus," she whispered and he was intrigued that she recognized the symbol. "But with dragons." She shuddered and pulled away, evading his gaze. "Why?"

"Because I thought it was cool," he said lightly, which wasn't entirely a lie. He watched her, noting how she tried to hide her revulsion.

"A symbol of the dead? Of the god who was the patron of *thieves*?" She shook her head. "Why would you think that was cool? And with dragons!" She drew back to look at him. "What kind of life do you live?"

Sloane was intrigued. Most people assumed the caduceus was the symbol of health care, although that was really the Rod of Asclepius, which featured only one snake. The caduceus did have a darker meaning, one he found appropriate for his inherited role among the *Pyr*.

It was also evocative of his father's warning, murmured so long ago.

He found himself a little troubled that Sam had spied one of his secrets. "You think dragons are more worrisome than snakes, maybe even more of a problem than thieves and the dead."

"Definitely." Sam was scurrying backward, slipping out of his embrace. She snatched her bikini bottom and pulled it on, her amorous mood clearly dispelled.

By the dragons in his tattoo.

Or the suggestion that he had a secret.

It was intriguing, given that she had plenty of them herself.

Sloane knew better than to pursue her. He remained where he was and watched her dress. "Why?"

"Don't you watch the news?" Sam's tone was hard, and she turned her back on him as she reached for her bikini top.

"Which news?" Sloane's kind had been in the news repeatedly over the past few years, not least because Rafferty's mate Melissa had aired a television special about the *Pyr*. There was another journalist named Maeve O'Neill who had also taken an interest in the *Pyr*, although her reports were far less favorable than Melissa's. Even Sloane, who wasn't that interested in public opinion, knew that Maeve had some rabid followers.

Was Sam one of them?

"The Seattle virus, of course! Dragons are responsible for that." Sam gestured wildly to his tattoo, her hands shaking. "To choose to have a tattoo like that on your body is an *abomination*." She was furious.

Clearly, he'd struck a nerve, without meaning to do so.

"You feel really strongly about this," he said, keeping his voice calm. "But many people think dragons are just myths."

"They're *not* myths! They're destructive killers, bent on exterminating the human race." Sam dressed with savage gestures, pausing to glare at him. "And making good progress with it, too." She pointed to his tattoo. "That *thing* on your arm is *not* cool." She turned and marched toward the gate, outrage in her every step. "And if you think it is, then we're finished forever."

Sloane wished he hadn't upset Sam, but he was intrigued by the vehemence of her reaction. "It's just a tattoo," he protested.

She spun at the gate to glare at him. "It's a permanent mark on your skin, a design that you chose and that was put there with considerable time, pain and expense. There's no *just* about it!"

"You can't leave already," he protested, keeping his tone low and calm.

"Why not?"

"Because you're angry." Sloane got to his feet slowly, noting how she surveyed him. Her stance softened slightly, and he knew she was as attracted to him as he was to her. He smiled a little and felt her heart skip. "It would be bad luck."

Sam laughed then, though the sound wasn't light-hearted. "Then I guess we're in for some bad luck, because I can't stay."

"Not even if I cover it?" Sloane put one hand over the tattoo, perfectly willing to put on a shirt if it appeased her.

Sam shuddered violently again and shook her head. "Not even if you have it surgically removed. The fact that you have it means we have nothing more to say to each other."

"I thought you didn't want us to talk anyway."

Sam glared at him, then pivoted and strode out the gate. "Let's forget this night ever happened."

Dragons were a problem for her.

Sloane watched her go, trying to be philosophical about it instead of disappointed. Maybe it was better that anything between them ended before it really began, given the truth of his nature. Sam wasn't going to take well to learning that he was *Pyr*—though he had no intention of confiding in her quickly, he was inherently honest. It would only have been a matter of time before he trusted a partner with such a secret.

Especially if he fell in love.

Could he fall in love with a woman who wasn't his destined mate? Sloane had never thought it possible, but there was something about Sam that touched him deeply. He leaned on the fence, watching her, more than his curiosity aroused.

Only when Sam was safely back in her own house, and after she turned out the kitchen lights, did he lock his gate and turn back to the house.

Maybe it was time he dug a little deeper into Sam's history.

Sloane might have done just that if his cell phone hadn't rung. In five minutes, he was booking a commercial flight to Chicago and throwing every unguent in his arsenal as the Apothecary of the *Pyr* into his bag.

Erik was seriously wounded, Boris Vassily was returned from the dead, and there was too much to do to ponder the contradictions of Samantha Wilcox.

CHAPTER FOUR

am was furious. Dragons! How could the one man who made her feel alive again admire dragons? How could the one intimate interval in her recent life have gone so incredibly wrong? She stomped back to her house and slammed the kitchen door behind herself, the lovely luxurious sense of well-being that had come from great sex completely dispelled.

She propped her hands on her hips and glared around her empty kitchen. The executed divorce agreement, the one that had arrived earlier in the day, taunted her from the end of the counter. Even though she'd known it was coming, even though she'd negotiated and agreed to the terms, seeing it all in black and white had been discouraging. Another failure to add to the growing list. Another reason to be glad her father wasn't alive to see what a mess she'd made of the promise of her life. Another reminder that she was alone, and maybe she deserved it.

She'd needed some reassurance, some human contact, some pleasure. She'd thought sex would be a simple solution. She'd thought that following impulse instead of planning every decision years in advance would be a positive change.

Simple sex, no complications, emotions or promises.

Ha.

Sloane Forbes was supposed to be candy.

He was supposed to feel good.

He was supposed to be *fun*.

He was supposed to ask no questions, make no emotional demands, and have no ability to make Sam remember what she'd come to California to forget. Sloane was supposed to be a gorgeous jock, who made love like a god and convinced her to forget all the stuff that was making her miserable. He was supposed to want nothing from her but sex.

He wasn't supposed to have tattoos that hinted at secrets.

He wasn't supposed to be curious about *her* secrets.

And he wasn't supposed to be so delicious that she slipped up. He wasn't supposed to *get* to her, much less to tempt her to lay open her life like a book just so he'd make love to her again.

And he sure as hell wasn't supposed to think anything positive about dragons. *Dragons.* That tattoo made Sam want to break something. It was disgusting that he had such an image on his body. She wasn't a fan of tattoos in the first place, but one with dragons was even worse. Two dragons! They weren't creatures that deserved to be venerated in any way.

But he thought the symbol was *cool.*

Sam seethed. He probably was one of those people who thought the caduceus was a symbol of healing, although the idea of dragons healing anything or anyone was more than ridiculous.

But wait. Sam took a steadying breath. Sloane was awfully perceptive for a man she'd expected to be all about muscles and good looks. After all, he'd seen right through the excuse that everyone else had accepted at face value about her occupation and her plans for the future. He'd even guessed that she was a scientist.

He didn't strike her as being impulsive, much less the kind of person who would go to the expense and pain of getting a large tattoo without being certain of its meaning. He seemed, in fact, to be very deliberate about his choices.

Thoughtful.

Not a dumb jock at all.

Just to be sure she was remembering the details correctly, Sam looked up the symbol. To her relief, she *was* right. The caduceus, with twin serpents twined around a staff—or dragons, in the case of Sloane's tattoo—was a symbol of the Greek god Hermes or his Roman counterpart Mercury, and thus the emblem of messengers of the gods.

She nearly scoffed aloud at the idea of dragons bearing messages from the divine.

She did nod at the note that the caduceus was confused with the Rod of Asclepius by many people, which was a symbol of healing and featured only one snake wrapped around a staff. Mercury was also the guide of the dead, and the protector of thieves, liars, gamblers and merchants. It could be used as a symbol for the planet Mercury or the element itself.

Sam frowned at the book, fighting her sense that Sloane's choice of tattoo wasn't a mistake.

What exactly did he *do*, other than grow herbs and give advice to gardeners? This hinted that there could be a dark side to his life.

Sam bit her lip. That could explain his affection for privacy.

Never mind his habit of checking out his neighbors and their history before they moved in. Did he do something illegal?

No. She didn't believe it. She had a strong sense that he was honorable and honest. Maybe he liked to appear dangerous. Some men did.

Sam fought the urge to look out the window. She was more intrigued by her neighbor than she knew was healthy. The fact was that Sloane Forbes wasn't at all what she'd anticipated. The dragon tattoo was the last surprise, but it hadn't been the first one. Winston Churchill had said that Russia was a riddle wrapped in a mystery inside an enigma, but he could have been talking about Sloane Forbes.

No wonder she was fascinated by him.

Could she figure him out? Guess some of his secrets the way he'd guessed some of hers? Something about Sloane made Sam want to try.

Solving riddles had always been her best trick, after all.

She checked the house and locked up, knowing she was too agitated to sleep. She returned to the kitchen to make herself a hot mug of milk. In the middle of filling the mug, she froze at the memory: she'd always made hot milk for Nathaniel when he couldn't sleep.

She'd never have the chance again. Sam put down the milk, blinked back her tears and fought to catch her breath.

Nathaniel. Just thinking his name hurt.

How would Sloane respond if she told him about her lost son? He'd feel sorry for her, that was for sure, but she wouldn't be able to bear his compassion any more than anyone else's. Not when she'd failed so very badly. Not when Nathaniel's death was all her fault. She put the mug in the microwave, turned it on and put the jug of milk away. She felt raw and bruised all over again, and couldn't decide whether it was better or worse than feeling as numb as she had for the past year.

Her gaze rose to the house several hundred yards away. Would Sloane discern Sam's secret conviction that she'd been a bad mother? She had a feeling that he might.

She thought he might try to console her, even so.

Or was she just seeing him as more of a hero than he was?

The microwave beeped and Sam stirred the milk. How sad was it that she couldn't even have simple impulsive sex, with no strings attached, without messing everything up? Their interval had been great and she'd felt wonderful—until she'd made an issue about Sloane's tattoo.

Which really was none of her business.

Especially given her terms for their relationship. She had no right to make judgments or demands of him, by her own stipulation. A magical night had been ruined by her reaction, and the best feeling she'd had in years had been dispelled for no good reason.

Sam owed Sloane an apology.

She sighed, recognizing a truth when she heard it, and wondered whether she should walk back immediately. Would he still be awake? She had to think so.

Maybe they could pick up where they'd left off.

Maybe she could make it up to him.

Sam was halfway across the kitchen when she saw headlights swing across the darkness. Sloane was backing out of his driveway and heading toward the road.

Leaving.

It was four in the morning. Where could he possibly be going?

Sam wanted to know, more than she'd wanted to know anything in quite a while. Surely, he didn't have another lover he was going to visit? The idea was more troubling than it had any business being.

For man candy and mindless amusement, Sloane was sure shaking her up.

She watched until the lights of his truck disappeared around the bend of the road. He didn't come back, not even by the time she'd finished her milk.

It had been a long time since Sam had gotten to the bottom of any mystery, but here was one that demanded her attention. She was going to find out more about Sloane while he was gone, however long he might be gone.

After all, he thought it was reasonable for a person to research their neighbors.

Fair was fair.

Drake had no doubt of the moment that Veronica's mind returned to practical matters. He had pleasured her three times and had two orgasms himself. The second time, he'd taken her in the bathroom, where the light of the candles and the heat of the bath water were reminiscent of the firestorm's touch.

They'd loved more slowly each time, yet desire still ran like molten honey in his veins. He was marveling at the power of the firestorm and the allure of his mate as he rinsed the bubbles from the tub and watched her brush her hair. He felt fortunate beyond all that he'd not only had a firestorm but been able to satisfy it without the intervention of *Slayers*.

He was thinking about having her again in her own bed, maybe about waking her up with pleasure in the morning. There was no question of him leaving his mate alone, not now.

Veronica had put on a voluminous terrycloth bathroom, though her feet were bare. Drake found it alluring how tiny her waist looked with the belt tugged tight, and the rest of her curves lost in the cloth. He was thinking of unknotting that belt and...

She put down her toothbrush so abruptly that Drake felt the change in her mood like the crack of lightning. She spun to face him, and he realized her mood was not nearly as amorous as his own.

What was wrong? Drake braced himself for the questions that hadn't yet been asked.

"We didn't use a condom," she said, her consternation clear. "I didn't think of it. I don't even have any!"

When Drake didn't reply, she flicked open the medicine cabinet and rummaged in its contents, then closed it. She went through the drawers in the vanity with the same haste, her expression revealing that she knew she wouldn't find what she sought.

She licked her lips and took a breath, as if trying to remain calm. She looked him in the eye and he knew she wasn't calm in the least. "I'm not taking any birth control, not any more."

"It does not matter," Drake said quietly.

Veronica exhaled, somewhat reassured. "I guess you can't have any diseases if you haven't been with anyone since Cassandra." There was a question in her tone, and Drake could well understand that this might trouble her.

"I have none," he admitted, seeing her instant relief.

"Neither do I." She smiled, and Drake had a moment to believe that all was well, then she bit her lip. "I'm not quite in the middle of my cycle, but it would be better to be sure. Maybe I can get one of those morning-after pills..."

Drake was confused by this. "There will be a child," he said, seeing no reason to deny the truth. Surely she knew this?

Cassandra had known from first spark what the firestorm's result would be.

Veronica hadn't asked about the firestorm. He'd assumed that she understood what was happening between them.

She had to be considering the repercussions and the impact on their lives, that was all. He would give her a moment.

Drake wrapped a towel around his hips and rubbed his jaw. He considered his reflection and frowned at the stubble on his jaw. He should shave and ensure he was smooth before he pleasured his mate with his tongue. He wondered if she had a razor.

He found Veronica staring at him, her displeasure clear.

"Excuse me?" she said, her tone a little more strident than it had been.

"There will be a son," Drake repeated calmly. "It is the result of the firestorm. Do not worry: I will not leave you undefended."

Veronica folded her arms across her chest. Her eyes snapped, and it was clear that she wasn't as reassured as he might have expected. Nor had she anticipated this development.

It was perhaps a bad time to ask her for a sharp implement like a razor.

"What's the firestorm?"

Drake frowned, a sick feeling dawning in his stomach.

He'd been wrong.

Veronica, it was clear, did not fully understand the import of the firestorm, or of what they had done.

Drake hoped he had the necessary diplomacy to explain it well. Talking was not his best skill.

"You will be the mother of my son," he said, turning to hold her gaze. "We have conceived a child this night."

Instead of reassuring Veronica, this seemed to alarm her. "That can't be true," she whispered, all the color leaving her face. She sat down on the lid of the toilet, as if her legs couldn't support her. "You can't know that." She shook her head, then glared at Drake. "Why are you saying this?"

Drake ran a hand over his hair, considering where to begin, then swallowed as he faced her again. "I am not like other men," he began.

Veronica's gaze dropped, then she looked into his eyes again. "I'm guessing you mean in a different way than that." He was relieved that she seemed to be recovering from the shock, though there was still wariness in her eyes.

"I am *Pyr*," he said, holding her gaze.

"*Pyr*? What's that?" Her lips parted in sudden realization before he could answer. "Those guys in the YouTube videos that Timmy watches all the time? Those dragon men?" She stood up, once again alarmed, and began to pace the length of the bathroom like a caged tiger. "But that's not real!" she protested as he watched her solemnly. "Men can't really change into fire-breathing dragons! Why would you lie to me about this?"

"I assure you, Veronica, that my nature is no lie." Drake nodded solemnly. "You saw the sparks of the firestorm."

"Those sparks! I thought that was an illusion."

"It is a truth and a hallmark. It means that one of my kind has found his destined mate."

"Oh." Veronica was slightly mollified by that. "That sounds romantic."

Drake shrugged. "It is our nature."

She was wary again, doubt in her eyes, and he knew he'd missed an opportunity to win her support. "Does that mean you'll be staying around?"

"It means that now the firestorm has been satisfied, you will bear my son," Drake said, sticking with the facts. He couldn't promise to remain with her, not when he knew that he would have to choose between his duties to the *Pyr* and his mate. They were in the last year of the Dragon's Tail Wars, after all. He had already vowed to defend her.

But that clearly wasn't enough.

Veronica scrambled to her feet. "You're sure of this."

Drake nodded. "The conception of a son is always the result of satisfying the firestorm." He lifted a hand toward her. "The sparks are gone. The firestorm is sated. You will bear my son."

Veronica was aghast. "Now? I'm thirty-five, Drake. I've just gotten my life sorted out. I have a good job and this townhouse and a car, and I'm building a future for Timmy."

Drake didn't know what to say. It had never occurred to him that she would be less than thrilled with this news. "But you have a son already."

"Yes, and he's growing up. I need to save enough money for him to go to college. I don't have time to be pregnant, Drake!"

"Yet you will be so."

"And you knew this when you came here." There wasn't really a question in her tone but Drake nodded agreement anyway. Veronica shook her head with exasperation. "You don't think we should have talked about this beforehand?"

"Destiny cannot be evaded."

She glared at him, lost for words for a moment, then she found plenty. She propped her hands on her hips, and her eyes flashed in a most beguiling manner. "So, you're telling me that you're a dragon shifter, that you've impregnated me without our discussing it first, and that now I'm going to have a little dragon son? Drake! I thought you were a man of honor! I thought you would treat me with dignity!"

"It is my intention to do exactly that."

"Then what happens next?" She marched toward him, shaking a finger in his face. "You just fly off and disappear for another four years or maybe forever, leaving me with this child to bear and raise? What if I refuse to have it?"

"Veronica!" Drake was shocked by the suggestion. "You could not deny me this son!"

She studied him again, clearly taking note of his horrified

reaction. Her lips set. "But I don't recall being asked about my participation."

"I thought you knew already." Drake rubbed his brow, knowing he had failed to fulfill this duty well. "I believed you understood the import of the flames, as Cassandra had done."

"I am *not* Cassandra," she snapped and he knew he had said the wrong thing again.

Drake dared to appeal to her. "I confess, Veronica, that our firestorm overwhelmed me with its power. I could not have dreamed for such good fortune, especially as it was with you."

She smiled a little and he dared to reach for her hand. "It *was* pretty awesome."

"Indeed." Drake held her hand and her gaze and hoped for the best.

"Wait a minute. Did this happen with Cassandra? Did you have a firestorm with her? Was Theo another of your kind?"

Drake bowed his head. "Cassandra knew of my kind. She understood the import of the firestorm's spark when she welcomed me. And yes, she bore my son, and yes, Theo was of my kind." He was impatient with these details of the ancient past. He was more concerned with the future, and with the son Veronica would bear. "What is of import is that they are lost to me forever." He could see that Veronica wanted to trust him, but that she also had doubts. This was the price of his failing to tell her of the firestorm in advance of satisfying it.

Drake couldn't imagine how they could have resisted its power long enough for such a conversation.

"I will tell you all," he vowed again. "Let us talk first of *our* son."

"Our son." Veronica looked around the bathroom as if not really seeing it and exhaled. "I don't believe it," she muttered as she marched into the bedroom. "A son. Now! After one night together." She was tugging on jeans and a sweatshirt when Drake followed her, that towel still slung around his hips. "I can't believe this. I *won't* believe this." She shoved her feet into soft boots, then spun to confront him. There was a light of challenge in her eyes and an enticing flush to her cheeks. "Okay, let's start at the beginning. If you're really like those guys in the videos, then prove it. Change into a dragon, right here and right now."

Drake considered the dimensions of the hallway and reasoned that there just might be space. He regarded Veronica warily. "There is a suggestion that humans may become insane if they witness the change."

Veronica folded her arms across her chest and scoffed, her spirit encouraging Drake. "Insanity might be an improvement over the last five minutes."

Drake debated the merit of doing what she asked, then there was no choice. There was a sliding glass door in the bedroom behind Veronica, with a small balcony beyond it. He saw a ruby and brass dragon on the other side of the glass. That dragon swung his tail and the glass panel of the door vibrated before it broke. Veronica spun and screamed as the *Slayer* erupted into her bedroom.

She, of course, only knew that the intruder was a dragon, but Drake could smell the toxicity of his black blood.

Drake shifted shape in a heartbeat and thrust Veronica behind him as he leaped forward to fight. He heard another intruder on floor below and knew it had been a mistake to command the Dragon Legion to leave him alone for his firestorm.

He hoped it would not be a fatal one.

It all happened so fast.

One minute, Ronnie was arguing with Drake, who seemed unmoved by her protests. His story made a treacherous kind of sense, but also seemed too far-fetched. It had taken her and Mark six months to get pregnant, and the doctor had said that was perfectly normal. He had, though, said that a second conception might happen more quickly. They'd used protection every time after that.

Demanding proof from Drake seemed like the only reasonable thing to do.

Ronnie wasn't expecting the proof she got.

There was a crash and she'd spun to find a red and gold dragon raging into her bedroom. He was breathing fire and tall enough that his wings brushed the cathedral ceiling. Ronnie might have doubted her eyes, but her bed erupted into flames and the dragon laughed.

Another dragon seized her from behind and pushed her into the corner. He was all shades of grey and black, like dark pearls, his scales far less elaborate and colorful than those of the intruder. For a moment, he shimmered pale blue around his perimeter, just the way the one guy in the video had shimmered before he became a dragon.

There was no sign of Drake.

Ronnie understood that this dragon *was* Drake, both by the level glance he granted her and the way he moved with the same deliberation Drake showed. He was protective of her, putting her out of the path of the intruder's breath of flame.

What had Drake said? That he would not leave her undefended? Maybe that wasn't such a small thing.

Ronnie willed her heart to slow its wild pace and backed herself into the wall. She was both afraid to watch and unwilling to close her eyes, lest she miss anything. She'd wanted proof and here it was in living Technicolor.

It defied belief, but it was real.

The two dragons roared at each other. There was a rumble like thunder, then they locked claws and breathed fire simultaneously.

The drapes caught fire, then the carpet. The red dragon swung his tail and broke the mirror on the far wall. The grey dragon bellowed and slashed at the intruder, ripping into his chest with sharp talons. The red dragon screamed as black blood flowed from the wound. It burned a hole in the floor, as if it were acid. The dragons battled each other, tossing each other into the walls and making the whole townhouse shake, even as the bedroom filled with flames and smoke. Ronnie coughed and backed toward the door.

A man with a cold smile stood there, blocking her exit. His eyes were very pale and his manner was menacing. Ronnie gasped and the dragon that she thought was Drake spun at the minute sound. He roared then spun back to destroy the first assailant in a flurry of blows. He burned that dragon and tore off his arm, moving so fast that his motions blurred. Then he cast the red dragon's body out the broken window and lunged at the second intruder.

That man shimmered blue and became another red and gold

dragon before Ronnie's eyes, one that could have been the twin of the first. Drake snatched up Ronnie and held her against his chest, even as he fought this second dragon. He was both gentle and strong, protective as she knew Drake to be. She was surprised to realize that she was glad he was a dragon shape shifter.

Otherwise, she would have been toast.

The battle took them down the stairs of the townhouse, leaving the railing ripped out, the roof falling in and everything erupting in flames.

Ronnie closed her eyes and prayed, thankful that Timmy was at his friend's house.

Against every expectation, there was another man in the living room, and he looked identical to the one who had become a dragon on the stairs.

He had both arms, so he had to be a third dragon shifter.

Ronnie blinked, wondering whether she was losing her mind. Could there really be three dragons who looked exactly the same in her house at the same time?

Was her life going to be filled with violent dragon shifters if she bore Drake's son?

Ronnie couldn't even think about it. The life she had carefully constructed would be in ruins, and worse, she wasn't the woman she once had been. She wasn't prepared to put all of her hopes and dreams aside to be whatever her partner wanted her to be. She wasn't prepared to be support staff to her partner's career again.

And Drake hadn't mentioned anything like marriage.

The man in the living room shimmered, then changed shape as well. Ronnie wasn't surprised that he became not only a dragon, but a red and gold one. How many of them were there? Would they just keep popping up like rabbits until Drake was defeated?

Instead of leaping into the fray, this one coiled on his haunches, his eyes glittering. He breathed slowly, exhaling in a long slow stream. Ronnie couldn't figure out his plan, and Drake was busy. He exchanged blows with the second dragon, who bared his teeth to breathe fire directly at Ronnie. Drake twisted to take the brunt of the flame, protecting her with one leathery wing, and she heard him inhale sharply at the pain of the burn. He trashed the other dragon with his tail, but his opponent only laughed.

Ronnie didn't know why, but Drake suddenly flinched. He

grimaced and shuddered, his grip upon her faltering. What was happening? The third dragon grinned as he continued to breathe slowly and the first one reappeared as he pulled himself on to the balcony outside the living room. That he could do so with one arm only was impressive. There was black blood running from the shoulder where his other arm should have been attached. He kicked open the door and began to breathe in the same rhythmic way.

Drake twitched. He flinched and shivered convulsively. He roared, and threw himself at the second dragon, thumping him with a flurry of blows that seemed desperate to Ronnie.

Her dragon was losing.

This couldn't be good.

The second dragon kicked Drake and when he fell backward, Ronnie slipped from his grasp. He opened one eye and regarded her. "Run," he whispered, his voice as deep and steady as Drake's in human form. Drake's economy with words suddenly made much more sense. "Take your car and flee as far as you can."

Run? And abandon him to these thugs? She wanted to argue with him, but his gaze turned steely. Ronnie understood that he knew more of dragons than she, even though she wanted to help him.

Maybe it would help Drake more if he didn't have to protect her.

At that thought, she nodded minutely, and Drake rallied with new vigor. She saw him throw himself at the second dragon and heard the walls of her townhouse shake with the force of impact. They roared and fought with ferocity, Drake tearing and slashing his opponent, then breathing fire at the other two. The third arrival had to abandon his slow breathing and join the fight, his gold talons flashing as he slashed at Drake. Red blood flowed from Drake's wounds, while black came from that of his opponents. Ronnie wanted to linger and help him, especially as he seemed to be turning the tide, but he flicked an intent look her way and she understood.

He was ensuring that she had the chance to flee.

Ronnie waited until the red dragons seemed to be ignoring her, then slipped down the stairs and out the front door. She could hear the emergency sirens in the distance and her neighbors were coming out of their townhouses in alarm. Ronnie remembered Drake's command and ran, trusting his advice above all.

Her car was in flames.

She stopped to stare in shock, but it would be a burned-out shell within moments.

She glanced back at the townhouse but knew what Drake would say.

She had to flee on foot.

As far and as fast as possible.

Even knowing it might not be enough.

Ronnie ran down the streets she knew, fearful of what was happening behind her. She could smell the smoke from her home and choked back her tears. Her heart was racing. Everything she had worked so hard to build was being destroyed. She prayed for Drake and she thanked God that Timmy was safe. She wasn't the least bit sure that she could run far enough, but she had to try.

When she couldn't run anymore, she halted, her breath heaving.

She'd only come a dozen blocks.

She wasn't truly surprised when a dragon appeared in the sky overhead, or that he was red and gold. She should have known that it would be impossible to evade him, although she tried. He swooped low and snatched her up, almost effortlessly. Ronnie struggled, knowing she couldn't escape the grip of his talons but needing to try. As he flew high into the sky, she stilled, not wanting to be dropped from such a height. She watched as her town disappeared beneath her, the dragon's strong wings beating hard as he flew higher.

She wasn't surprised when two more dragons joined his flight, but Ronnie was disappointed that they were red and gold. One of them was missing an arm, and black blood dripped from his shoulder. That must be the one Drake had injured first. He flew slightly apart from the others, but Ronnie was looking back, hoping for signs of pursuit.

There were none, although she could see the black smoke rising from her townhouse.

Had they killed Drake?

The *Slayers* left Drake battered but alive, of course. It would have been merciful to have killed him after abducting his mate.

But it was their nature to cause as much pain as possible to their victims.

It wasn't the most reassuring thought Drake could have had. Veronica was gone. She'd left as he'd commanded, but seeing the wreck of her car, he knew that she'd had to flee on foot. There was no way she could have outrun three *Slayers* in flight.

They had taken her. He knew it in his very marrow.

He hoped she wasn't dead. If they planned to kill her, though, they would have killed him. No, this was a game, one played at his expense and one intended to grant the greatest torment possible to him.

Veronica was alive but captive. And Drake had been left alive so he could try to save her. It was the perfect ploy, because even knowing it was suicidal to pursue her, Drake would do it.

He would do whatever was necessary for his mate.

He'd awakened in the parking lot outside her townhouse, which was being consumed by flames. He had a vague recollection of crawling out of her house after the *Slayers* abandoned him there and could still taste his own determination to survive. At least he'd shifted to human form before passing out.

Neighbors were gathered in little clusters of concern, whispering to each other as firemen tried to contain the raging blaze. Drake was sitting on the curb near the smoking remains of Veronica's car. He once again refused the assistance of the paramedics, who had nothing in their arsenal that could heal him.

"Suit yourself," the more persistent paramedic said with resignation and finally left him alone.

Drake touched the cut on his temple with tentative fingers and took a shaking breath. He was badly burned from the dragonfire, but it had been the dragonsmoke that had brought him down. He had felt it sapping his strength, cheating his power to fuel that of his opponents. He had known about the ability of some *Slayers* to use dragonsmoke as a conduit, but he'd never experienced it himself before. The sensation had been like being weakened and being compelled to witness his own demise.

Drake shuddered, hating that he had made such a terrible mistake. What would they do to Veronica? He didn't want to think about it, but he knew he had to. He'd vowed to defend her, but he'd erred thoroughly.

Even though he'd known that *Slayers* could disguise their scent. He'd been too confident, assuming that Jorge was the only *Slayer* remaining and that he could defeat that dragon if necessary. Drake was disgusted with himself and how the firestorm had addled his wits.

How could there be three *Slayers* who looked so similar as to be identical? He'd never seen that before and had a bad feeling about the development. He wondered how many more of those identical *Slayers* would have gathered, even if he had allowed the Dragon Legion to remain close.

Could there be enough of these *Slayers* that they outnumbered the *Pyr*?

Drake shuddered again. He had to tell Erik what had happened, and he needed the help of the *Pyr* to save Veronica. The Dragon Legion would assist him, those *Pyr* descended from his fellow Dragon's Tooth Warriors. They always treated him with honor, possibly because they wouldn't exist if the darkfire hadn't taken him and his companions back in time to their respective firestorms.

Drake caught a whiff of his fellows and spied three of the Dragon Legion in the shadows beyond the crowd, mingling with the onlookers. It was amazing to him that Theo, who led the Dragon Legion, looked just as Drake had imagined his own son, Theo, would have looked once grown. He supposed it wasn't that strange, given that this Theo was the descendant of Drake's own son.

Theo flicked a glance at Drake and looked annoyed. Drake should have anticipated as much. Theo hadn't agreed with Drake's insistence that he be left alone to satisfy the firestorm in privacy: they'd argued and Theo had been proven right.

Drake was relieved that they were there, but he wasn't free to leave just yet. He could, of course, have simply departed, using brute force against the human authorities, but it was prudent, in his opinion, not to cause more disruption.

A police officer had come to stand before him, his expression skeptical. He pulled out a notepad then fixed Drake with a look. "Want to tell me what happened?"

Drake decided to keep it simple. "I was with Veronica. She

offered to make dinner for us."

"Uh huh," the cop said evidently reading between the lines. Drake, after all, still had only a towel tied around his hips.

"A man came through the sliding glass door in the bedroom, then there were two more in the living room."

"Three intruders?" The cop scribbled. "And how did they gain entry?"

"The first one broke the glass," he said, then realized his mistake.

"He shattered an insulated sliding glass door?" The cop lifted a brow. "You sure about that? Did he have a crowbar or something?"

Drake shook his head and pretended to be confused. "I am not certain. It all happened so quickly," he murmured. "Suddenly he was in the bedroom and attacked."

"Attacked Mrs. Maitland?"

Drake nodded. "And he set fire to the drapes. I fought with him and Veronica tried to escape, but there was a second one in the doorway. He tried to seize Veronica." He frowned, not wanting to say too much. "I threw the first out the window and off the balcony to fight the second, but there was a third downstairs. And the house was burning."

"You're lucky you got out of it with that head wound. Sure you don't want the paramedics to stitch you up?"

"I will be fine. Where is Veronica?"

"I was going to ask you that."

"I told her to run when I knew I would be overwhelmed. They were three and I was injured." He swallowed, hating the truth of his own failure. She was his mate and he had failed to protect her.

"Any idea where she might have gone?"

Drake wished he knew. He shook his head, then had a thought. "She has a son. Timothy. He is with a friend on this night."

"When the cat's away," the policeman muttered and Drake stifled the urge to do him injury. His reaction must have showed in his expression because the cop took a step backward.

"I meant that perhaps she went to him."

"Maybe. You got a name?"

"I am Drake."

"Drake what?"

"Simply Drake."

"Let me guess: your identification is in the burning house."
The cop grimaced.

Drake let him believe what he chose. He inhaled, trying to
disguise it, and caught only a faint residue of Veronica's scent.
Would he be able to follow it after this police officer released him?

Time was of the essence. All scents dispersed in time, and the
Slayers might have managed to disguise Veronica's trail.
Impatience rose in Drake and he got to his feet with purpose.

"Easy there," the cop said, clearly discomfited that Drake was
a good bit taller than him. His gaze swept over Drake's muscled
torso and he scribbled some more. "How long have you been
seeing Mrs. Maitland?"

"Veronica and I have not seen each other for several years."
Drake averted his gaze, letting the cop make his own conclusions
about that. "We met four years ago."

A second cop joined them. "The neighbor says the kid is often
with a friend, Dashiell Patterson. I've got a number."

Drake closed his eyes, glad that Veronica was so organized. "I
would speak to the boy," he said, no question in his tone.

"You know him, too?"

"We all met four years ago." Drake held the skeptical officer's
gaze. "I believe Timothy will recall."

The cop snapped his notebook shut. "It's up to the kid. And
even if he does know you, you're not going to speak to him alone."
He met Drake's gaze. "We're going to need an address for you,
Mr. Drake, and I'd suggest you don't leave town."

Drake inclined his head in agreement, knowing it would be
futile to argue. Even if the police officer refused to let him speak to
Veronica's son, Drake would find him. He had to give Timothy his
assurance that he would do his utmost to find Veronica. If he had
to beguile the family taking care of the boy, he would do it.

He had to speak to Timmy.

He'd fabricate an address, because there was no choice. By the
time the police realized it was no good, Drake would be hunting
Slayers.

He'd begin by following Veronica's trail as far as it led.

Theo stepped forward with purpose, gesturing to Arach and
Kristofer, and Drake was glad he would have their help.

CHAPTER FIVE

hy wasn't Sloane older?

His age made no sense.

Sam had discovered that Sloane had bought his property over twenty years before. But he didn't look like he was much older than Sam, and she was thirty-three. People didn't buy extensive property in California in their teens or twenties, after all.

She'd checked three times, thinking there had to be a title transfer from father to son, or from some other relative he'd been named after, but there wasn't.

Was he older than she thought?

Sam had a hard time believing there was ten years between them. In fact, his physical condition was so prime that she had wondered whether he might be younger than her.

It was a mystery.

Which only made her more curious.

She'd casually asked about him, trying to slide her question into conversations as she ran her errands at the post office, the bank and the grocery story. The only thing she'd been able to discover was that everyone in the area liked Sloane. He was considered to be charming and reliable, but details about his life—let alone where he had come from—were sketchy.

In fact, people didn't seem to much care.

Mr. Privacy, all right.

He'd served on the Chamber of Commerce a few years before and had been active in local business organizations, as well as a charity or two. He was courteous and reliable, and she heard many endorsements of the plants he sold and his business practices. She was told repeatedly that she was lucky to have such a good neighbor.

Which didn't explain his age. Had she found another puzzle she couldn't solve? On principle alone, Sam was determined to work this out. How complicated could one man's life be? She returned home late in the evening, having consoled herself over her lack of progress with a delicious meal at a new restaurant in town. She stopped in the driveway beside her parked car, admired the stars, then opened the trunk to get the one bag of groceries she'd picked up.

The lights suddenly flicked on at Sloane's house. Sam frowned, because there was no sign of Sloane's truck. His shop hadn't been open when she'd left in the morning either.

Had Sloane just gotten home, from wherever he'd been?

Should she walk over now and apologize? Even though she knew it was the right thing to do, she was nervous about it. It was a bit late.

Although that hadn't stopped her the night before.

The thing was, she didn't recall his house ever lighting up like this, all at once.

Suddenly, the lights went out again. They'd only been on for a minute or two, and the house was completely dark once more.

Had someone broken into Sloane's house? Sam could call the police, but she hadn't actually seen anything or anyone. It might be Sloane, after all, having arrived home exhausted and headed right to bed. If so, he wouldn't appreciate her—or the police—knocking on the door now.

She decided that if there was any sign of life, she'd walk right over.

The house remained dark and silent.

Maybe the lights were on timers. Maybe they'd malfunctioned. Maybe there had been a power outage.

Maybe she should mind her business and get some sleep.

Still, it couldn't hurt to be a good neighbor. Sam would go for a walk in the morning, just to see if there were any signs of forced entry.

If Sloane turned out to be home, that would be a bonus.

Timmy couldn't believe it. He sat between Dashiell and Dashiell's mom on the couch in their living room while the cop gave him the news. Dashiell's dad paced behind the couch.

"My mom disappeared?" Timmy repeated, still trying to make sense of it. "She wouldn't do that."

"She might not have had a choice, dear," Mrs. Patterson said quietly. The cop and Dashiell's father gave her a look and she bit her lip.

"Was she kidnapped?" Timmy demanded.

"We're going to do everything possible to find her," the cop said, which wasn't the most reassuring thing Timmy had ever heard. "We have some leads and some eyewitness accounts..." His voice trailed away, which did just about nothing to build Timmy's confidence.

"I have to go home," he said, starting to rise to his feet. Dashiell's dad put a hand on his shoulder to keep him where he was.

"I don't think that's a good idea," he said with both kindness and resolve.

Timmy knew then that something really bad had happened. And his mom was gone!

"I should have been there," he said.

"You can't be home all the time, Timmy," Dashiell's mom said gently. "You can't blame yourself for a random event."

"Drake said I was the man of the house. Drake said I had to protect my mom since my dad was gone." He looked away, unwelcome tears rising in his eyes. "He was right, and I let Mom down."

"Drake?" the cop echoed, his gaze flicking to Dashiell's parents. "Who's this Drake?"

There was something about his attitude that made Timmy think the cop already knew the answer to his own question. "He's a guy who does covert operations, just like my dad did. He *finds* people. He found my dad, when no one would do anything or tell my mom anything. Drake's the whole reason we could even have a funeral. He's the only reason we *knew*."

The cop was surprised, but Timmy didn't care if he was insulted. He knew the cops weren't going to find answers for him, or help his mom.

"You should find Drake. He'd find my mom. He'd fix this."

The cop frowned and cleared his throat. "As a matter of fact, there was a man named Drake with your mother at the time. He was injured in the attack and left unconscious as a result."

Timmy was on his feet, unable to hide his relief, too quick for Mr. Patterson's hand. "Drake was there? Drake came back? I have to talk to him!"

"You have to recognize that Mr. Drake is being questioned..."

"He's not Mr. Drake. He's military. He's *secret* military," Timmy retorted hotly. "If you think he did anything wrong, you're totally stupid." The adults exchanged glances and Timmy guessed that they didn't believe him.

The cop appealed to Dashiell's parents. "If we can just give it a day or so until we check out some details..."

"Don't you understand? Drake's the only one who can find my mom!" Timmy cried. "She needs his help and she needs it now!"

"Timmy," Dashiell's mom said gently but Timmy didn't care what anyone said. He ran across the room, evading the grip of both Dashiell's father and the second cop—the one who was supposedly guarding the door—and raced down the front hall. He had to find Drake. He had to talk to Drake about his mom. He ripped open the front door and froze on the threshold.

Drake stood there, as if he'd been waiting for Timmy. He looked grim, more grim than he had the last time Timmy had seen him, and there were bruises on his face as well as a bandage on his hand. He stood motionless, waiting for whatever Timmy would do. He was dressed more casually than he had been the last time Timmy had seen him, but he would have known the older man anywhere.

Timmy didn't care if he looked like a baby. He was so glad to see Drake that he launched himself at him. Drake caught him up and held him tightly. "Timothy," he said, his voice hoarse.

"I should have been there," Timmy said. "I'm the man of the house, just like you said, and I should have protected her..."

"I *was* there," Drake said, interrupting him flatly. "And I couldn't protect her. There were three of them." He leaned back to meet Timmy's gaze, and Timmy was reassured by the cold resolve in the man's eyes. "It is better that you were not there, for they would have injured you."

Timmy swallowed. "They might have killed me, you mean."

Drake nodded minutely.

"But they couldn't kill you."

Drake winced and put Timmy down. He crouched down beside him and Timmy listened closely. He was well aware that Dashiell and his parents and the cops had come down the hall to listen, but he didn't care. "I will find her," Drake said, his gaze holding Timmy's. "I make this promise to you, Timothy."

"And you'll hurt them for hurting her."

Drake's eyes lit but he didn't smile. "What happens to them is of no concern to you. I want you to know that I will give my life for her, if it comes to that."

There was a lump in Timmy's throat. "Okay." It was a lame thing to say but he couldn't think of anything else.

"And you, you must be strong, so that when she returns, she finds you well."

Timmy nodded.

"You must excel in your studies so that she is proud."

Timmy nodded again.

"You must honor the memory of your father and do as he would have done."

"Yes, Drake."

"It will be her love for you that will give her strength. You must ensure that she is not disappointed."

Timmy nodded again, understanding that things didn't look good. Just knowing that Drake was looking for his mom made Timmy feel better, though. He trusted Drake to make everything come right.

The cop cleared his throat. "Where's your family, Timmy? In town?"

Timmy shook his head. "There's just us, now. Mom said we were family enough for each other."

"He can stay with us," Dashiell's mom said. "We'll be glad to have him."

"Awesome!" Dashiell said.

"I want to help," Timmy said to Drake.

"I have told you how to help." Drake lifted a brow and flicked a glance toward Dashiell's mom before looking at Timmy again.

Timmy understood. "Thank you, Mrs. Patterson, for letting me stay here. I really appreciate it."

Dashiell's mom smiled, and he saw that she was trying to hide how upset she was. "Oh, don't you worry. We'll find some chores for you, so you don't get too bored."

Timmy turned back to Drake. "I need your email or your phone number. I need to be able to call you."

But Drake shook his head. "I will find you each week and tell you what I can. In the meantime, I will send three friends to ensure your safety."

"Guys like you."

Drake nodded once. "They are named Kristofer, Reed, and Arach."

Arach. "That's a cool name."

"They will identify themselves to you, then fade into the shadows. Trust that they are always watching you. Kristofer will give you a cell phone number and a signal to bring him immediately to your side."

"Okay, Drake. Thanks."

"Wait a minute," the cop said. "We can post a protection detail, if we decide it's necessary."

Drake stood up and stared the other man down. "I have decided it *is* necessary. I will ensure his protection."

"Look, you don't know..."

Drake interrupted the cop, who didn't look nearly so much like a warrior as Drake even though he was younger. "I know that both I and the boy will be more comfortable knowing that every precaution has been taken."

The cop grimaced. "I'm not sure it's wise..."

Timmy turned around and interrupted him. He didn't realize that he stood exactly as Drake did, nor that they looked like partners. "Drake's going to find my mom, and Drake's going to protect me. I think that's wise enough."

He felt Drake's hand land on the top of his head, even as Dashiell's dad bit back a smile. "Show grace under pressure, Timothy," Drake murmured.

"But thanks anyway," Timmy added.

Mrs. Patterson was looking at Drake as if he was six kinds of awesome, and Timmy totally agreed with her.

"I don't see any harm in it," Mr. Patterson said. "It reassures

Timmy and that's good enough for me." He winked at Timmy.

"I'll have to get authorization," the cop grumbled, but he could say whatever he wanted. Timmy knew that Drake would send his friends, no matter what the cop said, and he knew that Drake would find his mom.

He felt movement and turned to see Drake offering his hand.

They were going to make a deal, like men of honor.

"I'll stay here and do what you said," Timmy said, putting his hand in Drake's much larger one. "I hope it doesn't take long to find her."

"As do I, Timothy," Drake said and he looked grim again. "As do I."

Ronnie awakened in an unfamiliar room.

There were bars on the windows and rubble on the floor. It smelled like mold. The walls were peeling, both plaster and paint coming off like large scales. There was a dark oily puddle on the floor on the other side of the room and the temperature was frigid.

She was lying on a mattress that appeared to be new, but had only a thin blanket. She shivered then got up, rubbing her arms to warm her skin as she investigated the confines of her prison.

Because that was undoubtedly what it was. There was only one door, which was steel and new, with a small viewing window at eye height. She didn't doubt that it was locked from the other side, but she checked anyway.

It was.

There was a small table beside the door and a straight chair. There was a pot in the far corner with a lid that looked new. Ronnie guessed it was a chamber pot. She wasn't in a hurry to use it, but the fact that it had been provided wasn't a good sign.

Ronnie looked out the window, discovering that the bars were on the outside of the glass. She rapped at the window hard, then pounded on it, but it must have been tempered glass. It barely even vibrated.

There was clearly no heat in the place, which might have been an old institution. The building emanated a damp chill. The glass in the window was grimy, but she could see scrubby trees, like an untended woodlot. They were devoid of leaves and she had the sense that the forest was reclaiming the territory. She listened and thought she could hear traffic at a distance. She might have been dropped into a forgotten corner of the world. The sky was getting dark, like it might be the end of the day.

Where was she?

What did these dragon shifters intend to do to her?

Ronnie could think of many options, given their assault on her home, none of which filled her with optimism. She supposed the townhouse was as trashed as her car. Everything she'd worked to build was in shambles, and if Drake was right, she was going to have a child. Ronnie pinched herself hard in the hope that she'd awaken from the nightmare, but nothing changed.

Surely the bad dragons hadn't gone after Timmy? She listened, but couldn't hear any other signs of life. Had they killed her son? Abducted him and drugged him?

Ronnie realized that any other prisoner listening to the building wouldn't be able to tell that she was there, either. She went to the door and peered out the small opening.

All she could see was a cinderblock wall, peeling with as much enthusiasm as the walls of her cell, and maybe ten feet away. It was covered with graffiti in bright colors. A corridor seemed to extend to left and right, but she couldn't see any other doors.

That didn't mean they weren't there.

"Hello?" she yelled. "I'm Ronnie Maitland. Is anyone here?"

The sound of her voice echoed back to her.

Then silence.

She realized she must be alone in this place and tried not to panic.

Had the attacking dragons killed Drake? Did he have any idea where she was? He'd said he would defend her and he certainly had tried, even with the odds so stacked against him. She had to believe that he'd try to save her, if he was alive, and if he could discover her location.

That seemed to be too many "ifs."

Ronnie began to pace her cell, her mind filling with questions for which she had no answers. She fingered her grandmother's pearls, a nervous habit that made her realize that she still had them, at least.

Even if everything else she owned was gone.

Ronnie's fingers closed around the pearls. Thank goodness Drake had asked her to leave them on. Of everything in her life, the only things it would break her heart to lose were the pearls and Timmy.

She paced the cell, praying that her son was well.

Ronnie wasn't sure how much later it was that she heard thunder. She returned to the window, but the sky was clear. It looked like early evening, because there was a smear of orange in the sky, off to her right.

That wasn't what made her catch her breath, though. A red and gold dragon descended from the sky, right outside her window. She saw that he was carrying another dragon that could have been his twin. That one was wounded, though, black blood flowing from the points where his wings should have been rooted.

To Ronnie's amazement, the injured one began to shimmer, as if surrounded by pale blue light. That reminded her of the light she'd seen before Drake and the intruders had changed shape. The light sparked and flickered, giving enough illumination for her to see that his eyes were closed.

He changed shape abruptly, becoming a stocky older man with fair hair. She gasped, because he could have been one of the intruders in her home.

He didn't appear to regain consciousness, but continued to shimmer. He became a dragon again, then a man, switching between forms with increasing speed even as that blue light faded in intensity. The dragon who had carried him watched impassively, his eyes glittering in the blue light. He stopped switching forms in his dragon form and was very still.

Ronnie heard a door slam and three men who also looked just like the intruders to her townhouse strode out into the wasteland. One had a bandage on his right shoulder, and she decided he must be Leftie, the one who had had his arm ripped off by Drake. They didn't help the fallen man, just stood and watched with as much disinterest as the dragon.

Leftie took a step forward, his expression alight with what

might have been anticipation.

There was thunder again, then the blue shimmer became brighter. The three men shifted shape, becoming red and gold dragons, and Ronnie heard them stomping down the dry growth of the forest. It was like looking into a mirror, because the three dragons appeared to be identical to each other—except for their various wounds, which were mostly superficial.

To her surprise, though, Leftie's right arm wasn't completely gone anymore. It seemed to be regenerating itself from the shoulder and had grown back to a stub. Ronnie knew it had been completely missing just the night before.

Even more worrisome, there were five very similar dragons outside her window, except one had no wings and one had only part of his arm. The wingless one also appeared to be dying, while the other four seemed to be indifferent to his fate. Leftie and the triplets, she decided to dub the ones watching. It sounded like the name of a band.

The wingless one's eyes opened and he moaned. He tried to crawl away from the others, and Ronnie wondered why.

Then the one that had carried him breathed a brilliant plume of orange fire, roasting the wingless one while he was in his dragon form. He howled in pain. The second dragon had flipped the wingless one over and was holding down his tail and legs.

Leftie threw himself at the fallen dragon, teeth bared, but a tussle ensued. Ronnie heard even louder thunder, and the dragon who had brought the wingless one fought with Leftie. The last dragon bit into their victim's gut, disinterested in the fight, ripping and shredding the flesh with relish. The wingless one groaned in agony as he was devoured alive.

He didn't protest for long.

Leftie snarled, apparently resenting that he was being denied a feast. His opponent flung him against the wall of the building, two dragons fighting while two savored their meal. Their victim was silent and still now. Leftie made another attempt to score a bite, but two of the triplets breathed fire at him. The other was too busy eating.

Ronnie blinked at a shimmer of blue light, then realized Leftie had vanished into thin air. At the same time, the first dragon spun and breathed fire to set the woods aflame. The forest was dry and the fire spread quickly up a network of deadened vines, lighting the gruesome scene. Did she hear a human shout? Ronnie pressed her face to the glass.

It started to rain then, which maybe explained the thunder. The rain started suddenly and fell in sheets, extinguishing the fire in the forest. The scales of the red and gold dragons glistened with water, but they appeared to be oblivious to the change in the weather.

She turned her back on the scene and leaned against the wall, shivering. Maybe nothing could have turned them away from that feast. As much as she hoped that Drake would come for her, she didn't want him to share that fate.

The third clone of Boris Vassily liked to think of himself as Boris IV. It had been a surprise to spring forth from an egg, his memories of his life as Boris as clear as crystal in his mind. His memory of his defeat at the talon of Erik Sorensson made him burn with a lust for revenge.

It was invigorating to be given a second chance.

It had been disconcerting to be flying with four mirror-images of himself.

It had been more disconcerting to have the *Slayer* Jorge seize them all and whisk them through space and time. Boris had enjoyed the sight of the terrified humans below them and would have happily indulged in a little ruthless slaughter. These were the beings responsible for the death of so many of his kind, after all, and his father's call to dragon shifters to defend themselves against humans still rang in Boris's memory. He could recite the entirety of the speech that had created the rift between *Pyr*, the division that had resulted in the kind known as *Slayers*.

His father had left his mark, and Boris wanted to leave his own.

It wasn't going to be as a minion of Jorge, that was for sure.

No, he was the only son of Mikhail Vassily, the first leader of the *Slayers*. He'd be the next leader himself. It was his birthright.

Boris IV knew what had to be done to win the Dragon's Tail Wars. A blood duel incited by the exchange of challenge coins was never left unfinished, so he would go to Erik. To his dismay, Jorge dispatched two of his fellow clones to hunt Erik. Boris IV had argued briefly with Jorge, but the younger *Slayer* hadn't listened to him.

Jorge wasn't even smart enough to heed good advice.

Boris IV had been dispatched to take the lead in destroying the firestorm of Drake. Jorge wanted to capture the mate, but Boris IV knew that was ridiculous. He'd intended to kill her outright, but Drake had severed Boris IV's arm and Jorge's more obedient minions had taken control of the battle. They would have left him behind if he hadn't recovered enough to fly with them, and Boris IV knew it.

Then Jorge had taken his vengeance, by ensuring Boris IV had none of the Elixir from the body of his fallen fellow.

Even though his injuries were more severe and the Elixir would help him heal.

Even though he was the only clone of Boris Vassily who seemed to remember the truth and the one best qualified to take command.

Boris IV seethed at the disrespect shown in this injustice. Boris had centuries of experience in leading *Slayers*, while Jorge had been alone or a minion. Jorge's ability to plan for the future had already shown his shortcomings as a leader: Erik had been saved, thanks to the intervention of Delaney and Donovan, while Drake and his mate had survived. To have only injured the *Pyr* in these surprise skirmishes was pathetic.

To attain his rightful place, Boris IV had work to do.

Disappearing, leaving Jorge with one less talon to serve him, had been the first step.

Next, he had to locate the second batch of eggs. He had almost six months to do it and a keen desire to find them. Being there at the hatching would give him first pick of the new clones. Eating one would restore him physically, given the infusion of the Elixir he'd consume. The newly hatched clone would be disoriented and easy prey.

After that, Jorge would pay.

And finally, once all the details were arranged, Boris IV would pay a visit to his old adversary, Erik, and finish what had been begun.

It was such a perfect plan that it couldn't fail.

Drake finally had to admit defeat.

Only when there was nothing else to be done immediately did he report. Erik, as leader of the *Pyr*, had to know about Veronica's abduction and the appearance of three *Slayers*. Theo was right that it would be news better delivered in person, but Drake didn't want to spend the time to fly to Chicago.

He borrowed Theo's cell phone instead and for once, he was glad of technological innovation.

"Gone?" Erik echoed, his displeasure clear. "There's no trace of her scent?"

"She might have vanished into thin air," Drake confirmed with frustration. "I followed her trail for six blocks and then it disappears. Theo has confirmed this and we have fanned out in all directions..."

"She's not there anymore," Erik said, interrupting him tersely.

Drake fell silent, knowing that the other *Pyr* was right. "They were *Slayers*," he said. "Three of them."

"They must have drunk the Elixir in order to disappear like that," Erik said. "Did you recognize them? What did they look like?"

"They all looked identical," Drake said. "That was the curious thing. Not similar, but identical. Like triplets."

Erik caught his breath and Drake heard Donovan's voice in the background. "Identical?" that *Pyr* asked.

"Indeed. Triplets."

"Quintuplets," Erik murmured. "There were two here, as well."

This was not good news.

"What about their scent?" Donovan asked.

Drake shook his head, forgetting for the moment that they couldn't see him. "I could only smell *Slayer* rot during the fight. There was no hint of it before their appearance, and there is only a slight whiff of it where Veronica's trail disappears."

"A taunt," Donovan said flatly from Erik's side, and Drake had to agree.

"How can we guess the location of their refuge?" Drake demanded in frustration. "We must retrieve my mate!"

"The firestorm is consummated?" Erik asked.

Drake nodded again, but Theo pointed to the phone to remind him. "Yes," he said simply.

"Then we have to hope they want the child more than your mate," Erik said.

The child! What would Jorge do with a *Pyr* son? Drake couldn't consider it.

"This is unacceptable," Drake protested. "I cannot fail her! I vowed to defend her, and her son..."

"And there has to be a smarter way of finding her," Erik said, with some temperance. "There is no trail, but that doesn't mean she's lost."

"I do not understand," Drake said with impatience.

"I'll ask Niall to seek her in dreams."

Drake shoved a hand through his hair, not liking that there was so little he could do. It reminded him all too well of how he had left Cassandra and never returned, how she had been compelled to raise their son alone, with no knowledge of his fate. He thought of all the things he had never told her, and ultimately never had the chance to tell her, and feared it was happening all over again. It made him sick that he was repeating his error of the past.

But there was nothing he could do.

"Defend the boy," Erik said crisply. "Niall may want to talk to you about him."

"To direct his hunt," Drake concluded, feeling some relief. "Timothy is the focus of Veronica's life. She will fear for him."

"And her concern may give Niall a trail."

Ronnie was shaken by what she'd witnessed.

The three dragons had consumed every fiber of the wingless one's body. There hadn't been a sinew or a talon left when they had straightened, shifted back to their human form, and strolled out of her line of vision. They walked as if there was nothing remarkable about what they'd just done. She heard thunder again, and that slamming door, then footsteps fading into the interior of the building.

She even heard a slight belch.

They couldn't have done that to Drake, could they? Ronnie didn't know, and she wasn't sure she wanted to know if they had.

Where had Leftie gone? It was spooky that he had vanished into thin air, which made Ronnie fear that he might be able to appear out of nothing, too.

She paced with greater urgency, desperate to find some way to escape and unable to think of one. She heard a vehicle coming closer and went to the window again. There were lights, as if a flashlight moved in the woods, and she heard a dog bark.

Ronnie guessed that wherever she was, there was a security team supposed to patrol the area. That encouraged her enormously.

At least until one of the triplets emerged from the darkness to the right, dressed in a dark jacket and heavy boots. He, too, carried a flashlight and moved directly toward the lights and sound of dogs. She heard him speaking to the other men, although she couldn't discern his words. His voice seemed very low.

And melodic, which was strange.

Worse, the security team retreated, not even coming into view of the building.

The triplet was smiling when he returned to the building and Ronnie didn't think she imagined the triumphant glance he fired toward her window.

It was much later and darker when she heard footsteps in the corridor outside and she spun to face the door.

One of the triplets looked through the door at her, his glittering eyes all the reminder she needed of his capabilities. Ronnie took a step backward and he smiled.

He had a deep cut in his cheek and she hoped it hurt. She thought of the wingless dragon and his torn up back and concluded that injuries followed these shifters between form. It seemed slightly more possible to injure one while he was in human form, so she'd keep that in mind.

He opened the door and she saw that another of the triplets hovered behind him. He carried a tray of covered dishes, which had a lantern on it, and Ronnie could see steam rising from beneath the lids. She could also smell the food. Her stomach growled as he set the tray on a table just inside the door.

"Where's Leftie?" she demanded.

"He's not so good with trays right now," the first dragon

shifter said smoothly. Ronnie sensed that this wasn't all of the truth, but the way these two smiled was unnerving. He indicated that the other should carry the tray into the room.

"You're probably going to poison me," she charged.

The first dragon shifter seemed to be elected to do the talking. "On the contrary. You'll only have a healthy son if you eat well during your pregnancy."

Ronnie regarded him in horror. There was the talk of sons again. These dragon shifters were so convinced that she'd already conceived. She'd been sure that Drake was wrong, but with repetition, it was starting to sound more plausible. "You can't be serious."

"I have no sense of humor," he said flatly and Ronnie believed it.

"I don't eat dragon," she said, the smell of the warm food tormenting her.

"That's good, because we didn't save you any." He gestured to the tray. "It's vegetarian." He made to close the door, but Ronnie had to learn more.

Could she already be pregnant?

Was that why she'd been captured and not killed? It made a treacherous kind of sense.

"What are you going to do with my son?" she demanded but the door closed resolutely behind the man. She heard him chuckle and raced to the door, pounding on it with her fists. "What are you going to do to me?"

He paused and glanced back. "Nothing."

"What about Timmy? What about Drake?"

He smiled, then came back to the grate. Ronnie instinctively recoiled from the coldness in his eyes. "All you need to know is that we're not going to kill you or torture you. That might affect the child, after all." He nodded in the direction of the tray. "Go ahead and eat. You've got nine months to discover our plans, and you don't want us to force you to eat for the sake of the boy."

Whether she was pregnant or not, their conviction of her condition was what was giving her a chance to live.

If she wasn't pregnant, would she be able to fake it?

If she was pregnant, though, the prospect was getting more horrifying by the moment. Ronnie looked around her prison, outraged that she could be confined in such a place for almost a year, never mind that she might have a child in this filthy hole. That might kill her in itself.

Had Drake guessed she would be in this peril? Her captors walked away, the sound of their footsteps fading, even as she heard that stupid thunder again. Maybe there was a subway near them.

Maybe she *was* losing her mind.

Ronnie shook her head, instinctively knowing Drake hadn't realized she'd be at risk. He wasn't irresponsible and he'd never lied to her. She closed her eyes and prayed that he had survived, that he was well and that he would come to save both her and their child.

She knew that so long as he drew breath, he'd look out for Timmy. Those two had a bond, one established the moment they'd met. Drake would take care of Timmy.

Her intuitive conviction made her feel better. Ronnie eyed the tray for only a moment before she removed the lid from the largest dish. It was lasagna, steaming hot. There was a green salad and some garlic bread, water, skim milk and a big mug of hot tea. If nothing else, these dragons understood human nutrition. The tea was probably decaffeinated because that would be better for the baby.

Did that mean they'd get her pre-natal care? She could only hope as much, because that might create an opportunity for escape.

They also understood that she might use anything provided to get away. The plates were plastic, as were the utensils. There was a small dish with a multivitamin in it, and Ronnie recognized both the shape of the pill and the logo on the side of it as the brand she took daily.

They even had the pink one, which was for pregnant and nursing women.

Dragons were nothing if not consistent. Given her circumstance, in a way, Ronnie was starting to hope they were right. Nine months would give her a lot more time to escape, or for Drake to rescue her, than the two months required to prove that she wasn't pregnant.

Her stomach growled and she pulled up a chair, sitting down to eat her dinner before the lantern went out or was taken away.

She might as well keep up her strength.

The lasagna was delicious.

By morning, Sam knew she couldn't bring herself to just walk up to Sloane's house, knock on the door and apologize.

She needed a story.

Her plan was to go to Sloane's shop first, then wander down the driveway after she "discovered" that it was closed. It would be as if she hadn't noticed him leaving and had a question about her garden. She had a thousand of them, actually, so it shouldn't be tough. There was a worm breeding on her roses, for example, dozens of the little pests gnawing away at the buds. There weren't as many buds on this late second bloom, of course, but she'd argue that made them more precious.

She probably could have found the answer online in five minutes, but she needed an excuse and this was going to be it.

Sam carefully clipped a branch off one rose bush, which hosted at least three of the little worms, and tried not to feel like an obsessed teenager.

She failed.

She tried to keep her pulse from racing in anticipation as she walked toward Sloane's shop, but failed in that, too.

There were no two ways about it—she couldn't wait to see him again.

She was even walking more quickly than usual.

Sloane's shop was near the road, with his greenhouses behind it. Behind them were rows of herbs, including several of lavender that reminded Sam of all those pictures of Provence. The shop was closed and dark inside, just as she'd expected, but her heart sank all the same. She peered in the windows of the shop to be sure no one was there, then began to walk down the driveway toward the house, carrying her excuse in one hand.

Sloane's house was located far back from the road, private and secluded behind the field of herbs. A seemingly impenetrable forest filled the land behind the pool that curved around its back side. Sam had a feeling the house was embedded into the hill and admired the solid impression it gave. It could have been there forever, except for its sleek, contemporary design. She was struck once more that no one could approach it without being observed, and that its location had much in common with a fortress. The house was both elegant and rooted, and Sam admired it all over again.

She would have bought it in a heartbeat, because everything about it seemed to scream that it was private and its occupants not to be disturbed. The real estate agent had laughed at her suggestion: evidently she hadn't been the first to covet Sloane's home.

Walking through the well-tended rows of his herbs, Sam found it easy to remember how she'd noticed Sloane on the first day she'd moved in—and cringe a little at the assumptions she'd made. Once upon a time, she would have appreciated the view offered by a man like Sloane but kept on going, seeking male companionship elsewhere. She was attracted to smart men, inquisitive men, men who delved into great mysteries and sorted them out—and they seldom looked like Sloane. She'd dated physicists and astronomers, research scientists and quantum theorists. She'd married a virus hunter and biologist.

But this was Sam's new beginning, her course correction, so she'd lingered.

And Sloane was different. He challenged her assumptions. She'd guessed the truth the first time he'd glanced up at her from his garden. She'd sensed even then that he was perceptive and intelligent. He'd strolled across the fields with that athletic grace and introduced himself, offering his hand to her.

She'd felt an awareness of him, even then, one unlike anything she'd experienced before. It had only heightened when he'd given her a small smile, his eyes glowing. She'd felt beautiful when he'd looked at her like that, with his appreciation clear. His grip was strong and his hand warm, and she'd seen that his eyes were a deep hazel, with green and gold lights in them. Beneath his perusal, Sam had felt something awaken deep inside her that she'd thought was dead forever.

He had her at hello, both her curiosity and her lust aroused.

That powerful impression had been reinforced with every exchange between them.

And her whimsical cover story, about being a tarot card reader and spell caster, had been put into immediate action. She feared that maybe he already had seen through her story. Sam had thrown herself into researching spells that used herbs, partly so that she had excuses to go to Sloane's greenhouse and seek his advice. She'd even planted a number of them, making a start of a garden around the house. She'd studied the cards that her sister read so easily and had been devouring books on their interpretation. Contrary to being something easily mastered, she found the detail almost bewildering.

Even with so much to do, Sam hadn't been able to stop thinking about Sloane. She hadn't been able to stay out of his shop. She'd been sure that seducing him would be the easiest way to cure her of the attraction.

Instead, she was even more intrigued by him.

It was those secrets.

She was on his porch, with a pathetic excuse at conversation in her hand, an apology composed in her thoughts, her heart skipping as she knocked on his door. He'd see right through the pretense, Sam knew it, but strangely enough, she didn't mind. She just wanted to see him again.

She wanted to make things right.

Sam couldn't deny that the house seemed empty. It was silent and dark. She knocked and called and rang the bell, but there was no reply. There was no one near the pool, either. She tried to peer into one window, but it was either tinted or the shades were drawn on the inside. She couldn't see anything but her own reflection.

The night they'd made love, she'd noticed that it had been impossible to look into his house, even from the pool area. Either the windows were tinted or blinds were closed, because the windows looked like dark mirrors. In earlier days, she might have dismissed his need for privacy as a quirk, but she thought again about that tattoo, and Sloane's insistence that there be no strangers in his house.

What *did* he do, really?

Why was he so private?

Mercury was the guide of the dead and protector of gamblers, liars and thieves.

Sam shivered, despite the warmth of the afternoon. She'd always found mysteries enticing. Her ability to shake the truth free, no matter how improbable it was, had been the basis of her entire career. The funny thing was that she hadn't felt much like solving riddles since her colossal failure.

But Sloane's tattoo rekindled Sam's almost-forgotten need to know.

She realized a bit late that a man so enamored of his privacy had to have an alarm system. She hadn't heard an alarm, though, and the police hadn't responded.

There was no crisis.

Sam walked home, more disappointed by Sloane's continued absence than she knew she should be. She tossed the branch of the rose into the field, well away from Sloane's meticulously tended gardens.

Her mother had always insisted that everything happened for a reason. If one night was to be the sum of her time with Sloane, what had been the point?

The mystery was the point, Sam decided. She was going to unravel Sloane's secret, no matter what it was, no matter how deeply buried it was, just to prove that she hadn't lost her mojo. There might be one riddle she couldn't solve, but there wouldn't be two.

Maybe that would push Sloane out of her thoughts for good.

CHAPTER SIX

hat's Erik!" Cassie was astonished to see the leader of the *Pyr* on the news in his dragon form. Erik was battling a red and gold dragon in the night sky.

"Our latest dragon sighting comes from Chicago, where these two dragons battled over the city, showing no care for the human residents sleeping in the vicinity," declared Maeve O'Neill. She was in a studio somewhere other than the battle itself, providing a voice-over, her image in a box at the bottom of the screen. Although she was a beautiful woman, with dark hair and blue eyes, Cassie found her perspectives irritating. "A flurry of dragon sightings coinciding with the blood moon and eclipse, as well as natural disasters in China, the Ukraine and Indonesia—never mind the unchecked progress of the Seattle virus—have this reporter wondering whether the end of the world really is near. Are the *Pyr* friend or foe? Call in now to share your views, as we watch this brutal attack unfold..."

Cassie turned off the sound so she could avoid another tirade by Maeve and watched Erik's fight. He was winning, and had torn the wings off the dragon who had to be *Slayer*, when another one popped out of nowhere to fight against Erik. It was strange how much he resembled the wounded *Slayer*. To Cassie's relief, Donovan showed up, and then Delaney, and the *Slayers* vanished into thin air.

She was in the large room of the Venetian palace she shared with Lorenzo di Fiore, her *Pyr* and the former Las Vegas illusionist. It was one of those rare moments when they were alone together and both of their sons were asleep. Antonio would be three in March. Bartholomew—Bart to all who adored him—had only been born the previous May. Cassie had been thinking that she was too tired to do anything about their moment of privacy when the fight had been televised. She was fully alert now.

Lorenzo was staring out over the canal, hands on his hips, apparently lost in thought.

Cassie knew better.

"You don't fool me," she said, turning off the television with the remote. "You have to be interested. It looks like Erik's wounded, and you know how he feels about being seen by humans."

"I watched the video online earlier," Lorenzo said quietly.

"And?"

"And?" He turned to face her, his smile no less enigmatic than his manner.

"And what have you concluded, planned or otherwise schemed without telling me about it?" Cassie softened her words with a smile. It was Lorenzo's nature to plan, but she couldn't resist teasing him about it sometimes.

Lorenzo came to sit beside her on the couch, his gaze intent. "I would never make a decision without consulting you."

Cassie rolled her eyes. "No, you just move all the pieces into place and ask me when it's too late to do anything different."

He was immediately contrite. "I thought it would be easier for you if I took care of details. You've been tired during your pregnancies and I wanted you to have every opportunity to work on your photographs."

"While you've had very little on your talons." She poked him in the chest and he sighed.

"I'm not used to retirement," he admitted ruefully.

"Regrets?"

His shrug was non-committal but his gaze was bright. "You?"

"The boys are so great," Cassie said, watching Lorenzo nod. "I wouldn't be without them."

"No." He arched a brow. "But?"

Cassie decided to be the one to voice her doubts first. "I miss living in the States. I worry about their schooling here, where there are so few other kids. I'm not sure I like seeing you prowl around the house, either, trying to find something to do."

Lorenzo took her hand in his. "We've been thinking the same way."

Cassie was glad to hear it. She gestured to the dark screen. "Talk to me."

He frowned, then nodded. "You're right that Erik doesn't like humans to see him in dragon form. That he was filmed and the video survived means that he was unable to beguile the person who shot the video."

"Because he was injured?"

Lorenzo winced. "I think Erik would defy death to beguile humans in defense of the *Pyr* and their privacy. I'm sure he, and the others, tried."

"Then what could be the reason?"

"Change." Lorenzo got up to pace the room. "You know that beguiling works best, like most kinds of hypnosis, when the person being beguiled wants to be convinced. Historically, people didn't want to see dragons. We were terrifying. We could destroy them, readily. And seeing a man change into a dragon was even more frightening. It challenged everything they believed to be true."

"Right." Cassie hugged her knees. "So it was easy to beguile someone into believing that he or she hadn't seen a dragon at all."

"It's *never* easy, Cassie," Lorenzo chided gently and she smiled, knowing she'd pricked his pride.

"Of course not. And you're the best at it because you've worked hard to be so."

He gave her a simmering glance, probably because she was teasing him. Cassie smiled at him, unrepentant, and patted the couch beside her. "You need to perform again. It keeps you more even-tempered."

He snorted and she practically saw a puff of smoke come out of his nostrils. "I wish you weren't so right."

"Come on. Tell me what's changed."

Lorenzo perched on the edge of the couch again, his restless energy tangible. His gaze collided suddenly with hers. "They *want* to see us now. Taking a video like that one of Erik, Donovan and Delaney is a ticket to fame, of a kind. Humans aren't afraid of us, and they don't want to be beguiled that their dream didn't come true."

"Could you have beguiled the person who shot this video?"

Lorenzo frowned. "I don't know. It would have been a challenge."

His uncertainty was unexpected. "You would have liked to have tried."

"Yes."

"Do you agree with Erik? Do you think the *Pyr* are in danger? This Maeve seems to want us to take up our pitchforks and battle you to extinction."

He turned a glittering glance upon her, one that could still make her simmer with desire. "We're all prey, Cassie, but the real hunters aren't humans. The real hunters are those other dragons."

"*Slayers?*"

"Not just any *Slayers*. The two in the video look just like Boris Vassily, who has been dead for several years. And they were indistinguishable from each other." He drummed his fingers on the couch. "I have to wonder what Jorge learned from Chen at the end, or what he's done."

"What does that mean?"

"It means that it's time for the illusion to end." Lorenzo eyed her, his manner regal. "I won't hide when I'm being hunted." He took her hand in his again. "And to my relief, that meshes quite well with what we've both been thinking."

Cassie smiled, knowing her dragon well enough to guess his choice. "You'll taunt."

He leaned closer, smiling with anticipation. "I'll taunt and I'll provoke and I'll find out the truth, so it can be used against them. This is the end of the Dragon's Tail Wars, Cassie. I didn't want to be involved, but our firestorm changed everything. I mean to survive this reckoning, and that means I need to fight in the only way I can."

"We're going back to the States," Cassie guessed, her excitement rising.

"The master illusionist Lorenzo is going to rise from the dead," her *Pyr* agreed with a nod. "And it will be the greatest show of all time." He smiled as he held her gaze with that familiar confidence. "The only way past the fire is through it." She could almost see him making lists and planning. "We'll start with a press conference to announce my return. You'll be there."

"Just another photographer in the crowd," Cassie guessed.

Lorenzo shook his head. "No, no. There will be no crowd."

"But don't you want as many reporters there as possible?"

Lorenzo's eyes danced. "I'm going to give Maeve O'Neill an exclusive." He sat back on the couch, lounging with a satisfaction that Cassie didn't understand.

"Why would she be interested in your illusion show starting up again, or even in your return from the dead?"

Lorenzo smiled. "Because you're going to tell her that I'm the *Pyr* you photographed shifting shape in the desert."

Cassie gasped. "I can't! Erik will be furious! It's a violation of the Covenant..."

"This is war," Lorenzo interrupted with resolve. His eyes glittered coldly. "I'll do whatever I need to do to win and secure the future of my sons."

Cassie still didn't understand. "But she'll broadcast the story and once everyone knows, you'll be in danger..."

"No, she won't." He leaned closer to her, his smile bright with anticipation. "Not after she's been beguiled into changing her views about the *Pyr*, and begins arguing in our favor."

Instead of condemning the *Pyr* with every broadcast. "Can you do it? Doesn't she want to believe you're evil?"

Lorenzo pursed his lips. "I think she's more interested in her own fame than any convictions about our nature. I think she wants a story, and the bigger the better. I just need to offer her a tempting one for the beguiling to work."

"Like what?"

"That's the challenge, isn't it?" Lorenzo smiled and Cassie knew that her *Pyr* had found a challenge to sink his teeth into.

She suspected it was one he would win, too.

"What can I do to help?" Just as Cassie had suspected, Lorenzo had a plan.

There was a ripple in the air of Ronnie's prison the next evening. It felt like a static charge had swept through the building, as if rubbing her hands together in its aftermath would be enough to make a spark.

What was going on?

She rose from bed cautiously and listened at the door. There was that thunder again, and the sound of footsteps. It was a man and he was in a hurry.

The lock sounded in the door and Ronnie had a heartbeat to wish she'd seized that chamber pot. She could have thwacked the new arrival with it.

Then she saw that it was two of the triplets. There was consternation in their manner, but she didn't have much chance to observe it. She was blindfolded and her hands bound behind her back, then she was spun in place. When she was dizzy, she was marched into the corridor, her captors holding her wrists.

Their skin was cold enough to make her shiver.

Reptilian.

She did shudder and one of them chuckled at her apparent fear.

"Where are we going?" she demanded, trying to sound brave.

"To meet the boss," one said.

"It's supper time," the other added. Ronnie couldn't help but think of the feast she'd witnessed the previous night and she inadvertently caught her breath.

When they laughed, she knew they'd let her see that on purpose.

They wanted her to be afraid. It made sense to be afraid.

Ronnie lifted her chin. But it didn't make sense to show her fear. She thought of Mark and she thought of Drake; she thought of all the service people who had been tortured and imprisoned; and she resolved to do her best to be strong.

She couldn't have been more surprised when her bonds were removed and she was left alone in a comfortable room. A man stood opposite her, watching her with a smile playing across his lips. There was electricity in this room, because the lights were on and a pair of refrigerators were humming on the far wall. There was a compact kitchen beyond the fridges, and in fact, it looked as if she were in a small and elegant apartment, outfitted with every amenity.

Except that it had no windows.

The man in front of her was tall and might have been considered handsome if not for the assessment in his eyes. She knew with one look that he liked hurting others, but she held his gaze to disguise her fear. He had blond hair cut very short and blue eyes and looked as if he worked out a lot. He'd be a powerful opponent. Was he a dragon shifter?

There was no upside to being coy. "Are you another one?" she asked warily.

"You could say I'm the only one," he replied, gesturing to a plush chair. "I *will* be the only one in a year."

Ronnie took a seat as he indicated, but didn't sink back into the chair. She perched on the edge, watching him.

"I shouldn't offer you a drink, although that might be appropriate otherwise," he mused. "What can I get you? Herbal tea? Milk? Sparkling water?"

"Tea would be great," she said tersely.

He snapped his fingers and one of the triplets appeared from behind the drapes, hastening to fill a kettle. Her host sat down opposite her, his gaze watchful. "I am Jorge," he said, his voice soft with menace.

"No surname?"

He smiled a little more. "My reputation is such that I no longer need one."

"Like Jack the Ripper."

He chuckled. "Something like that. Do you play board games, Ronnie?"

Ronnie was unable to hide her astonishment. "Board games?"

"Snakes and Ladders. Checkers. Monopoly." Jorge's eyes glinted. "You have a son. I was certain you would understand my meaning."

"I don't understand why you would want to play board games."

"Because they are an excellent time filler, and we have nine months to wait." Jorge leaned back. "I could hope for the sparkle of excellent conversation. I could yearn for many wild sexual encounters. But you are the mate of a *Pyr*, a cursedly principled lot, and so I suspect I will have to content myself with competition at board games." He widened his eyes slightly, and Ronnie bit back an unexpected and unwelcome urge to laugh.

Was he trying to undermine her resistance?

"I thought you were *Pyr*."

"No. I'm *Slayer*, as are my companions here."

"You bleed black instead of red," Ronnie said, guessing that wasn't the only difference between the triplets and Drake.

"How very observant." He opened the cabinet doors on the end table and lifted out a box. "Snakes and Ladders?"

Ronnie nodded, thinking it was both a consistent choice and an incongruous activity. The decor of this apartment looked like something out of *Architectural Digest*, every detail in place, and kids' board games really didn't seem to belong.

Jorge unfolded the board with care.

"Why?" Ronnie asked. He glanced up without understanding. "Why do you bleed black?"

"There's a physiological difference between us. One of the most obvious manifestations is the color of our blood."

"What are the others?"

"Perspective," Jorge said, then handed her the dice. "We have a fundamentally different view of the world."

Ronnie didn't take the dice. "How so?"

"The *Pyr* believe that humans are one of the treasures of the earth, which they are charged to defend. *Slayers* believe that humans are the pestilence that threatens the treasure of the earth itself, and must therefore be exterminated." Jorge smiled and there was dragon in his expression.

"You're going to kill me?"

"Not yet. You're more useful alive, at least for now." He smiled. "Give it nine months."

He'd kill her after this son was born.

What if she wasn't even pregnant?

Ronnie guessed he'd kill her sooner, then.

Jorge held out the dice again, and Ronnie took them, feeling numb and not knowing what else to do.

His thumb changed to a golden dragon talon before her very eyes. She gasped and drew her hand back, unable to keep from doing anything else, and Jorge chuckled, clearly pleased that he'd provoked the reaction he desired.

It was easy to believe he could become a dragon when his eyes glittered as they did then, and even easier to remember the fate of the fifth red and gold dragon shifter. Ronnie seized the dice and rolled, wondering whether it would be smarter to win or lose their game.

Sara gave one last push, just as her OB/GYN directed, and felt her son slip into the world. She fell back against the pillow, panting from her efforts, and Quinn pressed a kiss to her temple. Just like the other three times, he'd stayed with her, holding her hand and whispering reassurance.

Quinn was the Smith of the *Pyr* and was always protective when she drew close to the end of a pregnancy, but there had been something particularly intense about him this fall. He hadn't confided in her, probably because he hadn't wanted to worry her, but Sara was ready to know the truth. She had no doubt that it had something to do with the end of the Dragon's Tail Wars, which the *Pyr*'s prophecy declared would be resolved over the next year. She had no doubt which side she wanted to win, and to her relief, the *Slayers* seemed to already be out of the picture.

Quinn had probably just been worrying.

There was a fluster of activity, then the baby gave a cough and a cry. The attending staff in the delivery room cheered. Sara smiled without opening her eyes.

"Congratulations. Another perfect boy!" Dr. Mulholland said and Sara almost laughed that her doctor was surprised. *Pyr* only had sons, but Sara wasn't going to tell her doctor her partner's secret. "And just as healthy as the others. Blue eyes like his dad and his brothers. You are going to have a handsome bunch of teenagers one of these days." Sara opened her eyes to watch the doctor pass the swaddled boy to Quinn and saw Quinn's proud smile. "Soon you'll have delivered more babies than me, Sara."

Sara laughed despite herself. "No threats like that, please."

Dr. Mulholland gave her a twinkling glance, only now pulling down her mask. "You know what causes it. I've told you before that it can be managed."

"But Quinn was the fifth son in his family."

"Ah, so I'll see you again in the new year." The older woman smiled and shook her head. "You've had no complications and you're young, Sara. If you want to try for another, I'll be right here with you." She shrugged. "It might be nice for you to have a daughter to keep all these sons in line."

"One more, either way, then we're done," Sara said and Quinn nodded. The doctor gave her a thumbs-up and left them to admire their new arrival. The other boys were with their closest neighbors, whose sons were their playmates. That couple had no idea how thick and deep the dragonsmoke barrier was around their home. Quinn had been breathing it for weeks.

"Are you going to tell me his name now?" Quinn teased in a murmur. "I know you chose it a while ago."

"Are you going to tell me what's bothering you now?" she replied. "You don't fool me. Was there a firestorm with this full moon?"

Quinn sobered. "It was an eclipse. A blood moon."

"I suppose if any kind of moon is going to fill the maternity wards, it should be a blood moon," Sara said, then dropped her voice so low that only Quinn would be able to hear her. The staff were cleaning up and making themselves scarce, obviously intending to give the new parents a little privacy. "Was there a firestorm?"

Quinn nodded once and whispered in her ear. "It was Drake's."

"Oh good. I like Drake."

Quinn's gaze searched hers. "Have you received a prophecy about it?"

Sara shook her head. As the seer of the *Pyr*, she often did receive prophecies about firestorms, but not this time. That was why she hadn't been sure there had even been a firestorm. "I've been a little busy the past day or so." Quinn's smile was fleeting. "Why? Is something wrong?"

Quinn flicked a glance at the staff, then whispered in her ear again. "Three *Slayers* attacked and abducted Drake's mate."

Sara was outraged. "But there are no *Slayers* left, only Jorge."

Quinn shook his head and bent low over their new son. "There are suddenly more, all of whom look exactly like Boris Vassily."

Sara caught her breath.

"Two *Slayers* also attacked Erik in Chicago."

"Five new *Slayers*," Sara whispered. "Where did they come from?"

"No one knows." Quinn was grim. "Fortunately Donovan and Delaney were there to help. Donovan had a bad feeling and suggested to Delaney that they be in Chicago for the eclipse."

"I'm glad he did. Is Erik going to be okay?" Sara was relieved when Quinn nodded, then remembered. "Erik and Boris had a blood feud. He killed Boris years ago."

"And somehow that *Slayer* is back." Quinn was grim. "I don't understand it, but something's happening. We should all be together."

Sara felt a moment's panic. "The boys are okay?"

"Yes, I just phoned. All is well, but I'd like us to be together, and with the other *Pyr*."

They'd talked about this possibility as the end of the Dragon's Tail Wars loomed on the calendar and Sara was glad they'd already made a tentative plan. She wasn't glad that they had to use it. She looked at her new son and her heart squeezed. She'd been so sure that the *Pyr* were just finishing up the Dragon's Tail Wars, that Jorge would be killed by one of the others and their futures would be secure. Now she feared anew for Quinn and the boys.

"What happens to them if you lose?" she whispered, fighting against her urge to seize her new son and hold him tightly. "Will they just be like other boys?" Sara was asking whether they would fail to become dragon shifters at all, since that developed at puberty for the sons of the *Pyr*. She couldn't say the alternatives aloud. That her boys might be compelled to become *Slayers* or that they might die along with Quinn were horrific prospects.

Quinn bent and put his lips against her ear. "It won't matter," he murmured so quietly that no one else can hear. "Garrett is the oldest of the young *Pyr* and he's only six."

Sara felt sick and panicky. Her boys wouldn't even grow up if the *Pyr* lost? *Slayers* would hunt them down and slaughter them, and she wouldn't be able to do anything about it. Not without Quinn.

"California?" she mouthed and Quinn nodded.

"I've got a feeling that it's time," he said and she knew that the appearance of these new *Slayers* had changed everything for him.

"Portents are my department," Sara teased. She closed her hand over his when he didn't smile. "You should have told me."

Quinn shook his head. "I didn't want you to worry before the baby was born. I've been making preparations for my trip, though." He forced a smile and raised his voice. "Maybe since the baby came a bit early, you will be able to come along."

Fortunately, Quinn was an artisan blacksmith and traveled often to show his work at art shows. They'd first met at one in Ann Arbor. They'd planned to use his business as a cover story if it was necessary to join the *Pyr* during the last months of the Dragon's Tail War. They'd agreed to travel to Sloane's home in California, following Route 66 from Chicago, and stopping to show Quinn's work at shows along the way. Sloane knew about their plan, and Sara preferred the idea of being at his farm than in a city like Chicago, where Erik had his lair.

"Of course, I will," Sara said in a louder voice, assuming that the nurses would overhear. "It's like this one knew to come a bit early, so we could attend those shows on the west coast as a family. Next year, Garrett will be too busy in school to go to fall art shows and it will be good for the boys to see more of the country."

Quinn smiled with obvious relief. "Route 66, here we come." He stroked his son's cheek, then gave Sara an intent look. "With Garrett, Ewan, Thierry and..."

"Michael," Sara said. She watched Quinn catch his breath, having anticipated that naming their son after his brother would touch him. She worried for a moment that it was too soon, since Michel had returned as a shadow dragon and Quinn had been compelled to kill him.

But Quinn nodded once, his approval clear, and Sara was relieved about one thing, at least.

Niall Talbot, the Dreamwalker of the *Pyr*, was seeking Drake's mate.

It didn't help that Drake was pacing the living room of the apartment Niall shared with Rox, which was located over her tattoo shop in Manhattan. Relaxation was key to dreamwalking, after all. Theo, the leader of the Dragon Legion who seemed to have appointed himself as Drake's second, was standing guard outside the front door of the shop, on the street below, while another of his warriors guarded the back. Two more, whose names Niall hadn't caught, were on the roof, watching for trouble. They were still and intense, these *Pyr*, and Niall was glad to have their protection for his own mate and sons. They breathed dragonsmoke, all of them, weaving it together artfully as they kept a vigilant watch. They were accustomed to working together.

The twins, Kyle and Nolan, were asleep and Rox had stayed with Drake. Niall knew she intended to keep him from being disturbed, as much as she could, but Niall found it hard to ignore Drake's agitation.

The situation made Niall think of possibilities, dire ones. Rox had been snatched during their firestorm, and Niall had been equally agitated, even during those few moments that her safety had been out of his control. Veronica had been abducted by *Slayers* two days before. There were dozens of possibilities of what could have happened to her—or been done to her—in that time, not a one of which helped Niall relax.

That Rox was pregnant again made Niall only more protective than he usually was. That didn't help him relax either. He had to concentrate.

Niall compelled himself to close his eyes and tried to enter the necessary mental state. He felt the bed beneath him and smelled Rox's scent on the sheets. He hovered on the cusp of change, knowing it would sharpen his senses even further. He savored the trickle of power in his body, the faint glow of blue light, and let his mind float wider.

He heard the breathing of his sons, so deep in slumber, and sensed their awareness of each other. He and his twin Phelan had shared that bond once. He listened to Rox, as she offered Drake something to eat or drink, her presence in his lair both familiar and exciting. He heard the low rumble of Drake's voice, then his query to his fellows in old-speak, followed by Theo's low response.

All clear.

Niall felt the sparkle of the dragonsmoke they breathed, seeing it as frost in his current state and hearing it chime as another circuit was closed around the apartment. He returned to Drake's presence and inhaled deeply of the other *Pyr*'s scent. It was faint, more faint than that of modern *Pyr* and less distinctive. When the remainder of the Dragon's Tooth Warriors had been in these times, it had been hard to distinguish their scents. Now that only Drake remained of that company, his scent was still more elusive than Niall would have preferred.

But Drake had been the last to see Veronica.

Niall released his awareness of the physical realm, for it wouldn't help him at this task. He had to be intuitive and impulsive. He had to trust his instincts and follow scents and dreams wherever they led. They might take him to real places, or to imagined ones, but mapping the path of the dreamwalk to the real world was impossible. He might recognize locations, but he was more likely to find truths, to provoke change, to spark reactions, any of which might be more readily pursued in the real world than dreams.

He hoped for clues more than answers, but they were better than nothing at all.

In search of a dream, Niall followed Drake's scent, out into the world and far beyond the island of Manhattan. He felt as he did when he was flying, but it was effortless. There was no wind, although the stars shone high overhead. There was only the conduit of scent, glinting like a moonlit river, guiding him over Drake's recent path.

The scent crossed the streets of a small town in Virginia, over and over again, detailing Drake's obsessive search for some sign of his missing mate. Niall felt his anguish and sympathized, compelling himself to focus on the goal rather than wasting time in empathy. Finding Veronica as quickly as possible would be the best solution.

He concentrated on the location that Drake returned to time and again, the place that ultimately Theo had visited repeatedly. Beneath the scents of the *Pyr* tracking Veronica, there was a faint whiff of *Slayer*, a residue that smelled just like Boris Vassily. He'd been dead for years, but Niall remembered his scent. The scent of Boris was incredibly strong, too, as if it had been emitted in triplicate. Three *Slayers* who looked just like Boris had attacked Veronica's home. That they smelled just like him no matter how deeply Niall explored the scent meant that they *were* Boris, which made no sense at all. Still the evidence couldn't be denied.

Nor could Niall deny that the scent led nowhere. It just stopped cold right at that intersection, about fifty feet above the ground. Niall didn't like the only possible explanation for that. Veronica had been seized by *Slayers* with the power to spontaneously manifest elsewhere.

Slayers who had drunk the Elixir and were identical to Boris, but returned to life. Niall thought of his own battles during his firestorm with the shadow dragons that had been brought back to life with the Elixir—including his dead twin brother—and shuddered inwardly at this development.

The *Pyr* had learned how to ensure that these *Slayers* and shadow dragons stayed dead. Boris's body had been dismembered, incinerated and exposed to all four elements. He should have stayed dead forever. Niall didn't understand how Boris could be returned, never mind multiple times, but he knew enough to dread the implications of this change.

And to fear it. His awareness of the alternate realm slipped, shaken loose by his emotional reaction, and he had to concentrate again, breathing deeply and retracing his path.

Niall followed Drake's trail back to Veronica's home, identifying that trail by the scent of smoke and fire. The townhouse was burned to the ground, as was so often the case with a building exposed to dragonfire, and the burned-out wreckage of a vehicle parked in front of it revealed that her car had also been destroyed by the *Slayers*.

Niall fought a sense that they had wanted to take her alive and was revolted by the possibilities that created.

Drake's scent came out of the townhouse and Niall smelled the *Pyr*'s blood on the pavement. Again, he marveled that Drake hadn't been killed. Was Drake that powerful of a foe, or did the *Slayers* have a more complicated plan? Boris's scent erupted from three different points of the wreckage, meaning that the versions of him had departed the building in different ways.

Their trails led toward the point of abduction, just as Niall anticipated, and one was redolent with the scent of *Slayer* blood. Niall remembered that Drake had wounded one badly, by ripping off his arm.

He wished he knew where the *Slayers* had gone.

Niall floated around the site again, dissatisfied with what he'd learned. Fearing that he had failed and Veronica would be lost, he sought some hint he'd missed. That was when he caught it.

The tendril of a dream. It was faint, almost faded to nothing, so insubstantial that he'd nearly overlooked it.

Niall snatched the end of the dream and climbed onto it, like a magical carpet that would take him to another realm. He followed the dream, pulling himself along it as if he hauled his mind up a rope of glittering silver. He felt the anxiety of the dreamer, and guessed his identity before the dream unraveled in the upstairs bedroom of a nearby house.

He had no idea where it was, much less how close or far it was from the townhouse. Two boys slept there, each in one of the twin beds. One was dreamless and at ease. The other frowned as he fretted over the fate of someone else.

His mother.

Niall felt a surge of triumph that he'd located Veronica's son, Timmy. He hovered nearby, waiting and watching, listening to the course of the boy's subsequent dreams. Timmy dreamed of Drake and recalled his conversation with that *Pyr*. Niall was aware of the relief Timmy had felt in Drake's presence and how his fears had grown once Drake had left him. He might have tried to ease the boy's fears, more out of kindness than anything else, but suddenly he saw a flicker of the dream of another.

It was like a tongue of silver flame in the darkness, a dream wrought of worry but a tentative one, as if the dreamer feared to put a loved one in jeopardy.

Niall made an intuitive leap that it was Veronica, fearing for her son.

Then he made a Dreamwalker leap and seized the flicking tendril of that dream before it disappeared.

Ronnie had the strangest dream.

She was sleeping fitfully, worried about Drake and Timmy. She'd concluded that Timmy must still be with Dashiell. The Pattersons were responsible people and good friends. They'd take care of her son, she was sure of it.

But what was Timmy thinking? Was he afraid? What had he been told? She could easily imagine how shaken he would have been to have come home to find the townhouse burned, the car trashed and her gone. She knew how Mark's disappearance had given her son nightmares and made him fear that the world was an uncertain place.

She didn't want to make any of that worse.

Her conviction of Timmy's bond with Drake wavered then. If Drake was dead, he wouldn't be able to defend Timmy. Even if Drake wasn't dead, what would the Pattersons make of a stranger showing up to talk to Timmy? What if her son was tormented by nightmares again?

It was infuriating to be unable to do anything to protect Timmy or reassure him. Ronnie was sure she'd never sleep, but eventually she did.

Given her thoughts before she fell asleep, she wasn't surprised that she was restless.

She was surprised that she dreamed of a man she'd never seen before. He was a little taller than her but not as tall as Drake. He was muscular, like the boys she'd known in high school who wrestled, and he seemed to be looking directly at her. It was weird to have a dream like this, and Ronnie frowned, wondering whether her captors had given her some kind of drug.

"I'm a friend of Drake's," the man said, his voice low and pleasant.

Ronnie had heard claims like that before. She rolled over and tried to push him out of her mind without success. She felt as if she'd turned her back on a conversation, but that he was still waiting for her to answer him.

There was a blue shimmer at the periphery of her thoughts that was becoming increasingly familiar and Ronnie realized he had to be a dragon shifter. If he was *Slayer*, it would be stupid to ignore whatever he was doing. She granted her attention to him again, only to discover that in his place there was a large amethyst and platinum dragon.

Now that she'd seen a few dragon shifters, she studied him with care. He watched her with the same serene patience as the blond man, and she could see that he was muscled in a similar way.

"Cut yourself," she demanded in her dream and saw his shock. "*Pyr* bleed red."

He bared his dragon teeth in what must have been a smile, then drew the edge of his talon across his own belly. A thin crimson line appeared, then a few drops of red blood seeped from the wound.

If there were more divisions between dragon shifters than *Slayer* and *Pyr*, bad and good, then Ronnie knew nothing of them.

Did she dare to trust him?

"Drake is here." The dragon closed his eyes, and Ronnie wasn't sure what to expect. She was startled when a vision of an urban apartment filled her mind. A petite woman watched worriedly as Drake paced, his anguish so clear that Ronnie's heart twisted. She could see that he'd been injured in her defense because he had bruises and he moved more stiffly than he had before.

Even dragons were vulnerable, then. She drank in the sight of him, relieved that he was alive and worried about her. Her instincts about Drake were right.

But could she trust this dragon?

Or was this vision of Drake some kind of illusion, intended to trick her?

"My mate, Rox," the *Pyr* breathed and Ronnie took another look at the woman. She looked urban and hip, complete with tattoos and piercings, but there was genuine concern in her eyes as she watched Drake.

"We want to rescue you," the *Pyr* continued. It was the strangest thing. Ronnie felt as if he spoke to her, but the words unfurled in her mind, as if she thought them herself.

"I don't know where I am!"

"Maybe we can figure it out. Can you show me everything you've seen?"

"I don't know how."

"Think of it," the dragon whispered. "Fill your mind with it. Review your memories and they will become your dreams. I will follow your dream."

"How can you do that?"

He shifted shape, shimmering blue then becoming a man again. He smiled with a confidence she was coming to associate with the *Pyr*. "I'm Niall Talbot, the Dreamwalker of the *Pyr*. Show me, Veronica, and let's meet in real life." He sobered and she feared whatever he might say. "Drake says he's failed you, just as he failed Cassandra. It's tearing him apart. Whether you want to be with him or not, let us help you."

Ronnie sighed with relief at this proof. It wasn't just a trick.

He really did know Drake. He was calling her Veronica, just as Drake did, and he knew about Cassandra.

She was going to have to trust Niall Talbot and hope for the best.

"My friends call me Ronnie," she said.

"Ronnie it is then," Niall agreed. "Now show me what you've seen."

CHAPTER SEVEN

rake reviewed the notes Niall had made, determined to make some progress with what few clues they had. It was a pretty sparse beginning. "Somewhere in the forest," he read. "A ruined building. The distant sound of traffic." He looked up at Rox and Niall, unable to see what had been accomplished. "There have to be a thousand places like this in America alone!"

"But we know now, thanks to Ronnie, that Jorge is leading these new *Slayers*," Niall said then grimaced. "I don't much like the sound of that."

"Never mind that he wants the baby," Rox added. She folded her arms across her chest, which only drew attention to her own pregnancy. "As if I didn't hate him enough already."

"This has been a waste of time," Drake said, flinging down the notes with frustration. "It tells us nothing!" He paced the room. "I have failed her and the firestorm. I could have been searching for Veronica. I might have found her."

"Not since they've disguised her scent." Niall picked up the notes even as Drake acknowledged that he was right. "We have to work with this. Help me to figure out some questions to ask her, ones that might identify her location more clearly."

Drake sat down again, discontent. "Is she injured?" he demanded.

"I don't think so. She said they were feeding her well enough, though her prison doesn't look that comfortable. She dreamed of the place where she plays board games with Jorge. It's much nicer than her quarters, so at least she's there sometimes."

Drake inhaled sharply and stood up to pace again. His mate

was imprisoned and it was his own fault. He should never have insisted that Theo and the Dragon Legion stay away. He should never have assumed that it would be safe to consummate the firestorm in comparative privacy. He should have welcomed the firestorm in every way and corrected his errors of the past to ensure its smooth course.

He recalled the argument he and Veronica had been having when the *Slayers* attacked and wondered how that might have ended, if they hadn't been interrupted.

What if she didn't want to have his son?

Drake had to believe that she'd just been surprised. He had managed the situation badly, as he so often did when there were confidences to be exchanged and feelings to be discussed.

Her demand that he prove his story by shifting shape in front of her had been a surprise to him. Drake had a persistent sense that Veronica wasn't as vulnerable as she had been when he'd met her four years before.

That made him realize that he really didn't know his mate that well at all.

He'd never thought that an emotional bond between parents mattered very much, that the creation of a son was all that was of import. Certainly Cassandra had never demanded much of him emotionally. She'd welcomed him when he came home, she'd honored him in his household, she'd born his son and raised Theo in Drake's absence.

Would Veronica accept the same relationship? Drake had a feeling she might not, that more than technology had changed in several thousand years.

"Look what I found!" Rox said, returning to the main room with a cell phone in her hand. She tapped at it and Niall grabbed his laptop. In moments, a video was displayed on the small screen, and Drake hovered close to watch. It was created by an amateur, clearly, and one whose hand wasn't very steady.

And no wonder, because the film showed a dragon descending into the forest, crashing through the branches of the trees. He carried another wounded dragon and they were both ruby and brass. They looked just like the ones who had attacked Veronica's home.

"The *Slayers*!" Niall said and leaned closer to the screen.

"Where is this?"

"They don't say," Rox said. "Watch."

The wounded dragon was laid on the ground, the scene illuminated when he began to shimmer on the cusp of change. His wings had been torn off and he was bleeding badly. He shifted to human form while the other dragon watched. The dragon that had carried his body to the forest had his back to the camera.

"Wait," Niall said. "There's a building." He tried to zoom the image as three men who looked exactly like the fallen one came out of a steel door. There was a square of light framed by the open doorway, enough to silhouette the men and give a glimpse of the interior, then the door was slammed shut.

"That's the first one," Drake said, pointing to the one that had a bandage on his shoulder. "I ripped off his arm when he came through the window to attack Veronica."

"Five *Slayers* that look exactly like Boris Vassily," Niall murmured. "And Boris has been dead for years."

The fallen *Slayer* began to shift shape rapidly, rotating between forms. The new arrivals changed shape and watched his agony without much interest.

Niall caught his breath in realization. "Wait a minute. Veronica saw this," he whispered and Drake felt new encouragement. "The armless one made a play for the wingless one, the one who brought the injured one fought him off, the third held down the wingless one and the fourth ate him. The armless one disappeared, then the others finished eating the wingless one alive."

"You're kidding me," Rox said, as if she hoped it to be otherwise but didn't expect as much.

"It is the Elixir. They consume the fallen to suck the last of that vile substance from his marrow." Drake glanced up at Niall. "It must yet be in short supply, which means there may not be a new source."

"Or there's more of them wanting it," Niall said and Drake had to concede that might be the case. "She saw this from exactly the opposite side."

"You can almost make out a building there," Rox noted. "Although it's really overgrown."

The dragon that had carried the wounded one to the site

suddenly breathed dragonfire on him. The orange plume of flame lit up the forest and set some small branches ablaze. The armless one made his move, and the one breathing fire attacked him.

"Yes!" Niall said with excitement. "This is the same incident!"

Drake felt a surge of hope.

The camera wobbled as the person filming the scene gasped aloud as the wounded dragon was devoured. The armless dragon disappeared, then his attacker spun, evidently having heard the cameraman. He exhaled dragonfire into the forest. The trees lit into an inferno of flames and the image became jumbled as the person holding the camera ran for his life.

By the sound of the footsteps, he had a companion with him, and their breathing revealed that they were terrified. They ducked through a hole in a chain link fence and ran down a darkened road, the camera hanging upside down as if forgotten, then threw themselves into a car. The engine started, one of them swore, then the image went black.

"What do you think happened to them?" Rox asked in the silence that followed.

"They must have escaped to have been able to post this," Niall said.

"But there's no reference to where it was," Drake said with frustration. "Why not?"

"Because they're urban explorers," Rox said softly. Both *Pyr* glanced up in confusion at that. She smiled. "They go into abandoned buildings and explore. They're trespassing so they keep it hush-hush. I'll guess that they want to go back again and see if they can get better footage of the dragons."

"Do you have a hobby I don't know about?" Niall asked lightly and Rox laughed.

"Not any more. Remember when we went into the tunnels below the subway?"

"How could I forget? You had a friend, Neo, who knew the subways."

"Right. He wasn't the only one I knew."

Niall gave her a look.

"I dated the other one. You didn't need to know. Let's put this on the big screen. It looks a bit familiar. I might know where it is."

"But you've never been there."

"Not officially," Rox acknowledged. When the film was playing on the large television screen, she tapped a number into her cell phone. "I hope he's home," she managed to say before her features brightened. "Toad! How are you?" She nodded and paced the room, smiling as she listened.

"My wife dated a guy named Toad," Niall muttered good-naturedly. "And I never knew this." He played the video again, eyes narrowed as he searched the background of the image.

"There," Drake said, discerning a window in the darkness. He suspected it was only because of his keen *Pyr* vision that he could see it, and Niall had to stand right beside him for a moment before he saw it, too. "There's a reflection in glass."

"Have you seen it?" Rox asked the person she'd called. Drake tried not to eavesdrop on her conversation, though he wanted to know what she learned. "Well, yeah, I couldn't resist. You'd expect that, given that dragons are involved. Do I think they're real? I don't know. They sure look it." She listened for a minute. "Toad, do you recognize the location? It looks familiar to me, but I never really knew where we were...Yes, I know that was the point." She spun to face Niall, her eyes wide, and Drake felt a frisson of excitement between them. Niall took a step toward his mate. "Really? You're sure?" She reached for the laptop and tapped into the search field on Niall's browser. "I'll bet they're not talking. They must have needed to change their Jockeys." Toad laughed at that but Drake was too busy reading to share his amusement.

Seaview Hospital, Staten Island.

Drake was ready to fly there immediately, but Niall forced him to sit down. He pulled up a map on his laptop and winced at the size of the grounds. He pointed to the current hospital, which still existed, then ran a fingertip over the forest surrounding it. He found a satellite photograph and lined it up over the map. Peaks of old roofs from buildings no longer in use could be seen through the trees.

An abandoned institutional building in the forest, close enough to a road that traffic could be heard. Drake was excited, but Niall indicated the number of buildings that were potential candidates.

"They were lucky to escape," Rox said to Toad, but Drake shook his head.

It hadn't been luck. These two humans could have easily been tracked and destroyed. No. Jorge had let them go.

Why? It wasn't like the *Slayer* to show mercy.

Maybe he had been busy. Drake didn't trust that answer.

Rox kept talking to Toad. "No, I don't really want to meet a real dragon in the dark. I'm not going down there, even for the eye candy," she said with a dismissive laugh. "I'm a mom now, remember. I've got to think of the kids." She laughed again. "You're right, Toad. Niall is too uptight to be into that kind of sneaking around."

Niall glanced up in mock outrage, but Rox grinned at him, unrepentant.

"It just bugged me because I was sure I'd been there before. Uh huh. Uh huh. Maybe there *were* dragons there when we visited that time." She frowned as she listened intently.

Drake listened intently as well, unable to resist temptation.

The women's ward pavilion. That was what Toad said.

Drake leaned close to the screen, narrowing his eyes as he read the script, then put a finger upon the building in question. Niall nodded as Rox ended the call with various good wishes for other humans Drake didn't know.

"Got the map and location," Niall said. "This has got to be it."

Rox's eyes were shining, and Drake knew she hadn't told them everything. "You don't know the best part," she said, perching beside Niall. "It was a hospital, so there are tunnels beneath it, for moving laundry and patients."

"Patients?" Drake asked.

"Corpses," Niall clarified.

Rox was exuberant. "Toad only knows about them vaguely, but Neo took me to Seaview Hospital once."

"Mr. Subway."

"Mr. Tunnel. We only went once because it wasn't urban enough for him, but I remember how to get in."

Niall gave a hoot and pulled Rox down for a quick triumphant kiss.

Drake averted his gaze and scanned their comfortable abode. A city like Manhattan wasn't his choice of a place to live, but there was a feeling within these walls, an intimacy of home and affection. They were a team, Niall and Rox, and worked together not only to help the *Pyr*, but to raise their sons and to ensure each other's happiness.

What would give Veronica happiness? Drake had no idea. He didn't even know how she had earned a living these past four years. He knew almost nothing about her, except that he found her alluring and the firestorm had identified her as his mate.

Drake frowned and wondered for the first time whether the firestorm's spark might not be enough to secure his future with Veronica.

The truth was that she would have no future unless he saved her from Jorge. "We must go this night," he said tersely. "Those who made the film will talk, or be encouraged to do so, and others like this Toad will seek out the place in curiosity. We must retrieve Veronica now to ensure the safety of all."

"Exactly," Niall said, rising to his feet.

"No, no," Drake said. "You must defend your mate and sons. I will go with Theo and some of the Dragon Legion, leaving others here to ensure that Jorge does not retaliate against you. We must outwit him and surprise him in order to defeat him."

"I didn't realize you knew Jorge that well," Rox said, and Drake turned to her with cool confidence born of experience.

"I do not, but he is a viper, and they are all the same."

He did understand vipers, because he had tracked them, studied them and learned their deepest desires. He would defeat this one, using his knowledge against Jorge, using his experience and intuition to find the *Slayer*'s weakness.

And then, once Veronica was safe, he would use those same skills to woo her.

The firestorm did not lie.

The *Pyr* thought of Jorge as a *Slayer*, but he was acting like a viper.

With that realization, Drake understood. He spun slowly, scanning the various displays as the details all made sense.

"He *wants* us to come," he whispered and felt Niall straighten. "It's too easy because it's a taunt. He took Veronica to this place of comfort because he intended to beguile her. He has failed in that and means to undermine her resistance. He let those humans live so that this clue to his location would be revealed."

"But why?" Niall asked.

"I will guess that he intends to slaughter me before my mate to dishearten her."

"Then you'll stay away," Rox said, getting to her feet in turn. "You'll ignore the taunt."

Drake turned his gaze upon her and when she took a step back, he knew she saw the avidity of the dragon in his expression. Hunting and destroying vipers was what he did, and the stakes were higher than they had ever been before.

"On the contrary," he said softly. "We will do as he desires. If we fail to take the bait, it is the way of the viper to sharpen the hook." Drake surveyed the details again, reviewing all the vipers he had destroyed, seeking the one telling clue in this one's scheme. "He taunts us, which means he has prepared a trap. He will know his temporary lair far better than we can, and there will be snares to ensure his triumph."

"You have a plan," Niall said, his gaze assessing.

Drake nodded. "He hopes to draw us into his lair because he knows it, but we shall draw him out. The surprise will even the odds." He nodded at Niall. "That might be enough."

"And if it isn't?" Rox asked.

"Then I will be killed in the defense of my mate and son, and the *Pyr* will assume the responsibility of raising them." Drake smiled thinly. "But I do not intend to die just yet."

Ronnie was terrified that she'd inadvertently reveal her dream of the *Pyr* Dreamwalker to Jorge. He watched her so closely she was almost certain that he couldn't be fooled.

But she had to try.

The next night when she was collected for a visit to his apartment, she counted the number of steps she took. That might help Niall and Drake to find her. She tried to keep track of the turns they took as well, committing them to memory as well as she was able.

She knew when she arrived at Jorge's apartment because the air was warm.

When her blindfold was removed, though, Jorge was standing right in front of her. Ronnie's heart leapt for her throat and he smiled, as if she might make a nice snack. "You're nervous," he said, his voice low with suspicion. "Why?"

"I'm not nervous at all."

His eyes narrowed. It was interesting that she found it impossible to forget that Jorge could shift shape to become a dragon, yet she had struggled to accept the same truth about Drake. "Your heart is beating more quickly than usual."

Ronnie rolled her eyes. "Probably because my stomach is off," she lied. Inwardly, she marveled that she was giving him attitude, but she wasn't the woman she'd been when she met Mark. Ronnie realized with surprise that she was more accustomed to making choices, being in control, and dealing with the consequences.

Jorge couldn't hide the gleam of satisfaction that lit his eyes, or maybe he didn't try. "The food doesn't suit you?"

"Maybe I picked up something."

He practically smirked. "Yes, maybe you have." Ronnie wished these dragons would stop making references to her being pregnant. It wasn't even possible for her to have conceived this quickly!

"I'm not pregnant," she insisted.

"Don't you want a son?"

"No, not particularly."

Jorge smiled. "Then this provides the perfect solution. You'll bear the child and I'll keep him." She regarded him warily, distrusting how he smiled. "You do know that the *Pyr* just use human women as breeders, don't you? Either Drake will take the child and abandon you or I will, and trust me, I'll put him to much better use."

"That's disgusting," Ronnie murmured, hoping she wasn't pregnant.

Even though being so would let her live nine months more, which might give her more opportunities to be rescued. Surely Drake and his fellow *Pyr* wouldn't bother to rescue her just to abandon her after the child was born.

If there even *was* a child. Ronnie's stomach churned.

"What's your poison tonight?"

Ronnie glanced up and Jorge's smile widened. He had a lot of teeth. "Excuse me?"

"Which game shall we play?"

"Monopoly," she said on a whim.

"My favorite," Jorge agreed easily. "There's nothing like owning the best real estate to put me in a good mood."

He succeeded in that with alarming speed. He bought every property he could and in no time had two sides of the board under his control. He built steadily, chortling like a kid whenever Ronnie had to pay up for landing on one of his properties. She might have let him win, just because she wanted to see what a better mood looked like for Jorge, but he suddenly slid four properties, with their houses across the board to her.

"So you have a chance," he said with a smile. "I like a little challenge." He rolled the dice and bought Park Place.

"So," he asked, his tone oddly conversational. "I suppose you just met Drake during your firestorm."

Ronnie eyed her opponent. "Why do you suppose that?"

"It's usually how it works, from what I understand."

"Haven't you ever had a firestorm?"

Jorge laughed shortly. "Not in the cards for me, I'm afraid." He put a hand on his chest. "I have to make do with self-admiration."

Slayers didn't have firestorms, then. That was good to know. It followed that even if Ronnie hadn't seen Drake wounded and bleeding red blood, she could have been sure he was *Pyr*, just because they'd had a firestorm.

That meant he was one of the good dragons.

"You seem to get by," she dared to say and Jorge laughed, as if surprised.

"So, you met at the first spark of the firestorm, and its heat so overwhelmed you with a burning desire that you consummated it immediately." There was mockery in his tone. "I have to tell you that it's not a special story, not for the *Pyr*."

"Actually, Drake and I met years ago." Ronnie didn't know why she told him that, because he was obviously fishing for information, but his attitude irked her into telling him more than she should have done.

"Really? Now, that *is* different." Jorge applauded lightly. "Kudos to you for keeping the story fresh. Did he ravish you then, and just come back for more?"

Ronnie bristled at his mocking tone. "Drake was a perfect

gentleman when we first met. I'd been thinking of him ever since."

"Interesting." Those blue eyes gleamed with hunger. "How did you meet?"

"It doesn't matter."

"Maybe not, but we dragons do love our little secrets." Jorge winced. "Humans don't always think they're so little, though." He lifted a hand. "Maybe it's better that you had your night of passion then were separated. Otherwise, you might have learned something that you found...unpalatable."

"Drake has never lied to me."

"Oh, then he told you when you first met that he was *Pyr* and a dragon shifter?"

Ronnie couldn't hold Jorge's gaze. "Of course not."

Her opponent leaned over the board. "And did he tell you that satisfying the firestorm would leave you pregnant?"

Ronnie concentrated on rolling the dice.

"Yes, they do tend to omit that detail, in the heat of the moment, so to speak," Jorge murmured. "Of course, you've been a single mother for years..."

"I am *not* a single mother," Ronnie snapped, having confronted that particular conclusion more than enough times in recent years. "I'm a *widow* with a son."

Jorge shrugged. "But you still have to do everything, don't you? Whatever the history, all jobs fall to you when you're the only one parenting. I'm sure you aren't thrilled at the prospect of doing it all alone again." He winced. "At your age."

"I'm still young enough to take care of a baby," Ronnie retorted. "And there's nothing saying that Drake would have left me alone anyway, especially if you hadn't sent those other dragons to interfere."

Jorge used his get-out-of-jail free card. "I guess you'll never know," he said, as if rueful when Ronnie knew he couldn't be. "Even though he abandoned his first wife and son. I suppose that history doesn't *always* repeat itself."

"Cassandra and Theo died." Ronnie defended Drake, even as she wondered. Could there be truth in Jorge's story?

"Of course, they did! Everyone dies sooner or later. Well, mortals and *Pyr* do anyway. The thing is, he walked away from them, doing his duty to the *Pyr*, and never returned." Jorge met

Ronnie's gaze, feigning innocence. "Or did he forget to tell you that part, too?"

She dropped her gaze again. It couldn't be true. Drake would be a responsible father, and she knew he had loved Cassandra. He hadn't told her so, of course, but she'd seen his grief.

Jorge tsk-tsked. "These *Pyr* and their secrets. Come on, tell me, how *did* you meet? Drake isn't exactly a social animal."

"You're so determined to paint him in a bad light, but I know better," Ronnie said, losing her temper a bit. "Drake helped to find out what had happened to my husband, when he went missing and no one would tell me a thing. It's because of Drake that we even knew what had happened to Mark. For that, I will be eternally grateful to Drake and his men."

Jorge sat back to consider her. "Well, that does sound laudable." He pursed his lips and averted his gaze. "Unless, of course, he really didn't have to look."

"What's that supposed to mean?"

"That you are an attractive woman, Ronnie, and that Drake has been without the pleasure of a woman's company for a long time. Much longer than you realize." Jorge seemed to savoring a private joke, but Ronnie glared at him.

"By his own choice. That's honorable."

"But still." Jorge smiled and Ronnie trusted him even less than usual, which wasn't much at all. "If no one could find your husband, how did Drake find him? And was this Mark dead before or *after* Drake found him?"

Ronnie leapt to her feet. "How dare you make such an insinuation!"

"I'm just asking," Jorge said mildly. "Because you don't really know, do you?"

Ronnie tipped the Monopoly board so that all of the pieces scattered, then strode to the door of the apartment. "I'd like to go back to my room, please. The company is lacking a certain charm."

Jorge shrugged and gestured to his minions, then started to pick the pieces from the floor and pack them away. He moved methodically, as if he had all the time in the world, and Ronnie knew he was satisfied with himself.

He'd planted seeds of doubt in her mind, and he knew it. As

much as Ronnie would have liked to have argued otherwise, she really didn't know how Drake had found Mark or what condition her husband had been in when Drake found him. She really didn't know Drake's motives, or really, that much of his history. She certainly didn't know any of his secrets.

She knew, however, that Drake could become a dragon at will and slaughter any man he so chose.

And that was exactly what Jorge had wanted her to remember. One of the triplets blindfolded her and she felt that being plunged into darkness was a good metaphor for her current situation.

"Trust is a precious commodity, Ronnie," Jorge whispered just as she was being led to the door. "Don't be too quick to share it with those who don't reciprocate in kind."

Had she been too quick to trust Drake?

What else hadn't he told her?

The network of tunnels below the abandoned section of the hospital was more familiar than Drake would have preferred. The isolation and the smell of rot was consistent with the holes chosen by all the vipers he had ever hunted.

It was raining on the evening they selected for their attack. The cold October rain made the worn concrete surfaces slick and more dangerous than they usually would have been. There was rebar sticking out of the floors and walls where concrete had crumbled. Beneath the smell of mold and rot, of garbage dumped and toxic chemicals abandoned, there was a faint scent of Veronica.

She was here.

Her scent was warm, which meant she yet lived.

He exchanged a nod with the other three *Pyr*, each of whom went his own way as planned. Theo had asked for volunteers from the Dragon Legion. Kristofer and Arach, who were familiar to Drake, had come, which pleased him. They were good fighters and reliable *Pyr*. Three others, Rhys, Hadrian and Kade, were watching over Timmy. A fourth, Reed, was unknown to Drake, although Theo had assigned him to defend Timothy. Drake liked that *Pyr*'s resolute manner. The plan was that Jorge and his fellows would be flushed out with a fire set by the Dragon Legion in the tunnels beneath the building, and it would be left to Drake to rescue Veronica.

Drake found the spot in the forest where the dragons had devoured their fellow fairly easily, because the growth was charred from the dragonfire. That carried a faint scent of *Slayer*. He stood in the sheltered shadows of the trees and studied the spot while remaining hidden. He could discern the building on the far side, its walls and windows disguised by darkness and rampant vegetation. The roof had crumbled on one side, and most would have assumed it vacant. Drake surveyed the building with care. Only a *Pyr* could have seen sufficient detail at this distance, and Drake took his time to choose his point of attack.

There would be no time to correct a mistake.

He spied the steel door and knew from the smell of it that it was new. There was a faint residue of *Slayer* upon it, as if they had become sloppy in disguising their scent.

Or as if they intended to tempt him to enter that way. Drake would not make such a foolish choice.

He scanned the second story and almost missed the detail he sought, so concealed was it by grime and growth.

There were bars installed across a window, one of the few that seemed to still have intact glass. The bars were so perfect and similar that Drake recognized they were recently installed. The glass of that window was tinted, reflecting rain and forest like a black mirror, which meant he couldn't anticipate exactly what he would find behind it.

Veronica, certainly, but perhaps more than that.

He smelled the first match struck and then a prickle of awareness within the building. Jorge had heard it as well, Drake would wager, and he was glad they had chosen to light the fires with matches instead of dragonfire.

Jorge might guess that it was *Pyr* taking his bait, but let him learn the truth of it as late as possible. Drake didn't imagine the *Slayer* would be that readily fooled. He had baited a trap and was waiting for the *Pyr* to arrive. Drake smelled the gasoline ignite and felt the soaked cloth flare into flames.

Drake heard the *Pyr* stumbling in the tunnels, as if they were clumsy and human, lost and perhaps drunk. They joked with each other, like teenagers bent on making mischief, and Drake wondered whether Jorge believed the ruse.

Then he saw a flash of orange dragonfire in the basement of the building. It shone through slits in steel shutters that were locked over windows, and Drake understood that Jorge, like so many vermin, had chosen to secret himself in the earth.

He heard a roar and the hair stood up on his neck as his fellows shifted shape to fight. The building shook with the impact of their blows. Drake summoned his own change, lunging across the clearing as the blue shimmer raced over his skin. He bounded into the scrub on the far side and leapt up the side of the building, ripping the bars from the window with savage force and casting them aside. He shattered the window with a mighty swing of his tail and heard a woman gasp.

He saw Veronica and felt her relief when she recognized him, just before he heard humans in the forest behind him.

Trespassers, or urban explorers as Rox had called them.

Probably with cameras.

Drake exhaled in exasperation, guessing that the unexpected presence of humans might complicate events. Still, he had to focus. There were sudden footsteps outside the door to Veronica's prison and Drake beckoned to her to hurry. She was already running toward him and leapt into his embrace, the evidence of her trust enough to make his heart thunder. He spun immediately and took flight, propelling himself off the building wall with a mighty kick, even as he heard a *Slayer* swear behind him.

"Drake!" Veronica whispered and laid her cheek on his chest as he soared high. "I was afraid you were dead."

"Not yet," he muttered, flying high like an arrow shot at the stars. There would be pursuit and it would come soon.

"Don't say that!"

It was only as he held Veronica close that Drake wondered whether carrying her would hamper his ability to fight in her defense.

Drake had come for her, at no small risk to himself.

That said something about his reliability and determination to defend her. Ronnie ran her hands over his scaled hide, feeling his power as his muscles flexed. He flew straight up, his wings beating hard against the air. She was amazed by how quickly he moved, and how effortless he made his flight appear.

She was tucked under his chin, nestled against the pounding of his heart and sheltered from the cold rain. His scales were as dark as charcoal and he could have been made of chunks of night sky. They gleamed though, like black pearls. She felt how the scales layered over each other, making a coat of protective mail, and fingered the spurs on the bottom of each one.

Her dragon had thorns.

He was warm, too, which prompted her to curl against him. It was easy to recall how deliberate a lover he had been and even easier to want to survive this to make love with him again.

His wings were black and leathery, and their span was massive. His coloring made his dragon look to have been forged out of black pearls and iron, a massive sculpture come to life. His talons were a deep red, reminding her of iron heated at the forge and his eyes were the same inky dark hue as they were in real life. The iris was a vertical slit, instead of a round dot, but still there was something recognizable of Drake in the dragon.

She recalled how resolute he could be and how she felt his anger like a tangible force. There was something recognizable of the dragon in Drake, too.

She had so much to tell him and no notion of where to start. He had to know what she'd told Niall, but Ronnie wasn't sure.

She started with essentials.

"Jorge says he wants the baby," she confessed and felt Drake nod.

"I know." He spoke quickly then, as if in a hurry. "He is a viper, Veronica, much like the viper that killed your husband."

"I thought Jorge was a *Slayer*."

Drake was dismissive of the distinction. "In these times, wickedness has a different name. No matter the name, he is evil and thrives upon sowing doubt into the minds of others. He would turn you into his ally, convincing you that I am your foe. He would undermine whatever faith you might have in me and draw you into his scheme."

Jorge *had* tried to do just that. It was reassuring that Drake understood him so well.

She might have said as much, but Drake hurried on. Ronnie had never heard him speak so quickly or so much, so she kept silent and listened.

Time must be short for whatever he had to confide in her.

What did he anticipate?

"I erred in not telling you of the import of the firestorm." There was regret in his tone that made her want to forgive him. "I erred in not asking for your agreement in conceiving our son. I forgot that times have changed and I was overwhelmed by the fury of the firestorm. I am sorry, Veronica, and I would spend the rest of my days in seeing that mistake repaired."

Ronnie had to say it. "He said you killed Mark, that that's how you found him so readily."

She felt the surge of fury in Drake like a heat wave and when he looked down at her, his eyes were colder than they had ever been. "A viper will tell any lie necessary," he said with disgust, and she knew his anger was directed at Jorge.

It was interesting that she found it easier to read his reactions when he was in dragon form.

Or maybe she was getting to know Drake a little better. She'd thought him impassive and inscrutable once, but she was learning to detect the signs of his emotions. It didn't hurt that he seemed to invariably be on the side of honor and justice.

That was familiar and welcome.

In fact, Ronnie was reassured by his outrage. He would only have been so angry if Jorge had lied. "I didn't really think it could be true. I didn't think you had ever lied to me."

"I have failed to tell you *all* of the truth, for we have had little time for such confidences. I would improve upon my record."

"Starting now?"

"One never knows how matters will unfold," Drake said grimly. "Your husband was killed by a viper, much like this one, a malicious worm spewing his toxin into the world in the hope of gaining men to his side. Your husband battled him to his very last, and there is no more noble death than that."

Ronnie nodded. She spared a glance to the ground, now so far away, and held a little tighter to her dragon. Were there more dragons below? She thought so, although it was hard to pick their figures out of the darkness in the rain. She saw several plumes of fire and guessed that there were two pairs battling in the air. The building where she'd been imprisoned was in flames and she could hear sirens drawing closer.

"His death *could* be said to have been my fault," Drake admitted. "For I failed to kill that viper when first I hunted him. I was caught under his spell, and he did much evil before I could finish what I had once begun."

"And Cassandra? Did you truly abandon her?"

"Not by choice," he admitted, acknowledging the truth in the charge. "I left reluctantly, to do the service I owed." That was familiar to Ronnie, too: Mark had never wanted to leave when he was going to ship out, but he had believed in fulfilling his duty and in serving the greater good. That was the way of honor and justice. Ronnie liked that Drake had that trait in common with Mark. "That viper's spell held me captive until long after Cassandra had died. I cannot undo that she and my son never knew of my fate."

Ronnie thought of all the days and nights she'd been uncertain of Mark's whereabouts, or even whether he survived and wasn't nearly sure she was ready to sign up for that life again.

Drake's tone turned suddenly urgent. "Trust in the firestorm, Veronica. Unlike me, it never errs. That it has chosen you as my destined mate means that there is promise in our match. I know that to be so. I want *you* to know that is so, to have no shred of doubt, and to use that confidence to obstruct the charm of a viper."

Her grip tightened upon him at the implication beneath his words. "But you just saved me."

Drake shook his head. "I have stepped into his trap, but I did so to confide this truth in you." He cast a glance downward and his eyes narrowed. Ronnie looked down to find a furious gold and topaz dragon flying straight toward them very quickly, and she clutched at Drake in fear.

"And now comes the moment that I shall pay the price for provoking Jorge's wrath." His voice dropped low again, even as she realized the dragon in pursuit was Jorge in his other form. "Remember, Veronica. Remember and believe. He is powerless if there is no soil for his venomous seed to take root."

The thing was that Jorge didn't look very powerless to Ronnie at all.

"But..."

"He will let you live, because he wants the child."

"And you?"

Drake smiled, revealing a great many dragon teeth. "I shall have to earn the right to survive this night." He lowered his voice to a rumble, and Ronnie felt his words in the vibration of his chest as much as she heard them. "All is not necessarily as it appears."

Ronnie caught her breath, but Drake spun in mid-air. He held her fast against his chest with one great claw, even as he dove down toward Jorge. Clearly, she was going to have a front-row seat to this dragonfight. She could see the gleam of Jorge's cold blue eyes closing fast and saw straight down his gullet when he opened his mouth.

She hoped Drake wouldn't drop her into that maw, with all those sharp yellow teeth.

The *Slayer* emitted a plume of dragonfire, shooting it directly at them, but Drake elegantly moved aside so that it blew past him. The flames crackled and snapped, looking like the eruption of a volcano. Little sparks loosed themselves from the main torrent of fire to glow against the night then wink out.

Before Jorge could stop breathing fire, Drake darted down and seized the *Slayer*'s tail. He sank his teeth into it and tore the flesh with a vicious gesture. Ronnie saw the wound, up close and personal. Jorge howled as the end of his tail was torn off, and Drake flung it downward, leaking black blood.

Drake spat the residue from his mouth and Ronnie smelled the vileness of that black blood. She felt a drop of it burn the back of her hand where it fell. Drake roared and snatched at Jorge's genitals with his spare claw, ripping open the flesh. Jorge bellowed and belched flames again, snatching suddenly for Ronnie. She felt the golden talon slide through her hair, then Drake rolled in the air, turning his somersault into a dive.

Jorge, of course, was fast behind him.

Breathing fire.

Ronnie held on for dear life.

CHAPTER EIGHT

loane returned home from Chicago, exhausted.

There was nothing like healing other *Pyr* to wear him right out. There was an emotional component to the best healing practices, a need for him to pour his own energy into the treatment of the wound. Erik had been torn up pretty badly, and it hadn't helped that the leader of the *Pyr* was a bad patient.

Erik never wanted to rest or take a break, especially when there was fighting to be done and *Slayers* on the rampage. In a way, Sloane couldn't blame him for that. In another, he wished Erik would learn to delegate a bit more. It would have been far better for the older *Pyr* to have rested, rather than characteristically pace the floor.

Maybe Erik's determination to be fighting as soon as possible would help facilitate his healing. Sloane had grown tired of arguing about it and had left Chicago, surrendering Erik to Eileen's care.

His healing had begun, and she was more accustomed to charming him into appropriate behavior. Sloane had too much to do to linger where he wasn't needed.

It was late by the time he got his truck out of the paid parking at the airport and drove home. There were a ton of messages and texts on his phone, but he needed some down time to recover his balance. Whatever battles the *Pyr* were fighting on this night, they could fight without him.

Sloane found the gentle roll of the land reassuring and took his time, savoring the sense that he returned to his refuge as well as his lair. He indulged himself in a memory of that hot night with Sam and wished he hadn't made her so angry.

He knew exactly what would be the best down time—another night with her, exploring and pleasing each other.

He wondered how—or if—he could make things right again. He could accept her terms, ask no questions and make no emotional demands.

He could apologize for researching her acquisition of the house, though he didn't think it was wrong to check on new neighbors. He certainly hadn't meant to offend her. Maybe tarot card readers thought that people should just all trust each other and get along. It wasn't a bad idea, but people certainly didn't always turn out to be trustworthy.

He could cover his tattoo, if that put her concerns at ease.

Sloane parked the truck in the garage, then walked back to the shop. He had a faint sense that something was wrong, but couldn't see anything amiss. The alarm system registered no entries since he'd left. The greenhouses were intact and the automated watering system was on, right on time, the water rising from the beds to fill the greenhouses with a faint mist. He walked through the rows of herbs behind the greenhouses, savoring the scent of the rosemary and lavender and the feel of the earth beneath his boots. His dragonsmoke boundary was intact and still resonant, barely faded during his absence.

To Sloane's surprise, he caught a whiff of Sam's perfume on the front porch of his own house and his body responded with immediate enthusiasm. He wondered when she'd come to his door—then he wondered why.

Maybe she'd wanted to make up. Maybe she'd been hot again. That was more than distracting and he turned to stare across the fields at her house.

Was that a light at one window? It looked like a candle flickering. Maybe he'd go over and check.

First, he needed a shower and something to eat. He could hardly argue his case when he looked as he did.

Filled with new purpose, Sloane unlocked the door and strode into his home, entering the code into the alarm system by rote. Everything looked as it should, but he had a sudden sense that something was wrong.

Very wrong.

He locked the door behind himself and took the stairs two at a time to the basement. Sloane had upgraded, at considerable expense and in almost complete secrecy, the laboratory that had long been in his basement. In his quest to isolate this virus and create an antidote, he had added new equipment that he'd never needed before for his herbal cures, as well as containment for biohazards. He'd implemented protocols for containing dangerous toxins, which was part of the reason that only *Pyr* were permitted into his house: they couldn't catch the virus.

There was a glass wall opposite the base of the stairs, the first barrier and airlock before the lab. There was a hum of the generator that kept the reverse air pressure constant and the lights were dim. The control panel showed that the door had been sealed since before his departure, but even through the protective barriers, Sloane could see the broken glass on the floor of the lab. He leaned against the glass, unable to believe his eyes. Everything inside the lab itself was broken, shattered, stomped, torn or burned.

His lab had been trashed and the fact that no one had passed through its door made it easy to guess whom.

A *Slayer* who had drunk the Elixir.

Sloane suited up in a hurry and tapped his toe with impatience as he worked his way through the airlocks to the lab itself. Finally, he was inside. It was before the line of refrigerators that he was assailed by one pungent punch of *Slayer* scent.

Jorge.

Sloane guessed the truth then. The seal that he'd left intact on the fridge was broken, which was bad news. He opened the fridge, fearing that he knew exactly what he'd find.

Or more correctly, what he *wouldn't* find.

It was no consolation to be right. The vial of infectious blood, the sample from which he was trying to isolate the Seattle virus, was gone.

As if it had vanished into thin air.

Jorge must have spontaneously manifested inside Sloane's lab, just to steal it. Given that Jorge had been the one to introduce this plague to Seattle in the first place, there couldn't be a good reason for him to need more of the virus.

Plus, he'd evidently known that Sloane would be gone, which meant Jorge knew about the *Slayers* who had attacked Erik. Maybe he'd even sent them. Maybe the whole point of the attack had been injuring Erik badly enough that Sloane had to leave California to tend him.

Sloane didn't even want to think about why Jorge wanted more of that virus.

How was he even going to be able to find a cure, without having a sample to test against? His research was completely stymied by this. He had a back-up of his notes and hoped that was intact, but without the virus to test against, he'd never know if any antidote worked.

And he had no idea how he'd get another sample. The first had been collected by luck and bravado, before the officials had mustered their resources and put containment measures in place. It would be much tougher to get another now.

Deeply frustrated, Sloane pulled out his phone and called Erik, feeling more than sick over the tidings he had to confide.

The phone was ringing when he wondered whether Sam had been at the door while Jorge had been in the house. Terror slid through him and he knew he had to check that she was okay.

He didn't trust Jorge not to take more than his due, after all.

He updated Erik quickly as he ran to Sam's house and ended the call in her driveway.

Sam nearly jumped out of her skin when someone hammered on her door. She sat bolt upright at the noise, her heart hammering. Her mind was filled with memories of Nathaniel and there were wet tears on her cheeks. For a moment she wasn't sure where she was.

"Sam!" a man shouted. "Are you there? Are you all right?"

Sloane!

Relief flooded through Sam, then concern as he kept knocking hard. It sounded like he was going to come through the door.

"Sam!" he called again, his urgency making her heart leap.

"I'm coming!" Sam hurried to her front door, wiping her cheeks as she went. Last thing she remembered, she'd been drilling herself on the meanings of the individual tarot cards with a new reference book. The clock in the kitchen told her that she must have dozed off, because it was later than she remembered. Thank goodness the candle she'd lit was in a glass votive.

She unlocked the door to find Sloane looking agitated. There was a shimmering blue light around him, like an aura, but when Sam blinked, it disappeared. She must have imagined it. Relief flooded his features and he surveyed her quickly, as if to prove to himself that she was all right.

"What's wrong?"

"I just got home. I thought maybe you'd been hurt." He shoved a hand through his hair, leaving it disheveled. He looked tired and his shirt was wrinkled. She knew he noticed the tracks of her tears, because his voice softened. "Are you all right?"

"Fine," Sam said, folding her arms across her chest. There was no way she could confide in him right now, not with those memories so bright in her mind and her heart aching as if it had been shredded before her eyes.

It pretty much had. There was a lump in her throat and Sam felt vulnerable, which she didn't like one bit.

Sloane seemed to recognize her reaction because he took a step back. He pinched the bridge of his nose and took a steadying breath. "Sorry I disturbed you. Long flight." He might have walked away, but Sam did appreciate his concern.

And she wanted him to linger.

"Why did you think something was wrong?"

He gave her an intent look. "Someone broke into my place. I was afraid he might have come here next."

Sam supposed it was reasonable to assume that the intruder was male, as most burglars were, but it sounded almost as if Sloane knew who it had been.

That was crazy, though. She was tired and making stuff up. "Was it last night?"

Sloane met her gaze, a question in his eyes.

"I saw lights at your house. They came on then went off again just a few moments later. I figured you had to have an alarm system..."

"I do."

"Well, it didn't go off. So, I thought maybe you'd just come home."

"No." He turned as if he'd leave and Sam kept talking, just to have him stay a little longer.

"I had a funny feeling, so I walked over today, but it just looked like you weren't home."

Sloane gave her a steady look. "Is that the only reason you came over?"

It was the best opening she was likely to get. Sam took a deep breath. "No. I owe you an apology," she admitted. "I'm sorry that I reacted so strongly. If you have a tattoo, it's your business, not mine."

Sloane shook his head and looked down at his shoes, but not fast enough to hide the twinkle in his eyes. Sam's heart leapt, because she suspected he *was* giving her a second chance.

"Damn," he muttered. "I was hoping you were hot again."

Sam laughed despite herself, glad that he didn't seem to be holding a grudge. She leaned in the doorway. There was something in his manner that tempted her to flirt with him. "Come to think of it, maybe I am a bit warm. Would you like to come in and talk about it?"

"Talk?" Sloane echoed, the sparkle in his eyes indisputable. He braced a hand on the door frame and leaned closer, his amusement clear. "What about no confessions, no questions, and no commitment?"

"Okay, so we can find something other to do than talk," Sam said, smiling back at him. The air warmed between them and Sloane lifted a hand to wind a tendril of her hair around his fingertip. His eyes glowed, just the way they had that first day. Sam felt alive, admired, aroused, and didn't want the moment to end.

Sloane's cell phone, which was in his hand, gave an alert. He flicked a glance downward at it, clearly a habit, but then frowned at the text message. He excused himself and read it, his expression telling Sam that it wasn't good news.

"Something wrong?" she asked.

Sloane sighed. "Only that as much as I'd love to take you up on that offer, I have to go."

"You said you just had a long flight. You must be tired."

"That and now, I've got to catch another flight." His expression was rueful and if anything, he looked more tired. "Chicago, then New York."

"It would have been easier to go from one to the other."

"If I'd known this morning that I had to go to New York." He shrugged, even as Sam wondered what kind of emergencies could make him hurry across the country twice in rapid succession. "Isn't that what friends are for?"

"Can I help?"

Sloane smiled a little, then bent to brush his lips across hers. The fleeting touch left Sam tingling and hungry for more. "That would require a confession, I think."

Sam felt herself blush a bit, but she knew he was teasing her. "Maybe I wouldn't mind knowing a few of your secrets."

"Maybe you're better off *not* knowing them," he replied, to her surprise. She opened her mouth to ask, but Sloane dropped a warm fingertip to her lips. "I'll call you when I get back," he promised. "We can pick up right here." She had no chance to agree because he kissed her more thoroughly.

Sam wound her arms around his neck, wanting to give him something to remember—or a reason to hurry back. Sloane caught her close and deepened his kiss even as Sam knotted her fingers in his hair. She rose to her toes, opening her mouth to him, and Sloane groaned even as he pressed her between himself and the wall. He felt so good that Sam was wondering whether it was possible to convince him to stay.

Then he lifted his head and smiled down at her with satisfaction. "You make a persuasive argument," he mused and Sam smiled.

"How *did* someone break into your house without setting off the alarm?"

Sloane's gaze slid away from hers. "I guess he knew what he was doing." He eased his fingertip across her cheek, leaving tingles in its wake. His expression was very serious, though. "I'm glad you didn't decide to go and check. Promise me that you won't, if it happens again."

"Will it?"

"Probably not."

"Was anything taken or damaged?"

"It doesn't matter," he said with a grimness that indicated it did. "Not now." He looked worn out again, and Sam wanted to make him smile before he left.

She kissed the corner of his mouth.

But Sloane's gaze darkened and his voice dropped to a whisper. "I wish I could stay, Sam. Don't make it harder to leave than it is, please."

The entreaty tore at her heart. Sam kissed him again to leave him in no doubt of his welcome and stepped back. Sloane turned to walk home, resigned to whatever errand he had to run. "Thanks for checking on me," she said.

He cast her a smile. "I couldn't do otherwise."

She liked that he was protective, but sensed there was a lot he wasn't telling her. She bit her lip, then dared to ask: "Why a caduceus?"

"Is that a question?"

"You know it is."

"Are you changing the terms of our agreement?"

"Maybe a little."

A challenging glint lit Sloane's eyes. "Okay, I'll meet you halfway then. It's because I'm the Apothecary."

Sam shook her head that she would have confused the two. "But it's not the Rod of Asclepius..."

"No, it's not." Sloane hesitated before leaving her porch and she sensed that he was deciding whether to confide more in her. She was glad when he glanced back, and even more glad when he spoke again. "'It is said the wand would wake the sleeping and send the awake to sleep.'"

"That sounds like a quote."

"It is. William Godwin, *Lives of the Necromancers*."

Sam took an involuntary step back. "Necromancers? Doesn't that mean raising the dead?"

Did he believe in that kind of nonsense?

Sloane sighed theatrically, making Sam wonder whether he was just teasing her. "Sometimes it feels that way. Mostly the quote reminds me of my father." He saluted her with his fingertips, then strode into the night, before she could ask him anything else.

Not that it mattered. His answer had just left Sam with more questions than she'd had before. She folded her arms across her chest and watched Sloane go, even more interested in him than she'd been before. The man had a gift for fascination, that much was clear. Sam had to wonder whether she'd ever figure him out.

She certainly wasn't going to stop trying.
William Godwin.
Sloane had given her a clue.

Drake was glad to see that Theo had chosen competent warriors for this mission. Two *Slayers* had erupted from the burning building, each identical to the other with their ruby and brass scales and trailing red plumes. He recognized his allies by their colors: Theo was carnelian and gold in his dragon form and his scales glittered in the rain. Kristofer was peridot and gold, while Arach was aquamarine and silver. Reed was smoky quartz and silver.

Theo and Reed had engaged one of the *Slayers*, while Kristofer and Arach fought the other. Drake didn't mind those odds at all and was convinced that he could defeat Jorge, even with Ronnie in his grasp.

Certainly his reactions were more vehement than they might have been if he had battled alone.

Jorge raced after him, his stream of dragonfire stinging Drake's tail. Drake turned sharply over the forest, so that the dragonfire set the trees aflame. He liked having more light for the battle. He spun suddenly and ripped at Jorge again. The topaz and gold *Slayer* leapt upon Drake and sank his teeth into the side of Drake's neck. The pain was excruciating, and it only grew when the *Slayer* gave Drake a mighty shake. He would have torn at the *Slayer*'s chest, but he cupped his claws over Veronica to protect her instead. He kicked upward and Jorge roared as he released Drake's neck, breathing fire on the open wound even as Drake fell.

Veronica whispered his name, but reassuring her would have to wait. He raged dragonfire himself, singeing Jorge's scales so that they blackened. Jorge screamed, then retreated to hover in the air facing Drake, his eyes shining with malice.

Drake was immediately wary. What had changed?

"Such a feeble species," Jorge murmured in old-speak. He gestured to the ground below them and Drake belatedly remembered the urban explorers. There were a good dozen of them, hoodies pulled over their heads as they stood in the rain.

Holding up cell phones and cameras.

Veronica gasped as she evidently saw them as well, and by the time Drake looked back at Jorge, that *Slayer* had produced a small gleaming vial. It was glass and its contents were red. Liquid. Drake's eyes narrowed and he inhaled deeply, discerning immediately that this was blood infected with the Seattle virus.

"The perfect sample," Jorge said, speaking aloud. "The Seattle virus is even concentrated in this blood, thanks to the skills of the *Pyr*'s own Apothecary. There's something satisfying about the *Pyr* having a part in this mayhem." He cast a glittering glance down at the human spectators. "Shall we watch history repeat itself?"

"No!" Veronica shouted, even as Jorge dove toward the spectators, the vial held aloft, as if he would cast it down and make it shatter in the small crowd.

Drake hesitated for a heartbeat, guessing this was the viper's trap.

"Drake!" Veronica cried. "You have to stop him!"

Of course, she had compassion for others. Of course, she believed that she could change the world with her choices. That optimism was a trait he admired in Veronica, and he couldn't find fault with her conviction that he would act out of honor and duty.

If he failed to do her bidding, that might ensure the safety of both of them, but his refusal to defend nameless strangers would compromise Veronica's opinion of him.

It might doom their future.

The situation was the perfect bind, a choice that revealed a viper's talon.

In fact, there was no choice to be made. Drake spun in the air, feeling Veronica's grip tighten upon him. He felt a scale loosen on his chest even as he dove after the villain at his mate's command, fearing the worst and hoping for the best.

It was a sight Theo had never wished to see.

He admired Drake more than any of the *Pyr*, for he knew that warrior's story and recognized that his own life and his command were the result of Drake's sacrifices. Drake was mentor, comrade and—oddly enough—ancestor. In fact, Theo had been named for

Drake's son, just as the first boy born in every generation of his lineage had been named in tribute to their forebear and his son.

It was an honor to serve with a *Pyr* that had made such a contribution to the survival of their kind.

Given the blood link, it didn't surprise any of the *Pyr* that Theo was eager to help Drake whenever possible and was always ready to put his forces in Drake's service. Drake wasn't much of a talker, and they'd never exchanged confidences, but Theo felt it was his role to try to make up for Drake losing his son.

He didn't think it could be easily done, and he'd been glad to come to Drake's second firestorm.

Theo had dared to hope that Drake was mistaken about Jorge's scheme for this night, especially when he and Reed beat one *Slayer* so that he fell out of the sky. That dragon hit the ground hard and began to rotate between forms. Some of the kids began to photograph the transition, which made Theo frown.

Erik wouldn't like that.

Theo dispatched Reed to help Kristofer and Arach against the second *Slayer*, then looked for Drake. The last time he'd seen the older *Pyr*, Drake had had his mate firmly in his possession and had been fighting well against Jorge. Now Jorge dove low, like a gold and topaz comet, something sparkling in his grip. Drake gave hot pursuit as his mate urged him on.

The third *Slayer* came out of nowhere. One moment, the sky was clear. The next, there was a third ruby and brass *Slayer* in the air behind Drake, out of his field of vision. Theo roared in old-speak, but the *Slayer* was fast. He fell upon Drake from behind and ripped his wings, practically tearing them from his back.

Theo bellowed and raced toward his mentor, fearing he couldn't get there in time.

Drake roared in pain, his blood flowing like water. His wings fluttered, then collapsed, too damaged to be of aid in keeping him aloft. The mate screamed as Drake fell.

Jorge proved that he was a viper after all, because he pivoted in mid-air and launched a conduit of dragonsmoke at Drake. Theo could see its icy glitter in the air and he knew the moment that it latched onto Drake. The older *Pyr* twitched convulsively, then shuddered.

That his grip loosened on his mate said it all. Mate and *Pyr* fell separately toward the ground. The second *Slayer* continued to fight hard against Kristofer, Reed and Arach. Kristofer might have abandoned their battle to help Drake, but the *Slayer* who had attacked Drake descended to join their fight. Their battle became vigorous as the two *Slayers* fought against three *Pyr*. The humans began to shout encouragement to one group of dragons or the other and Theo heard them making bets. He flew straight for Drake.

Theo heard Reed shout in pain, but he had to get to Drake. He eyed the falling mate and guessed that she would break a leg when she fell but no more than that. Jorge wasn't pursuing her: he was too focused on draining Drake's life force.

And he was succeeding brilliantly. Theo could see Drake's vigor fading fast.

Theo had to choose between mate and *Pyr*.

It wasn't much of a choice.

He raged into battle, wincing as he flew through Jorge's dragonsmoke. He heard his scales sizzle as they burned and felt his own energy dip as Jorge stole power from him as well. But he broke the tendril of dragonsmoke, scorching his tail painfully. He then snatched at Drake, carrying him aloft and away from the villains. Drake's breath was shallow and his wounds were deep.

When Theo looked down, he saw that Reed had fallen to the ground and shifted to his human form. All of the *Slayers* were gone.

Worse, there was no sign of the mate. Kristofer and Arach snatched up Reed and flew away with him, lifting him away from the curious humans.

The crowd of onlookers was filled with excitement. The sirens grew louder and dogs could be heard barking. Searchlights were shone into the forest and the humans scattered into the darkness like mice into tall grass. Theo saw a fire truck making its way along an overgrown access road toward the burning building, but guessed the rain would extinguish most of the fire.

Drake stirred, his eyelids flickering. *"Veronica?"* he whispered in old-speak.

"They took her," Theo replied, fearing that the other *Pyr* would be angry at his choice but not seeing what else he could have done. *"But I couldn't let you die."*

Drake shook his head, his disappointment evident to the

younger *Pyr*. To Theo's surprise, though, Drake didn't blame him.

"Of course not," he murmured. *"It is the way of the viper to use our own natures against us."* His eyes opened then, and Theo was surprised to find them filled with more resolve than he could have expected. *"Fear not, Theo. This battle has only begun."*

Ronnie found herself in a cave, with burning torches on the walls. Unfortunately, her companions were Jorge and the triplets. One of them was dripping black blood and Ronnie hoped he died a painful death.

Maybe he could take the others with him.

It was dark enough when they arrived that Ronnie had a moment to hide her prize from view. She'd examine it later. The flames in the torches flickered at their arrival, then settled to burn brightly again. By then, whatever she'd taken from Drake was safely tucked beneath her sweatshirt.

That Jorge released her from his grip was a clear sign that there was no way to escape, but Ronnie studied her surroundings with care all the same. There was a lot of rubble underfoot and the ceiling of the one cavern was cracked. Ronnie thought that someone had cleared this space after some kind of collapse.

The wounded dragon was flung down hard by his fellows. The injured *Slayer* was shimmering blue, shifting from human to dragon repeatedly, and his breathing was shallow.

No wonder, given how torn up his body was.

"A sign of distress," Jorge said, noting the direction of Ronnie's gaze. "And an indication that he is near death. He *could* still heal, though, if given the chance."

The dying dragon's eyes opened for a moment, his lids flickering and his claw lifting as if he would appeal to Jorge for mercy. Ronnie had to think that was a long shot, and Jorge turned away, as if he hadn't even seen the gesture.

Jorge was clearly indifferent to the fate of his minion and more interested in the other dragons for the moment. Tweedle-Dee and Tweedle-Dum were scratched up, but not shifting compulsively in the same way. They dropped their gazes when Jorge approached them. Ronnie assumed it was a submissive gesture, but then wondered when Jorge seized one *Slayer*'s chin and compelled him to meet his gaze.

Ronnie heard rumbling as if there was an earthquake. She scanned the cavern again, fearing she'd be buried alive, but the dragons showed no similar concern. As she watched, Jorge bent his attention upon the *Slayer* whose chin he held. His grip was tight enough that the tips of his claws pricked the *Slayer*'s chin— Ronnie could see black blood leaking from those points. The *Slayer* thrashed a little in Jorge's grip, struggling to keep from looking up at Jorge, but Jorge was relentless.

And he triumphed. Once the ruby and brass dragon stared up at him, it seemed he couldn't look away. He was apparently transfixed, his eyes wide. Ronnie wondered what was happening. After a lot of low murmuring, Jorge released that dragon and seized the third. This *Slayer* twitched and struggled, but went limp when he looked into Jorge's eyes.

What was Jorge doing?

It wasn't anything good. Ronnie could see that. She didn't trust how Jorge relinquished his grip then stood back to watch, his anticipation clear.

The first *Slayer* he'd spoken to was fumbling beneath his scales and Ronnie saw him flicker quickly between forms. When he was in dragon form again, there was something small and gold in his talons.

A coin.

"We call it a challenge coin," Jorge said, his manner unctuous.

The *Slayer* clumsily tossed the gold coin at the second *Slayer*, as if he would have rather not but was compelled to do so. With shaking talons and some resignation, the second *Slayer* picked up the coin from the floor of the cavern. He stood then, unsteady on his claws. The pair eyed each other, then there was a rumble of thunder again. They leaped at each other with talons bared. They locked claws and struggled for ascendancy, then took flight in the cavern. In a heartbeat, the dragonfight was on, as they bit and breathed fire at each other with increasing fury.

Jorge turned away from the erupting battle with satisfaction. His gold and topaz form seemed to slither as he returned to Ronnie.

"A blood duel," Jorge informed her amiably. "It's traditional that with the exchange of challenge coin, we dragons will fight to the death." He shrugged as he settled beside her, clearly indifferent to the result of the fight behind him. Jorge smiled. "Not their idea, of course, but I only need one of them now. It might as well be the stronger one."

He considered the injured *Slayer* for only a moment, before he bent and bit into his guts, tearing the flesh from the bones and consuming it. Ronnie knew she shouldn't have been surprised, much less disgusted, but she was both.

She averted her gaze.

Jorge chuckled. "One can't be too particular about new sources of the Elixir," he murmured. He watched the fight almost absently, gnawing the fallen *Slayer*'s flesh with such vigor that the black blood dripped from his chin and down his scales. He chewed with gusto.

The stench was disgusting.

Ronnie supposed her revulsion showed.

"Care for a bite?"

She shook her head and backed up, finding only the stone wall behind her.

"Probably wise on your part. There's no telling what the Elixir might do to a human, let alone to the child."

"What if I'm not pregnant?" Ronnie had to ask.

"You are," Jorge said with confidence. "I can smell it on you."

"That's impossible!"

Jorge shook his head as he chewed. "Not for a dragon shifter. Our senses are keener than those of humans. We discern more of the physical world, which is a sign of our superiority."

"I don't think it's superior to cannibalize your dead," Ronnie said.

Jorge laughed. "We don't usually. This is a necessary adjustment." He grimaced. "And really, there's little to recommend a meal of fallen *Slayer*. Dragon meat is tough and sinewy, by and large. I had hoped that this one might be more tender, given his age, but alas, that's not the case." He took another bite, his manner philosophical. "It must be our nature to make poor eating."

"Why is it necessary to eat him? Isn't there anything else to eat?"

Jorge's cool gaze landed upon Ronnie again and she was afraid she'd given him an idea of an alternative. "We don't eat humans," he said, and she wondered why he confessed anything that might reassure her. "There is a pungency about your kind that I find distasteful." He returned to his meal. The battling dragons thrashed and struggled for supremacy, one slamming the other into the rock wall so that the whole cavern vibrated. Ronnie wasn't surprised when black blood flowed down the wall, or when the battered dragon went limp.

She'd learned to expect the victor to eat his kill, but averted her gaze when he did.

Ronnie found Jorge watching her with undisguised amusement. She knew enough about him to understand that he was lingering—and chatty—for a reason. There had to be a point to this display, never mind his smug manner.

Maybe she could find out something. If he wasn't going to eat her, then it didn't look as if she had a lot to lose. If Niall dreamwalked to her again, she could confide what she'd learned and that might help the *Pyr*.

"So? Why eat this one?"

"It's the Elixir," Jorge repeated, his voice dropping to a hiss. "The Elixir confers something close to immortality upon those who consume it and makes us more vigorous." He flicked his tail and she saw to her horror that it was already growing back. "It's a substance that needs to be replenished in one's system, however, and there is no longer a source, thanks to the *Pyr*."

"They claimed it?"

Jorge's eyes glittered. "They destroyed it, and so I have been compelled to find Elixir wherever I can." His gaze remained fixed upon her as he ate another bite, and Ronnie realized the implication of his words.

"Those *Slayers* had taken the Elixir, too! That's why you eat the corpses."

"Waste not, want not," Jorge said easily. "The *Pyr*, of course, will honor their dead," he continued, his disdain clear. "But then, warriors like Reed and Drake are no good to anyone once they're dead." And he smiled, his satisfaction so clear that Ronnie wanted to kick him. "Of course, this one didn't exactly choose to take the Elixir as I did. He was given it, before he was hatched."

"Hatched?" Ronnie asked. "Is that how *Slayers* are made?"

Jorge smiled, showing all those teeth, a sight made less appealing by the bits of flesh and black blood adorning them. "It could become so, certainly."

"That's enigmatic."

"Yes, I apologize. There is an old saying that *Pyr* are born but *Slayers* are made, a reference to the fact that we choose our path." Jorge chewed steadily. "But matters are in flux, since the darkfire was released." He looked around, then nodded. "In this very cave, actually."

"I don't understand." Why was Jorge so confident that he needed only one *Slayer* to guard his back? There seemed to be a lot more *Pyr* in the world and Jorge didn't strike her as a dragon who liked to have odds stacked against him.

Ronnie had a bad feeling about that.

Hatched.

"Where are *Slayers* hatched?"

"You don't need to understand that," Jorge said, his tone turning harsh. Apparently the time for confidences was coming to an end. He fixed a glittering stare upon her. "What you need to understand is that Drake is dead, and that he died because you appealed to him to save the humans." Jorge shook his head with amusement. "I really couldn't have planned it any better. Sometimes humans do inadvertently improve upon the best scheme."

"You planned for them to come." Ronnie was disappointed to realize that Drake had been right. Jorge had baited a trap.

"They wouldn't have found you otherwise." He wagged a talon at her, his confidence supreme. "They won't find you here. I've ensured as much. There will be no more dreamwalking." He said the word with scorn. "We will simply wait in cozy, if isolated, comfort." He heaved a sigh and considered the shredded corpse. "Perhaps after my meal, I'll hibernate until the spring. You'll believe me about the baby by then."

She spun away from him and his disgusting meal, her tears rising even though she would have preferred otherwise. He'd killed Drake. She'd seen her dragon injured and falling from the sky.

Worse, Drake had died because she had urged him to protect those humans from the contents of the vial. It was her fault, just as

Jorge had gloated.

The *Slayer* had planned it all so well. Had they ever had a chance?

But then Ronnie remembered Drake's last words to her. *Appearances are not always what they seem.* Was it possible that Drake was alive? Or that he had tricked Jorge? She could only hope as much and cling to that hope to get her through this ordeal.

It wasn't much, but it was all that Ronnie had.

It was only then that she realized she didn't know what had happened to the vial of blood. She sensed that she had missed a critical detail in that. And there was another dragon missing. "What about Leftie?" she asked. "Did you eat him already?"

Jorge snarled, his eyes flashing, and waved a talon as if to dismiss her from his presence.

Ronnie found herself abruptly alone in a cavern with no visible exit.

She thought about Jorge's reaction to her question and had to think that Leftie had somehow gotten away. She wished that she could vanish into thin air herself.

Otherwise it seemed unlikely she'd be leaving this new prison any time soon.

The *Pyr* carried Reed's broken body out over the Atlantic. Drake watched from the beach at Great Kills Park with Theo standing guard over him. In other circumstance, Drake might have protested that he didn't need a sitter. On this particular night, he was glad Theo had assisted him and welcomed a *Pyr* at his back. He'd watched as Theo sent a summons to Sloane earlier, and once again, felt a grudging admiration for technology.

There was no doubt that he had need of the Apothecary's aid. Drake's back was bleeding and sore, and the dragonsmoke had left him weakened.

He needed his strength to save Veronica.

The beach was deserted at this hour of the night. The rain and the chilly air of October no doubt also contributed to the solitude. Drake waited in his human form where Theo had placed him, not having the energy to move.

He watched Kristofer and Arach in flight, their figures dark against the overcast skies. At least the falling rain made them slightly less visible. Drake didn't doubt that there were half a dozen humans filming the progress of the dragons from somewhere on the island, but he didn't care. He had failed Veronica again.

At least, the *Pyr* would not fail their dead.

It was important to ensure that Reed couldn't be raised from the grave by the Elixir. Drake watched as the *Pyr* released Reed's body, then breathed dragonfire upon it as the warrior fell toward the sea.

Reed had been exposed to earth when he hit the ground right after his death, to air as they flew, to fire as they cremated his remains. Kristofer and Arach seized his body just before it splashed into the sea and flew high again, repeating the exercise. Three times they turned their flames upon him, until finally only ash fell to touch the ocean's surface.

Drake bowed his head and asked the Great Wyvern for mercy for his lost comrade.

Then he got to his feet with a grimace and braced himself to be carried back to the city by Theo and his team. No doubt Sloane would arrive as soon as he could.

Drake thought it encouraging that the *Slayers* hadn't collected Reed's body, or even to have appeared to be interested in doing so.

That they'd taken their own injured dragon hinted to him that there wasn't a new source of the Elixir, that they were compelled to harvest it from those fallen *Slayers* who had consumed it during their lives.

Drake would take encouragement where he could.

He wasn't a superstitious *Pyr*, but he was beginning to think that his second firestorm was challenged because of his own choices. He feared that the Great Wyvern had found him unworthy, and that Veronica would be the one to pay the price.

Which meant only that Drake had to change, and do so as quickly as possible.

CHAPTER NINE

loane arrived at Niall's apartment the next afternoon, knowing that his disgruntled attitude showed and not caring much about it. Niall gave him a quick survey, said nothing, then led the way to Drake. The apartment stunk of *Slayer* and Elixir, filthy dark smells that turned Sloane's stomach. That could explain Niall's quiet manner, and Sloane supposed the residue had been carried on the *Pyr* who had fought Jorge and his minions.

Still it was revolting.

First things first. Sloane didn't doubt that Niall would have questions, once the business of being the Apothecary of the *Pyr* was done.

Drake was in bad shape, but as stoic as Sloane would have expected. He commanded the grim *Pyr* to shift shape, then cleaned and stitched the gaping wounds in Drake's wings. He sang the song of the Apothecary softly but with vigor, watching as the traditional chant had its effect. Drake was breathing steadily, and his eyes were narrowed slightly against the pain, but he was already at greater ease.

"If the wounds had been deeper, you'd have lost them," Sloane noted.

"I shall have to thank Jorge for the courtesy when next we meet."

Sloane smiled at Drake's dry humor. It was a good sign. "You'll probably have a lot to talk about then anyway."

Drake exhaled a puff of smoke but said nothing more.

"You're not the only one who has issues with that *Slayer*," Sloane admitted as he treated the wounds with an unguent that he had formulated for the *Pyr*. He couldn't push the destruction in his lab out of his mind. That he'd had to walk away from Sam just when things had looked promising again didn't help his mood. "I wouldn't mind ripping his wings off myself, but I'd finish the job."

"It is the way of the viper to torment his victim with possibilities," Drake said.

"Good to know that was his plan," Sloane replied shortly. "Although right now, they're more like impossibilities."

"Why? What happened?" Niall asked. He was standing in the doorway, watching. "What else did Jorge do?"

Theo was pacing, obviously trying to resist the urge to fret like a mother hen and losing the battle. Drake spared him the occasional glance. Sloane resisted the urge to snap at him to be still. He knew the other *Pyr* was just worried, or maybe felt responsible. He also knew his own frustration was coloring his reactions.

"Jorge pretty much destroyed my research, and my hope of finding a cure for the Seattle virus." Sloane shook his head. "I should have seen it coming, but he manipulated me easily. Maybe I deserve to fail for that."

"How?" Niall asked.

Sloane heard his voice rise. "He sent those *Slayers* to attack Erik because he knew that if Erik was wounded but alive, I'd go to heal him. That meant my lab was empty, defended by dragonsmoke—but that's no more of a barrier to him than the alarm system. He knew he wasn't going to be interrupted." He shook his head with disgust.

Drake's eyes opened. "Jorge had a vial of blood tonight that he said was infected and stolen from the Apothecary of the *Pyr*."

Sloane raised a hand and spoke with some bitterness. "That would be me."

"He threatened to spill it over the humans gathered to watch the dragonfight," Theo supplied.

"It would be consistent with what he did in Seattle," Niall said.

"Yeah, well, it also ensures that I can't stop him," Sloane said with frustration. "Even if I come up with an antidote, I can't test it without having a sample of the virus in my lab." He flung out his hands. "Everything I've done is trashed."

No one had anything to say to that.

Theo, Kristofer, and Arach had sustained minor injuries that didn't really need his attention, but since Sloane was there, he took care of them anyway.

"Cup of tea?" Rox offered with a smile. "I've got some chai that will put a smile on anyone's face."

Sloane nodded agreement, smiling a little because he knew where Rox got her chai.

From him.

He sat in their small kitchen and sipped the tea, filling his nostrils with the scent of his own gardens.

Niall sat opposite him, concern in his expression. *"You're never grumpy,"* he said in old-speak.

Sloane gave him a look.

Niall laughed at that, then sipped his own tea. *"Want to talk about it?"*

"I just did," Sloane cleared his throat, then spoke aloud, seeing Rox hovering in the doorway and not wanting to be rude. It wasn't as if Niall had any secrets from his mate. "The only thing I seem to be getting accomplished is cleaning up after Jorge. I never wanted to be *Slayer* staff, that's for sure."

"What about your research? Had you made any progress?"

"Some, but it doesn't matter now." Sloane shrugged, his exasperation impossible to hide. "There's nowhere to get any more of the virus, at least not legally. I can't help the sense that Jorge is trying to provoke me into doing something stupid."

"Or he just wanted the virus for some scheme of his own," Drake said from the doorway. That *Pyr* claimed a chair at the table, grimacing as he sat down.

"You should rest for a few days," Sloane said.

"I will rest when I am dead," Drake replied, but there was no heat in his tone. "My mate has been stolen, *again*, and it is impossible to know when Jorge will tease us again. I must be vigilant."

Sloane and Theo exchanged a glance and he knew the younger *Pyr* would defend Drake's back.

"I must tell you exactly what Jorge did this night," Drake said and recounted the taunt with the vial of blood.

Sloane muttered a curse under his breath. "So, it was used to torment you."

Drake gave him a solemn look. "I would not be surprised if he had a second purpose in mind. He did not intend to spill it last night, just to compel me to choose."

"He must have another plan," Theo said.

"And it involves making things worse," Sloane agreed. "Thank the Great Wyvern that he didn't pull the stopper and break the seal, because he might have spilled it inadvertently."

"I do not believe he would risk using his advantage too soon," Drake said softly.

"Then when?" Theo asked, but none of them had an answer.

"So, what are we going to do?" Sloane asked with undisguised frustration. "There's no telling where Jorge has gone."

"If he doesn't want to be found, he'll disguise his scent and Veronica's," Theo contributed.

"I'll try to dreamwalk to her," Niall said, obviously anticipating Drake's request. "But it might not work."

"Jorge might have let you find her before," Theo said and Niall nodded reluctant agreement.

"I despise that we must wait for his move," Drake murmured, and a familiar glitter lit his eyes. "There must be a way to change the course of events."

"Well, I'm going to head home and clean up my lab," Sloane said. "Try to stay out of fights for a while, so I can get some work done."

Drake surveyed the kitchen. "I must speak to the boy," he said softly.

"He's safe," Theo said. "I checked with the *Pyr* guarding him."

"At least rest until tomorrow," Sloane said, doubting that Drake would do any such thing.

"If he's been left alone this long, then Jorge has no interest in him," Niall said.

"And why should he?" Drake murmured. "He has won this round, and the boy is not *Pyr*."

"It's not over yet," Theo said with false cheer. "The Dragon's Tail doesn't turn for almost another year."

Sloane dropped his gaze to his steaming cup as the kitchen fell silent. He guessed that he wasn't the only one with doubts about their collective future. He'd never known of a mate being lost like this, and he couldn't help thinking it was a very bad sign.

What if Jorge *did* eliminate them all within the year?

"It's so strange to have all these replicas of Boris Vassily appear at once," Niall said. "It's like Jorge has a photocopier someplace, one that makes *Slayers*."

Sloane looked up from his tea. "Clones," he said suddenly. "What if they're clones?"

The other *Pyr* glanced at each other, then back at him. "How would we find out?"

"I don't know," Sloane said. "Maybe by dissecting one. Or two."

"Good luck," Theo said. "Didn't you see that video? They've all had the Elixir so the survivors ate the dead one to get more."

"Still, we might manage it," Drake mused. "It would be worth a try, as doing so might weaken Jorge further."

"One of them did disappear," Sloane said. "Maybe we could find him."

A ripple of excitement passed through the room.

"We can talk to Erik about it, spread the word," Niall said. "We don't know when they're going to pop up, but when they do, we can try to keep a corpse."

"We just have to get one to Sloane," Theo said.

"I'd better order a chest freezer, just in case," Sloane said, feeling a new optimism. "And do some research." He didn't know much about cloning, although he remembered the story of Dolly the sheep.

If a sheep could be cloned, why not a *Slayer*? It was horrifyingly plausible.

It was also possible that cloned *Slayers* might share a common weakness.

"So, let's review the count," Niall said. He pulled out a sheet of paper. "Two attacked Erik in Chicago, and one had its wings torn off before they disappeared. He was later eaten by the others, according to Veronica and that video."

"Three others attacked Veronica's home," Drake contributed.

"And the one who lost an arm has vanished from the feast," Sloane added. "We saw that in the video, too, although he could be anywhere."

"That makes four survivors," concluded Kristofer.

"We fought three last night," Theo confirmed.

"And they all had both arms," Drake concluded.

Niall tapped his pen on the paper. "I wonder about the other one. Do you think they've split ranks?" No one had an answer to that, although Sloane liked to think it was the case.

"They could have eaten him, too," Kristofer noted.

"They've had the Elixir," Theo agreed. "But that would also help him to heal. How quickly do you think his arm could grow back?"

"Not instantly," Sloane said. "A major injury like that would take *some* time. I'll guess he's hidden somewhere, healing, or eaten." The others nodded agreement.

"I wonder how many more clones Jorge has in the works," Kristofer said.

"If Erik's dream is right, we'll find out on the next eclipse, when the blood moon ripens the eggs," Theo concluded. "Whatever that means."

That it was the obvious conclusion didn't make it any more palatable. If nothing else, it renewed Sloane's sense of urgency. "I need to get home," he said. "If any of you can think of a way to get me the corpse of one of these clones or a sample of the Seattle virus, it might provide a clue. In the meantime, I need to restore my lab."

But it was the prospect of paying a visit to Sam that made him want to hurry back to California.

For once, Timmy didn't want to watch a movie with Dashiell or play a game. He watched the video of the dragons at Seaview Hospital repeatedly and compulsively. The video image was grainy and the quality was poor. The camera shook a lot and it had been filmed at night in the rain. Still, it held the answers to so many questions.

First, there was his mom. And she was okay, just like Drake said. Scared and unhappy, but alive. That was good.

Second, there was a dragon trying to save her. A big dark dragon who was even more awesome than the ones he'd seen in other videos. That was cool. He looked like his scales were made of black pearls but were thorny at their edges. Timmy hadn't realized that his mom knew dragons and hoped he had a chance to ask her about them soon.

Third, there was a dragon fight. That wasn't so awesome because the dragon carrying his mom got beaten up. Even after watching the video a hundred times, Timmy winced in sympathy with every blow the grey dragon endured. The red and gold dragon practically ripped his wings off, and the gold one did something nasty that hurt the grey dragon a lot. It must be magic or invisible, but the grey dragon's pain was real. Timmy's heart leapt when his mom fell, and he wanted the fight to end differently.

But the fourth thing was the coolest part. His mom called her dark dragon 'Drake,' which explained *everything*. Drake was one of the *Pyr*, one of the dragon shape shifters in the videos Timmy watched over and over again. That was why Drake had been able to find Timmy's dad, when no one else had been able to. Dragons unearthed the truth, no matter how deeply hidden it was, and they faced it, no matter how ugly it was. Dragons solved riddles, everyone knew that. Dragons were noble and honorable.

The gold dragon that Drake was fighting in this new video looked *exactly* like the one in Seattle who had introduced the virus.

Obviously, the gold one was an evil dragon. That Drake was fighting him meant that Drake was a good dragon. Timmy watched again, and noticed that the red and gold dragons seemed to be on the gold one's side. There was a green one and an orangey red one who fought with Drake, as well as the smoky gold one that seemed to have been killed by the bad dragons.

That the gold dragon snatched Mom out of the air and disappeared meant that he had big bad plans for her.

It was just the way that reporter Melissa Smith said: there were *Pyr* and there were *Slayers*.

Drake was *Pyr*, and that meant he'd save Mom. He wondered then at the identities of the other dragons who fought with Drake. Was it possible that they were his fellow warriors? Could one of them be Theo, who was keeping an eye on him? Kristofer and Arach hadn't been around the night this fight had happened, but had introduced him to a couple of other guys. Were any of these dragons Kristofer or Arach?

Who had died? He hoped it wasn't one of the dragons he

knew.

One thing was for sure: Timmy really liked the idea of dragons keeping vigil over him and his mom. He was pretty much positive, though, that being *Pyr* was Drake's big secret, as well as that of his comrades.

Timmy wasn't going to be the one to reveal them.

He'd just have to wait for them to confide in him, or the chance to ask Drake.

There was no longer a clean mattress in Ronnie's prison, much less a single blanket.

There was no window, and the chamber pot had been replaced by a hole in the floor big enough only for a mouse. As time passed, it became clear that there would be no visits to a fancy apartment and no more board games. This cell was warmer than Ronnie's other prison had been, but still claustrophobic. There was a faint light, just enough to keep it from complete blackness, but Ronnie never could figure out its exact source. It seemed that the hewn rock floor beneath her feet glowed slightly.

She hoped it wasn't radioactive.

She had nothing to do and no one to talk to, nothing to watch and no way to tell the passing of the time with any accuracy. There was only the rhythm of her body.

And Drake's scale. That was what had come off in her hands when she'd grabbed at him that last time, then she'd fallen with only it in her grip. She'd hidden it from Jorge, which had to be some kind of miracle, and only removed it from under her sweatshirt when she knew she wasn't going to be interrupted.

The scale was a remarkable thing, all the more amazing because it was a part of Drake.

Ronnie studied it often, seeing a thousand colors hidden in its hard surface, a surface that appeared to be dark grey until she looked closely. She pressed it between her palms, letting the thorny extrusions on the lower edge dig into her palm, proving to herself that it was all true.

Her destined lover was a dragon shifter.

As time passed, it became more evident that she *would* bear

Drake's child. Her body was softening and rounding, her breasts were heavier and the veins around her nipples were more visible. She felt moody, on the verge of tears sometimes, and angry others.

Mostly, she felt alone.

Time slid away, time she could only measure by the development of her pregnancy, and Ronnie feared the future. Would she be compelled to have the child in this prison? Would she be allowed to see him at all? What would happen to her after the baby was born? There were few good possibilities that she could anticipate.

She fiercely wanted her future to be different, but there wasn't much she could do about it. She had to keep her faith and keep up her strength. She did exercises in the cell and tried to force herself to remain positive. She tried to convince herself that Drake wasn't dead, that he had tricked Jorge, that he was taking care of Timmy and that everything would be fine.

She never really managed to believe it.

There were no more hot meals for Ronnie, either. A yellow dragon claw appeared in mid-air each day with a bowl of some kind of gruel, a pink multi-vitamin perched atop it. She'd learned to snatch it quickly from Jorge's claw because otherwise he dropped the bowl before his claw disappeared. It was barely warm and almost completely devoid of flavor. It was much worse eaten off the floor.

But the gruel was all that was offered for her to eat. Ronnie ate it so her baby wouldn't starve.

It must have had something mixed into it, because after the dragonfight, no matter how much Ronnie slept, she no longer dreamed.

It did not promise to be easy, but Drake had to tell Veronica's son what had happened. He would have to talk, and talk about feelings, with his mate's son.

He supposed it was time he mastered such feats.

He waited until after school, at the time that Timothy and his friend Dashiell walked home from school together. Theo's team knew their schedule well and had quietly ensured their safety.

Drake did rest for one day, but no longer.

The boys had just left the school yard and turned the corner when he joined them. He moved silently out of the shadows and matched his steps to theirs. To his pleasure, Timothy noticed his presence immediately and wasn't surprised, while Dashiell jumped at the sudden sight of him.

"Drake! Did you find my mom?" There was something in the boy's eyes, as if he already knew how Drake would reply.

"Yes and no," Drake acknowledged heavily.

"You spoke to her, though?"

"I did. She is concerned for you."

"I'm more concerned for her." The boy nodded with a confidence Drake didn't quite feel. "You found her once, so you'll do it again."

"Indeed. I shall not surrender this battle."

Timothy surveyed him, clearly unsurprised by Drake's wounds. "You're hurt."

"There was a fight." Drake shook his head. "I was injured in your mother's defense, and one of her captors was wounded, as well."

Again, the boy seemed unsurprised. "Excellent," Timothy said with approval. "They should all die for even touching her."

There was little Drake could say to that, for he agreed heartily. He would like to do the honors himself.

"I know you can't tell me anything, because it's probably a secret, but I'd do anything I could to help." Timothy looked up and held Drake's gaze so deliberately that Drake understood the truth.

Timothy had discerned his secret. It made the conversation easier, in a way, because Drake didn't like to deceive. He spared a glance at Dashiell, but Timmy shook his head. He nodded approval that the boy had not shared his conclusions, then smiled down at Veronica's son. "You do all that is necessary in being strong and remaining vigilant." Timothy walked a little taller beneath Drake's approval and Drake wondered how it had influenced him to have been without his father.

"Where do you live, Mr. Drake?" Dashiell asked after they had walked in silence for some moments.

"It does not matter," Drake said with care. He was watching Timothy and thinking of the boy's home being destroyed. Timothy kept his gaze fixed on the sidewalk. Impulsively, Drake confessed his feelings. "The truth is that I have had no real home since the loss of my wife and son."

Timothy looked up at that.

"But you have to live somewhere," Dashiell insisted.

Drake shrugged. "It is but a place to sleep. That is not the same as a home."

Timothy was shuffling his feet. "Mom said we lost our home when Dad died. We had to move from the base and find another place to live. We had a little apartment and no car because she went to college. She said we both had to go to school to make a better future."

"And so she is wise in that. There is no replacement for a good education."

"But you have to *make* a home, Drake," Timothy insisted. "It doesn't just happen. That's what Mom said."

"In my time, it was the task of women to make homes."

The boys laughed at this. "Drake! That's ancient history!" Timothy protested. "Even I can make supper, when Mom's working late."

"He makes the *best* spaghetti," Dashiell added. "I make the garlic bread."

"Indeed?" Drake said, amused by the pair of them. "Does your mother often work late?"

"Sometimes. She has a job at the library doing research. She does some freelance research, too, and that's usually in the evenings at home. I make dinner sometimes, when she has a deadline."

"That is teamwork of the best kind," Drake said, admiring his mate's work ethic, and the boy beamed. On impulse he said more. "Perhaps you could teach me to cook spaghetti. I would not like your mother to think me a relic of ancient history."

Timothy turned shining eyes upon him. "Then you're staying?"

"It was always my intent."

That this pleased Veronica's son was evident, and Drake thought that perhaps there was much he could do, even while he remained vigilant. "Food alone does not make a home, though. There must be more."

"Like?"

"Good company. Comfort." Drake gestured vaguely. He thought of Veronica's lost home and how he had been struck by its comfort and elegance. It had been uncluttered, but welcoming. He didn't know how to create such an ambiance, but he recognized it when he saw it. "A home should be a place of refuge."

"Mom says a house is a home when it's filled with love." Timothy gave him a sidelong glance as Drake considered that. "Maybe you shouldn't live alone, Drake."

"Maybe not." Drake found himself thinking about homes, as he never had before. He had traveled constantly, resting where he needed to, carrying his belongings with him at all times. Now he looked at the town where Veronica had chosen to make her home and was tempted by permanence.

Maybe he could learn more of his mate from her son.

In a year, the Dragon's Tail Wars would be over, one way or the other. If he survived, he might make a home with Veronica and Timothy. He liked the prospect of that, though he knew there was much stacked against him.

"I do not share your mother's skills in understanding how to make a home," Drake acknowledged.

"But you have other skills."

"Each to our own specialty," he agreed with a smile. "Yet, there is no fault in learning new abilities. Perhaps, with your help, I can begin to make a home here."

"For when Mom comes back," Timothy said with conviction. "We'll need somewhere to live after you rescue her."

"That would be my goal." Drake recognized that Timothy must have had concerns for the future. He resolved then and there that the best thing he could do for Veronica was to ensure not just the safety but the welfare of her son.

"My abode is simple," he said, when in fact he had yet to find one of his own. "Perhaps you might help me to make it more like a home." He was aware of the concerns that humans might have of a man unrelated to Timothy taking the boy into even temporary custody. "Both of you."

"Do you have a television?" Dashiell asked. "A really big one?"

"Alas, no. I shall endeavor to see that resolved before seeking your further assistance."

"You need a computer, too," Timothy said. "A really hot box for playing games."

"I play no games."

"What do you do, Mr. Drake?" Dashiell asked. There was a light in the young boy's eyes that made Drake wonder what Timothy had said to his friend. That Timothy caught his breath convinced Drake that he had to concoct a cover story.

Drake said the first thing that came to mind, the last thing he had done that humans would understand. "I coached a soccer team. We traveled in Europe in a bus."

He referred, of course, to the Dragon's Tooth Warriors and the disguise they had undertaken to seek out shreds of their lost past. Thanks to the darkfire crystal and its unpredictable sorcery, those *Pyr* had been scattered throughout time, each at the location of his mate, for his firestorm.

Drake supposed that Veronica was the reason he alone had been returned to these times and felt frustration again that their destiny should be so challenged.

"They call it football there," Dashiell contributed. "That's what my dad says."

"Mr. Patterson coaches *our* soccer team," Timothy confided.

"I see. Do you both play, then?"

The boys nodded enthusiastically. "Dad says we might make the play-offs this year."

"Those guys you were with when I met you," Timothy said. "Were they the players you coached?"

"Indeed."

"Are you going back to Europe then?" Dashiell asked, to Timothy's obvious consternation.

Drake shook his head. "They have all ceased to play the sport," he said, keeping matters simple. "In fact, I have not coached a team in a while."

"Then you should help coach ours," Dashiell said. "Mr. Quigley had to quit coaching because he started to work afternoon shifts, and Dad was saying the other night that he could use some help."

"Indeed." Drake nodded, liking the sound of this very much. "Then I shall speak to your father and ask if my aid would be welcome in this matter."

The way that Timothy looked up at him, his eyes shining, told Drake that he had made exactly the right choice.

He would need an apartment, a place where he could begin to make a home to welcome his mate and her son. Drake felt a new surge of optimism, for he believed that the future promised by the firestorm might fall within reach, after all.

It was late in England when Melissa Smith's cell phone rang.

Or it was early, depending how she looked at it. The bedroom was dark, Rafferty was gone, and the bed was chilly. The phone rang again and she remembered that it was in her purse, which she'd left in the foyer. She got out of bed quickly, intending to run, but Rafferty walked into the bedroom with her purse.

"I knew you'd want to get it," he said and she dug into the bag.

She answered on the fourth ring, which wasn't all bad considering that it was 3:30 in the morning. "Hello?"

"Are you seeing this?" Doug, her producer, demanded. His voice was hoarse, as if he'd been awakened from sleep, too. There was an edge of excitement to his voice, a sign that an interesting story was breaking.

Rafferty must have heard that, because he took the stairs three at a time to hurry down to the office and boot up his computer. Melissa recognized Maeve O'Neil's voice from the broadcast Doug was watching and cringed inwardly.

What had that witch dug up on the *Pyr* this time?

An older woman was talking by the time Melissa got to Rafferty's office. She looked as if she were on Skype. "They were right there, right in front of us, Maeve," she said, talking as if the reporter was her oldest friend. "I've never seen anything like it. Arthur and I always thought it would be wonderful to visit Easter Island and see its marvels, but we never imagined we'd see dragons hatching!"

"What?" Rafferty murmured, his eyes glittering as he leaned closer.

"It must have been terrifying for you," Maeve said in her smooth Irish accent. "It's just another sign of the gross indifference these creatures show to humans, the rightful residents of this planet..."

Melissa stood behind Rafferty, her phone forgotten in her hand, and wanted to injure the journalist who'd apparently made it her mission to turn public opinion against the *Pyr*. She could hear the same broadcast coming through the phone, because Doug was watching it, too.

The woman kept talking, but her pictures really did say it all.

"I know exactly what you mean, Maeve. They couldn't have cared less about us."

"Tell me exactly what happened, Peg," Maeve purred. "You're doing such a wonderful job."

Peg preened. "Arthur didn't even want to go and see *Ahu Te Pito Kura*, but I thought we should see the largest statue, even if it hasn't been restored, and while we were there, we could see the navel of the world, *Te Pito o te Henua*. We had to get up terribly early and the light was odd, with the blood moon, but the guide thought the photographs would be good..."

The photographs, in fact, were creepy. They were displayed in succession on the screen, the woman reduced to a voice-over. The first shots were clearly taken from a truck and must have been taken as it was moving because some of them were blurred.

Still there was no mistaking the dragons taking flight.

They were *Pyr*. Their figures were silhouetted against the strangely lit sky and became clearer as the eclipse passed. Once the moon was shining white again, it was evident that the dragons in question were red and gold.

In fact, they were just about indistinguishable from each other. It was hard to get a good count of them from the photographs, each of which showed one or two.

Melissa and Rafferty exchanged a glance, and she worried about the import of his consternation. What did he know that she didn't?

"Dragons, Maeve!" the woman said. "Real live *dragons*! Who would have believed it? And not just one, but many of them, one after the other. They were red and gold, we could see that when the moonlight returned to normal, and they flew straight up." She cleared her throat. "And then they just disappeared, as if they'd never been there at all. They were snatched up by that gold dragon."

"Do you think it was the one from Seattle?" Maeve asked. "The one who infected thousands of innocent people and launched a new plague?"

Melissa caught her breath. There was a blurred shot of the gold dragon, and it sure looked like Jorge. He breathed fire back at a group of watching tourists, who fled from him. Several fell, not as steady on their feet as they had been in their younger days.

Rafferty frowned.

"That would make sense," the woman said, her voice rising. "And these ones sure didn't care what happened to us! Our driver nearly went into the ditch in his shock, and one of the people already there broke a leg trying to run away. Roger's angina began to act up, especially once the dragons began to disappear." She huffed. "But we went on to find out where they were coming from and we found *this*!"

Her tone was triumphant as the next series of photographs were displayed.

"A dragon nest!" Maeve breathed. "Why, Peg, I believe you're the first to ever photograph one!"

Melissa had seen pictures of the round stone referred to as the navel of the world on the north side of Easter Island and had always wished there hadn't been four smaller stones added around it. It made the stone, which was supposed to have mystical powers and was magnetic, look like a table in the middle of a patio set.

The mystical stone was centered in a round platform beside the ocean, with a low fitted stone wall around it. Nearby was one of the large funerary platforms known as *ahu*, though the statue that had once stood upon it was toppled.

In the moonlight, the stone looked a bit like a huge egg.

Albeit one that was cracked open, with four cracked stones around it.

Eggs in a nest.

"There must have been five broken eggs," the eyewitness continued. "We tried to fit the shells back together to be sure, but they were heavy and hard to move. Arthur said we should leave them alone, but they were disintegrating right before our eyes!"

It was true. Melissa could see the big egg shards crumbling as the group of older tourists examined them, and the dust itself seemed to disappear when it touched the earth. By the time the sun came up, the tourists were standing in that circular platform with dust gathering around their shoes.

"I knew I couldn't get a satellite connection, not from there, but I took all the pictures I could, before they disappeared from sight. I filled the memory card on my cell phone, and Arthur practically filled the one on the digital camera. I knew that we could send them once we were back on the mainland."

"I'm so glad you contacted me, Peg McKay, to share your experience," Maeve said. "Even though it's terrifying to see five more dragons appear in the world overnight, as hungry, violent, and rapacious as their fellows. How many more will infest the world?"

Peg grimaced. "Do you think that gold one from Seattle was their parent?" she asked with obvious distaste and Rafferty inhaled sharply.

"It's clear that there are more dragon shifters breeding," Maeve said. "All around us. Will they outnumber us all? Will they spread more disease and kill more people?" The image changed to Maeve, comfortable in a studio somewhere and as beautifully dressed as she always was. She looked into the camera, appearing utterly trustworthy and concerned. "We are under assault, my friends and neighbors, under attack by an alien species, who intend to make their world their own. They mean to exterminate us, and we can't just stand by and watch. Please protect yourself and your families...."

Rafferty turned off the sound with a savagery.

"I need to interview this Peg McKay," Melissa said into her cell phone. "I want to interview all of them, preferably before anyone else does."

"Maeve probably tried to convince her to sign an exclusive," Doug said.

"Then one of the others in her group. There's more to this story than Maeve is telling and our audience deserves to know."

"Exactly," Doug said. "This tour group has gone back to Santiago, which is where they submitted these images. Luck is with us: we've got a crew there doing a follow-up story on the last earthquake. I've asked them to try to talk to the McKays and convince them to give you an interview. Your series on the *Pyr* might help close the deal."

"I hope so," Melissa said. "In the meantime, I'm on my way."

"Do whatever you need to," her producer said, his code for sparing no expense. "We need you there as quickly as possible."

Melissa ended the connection to find Rafferty watching the sequence of images again, with the sound turned off. "Are they *Pyr*?" she asked and he shrugged.

"They can't be true *Pyr*, not hatching from eggs." His disgust at the notion was clear.

"Then what are they?"

"I don't know." He sighed. "They look exactly like a dead *Slayer* named Boris Vassily."

"Back from the dead?"

Rafferty shook his head. "Not by any means I know. This is new."

"Are they dragon shifters at all?"

Melissa won a skeptical glance for that question, which she supposed she deserved. Rafferty arched a brow. "Don't tell me that you believe in dragons who aren't shape shifters? They're a myth, Melissa."

"Then?"

Rafferty frowned. "I fear they are *Slayers*, but this hatching isn't right." His voice dropped. "What has Jorge learned?"

"Will you come with me?"

"Not just yet." Rafferty spoke slowly and she knew he was weighing his options and his responsibilities. "Whatever they are, they aren't there anymore. I'll take Isabelle to Chicago, so she can stay with Erik in case I do need to be with you. She'll be safer there with the other children." He nodded once and caught her hand in his. "I think that's the best choice for the moment."

"What else?" Melissa whispered.

"What do you mean?"

"There's something else bothering you about this. Tell me."

Rafferty sighed. He replayed the video, freezing it where the dragons had suddenly disappeared. They hadn't faded from view, Melissa realized belatedly. They had vanished.

She caught her breath. "Spontaneously manifesting elsewhere," she murmured and Rafferty nodded.

"Which makes them not just *Slayers*, but *Slayers* who have drunk the Elixir and have no scent." He sighed and spun in his chair before getting to his feet with purpose. "That explains why we knew nothing about them. Erik wouldn't even have sensed them in advance. The question is how many of them are there in total."

"And where did they go?" Melissa asked.

"Oh, I think I know where they went," Rafferty said. He indicated the stairs. "I'll find us flights. Go and pack."

Melissa didn't move. "Where did they go? What do you know?"

"Two ruby and brass *Slayers* attacked Erik's lair after the eclipse, and three targeted Drake and his mate, just after his firestorm was satisfied."

"The eclipse sparked his firestorm," Melissa guessed and Rafferty nodded. Then she had a feeling why he hadn't told her about this. "What happened to her? What did they do with Drake's mate?" When he hesitated, she heard her voice rise. "Rafferty! You have to tell me!"

By way of answer, he started another video, one she hadn't seen. It showed a dragonfight, with Jorge and the red and gold Slayers. "Is that Drake?" she asked, then gasped as the dark dragon was wounded and the woman snatched up by Jorge.

Before he disappeared.

Melissa swallowed hard. "Is there more?" she asked, fearing the answer.

Rafferty came and stood before her, the weight of his hands landing on her shoulders. "She is gone, without a trace." He held her gaze. "I would prefer that you come to Chicago with us."

Melissa shook her head, even before he had finished speaking. "I have to do this. I have to cover this story. She's already blaming the *Pyr* for this Roger's angina attack and that other person's broken ankle. You guys need to turn public opinion in your favor, and I can help."

Rafferty smiled just a little. "I knew you would say that."

She smiled back at him then gave his fingers a squeeze. "I like that you want to protect me, but it's better if you protect Isabelle." Their adopted daughter had to be defended.

"There are no good choices." Rafferty nodded once then. "See if you can convince them to return to the island for the interview."

"It will be better for the video if they do."

"It will be better for many things." Rafferty's tone was ominous and expression was resolute. "I will meet you there."

It was clear that he didn't expect anything good to happen. Melissa shivered, knowing she'd be glad to have her *Pyr* at her side. She would have liked to have been selfish and not parted with him at all, but Melissa was the only one who could secure that interview, and time was of the essence.

She had to choose between her own defense and that of Isabelle, and it was no choice. Isabelle was still young, and Melissa had fought dragons on her own before she'd met Rafferty.

She'd beat cancer, after all.

These dragons weren't metaphorical, but she'd do it again anyway.

It was the only way to ensure that Isabelle had the future she deserved: a future with *Pyr*, not *Slayers*. A future with dragon shifters defending the human race.

Preferably a future without people like Maeve O'Neill.

CHAPTER TEN

ac read Sigmund Guthrie's book three times from cover to cover. It was written in a convoluted style that wasn't as accessible as would have been ideal. In fact, she had a definite sense that there were secrets hidden between the lines, like it might have been in code. She wasn't nearly as good at solving riddles as her brilliant sister, but she was determined to figure out this one alone.

If nothing else, this book might be the key to making her dream happen. She'd always tended to others and put her own dreams aside in favor of theirs. It was time for that to change, and Jac had been determined to start by avenging Nathaniel. That was her goal and no one else's.

That meant hunting dragons—well, dragon shifters—and returning the favor of doing them injury. She'd moved to Seattle to be at the source, the place closest to ground zero. She'd tried to find out more about that gold dragon, even to find some hint of his presence, but without any luck.

Until she'd received this book, she'd feared she would fail.

Knowing more about her prey made the difference.

When she was done reading the book for the third time, Jac made a list. As far as she could determine, these dragon shifters had a few weaknesses.

First, they could lose a scale because they loved someone. That would leave a bit of their skin unprotected, and that—obviously— was the place to strike to give the greatest wound. Jac wasn't at all sure she'd have the time to search for missing scales if confronting a fire-breathing dragon intent upon defending himself—or destroying her—but it was good to know. She also wasn't convinced that she'd be able to reach the vulnerable point—that would depend upon its location and their relative positions in the fight—but still, even discovering they *had* vulnerabilities was good.

Secondly, they hid their clothes when they shifted shape and evidently could only change back to human form if in possession of those clothes. Jac would have preferred that they could have been stopped from changing into dragon form, but she supposed beggars couldn't be choosers. Finding the clothes and taking them—or better, destroying them—could compromise a dragon shifter's ability to shift.

Thirdly, they mated once in their long lives, always with a human woman. The woman would be a point of weakness, Jac had to believe, because humans were easier to kill than dragons. She didn't think it right to avenge herself upon dragon shifters by injuring the women they loved, though.

She wanted to injure dragons.

But what kind of a woman would a dragon love? Maybe she'd be a human as rapacious, greedy and destructive as a dragon shifter. Maybe she'd deserve to die, just as much as her lover.

Especially if the woman loved the dragon in return.

Jac considered her list and wished it was longer. She flipped through the book again.

The truly strange thing about the book was that it seemed to be written for other dragons. Its instructions about the protocol for a dragonfight, for example, insisted that one should lock talons first "in the customary fighting pose," but slip out of the other dragon's grip early, or thrash the other dragon with one's tail before he was ready for an assault. Jac didn't have those options at her disposal.

She considered the title of the book for the umpteenth time. *The Compleat Guide for Slayers.* Was it true that there were two kinds of dragons: good dragons and bad dragons? That's what Melissa Smith said.

Were they all dragon shifters?

Did dragons slay each other?

Jac didn't know how she would find out.

If nothing else, she had more to add to her notebook of details about dragons. She'd already spent days on her computer, trolling through all of the video footage of the *Pyr* on YouTube. From each short film, she'd slurped one good image of each dragon and printed it out. Her compilation of known dragons included the date and location of their appearances. She tried to augment it with weaknesses and information from this old volume on hunting dragons.

There was the opal and gold dragon that appeared in Melissa Smith's documentary. There was the huge moonstone and silver dragon that had shifted shape in a crowd in Washington, D.C. There was a trio of them filmed fighting near a roundabout in England, an opal and gold dragon and a moonstone and silver one pitted against a jade and gold one.

Jac bit her lip as she watched that one again. Clearly, there could be a dispute between dragons. It was possible that the opal and gold one was the same dragon as the one in the documentary, and that the moonstone and silver one was the same dragon as shifted shape in D.C. Jac couldn't see any differences, so she concluded that they were the same dragons in different places.

Shortly after that, three dragons had closed the Thames Barrier in London. One was ebony and pewter, while the second was tourmaline and gold, his scales shading from green to purple and back again. The third had scales in vivid hues of orange and yellow, edged with gold, and was so vivid that the sight of him was like looking into the sun. Jac watched the video several times, listening to the commentator's remarks that the closure would save the city from flooding and keep thousands of people from dying.

Jac tapped her pencil. She was back to good dragons and bad dragons, but still skeptical. The three closing the Thames Barrier had kept the city of London from flooding. That might mean they were good—or it might mean that they had another agenda, one that had nothing to do with the survival of humans.

She wasn't yet convinced that any of the dragon shifters deserved to live, but she put a divider into her notebook and put these three dragons on the other side of it.

Of course, there was the video of the incident that had changed her own life. She could barely watch the topaz and gold dragon as he shook blood over the crowd, because her gaze was snared by Nathaniel and his excitement. God, she missed him. And she hated feeling responsible that he was gone. Her heart clenched that she'd taken him there, instead of to the Space Needle yet again, and Jac fought her tears as she pasted that dragon's image into her book.

The topaz one was obviously evil.

Jac dug deeper and found an interview with an eyewitness about the Thames Barrier. He'd observed a fight between two dragons over the controls. One was jade and gold, the other opal and gold. That had to be two of the ones who had fought by the roundabout, shortly before that. So, if the jade one had been evil, was the opal one good as Melissa insisted? Was the moonstone one good, too?

Jac didn't have nearly enough information. The videos were years old.

Where would she find these dragon shifters now? Where were their lairs?

And what would she do once she did find one?

Jac set the book aside in frustration and turned on the television. To her horror, there was a story breaking on the news, and more pictures of dragons.

These dragons had been over Easter Island.

Jac watched in disgust and revulsion as the photos of the dragons were shown over and over again. They were red and gold, and they looked so similar to each other that they could have been siblings. She guessed they probably were, because they'd been hatched out of the same nest. She winced as the eggs were shown, the way they disintegrated almost immediately revealing why dragon eggs had never been found before.

Her heart stopped cold when a topaz dragon appeared out of thin air, snatched the red and gold ones, and disappeared. That was the dragon from Seattle again!

The evil one had claimed these newborns.

Did that make them minions or captives?

Did they have a choice about their allegiances? Or would he force them to be evil just like him? Jac could only guess. She put the red and gold dragons on the "evil" side of her divider.

Guilty until proven innocent.

The helpful links on the screen took her to two other recent videos she had somehow missed, probably because she'd been so absorbed in reading Sigmund's book. The first showed a red and gold dragon, exactly like the ones hatched, battling an ebony and pewter one over Chicago. She added another image and sighting notes for the ebony and pewter one. He'd been one of the dragons at the Thames Barrier, she was sure.

So, did being attacked by evil dragons make him good? It was possible. Her notebook gained a third section: now she had Evil, Good and Unknown. The guy shifting shape in the desert went in the Unknown section too. He hadn't hurt Cassie Redmond, but that wasn't enough to make him a good guy.

The second linked video was blurry, as if shot from a cell phone by a shaking hand, and showed four red and gold dragons with a fifth red and gold one who was injured. Other than the injuries, they were identical, as far as she could see, just like the ones on Easter Island. Did they all look the same when they were hatched and develop differences later? These ones fought with each other, one—that seemed to be missing an arm—vanished, then the others consumed the last one. That said something horrible about sibling rivalry, and Jac was glad that her relationship with Sam had never disintegrated that much.

Were these the dragons just hatched at Easter Island? They sure looked similar, and the timing was right. Jac grimaced as she added a note to the Easter Island dragons, then wondered where those dragons were now. One was dead, but what of the others? They definitely belonged in the Evil category.

Were there more dragon eggs in the world, just waiting to be hatched? Jac was on her feet at the very idea. That would be the easiest way to destroy dragon shifters, she was sure of it. Maybe the eggs could be broken before the dragons were ready to hatch. Maybe they'd be weaker then and easier to kill.

Of course, these eggs had looked like round rocks before they hatched, and who knew how long they had been there, incubating. Checking every round rock on the planet seemed like an insurmountable challenge, but there had to be a way to stop these monsters.

Maybe Marco knew more than he'd revealed to her.

Maybe the package hadn't been misdelivered.

Maybe it had come from Marco.

The idea stopped Jac cold. Her new neighbor certainly was mysterious. There was something alluring about his patience and stillness. Jac liked that she could see his admiration in his eyes, but he didn't rush to make a move on her. If anything, he seemed to be waiting for an invitation. She had no doubt of his orientation—the heat in his eyes when he surveyed her said it all, and set her simmering, too. Jac had the feeling that she only needed to crook her little finger to have an awesome night with him, or even more.

She was giving serious consideration to crooking her finger.

If nothing else, Jac recognized a conversation starter when she found one. She wasn't sure if her hot new neighbor was home, because his apartment was really quiet. It always was. The only way to find out for sure was to go up there.

And ask him about dragons and their eggs. Either he'd reveal that he knew more and they'd find a common interest, or he'd think she was insane. Jac hoped for the former, but feared the latter.

Either way, she'd get to see him again. She could decide whether he was just as attractive as she remembered, or whether she'd imposed her own hope on the view. Jac was pretty sure she knew the answer, which was why there were butterflies in her stomach when she decided to go.

She brushed her hair and put on her favorite shirt for luck. Lipstick would be overkill, she knew, especially as she was trying to look casual. Just dropping by with a question. Jac checked her reflection in the mirror, picked up the book, then headed upstairs to knock on Marco's door. It was time to find out whether her sense that he knew more about the parcel than he'd admitted had any justification at all.

Would he tell her the truth?

Show her where to find dragons?

What about their eggs?

It sounded silly when Jac even thought those questions, but she had to find out.

Nothing ventured, nothing gained, after all.

She took a deep breath and knocked on his door.

Marco heard Jac coming.

He was thinking about the news story he'd overheard through the floor and wondering whether he could use it to draw as close to her as the darkfire desired.

Easter Island.

He liked islands.

But five new dragons hatched from eggs. That made no sense at all. Had someone been fooled? Or was this a manifestation of the darkfire loose in the world? Were they *Pyr* or *Slayer*? Marco couldn't be sure.

Not without going to the island himself. The scent of those new dragons would linger, and it would tell him a great deal.

As would any other lingering scents.

He would go.

He heard Jac's approach and decided he might not go alone.

Marco's eyes opened and he shifted shape leisurely, savoring the blue shimmer of light in his apartment. He loved the feeling of shifting shape, the way it made his body tingle. He felt as if he were filled with starlight when he changed to human form, and as if he were filled with fire when he shifted to dragon form. Either sensation was wonderful, and he savored the rightness of letting his body do what it did best.

It was dusk outside and he wondered if anyone in a nearby building might have seen the evidence of his shift. He smiled, wondering what they would make of it.

Unlike Erik and many of his fellows, Marco felt no threat from humans and little concern as to what they thought of the *Pyr*. They were treasures to be defended, no more than a task. He had slept through the hunting of dragons that so haunted Erik and could only be fascinated with the blend of weakness and strength that characterized humans.

Like his enchanting neighbor. Marco heard himself growl deep in his throat at the possibility of learning more of her weaknesses and strengths.

As well as what kind of pleasure would make her moan aloud. He wanted to see her wild with desire, incoherent with need, and demanding satisfaction.

From him, of course.

One day, he might have a firestorm, but to date, he'd been content to live alone, outside the perimeters of expectation. He'd been happy with the darkfire as his companion and fleeting connections with human women.

Jac enticed him as no woman had in a long time. Was it

because of her interest in dragons? Or his sense that the darkfire had led him to her?

Marco suspected that his firestorm would be in the old style, that he would satisfy it and leave his mate pregnant then disappear again. It wasn't in him to commit to anyone, not even to pledge to follow his fellow *Pyr*. Marco carved his own path and believed he always would. He had slept away too many centuries to fret about the short term. He considered the merit of satisfying his fascination with Jac, knowing that a night—or a taste—would likely be enough to sate him.

He probably should ensure that he wasn't distracted, in case the darkfire brought even more unexpected challenges in the year ahead.

The idea was so appealing that he strode to the bedroom with new purpose. In his human form, Marco was wearing just jeans and a T-shirt. The sound of the fridge echoed loudly in the apartment's emptiness. He would have unplugged it, ending its rhythmic noise, but he had some food in it, as much for the sake of appearances as anything else. The landlord had proven to be curious.

The darkfire crystal was on the windowsill, the blue-green light of the darkfire crackling within it, like a spark of lightning. It had become more agitated since the eclipse, as if it had drawn power from the blood moon. The darkfire in the gem was the only illumination in the room, and Marco chose to leave it in view.

He got the backpack from his closet and put some clothing into it. He tugged on a sweatshirt and set a jacket at the door beside his boots. He had a toothbrush and razor, a few toiletries and added them to the backpack's contents. He had a passport, which made him smile, because he didn't need anyone's permission to go anywhere. Erik had arranged it for him, 'just in case,' as well as some human affectations like credit cards and bank accounts. Marco had been amused, but was glad of those preparations now.

Perhaps the foresight of the leader of the *Pyr* had its uses.

He was keenly aware of Jac's approach and he timed his actions so that he'd, once again, meet her at the door. He had just laced his boots and tossed the pack over his shoulder when she arrived.

Jac knocked at the door, and her rap sounded loud. He could

smell her trepidation and her interest in him, a reaction that echoed his own fascination with her.

Maybe there could be a kind of kismet, even without a firestorm.

Marco opened the door to reveal Jac standing there, Sigmund's book clutched against her chest. She was wearing black jeans and boots, a wide belt around her hips and a black tank top that showed her curves to advantage. Her red linen blouse hung loose and open, the color suiting her well. She had dark hair and blue eyes, but wore neither make-up nor jewelry. Her long hair was drawn up in a ponytail, which made her neck look long, bare and delicious. He wanted with sudden fervor to caress the spot beneath her ear, even to kiss it.

"Hi," she said, summoning a nervous smile. "I wondered if you had a minute."

"I have all the time in the world," Marco replied.

Her gaze flicked over him, landing on the backpack. "You look like you're leaving."

"I am, but we can talk first."

She eyed him uncertainly, hesitating when he invited her into the barren apartment with a gesture. She stepped inside and he felt a primal surge of satisfaction that the woman he desired had entered his lair. The vigor of his dragon's response surprised Marco, but that only convinced him that his scheme was right. Jac looked around, and he felt her surprise when she saw the prophecy he'd written on the walls.

He waited for her to read it and noticed how her pulse quickened.

Great Wyvern, he could hear the beat of her heart and feel the rhythm of her breathing. He closed his eyes, savoring his awareness of her vitality, of the blood rushing through her veins, of the uncertainty in her stomach.

Of the desire burning a little lower. He inhaled slowly, wanting and fearing he would move too quickly.

Jac turned to him abruptly, her confidence fed by the presence of the prophecy, or maybe because of its contents. Marco was content to wait to find out.

Her eyes widened as she surveyed him and Marco knew his desire showed. To his delight, though, she didn't run.

In fact, she stepped closer, her choice making his blood hum with need.

Jac cleared her throat with purpose. "The thing is that this book was in the parcel you brought to me the other day, and I was wondering if you knew anything more about it."

"About the book or its contents?"

"Well, both."

"You think I opened your parcel?" Marco asked the question in a mild tone, not insulted but wanting to know how much she had guessed about him.

She blushed. "I thought maybe you'd sent it." Her color deepened. "I'm sorry. That's rude, but—" Her gaze trailed back to the prophecy and she bit her lip, the sight of her teeth on that ruddy bottom lip making him want to kiss her. "But maybe it's not crazy."

"Not crazy at all," Marco admitted, holding her gaze when she fell silent. "I did give it to you."

"Why not say so?"

"I wasn't sure you'd accept a gift from a stranger." He watched her swallow, noted how she was physically aware of him. As much as he wanted to taste her, he sensed a little trepidation in her attitude and was content to wait for her to come to him.

"Why?" Her voice had turned husky, which was promising.

"Because I thought you needed it, of course."

Her lips parted in surprise. Their gazes held for a potent moment, and Marco's desire for her redoubled. He held her gaze unblinkingly, letting her see his simmering desire. She caught her breath and licked that lip, then took a step closer. Her fingertips landed on his forearm and Marco was the one to catch his breath.

"I've been thinking about you," she whispered, her eyes wide.

"I've been thinking about you," Marco admitted in turn, which obviously pleased her.

The darkfire was crackling in the crystal, alive with possibilities.

The air seemed to crackle between them in the same way. It had been so long—that must be why his reaction to her was so powerful.

"I hardly know you," Jac said and abruptly looked away, surveying his apartment again. Her nervousness was interesting and made Marco wonder about her past. He certainly had done nothing to frighten her.

"There's an easy way to remedy that," he murmured and she flushed a little.

She gestured to the apartment. "There's nothing here," she said, as if that was a problem.

"Yet it is sufficient for my needs." Marco eyed her, then walked to the kitchen.

Her gaze followed him, then she did, too. "You don't even have a television."

"No."

"How do you know what's going on?"

Marco considered the merit of telling her that he listened to her television, but given her uncertainty, decided against such a confidence. He shrugged. "News is on every corner, in every restaurant, even at the gym. I prefer to have a place of refuge and silence."

She nodded, even as she scanned the emptiness of his kitchen. "Are you some kind of minimalist? Do you follow an eastern religion?" Jac's gaze flicked to his. "Or don't you really live here?"

"I stay here, for now," Marco conceded, intrigued by her insistence that he should have his home filled with possessions. "I have water to offer, but nothing else."

After he'd caught a whiff of the landlord's first prowl through the apartment, Marco had made an effort to appear more human. He'd bought a starter set of dishes with four plates, four mugs, four glasses and four bowls, and they were still in the box on the counter. He'd also bought those toiletries and some clothes to put in the closet.

Jac bit back a smile. "Because there's a tap included in your rent?"

Marco smiled and she actually laughed.

"Thanks. I'm fine." The sight of the dishes seemed to reassure her, although Marco couldn't imagine why. She walked back into the living room, her heels clicking on the hard wood floor. "Just like college," she murmured. "Living on pizza and beer, eaten out of the box and drunk from the bottle."

"That's not my diet," Marco said, leaning in the doorway to

watch her. He liked the way she walked, as if keeping time to music he couldn't hear. There was a rhythmic swing to her hips that he could have watched forever.

She stopped in front of the darkfire crystal, just as he had anticipated and was staring at it in fascination. "What's this?"

"It's called a darkfire crystal."

"Does it have a battery?" She bent down to peer at it. "What makes the spark?"

"The darkfire illuminates it."

She glanced back at him, her confusion clear. "I've never seen anything like it."

"I'm not surprised. It's the last one remaining in existence," he said, then strolled to her side. He picked it up, turning it in his hand while he savored the scent of her skin. The quartz crystal was large, several inches across and long enough for the points to protrude beyond his palm. The blue-green spark of the darkfire brightened at his touch, as it always did, and illuminated the apartment more brightly.

Jac caught her breath. "Can I touch it?"

Marco handed it to her, noting how the spark did not dim. It changed color, becoming greener when she held the stone, and flared wildly, as if it would force its way out of the stone. He dared to drop his hand to the back of her waist, felt her pulse leap, and liked that she didn't move away.

No, she took a little step closer, as if she wanted to be in his arms.

"I guess if you're only going to own one thing, it should be remarkable, like this." Jac smiled up at him and made to hand it back to him.

Marco instead closed his hand around hers, leaving the stone in her grip. The darkfire snapped and jumped when both of their hands were folded around it, illuminating the room with its strange light. Jac caught her breath. "It likes that," she whispered.

"It's not alone," Marco murmured and bent to touch his lips to that spot below her ear. He felt Jac shiver, then she turned to him without pulling her hand away.

She stared up at him, then reached to brush her lips across his. "I wish you weren't going," she confessed, then a twinkle lit her eyes. "Not when things are just getting interesting."

Marco smiled and bestowed a light kiss on her lips. She tasted sweet and hot, and it took everything in him not to claim her mouth in a possessive kiss. His heart thundered when she put her free hand on his shoulder and leaned against him, lifting her face for more. Then he kissed her deeply, partaking of the feast she offered. Her kiss fed the fire within him, driving all thought from his mind except the pleasure they could give each other.

When he lifted his head, her cheeks were flushed and her eyes sparkled. He couldn't evade the thought that the darkfire had lit her gaze. He kept her close, but lifted the crystal in his hand, noting how she watched him turn it in his grip. Its color changed back to its regular hue when she wasn't touching it anymore, and Marco doubted he was the only one to have noticed that.

"I don't own the darkfire crystal," he confessed, remembering her earlier comment. "It's here, but it's not my possession."

Jac eyed him warily. "Is it stolen?"

Marco shook his head. "No one can own such a thing. It exists and I'm fortunate that it's here, but it has its own destiny to fulfill." He held her gaze, his own falling to her lips once again.

Jac nestled a little closer. "Why? What's it for?" She dropped a fingertip to the stone and smiled when the spark leapt at her touch. Marco wondered why it responded to her, and concluded that he and the darkfire, as usual, were in agreement.

"It has many purposes," he admitted. "But you will probably be most interested in its ability to kill a dragon shape shifter."

Jac caught her breath, her eyes wide as she stared at Marco. "How do you know that?"

"Guess." He held her gaze and smiled slowly, willing her to make the obvious conclusion. When Jac glanced to the backpack he'd left by the door, Marco was sure she'd done just that.

But she made a different conclusion than he'd expected. "You're a dragon hunter," she whispered, and Marco had to admit that in a way, it was true.

He did hunt *Slayers*.

"Where *are* you going?" she asked with new urgency.

"Easter Island." Marco wanted more than anything for Jac to go with him. He was concerned, though, that asking her outright might seem too forward for her. That nervousness was gone, but he was aware that some of her uncertainty lingered.

He held her gaze for a long moment, then released her, letting his reluctance to do so show. He crossed the floor to pick up his backpack, feeling her gaze follow him. He put the crystal into the bag with care, ensuring it was rolled into a T-shirt for protection, then glanced up to find Jac still watching him. She gripped the book tightly, but there was a new fire in her eyes.

"Can I come with you?" she asked and Marco nodded.

"I was hoping you would," he admitted and was rewarded by her brilliant smile.

Jac knew what her sister would say: she was out of her mind.

Actually, pretty much everyone Jac knew would have said the same thing. Going on a whim to Easter Island with a neighbor she knew just about nothing about—except that he kissed like a god and that he hunted dragon shifters—was the most impulsive thing she'd ever done.

Which was saying something.

On the other hand, passing up the opportunity to join ranks with a guy who was obviously experienced in the art of hunting dragons would have been even more crazy, especially as she wanted to kill dragons and hadn't a clue where to start.

Granted, she'd never seen Marco take down a dragon, but he'd had the book and he had this darkfire crystal, and there was that verse on his wall. Something about three blood moons and darkfire and firestorms. Firestorms were discussed in this book he'd given her.

The fact that he'd written a poem on the wall of his apartment with a marker was enormously compelling to Jac. It indicated an artistic flair and a disregard for the rules that she admired. The emptiness of his apartment showed a disinterest in conventionality and the expectations of others that she liked, too. She felt as if they were kindred spirits and was certain she could trust him. He was clearly as serious about hunting dragons as she was, and she admired the dedication shown by his focus. She liked that he had immediately decided to go where the dragons were. She was glad she'd knocked on his door and caught him before he'd departed.

And she was thrilled to be going along.

Jac didn't really want to talk to her sister, but she couldn't just disappear either. Irresponsibility was one trait Jac didn't possess. Fortunately, her sister had taken to turning off her phone since leaving her job. Jac called Sam, her fingers crossed and figured it was a sign of everything going her way that the call was immediately directed to voice mail. She left a message, explaining that she was going to a retreat. It was a lame excuse but Sam would probably accept it.

Jac packed in five minutes flat, grabbed her passport and credit cards. She debated the merit of taking the book and decided it was too risky. She really didn't want to lose it. Instead, she tucked it under the loose floorboard in her closet, and piled shoeboxes on top of it, thanking her lucky stars that she lived in an old building filled with idiosyncrasies. She took her notebook on dragons, though, even though it wouldn't fit in her purse. She grabbed a bigger purse from her closet and dumped the contents of her smaller one into it, then jammed the notebook in the side. No doubt she'd have time in an airport somewhere to restore order to the contents so that she could find everything quickly.

Jac was out of breath when she met Marco in the lobby of the apartment building and knew her relief that he was still there showed. He had a cab waiting and took her bag to put it in the trunk beside his own. He held the door for her, too, and Jac felt like a queen when he settled beside her.

He offered his hand, palm up, and she glanced up to find that simmer in his eyes and that slow smile curving his lips. She put her hand in his, liking how he closed his fingers around hers. His grip was proprietary, but she knew he'd release her at the slightest sign she'd prefer he do so. Jac had no intention of giving such a sign. He was so different from men she'd dated before. He waited for her to show her preference, but still managed to make his interest clear. Finally, impulse was steering her in the right direction. She eased closer, so that her thigh was pressed against his and felt Marco give her hand a minute squeeze.

God, he was hot.

She had to hope that the next time he kissed her, it was in a place where they could get naked.

"What's with the verse on your wall?" she asked once the cab was headed to the airport. "What does it mean?"

He shook his head, appearing to be untroubled. "I don't know."

"So, it's a clue." Jac nodded, excited to be closer to the action. "Do you have it written down somewhere?"

Marco tapped his temple, then bent toward her. He whispered the verse into her ear, his breath making her skin tingle. Jac felt that it was impossibly intimate to be in a cab at night with this man murmuring so low that only she could hear his words. She discovered that her fingers were trembling as she wrote the verse in her notebook. Her heart was racing, too.

> *Three blood moons mark the debt come due*
> *Will the* Pyr *triumph or be hunted anew?*
> *Three eclipses will awaken the spark*
> *In thirteen monsters breeding in dark...*

Jac was so consumed with the recollection of Marco's kiss and the desire for another that she barely understood the rest of the words as she wrote them down.

There'd be time for that later, Jac was sure.

For now, there was the muscled heat of Marco's thigh, the warmth of his breath in her ear, the tightness of his grip on her hand, and the knowledge that they were embarking on an adventure together.

That was more than enough.

Sam's first day of having a booth for her readings was clear and sunny, a perfect California afternoon. She set up her canopy at the local farmers' market and was a little bit nervous about taking money from people for readings when she was so new at it. She had to make a start, though, and the other vendors were very friendly. Sam sat at her table, enjoying how the tablecloth adorned with moons and stars fluttered in the breeze. The sunlight came through her canopy, and she didn't mind at all that she had no takers as yet.

She felt good.

It had been a long time since she'd stopped to smell the

proverbial roses.

She had Sloane to thank for that change.

And her perspective had improved even more since she'd apologized to him. His parting kiss and promise to call her had given her an optimism that made everything seem possible again. Strangely enough, her excursion into town to delicately enquire after him had sent some new customers her way. She'd looked up the quote he'd given her and had requested the book through the library, liking the sense she was making progress on solving a mystery.

Thanks to Sloane, she was doing better at enjoying the view, instead of condemning herself for her failures. She was even managing to remember Nathaniel a little bit, the good times, in a way that she knew was healthy. She'd unpacked an old photo album the night before and smiled at his birthday parties.

Well, she'd cried a bit, too.

At least she wasn't numb any more. Something was healing within her. Going to Sloane's house that first time on impulse had started her on a good path. Sam had to think that impulse might be a good thing. She'd definitely under-rated its advantages.

She wished that her sister was a little less impulsive, though. It seemed that Jac was looking for things to do, maybe to avoid thinking about Nathaniel—or maybe to avoid talking to Sam. Maybe to avoid growing up, or having a life of her own. Sam didn't know.

Jac had moved across the country on a whim. Why did she even want to be in Seattle? And now this. Sam thought of the message Jac had left on her voice mail and irritation stirred. How like Jac to give half of the information and leave no way to contact her. Sometimes it seemed that Jac took being a free spirit a bit too far.

Their father had always said that Jac had to make her own mistakes and follow her own path, that saving her from herself wouldn't accomplish anything, given how stubborn she was. He'd said that only Jac could find her way, then had rolled his eyes to show his expectation that Jac never would.

Sam couldn't help wishing that their father hadn't been so right, or that she was better at taking her sister's nature in stride. She wished that she and Jac could really talk, although they never had. It was worse since Nathaniel had gotten sick. Sam hadn't wanted to blame Jac or say anything accusatory out loud. She knew her sister blamed herself for what had happened, but also that Nathaniel had been in the wrong place at the wrong time. She hadn't been able to talk about him at all, and the tension between them had only grown. Now that they were both alone, Sam found herself wishing for a stronger bond with her only sister.

She didn't even know how to start, though.

Sam stirred in her chair with some impatience, disliking that her serene mood was being disturbed. She considered the sunlight again, the happy crowds, the light breeze, and forced herself to feel content. She thought about how good she felt when Sloane touched her, how the way he looked at her made her feel beautiful and powerful, and couldn't wait for him to come back.

He'd promised and she knew he was the kind of man who kept his vows.

Sam liked that, a lot.

But what had he needed to do in Chicago and then New York? As much as she wanted to keep things simple between them, Sam couldn't deny that she wanted to know.

That quote was creepy, after all, and what she'd read of the book was worse. Necromancers. Sam shivered. That was hardly better than dragons.

What would she say if he asked more about her reaction to his tattoo? That she had a pathological fear of dragons? That sounded stupid.

Telling him the truth was out of the question.

What if he figured it out for himself?

The prospect of him guessing her big secret nearly gave her palpitations.

Sam took a deep breath. She supposed that Sloane's absence gave her too much time to think about it. She'd always over-analyzed everything, that's what Jac said, and maybe it was true.

Sam smiled at the people strolling past her booth, pushing strollers and carrying baskets stuffed with fresh produce, artisan bread and cheeses from the local creamery, as she tried to let her worry go. It was starting to work, much to her surprise, and she pulled out her tarot card book for a bit of studying.

"How much for a reading?" a man asked, his voice low enough

to give Sam shivers.

She glanced up, only to find the man who had been filling her thoughts leaning against the corner pillar of her booth. Sloane was wearing jeans and desert boots, a red T-shirt and had an untucked chambray shirt open over top. He carried a bulging canvas tote bag, the end of a baguette protruding from it and was wearing a battered straw hat. He took off his sunglasses and smiled at her, making Sam glad she was sitting down.

The man was hot enough to melt her knees.

Never mind her reservations.

CHAPTER ELEVEN

wenty bucks," Sam said.

"That's cheap."

"Neighborhood discount," she replied, picking up her cards before she realized the import of what he'd said. She paused to consider him, liking how he seemed to have been waiting on that. "How do you know the going rate?"

"Call it a weakness," he said easily and sauntered into her booth. Sloane sat down opposite her and tipped back his hat, that smile even more potent at close proximity. Sam had thought it a temperate day but she got shivery chills when his knee bumped hers under the table. He put a twenty dollar bill on the table, then took the cards from her hand. She knew she didn't imagine that he ensured their fingers brushed. He shuffled the cards easily, despite their large size.

"You must have just gotten back," she said.

He feigned surprise. "And you haven't even dealt the cards yet. Wow."

Sam laughed and plucked the shuffled deck from his hand. "I noticed that your truck wasn't back this morning and you know it."

His eyes twinkled in a way that made her feel feminine and desirable. "I'm glad you noticed." His gaze locked with hers and Sam felt the awareness rise between them.

She said the first thing that came to her lips. "You didn't mention why you had to go to Chicago and then New York."

"No, I didn't." Sloane leaned over the table and changed the subject before she could blink. "I'm guessing that asking why you hate dragons so much would be a violation of the rules?"

"It seems like we're renegotiating the rules."

His smile turned wicked. "Now, that's intriguing. So, you'll explain about dragons if I tell you why I had to go?"

Sam's heart was racing. "Maybe we should go back to the rules, after all."

"Chicken." Sloane's gaze warmed as he surveyed her. "What makes you think you're the only one who likes to unveil secrets?"

"I'm guessing I'm not."

Sloane shook his head. "Maybe it's something we have in common."

"Maybe," Sam acknowledged, liking that idea a lot more than the possibility of him figuring out her secrets. "Maybe it's healthier to let some secrets stay buried."

He eyed her for a long moment, and Sam couldn't guess his thoughts.

Once it wouldn't have bothered her, but with this man, in this moment, she really wanted to know what was in his mind.

It might even be worth sharing one or two of her own secrets.

"Maybe we should start again." Sloane offered his hand, which looked just as strong, warm and welcoming as it had that first day. Sam was relieved by the gesture, and even more by his words. "I'm Sloane. Would you like to have frequent and enthusiastic sex, with no commitment, and just the occasional question?"

Sam found herself laughing. "I would," she said and put her hand in his. Sloane closed his fingers over her hand, the possessive gesture making her heart pound, then pressed a kiss to the back of her hand.

"Deal," he murmured, the low sound of his voice making everything inside her flutter. She wanted to ask what he'd done, when he'd leave again, everything about him—but that was more like an interrogation than an occasional question. She pulled her hand from his and shuffled the cards.

"We should ask the cards about those secrets," she said and Sloane grinned.

"My thoughts exactly. Do what you do, neighbor of mine."

Sam sat straighter in her chair, feeling that it was portentous that Sloane would be her first reading, and turned over the top card.

"Just a three-card layout for that discounted price," Sam said, as if she did this all the time. It was her first official reading and she was well aware of how closely Sloane was watching her. "Past, present and future." She set the first card down. "This is about your past." It was The Hermit. "Um, this is a card about learning..."

"Is it?" Sloane drawled, and Sam realized she must have it wrong.

He watched her, inscrutable, and didn't offer a single clue.

Except for her conviction that he was enjoying himself. His eyes weren't just twinkling. They were dancing.

"Yes," she insisted, trying to brazen her way through it. "It means that you'll live to a very ripe old age and become very wise."

"But I thought it was the card for my past."

"Then you come from a family with a lot of longevity. You'll live long because it's in your genes." She nodded as if certain of that, although she had a feeling she'd mixed it up with another card. Sloane seemed to be biting back a smile. "And your present," she said, turning over the next card quickly.

Sloane couldn't fully hide his surprise. "The Nine of Wands," he said.

It was hard to remember the meanings of seventy-eight cards anyway, and tougher still with Sloane watching her so intently. "A blond messenger has sent you an announcement," she decided.

Sloane leaned an elbow on the table, bringing his steady gaze even closer. "I thought the cards that had pages or squires were male messengers."

Sam became flustered, because it seemed that he knew more about doing a reading than she did. He certainly wasn't pleased with this card. "Give me a second," she said tightly and dug her reference book out from beneath the table. She looked up the card, then smiled at Sloane. "You're being tested in your job."

He leaned back. "By a blond messenger?"

Sam resisted the urge to consult the book again and decided to go for it. "Maybe. Yes! The third card will reveal the result." She turned it over quickly, then couldn't utter a sound.

It was The Lovers.

Sam supposed it was a statistical probability that sooner or later, a card would be right.

"Me and the male messenger." Sloane winced. "I'm thinking that's a long shot." He bent closer, his eyes gleaming. "I'm definitely heterosexual."

Sam felt like her body was on fire. She knew his orientation, without a doubt. "Well, it could be someone else who is blond," she said quickly. "It definitely is a card about physical union."

"I don't work in that kind of a place, though," he said, his tone teasing again. "I mean, I'd frown on that kind of intimacy at the shop, even if I wasn't the only one working there."

"It could be a close associate," Sam said, knowing she sounded desperate. She realized that Sloane was looking at her hair, which was indeed blond, and felt her cheeks heat.

Sloane chuckled. "You really do stink at this, don't you?" he said, his tone so affectionate that she couldn't take offense. "What made you think you could pretend to be a tarot card reader?" He shook his head, not seeming to expect an answer.

Sam impulsively chose to give him one.

Even though it was only part of the truth.

"I'm not pretending."

"At the very least, you're learning."

Sam blushed. "I needed something to do, something that was new and different. A fresh start." She paused. "And I thought it would be easy." She winced at the admission but Sloane smiled. He was clearly pleased that she was confiding in him, so Sam told him a bit more. "How hard could it be to memorize seventy-eight picture cards? I've done more than that, a lot of times."

The periodic table, for example.

"There are lots of other things you could have done."

But nothing so opposite to everything she'd done with her life to date. Sam didn't want to admit that. Yet. "You need credentials to be an architect or a chef or a lawyer."

"But not a dog walker."

"I don't do well with small creatures."

"It doesn't look like you're playing to your strengths with tarot cards."

"But I've always wanted to be able to do this. Call it a dream.

My sister reads tarot cards, and she makes it look simple."

"Aha!" Sloane smiled. "Sibling rivalry. You thought you could easily do something she does easily."

"Pretty much." Sam grimaced at the truth in that. "But it isn't working."

"Are you that similar?"

She laughed despite herself. "No."

"Maybe she listens to her intuition more than you do."

"She's a lot more impulsive than I am."

Sloane gave her a look. "Is your sister lucky in love?"

"No." Sam shook her head at the very notion. "She has the very worst luck with men. It's so sad."

"Why?"

"Because she's always wanted to have kids, a husband, a home, all the traditional bells and whistles, but no luck." Just saying that aloud was depressing. Sam feared that this retreat Jac was on somehow involved another loser of a man who would leave her broken-hearted, far from home and out of cash. Had Nathaniel's death left Jac afraid to reach for her own dreams, lest they be torn away? Sam sighed, only realizing after she did that Sloane hadn't missed a bit of her reaction.

"So far," he said. "She can't be that old."

"Tick tock," Sam said. "Women can't have kids forever."

He frowned at the cards, and she realized that she might have inadvertently revealed that she'd had all those things—if only for a while. "Is that what's making you think we can only have sex? You were being impulsive like your sister, but she's unlucky in love?"

Sam regarded him with disapproval, trying to look more annoyed than she was. It was far too easy to confide in Sloane, that was for sure. If she didn't watch out, he'd know everything about her—and still be a mystery to her. "What happened to the *occasional* question?"

Sloane was unapologetic. "You're right." He snapped his fingers. "I forgot." His mischievous smile, though, proved that he hadn't.

"I need to figure out how to get you to answer my questions so readily," she said under her breath and his grin was bright enough to steal her breath away.

"Let's try this the other way around, then." Sloane scooped up the three cards and handed them back to her. "Go ahead. Shuffle."

"What? *I'm* doing the readings." Sam felt agitated, not just because she'd been outed, but because he seemed to find it endearing that she couldn't give him a reading.

She wasn't *cute*.

"Not this time. Let me do yours."

"Well, I doubt you'll be any better at this than me..."

He interrupted her smoothly. "So, what's the harm?" He widened his eyes slightly. "Afraid the cards will reveal the real truth of who you are?" He held up the cards. "Go on, take a chance." Again, his manner was teasing, but Sam caught the challenge in his tone.

She picked up the cards and shuffled vigorously, wanting to get this over with. It was irrational to suggest that pieces of cardboard could give away any of her secrets.

Much less to be worried about it.

"No, no, no," Sloane said, his voice low and melodic. "You have to get into the spirit of it. This isn't a mission to be completed, or something to strike off your job list. It's an exercise in opening your mind to possibilities."

"Is it?"

"Sure. Think about your situation and your question. Close your eyes and pour your energy into the cards."

"You *have* done this before," Sam accused, but he gave her an intent look. Pour her energy into the cards. That was just the kind of flakey thing she'd expect Jac to say. Well, they were in California and Sloane had lived here for a while. And really, she should learn how to say those sorts of things. If nothing else, she could take some performance tips from Sloane.

She took a deep breath and closed her eyes, shuffling more slowly. She tried to believe. She tried—incredibly—to channel some of Jac's ease with matters illogical and intuitive and had a strange feeling that she was making a bit of progress.

"Give them to me when you feel that they are ready," Sloane advised, his voice spellbinding.

Sam had to remember to speak just the way he did for her clients.

Then her eyes flew open as she realized what he'd said.

"When they're ready?" she echoed, unable to keep the skepticism from her voice. "Like eggs in the frying pan?"

Sloane's quick smile made her heart skip a beat. "You're supposed to believe in this," he murmured, his eyes twinkling. "Close your eyes and shuffle. Stop when your intuition tells you the cards are in the right order, when they're ready."

"There should be an indicator light."

"There is. It's in your mind."

Sam decided to believe. She breathed slowly, thought about pouring her energy into the cards and tried to focus on them to the exclusion of everything else. That was a challenge with Sloane's knee pressing against hers, but she gave it her best shot.

If only to win his approval.

Sam shuffled slowly, feeling the weight of the cards in her hand, hearing the way they brushed against each other. She felt the wind and smelled Sloane's skin, and shuffled. Suddenly, she had the distinct feeling that she should stop shuffling. It was a lot like the impulse that had sent her to his pool originally and she chose to trust it.

"There." She handed the cards to him, again feeling the warmth of his skin brush against her own.

"Good job." Sloane smiled at her, as if she'd climbed Mount Everest, and she couldn't take a breath.

"How do you know?"

"I can feel your energy in the cards," he murmured, and Sam didn't know what to say to that. Could he?

"Past," Sloane said softly, and she leaned forward as he turned over a card. "The Magician." He nodded approval. "A card governing those who create, who investigate, who are energetic, devoted to their lifework and effective. These are people with demanding careers who solve issues of import to more than themselves. This is what you left behind when you came to your current situation."

Sam blinked. He really did know this stuff. She was sure that must be exactly what the book said.

But wait. The Magician was about *her* past.

It was a bit spooky to have the first card be so right.

Sloane smiled with satisfaction. "I knew you'd run away from something, and it wasn't a busy practice reading tarot cards."

"But..."

He waved his hand. "You don't have to tell me. I like following the breadcrumbs and trying to figure it out."

Sam smiled. "I like solving riddles, too."

Sloane's answering smile was warm enough to set her on fire. "And you are one serious riddle, Samantha Wilcox." She couldn't take a breath when he looked at her like that. There seemed to be an electrical charge between them as their gazes locked and held. His voice dropped. "I could Google you, but that would be cheating."

Sam's heart stopped cold then lunged for her throat.

Sloane wagged a finger at her, obviously having noted her reaction. Then he cleared his throat and tapped his finger on the card. "Must have been an important job. The problem with that kind of job, though, is that there's always a lot of pressure that goes with it. It's tough to balance the challenge and the responsibility with your own needs." He seemed to see right into her heart. "People with demanding careers have to make choices and strike balances. They have to give things up and hope they choose right for the greater good."

She swallowed, not knowing what to say. "I didn't realize you'd know about those kinds of jobs."

"There's a lot you don't know about me," Sloane said.

That was for sure.

"'It is said the wand would wake the sleeping and send the awake to sleep. If applied to the dying, their death was gentle; if applied to the dead, they returned to life,'" she quoted.

"You found William Godwin." He was clearly pleased that she'd looked up the citation.

"You invited me to." Sam watched him. She couldn't ask him if he was a necromancer. That was crazy. "Why do you really have that tattoo?"

"I told you already." It was interesting that even though Sloane's posture hadn't changed, she had a definite sense that he'd just shut a door against her and thrown away the key. He turned over another card. "Your present. The Knight of Cups."

"I know this one!" Sam said, triumphant. "It's the dark-haired stranger sweeping into the questioner's life. See? It's the suit of cups, which means true love." She sat back, proud of herself, not troubling to hide that her gaze lingered on his dark hair.

Could the cards be right about her present, too?

"Maybe he's just a lover who arrives with a bottle of wine," he teased, but Sam understood the warning. "Remember: it *is* just the card for the present, not the future."

Sam exhaled but didn't break his gaze. "Maybe great sex is good enough for the moment."

"Maybe. Maybe not." Sloane turned over the next card. "And your future. Justice." He leaned back and considered her, his gaze warm. That slow smile was turning her to jelly and making it hard to concentrate on the cards. "A card about weighing all the variables and making decisions."

"A card about admitting the whole truth," Sam added, remembering that bit. She braced her elbows on the table and leaned toward Sloane, impulsively taking the advice of the cards. "So, maybe sex *isn't* enough."

"Future," he reminded her.

"Or it won't be." Sam found that surprisingly likely.

Maybe she should tell Sloane so.

"Here's the thing," she confessed on impulse. "I thought that having sex with you once would be enough." It wasn't that hard to admit, not once she decided to do it. Everyone always said that she couldn't talk about her feelings, but maybe Sam could learn something new.

"We did it more than once," Sloane noted, his gaze simmering.

"And still it wasn't enough."

"Imagine that."

"I do."

His smile was quick. Sloane leaned forward, echoing her posture and dropping his voice low. "Here's another thing," he said softly. "I've been wandering around this market today, working up my nerve to seduce you the way you deserve."

Sam shook her head, her heart racing. "I don't believe it. You don't need to work up your nerve for anything."

Certainly not seduction.

"You might have changed your mind since the other night. It might have been a dream, or wishful thinking. I *was* exhausted."

"But not any more."

"Not any more." Sloane glanced down at his bag. "And, now I

have this bottle of local wine, a loaf of fresh bread, some cheese and fruit, and if you've changed your mind, I'll have no one to share it with."

"Good thing I haven't," Sam said, fighting her smile.

Sloane nodded agreement. "It certainly is." He leaned back in his chair, his thigh against hers under the table.

Sam took a breath, feeling very bold, then leaned across the table to whisper. "The thing is that I have a small problem."

"Really?" Sloane pressed his leg against hers a little more firmly.

It took everything in Sam to not jump into his lap. Instead, she chose to tell him just what she was thinking. "I like sex in the afternoon, and it's a perfect day, in my opinion, for sex in the afternoon."

Sloane's gaze brightened. "That's a problem?"

Sam tapped the card. "I'm not sure when my Knight of Cups will turn up."

"Bearing wine or not?"

"Exactly."

Sloane pushed the card across the table in a deliberate gesture, watching its progress. "The card is supposed to represent your present," he noted, apparently not at all shocked that she'd been so blunt. He glanced at his watch. "And it's 2:15." He laid his hand flat over the card and closed his eyes. Sam fought her laughter as he pretended to channel a message from the card, and his eyes flew open in time to catch her expression. He leaned close and whispered. "The cards say he might turn up anytime."

Sam laughed aloud, feeling playful and happy. There was a lot to be said for flirting with Sloane.

There was more to be said for spending the afternoon having sex with him.

She pretended to be serious then. "I should get home, so I can welcome a dark-haired lover to my door."

"Make sure he's the one bearing wine," Sloane added with a shake of his finger.

"I will."

"What about your customers?"

"There's not exactly a line. And I think I should study the cards more." Their gazes locked and held for a potent moment.

"Know anybody who might help me take down this canopy?"

"I think I just might," Sloane said and got to his feet with a speed that convinced Sam that their thoughts were as one.

"Who knew I'd end up with such a helpful neighbor," Sam teased, feeling lighter and happier than she had in quite a while. She still didn't know his secrets, but right now, it was hard to care.

Sloane turned to give her an appreciative smile. He caught her around the waist and whispered in her ear. "Maybe it was in the cards."

Sam laughed only a little before Sloane silenced her with a kiss.

Easter Island.

It was one of the zillion places on Jac's bucket list. Being here with Marco was incredible. She lay in bed in their hotel room, watching the night sky beyond the window, and marveled that she was here. Her sense of time was all messed up after the journey, and even though they'd tried to stick to local time, she was wide awake when she should have been falling asleep.

The trip had been long. To Jac's amazement, they'd had to fly to Chile, hopscotching practically all the way to the South Pole, then back north and west to the island. They'd connected in Miami, in Rio, then finally caught the flight to Easter Island from Santiago.

They'd arrived just after noon and had rented a 4x4, which didn't seem very environmentally friendly to Jac, but one look at the roads had convinced her of its practicality. They'd found a hotel and booked a room, gone for a late lunch and then crashed. Their host had assumed they were a married couple and put them in a room with a queen-sized bed, and neither she nor Marco had corrected his assumptions.

They were both exhausted, she was sure, and had slept like the dead for a few hours after eating.

Now Jac was awake, listening to the deep rhythm of Marco's breathing. She loved that they were in bed together, that he was practically naked beside her, and yearned to take a good look at him. Although they'd fallen asleep lying flat on their backs beside each other, Jac had awakened to find them spooned together, with Marco's heat curled protectively behind her. It felt good enough that she didn't want to move.

Even to check him out.

There was a huge window opposite the foot of the bed, which showed a square of night sky. The stars were brilliant and so numerous that she couldn't believe it.

His darkfire crystal was on the sill, the blue-green light within it dancing like a miniature bolt of lightning. Marco's body was warm against her back, and it was both comforting and sexy to be nestled against him like this.

Jac had learned a lot about her mysterious neighbor on their journey, and she made a mental list as she snuggled beneath the weight of the arm he'd thrown around her waist. He was vegetarian. He was calm in any situation. He was unfailingly polite. He slept very little, and he always looked composed. He didn't touch her a lot in public, and Jac was glad about that. She preferred that intimacy be private and that a man be a gentleman. But there was no doubting his interest, which she supposed was why the hotel owner had assumed they were a couple. Marco held her hand and he whispered in her ear and he leaned his leg against hers. When she'd dozed in airports or on flights, she'd awakened to find herself tucked against his heat, like he was her guardian angel.

And the heat of desire lingered in his eyes. Jac wiggled a little when she remembered that.

Plus he never lost sight of that crystal. He cradled it in his hands whenever they had to go through security and passed it with care to attendants along with his passport. His reverence for the stone and his solemnity were so great that they invariably showed the same care for the stone as he did. The strange thing was that there was no spark in it whenever they passed through security checks.

Even stranger, Jac caught him whispering to it a few times.

Then he'd smile and wink, his mischievous expression making her heart skip, and tuck it away in his pack again. She liked that playfulness about him, that sense that he didn't assume that all the rules were correct. She suspected that he was unconcerned with convention, just like she was—except more so.

He could drive a manual transmission, which was intriguing to Jac. She wondered where he was from.

The light in the crystal flickered more quickly, and she glanced over her shoulder at Marco, only to find him watching her in silence. He smiled and his eyes glowed.

Did the stone respond to his mood or his state?

"Did it know you were awake?" she whispered.

"It's just a stone," he whispered back, but she could tell by the glimmer in his eyes that he didn't believe that any more than she did.

She twisted a little to see his face better and felt his arousal against her hip. "Where did you get it?"

"I inherited it."

"From your parents?"

He shook his head minutely, his gaze darting to the stone and back to her. "From the man who raised me. I thought he was my grandfather, but it turned out he wasn't."

"Who was he?"

"His name was Pwyll."

Jac tried to say the name herself, which made Marco smile. He corrected her until she managed a decent approximation. "What kind of name is that?"

"Welsh."

"Are you from Wales?"

He nodded, his gaze fixed upon her. Jac braced herself on her elbow to look down at him. "But Marco isn't a Welsh name. I thought you were Italian."

"My mother was from Rome."

"But she didn't raise you?"

"She died," he admitted quietly, his regret obvious. "I never knew her."

"My mom died, too," Jac found herself confessing in a whisper. "When I was twenty, she died of breast cancer."

"But you knew her," he whispered.

"I did," Jac admitted, feeling sorry for Marco that he'd never had the opportunity to know his own mom. "I loved her." She smiled sadly. "I miss her."

Marco reached up, and Jac realized she'd shed a single tear. He lifted it from her cheek with a fingertip, then touched his finger to his own lips, swallowing her tear. She found her fingertips on his cheek, her fingers fanning out to frame his face. It seemed the most natural thing in the world to touch her lips to his again.

And what happened after that felt even more right. Marco's fingers speared into her hair and he drew her closer, making no effort to disguise his desire. Jac's fingers were in his hair and her breasts crushed against his chest as his kiss turned possessive and hungry. She responded to him in kind, loving how he made a little growl beneath his breath. His eyes were glittering when his hands swept over her, removing her T-shirt in one smooth gesture. He surveyed her, smiled, then bent to kiss her taut nipple. Jac sighed with pleasure, savoring the weight of his hand as it slid over her waist, across her stomach, and his fingertips eased between her thighs. He conjured a wonderful heat beneath her skin, one that felt both natural and right.

Inescapable.

Jac didn't notice how the darkfire in the crystal burned with new fire, crackling and snapping with vigor as she and Marco made love with slow fervor in the night.

It was early evening, after several rounds of lovemaking, and Sam had disappeared into the washroom. Sloane was on the prowl, curious about his partner even though he knew he shouldn't be. His interest in her wasn't that easily contained.

Sam's house was impersonal to the point of carelessness, as if she really didn't intend to stay. There were boxes stacked against the walls in several rooms, and quite a few rooms were empty. Maybe she couldn't be bothered to unpack. The cupboards in her kitchen had the bare minimum of dishes and implements. The few pieces of furniture she possessed were comfortable and built to last, but the house was, at the very least, austerely furnished.

Sloane was intrigued. Had she lost all of her treasures in that divorce? Or was she indifferent to material possessions? With Sam, answers only seemed to breed more questions. Sloane wondered whether he'd ever figure her out completely.

Was that why she intrigued him so much?

The house itself was one he'd always admired. It was probably the oldest house in the region, a Mission-style fortress of high ceilings, dark wood and white plaster walls. The floors were tile and he liked the blue and yellow Mexican tiles used on the kitchen counter and backsplash. The house was in need of all the usual updates, plumbing and wiring, and it could use a new roof, as well as some landscaping. He wasn't sure whether Sam had a renovation vision for it or not. She just seemed to be camped in as little of it as possible.

The exception was the dining room of the house, which she had converted to a study. There were teak bookshelves along one wall, their modern lines a bit incongruous with the house, and they were crowded with books. He recognized that she was a fellow reader by the careful organization of her library. This was one bit of unpacking she'd not only done, but spent time getting right. Two old leather armchairs were in the same room, their oxblood upholstery wrinkled with use and the brass studs that lined the edges a bit tarnished. There was a large end table of glass and wrought iron between them. Even though the furnishings were of different styles, he guessed that she liked all of the pieces.

The room's eclectic look appealed to him. It looked comfortable, like a refuge. It had character.

There were two books on the table, a Minette Walters mystery and a guide to reading tarot cards. The second book made Sloane smile.

There was a lonely cactus on the sill in need of water, so Sloane gave it a drink, then perused the bookshelves. Sam liked mysteries, when she read fiction, it was clear, because there was a good selection of them on the shelves. She had a lot of non-fiction as well, mostly books about cell biology, viruses, diseases, and virus hunters, mixed with a few volumes on reading cards and telling fortunes. He was running a finger along the science books, comparing her collection to his own, when he found a book that seemed to be made of silver metal.

It wasn't a book. It was a framed picture that had been slid between the books.

So it wouldn't be seen.

It was as if Sam couldn't bear *not* to have the picture, but didn't want to be confronted with it all the time. There was a box beside it, a gold gift box, but Sloane ignored that. Sam wanted to know where the picture was, he guessed, and to consider it when she chose.

That was enough to prompt Sloane to pull it out.

A young boy smiled out of the frame. It was clearly a school picture from an early grade and the boy was missing one of his front teeth. He was a handsome kid, all the same, and his smile was brilliant. Sloane traced the frame with a fingertip, hoping this wasn't one of the small creatures Sam had said she didn't manage well.

On the back was a notation in neat letters: *Nathaniel. Grade One.*

That this was the only personal photograph he'd noticed in Sam's home—never mind that she'd hidden it from view—told Sloane how important it was. Was it a nephew? A brother? Her son? Had she lost custody of a child in the divorce? Or had something terrible happened to this boy?

Nathaniel.

Sloane looked more closely. Nathaniel Sullivan had been the first victim claimed by the Seattle virus, the young boy whose face had been shown all over the world, both when Jorge had infected that crowd and when Nathaniel had subsequently died. It was impossible to forget the kid's brave smile. It had been only about six months since he'd succumbed.

Although this boy was photographed at a younger age, Sloane could see similarities.

Or was he imagining them?

He remembered that there had been a bitter irony in the story, because Nathaniel's parents had been biological researchers. Virus hunters. Sloane recalled now that mother and son hadn't had the same surname, but he hadn't paid much attention to it at the time.

Sloane guessed that when he did Google Sam, he'd discover that she was Nathaniel Sullivan's mother.

And The Magician. He guessed she had burned out in that last desperate hunt for an antidote. She'd lost her son, her marriage and her desire to work. She felt she was a failure, and quite reasonably, she despised dragons.

The collection of books along with this picture told him Sam's secret and the source of the emotional wound he'd sensed in her. He wondered what he would do if he ever had a firestorm and a son, one who developed an ailment he couldn't cure, and felt a surge of sympathy for Sam.

His desire to help her to heal redoubled.

Sam came into the room then, wearing jeans and a loose shirt, as she rubbed a towel over her hair. At the sound of her footsteps, Sloane returned the picture to its hiding place. He thought he managed it just in time.

"I thought you might join me in the shower," she said, then caught her breath when she saw where he was standing.

The way she froze and stared told Sloane that he was absolutely right about her secret.

"Do you always go through people's books?" she demanded. It wasn't about her books, though.

Sloane smiled at her, as if he hadn't noticed anything important at all. "I can never resist a good library."

"I'm not sure you'll find it that good," Sam said, her smile tight. "They're mostly reference books at that end, and intense reads for the lay person."

"And a tarot card reader wouldn't be a lay person when it comes to microbiology and germ warfare?" Sloane prodded gently.

Sam bristled, but recovered well. "You've already guessed I'm not a mystic."

"And what do you think you know about me and my reading tastes?"

She softened her tone. "I'm sorry. I don't mean to be insulting, but a lot of them are written at a very specific and detailed level. They're not accessible reads."

Sloane turned his back on her, needled even though he knew he shouldn't be. He reminded himself that he was learning things about Sam that she wanted to hide and that made her prickly.

On the other hand, he wasn't without feelings himself.

"I don't know that I agree. I thought this one was pretty readable." He laid a hand on one volume and lifted his gaze to meet hers in challenge.

A frown of confusion touched Sam's brow. "You read that book just now?"

"I have it in my own library," Sloane said, noting her obvious surprise. He ran a finger along the book spines. "I have most of these, actually."

Sam's surprise was clear. "And you've read them?"

"Cover to cover." He gave her a cool smile. "We maybe should start a neighborhood loan program. These books are pretty expensive and if we shared the ones we both want to read, we could save some money."

Sam blinked. "It looks like there's a lot I don't know about you," she said.

"That's probably a hazard of sex with no questions," Sloane replied. Before Sam could answer, he went to the kitchen and opened the bottle of wine.

If he pulled out the cork a little more emphatically than was necessary, he didn't care whether Sam noticed.

Sam once again had the sense that Sloane wasn't who—or what—she thought he was. He'd read books about microbiology? And understood them? He should have a couple of graduate degrees for that, and if he was an enthusiast who read such works in addition to running his business, he should have been a lot older than he was.

There was no doubting that he was offended by her assumptions, though.

And he *had* called himself the Apothecary. What did that mean, exactly?

She followed him to the kitchen, knowing she'd made a mistake and not knowing how to set it right. It wasn't as if Sloane was in a hurry to answer *her* questions about him. The thing was that if both of them kept their walls in place, this relationship would end, probably in the next hour or so. Sam wasn't ready for that.

Maybe she should take the first step.

He'd already found her wine glasses and had opened the bottle of wine he'd brought. He checked the cork, set it aside, then swirled the wine in the glass with the ease of doing a familiar task.

He was ignoring her so pointedly that she knew she'd hurt his feelings.

"I'm sorry," she said, because that was always the best start. "I'm not used to meeting people who read the same kinds of books as me."

He shot her a look. "Clearly."

At least he'd answered her. "Don't be angry when I'm trying to understand. It's unlikely to meet anyone interested in this stuff outside of the lab, a danger zone or a specialist conference."

Sloane gave her a hard look. "The herb farm was my dad's choice. I always wanted to go to medical school."

"That explains everything!" Sam was intrigued by this confession and the possibility of them having more in common. "It sounds like you didn't go. Why not?"

Sloane shrugged and she sensed that he was ducking the question. "It just didn't come together." He sipped, giving his attention to a tasting sample of the wine, then nodded approval and poured. "My dad wasn't enthused about the idea."

"What did he do?" Sam assumed that he was someone who didn't think much of the medical profession and that Sloane's ambitions had been obstructed early.

"He was the Apothecary."

Sam thought again about the quote that gave her the chills. "That's what you said you were, although I didn't understand it at the time."

Sloane gave her an intent look. "It's a hereditary role."

"So, he preferred traditional cures?"

"You could say that."

Sam felt that there was something she was missing. "The Apothecary," she repeated. "But he can't have been the only one. Not unless you grew up in a small place."

In another century.

"I did." Sloane said and she noticed how he dropped his gaze. "A little town in Ireland. It was a long way to medical school, even if I'd had the opportunity to go."

"There's a school in Dublin."

Sloane shook his head. "I would have gone to London."

Sam watched him, trying to make sense of his confessions. "Are you really from Ireland? You don't have an accent."

"Not any more. It fades over time."

Sam wasn't so sure about that. She'd had colleagues whose families had emigrated from Europe while they were children and most of them still had accents.

"How old *are* you?"

His gaze locked with hers so abruptly that she jumped. "Now who's asking the questions?" His tone was low and Sam had the definite feeling that he was warning her.

"Me. I made the rule and I'm discarding it because so far it only seems to apply to you." She smiled at him. "Here's one question that's been puzzling me. Can people even buy real estate in California before they're twenty-one?"

Sloane looked startled, then she knew he realized what she'd done. "The title?" She nodded and his lips tightened. His eyes were bright. "Fair's fair?"

"Something like that."

"I guess I'm older than I look, then."

It wasn't much of an answer, but it was apparently the only one she was going to get.

Before she could ask for clarification, Sloane pointed back to her books. "I see you have that autobiography by the virus hunter, the one who did all the talk shows a few years ago."

Derek's book. Sam nodded, ignoring the lump in her throat.

Sloane shook his head. "I passed it along to the charity shop. I knew I'd never read it again. His experience was interesting, but he was a bit too convinced of his own brilliance for me."

"He pretty much is," Sam said before she could think better of it.

"You know him?"

Sam blushed. "I just had the same impression, that's all."

Sloane's gaze locked with hers. "Oh. I thought maybe he was your ex."

Sam stared at him, stunned that he could have guessed the truth so easily. Was Sloane psychic? Or just very observant? She tried to cover even as her cheeks heated. "Why would you think that?"

Sloane shrugged. "It would explain your having such a book collection. You might have taken them all, just because they were his."

Sam had to admit that might have been tempting.

Although by the time she'd moved out, she hadn't cared enough to be angry with Derek any more. She'd been too devastated by Nathaniel's illness, and her own inability to cure him.

Sloane raised his gaze to meet hers. "What is it that you do?" He arched a brow. "Or used to do, as The Magician?"

"Does it matter?"

"I'm just curious."

"I'm curious, too." Sam leaned across the counter. "Do you really read these books for fun?"

Sloane grinned. "Living vicariously, I guess, more than fun. It's a glimpse into another world, or maybe the path not taken." He sobered and trailed a finger down the stem of a wine glass. Sam watched the gesture, remembering how it felt for him to drag that finger down her spine.

Why were they arguing?

"I don't want to fight with you," she said quickly.

"But you don't want to confide in me either." Sloane held her gaze, then shrugged. "You're more than private, Sam. You want me here for sex, when you want it, and no more. I'm finding that less appealing than I might have expected."

Her heart skipped. "You can't be talking about marriage."

He shook his head, yet oddly she wasn't reassured. "That's not in my near future and you said it's not in yours. I'm talking about something in between. We can talk to each other, we can know things about each other, and we can enjoy each other's company." He grimaced. "If it's just physical, I don't see the point."

Sam thought there was a lot to be said for the past few hours they'd spent, in terms of pleasure given and received. "I understand what you're saying. It's just not easy for me."

"Now or ever?"

Sam looked up at him. "What's that supposed to mean?"

Sloane shrugged easily, but his gaze was bright. "Is privacy your habit, or a reaction to something?" He sipped his wine. "Something like a divorce?"

Sam nodded reluctant agreement. "Okay. Maybe I *am* more prickly than I used to be. And maybe I'm not used to talking to people about that. Especially not about my feelings."

"To quote a friend of mine, fair enough." Sloane said and touched his glass to hers.

Sam took a sip of wine.

"I have to wonder what it's like to have a job like this Derek guy," Sloane mused. "It would be a challenge, but I wonder if it would feel like a huge responsibility."

"What do you mean?"

He pursed his lips as his finger moved up and down the stem of the glass. Sam found herself watching his gesture. "I mean that a virus hunter would have to have contact with people who had contracted illnesses that had no cure. I have to wonder that in his place, if I didn't find a solution in time for any given person, whether I'd feel like a failure, or like that person's death was my fault." He met her gaze so steadily that once again Sam's heart pounded so hard she thought it might burst.

She couldn't talk about that, not yet.

Even if she was getting the feeling that when she did talk about Nathaniel, it would be with Sloane.

"I have no idea," she said brightly. "Want to try that bread? It smells delicious."

CHAPTER TWELVE

am and Sloane were sitting at her kitchen table. They'd made a meal together, working in the same space and anticipating each other's choices in a way that Sloane found both easy and hot.

Sam had lit candles and the light flickered warmly as they enjoyed the simple meal of pasta with grilled vegetables, wine and a green salad. Her hair had dried into loose curls around her face and glinted in the light, and Sloane liked how her eyes sparkled. Something in her had loosened up after their argument, and he appreciated that she was making an effort.

Maybe he wasn't the only one who wanted this to continue.

They'd talked about the books they'd both read, comparing their reactions and discussing a subject thoroughly when they disagreed. The conversation had been one of the best he'd had in a while, ranging from antibiotics in food to clinical tests on medicinal herbs, to plagues, pandemics and pollution. It had flowed organically and effortlessly, but thrummed with sexual awareness. Sloane had lost track of the time. He'd carefully avoided any more personal references or any discussion of the Seattle virus, and had just enjoyed being in the company of a beautiful intelligent woman.

Maybe it was good that Sam had so many emotional barriers. If she had shared her personal stories and pain readily with him, Sloane suspected that he might fall in love with her. As she wasn't his mate, that could lead to disaster in the future.

That was a sobering thought. He wondered if he was already in too deep.

"Tell me about your dad," Sam invited suddenly. "The

Apothecary who gave you his job and inspired you with creepy quotes."

Answering her question was the antithesis of what Sloane felt he should do, but he couldn't shut her out. Maybe sharing some of his own history would help to heal Sam's wounds. Maybe that was the point of their relationship.

He found himself smiling in recollection of his father. "He was a romantic and an idealist," he admitted.

"Even though the quote reminded you of him?"

Sloane avoided her eyes. "He meant it as a warning, I think." To his relief, Sam seemed to accept that at face value. "About dabbling where you shouldn't."

"Was his romanticism why he didn't want you to go to medical school?"

"Partly." Sloane saw no reason to confide his father's conviction that a *Pyr* had no business in a place of learning run by humans, or his certainty that Sloane's true nature would be revealed. He didn't want to think about the arguments they'd had, or his thirst for knowledge, his own conviction that the traditional healing processes of the *Pyr* practiced by his father were in need of updating. "Partly he wanted help."

"Growing the herbs for his practice?"

"It's a lot of work. It was harder there because of the climate. Many of the herbs I grow outside had to be cultivated in the greenhouse in Ireland, which made them susceptible to germs and disease. Greenhouse plants just aren't as vigorous."

Particularly centuries in the past, when there weren't the same climate controls as the ones installed in Sloane's greenhouses.

"He could have moved here, like you did."

Sloane smiled and went with the simpler answer. "My father was determined to live and die in Ireland. He said it was bred in his bones."

"Is he gone, then?"

Sloane nodded once. He didn't want to think of the shadow dragon that Magnus had raised of his father, or of the brutal way that he and Donovan had been required to ensure that Tynan Forbes died and stayed dead. He didn't want to think about his father's warning, the tattoo he'd gotten to ensure he remembered it, or his awareness that his task to guide the living to their final rest might never be done.

Sam was studying him closely. "You miss him."

Sloane exhaled. "Every day."

"What about your mom?"

"I never knew her. She died in childbirth."

"How medieval!" Sam said with surprise. "That's pretty rare now."

It hadn't been rare in the seventeenth century. Sloane shrugged.

"Brothers? Sisters?"

Sloane shook his head. "I was first and last. My father never married again. He raised me, but otherwise buried himself in his work and his research into the properties of the healing plants."

Sam was studying Sloane. "Sounds like a lonely childhood."

"I didn't know any different. He was interesting when he'd get talking about plants." Sloane leaned forward, intent on removing the sympathy from Sam's eyes. "He used to say that if you listened to a plant long enough, it would confess all of its secrets to you. It would tell you what it could heal and how and when."

Sam's eyes were dancing. "I've never had a plant tell me anything."

"Maybe you don't listen long enough." Sloane winked and gestured to the cactus in the library, the one she'd clearly forgotten. "That one was screaming for a drink of water. I heard it clear across the room."

Sam blushed. "Okay, so I'm not very good at domestic details."

He gave her a look.

"Or at listening to tarot cards or plants," she admitted. "You make me feel lucky, even though my sister makes me crazy sometimes. At least there's some family in my life."

"Why does she make you crazy?"

"Oh, she's an artist. At least that's what my father used to say. She's not supposed to live within her means, or make sensible choices. She somehow escaped his expectations and, as infuriating as I find her, I've been jealous of her sometimes, too."

"How's that?"

Sam put down her fork and shoved a hand through her hair. "I'm the oldest. I was the bearer of the dream, the one who had to fulfill every ambition. My father had wanted to go to medical school, but his family was poor, so he went to work. I had good marks, and he pushed me to make them better."

"You were supposed to go to medical school instead of him."

Sam shrugged. "Do people really think of it that way? I'm not sure. I know my dad had tons of aspirations for me, more than I had for myself, and in a way, his clear sense of purpose made it easy for me to decide what to do. I went to medical school. I went into research. I hunted viruses, but mostly I hunted cures and antidotes." She swallowed, frowned and gestured to the bookshelf. "That egomaniac was my first boss." She swallowed. "Then my husband, for a while."

Sloane decided to push her just a little bit. "And the boy in the picture?" he murmured.

Sam caught her breath, but her gaze didn't swerve from his.

Sloane nodded, finding his throat tight at the sight of her dismay. "The cactus told me that you loved him," he said with a shrug. She swallowed and her gaze trailed to the photograph.

"You know," he said, leaning across the table. "I thought I'd die when I lost my father. I couldn't imagine the world without him. In a way, I didn't want to go on, and I didn't want to try to fill his shoes."

"That's why you came to America," Sam guessed and Sloane nodded.

"I had to do something different. I wanted to forget. I needed to start fresh in a new place."

"I can understand that."

"But the funny thing is that I couldn't forget, and I ended up doing pretty much the same thing as he did. Ireland was bred in his bones, but I guess his love of the helpful plants was bred in mine."

"Is that why you said you're the Apothecary now?" Sam asked softly. "Because it keeps his memory alive, or what he instilled in you?"

Sloane found himself smiling. "Maybe. I never thought of it that way. I do like continuity and tradition. I remember so many good times with him, and I guess I don't want all of that to be gone." He shrugged even as his mind filled with memories, though they probably weren't the ones Sam might have expected. He recalled the first time he'd watched his father shift shape, the way his father's scales had gleamed in sunlight, the way his father's smile had been so similar in either form. Tynan had had a puckish sense of humor and a love of practical jokes.

Sloane smiled even as his voice dropped low. "And I know now that no matter how much it hurts to lose someone I love, it'll never be enough to make me believe that loving isn't worthwhile."

"Will you ever go back to Ireland?"

"I don't need to." Sloane tapped his chest. "I have him right in my heart, all the time."

Her eyes filled with sudden tears and she bit her lip. It was disconcerting to Sloane to see Sam overwhelmed by emotion, because she seemed always to be in control.

Or always to have a barrier between herself and the world.

Sloane lifted his glass to hers. "To love, to loss, and to what we learn from both."

Sam swallowed hastily and lifted her glass to his, her hand shaking slightly. They sipped the wine, then she abruptly put down her glass and leaned over the table, catching his face in her hands.

"Thank you for that," she whispered. "You make it easy to tell you things."

And when she leaned forward to kiss him, Sloane tasted the wine upon her lips mixed with the salt of her tears. Her strength and vulnerability was irresistible and he eased around the table, catching her up in his arms. He deepened his kiss and when she drew him closer, he carried her to the bedroom once again.

It would be a slow loving this time. Sloane had a sudden understanding of the reason behind this relationship. He was right that he was the one who could heal Sam's wounds, because he was the one who could persuade her to talk about her pain. Once Sam had told him her secrets, once she'd bared her soul and healed, he knew she'd be gone from his life for good.

He wanted to savor every moment of their time together. Theirs would be a good relationship, a powerful one, but not one destined to last.

Sloane was glad to be having it at all.

Marco trusted the darkfire.

He'd learned from Pwyll to follow the darkfire's lead, and his connection with it ensured that he knew its will better than he knew his own. It had brought Jac to him, and their lovemaking left him feeling replete as he hadn't in a long time.

They drove to the site where the dragons had been hatched, parked the 4x4, and walked closer, hands locked together. Even after their night of passion, he tingled with desire for her. He was keenly aware of the curve of her cheek, the fragility of her fingers in his, the treasure of her smile. He wanted her again and again and realized that he wouldn't be easily sated this time.

She cast him a smile of anticipation and Marco liked that their minds were as one in this.

To his surprise, when he and Jac approached the site where the eggs had hatched, a television crew was set up to film there.

He supposed he shouldn't have been surprised to recognize that the reporter was Melissa Smith. It was true that she had done the other television reports on the *Pyr* that had aired in recent years. Melissa was the mate of Rafferty Powell, the *Pyr* who really was the grandson of Pwyll, the *Pyr* who had been Marco's guardian for centuries and had kept the darkfire crystal in trust for him.

Marco marveled that he hadn't anticipated Melissa's presence, but then he'd been distracted by his desire for Jac. Such distraction could be dangerous, though, and his awareness of how careless he'd been made him doubt the wisdom of the darkfire.

Still, he couldn't question it. It had to be attuned to the greater good.

"Oh, it's Melissa Smith," Jac said as they walked closer. "She's the one who does those specials about the *Pyr*." Jac wrinkled her nose. "The ones where she says they're good dragons. As if there's any such thing."

Marco didn't reply, though his sense of unease grew. He could feel the darkfire crackling in the stone he had shoved deep into his pocket. It cast a heat into his palm that felt like stabbing ice and he shivered.

"Do you think we can still get a look at the nest?" Jac asked.

Marco shook his head. "They have it barricaded off. Maybe we should come back tomorrow."

"Are you kidding? There's the woman who took the pictures.

Wow. Maybe Maeve O'Neill is even here!"

Marco didn't want to see that reporter, ever.

But Jac was excited. "The *Pyr* might show up, because Melissa is filming this. They have in her other shows." She scanned the sky with obvious anticipation. "It could be the opportunity we're waiting for."

Before Marco could protest, Jac ducked into the crowd, making her way to the front with smiles and apologies.

His sense of foreboding redoubled, and he tried to catch up with her. Marco kept his hand locked around the crystal deep in his pocket. When he caught Jac's elbow with his free hand, he felt the heat of the darkfire redouble.

Jac turned in time to see him wince in pain. "What's wrong?" Her gaze fell to his pocket, where he obviously held something, and her eyes went wrong. "It's the stone, isn't it?" Her excitement was tangible and Marco nodded, sparing a glance for the people surrounding them. "It's ready to take them out. Maybe it knows they're coming!"

"I can't show you here," he whispered, feeling that the situation was spiraling out of his control. It was a strange sensation for Marco and he didn't like it. He was relieved when Jac nodded agreement.

She tugged him out of the crowd and a little further down the coast. They hunkered down behind the rocks along the shore, out of view of the people gathered to watch the broadcast. He felt better when they were alone together and when Jac was away from whatever was happening.

At her urging, Marco removed his hand from his pocket, and they blinked in unison, shielding their eyes against the brilliant fire in the stone. The darkfire burned so brightly that it was almost white and impossible to look at.

"Wow," Jac whispered. "Something *is* going to happen."

"Stay close and stay down," Marco advised, then he heard the rumble of old-speak.

"Thunder!" Jac said, scanning the sky. "No, it's old-speak. They *are* coming!" Her eyes lit and Marco was afraid.

"Stay here," he commanded, but Jac seized the crystal from his hand and leapt over the rocky barrier.

To his dismay, she ran directly toward Melissa Smith and her crew, her gaze fixed on the dragon regally descending from the sky.

It was Rafferty, come to his mate.

"This is for Nathaniel!" Jac roared.

No. She couldn't.

She *wouldn't*.

But she did.

Marco watched in shock and horror as Jac shot Rafferty with the darkfire crystal. She hit Rafferty in the lower gut and the darkfire exploded into blinding light on impact. Then it crackled all around the wounded *Pyr*, like an electrical shock finding a hundred answering sparks. Rafferty lost the rhythm of flight and fell toward the earth, his massive opal and gold dragon form emitting a shimmering blue light.

Marco knew what would happen next. Rafferty would shift shape involuntarily, and the camera crew would broadcast it. Rafferty's human identity could be revealed, and the Covenant would be broken.

He had to intervene!

Marco shifted shape and leapt into the sky, snatching the crystal from Jac's outstretched hand as he flew past her. He plucked Rafferty out of the air, shielding his body from the view of the cameras just as the unconscious *Pyr* shifted to his human form. The crowd on the island shouted and cried out, but Marco was deaf to their cries.

It was Marco's worst nightmare come true. Rafferty was out cold and injured badly. And it was Marco's fault, because he'd been careless.

Because the darkfire had led him astray.

Marco soared into the sky, thinking furiously of what he should do. He heard the crowd roaring behind him, and he heard Melissa's cry of anguish.

He was shaken to his very marrow that the darkfire could have betrayed him like this and unable to even think straight.

Rafferty was injured, perhaps fatally so. His guardian, mentor and friend might die, because of his mistake.

It was up to Marco to make this mistake come right.

Marco closed his eyes, exhaled and used the treacherous darkfire to journey immediately to the home of the Apothecary of the *Pyr*.

"It's Mum!" Isabelle shouted, racing through the loft apartment in Chicago. She flung herself onto one of the leather couches in the main space and Zoë was right behind her. The younger girl snatched up the remote and turned on the television, and Eileen heard Melissa's measured tones.

"I'm Melissa Smith and we're here on Easter Island. There was a sighting last week of dragons taking flight from the island, early one morning."

Eileen came out of the kitchen and perched on the end of the couch with the girls. The familiar pictures were now being displayed as Melissa spoke. She made no mention of Maeve O'Neill and Eileen didn't blame her.

"Do you know them?" Zoë asked Erik as he joined them. He folded his arms across his chest and didn't answer, his gaze locked on the television. He was still pale and even more forbidding than usual.

Zoë studied her father for a moment, then took his mood in stride, turning back to the television.

"These images were taken by a tourist, who has joined me here on the island again today. Welcome, Peg McKay. Can you tell us what it was like that morning? What did you see first, and how did you feel about it?"

"Well, as I told Maeve O'Neill, we were terrified, of course..."

As Peg repeated her story, obviously reveling in the attention, the camera widened the view. In the distance could be seen an opal and gold dragon, flying closer with leisurely speed. The sunlight glinted on his scales and he looked so majestic that Eileen found herself smiling in admiration.

"Dad!" Isabelle said with delight. "Rock it, Dad!" She and Zoë bumped fists then turned to watch again.

"Why do we even have a Covenant?' Erik muttered with irritation. "How many videos does this make now? The two of Thorolf, the one of Rafferty and Thorolf battling Magnus during Rafferty's firestorm, the one of these new *Slayers* consuming one of their own, the one of Drake trying to rescue his mate with the

Dragon Legion but being fought by Jorge and the *Slayers*...”

“The one of you and the *Slayers* from last week, Dad,” Zoë contributed. “Don’t forget that one.”

Her father’s gaze simmered. “Rafferty in London during his firestorm,” he added, trying to hide his annoyance that the girls were recalling that he had been filmed as well. Eileen knew it annoyed him.

“Plus the one of you, Sloane and Brandt closing the Thames Barrier during Dad’s firestorm,” Isabelle added.

“Melissa’s first television special,” Erik continued.

“You know Rafferty won’t shift on camera,” she chided. “He’s supporting his spouse, defending the *Pyr* and keeping the Covenant.”

Erik gave her a dark look for that. “I still don’t like it.”

“You never do.” Eileen gestured to the television. “If he makes the distinction clear between *Pyr* and *Slayer*, it wouldn’t hurt your PR. Maeve sure isn’t doing you any favors.” The camera panned the crowd, many of whom had placards calling for the *Pyr* to die.

Too late, Eileen wished the girls hadn’t seen that.

“They won’t listen,” Erik replied and scowled at the television. “Humans have an infuriating ability to see only what they want to see.”

Eileen propped a hand on her hip. “And we can’t say that about the *Pyr*, can we?” she demanded and might have said more, but there was a commotion on the screen. She pivoted in time to see blue-green light crackling all around Rafferty’s body, even as he twitched convulsively. He lost the rhythm of his flight and his body started to fall. Melissa cried out, even as Isabella and Zoë did. The girls fell on their knees in front of the television, transfixed. Erik was on his feet, shimmering on the cusp of change.

A dark dragon swooped in from off-camera, a familiar crystal clutched in his claw.

“The stolen darkfire crystal,” Erik whispered. “It’s alight again.”

“Is that Marco?” Eileen asked and felt her partner’s nod as much as she saw it.

Isabelle started to cry and Eileen reached to reassure her. Erik caught his breath as Rafferty began to shimmer with blue light. Eileen knew Erik feared that Rafferty’s human identity would be revealed. Marco flew directly for Rafferty and blocked him from view, either by accident or design. He then flew straight up and away from the island, Rafferty in his grasp.

He glittered with the blue-green light of darkfire against the morning sky, then disappeared, as surely as if he'd never been.

"Just like the other ones!" Peg cried, and Erik turned off the sound.

Isabelle screamed and threw herself at the television. Melissa was talking quickly, her agitation apparent as she tried to end the broadcast. She was holding her ear and looking distressed, the conflict in her posture telling Eileen that her producer was demanding that she not stop broadcasting.

Even though she'd seen her husband shot.

Erik sat down heavily, his shock clear. "Marco's abducted Rafferty," he whispered, his gaze lifting to Eileen. She could see how badly shaken he was. "Who could have anticipated such a betrayal?"

Eileen hugged Isabelle close and worried. If Marco and the darkfire had turned against the *Pyr*, were they doomed to lose the war?

Thorolf was running his regular class in Bangkok, teaching kids and women how to defend themselves with simple physical moves. He liked showing the people in his neighborhood how to keep themselves safe. He'd done it in New York and he continued doing it here. There were some in his informal class who had been abused in intimate relationships, and he liked watching their confidence grow in steady increments.

His lessons had started organically, when the little lady who lived below them had been robbed and had come to the door asking for help. Thorolf had thought she had wanted the perpetrator hunted down and injured, but she wanted to make sure it didn't happen again.

Chandra had taught her some moves—and Thorolf *had* hunted down the perpetrator—and slowly word had gotten around. As Chandra had become more visibly pregnant, Thorolf had taken over the classes. As the number of students grew, they'd rented a hall from a martial arts school to hold the classes. Cops were sending people to them now, because Chandra and Thorolf taught for free. It had cemented their relationship with their human neighbors and Thorolf found it incredibly rewarding.

The regular class also helped him to keep from fussing over Chandra, who didn't always welcome his protectiveness. He was terrified by her pregnancy, not only because it was the result of their firestorm and her condition was thus his fault, but because he couldn't imagine being without her. That Chandra wasn't inclined to take it easy didn't help. He didn't want to argue with her when she was pregnant, but she seemed to forget that she wasn't an immortal goddess anymore, never mind one who had been able to do pretty much anything imaginable.

On this day, there were three kids in the back who weren't paying attention. They were huddled around a cell phone, whispering and distracting the class.

"Hey, if you don't want to practice today, take it outside," Thorolf said.

One of the kids pointed the cell phone at him, as if he'd fire it like a weapon.

Thorolf stopped cold, remembering how Marco had fired the darkfire crystal, just like that. "What are you watching?"

"A dragon getting his ass kicked," the biggest kid said.

Unfortunately, they were also learning English from Thorolf and he resolved—again—to clean up his language.

The video didn't help.

"Can I see, please?" he asked.

The kid came to Thorolf and proudly displayed the screen. The video played again, and Thorolf's heart sank to his toes. Rafferty had been shot down by the darkfire crystal, and on camera! It wasn't clear who had shot the crystal, but when Marco appeared, he had it in one claw. He snatched up Rafferty, soared high into the air, and disappeared.

"What the fuck," Thorolf whispered and the kids immediately began to echo his words.

"Poof," said the kid with the phone "He's taking him somewhere else to kick his sorry dragon ass."

Where was Marco taking Rafferty?

Had he really shot him?

There was no one else who could shoot a darkfire crystal, well, except Liz.

Had she done it? Thorolf couldn't believe it.

He pivoted to find the class watching him. "Hey, we've got to cut it short today," he said, then repeated that in Thai. He held his stomach. "I'm sorry. I don't feel well."

"Too much kim chee," accused his neighbor with a smile.

Thorolf nodded and bowed. "I think so." The truth was that Chandra couldn't get enough of the stuff since she'd become pregnant. She was going through their neighbor's homemade kim chee like nobody's business. He never even got a bite. It was an excuse but he'd take it.

The truth was that he did feel sick.

He had to get back to the States and find out what was going on.

He had no idea how he was going to convince Chandra not to go with him—because at six months along, she shouldn't really be flying so far—much less how he'd persuade her to be careful while he was gone.

There had to be a way.

Sam awakened with one thought resonating in her mind: she could confide in Sloane. She was alone in bed, although she could hear Sloane leaving the bathroom.

Confiding in him was both a terrifying prospect and one that felt right. She knew he'd be kind and compassionate, and she suspected she'd feel better just by saying the words aloud. Maybe it would hurt less if she admitted to missing Nathaniel, if she said out loud that she'd failed her son as a mother and as a doctor, if she admitted that she'd thought she had everything right when really she'd had a lot of it wrong.

It sure as hell couldn't hurt as much as keeping it all inside.

Sam rose from bed with purpose and looked out the window. The night sky was filled with stars and Sloane was checking out something on his phone on the patio. She studied him with a smile, knowing his gentle persistence had helped her to start talking.

His confession about his father had cracked some resistance

inside her, making her see that it was possible to embrace the vulnerability of love and its scars, yet still be strong. There was no doubt in her mind that Sloane was like a rock, but he also had such tenderness. Her smile broadened as she remembered their conversation the night before and she knew she wasn't going to be able to keep her emotions out of this for much longer.

It might already be too late.

Was it possible that there was a man in this world who had it all?

If so, he was on her patio.

Even if Sloane didn't have it all, he had plenty to suit Sam.

She joined him under the stars, running an appreciative fingertip across his bare back, then lit candles on the patio. "We could go for a swim at your place," she said, glancing up at the clear sky overhead. She could tell him there, where they'd started, after they made love.

Or maybe before.

Sloane made a noncommittal noise and kept tapping at his cell phone.

"Oh, put it away, please," she urged, unable to remember when she'd last bothered to look at the news. "It's been such a good evening. Who needs the world and all its troubles?"

Sloane frowned. "Sorry." He cast her an apologetic smile. Sam heard thunder in the distance, but more importantly, she knew that she'd lost Sloane's attention. "I've got to go," he said, his smile not quite reaching his eyes.

"What's happened? Is something wrong?"

"No, I got a message from a friend who needs a hand," he said, and she had an awful feeling that he was lying. "Occupational hazard."

"Of running an herb farm?"

Sloane looked disconcerted at that, and Sam saw color rising on the back of his neck. What wasn't he telling her?

"Or of whatever else you do that compels you to fly out suddenly?"

Sloane frowned. "I was just distracted by this video that's going viral."

"It seems that the only videos that go viral are the ones featuring those dragons." Sam didn't say any more. She knew better than to vent about dragons in front of Sloane again, because she wasn't going to mess with a good thing. Let him believe what he needed to.

She knew dragons were evil.

"So was this one," Sloane said with visible impatience. "They appeared in the middle of Melissa Smith's broadcast from Easter Island."

"Easter Island?"

"There were eggs there, that hatched into dragons."

Sam shuddered. "I'm glad I haven't looked at the news." Sloane didn't reply, just tapped away on his phone. "Doesn't she get tired of insisting on the goodness of dragons all the time? Maeve O'Neill makes a lot more sense." Sam might have said more but Sloane gave her a look that she took as a warning. She thought of his tattoo and forced a smile. "What's the video?"

Sloane came to stand beside her. Sam watched the image on the small screen, feeling the heat of his arm against her own. He smelled good, too. She didn't much care about Melissa Smith's latest dragon broadcast, or the opal and gold dragon appearing on the display. She'd seen him in these videos before and was about to say as much when a woman shouted off-screen.

"This is for Nathaniel!" that woman cried just before the blue-green lightning was shot at the dragon.

Sam caught her breath.

What the hell was Jac doing on Easter Island?

It couldn't be her sister. Sam had to be wrong. Her amorous mood was completely shattered, all the same. Sam dug in her purse for her own phone, then listened again to Jac's message on her voice mail.

A retreat? Had Jac lied to her?

Had she gone to Easter Island in search of dragons?

If she had, Sam had a lecture for her baby sister about risk that would take a while...

Sam heard the gate in her backyard fence clang and looked up to realize that Sloane was striding home. He looked, actually, as if he had broken into a run.

And to Sam's surprise, there were lights on in his house. They hadn't been on before.

Maybe he *had* installed timers. It seemed like a reasonable explanation, but Sam couldn't help thinking that both Sloane and her sister weren't telling everything they knew.

Sloane burst through the door of his house, halfway afraid Sam would follow him. She hadn't, but he locked the door behind himself and pulled down the blinds. He tossed his keys on the kitchen counter and strode into the great room.

"Great Wyvern," he whispered when he saw Rafferty sprawled on his floor.

The older *Pyr* was on his back, his eyes closed. His gut was badly burned and Sloane found it telling that he'd only managed to pull on one leg of his jeans when he'd shifted shape from dragon form.

Marco was crouched beside Rafferty, shaking his head. "I didn't mean for it to happen. I didn't know she'd do it."

Sloane had never seen the Sleeper agitated about anything.

Not that it was going the help Rafferty any.

"What happened?" Sloane demanded. He bent over Rafferty and listened to the *Pyr*'s breathing, put his hand on his chest to feel the beating of his heart. The beat was faint, too faint for Sloane's taste, and the burns were extensive. They seemed to be crackling with blue-green light before his eyes, as if the darkfire had slipped beneath Rafferty's skin and continued to burn.

"I listened to the darkfire," Marco confessed. "I trusted its counsel." He raised his gaze to Sloane. "But the darkfire lied."

"Rafferty was hit with darkfire," Sloane said, recalling the blue-green light in the video. "Where did it come from?"

"From the crystal that had been extinguished. It lit again." Marco put the crystal on the floor beside Rafferty, his hand shaking. The flame within it had died to a tiny point of blue-green light, as if its power had been transmitted to Rafferty. Sloane didn't understand darkfire well, none of the *Pyr* did except Marco, and he felt out of his depth.

Again.

"It betrayed me," Marco whispered.

It wasn't the time for regret, in Sloane's opinion, but for action. "Do you remember the Cantor's songs?" he asked urgently.

"The ones that harness the darkfire? We might be able to conjure the darkfire out of Rafferty's body, if you taught me the songs that command it."

Marco got to his feet, his expression horrified as he stared at Rafferty, and Sloane wondered whether the other *Pyr* had even understood the question. Marco looked shell-shocked. "He only ever did good for me. He saved me from Magnus before I was even born. He guarded my sanctuary at Bardsley Island, and he took custody of the crystal until I could claim it. He awakened me from my slumber, trained me and taught me." His expression turned bleak. "And now he's going to die because of me."

"Rafferty doesn't have to die. You can help me," Sloane appealed. "Help me with the Cantor's songs!"

But Marco was backing away. "I don't trust the darkfire any more. I don't trust it to do any good at all."

"Wait! Where are you going? I need your help!"

"I'm going back to finish what I started," Marco said with grim resolve. Then he closed his hands into fists, tipped back his head, and shimmered vivid blue.

"No!" Sloane bellowed, but it was too late. He blinked once, and then Marco was gone.

He had to solve this alone.

Somehow.

Sloane looked down at Rafferty, then flattened his hands against the older *Pyr*'s chest. He had only the Apothecary's healing songs at his disposal, and maybe that was best if the darkfire had turned against the *Pyr*. Darkfire was unpredictable and turned situations upside-down for the *Pyr*, making improbabilities into reality.

Maybe Rafferty's condition counted. Sloane had to think that saving the older *Pyr* was a long shot.

Maybe his songs would be enough. Sloane began to sing softly, putting his heart into his chant because he couldn't imagine a future without Rafferty Powell in the ranks of the *Pyr*. He could feel a crackle beneath Rafferty's skin, one that made the hair on his arms stand up and he had a hard time believing it was a good sign.

Sloane had his eyes closed and his focus on his task was so complete that he didn't see the darkfire flicker and snap in the crystal, burning more steadily as he endeavored to heal the

Cantor's grandson.

Jorge felt darkfire ripple over his scales and lifted his head to survey the ruined cavern that had once been Chen's lair. There was no mistaking the sudden appearance of blue-green sparks where the darkfire crystal had been broken by Marco the year before. The Sleeper had used the crystal to free Lee from his brother Chen's spell. The darkfire bounced around the cavern now, its activity interrupting Jorge's feast of the fallen clone.

Jorge had a hearty respect for darkfire. It was unpredictable, to be sure, but since first one crystal had been broken by Chen and the second by Marco, he'd been able to make improbable things happen—like animating those thirteen clones of Boris Vassily that Sigmund had left. Although the *Slayer*'s experiment had been left unfinished by his death, and although Jorge knew little of such biological feats, just bringing the eggs to the cave seemed to have helped. Jorge had watched the darkfire slide over the shells until he had dreamed of them hatching, beneath the light of a blood moon.

It couldn't be a coincidence that the turn of the moon's node from Dragon's Tail to Dragon's Head would be marked by four lunar eclipses in a row that were blood moons. He'd failed to understand the importance of location early enough to take advantage of the first blood moon. He'd moved the thirteen eggs since then and was glad that five had hatched, exactly as he'd planned. He knew the rest would do the same.

But the darkfire's abrupt activity made him suspicious.

What was happening in the world above? The mate he'd captured was securely imprisoned, and she was of little more use to him until her pregnancy was confirmed. The fourth of the Boris Vassily clones hatched in this batch was dozing contentedly after his meal, one eye on Jorge with a wariness that was appropriate.

What about that missing clone? Jorge had thought him too injured to cause trouble, but the darkfire made him reconsider the possibility.

"*I have an errand,*" Jorge said in old-speak to his minion. "*Guard the woman. If anything happens to her, it will be your fault.*"

The ruby and brass dragon exhaled slowly, his eyes glinting in comprehension.

Jorge was glad he'd eaten well. He had the energy to spontaneously manifest elsewhere and chose a bar in Sydney that was a favorite of his. The news was always shown there, on at least ten televisions, so it was easy to catch up on world events. The bar was near the port and frequented mostly by men of the type who minded their own business and asked no questions. It was always crowded, smoky and dark, too, which meant that he could appear suddenly in the corridor to the men's room and probably not be seen.

Any humans who did witness his sudden appearance would likely be drunk enough to think they had imagined it. In all the times that Jorge had popped into this place, he'd only had to beguile a human once.

His luck held.

Within moments, he was rubbing elbows at the bar with a variety of unsavory humans, most of whom were rough and prepared to sell anything for the right price. They were universally transfixed by footage shot on Easter Island, which was being played over and over again on at least five of the televisions.

Jorge recognized the *Pyr* in question immediately. Rafferty was shot down by what had to be a blast from a darkfire crystal. Jorge was intrigued, as he hadn't been aware there was one remaining. Chen had broken one deliberately to loose the darkfire. A second had been taken by Drake from Lorenzo's hoard and had scattered the Dragon's Tooth Warriors through the centuries, sowing them in the times of their respective mates. It had gone dark and disappeared after that feat, presumably vanishing into the hoard of one of the *Pyr*. The third crystal had been broken by Marco in Chen's cave to release Lee.

Had the spark lit again in the darkened one?

How perfectly unlikely.

And intriguing. Jorge had a bit of a fondness for darkfire and the way it turned assumptions on their heads.

As he watched, Marco swept into the shot and carried Rafferty high into the sky, disappearing as abruptly as Jorge had appeared in this bar.

No doubt Marco had taken Rafferty somewhere to be healed.

Perhaps to Erik's lair in Chicago. Perhaps to Rafferty's lair in London. Perhaps to the lair of Sloane the Apothecary in California. Truth be told, Jorge wasn't very interested in that detail. Rafferty had been injured by darkfire and might die.

The darkfire was the interesting bit.

As well as the fact that a woman had shouted "This is for Nathaniel" before the bolt of darkfire had struck Rafferty.

Who had fired the crystal? Jorge felt it must have been the woman who had shouted. Humans were so strange about making such declarations. But who was she? There was no footage of her. Jorge had only been aware of Marco using the crystal as a weapon and the Firedaughter Liz, who was the mate of Brandon. Last Jorge had known, that elemental witch had been in Hawaii with Brandon, having sons, as mates of the *Pyr* usually did. Jorge wasn't keen to battle with Liz again, given how she'd summoned Pelé to drag him down into the fiery depths of the earth, so he watched the video again for more clues. It was impossible to tell if the shout was in Liz's voice.

Was Liz on Easter Island?

Had she fired the crystal?

Or were there more Firedaughters on the loose?

Where was the crystal now? Marco had been holding the crystal at the end of the footage, but he'd entrusted one to Liz before. He could have given it back to her.

Who was Nathaniel? Perhaps one of Liz's sons, but why would she be angry with Rafferty? It made no sense to Jorge, but then, humans seldom made much sense.

The point was the crystal. Jorge was sure he could put its power to use, somehow. If nothing else, his possession of it would mean that no one could use it against him. The crystal, or the beginning of a trail to its location, had to be on Easter Island.

His decision made, Jorge returned to that dark corridor and abandoned Sydney for Easter Island.

CHAPTER THIRTEEN

ac was flushed with triumph and ready to celebrate, but she hadn't been able to find Marco. It was like he'd disappeared. She could have used that gift herself and recognized that he knew more about what to expect after shooting a dragon than she did. She'd ducked into the crowd and managed to evade the reporters, including Melissa Smith. That woman had practically passed out after the dragon was hit, and her crew had been primarily concerned with her.

Jac wished she could have known for sure that the dragon was dead, but that other dark dragon had interfered.

She'd have to add him to her notebook.

He definitely belonged in the Evil section, if he saved dragons.

She'd looked and waited for Marco, then figured they must have been separated in the crowd. The 4x4 was still there, but Marco had the keys, so she started the long walk back to their hotel. The sun was setting and she was feeling good about what she'd done.

Her first dragon hit, maybe even a kill. She was avenging Nathaniel. This totally rocked. She wished there was someone she could tell and hoped Marco would turn up. She didn't have a lot of cash left, but she'd blow it on a celebratory dinner in a minute.

Maybe they could celebrate in another way afterward.

That prospect made Jac smile and walk a little more quickly.

She heard the truck before she saw it and stepped off the road as it came closer. Marco was driving, but he looked annoyed.

She assumed it was because he'd spent time looking for her and was disappointed to see that he was acting more like other men she'd dated. Maybe she should have expected the change, since they'd had sex.

There was a depressing thought.

"I couldn't find you," Jac said cheerfully when he halted the truck beside her. He said nothing, just glowered at her and kicked open the passenger door.

It wasn't like him to be so abrupt.

Of course, Jac didn't know him that well. Maybe he was routinely grumpy, but she'd just been lucky enough to have missed out on it. She did think it strange that his mood was the exact opposite of hers, given that they were both hunting dragons and she'd scored a hit.

She got in and they were moving before she realized what the issue had to be.

"I'm sorry that I don't have your crystal anymore. The dark dragon ripped it right out of my hand."

He gave her a look that chilled her to her marrow. It was worse because he didn't raise his voice. "You took the thing most precious to me."

"I didn't mean to," Jac protested.

"And yet it's gone all the same."

"But I shot a dragon! I'm a hunter now, too."

Marco said nothing. He ground the gears as he pulled into town, then braked so hard in front of the hotel that Jac thought she might be thrown through the windshield.

Jac wondered whether he didn't like that she'd made the hit instead of him. She never would have thought he was the kind of guy who kept score, but she was seeing a new side of Marco. She reached out and put her hand on his arm.

He flinched.

"I'm sorry. We could try to find another."

"There is no other," Marco said through gritted teeth. It was hard to believe this cold stranger was the man who had sweetly made love to her the night before. Jac would have found it easier to believe that *he* could become a dragon, given the glitter of his eyes.

"Come on. Don't be angry." She tried to cajole him into a better mood. "There's one less dragon in the world."

His eyes narrowed slightly. Jac could have sworn that a puff of smoke came out of his nostril, but it had to be a trick of the light.

She kept trying to improve his mood. "Let's celebrate and decide where we go from here," she continued. "After all, you have that verse, and there are two more blood moons coming. Even without the crystal, maybe we can solve the riddle. Maybe there are more dragon eggs just waiting to be discovered..."

Her voice faded beneath his steely gaze.

"There's *nothing* to celebrate," Marco said softly. "I made a mistake."

"A mistake? I don't understand."

"I trusted when I shouldn't have." A muscle worked in his jaw and she sensed that he was trying to control his emotions. It was remarkable to see, because he'd always been so composed before. Even when they'd made love, she'd had the sense that he was in complete control. How was it possible that she'd made him this angry? "I want the page out of your book, the one where you wrote down my poem."

"But..."

Marco's eyes flashed with dangerous heat.

Jac tugged her notebook out of her purse and ripped out the page. She thought he might shred it or fling it out the window, but he folded it carefully and put it in his pocket. "I'm leaving the island now."

"But there's only the one flight, tomorrow afternoon. Let's talk about it tonight."

His look silenced her again. "Do you want the truck? Or will you take a cab to the airport when you go?"

"I'll take a cab," Jac said, not certain she'd be that quick to head back to Seattle. There might be more dragons here or more eggs. She might have another chance to take one down.

"Then it's goodbye," Marco said, as if he couldn't have cared less what she did.

Jac was stung. Why were all the guys she met such jerks? She'd really liked Marco and the way they'd made love had convinced her that he was different. This side of his nature was an unwelcome change, though, so maybe it was best if they parted early.

Still, she wondered what had happened to Dr. Jekyll.

Ever the optimist, Jac got out of the truck and smiled at him.

"I'll see you back in Seattle, then?"

"Probably not," Marco said grimly, then gunned the engine and left her standing there.

So, that was that. Jac exhaled. Another relationship that seemed to have great promise had come to a grinding halt. Jac had to have the worst romantic luck of any woman on the planet.

But she'd at least wounded a dragon.

And she *had* memorized Marco's verse. Jac dug out her journal and turned to a fresh page and wrote it down again.

> *Three blood moons mark the debt come due*
> *Will the* Pyr *triumph or be hunted anew?*
> *Three eclipses will awaken the spark*
> *In thirteen monsters breeding in dark.*
> *Three times the firestorm will spark*
> *Before darkfire fades into the dark.*
> *Firestorm, mate or blood sacrifice*
> *None or all can be the darkfire's price.*
> *When the Dragon's Tail has turned its bore*
> *And darkfire dies forevermore*
> *Will the* Pyr *be left to rule with might*
> *Or disappear into past's twilight?*

Perfect. She'd recalled it exactly. Maybe getting the verse had been the whole point of the relationship. Maybe meeting Marco had just been a way to get her on the path to dragon hunting.

Either way, she was going to figure out this poem.

Then she'd take down more dragons, with or without the crystal.

She'd made a start and that was worth something.

Even if she didn't feel very celebratory any more.

The rumble of old-speak was impossible for the *Pyr* to ignore, because it emanated from the leader of the *Pyr* himself.

Where is Rafferty?

Sloane heard the fury in Erik's old-speak and the growing consternation of the older *Pyr*. He must have been receiving a flurry of replies from his fellows around the world but not the news he sought. If any of the other *Pyr* had known Rafferty's location, Erik would have replied with relief.

Sloane had to finish the verse of his chant and couldn't hurry it, not when Rafferty was in such poor condition as this, not even when Erik demanded answers. The older *Pyr* had shifted back to his dragon form, his opal and gold figure limp on Sloane's tile floor. He wasn't sure whether the shift was a good sign or not. Usually the *Pyr* shifted to human form when they died, but there was nothing usual about Rafferty's condition. His pulse was barely discernible.

His scales looked as if they were lit by darkfire from the underside, which gave him a strange blue-green glow. When the chant was done, Sloane had a hard time believing it had made much difference.

"He's here," he responded belatedly, guessing that his tone would reveal Rafferty's state. Sloane closed his eyes, feeling like a failure. He recalled his father's warning, that he would have to choose one day who lived and who died, and hoped that time hadn't arrived.

Where is the traitor? Erik demanded next.

He brought Rafferty to me, Sloane admitted and Erik's relief was almost tangible. Sloane was glad he didn't have the power to hear all of his fellows, because the thunder would have been deafening.

His cell phone rang and he answered it, guessing it would be Erik.

But it was Eileen. "Rafferty's there with you, then?" she asked. "How is he?"

"It's bad," Sloane said. "I'm not sure what to do for him. The darkfire is so unpredictable, and it seems to be beneath his scales."

She obviously repeated this to Erik who growled a reply.

"Marco brought him to me and left. He was pretty shaken up."

"He should be!" Erik fumed, his words audible even though he wasn't holding the phone.

"He's not healing quickly," Eileen whispered and Sloane understood why she'd called.

"I'm healing," Erik protested and Sloane shook his head. There was no creature so stubborn as a dragon who needed to rest when there were battles to be fought.

Sloane became authoritative, because as Apothecary he knew best.

"Can you call Melissa? She must be worried sick. I expect she'll come here," he said. "If not, could you suggest that to her? I need to keep singing but Rafferty's bond with her is so strong that her presence might help." He thought of how their firestorm had been tinged by darkfire and wondered if having her here might help in other ways.

"Of course. And we should bring Isabelle, too," Eileen said, clearly understanding his plan. "We'll rent a van and head out as soon as possible."

"I can fly!"

Eileen covered the phone, but Sloane still heard her reply to her partner. "You're not flying all of us, not in your condition. And you're not getting on a commercial airliner with those wounds still healing."

Erik grumbled but conceded the point.

Eileen spoke to Sloane again. "Your song might help Erik's wounds to heal faster, too. If we drive straight through, we should be there in two days."

"Thorolf will be there sooner," Erik contributed, speaking closer to the phone. "He and Chandra are on their way."

"And Quinn should be arriving any time," Sloane noted. The Smith had left a message while Sloane was in New York. He and Sara weren't rushing their journey, because Sara was finding the travel tiring.

It looked as if Sloane was going to have a house full of *Pyr*. There wasn't nearly enough to eat, but Thorolf could fix that when he arrived.

Sloane needed to focus all of his energy on Rafferty.

For someone who was supposedly so private, Sloane was having a ton of company.

Sam couldn't help but notice the lime green Mustang, because it raced down Sloane's driveway as if it was on the freeway. It stopped in a cloud of dust and two people got out in a hurry, as if they were racing to put out a fire.

She watched, wondering whether something was wrong. The guy, who had been driving, was tall with long blond hair. He looked like a body builder. The woman was almost as tall as him and had long ebony hair. She moved with such speed that Sam was surprised to see that she was visibly pregnant.

A navy sedan came down the driveway almost immediately after that, and the newly arrived pair glanced back when they were almost at the door. This car was driven more sedately, and a woman got out of it alone. She was dressed more conservatively, and her appearance contrasted with that of the other two. She was in a hurry, too, though. The three embraced warmly, evidence that they knew each other, then walked straight into Sloane's house.

Without even knocking.

Sam had to guess that they were Sloane's friends.

While she, evidently, was not. That burned after the intimacy they'd shared, but she had to hope that Sloane would have been more welcoming if she'd gone to his door now. She was giving the idea serious consideration, even though he had company and she might be interrupting, when her phone rang.

To Sam's relief, she saw that it was Jac. She answered immediately, Sloane's guests forgotten. "Where are you?" she demanded by way of greeting. "And where exactly is this retreat? I've left you a hundred messages!"

"Well, that's the thing," Jac said. "I'm not at a retreat."

"No kidding." Sam saw no reason to beat around the bush. "Was that really your voice on the news video from Easter Island? Are you really in *Chile?*"

"You heard me?" Jac sounded ridiculously pleased by this, which only made Sam angrier.

Her sister was in the middle of the Pacific and had never told anyone where she was going! It was classic Jac—impulsive and irresponsible.

"You recognized my voice?"

"That *was* you! You're the one who shot that dragon shifter!"

"Yes! Wasn't it cool?" Jac was clearly proud of herself. "I don't know if he died or not, but..."

"Are you out of your mind?" Sam demanded. "What were you even doing there? And what makes you imagine that hurting someone else changes anything?" She took a deep breath. "Nathaniel is dead. He's going to stay dead, no matter how you try to avenge him."

"Well, at least you finally said his name," Jac replied. "I was starting to feel as if you'd forgotten you ever had a son."

Sam bristled at her sister's unexpected censure. "It's not up to you to tell me how to mourn..."

"And it's not up to you to tell me how to deal with my grief, either," Jac retorted. "Honestly, Sam, you're such an icicle. Did you even care that Nathaniel died?"

"Of course I cared!"

"And that's why you spent so much time with him as he died," Jac said bitterly. "As always, you chose work over family."

"I was trying to find a cure..."

"You were ducking any display of emotion," Jac replied. "Just like you always do." Her voice wobbled a bit. "Why do you get everything so easily when you don't even want it?"

Sam exhaled and rubbed a brow, not wanting to fight with the very last surviving member of her family. She tried to sound calm. "I thought you'd plant a tree to mourn him, or something like that." She winced, having heard the bitterness in that last sentence.

"Not this time," Jac said grimly. "This time, I want to *do* something. I want to make a difference, and I have."

"You could have died," Sam said.

"It would totally have been worth it." Jac's voice turned bitter again. "Besides, who would have missed me?"

Sam realized they weren't getting anywhere and she thought of her exchange with Sloane. Something was bothering Jac, because Sam had never heard her so irritable. She loved her sister, even though they'd fought all their lives. Would it hurt to admit her feelings out loud?

"It would have mattered to *me*." Her voice softened as she dared to admit the real reason for her concern to her sister. "They're dragons, Jac, not bunnies," she continued, finding that the confessions got easier to make. "You could have been killed, and then where would I be? What would I do without you?"

There was silence between them then, a silence punctuated only by the crackle of a bad connection. When Jac spoke, her voice was hoarse. "You've never said anything like that to me. I always figured you'd be glad to be rid of me. The new baby stealing your spotlight and all that."

"Well, there has been some truth in that." Sam tried to make a joke. "It would be cheaper to be without you," she teased, and they laughed together for the first time in a long time. "You could go crazy and get a paying job, you know. How did you afford to go to Easter Island anyway?"

"Well, that's just it," Jac said with some hesitation, and Sam rolled her eyes in anticipation of the inevitable request. "I bought a one-way ticket because that was all I could afford."

Sam shook her head and bit back the comment she would usually have made. She and Jac only had each other, so it was time they improved their relationship. Sam wasn't afraid to make the first move.

Not any more.

She figured she wasn't going to see much of Sloane since he had all that company and it was time she and her sister mended some bridges. "How about this? I'll send you the money, if you stop here on your way back to Seattle. It's time we talked."

"About Nathaniel?"

Sam knew that the death of her son, and his infection while he was in Jac's care, was only the tip of the iceberg. "About everything."

"Deal," Jac said, her enthusiasm encouraging Sam that she wasn't the only one who wanted to make a fresh start.

Sloane was singing the Apothecary's song for the umpteenth time when he heard Thorolf, Chandra and Melissa arrive. He'd already changed the permissions on his dragonsmoke and got up to unlock the front door before returning to his song. *"It's open,"* he told Thorolf in old-speak even as he knelt beside Rafferty again.

He scanned the *Pyr*, seeing no visible improvement in his condition. The light within the crystal was brighter, though, and the glow beneath Rafferty's scales seemed to have diminished. But Sloane was so tired that he might have been seeing things.

"Rafferty!" Melissa cried and flung herself at her husband and mate. Sloane noted a slight increase in Rafferty's pulse and was glad she had come. She ran her hands over his scales, then froze when she found the main burn on his belly. It looked as awful as it was.

"Will he live?" she asked Sloane and he wished he knew the answer.

"I'll hunt Marco down and finish him off," Thorolf said as he dropped to his knees beside Rafferty, his concern clear. "What can I do here?"

"I'm getting tired," Sloane admitted. "Help me with the healing chant."

"Even though he's tone deaf," Chandra teased. Her worry was clear despite her manner and her eyes narrowed as she reached out a hand to Rafferty. She, too, ran a hand over his scales. Thorolf grabbed her a chair and pulled it closer so that she could sit down. Sloane saw that she was tired, undoubtedly because of the long air journey when she was seven months pregnant. He didn't want to think of how these two had convinced an airline to let her on board. Thorolf's beguiling must have improved.

"Marco was here," Sloane said. "He brought Rafferty to me. He was really upset."

"And so he should be," Thorolf said.

"He said he'd trusted the darkfire but that it had betrayed him."

"What does that mean?" Chandra asked.

Sloane shrugged. "The most important thing is that he refused to try to sing the Cantor's songs, which control the darkfire, because he no longer trusted the darkfire."

"And Rafferty is the only other one who knows them," Melissa said, biting her lip as she considered her fallen mate. There was tenderness in her caress and fear in her eyes.

"I'm trying to remember," Sloane said. "I was there when Marco was awakened. Rafferty sang the Cantor's songs to do it."

"Who else was there?" Chandra asked.

Melissa bit her lip as she recalled. "Erik, Eileen, Zoë, Isabelle, and Brandt."

"Erik and Eileen are on their way with the girls," Sloane told them and Melissa wagged a finger at him.

"Erik could see Pwyll that day," she reminded him. "He said that the darkfire had opened the conduit for him to talk to the dead. Rafferty was able to remember some of the Cantor's song, but Erik prompted him as to how to use it."

"With Pwyll's advice," Sloane agreed, remembering. "Maybe he'll be able to talk to Pwyll when he gets here."

"In the meantime, what can we do?" Thorolf asked. "Who fired the crystal? Was it Marco?"

"I don't know," Melissa said. "Of course, we have tons of footage of Rafferty falling and Marco carrying him away, but no one turned a camera on the crowd."

"I might have to go there," Thorolf said.

"Isn't Brandt in Australia?" Chandra asked and Sloane nodded.

"Why?"

She frowned. "I feel something there. Like a ripple in Myth. It must be strong because I'm not as sensitive as I was, and I don't have the power to visit anymore."

"What kind of ripple?" Melissa asked.

"Words." Chandra shrugged, then recited something. "'Once there were twin boys, each indistinguishable from the other, except that pearls dropped from the lips of one whenever he spoke and snakes leapt from the mouth of the other whenever he spoke.'" Chandra shook her head. "I keep dreaming of Australia and hearing those words."

"Anywhere particular in Australia?" Melissa asked.

Chandra bit her lip. "The dream is always red. Like the world is on fire."

"Kim chee," Thorolf muttered. "The volumes you've been eating would give me bad dreams. Great blazing red ones." He shook his head. "Our neighbor does make it hot."

Chandra poked him. "But I'm dreaming it, not you. And this is new."

"The red could mean a firestorm," Melissa suggested, but no one else had other suggestions to make. Sloane was too tired to think about it.

"Erik should be here tomorrow," he said. "He might know more. For the moment, maybe you could all help me with the Apothecary's song." He shifted shape, hoping that the song would be more powerful in his dragon form. He remembered his father doing that on occasion.

He placed the crystal between himself and Rafferty, then

reached out and took Chandra's hand. Melissa came and took his other claw, then gripped Rafferty's claw. Thorolf shifted shape in a shimmer of blue, becoming a massive dragon of brilliant silver and diamonds. It was a good thing they were friends, because the large space was crowded. Thorolf closed the circle, taking Chandra's hand and Rafferty's other claw.

Sloane began the slow chant he'd learned from his father, the healing tune passed down from father to son in the line of the Apothecary. The darkfire in the crystal leapt as if in response, and he tried to believe that Rafferty could be cured.

There was a kind of irony in the fact that Jac had finally succeeded at some goal, and no one noticed or saw fit to congratulate her. All of her life, she'd been compared to her super-successful sister and knew she'd come up short.

Now she'd shot down a dragon to avenge Nathaniel, but only Sam knew she was responsible—and Sam didn't seem to care. She had–oddly enough–been concerned for Jac's safety. That was new and a bit difficult to think about so Jac didn't.

Marco should have been celebrating her triumph with her, but he was gone.

She went to a little local restaurant and ordered a salad and a glass wine to celebrate by herself. She tried not to think too much about Marco's sudden departure, but to focus on her plan going forward.

The poem was her only clue, so she had to make it work.

The salad was delicious and the restaurant was filled with people who seemed to know each other. She savored the meal and the atmosphere.

Jac noticed that the group of people at the corner table were a bit loud, but it was only when the woman laughed that she recognized her voice. She peeked over her shoulder to find Maeve O'Neill holding court. The others must have been her crew. She was even more gorgeous in real life and slimmer, too.

Jac was trying not to stare—and wondering whether she should confess to Maeve that she'd shot the dragon—when a guy came into the restaurant. He looked like a commando, or a model for a recruiting poster. He was tall and really muscled, his blond hair buzzed short and his eyes such a bright blue that she could see their color from across the restaurant. He was dressed casually, but looked ready for anything. He surveyed the occupants of the restaurant–who stared back at him in silence–and Jac thought of a laser being sighted.

Maeve checked him out so openly that Jac averted her gaze.

Even when she returned her attention to her companions, Maeve's gaze flicked to the new arrival.

Incredibly, his gaze landed on Jac and he marched toward her with such purpose that she thought she might have heart failure. Maeve watched as the guy pulled out the chair opposite Jac and sat down, fixing that intent blue gaze upon her. "You're the one," he said, his voice low. He didn't even blink as he studied her. "You're the one who did it."

Jac's heart was fluttering and she felt the need to get up and run. That was irrational, though. They were in a public place. "Did what?" she asked, and her voice was higher than usual.

His smile flashed and she wasn't surprised that he had perfect, straight white teeth. He leaned over the table, his gaze pinning her to the spot. "Shot the dragon, of course."

Jac wasn't sure whether to admit her deed or not. She was so shaken by her intuitive reaction to him that she couldn't decide if he was friend or foe.

Then he offered his right hand to her. "Welcome to the league of *Slayers*."

Jac felt her eyes widen. "You've done it, too?"

He nodded, as pleased with himself as he should be. "All the time. I've lost count." He shook his head and his lip curled. "But there always seem to be more of them." He smiled again. "I'm Jorge."

"Jacelyn." Jac smiled and put her hand in his. His skin was surprisingly cold, but his grip was firm as he shook her hand. Maybe a little too firm. Jac wondered whether the bones in her hand would crack. She must have caught her breath because Jorge glanced down, then grimaced and apologized as he released her hand.

"Sorry. I forget my own strength sometimes." He winked. "I'm usually battling dragons, after all."

Jac smiled at his apology. She had a strange sense that she should be charmed by him, but the hair was pricking on the back of her neck. She supposed that Marco's abrupt change of attitude was affecting her reaction to Jorge. Men were so difficult to read.

"You must know Marco then," Jac said, and Jorge's gaze fixed upon her with new intensity.

"Marco, whose real name is Marcus?"

Jac nodded, encouraged that he knew this detail.

"Was he here?"

"We came together. He had the darkfire crystal that I used to take down the dragon."

Jorge nodded sagely. "I thought it looked like darkfire," he murmured. "There's really nothing more effective." He glanced up, his eyes alight with a raw hope that startled Jac. "You must have the crystal then."

She shook her head. "No. The dark dragon took it."

"Figures," Jorge said and sighed. "They know it can be used against them, so try to keep track of it."

"Marco said it was the only one."

Jorge nodded. "There used to be three, but the other two were broken." He shrugged. "I actually thought that this one was worthless."

"What do you mean?"

"Well, I had heard that the darkfire within it was extinguished, and the stone was dead." He pursed his lips. "I wonder how it was revived. Maybe Marco could tell us."

Jac shook her head. "He's gone, and I don't know where he went."

Jorge glanced up, his curiosity clear.

Jac blushed a little as she confessed what had happened. "He was angry with me for using the crystal. We argued and he left."

Jorge surveyed the half pizza and the part bottle of wine. "And so you have to celebrate alone," he mused, then shook his head in apparent disapproval. Then he smiled at her. "How about sharing your victory dinner? I'll order another bottle of wine and a second pizza."

Jac felt a strange suspicion of his motives and found herself beginning to decline. "I already ate..."

"Then share the wine with me. My treat," Jorge said,

interrupting her protest. He leaned across the table. "And I'll even tell you why Marco was so angry with you."

"How can you know that?"

Jorge smiled and leaned back in his chair, looking like the hungry predator she supposed he was. "Because I've been stalking *Pyr* for a long, long time."

"Deal," Jac said, even though it was against her better judgment. "But we'll split the bill." She didn't want to feel that she had to be intimate with Jorge, but she did want to learn what he knew.

His smile broadened, his gaze sweeping over her, and she shivered when she saw how his eyes glittered. Her bad feeling about him intensified and she almost got up to leave the table. Then he turned to gesture to the waiter, his manner so easy that she wondered whether she'd imagined the glitter of his eyes.

Maybe she was just shaken up by the day's events.

Maybe she was too skittish.

Maybe she should welcome the chance to learn what she really wanted to know.

It was remarkable to Jorge that such a weak species had managed to survive for so many eons. It must be simply because humans bred with such abandon. Raw numbers made up for the inadequacies and misjudgments of the individuals.

This one, for example, this Jacelyn, had absolutely no clue that Marco was *Pyr* and that Jorge was *Slayer*. Even better, she was unaware that the dragon she sought to destroy was sitting right across the table from her. Her obliviousness to the truth made Jorge want to laugh out loud.

He had recognized her scent, of course, as being the woman with the boy in Seattle all those months ago. She had lost some weight, but it was the same woman. There were shadows in her eyes and her lips were tight, and she dressed more athletically than she had. Clearly the boy's death had changed her, giving her new purpose.

Jorge could work with that.

He was keenly aware of the woman on the far side of the

restaurant, a real beauty, who was watching him. There was a
confidence and a hunger about her that Jorge found remarkably
appealing. He had little time for the wiles of women, but liked how
intently she watched him.

At least she could appreciate quality.

Jorge could almost taste Jac's curiosity, but he let her wait for
the morsel of information he could share. The wine was opened
and poured, and the alcohol put a flush in her cheeks. The hum of
conversation resumed all around them. Jorge asked her questions
and the more wine she drank, the more readily she replied.

She had moved to Seattle recently although she didn't say
why. Jorge could guess.

She had wanted to be an artist, but had put aside her goals and
opportunities to take care of her sick mother. In fact, she seemed to
be one who frequently put aside her own goals to help others.
She'd taken care of her sister's son frequently, too.

The details of her life were excruciatingly boring, but Jorge
smiled and listened as if fascinated. He believed that he even
managed to appear sympathetic at the right moments—like when
she confessed to providing palliative care for her mother.

All the while, he schemed as to what he would tell her. There
was so much he knew of Marco, but most of it would show Jorge
in bad light. He selected one key detail.

"So?" Jac asked when the pizza was served. "What do you
know about Marco?"

"Just enough to guess why he might have been angry with you
today."

Jac's manner was expectant.

"The dragon you shot today..."

"The opal and gold one," she interjected. "There's video
footage of him fighting a green and gold dragon near London, and
he was in that television special that Melissa Smith did about the
Pyr. At least, I think it was the same dragon."

"It was," Jorge said with authority. "His name is Rafferty. He
killed Marco's uncle a few years ago, and Marco witnessed the
attack." Jorge shook his head sadly, even though he knew that
Marco hadn't mourned Magnus for a second. "Marco had no other
surviving family."

Jorge chose not to tell her that Rafferty was only wounded, not dead.

Jac's dismay was evident. "Then it was personal for him, too," she whispered and bit her lip. "He must have been stalking that dragon. He was the one who wanted to come here. Maybe he heard that Melissa Smith would do an interview here and guessed that Rafferty would make an appearance."

Jorge nodded and ate pizza.

"But I ruined his plan!" Jac took a gulp of wine. "No wonder he was angry with me." She shook her head, her disgust with herself clear. "I don't blame him for being furious. He must have planned and prepared, and I ruined everything by being impulsive."

"Don't be too hard on yourself," Jorge murmured. "It's easy to be overwhelmed by enthusiasm."

"But it's the mark of an amateur," Jac said with such despair that Jorge had an idea.

Time would be heavy on his talons for the next few months. He had to wait to verify that Drake's mate was pregnant and also for the next blood moon to ripen the next batch of clones. In Jac, he saw an opportunity to create more trouble for the *Pyr*, which might give him an unexpected advantage.

"Wouldn't it be great if you could make it up to him?" he asked, and Jac looked up at him, her eyes wide.

"How could I do that?"

"What if you continue with what you started?"

"You mean kill more dragons." She nodded with vigor. "I'd do it, but I have no idea how. The crystal was the only weapon I knew about."

"There are others," Jorge said, eating the last bite of pizza. He forced himself to sound casual, but really, the idea of having a human in thrall to him was exciting. And he still had the option of beguiling her. "If you like, I can teach you." He pushed a napkin across the table to her. "I live in Portland," he lied. "Give me your address in Seattle and I'll call you when I get home. It could be a week or two."

"Me, too," Jac said, writing her address on the napkin. "I want to check out the nest where those eggs were."

"Really?" Jorge asked idly, guessing that she knew more than she'd told him. "I'm more interested in finding out where the others are."

"There are more?" She glanced up, her gaze darkening when Jorge smiled. "Because there were only five," she said softly. "Which means there have to be eight more to make thirteen."

Jorge was startled but he hid his reaction. He nodded. "How did you know?"

"Marco has a verse on the wall of his apartment that talks about them."

"You've visited his apartment?" Jorge asked.

Jac smiled. "It was how we met. He lives in the apartment right over mine. There was a parcel delivered to him instead of to me." She frowned then. "At least that's what he told me at the time. Later I guessed that it was really from him."

"How so?"

"Oh, it was a book about slaying dragons, by someone named Sigmund Guthrie."

A jolt ripped through Jorge at that detail. Sigmund, of course, had contrived the cloning of Boris Vassily, and Jorge would love to have had more than thirteen clones at his disposal.

Had Sigmund written his process down in that book?

"Really?" he asked, striving to appear casual. "I don't know it."

"I think it's the only copy," Jac confided. "It has tons of detail, although it's kind of old-fashioned."

"I assume you've put it in a safe place."

Jac laughed. "Of course!"

So, the human had usefulness, and Jorge had a reason to let her live. "That was good thinking," he said with a smile and topped up her wine. He let her chatter on about her plans, paying only slight attention while he concocted his own.

He eyed the dark-haired woman, who smiled at him openly. She had fabulous legs, and Jorge let her see his appreciation.

She let him see her pleasure in that.

A trip to Seattle was in order, Jorge decided. He wanted that book, as much to keep the *Pyr* from having it as anything else. He wondered whether he could make it appear that Marco had turned *Slayer*, just to cause confusion in the ranks of the *Pyr*. They would have doubts, after all, given that Rafferty had been injured by the darkfire crystal. He sipped his wine and decided it was definitely worth a try.

If nothing else, it would fill his time.

He winked at the brunette, who smiled in invitation, then focused on his scheme.

CHAPTER FOURTEEN

 arco had trusted the darkfire and the darkfire had lied.

He couldn't really accept it. In fact, he couldn't understand it. He nearly stalled the 4x4 as he drove it back to the rental place. All he knew was darkfire and its ways. All he heeded were the urgings and whispers of darkfire. All he believed was that darkfire, even with its propensity for turning everything upside-down, was good.

The injury of Rafferty was not good, no matter how he looked at it. The death or disfigurement of that *Pyr* could never contribute to the greater good of anything, as far as Marco could see.

Had something tainted the darkfire? Had Jorge somehow found a way to turn the ancient force to his demand? The very idea made Marco sick at heart.

What would Pwyll have thought of this development? Marco could only imagine. That Rafferty had been struck down, and would possibly die, because of Marco's actions was an abomination. He didn't dare trust the darkfire to heed Pwyll's chant, not without subverting it to something else.

Something worse.

If nothing else, this incident showed Marco to be a poor custodian for the last crystal containing darkfire. That was why he'd left it with Sloane.

Oh, Jac had fired the crystal, but that didn't absolve Marco from responsibility. He had approached her. He had misled her. He had invited her to Easter Island with him. He had made love to her and trusted her, even been enchanted by her. He had certainly been distracted by her.

He had told her that the crystal could be used to kill dragons and had been by her side, with the crystal, when Rafferty appeared. He had known that she was determined to hunt dragons. In hindsight, his choices seemed naive, if not stupid.

His only excuse was that humans weren't supposed to be able to command the darkfire. Jac shouldn't have been able to fire the crystal. She wasn't a Firedaughter, like Liz.

Why had the darkfire responded to her desire?

The only possible explanation was that the darkfire had responded to the desire of a *Pyr* or *Slayer* in the vicinity, not to Jac at all.

Marco parked the truck and considered that idea. He couldn't smell any *Pyr* or *Slayers*, but the *Slayers* who had drunk the Elixir could disguise their scent. The island could be crawling with them, and he wouldn't know. How many were left? There was Jorge, of course, and the five that had hatched from these eggs. Were there other eggs? Other hatchlings? He recalled the verse and assumed these were five of the thirteen "monsters" that would emerge into the world.

Was Jac in danger? He sat in the car, letting it idle.

He only thought of the possible danger after their last exchange, which in itself was remarkable. Marco couldn't recall ever having been so angry as he was with Jac. He never lost his temper. He was always serene and composed, always observant but somehow outside of events.

Not this time, though. This time, he was embroiled in Jac's choice and Rafferty's injury. Had the darkfire changed him, too?

Or had it been Jac herself? Marco closed his eyes and took a deep steadying breath. He hadn't been able to believe his luck when she'd turned to him with that small smile the night before, or the light sweep of her hand over his chest. He'd been struck by her fragility, the very vulnerability of being human, in contrast with her determination and spirit. Her resolve to avenge her nephew, regardless of the price, showed a nobility that Marco found admirable.

He hadn't been able to resist her.

He'd let down his guard for the first time ever, and Rafferty had paid the price.

What was his responsibility to Jac from this point forward?

Had he put her in danger by creating the possibility for her to injure Rafferty? Marco had to think so. It was his creed to defend humans, after all, and while a small part of him thought she deserved to be abandoned to her fate for such a foul deed, another part of him knew that the greater responsibility was his own.

She hadn't understood what she was doing.

Pwyll would have said that it was up to him to make the distinction clear. Marco backed the car out of the lot and turned around, heading back toward the small hotel where he'd shared a room with Jac. He waited when he discovered that she was out and spent the time wondering whether she would even speak to him again.

When he saw her strolling back to the hotel with another guy, he couldn't believe his eyes. When he took a deep breath and smelled *Slayer*, Marco was incredulous.

It was Jorge. The one *Slayer* Jac was determined to remove from the face of the earth. Marco knew he should disappear to keep Jorge from catching his scent, but he couldn't leave. He watched from the shadows as Jac laughed at something Jorge said and he could practically smell her discomfiture. She didn't really like Jorge, Marco guessed, much less trust him, but somehow the *Slayer* had established a bond with her.

Had he beguiled her? The very idea sent rare fury through Marco.

Jac pivoted quickly and walked away as the *Slayer* watched. Marco saw Jorge take a deep breath, saw him smile, and knew he'd been discerned. To his relief, Jorge turned and strolled in the opposite direction.

Indifferent to the fact that Marco was there.

It was dismissive, a slap in the face in dragon terms, but Marco didn't care. He didn't want to fight, not right now.

Jac glanced over her shoulder and relaxed slightly to see Jorge retreating. She didn't know who the *Slayer* really was. Marco was sure of it.

Which meant that Jorge was trying to charm Jac, undoubtedly for some dark purpose of his own. What did he want from her?

How could Marco find out? Somehow he had to guard Jac, find out Jorge's plan, and keep from being discovered by that *Slayer*.

That sounded like the kind of long shot the darkfire might favor.

Marco lingered until Jac was securely in the hotel room. He breathed a barrier of dragonsmoke around the hotel, knowing it wouldn't stop Jorge but hoping it might defend her a little. As he breathed, he considered his options.

He had inherited the role of the custodian of the darkfire crystals.

But he didn't trust the darkfire anymore.

Marco wove in the ends of his dragonsmoke, then checked for the resonant ping of a completed barrier. He knew he could go to Sloane's home and retrieve the crystal, but that would mean using the power of the darkfire to spontaneously manifest elsewhere. He wanted nothing more to do with darkfire.

No, he'd stand vigil over Jac and do it the old-fashioned *Pyr* way. No more spontaneous manifestation, not if it meant using the darkfire. He'd live like the other *Pyr*, bound to the world and limited just as they were. If he travelled, he'd fly himself or journey amongst humans. No more easy fixes.

Marco had to consider that the power of the darkfire wasn't his to command, not any longer. Maybe that was what it was turning upside down, taking his hereditary responsibility and blessing, then turning it into a curse.

Either way, he wasn't going to play darkfire's game.

Rafferty's unconscious figure in the middle of the great room of Sloane's home was enough to sober all of the *Pyr*. Sloane kept humming the Apothecary's song beneath his breath, unable to stop himself even though it hadn't helped much.

Rafferty seemed to be in a coma, neither recovering nor getting worse. Even in dragon form, his breathing was so shallow that Sloane found it hard to hear.

"At least he's stable," Erik said, and Melissa shot him a look. The leader of the *Pyr* was seeking a positive detail, and there weren't many candidates. Sloane knew that Erik was disheartened by his own inability to see Pwyll's ghost, much less hear the Cantor's song. He kept flicking glances into the corners but his strained expression revealed that nothing had changed.

"For how long?" Melissa asked. The darkfire crackled under Rafferty's scales, and Sloane found it easy to imagine that the unpredictable force was wreaking havoc in Rafferty's body.

Havoc that Sloane apparently couldn't halt. It was another failure to heal on his part, and he was getting sick of failure. It seemed that the darkfire had inverted any potential success by the *Pyr*.

Or maybe just by him.

"How can there not be a prophecy?" Thorolf demanded. He was rubbing Chandra's feet where they sat together on the loveseat. "It could help us understand Chandra's dreams."

"Have you had any more?" Erik asked.

Chandra shrugged. "Two more versions of the story, if it *is* the same story. I keep seeing the same twins."

"One with serpents falling from his mouth," Eileen said with interest. "And one with pearls?"

Chandra nodded. "I see those two brothers coming to eat together in peace, but they end up fighting over the affections of a beautiful woman who is sleeping there and kill each other."

"What happens to the woman?" Erik asked.

Chandra shook her head. "I don't know, but there's a kind of earthquake afterward."

Eileen exhaled. "The woman is a prize in this story, not a character. She might as well be a fortress or a gem or even a pile of money. The taboo against fighting while eating exists in many cultures and is reinforced in many stories."

"Like attacking your host or guests," Melissa added.

"But it doesn't help much in this case," Erik nodded, and his mate nodded agreement.

"What else?" Eileen asked.

Chandra winced. "The guy who has snakes falling from his mouth throws something. It's something he's made and I can't tell what it is. He seems to expect it to come back."

"A boomerang," Thorolf said, leaning forward. "That's the only thing I know that comes back when you throw it."

Eileen snapped her fingers. "Does he go hunting for it?" she asked, with obvious excitement.

"Yes," Chandra said, "but he ends up at a mountain of some

kind and tries to pry it from the earth. He doesn't succeed."

Eileen laughed. "It's a creation story. Alinga, the lizard man, makes the biggest boomerang he's ever made, but when he throws it, it doesn't come back. He goes in search of it and discovers that it has buried itself in the desert and become Uluru."

"Uluru?" Erik asked with obvious confusion.

"They used to call it Ayer's Rock, until custody reverted to the aboriginal peoples of Australia," Eileen said. "That's one of the traditional stories explaining its creation." She smiled. "The other involves twin brothers." A ripple of excitement passed through the room.

"Uluru sounds like a great place to hide eggs that look like rocks," Thorolf said.

Erik nodded, tapping away on Sloane's computer. "And it will be in the full shadow of the next lunar eclipse."

"The blood moon will ripen the eggs," Eileen repeated softly.

"Not if we find them first," Erik said with resolve. "Liz said she felt the quickening in the eggs on Easter Island."

"But they won't appear any different from other rocks, not before the blood moon and that quickening," Sloane protested. "How will we find them?"

"Liz might be able to sense a difference when she's closer to them," Erik said. "And Chandra might be able to home in on them with the help of her dreams."

"Brandt and Brandon are both in Australia already," Thorolf said. "They could start the hunt and we'll join them."

"Wait a minute." Sloane raised a hand. "I don't think Chandra should go anywhere before the baby is born. It's too long of a commercial flight for a woman entering her third trimester. I don't know how you managed to get here, but you should *stay* here."

He saw the hot look that Thorolf and Chandra exchanged and recalled that she'd surrendered immortality to be with him. He could see that Thorolf was ready to depart, yet also wanted to remain with Chandra. Sloane wondered whether she had regrets, but she reached out and took Thorolf's hand, then gave it a visible squeeze.

"You're going to Easter Island, to track the attacker's scent first," she reminded him and he glanced to Erik who nodded approval. "While you do that, I'll stay here with Sloane and try to help him."

Thorolf nodded. "We've only got five months, so we need to start the hunt."

"Follow the trail and kick some butt," Chandra said. "When you're done, you can fly me to Australia to search for clues."

Sloane winced, as Chandra would be even further along in her pregnancy by then.

She gave him a stern look, as if reading his thoughts, and Sloane was reminded that she had been a warrior goddess. Compromise wasn't in Chandra's vocabulary, but he hoped she wasn't forgetting that she had made a sacrifice. "It's the final challenge to your kind," she said with force. "A little discomfort is a small price to pay."

"You're mortal now," Sloane reminded her, because she seemed to be forgetting that bit.

Chandra dismissed his fears. "I'm not nearly done here." She held Sloane's gaze with such steely determination that he knew she understood the risk.

She just thought it was more important for her *Pyr* to survive this war.

As much as Sloane could relate to that, he felt a portent of doom.

What he needed was a success of some kind to feel his usual optimism restored.

He longed to visit Sam and forget his troubles for a night, to lose himself in passion, but he had to think of others before himself. He had to cure Rafferty of the darkfire's touch.

The problem was that he didn't know how.

Almost a week had passed after their call by the time Jac got to California, but Sam hadn't really expected much different. Jac ran on her own schedule, without regard for anyone or anything else, just as their father had always insisted. The flight was even late, which made Sam fume, believing as she did that somehow Jac had to be responsible for that, too.

Hunting dragons. Honestly! What was in her sister's head? The more Sam thought about it, the more determined she was to sort out Jac's misguided ideas for once and for all.

The fact that she hadn't seen Sloane again wasn't helping her mood. Her tarot card readings had improved since his advice, but her mood was worse. What was probably most annoying was that by disappearing, Sloane was giving her exactly what she'd insisted she wanted. Great sex with no strings attached and no emotional commitments.

Sam didn't like it nearly as much as she'd expected she would.

She wanted to talk to him.

She was tapping her toe by the time Jac sailed into the arrival lounge, smiling, tanned, and relaxed.

She knew that look.

This wasn't about hunting dragons. It was about some guy.

Sam forced a smile. "Who is he?" she asked when Jac stopped in front of her.

Jac smiled. "My new neighbor. Well, he was." She winced. "We had a bit of an argument, but I understand why now."

"And before that?"

Jac sighed. "Awesome."

"So where has Mr. Dreamy gone?"

"Hunting dragons." Jac said, hefting her bag as they headed for the parking garage.

That explained it. Jac had a tendency to take on the causes of the men she dated. If the dragon hunter was gone, then Jac wouldn't be hunting dragons any more. It was good to know that she'd be safe.

"It was his crystal I used to shoot that dragon, you see," Jac confided as she dumped her bag into the trunk of Sam's car. "I found out later that the dragon I shot had killed his uncle."

Sam slammed the trunk. "Then there can't be too few of them." She really didn't want to talk about dragons, but it seemed that Jac did.

"But we have something in common," Jac said. "Both of us lost someone important to a dragon shifter on the hunt." She gave a little shiver of delight as she settled into her seat. "Like you and what's-his-name, and your science thingy."

Jac didn't refer to Derek by name, not since Sam's divorce.

"And we saw how well that worked out," Sam retorted, not wanting to talk about her ex-husband either.

Jac turned to study her. "The weird thing is that I thought you had a good marriage for the longest time."

Sam laughed because she couldn't stop herself.

"Dad always held your marriage up as a shining example of perfection."

"Yes, well, I guess he saw what he wanted to see." Sam paid the parking attendant and couldn't believe how expensive it was to park for so short of a time. That made her wonder how much money she'd be lending to Jac, and whether she'd ever see it again.

"Ever thought about getting a job?" she asked, hearing her father in her voice. She frowned and pulled out into traffic. She'd wanted to start fresh with Jac but it wasn't working out that way.

"I haven't noticed that you had one lately," Jac replied. "What's the deal with this retreat to the hills, anyway? It's not like you to run away from anything."

"I'm not running away!"

Jac gave her a look. "Uh huh. You've always wanted to leave the cares of the world and the rigor of science behind to read tarot cards for strangers." Her tone showed all of her skepticism. "Who are you and what have you done with my sister?"

"I just got burned out," Sam said, hearing defensiveness in her tone. "I needed a break."

"That's a first," Jac muttered.

"There's nothing wrong with doing something for the first time."

"No, but you don't usually."

"I'm trying to change that." There was silence between them for a moment, and Sam finally spoke. Expressing her feelings aloud had worked with Sloane. Maybe it would work with Jac. "Like this. I want us to get along better, but we're just continuing as we always did."

"Maybe we should just toss out all the shit that's been simmering and get rid of it, for once and for all," Jac said.

"Who'll pick up the wounded?" Sam asked, sparing a smile for her sister. Jac was right about unspoken thoughts having power.

"Chicken."

"You bet."

Jac grinned back at her. "Are you any good at reading tarot cards? You could tell my fortune for me."

Sam couldn't bring herself to make a pronouncement. She didn't want to sound like her father, even if she heard his commentary in her thoughts all the time. "Why don't you tell mine instead?"

"Just to prove you aren't chicken?"

"Exactly."

Jac straightened in her seat. "All right. You're going to find a new goal, even without Dad to give it to you, and you're going to pursue it with such dedication and devotion that there won't be one second in your life for anything or anyone else. The people you supposedly care about will have needs, but you'll be too busy working to even speak to them, much less to help them out. You'll become a stranger to all of them, although maybe some—like Dad—will keep the candles burning on the altar of St. Samantha. Those of us left to clean up the mess might be a little less impressed."

Sam exhaled slowly, astonished by her sister's words and tone. "Well, thanks a lot."

"That's the view from here."

"Ouch. Maybe I should have been more afraid." Sam glanced at her sister, seeing strain in the line of her mouth. "Tell me."

"Everyone thinks I don't have ambitions, instead of realizing that I give them up for the team," Jac said, her words making Sam see the situation from a new perspective. "Just what kind of job do you think I could have had that would have allowed me to give palliative care to Mom for two years? Just what kind of job would have paid me for running to drive Dad everywhere when he gave up the car and refused to bother Number One Daughter, the superstar scientist? Just what kind of job would have let me take care of Nathaniel at a moment's notice while you and what's-his-name argued over whose turn it was *not* to work late?"

"That's unfair!" Sam protested, though in her heart, she wasn't sure.

"It's not!" Jac retorted, glaring out the window. "I left college to nurse Mom, abandoning my degree and my chance at a gallery show," she whispered.

Sam was shocked. "You never said you had a chance at a show. I thought you didn't like the program."

"It doesn't matter. It was an easy choice to make, but there's been no getting back on track since."

"That's not entirely fair," Sam had to point out, even as she wished she'd been more perceptive sooner. "Every step has been your choice."

Jac sighed. "I guess it has been."

"You should have talked to me."

"We weren't exactly exchanging confidences." Jac shook her head and said something unlikely, as was her way. "What's really unfair is that we're on the freeway so I can't just get out of this damn car and walk away from you." She made a sound of frustration. "What's stupid is how tempting it is to do it anyway."

They *were* on the freeway, in the midst of four busy lanes of traffic, hurtling along at the limit, but Jac sounded serious.

"Am I really that bad?" Sam asked gently.

Jac exhaled. "You could be a *little* less perfect."

"Then you'll be glad to hear that I'm on top of that these days," Sam replied. "Maybe you should let me read your tarot cards. I'm so pathetic at it that you'd laugh."

Jac gave her a considering glance. "Oh no, you don't." She folded her arms across her chest, making a joke. "You'd better rethink this plan, Dr. Samantha Wilcox. I'm not ready to share the throne of Loser Daughter just yet."

"Mom and Dad are both gone, Jac. Do we still have to compete?"

"I never competed."

"No. You just abandoned the field completely." It was only now that Sam saw that her sister's apparent lack of ambition wasn't that at all. She put her family and friends first, partly because she'd refused to compete with Sam. She had to think about that for a minute, and negotiated the exit with more care than was necessary.

"Is that why you're here?" Jac asked gently. "Because without Dad telling you which mountain to climb next, you're not sure what to do?"

Sam was startled by her sister's insight.

Then she realized it was right on the mark. "Something like that," she admitted and there was silence in the car for a long while. "He never expected results from you," she added, keeping her tone mild. "And oh, there were times I hated you for that."

"He only ever gave a shit about you and your achievements," Jac replied in the same mild tone. "And oh, there were times I hated you for that."

Sam stopped at the traffic light in town and they turned to eye each other. She realized that their father's dismissal of Jac had been a knife that cut both ways. By expecting nothing, in a way, he was suggesting that she wasn't capable of anything of importance.

"You were right," Sam said. "It was good to let go of all that crap." She opted for Sloane's strategy. "Can we start fresh now?" Sam offered her hand. "I'm your sister, but maybe we could be friends, too."

Jac smiled, never one to hold a grudge. Sam had always admired that about her sister. "It's worth a shot," Jac said as she shook Sam's hand. The light turned and the driver behind honked his horn.

Jac shook her head as they continued, as if amazed. "You know, I never thought you'd be the one to offer the olive branch. I thought that would be up to me, too. You've changed. Thawed maybe."

Sam drove for a bit while she considered her words. "Well, I met this guy..."

"Met," Jac echoed in a teasing tone. "I'm thinking you did more than shake hands."

Sam felt her cheeks heat. "I met this guy, and we had dinner..."

"Here?"

"Here."

"Now things are getting interesting. Suddenly this staying-in-California stuff is making a lot more sense." Jac shook her head. "Imagine my ambitious sister making a decision to stay in a place because of a *guy*."

"It's not like that!" Sam protested.

"Your blush says it is." Jac leaned closer, her eyes dancing. "Or maybe you want it to be. What do the cards have to say about it?"

Sam cleared her throat, thinking of The Lovers card. "The point is that while we were having dinner, he said something that made me think. He said that no matter how much it hurts to lose someone you love, it's never enough to make you regret having loved them." Sam found her tears rising. "He's right."

Jac's teasing manner was dismissed and her surprise was clear. "You actually told him about Nathaniel?"

Sam shook her head, feeling disappointed in her own choice. "He was talking about his dad." She felt Jac turn to study her, but didn't meet her sister's gaze. Instead she concentrated on driving. They'd never talked so bluntly to each other about their feelings, and Sam was both relieved and flustered.

"Did you really love Dad?" Jac asked, no charge in her tone. "Or was he just kind of a hard habit to break?"

Sam cast a smile at her sister then sobered. "I loved how sure he was," she admitted, as she turned into her driveway. "I loved that he never had any doubt of what to do next, of what anybody should do next."

"Even if he was wrong."

"Was he?" Sam shook her head, haunted by old arguments and resentments. "There's something to be said for acting without hesitation, for being decisive."

"I guess." Jac sounded less convinced. Sam pulled into her driveway, her gaze trailing to Sloane's house. There was a black pick-up truck there with a trailer. She narrowed her eyes but she wasn't imagining that the words 'Here Be Dragons' were emblazoned on the side.

Dragons *again*?

Before Sam could say anything, her sister was leaning forward, peering at her own house. Her eyes were wide with surprise. "You bought *this* house?"

"Well, I didn't bring you to somebody else's."

"Ha ha."

"Why? What's wrong with it?"

Jac got out of the car and stared at the house, walking up and down one side as she checked it out. "It's a fixer-upper. It has charm and character, maybe a few idiosyncrasies."

"It has idiosyncrasies by the bucket," Sam replied. "Don't have fantasies about your shower water staying the same temperature. We won't even talk about the electrical. Or the mice."

Jac turned to face her. "Again I ask: who are you and what have you done with my sister?"

"What's that supposed to mean?" Sam opened the trunk and Jac came to get her bag.

"It means that this looks like a place Mom would have bought," Jac said, much to Sam's surprise. "Or maybe me. It's the kind of place that charms you and catches at your heart so that you look past its issues."

"Is it?" Sam glanced over the house again.

Jac nodded, her approval clear. "Yes. This is the kind of house that would haunt a person, tempt them with possibilities. It's a dreamer's house."

"And you're surprised I bought it because..."

"You always live in places that are sterile and contemporary, all steel and glass and yawning emptiness." Jac grimaced. "White and silver. Stainless steel counters. Floors so cold you can get frostbite, and surfaces so clean that you could do surgery anywhere in the house. Practical houses." She shuddered visibly.

"Be serious. The place in Atlanta wasn't that bad. I liked it."

Jac grimaced. "Exactly my point. It was as welcoming as a morgue. How on earth did you end up with *this* place?"

Sam considered the house from her sister's view. "I liked how far it was out of town. Close enough for shopping, but far enough not to have nosy neighbors."

Jac shook her head, amused, then turned and looked at Sloane's house. It was the only neighboring house in view. Sam felt herself stiffen, but her sister just smiled and headed for the front door. "That is far away. Come on and show me what you've done to the place."

"Nothing," Sam admitted. "My stuff is here and that's it."

"Oh good." Jac feigned relief. "You really *are* my sister, then. I was getting worried." She smiled to soften the words. "Maybe I can help you make it look as if you live here, instead of like you're renting for an hour or two."

Jac did have a gift for making a house into a home. It was a knack that Sam didn't possess and she knew it. It had never been important to her before. She'd always had more important things to do, and had known that she might have to fly out to another corner of the world at a moment's notice.

But maybe, just maybe, this time she'd stay. She didn't want to think about the influence Sloane Forbes could have on that decision.

She also didn't want to think about the fact that she'd been inspired by her father, driven by him most of the time, but she'd always gone to her mom for solace.

Maybe that was why she'd bought this house.

"That would be great," Sam said with a smile and meant it.

In the great room of Sloane's house, three dragons slumbered side by side. The tourmaline and gold one was on one side, the sapphire and steel dragon on the other. The opal and gold dragon was between them. Sloane was dozing, breathing dragonsmoke and weaving it with Quinn's, and monitoring the older *Pyr*'s vital signs. He'd sung the Apothecary's song until he was too exhausted to sing it again, and he believed that Rafferty's state was stable. Quinn's strength was a big help, as was the fact that he shared an affinity with earth with Rafferty. Sloane hoped that Quinn was able to reach Rafferty in different ways than he could. He had to hope that the fact that his house was partly underground, meaning that the influence of the earth was strong, would help Rafferty.

Rafferty wasn't improving though, and the darkfire still glimmered beneath his scales, like a lightning storm gathering in the distance. Sloane had no idea what that meant, but he didn't trust it.

Still, he had to restore his own strength.

Sloane was more than aware of Chandra and Thorolf in an upstairs bedroom, and Melissa and Isabelle sleeping in another. Sara was sleeping with the boys in a third bedroom while Eileen had retired to a fourth bedroom with Zoë. Erik had only joined his family at Sloane's insistence that he rest. It was discouraging that Erik couldn't see Pwyll's ghost, and he knew that Erik was disheartened by that as well. It had to be just exhaustion, not the loss of Erik's abilities. Sloane suspected Erik would have argued with him more if Quinn hadn't arrived.

Sloane cast his thoughts more broadly and felt Sam's presence in her house next door. She was talking and he could almost discern her words. There was someone visiting her, someone whose presence clearly made her happy, and Sloane was glad.

He could have used some of her company himself. He sighed and let his eyes close again, trying to will his strength to rebuild.

Rafferty stirred suddenly and Sloane was immediately awake once more.

"*She's here*," the older *Pyr* murmured in old-speak, his words so low as to be almost indistinct, even to Sloane.

"*Melissa is upstairs*," Sloane replied. "*I'll call her.*"

"*No, no. She's here*," Rafferty repeated with some agitation. There was an edge in his next words. "*I smell her.*"

Who did Rafferty mean? He inhaled deeply of the evening air but didn't smell anyone other than his sleeping guests. He shifted shape and went to look into the night, but there was no movement on the driveway or the road beyond.

He looked at Sam's house, unable to restrain his curiosity about her guest. The lights were on in her kitchen. He inhaled again, unable to stop himself, and recognized that two human women were in Sam's house. One was Sam, the other a stranger.

A woman. A girlfriend, a sister, an aunt or a niece.

Not a lover.

Sloane shook his head at the power of his own relief. He wasn't quite ready to be replaced.

He turned back, only to find that Rafferty had slipped into a deeper sleep again. Quinn's eyes shone, his lids almost but not quite completely closed.

Who had Rafferty been talking about? Was he just confused? Who had he thought was here?

Marco went back to Seattle, for lack of a better destination. Time had given him a bit more perspective. He hated that the darkfire had betrayed him, and he despised that he had had any part in Rafferty's injury. He hoped that *Pyr* would recover from his injury and wished there was something he could do to fix his miscalculation.

Other than give voice to Pwyll's song. He just didn't trust the darkfire. He couldn't summon it or try to control it, not now.

Marco couldn't, however, blame Jac for her choice. He'd known she wanted to strike down dragons. He'd known she needed to avenge her nephew's death. He hadn't made any effort to explain distinctions between *Pyr* and *Slayer* to her. The fault was his, not hers.

He was responsible for her trusting Jorge as much as she did, as well.

He'd followed her to California and been startled that her destination was so close to Sloane's home. The air was thick with the scent of the *Pyr*, and he'd quickly departed, knowing that Jorge wouldn't attempt any attack when there were so many *Pyr* in the vicinity.

Not alone, anyway.

Instead, he returned to Seattle, wanting to be there when Jac arrived. Maybe they could talk about it. Maybe he could make amends. Maybe he could figure out Jorge's scheme.

As soon as he unlocked the door to his apartment, Marco knew something was wrong. First he saw the mark on the hardwood floor in the living room. A spiral had been burned into the floor, the smell of its creation faded but still clear to him. He stepped into the darkened apartment and saw that the wall where he'd written the verse had been scorched. It was black, the words burned to oblivion. His body hovered on the cusp of change and the blue shimmer of his pending shift lit the apartment.

He took another step before he smelled *Slayer*, and then he froze.

He saw the golden salamander at the middle of the spiral and knew it was Jorge. The salamander was perched on a book, an old book, and Marco knew it was the book he'd given to Jac. The spiral reminded him of the one in Chen's cavern.

Jorge glimmered blue.

Marco shifted and leapt at the intruder, talon outstretched. Jorge laughed and disappeared, vanishing along with the book as if neither had ever been there. Marco's claw closed on empty air, but he was too consumed by pain to care that the *Slayer* had escaped.

He was snared in a coil of dragonsmoke, his scales burning all over his body with savage fire. He cried out, even as the spiral in the floor seemed to spin around him, drawing him down to its center with inexorable force. He was trapped, snared, and hooked, his struggles only pulling him closer to the eye of the spiral.

Once there, he felt the dragonsmoke slide beneath his burning scales and spear his heart. He felt the strength leaving him, as Jorge's dragonsmoke sapped his power. He tried to summon the darkfire so he could manifest elsewhere, outside of the trap, but it was too late. He rotated helplessly between forms, then felt consciousness ebb away.

Even then, he knew that if he awakened from this slumber, it would be because Jorge still wanted him alive.

Marco didn't even want to think about why that might be. He groaned at his own mistake, then closed his eyes in anguish.

How could the darkfire have led him so far astray?

Sam drove Jac back to the airport at the end of the week. Their relationship was much improved, to her thinking, and was both warmer and more honest. Sam knew it would take many more such visits to remove all the barriers between them, but they hugged at the airport and promised to keep in closer touch, which was a good start.

She was thinking about Sloane as she drove home, wondering how she could drop in on him without being too obvious.

Maybe being too obvious wouldn't be a problem. It hadn't been, that first time.

She missed him in a way that had nothing to do with sex. And she missed the sex, too. She smiled at herself, thinking that she was being more honest with herself as well as Jac, and turned onto the road out of town. There was a man walking along the shoulder. He looked tired, because his footsteps were dragging.

There was nowhere he could be walking within easy proximity and the day was getting warm.

On impulse, Sam stopped the car and opened the passenger window. "Can I give you a ride somewhere?"

To her surprise, he was younger than she'd expected. He looked to be about thirty-five, a handsome Asian man with weariness in his eyes.

"I'm going to the Apothecary," he said by way of reply.

So, there *were* people who called Sloane by that title.

"Sloane Forbes," she said and he smiled. "I know where he lives. I'll give you a ride."

"I wouldn't inconvenience you."

"He's my neighbor," Sam said with a smile and unlocked the

door. "It would be no trouble to give you a ride."

"Thank you very much." He got into the car and sighed. "I've come a long way."

"It's a good hike yet." Sam pulled out and drove as her companion looked out the window at the passing scenery. "Have you visited Sloane before?"

Her passenger shook his head. "Never. It's very beautiful here."

"It is nice," Sam agreed. They rode in silence the rest of the way, then Sam pulled into the parking lot in front of Sloane's shop. Her passenger, to her surprise, inhaled deeply, then nodded with satisfaction before getting out of the car. He looked taller and more alert.

He must have been smelling the herbs. Sam could always smell the lavender when she drove down her driveway and she took a deep breath of it, too. She associated it with coming home now.

The shop was open, which was a relief, so Sam seized the excuse of delivering Sloane's guest and got out of the car, too. They went into the shop, her passenger's curiosity more than clear. There was a big blond guy behind the counter, and Sam realized he was the one who'd arrived in the Mustang.

He was wearing a blue T-shirt but Sam noticed the large and detailed dragon tattoo on his forearm. The dragon coiled around his arm, its head and open claws on the back of the man's hand. The tail disappeared beneath the sleeve hem and Sam shivered a little. How weird that there seemed to be so many dragons in Sloane's vicinity.

"Lee!" The blond guy said with obvious delight. "How great to see you!" He shook the other man's hand and even gave him a hug, the enthusiasm of his greeting making Lee appear a little discomfited. Then he glanced at Sam. "Can I help you?"

"I was looking for Sloane," Sam said, feeling herself blush a little.

"Present and accounted for," Sloane murmured. He stepped out of the small office in the shop, his gaze warm as he smiled at her. Sam's blush deepened, even as she noticed that he looked exhausted.

"I haven't seen you in ages," she said. "But then, I guess

you've had company, too. My sister just left."

Sloane nodded. "Nothing like a full house to wear out the host or hostess," he agreed. "I hope you had a good time with her." Even though they were making small talk—and both the blond guy and Lee were listening—Sam could detect the questions beneath his words. It was funny that she hadn't wanted to talk about her life before, but now she was more than ready to do so.

She had a strange sense that all three men were waiting for her to say or do something. It made her feel more self-conscious than she might have been otherwise.

"It *was* good to catch up." Sam glanced at that big tattoo again, and the words fell out of her mouth. "Does everyone you know have a dragon tattoo?"

Sloane smiled and shook his head. "Not you."

"Hey, you don't know that for sure," the blond guy said heartily. "She could have a back piece or..."

Sloane silenced him with an intent glance.

The big guy stammered to silence, as if he was used to putting his foot square in it. Lee averted his gaze and seemed to be hiding a smile. "Or, uh, maybe you do know. Look, I'll take Lee up to the house."

Sloane held his ground, watching as the other two departed. The shop felt small and empty after the back door slammed, intimate in a way that Sam hadn't anticipated. Sloane stepped closer, his gaze warm enough to set her on fire. "I've missed you," he murmured.

"I've missed you, too." Sam put her hand on his arm, liking the solid strength of him. "Maybe you could come for dinner tonight."

Sloane closed his hand over hers. "I'd like that. And I think I can leave my guests to their own devices for one meal."

"I actually have a devious plan," Sam admitted and Sloane lifted a brow. "My sister says my tarot card reading still needs work. You seem to have such a knack for it. Maybe you could help me study this evening."

"Maybe I could. It would take a long time to get through all seventy-eight cards, though."

"I think I'm ready for an intense session," Sam whispered, her gaze locked with his.

Sloane leaned closer and dropped his voice to a whisper. "It might take all night."

"God, I hope so." Sam closed her eyes as his lips touched her cheek and she leaned against him, needing to feel his heat against her. She ran her hand over his chest, savoring his strength. "Your guests have been here long enough to fix their own breakfast, I think," she said and Sloane's smile flashed.

"I think you might be right," he murmured. "After all, it would be for a good cause." They stared into each other's eyes for a long moment, until Sam's heart was racing and her mouth was dry with anticipation. Then Sloane slowly bent his head to capture her lips beneath his own. Sam wound her arms around his neck and kissed him back, more than ready for all he could give.

CHAPTER FIFTEEN

February, 2015

t was pathetic, really, that the *Pyr* had to mate with such an inferior species. Jorge watched Veronica Maitland fight against the drugs in her system, apparently too stupid to know that she couldn't succeed.

She'd become more troublesome since her stomach had started to round.

But the changing shape of her body had told Jorge all he needed to know. The firestorm had been consummated, just as Jorge had hoped, and this woman would bear Drake's son. He had one final touch to make before releasing her, one flourish that would ensure his success.

Ronnie was conjured out of her prison only when she was drowsy. A sedative had been put in her last meal and she was already under its influence. Though she had started to eat more since she realized she was with child, she still did not eat much. The drugs were so much more effective this way. Jorge manifested in the crude operating theater he had arranged in yet another abandoned hospital facility. Jorge's last minion strapped her to a gurney. Ronnie struggled beneath the bright lights, as if anticipating her fate. Jorge could have given her more sedative, ensuring that she was completely under, but it was more amusing to let her be aware of what he did.

He leaned over her, smiled when her eyes widened, then ripped open the neck of her sweatshirt. It wasn't particularly clean after all these months and he grimaced at the scent of her body.

She shivered convulsively when her skin was revealed to his view, but there was little else she could do.

"We have a little job to take care of, before you're released," he said, his tone silky as he chose a spot.

"You're not going to release me." Ronnie's words were slurred.

"Actually, I am." Jorge smiled. "You'll be my gift to the *Pyr*."

Her eyes narrowed with suspicion, then she gasped when the *Slayer* assisting Jorge allowed his right index finger to change to a golden dragon talon. He hovered between forms with impressive ease. Ronnie eyed the talon and swallowed, writhing against the strap once more.

"There," Jorge said in old-speak, and this version of Boris Vassily sliced open Ronnie's skin. She blanched as her blood flowed from the wound right over her heart. Jorge thought the location of the cut a poetic touch.

He unstopped the test tube, taking his time.

Ronnie's shock was clear and he knew she had guessed what it contained.

"Blood from a victim of the Seattle virus," Jorge confessed. "It's highly infectious."

She gasped when Jorge held open her cut, then poured a measure of the infected blood into it. He liked that the cut was good and deep, and ensured the blood was mixed with her own.

"Sew her up," he instructed this Boris, who had already changed his talon back to a finger. He smiled at Veronica. "We'll give it a week, then test you to see if you're infected."

Mutiny lit her eyes. "And if I'm not, you'll do it again," she guessed.

Jorge turned to leave.

"What about my child?" Ronnie cried, her agitation clear.

"Mothers share blood across the placenta," Jorge said. "I'm sure he'll be infected as well, sooner or later." He could, of course, have injected the infected blood into the womb itself, but he didn't want to threaten the pregnancy. No, Veronica Maitland had to return to the *Pyr* both pregnant and contagious for his plan to succeed.

He'd have to rely upon the biology of humans to infect the boy. Such a ridiculously weak species. The world would be far better without them.

Ronnie anticipated they would come for her a week after she'd been cut. She didn't know whether Jorge had told her the truth about the blood or whether he was just trying to undermine her confidence. It seemed unlikely to be something he'd lie about, even to play mind games.

She developed no outward signs of illness during that week and paced her cell, wondering whether she should fake some. She sure didn't want to be tied down and cut again. If she'd been lucky enough to not contract the Seattle virus from infected blood, she couldn't count on being that lucky again.

When her lunch was delivered, Veronica didn't eat it. Last time, she'd become sleepy. They must have put a sedative in her meal, and she was determined to be able to fight. She hadn't eaten breakfast either and her stomach was growling. It was hard to decide what was the best choice for her son, when all of the options were such bad ones.

Her son. Ronnie's hand slid over the roundness of her belly. Drake had been right about her conceiving. Had he been right that it would be a boy? For the umpteenth time, Ronnie hoped that he was alive, even if he wasn't hunting for her. She couldn't bear the thought of him being dead, that he could have paid such a price for following her impulse.

She wanted to give Drake a son and see that shadow diminish in his eyes.

She pulled out Drake's scale from the hiding place beneath her bed and ran her fingers over its dark surface. It seemed to have dulled a little over time, and she worried it was disintegrating. Or did the scale mirror Drake's wellbeing? She feared that she might not have any token from him soon. She'd readily surrender the scale, though, if it made a difference to Drake's survival.

The air moved suddenly in her prison and Ronnie spun, knowing she wasn't alone any longer. The two of them were in the cell with her, having appeared out of thin air. Jorge held out a test tube. The *Slayer* held her down, then did that trick of letting his nail become a talon again, using it to slice the inside of Ronnie's wrist.

A dozen drops of her blood fell into the test tube, mingling with some substance that was already within it. Jorge swirled it, then held it up to the light.

The contents had turned black.

The malice in his smile told Ronnie what that meant. She was infected. "Bastard!" she cried. "I hope you get it first. I hope I get to see you die!"

Jorge laughed. "My kind is impervious to this virus," he said and Ronnie fell silent at the import of his words.

"*Pyr*," she whispered. Dragon shifters couldn't get it.

Jorge struck her hard across the face, his eyes glittering even as Ronnie's face snapped to one side. She feared for a second that he could have snapped her neck, for she had never imagined a man could strike anyone so hard. She saw stars and knew the other was holding her upright.

Jorge leaned into her face, his hatred making her shiver deep inside. "I am *Slayer*," he snarled. "A higher evolution. My kind will be the survivors."

He stepped back then and snatched at the scale she'd forgotten she was holding. His smile was cold as he tucked it into his pocket and Ronnie knew there was no point in asking for its return. She wondered whether he'd known all along that she had it. He nodded to the *Slayer* who then released her arms. Ronnie didn't know Jorge's plan but she was pretty sure she wouldn't make it to the door.

"Catch," Jorge said and tossed the test tube at her.

Ronnie guessed he wanted to know which hand she favored. She snatched with her right hand for the test tube but missed. Had she revealed that she was left-handed? The test tube fell and shattered on the floor of the cell. Jorge seized her right hand, his grip closing over hers as he crushed her fingers within his grip.

Tears rose at the pain, but Ronnie knew by the look on his face that he wouldn't respond to any pleas for mercy. In fact, she refused to beg this *Slayer* for anything. She held his gaze, her own resolute, even as the pain built.

She heard the bones in her fingers snap, one at a time.

He smiled as he released her hand. Ronnie regarded its limp state and wondered if it could ever be healed. Thank goodness she had deceived him...

Jorge seized her other hand and did the same thing to it, but this time Ronnie cried out. "Yes," he whispered with a chilly smile. "Even your attempts to trick me are pitiful."

Jorge closed his hands around her neck then, his eyes only inches from her own. Ronnie swallowed, then felt him begin to squeeze. "You see, Veronica, it's important that you be unable to communicate the fact that you are infected. You will be released. The *Pyr* will hasten to collect you." He squeezed and Ronnie couldn't take a breath. She struggled, but she couldn't make any change in her circumstance.

Jorge tightened his grip, talking all the while in his calm tone. "They will take you to a refuge, where you will be safeguarded, probably with the other mates and children of the *Pyr*." He smiled and Ronnie's view of the room shrank to his face. "Of course they will. While *Slayers* are impervious to this disease, humans are not. You will be the vehicle to kill all the mates of the *Pyr*, Veronica. You might even kill the *Pyr*. We'll find out about their resistance. Isn't that a tidy way to end the Dragon's Tail War?"

She made an incoherent sound of protest, but he simply tightened his grip even more.

"I'm not certain whether their children will also sicken and die, but the loss of their mates will destroy their spirits."

Ronnie felt faint, her view of the room darkening as she struggled for air.

"You won't be able to tell them anything," Jorge murmured, even as he crushed her throat.

Ronnie made a gurgle of pain and the room went black around her.

"Such a feeble species," she heard her tormentor say, then click his tongue in disgust.

Ronnie awakened in a park.

She sat up too abruptly and her surroundings spun around her, but she blinked and forced herself to her feet. It hadn't been a bad dream. Her hands were shattered, covered in blood and useless, her throat burned with pain and her belly was still round. She was starving and filthy...

But she knew this park. It was the little creek beside the hospital parking lot in the town where she lived with Timmy. Her heart leapt with hope and tears sprang to her eyes. She stumbled into the parking lot, hailing a passing car for help.

The woman squealed the tires as she brought the car to a halt, and she leapt out of the car to come to Ronnie. "Oh my God!" she exclaimed. "You've been hurt."

Ronnie tried to explain, but no sound came out of her throat.

The woman swore and waved at an ambulance parked at the entrance to the Emergency. "Help! This woman is injured!"

The paramedics leapt into the ambulance and raced toward them, lights flashing. It was only then, when help was so close at hand, that Ronnie realized how diabolical her captor had been. She was infected with the Seattle virus, and Jorge had left her outside a *hospital*.

She'd pass the infection along, but wouldn't be able to tell anyone the truth. She saw her own blood on the sleeve of the woman who was trying to help her and despair welled inside her. Ronnie tried to shout, she tried to warn the woman, but she couldn't make a coherent sound. She rubbed at the blood on the woman's cuff, her tears falling in her consternation.

"She's panicking," one paramedic said and opened his bag. Ronnie saw the syringes and tried to run, but the other paramedic held on to her shoulders.

"Poor thing," the woman who had stopped her car said, her sympathy clear. "God only knows what she's endured. She's filthy and look at her hands!"

"It's all right, we've got you now," the second paramedic said, his tone soothing. He held her so tightly that she couldn't get away. He was trim and strong, just her luck.

At least they were both wearing latex gloves.

Ronnie struggled and tried to kick him in her efforts to escape. She couldn't be the vehicle for Jorge's plan of destruction. She just couldn't help him win.

"Hurry up!" the paramedic said to his partner, who turned with a loaded syringe.

Ronnie moaned in protest, but it made no difference. The needle slid under her flesh and once again, she lost consciousness.

"Poor dear," the woman whispered, patting her shoulder.

Something rippled in the air, a taunt in old-speak that was at such a distance that Drake barely discerned it. He was on his way to soccer practice, where he coached the boy's team, when he felt it. His whole body tingled with sudden awareness and he was immediately alert. He caught a whiff of *Slayer*, the same whiff of *Slayer* that he'd smelled on the night that Veronica had been taken, and leapt into action.

He knew it was a lure, that the *Slayer* in question had deliberately revealed his presence.

On the other hand, Drake smelled a familiar woman—as well as her fear—and couldn't turn aside from the hint of Veronica's presence. He summoned three of the best of the Dragon Legion with a mere word of old-speak, and they appeared beside him immediately. They'd obviously been waiting for any summons from him.

The four of them honed in on the location of the scent, and Drake wasn't surprised that there was no sign of the *Slayer*. The four *Pyr* spread out, their senses attuned to any hint of an enemy's presence.

They were near the hospital, in the town in Virginia where Veronica had made her home and Drake had begun to create his own. He had rented an apartment, and he had a large television mounted on the wall—much to the delight of Dashiell and Timothy, who came now to watch movies with the Pattersons' approval. He had taken a cooking class, where he had become the darling of both teacher and students when he had admitted that he wanted to better share the tasks of running a home with his mate. He had taken Timothy shopping and they had collected new copies of both the boy's favorite books and the ones that Veronica relied upon in her research. He had learned much about his mate from the boy, and he felt his bond with her grow stronger each day.

All that was missing was Veronica herself.

The teasing scent was greatest in the parking lot of the hospital.

But where the *Slayer* scent was just a drop, the scent of

Veronica was strong and sure. Drake landed in the darkened parking lot and shifted shape, discerning that the trail led to the entrance to the Emergency ward.

Did he dare to hope that she had been released?

He left the others with a nod, knowing they would defend his back, and strode into the hospital. He walked right past the receptionist, following Veronica's scent with greater urgency once he smelled her blood.

No! She could not be injured!

She could not be *defiled*!

Drake began to run, terror driving his steps.

"Sir. Sir!" A nurse ran after him. "Sir, you can't just walk in here!"

But they couldn't stop him. Drake lunged into the room that seemed to be the source of Veronica's scent. There was a woman in the hospital bed, her hands bandaged and her throat bruised. She was pale and emaciated and — he inhaled deeply — pregnant with his son.

Veronica. Alive!

Relief nearly took Drake to his knees.

Drake!

Ronnie wanted to cry out with joy when she saw him on the threshold of the room, both familiar and changed. If anything, he was a leaner and tauter version of the man she had known. He had lost some weight, and there was more silver at his temples than before. While once he had been resolute, or even grim, he looked haggard.

Because he had feared for her. Ronnie hoped that was the case, but when she saw the relief surge into his eyes, she had no doubt.

Drake had come. Suddenly the obstacles seemed less insurmountable.

"Hey!" the doctor said, turning from the nurse he'd been consulting to address Drake. "You can't just march in here..."

But Veronica made a sound of joy that didn't need any translation. She reached for Drake and he hastened to her side, seizing her damaged hands in his. He kissed the back of her hands reverently, obviously relieved to have found her, and she exhaled shakily as she wept silent tears.

"I do not die so readily as that," he murmured to her and she smiled that he had read her innermost fear. She clutched at his hand as well as she was able and wished he would stay by her side forever.

He smiled slightly, then bent and brushed his lips across hers gently. "Timothy is teaching me how to make a home," he murmured and with that small confession, Ronnie knew the truth.

Drake had protected her son.

And better, he meant to stay.

"I take it you know each other then," the doctor said drily. "Perhaps you could tell us who she is."

"Her name is Veronica Maitland," Drake said crisply. "She was kidnapped on the 8th of October and has been missing ever since. She has a son, Timothy, who is staying with his friend, Dashiell Patterson."

It was wonderful to know that he had resolved details in her absence, and Ronnie felt a new sense of sharing the burden of parenting. A weight she hadn't even realized she'd been carrying slipped away.

Drake's voice dropped lower, and he shook his head. "Her condition is my fault."

"How so?" the doctor asked, suspicion in his tone.

Drake turned on the other man. "I failed to defend my mate from assailants." He shook his head. "I failed to protect her from harm."

The doctor tapped his pencil on the chart, his gaze considering. "You wouldn't know anything about her state, then?"

Drake's eyes narrowed. "Veronica is pregnant with my son. She conceived on October 8th." Anxiety touched his tone as he evidently thought of Jorge again. "Is the boy well?"

The doctor was visibly surprised. "But if she was kidnapped on the 8th, how could you know that she conceived, and that it's a boy? We haven't done any tests other than confirming the pregnancy..."

"It's my son." Drake spoke flatly, even as Ronnie's hand shook within his.

The doctor noted her trembling as well and gestured to the

hall. "She is very tired. Would you like to confer about her condition in private?"

"I see no reason why Veronica should not know the details of her own condition."

Ronnie nodded vehemently.

The doctor sighed and exchanged a glance with the nurse, then spoke in a monotone. "As you apparently know, or at least suspect, she is about four months' pregnant. She's not eaten particularly well lately and her hemoglobin count is lower than I'd like. She's also not been exposed to any sunlight. She's had all four fingers broken on each hand and her throat is so badly bruised that she can't talk. Other than that, she's doing reasonably well, considering, and can be expected to make a full recovery."

Ronnie shook her head. That wasn't half of it. She tried to clutch Drake's hand but the casts on her fingers made it impossible. He eyed her, and she knew he realized she was trying to tell him something.

He looked down at her hands, then at her throat, his eyes glittering. "Someone wanted to ensure that she could not confide a key detail to us," he mused and Ronnie nodded.

"Probably whoever did this to her didn't want to be identified," the doctor said. "Kidnappers can be brutal."

Ronnie shook her head and Drake caressed her hand. "If that were the case, her injuries would be permanent," he argued softly. "She was released for a reason, and the fact that her injuries will heal is an indication that time is of the essence."

Ronnie held his gaze and nodded again.

The doctor cleared his throat. "Well, the police will figure that out. We should send for her son. He must be worried about her."

Not Timmy! Not here! He couldn't be exposed like that kid in Seattle! Veronica nearly came out of the bed at the suggestion, because her agitation was so great.

"Nurse! It looks as if she needs sedation again."

"She needs no sedation," Drake said flatly, placing himself between the nurse and Ronnie. She heaved a sigh that he was so protective of her.

"You don't know what she needs..."

But Drake ignored him, pivoting to face Ronnie again. "Why don't you want to see Timothy?" he murmured. "What is your fear?"

She tugged at the neckline of her hospital gown, so clumsy with the casts that she wasn't sure he'd understand.

"She has a cut there, but it's healed," the nurse said. "It's the least of her injuries, but she keeps picking at it."

"There must be a reason why. Veronica is trying to tell us something." Drake reached behind her, unfastening the gown with gentle fingers. She knew when he exposed the scar to view because his lips tightened and his nostrils flared. She knew he was thinking about Jorge, and how he'd like to retaliate for this injury.

Then Drake leaned closer as if to kiss her skin. Ronnie heard him inhale deeply and her eyes widened. What would he be able to smell?

He straightened abruptly and she saw a quick flick of pale blue light around his body. It was there for the blink of an eye, no longer, but was an accurate reflection of his angry reaction.

He knew!

"What if she had been infected with the Seattle virus before release?" Drake demanded of the doctor, who looked astonished.

He *could* smell it. Ronnie nodded emphatically, tears leaking from her eyes again.

"The Seattle virus?" The doctor stepped forward in consternation. "But that's crazy. That would be an act of terrorism. No one would do that..." He fell silent at Ronnie's fervent nodding.

"Yet she believes this is what has been done to her," Drake said with his usual resolve. "Would it not be prudent to be certain?"

The nurse swore and ran from the room.

The doctor suddenly looked less confident. "I'll get a test kit from the CDC. We'll have to move her into isolation, and get the staff into HazMat suits..." He glanced up at Drake. "You, too. Everyone who has been in contact with her has to go into isolation. I'll have to check with the CDC about the timing."

"I will first have a moment of privacy with my mate," Drake said, and Ronnie bit back a smile. They wouldn't blast him out of here without dynamite, not before he wanted to go.

She could get used to having a dragon shifter in her life.

"But you can't... You shouldn't..."

Drake turned his back on the doctor, who fled the room, shouting orders.

He slid an arm beneath Ronnie's shoulders and drew her into his arms, the reverence in his touch making her feel treasured and precious.

She touched him, though, fearing that he would become infected, but Drake only drew her closer. "I do not care," he whispered. "I must be close to you in this moment."

Ronnie nodded understanding, her tears flowing as she leaned her head against his shoulder. She had so much to tell him, but it would have to wait.

He whispered into her ear. "I am sorry that I failed you, Veronica, but I will not let this insult pass. I will find them."

She nodded once, unsurprised.

"I promised Timothy as much, after all," he added, knowing it would make her smile. When she did, he bent and kissed her gently, feeling her relief. "You have been strong and you are safe. Sleep now, knowing that you are defended, not just by me but by more of my fellows." He held her gaze until she nodded again. "I will speak with Timothy."

Ronnie smiled, so relieved that she thought her heart would burst. In this moment, she believed that Drake would somehow make everything come right. He wiped her tears with a fingertip, then sighed. "I will even let them inflict this isolation upon me," he whispered. "Once I would have shifted and seen myself free, but no longer."

Ronnie met his gaze in confusion.

"I would build a home here, Veronica, with you, and that means ensuring that some secrets remain our own."

He kissed her one last time, a lingering sweet kiss that put fire in her veins all over again, then surrendered himself to the custody of the nurse waiting outside the door. Ronnie closed her eyes, sighing with relief, and wondered when she heard that distant rumble of thunder.

The sky, after all, was perfectly clear.

Sam answered the phone, halfway wondering whether Jac had run out of money already. "Hello?"

"How long are you going to hide in the hills and pout?"

She straightened immediately at the familiar sound of her former supervisor, Isaac. Then she bristled. "What difference does it make?"

"What difference can *you* make? That's the real question." Isaac was terse and impatient as always. He was a brilliant researcher, pushed into management against his will. He never sugar-coated anything that had to be said, and he was always in a rush to get back to his lab. The very fact that he'd called made Sam more alert.

"None," Sam said. "I failed."

"You failed *that* time. Since when does a setback mean you give up completely?"

"I don't think I have it in me to come back to work," Sam started to protest.

"Bullshit," Isaac said, interrupting her. "You're almost as good as me."

Sam covered her mouth as she bit back a laugh. "Don't go getting all modest, just because I'm not around to give you a run for your money anymore."

Isaac snorted and gave as good as he got, just like old times. "You're intuitive in a way I'm not. That's how you make up the difference for not being as smart."

Sam found herself very pleased by his choice of compliment. Being intuitive suited her well. "Thank you very much."

"Sam, what the hell are you doing? Of course you had to grieve for Nathaniel, but it's been months. This is the plague of our century. This is the opportunity to make a difference that every serious researcher wants to confront. This is a chance to preserve your name forever..."

"I don't care about fame."

"Well, you've got to care about something other than your son, but I don't know what the hell it is." Isaac dropped his voice. "How about this? We've got a new victim, a woman deliberately infected with the virus by one of these dragon shifters."

Sam exhaled, ignoring how the story tugged at her heartstrings. "I saw on the news. She's pregnant."

"Here's what you didn't see. She's a widow with a young son, who might not be much older than Nathaniel was. You want to tell that kid that you're not going to try to save his mom? I can get him on the line, if you want."

"Not fair, Isaac. That's not my battle."

"A rampant virulent virus, claiming lives unchecked *is* your battle!" Isaac raged, then his voice dropped low. "At least that was the fight of the Samantha Wilcox I knew. Her son told me once that his mom was a superhero."

Sam's tears rose at that. "Don't, Isaac."

"Oh, right. You're not interested in fighting the good fight anymore. You're too busy picking daisies." Isaac's disdain was clear. "Sorry to have troubled you. I can use all the help I can get on this one, because I don't want Veronica Maitland or her unborn son to die. I promised her son Timmy to do my best, which meant calling you to grovel."

"You don't grovel."

"That's as close as I get. Derek, by the way, has been back at work for five months."

Sam ground her teeth at the deliberate prod, but kept herself from saying anything.

"Enjoy your daisies." And with that last scathing remark, Isaac terminated the connection.

Samantha looked at the receiver, everything within her churning. She'd failed. She'd failed the only time it had really mattered. She'd paid a high price for that failure in the loss of her son. She didn't think she'd ever get over it. She put down the phone and glanced out the kitchen window, toward the haven of Sloane's house.

Sex in the afternoon was what she needed, not daisies, and certainly not challenges from Isaac.

Especially when they struck a chord.

She called Sloane.

Something had changed.

Sloane had known it as he and Sam made love. She'd been more vulnerable and more passionate, as if an irrevocable change had taken place.

As if this would be the last time.

He wasn't surprised when he awakened alone in her bed. He

wondered whether she would confide in him, or whether he'd have to tease the story from her lips. If she was hurting, he knew he'd do whatever was necessary to help.

Sam was in her library, and Sloane noticed immediately that she was holding the picture he'd found the first time he'd been in her home.

She spoke, aware of his presence, without looking up. "You're right to call yourself the Apothecary," she said and her voice was husky. He watched her slide her thumb across the image of the boy. "I'd never have started to heal without you."

She turned, her heart in her eyes, and said the words Sloane had never expected to hear. "This is my son. I'd like to tell you about him."

"I'd be honored to listen," Sloane said and meant it.

She gestured and he sat in one of the chairs. To his pleasure, she came and sat beside him, perched on the edge of the seat. The chairs were wide but he pulled her into his lap. She tucked up her legs and put her cheek on his chest, the picture cradled in her hands, along with the small gold box. Sloane closed his arms around her, wishing he could protect her from every hurt in the world.

"I never thought I'd be a mother," Sam said quietly. "I never imagined that would be my life, and it certainly wasn't something I ever believed I'd be good at. I'm the driven one, the rational one, the scientist, and the one destined for great things. It was my sister who was always going to have a big family, nurture them all and fill her home with love. I was going to work." She swallowed. "I suppose that's why I wasn't prepared. It was my first assignment, on a small team in Africa. We were tracing new outbreaks of something we thought was a strain of Ebola, and ended up in small teams, camping outside remote villages. Derek was my boss. Brilliant, driven. I admired him."

She pursed her lips and Sloane's heart squeezed. Was this the part where she admitted that she'd never stopped loving her ex-husband? He both wanted to know and could barely stand to listen.

"I didn't love him, not like that. It was pure hero-worship." Sam shook her head. "But there's a funny thing that happens in close quarters, when you're tired and stressed and striving for the same goal. Impulses become realities, and not always ones that look good the next morning. We both agreed that we'd made a mistake, and it wouldn't happen again. Turns out once was enough for a miracle."

She paused and Sloane waited. "As soon as I knew, I told Derek, and we agreed to do the right thing, for the baby's sake. I wasn't sure we could really make a go of it, because my mom always insisted that it was love that made it possible to get a marriage through the inevitable tough bits, but I was willing to try. We got married at city hall and moved in together, and you know, when Nathaniel was born, he was so perfect and so wonderful that it seemed it might work, after all. One thing is for sure: we both adored our son."

"What was he like?"

Sam smiled. "Oh, he was the sunniest boy ever. He always had a smile on his face. Even as a baby. It was as if he was amazed by the world and delighted to be in it. We realized quickly that he was really clever, and he was put in gifted classes at school. He liked puzzles and riddles. He collected books of jokes, terrible puns most of them, and he was convinced that anything could be built of Lego. We had tons of it. Derek used to say that we should have bought stock in the company."

She sighed. "My sister loved him, too, and she moved to Atlanta to be closer to us—but really, to Nathaniel. They were buddies, if not partners in crime, and it was wonderful to see them together. She picked him up after school, and had him over for weekends when both of us had to work. She insisted it wasn't an imposition, and I believed her. I felt glad that I was able to share him with her. He wasn't her son and it wasn't her dream of a large family, but it was better than her being all alone. He was crazy about her, too."

"Weren't you a large family together?"

Sam shook her head. "No. Derek and I were both working a lot, so the rift between us grew. We really only had common ground with Nathaniel. Derek was still traveling, mostly to Africa, so he was often gone. Before Nathaniel was born, I'd transferred departments and worked for Isaac in the research labs." She grimaced. "That was about the closest I got to being a doting mother."

"There's more than one style of parenting."

"My way still felt wrong. Derek and I were supposed to take Nathaniel to Seattle on a family vacation. In hindsight, I guess it was a last attempt to get it right. But there was a new outbreak in the Congo, and Derek was gone in the blink of an eye, determined to fight the good fight. The samples were coming into the lab fast and furious, and Isaac thought we were close to isolating the cause. I chose to stay and work, for the greater good. Jac took Nathaniel to Seattle, so he wouldn't be disappointed."

Sloane knew what had happened after that.

Sam took a deep breath. "When I arrived here, I wished I'd been the one who'd died. I didn't want to think about Nathaniel and how I'd failed him. I couldn't even look at his picture. I believed that I'd been a bad mother, maybe the worst mother possible. I believed that I'd let my son down and really, I couldn't see the reason why I'd been left to live when he was gone. He was innocent, and I was very guilty."

She looked up at Sloane. "Until I met you. Until you refused to take my terms and kept asking questions." She smiled, although it was a pale approximation of what her smile could be. He saw her throat work. "Thank you for helping me start to heal."

"Why does it feel like you're saying goodbye?"

"Because I am. Isaac called me earlier today. He wants me to come back to work."

It wasn't any consolation that Sloane had been right: now that Sam was healing, she was going to leave. Their relationship had served its purpose and come to its end, and done so far before he wanted to let her go. He changed the subject a little, because he didn't want to say goodbye. "I'll guess that you're good at what you do."

Sam looked down at the picture of Nathaniel again and her voice softened. "The thing is that there's a woman who's been infected with the Seattle virus by those dragons. She's pregnant, and she has a son not too much older than Nathaniel was." She looked up at Sloane. "I want to help her."

"Not just her."

"No, not just her, but Isaac's right. I *am* hiding. I am refusing to help, and that's not like me. That's not why I went to school. That's not why I worked so hard. Giving up is certainly not what Nathaniel would have expected me to do."

She revealed that she was holding the gold box that Sloane had seen beside the picture on the shelf. "Jac told me that he admired what I did and that he was so proud of me. So did Isaac. He said that Nathaniel called me a superhero. I never knew that. We never talked about it. Maybe I couldn't see it for my own guilt." She opened the box to reveal a gold necklace. It had a gold charm on it, a replica of the Space Needle in Seattle. "He saved his money and bought me this on that trip. Jac gave it to me at his funeral, and I could only see it as an accusation." She shook her head and her tears fell. "But that's not what he meant. He wasn't like that."

There was a card in the box. Sloane tilted his head to read the childish script.

> *For Mom -*
> *Wish you were here!*
> *Love Nathaniel*

"It doesn't belong in a box on the shelf," Sloane murmured.

Sam shook her head, scattering tears. "No. It doesn't."

Sloane lifted the necklace out of the box and unfastened the clasp. Sam bent her head and he put it around her neck. The charm fell into the hollow of her throat and she touched it with her fingertips.

"Thank you, Sloane," she whispered.

"Thank you for confiding in me." They smiled at each other then he kissed her sweetly and thoroughly.

Sam ran her fingertips down his cheek. "Do you want to buy the house?" His heart clenched as she hurried on. "You said once that you'd thought about buying it, so I thought I'd ask you first."

Her departure was both quicker and more final than he'd hoped. "You won't be back?"

Sam shook her head. "I have to go where the work is. Fresh samples and all that."

"Did you know that you were leaving when you called me today?"

She shook her head again. "No. It just all became very clear to me. I know what I have to do." She winced. "I've been the Magician before, and I know it takes everything I have. I don't want to make promises I can't keep."

Sloane nodded reluctant agreement.

He wanted to offer Sam a reason to stay, but knew he couldn't. He wanted to invite her back to visit, to come to his home whenever she wanted, to continue their relationship, but he knew it wouldn't be fair.

For all he knew, his firestorm could spark next.

He felt her waiting on the invitation and knew the conclusion she'd draw when he didn't make it.

Maybe it was easier this way.

Maybe it was best.

"When are you leaving?" he asked.

"In the morning, I guess. It's a bit late to get a flight now, and I have to pack." She surveyed the room. "You have my email and phone. Let me know about the house. I'll wait before calling a real estate agent."

"Thanks." The silence grew between them and began to turn awkward. Sloane wondered whether Sam had expected more of an argument from him and wished he could have made it. He bent and touched his lips to her temple, and she didn't pull away. She closed her eyes and leaned against him, one last tear sliding from beneath her lashes. He curled a tendril of her hair around his fingertip, telling himself that it couldn't be the last time ever, but suspecting that it was. "I should go home," he murmured. "My guests will be wondering where I am."

She nodded once. "Thank you," she whispered again.

Sloane knew what he could promise and what he couldn't, even if he didn't like the truth of it. He sighed, then left Sam, aching that he had to walk away from the most promising relationship of his life. Because it wasn't his firestorm and, just like Sam, he wasn't going to promise what he couldn't deliver.

He'd made a difference to her, and maybe that had been the point.

Funny that helping Sam to heal didn't feel that good to Sloane.

Fortunately, he had work to do.

CHAPTER SIXTEEN

t was when Drake was discharged from the hospital, apparently clear of any infection, that he became a thief.

He had time to think in the isolation ward, time to consider his options. It was clear that Jorge had stolen the virus from Sloane in order to infect Veronica. It was equally clear to Drake that he had foiled the *Slayer*'s scheme before it could do its worst. If he had not discerned the virus so early, Veronica would have been discharged and the *Pyr* would have gathered her protectively into some private lair. He did not doubt that the mates of the other *Pyr* would have surrounded her in a gesture of support, and that they would have subsequently become infected. Possibly the children of the *Pyr* would also become infected, and the *Pyr* themselves. These illnesses and any deaths could only dishearten the *Pyr* in this final battle, if not lessen their numbers.

The plan made sense to Drake and was consistent with what he knew of vipers.

The thing was that even though he had kissed Veronica, he had not contracted the illness. They could find no sign of it in his blood. The nurse who had tended to Veronica upon her admission was infected, but not the doctor–the difference had been attributed to the fact that the nurse hadn't worn gloves in her initial contact with Veronica's bleeding fingers. The exchange of body fluids had been proven again to be key to the spread of the virus.

The most pertinent fact was that his mate was infected with a fatal virus, as might his son be. There was no cure or antidote, and Drake had a feeling that the one best qualified to find such a cure was the Apothecary. Sloane's research, however, was hampered by his lack of a sample of the virus. Drake had tried to visit Veronica while he was in isolation, in the hope that he could obtain a sample by stealth, but the staff were determined to keep the isolated patients separated even from each other until it was clear who was infected and who wasn't.

Since he wasn't, he'd been evicted from the ward.

Drake watched through the glass as the staff gathered Veronica's blood. They were still establishing the protocol of isolation at this hospital and the management of the hazardous fluid that was infected blood. The lab was in the basement, and the samples had to be taken there. He wasn't as skilled with beguiling as many other *Pyr*, but he had convinced the attending doctor to destroy the rest of Drake's blood sample after it was tested for the virus, a small victory in breaking protocol. When these blood samples were moved to the lab, there might be an opportunity to see Sloane equipped with what he needed.

And if there was not an opportunity, Drake would create one.

The survival of his mate and son hung in the balance, after all.

The orderly got into the elevator with the cart of blood samples, feeling a little creeped out that he'd ended up with this job. He'd worn a HazMat suit to collect them from the nurse and had sealed them into the trolley, and was still wearing three layers of latex gloves and a mask, but still.

This shit might as well be Ebola.

He jumped when a muscular guy stepped into the elevator, just as the doors were closing. It was that partner of the woman who was infected, the guy who looked like a commando and had been in isolation himself for a week.

The orderly took a step away from the man as the doors closed. His tests had come back clear and he looked vital, but the orderly didn't trust this infectious shit.

It came from dragons, after all. It might be magic.

The guy exhaled slowly and the orderly couldn't help but hear the sound of it. He seemed to exhale forever, as if his chest was the size of the whole elevator. The orderly glanced at the other guy in curiosity, only to find that man's gaze fixed upon him.

It was weird. It looked as if there were flames burning in the guy's pupils.

"A pestilence," the guy said, his voice oddly low and melodic.

The orderly nodded agreement.

"A plague carried by vermin."

"A plague," the orderly agreed, unable to look away from the guy's eyes. The flames seemed to burn brighter in his eyes, which was some kind of weird illusion. The orderly found himself leaning closer, as if he'd be able to see how it was done. No luck: the flames were brilliant orange and the guy didn't seem to blink.

"So many samples," the guy said softly.

"So many samples," the orderly agreed.

"Toxic samples that must be counted."

The orderly nodded. "Toxic samples that must be counted."

The guy gestured to the cart and counted aloud. The orderly found himself counting along with him, under his breath. "One, two, three. Four, five, six. Seven, eight, nine." The man nodded. "Nine samples, safe and secure."

The orderly frowned. There had been ten. He was sure of it. He looked down at the cart and counted, but there were only nine.

And the lid that should have been locked over the cart didn't look right either.

He caught his breath but the man hit the stop button on the elevator. He seized the orderly's chin and compelled the smaller man to look into his eyes. Those flames burned like an inferno and once he looked at them, the orderly couldn't avert his gaze.

"Nine samples, safe and secure," the man said.

"Nine samples, safe and secure," the orderly found himself saying, even as his mind fought against that conclusion.

The man widened his eyes. "If one's missing, it's not your fault."

"Not my fault."

"The nurse gave you the tray, just this way."

Relief rippled through the orderly. "The nurse gave me the tray, just this way."

"You just do what you're told."

"I just do what I'm told."

The man started the elevator on its descent again. "The nurse is to blame."

"The nurse is to blame," the orderly concluded.

The man smiled. "You were in the elevator alone."

"I was in the elevator alone."

"It's not your fault."

"It's not my fault."

"The elevator stopped for no reason."

"The elevator stopped for no reason."

The elevator stopped on the next floor and the man got out. There was no one in sight and he disappeared so quickly that he might never have been there.

The orderly frowned at the control panel and the empty corridor. Why had the elevator even stopped on this floor? He was alone in the elevator, and it had stopped for no reason. He pushed the button to close the door and it continued to the basement where the lab was located.

When he pushed the cart out of the elevator, he noticed that the seal was broken on the tray. It wasn't his fault. The nurse had given it to him this way. He just did what he was told.

All nine vials were still safe and secure.

Sloane was washing up the dishes after his solitary dinner, listening to jazz, drinking wine and indulging in a little self-pity. He'd staked out a private corner of his own house, and wasn't inclined to share on this night. His lover was gone. His research was lost. His mission was impossible. His fellow *Pyr* were becoming injured on a regular basis and he couldn't help feeling that this was the beginning of the end for his kind. Drake's mate was in isolation and infected, and Drake was being held for tests. Sloane had asked Theo to see if he could get a sample of the infected blood, but that *Pyr* had had no luck.

Sloane had a persistent sense that Jorge held all the proverbial cards. The Seattle virus was killing more people all the time, and the media blamed the *Pyr* for it—despite Melissa's broadcasts.

And all they could do was wait to see what Jorge intended to do next.

The situation stunk, no matter how Sloane looked at it.

He supposed he shouldn't regret that his house was full of his fellow *Pyr*. He realized how accustomed he'd been to his own company and how much his privacy meant to him just when it was gone. Erik was more grim and irritable than usual, Melissa was worried, and Eileen was researching on Sloane's computer. Rafferty still hadn't awakened. Quinn and Sara were outside with the boys and he could hear them playing a game that had to be intended to tire them out. Donovan and Alex had taken their boys to Delaney's farm in Ohio, as had Niall and Rox.

Thorolf had been to Easter Island, without finding much, and had gone to Australia afterward at Chandra's insistence. Sloane was glad that she'd agreed to remain at his house until the baby was born. Maybe Thorolf had a gift for talking sense into her. Despite all of them being together, Brandon, Brandt, Liz and Thorolf hadn't been able to distinguish any rocks on Uluru as better prospects than the others.

Chandra was getting closer to her time. She'd eaten an impressive variety of pickles while at Sloane's home, showing a real taste for hot and sour varieties. He wondered whether he'd have much to do when she went into labor — she was remarkably strong and self-sufficient. Sloane doubted that he'd be able to convince Chandra to linger long after the delivery.

Everyone was busy, but nothing was being resolved.

Sloane felt responsible for that. He had bought Sam's house in the end, and Quinn and Sara had moved into it for the time being, which at least took their family out of Sloane's house. If Niall hadn't been so busy trying to dreamwalk to Rafferty — and Rox hadn't been as pregnant as Chandra — they'd probably all be in residence here. While his house was generously proportioned, it wasn't a hotel. He already wished it had a few more bathrooms.

Sloane hadn't heard a word from Sam since her departure, just one short email from her lawyer acknowledging the transfer of the title. He looked across to the house that had been hers, remembering her words about dragons, and winced.

It was probably just as well that she was gone. There could be no future with a woman who hated what he was.

No matter how many times he assured himself that this was true, it remained a depressing thought.

And a situation he wished he could change.

Sloane supposed he should have been glad that Sam wasn't his mate, but he didn't find a lot of joy in that thought either. He emptied the last of the bottle of wine into his glass, grimacing that he'd hoped to share this one with Sam, then heard an exchange in old-speak.

Sloane spun and inhaled, his gaze searching the shadows outside his kitchen window.

Then he felt relief, and the shimmer he emitted when on the cusp of change faded away again. Two large dragons landed on his patio with the unison shown only by the Dragon Legion. They were precision flyers, all of them.

They shimmered blue as they shifted shape, becoming men just as their feet touched the ground. They strode to the door, in step, without missing a beat, and Sloane recognized Drake and Theo.

He changed the permissions on his dragonsmoke barrier, wondering what they wanted.

Drake, true to form, said nothing. He just held up a stoppered vial of blood and Sloane guessed what it was.

He threw open the glass door. "Where did you get it?"

"The first theft of my life," Drake said grimly even as he offered the vial to Sloane. "But I believe my mate would have given it to me willingly if she'd known my intent."

"How is she?" Sloane asked.

Drake bowed his head. "They say it is the latent phase, and its duration cannot be anticipated." At Sloane's gesture, the two *Pyr* stepped into his home. Theo glanced around with curiosity, while Drake kept his attention upon Sloane. "They appear to believe it significant that I did not become infected. The attending doctor did not either, but he wore gloves, but the attending nurse did." He arched a brow when Sloane looked up. "And I kissed Veronica, as surely they did not."

"Did you, um, exchange body fluids?" Sloane asked, wishing he didn't have to.

Drake's eyes glittered. "It was a passionate kiss, as befits a reunion." He frowned. "They wish to run more tests upon me, in case the secret lurks in my physiology."

Sloane winced. "Bad idea. I don't even like that you had a blood test. They could look deeply and notice significant differences."

Drake shrugged. "I knew they would only test for infection."

Theo grinned, and Sloane guessed that Drake had done a bit of beguiling. "Nothing like the power of suggestion."

The older *Pyr* bristled a bit, and Sloane recalled that he was not fond of beguiling. To Drake it seemed deceptive. "It had to be done, so that I could be both compliant with their expectations and leave that place," Drake said with patience.

"You could have just shifted shape and gotten out of there with brute force," Sloane said, wondering that his fellow *Pyr* hadn't done as much.

"This town is Veronica's home, and she is my mate." Drake straightened and held Sloane's gaze. "Great Wyvern willing, it will be my home as well."

Sloane lifted the vial and turned it in the light, thinking. "You don't have it at all? Not even in latent phase?"

Drake shook his head. "This is their conclusion. Is it of import?"

Sloane set down the vial with care. "I knew that Jorge hadn't been infected. I assumed that was because of the Elixir in his veins."

"Because the Elixir allows for near-immortality," Theo guessed.

"And ensures prompt healing," Sloane added. "I was thinking that the Elixir's ability to repair cells at high speed was undoing the damage of the virus, pretty much in real time. That was my theory as to why Jorge wasn't becoming ill."

"Although it wouldn't have broken any hearts if he had," Theo concluded.

"But why do I not have the infection?" Drake asked.

Theo cleared his throat. "Maybe there's something special about Drake's blood."

Sloane nodded with excitement. "Drake's the last of the Dragon Tooth Warriors!" He grinned as he realized the key. "You've come from the same era as the virus! Of *course*, you have antibodies to it!" He gripped Drake's shoulders, filled with new optimism. "You're the only surviving creature who does."

"And so my firestorm was with Veronica because I literally can heal her?"

"Great Wyvern, I hope so," Sloane said with fervor. "It's so elegant in theory." He picked up the vial again. "We just have to figure out what it is in your blood that makes the difference, isolate it, replicate it, test it and create a vaccine."

"Can you do all this in time to heal Veronica?" Drake demanded.

"I don't know. But I'm sure as hell going to try." Sloane eyed Drake. "How do you feel about giving me a great big blood sample?"

Drake pushed up his sleeve. "Take as much from me as you need. Take it all. Show no regard for me. My mate's fate hangs in the balance, after all."

"As well as that of your son," Theo said, which earned him a considering glance from the older warrior.

Sloane was too busy planning the sequence of tests he'd do to pay much attention.

In a way, it was reassuring to be back in the world of humans and in a hospital as well. A part of Ronnie felt that she could finally relax and concentrate on getting well. She'd seen Timmy and he'd been relieved to see her, even though the glass. He looked well. She was glad that Drake had not only stayed in town but had endeavored to build a bond with her son.

That was a good sign for Timmy's future, whether she was part of it or not.

In another way, Ronnie was waiting for the other shoe to drop. She knew *Slayers* could materialize out of thin air, and that left her jumpy. She wasn't happy to be stuck in an isolation ward, much less that no one was telling her anything about her test results.

That couldn't be good.

She hoped the doctors were being cautious and Jorge had just lied to her, but with every day that passed, her hope faded. When they let Drake leave, though, and she heard the nurse who had treated her was infected, Ronnie knew. How could she feel so good when she had a fatal illness?

More importantly, how long would she feel good?

Long enough for her son to be born?

Was he infected, too? The prospect of Jorge's plan succeeding at all was just wrong.

Ronnie had taken to pacing the room and continuing the exercises she'd begun while in captivity. It wasn't like her to sit still, and she wanted to be as strong as possible for the birth of the baby.

She wanted desperately to talk to Drake. His kiss and his vow had been great, but she had too many questions. Now that she knew for sure she was pregnant, she wanted to hear how he envisioned their future together, or the future of her sons without her.

But Drake was gone.

She had to trust him.

Ronnie was doing Kegel exercises when the airlock hissed. She glanced up as someone in a HazMat suit entered the room, and concluded it was time for more blood work. The person turned, revealing her face to Ronnie, and waved a friendly greeting.

Ronnie didn't know her.

"Keeping active, I see. That's good. I'm Dr. Wilcox," she said, offering her gloved hand. "I'm a virus hunter, specializing in the Seattle virus. I'm hoping we can work together to find a cure."

Ronnie shook her hand. This doctor's arrival answered so many questions. She swallowed and frowned, but when she tried to speak, her words came out in a hoarse croak.

Dr. Wilcox gave her the tablet and a stylus.

Ronnie fitted the stylus into the brace on her right hand, then tapped out her question with care. She was relieved that the doctor didn't seem to be in a hurry.

In time for me and my son? She knew her heart was in her eyes when she turned the screen to face the doctor.

"I hope so," Dr. Wilcox said with a candor that Ronnie found reassuring. "That would be my goal, although you have to understand that this isn't a process in which promises can be made."

Ronnie liked that the other woman didn't tell her comforting lies. *What can I do to help?*

Dr. Wilcox was reading over her shoulder, answering the question before Ronnie had finished pecking out the letters. "You need to stay as healthy as possible. Eat well, although I'm sure they're taking care of that here. Exercising in this space is a great idea. We've run all the tests we have on your blood..."

And I have it? Ronnie wanted to ensure that their relationship was totally open.

The doctor met her gaze. "You are infected, Mrs. Maitland, but the virus is in its latent phase. That means you have no symptoms, but you are infectious. There is no firm timeline on this phase. It can be hours. It can be months. It seems to depend very much on the health of the infected individual, and truth be told, the virus is mutating constantly. It seems to be trending toward a longer latent phase than when it first appeared."

Like HIV. Ronnie's chest tightened at this. If the virus waited for a weakness, she had to believe that pregnancy would count.

Given how she'd been eating in Jorge's prison, her usual good health might already be compromised.

Dr. Wilcox nodded slowly, her gaze assessing. "Possibly. We don't have enough observations of its development to be sure. We're usually alerted *after* a person exhibits symptoms. By then, the latent phase is over and whatever was going to trigger the active propagation of the virus has done so. That's why we know so little about the triggers or about the latent phase itself. In fact, we initially didn't know there could be a latent phase. Those earliest infections blossomed very quickly."

Then it's too late.

Dr. Wilcox averted her gaze for a moment. When she looked back, she changed the subject slightly. "You seem to know a lot about infectious disease," she said with care. "Do you have a biology background?

Ronnie shook her head. *Research librarian,* Ronnie tapped out. *Custom research for authors. Character with HIV and AIDS.*

The doctor leaned over her shoulder to read the words as Ronnie wrote them. "I see," she said. "So you do know a fair bit about what we're dealing with. Any characters with Ebola or Marberg?"

Ronnie nodded. *Ebola.*

The doctor held her gaze unswervingly.

Symptoms? Ronnie wrote. *Fever?*

"That's often the first or at least the most obvious symptom. We hear subsequently about aches and pains, lethargy, lack of appetite or nausea..."

Pregnancy symptoms. Ronnie tapped and the doctor smiled.

"Yes, among other conditions, like age. Detection can be elusive." She paused, then spared an assessing glance around the room.

Mortality rate?

The doctor wouldn't look at the screen, which was a bad sign. She fussed with the readings on the monitors and seemed not to notice Ronnie's gesture. Ronnie knew better. She shoved the tablet in front of the doctor's helmet and shook her arm.

Dr. Wilcox read the question then heaved a sigh. "How much do you want to help, Mrs. Maitland? I could get you a laptop, and there's a WIFI node here at the hospital. You could put your research skills to work, maybe find something we've missed." She held Ronnie's gaze. Her words were husky when she continued. "Maybe Skype and email with your son, Timothy."

While you can. Ronnie heard the unspoken words. It *was* fatal, then.

100% mortality, she tapped out.

The doctor nodded, though she didn't look happy about it. "That's been the case to date. Once symptoms develop, it's a predictable trajectory. *But* bear in mind that we know very little about this virus. It's entirely possible that there are people who will live their entire lives as asymptomatic carriers without getting the actual disease."

Ronnie saw that Dr. Wilcox had her doubts about that. *Are carriers infectious?*

Dr. Wilcox raised her hands. "I've thought they must be, but we had no way of knowing until now."

Because the nurse had caught it after helping Ronnie.

"You're already helping, Mrs. Maitland."

Ronnie's eyes widened in her dismay. *Drake?*

"The father of your child?" At the question, Ronnie nodded emphatically. "That's the intriguing thing. Even though his exposure was more intense, by all accounts, than that of the attending doctor and nurse, he's the only one who was unprotected and didn't contract the virus from you."

Ronnie blushed in recollection of that very public kiss.

Dr. Wilcox checked a list she carried. "The attending doctor wore latex gloves, which meant that he didn't come in contact with any body fluids. It makes sense that he didn't become infected."

Ambulance and pedestrian. Ronnie tapped out.

"Good question. The emergency workers who found you first were also wearing gloves as a matter of procedure. The woman who spotted you first had a bit of your blood on her cuff, by all reports, but didn't touch it, fortunately. It dried, we notified her, and the coat was destroyed."

Dr. Wilcox mused. "But your Mr. Drake gave you that kiss and did not become infected. It's a first. Every answer brings another question." She eyed Ronnie. "We'd like to talk to him about that, actually, but he seems to have disappeared. Any idea where we might find him?"

Ronnie shook her head.

Drake hadn't disappeared. He'd gone to solve something. Ronnie knew that in her heart and she knew she could rely upon him to return to her.

He'd certainly do whatever he could to try to save her.

And he would take care of Timmy.

Timmy might know where Drake was, but Ronnie wasn't going to hint as much to these people. It would upset Timmy if he had to choose between defending Drake, who was pretty much his hero, and honestly answering the questions of the authorities.

"The police want to talk to you about the destruction of your house and the abduction," Dr. Wilcox said. "But I told them you have to rest for a few more days after your ordeal."

Ronnie nodded and smiled her gratitude.

"They can wait until your throat heals." The doctor seemed to be waiting for something, so Ronnie tapped out one last sentence.

I'd like that laptop, please.

Sam went through the protocol of leaving an infected zone by rote, enduring the chemical showers and shedding the HazMat suit once she was all clear. There was nothing worse, in her estimation, than telling a person that he or she was going to die. She'd always tried to get out of that job, actually, either going for cheerful optimism or avoiding direct conversation with the infected individuals. She routinely let more senior doctors deliver the bad news, taking refuge in her lab.

Viruses didn't have hurt feelings. They didn't feel disappointment or despair. They didn't have children, and they sure weren't ever pregnant.

This time, though, Sam didn't want to avoid it. The way she saw it, Veronica Maitland needed as many friends as she could get, because her situation stunk.

The interactions Sam had had as a tarot card reader had made her feel more connected with those around her. Being honest with Sloane and then with her sister had given her a taste of the emotional bonds that made her want more. She didn't want to be the cold and clinical one, much less the ice queen. She wanted to be the compassionate doctor, the shoulder that the patient leaned on.

She wanted to be more like Sloane, the way he listened with patience as someone confided the sorry state of her roses, then made a few gentle suggestions.

In fact, there was nothing she'd like better in this moment than to talk to him. It was funny, because she'd expected their relationship to be just physical and had tried to insist upon that paradigm. She missed the feel of his hands upon her body and the pleasure they shared together, but she also missed the way he teased her and the way they'd talked.

Careful what you wish for.

Sam had wanted just sex, but Sloane had said he wanted more. In the end, though, her leaving California had proven that he wanted simple sex, too. Why else wouldn't he have offered to keep in touch, to meet somewhere, or to have a long-distance relationship?

A little bit too late, she knew she wanted more. She missed how well Sloane listened, though. It was his fault that she'd finally had the nerve to open the box stored beside Nathaniel's picture, never mind that she'd put her son's picture on her desk again and wore his last gift to her.

Not that it mattered now. The house was sold. Her life was in the lab again, and she'd slipped back into her familiar rhythm of working and sleeping to the exclusion of everything else.

The difference was that this time, Sam was dissatisfied. Work wasn't enough. The intellectual challenge wasn't enough. She wasn't sure that living her life alone, focused on her work, was going to be enough either.

Sam realized that Sloane had taught her to hope for more.

For the moment, though, she had to do her son's memory proud.

She'd demanded that she be put in charge of Veronica Maitland's treatment, as a condition of her return. She hoped they could wrest something from this rare opportunity to learn more about the latent phase of the Seattle virus. Sam didn't think it was going to end well for Mrs. Maitland, but she admired the woman's determination to know the worst.

She'd gone to see the patient, expecting her to be unable to hear hard facts, but Mrs. Maitland wasn't having anything to do with glossed truths. Sam respected that. She'd want to know the truth, too. And she'd seen the gleam of determination in the other woman's eyes, the resolve to make a difference as well as to protect her unborn child.

Sam could relate to that, too, and respect her patient for it.

It didn't mean, however, that Sam's respect for the ruthless efficiency of the Seattle virus was in any way compromised. She suspected the end result would be exactly as anticipated, because the human spirit wasn't enough of a barrier against diseases like this one. She knew that as soon as Mrs. Maitland exhibited any symptoms, her care would be escalated out of Sam's hands.

She'd be shipped to Atlanta, so the evolution and final inevitable stages of the disease could be observed more closely. Probably Isaac would handle the final days, as he had the keenest eye for detail.

The real hope was that they would learn something from Veronica Maitland's death. No one seriously expected that her life could be saved.

But as Sam returned to the lab, she found herself hoping otherwise and wondering if harder work could lead to victory. She'd wondered that before. She'd nearly destroyed herself trying to find an antidote to this virus. She had failed.

That didn't mean she'd fail this time. One interview with Veronica Maitland was enough to fire Sam's determination to kick this virus's sorry ass.

And to do it in time to save this patient and her unborn son.

Chandra was glad Thorolf had made it back to California before the baby arrived. She'd had a feeling the baby was going to come, but had only a single contraction before she heard the rumble of old-speak and the beat of dragon wings. A heartbeat later, he'd strolled to her side and given her a crooked grin.

Not a minute later, another contraction ripped through her belly and she closed her eyes, panting the way Sara advised, until it passed.

"Okay?" Thorolf asked with concern.

Chandra nodded. "This part of being mortal is the least fun." She smiled at him. "I guess it's only fair, given how much fun it was starting this pregnancy."

Thorolf didn't smile. In fact, he looked worried. "It'll get worse before it gets better," he said with sympathy. "Look, one son is good for me. Get through this, and we're good to go."

"Don't be ridiculous," Chandra countered, indicating Sara, who was nursing her new son beside the pool. "If Sara can do it four times, I can do it at least twice."

"But you don't have to..."

"Our son needs siblings, rivals and friends." And Chandra kept dreaming about those two boys. Whether her first son was angelic or found trouble everywhere he went, he'd need a brother and counterpart to help him find a balanced path.

Thorolf wrapped his arm around her shoulders and encouraged her to walk some more. "So he doesn't turn out to be a stubborn loner, like me?"

"Exactly," she agreed and they grinned at each other, both more than content to no longer be alone. "You worked out all right in the end," she teased.

"I had a goddess kicking my butt."

"And I don't have any more divine connections," Chandra teased. "I think we'd better go with brothers."

She'd had doubts about joining the tight group that was the *Pyr*, but Chandra had come to like their camaraderie and support of each other. There hadn't been any loss of privacy, which was what she'd feared. The *Pyr* were just there for each other, and she liked that. Chandra had hunted alone for millennia, and she knew that Thorolf had been solitary for centuries. Maybe that was why the *Pyr* felt like a warm and loving family, and it was one she was determined to defend.

"I'm glad the baby's finally coming," she whispered to Thorolf. "I want to be ready to fight again by the eclipse."

He nodded, his grip tight on her, and she knew he understood. "Let's get through this bit first," he advised, and Chandra wondered if he was more afraid that she was.

"Just because I'm not immortal anymore doesn't mean I plan to leave you anytime soon," she whispered. Thorolf had no chance to reply because Chandra caught her breath at the next contraction.

This one was deeper and stronger, as if the baby was in a hurry to arrive. She was glad to be at Sloane's home for the delivery of Thorolf's son, and even more glad that Sara was with her. The two women couldn't have been more different in appearance or nature, but they shared a gift for seeing things beyond the mundane.

Sara joined them now, leaving her newest arrival to be burped by his dad. "Five minutes apart," she said, and Chandra knew the other woman had kept an eye on her watch. "If you're going to change your mind about the hospital, this would be a good time to do it."

"No." Chandra shook her head. "None of this modern stuff for me. Sloane will take care of everything."

"Have you chosen a name yet?" Sara asked.

"I was thinking Kim Chee," Thorolf said with a straight face, then laughed when Sara poked him. "Seriously, it's up to Chandra."

Chandra smiled. "Raynor. I dreamed it last night."

"Warrior from the gods," Thorolf mused. "I like it."

"He'll take after his mother and his father then," Sara said, then Chandra gasped at the vigor of her next contraction. She felt her water break and looked down in horror at the puddle of fluid.

Sometimes being mortal was a bit more earthy than Chandra preferred.

She might have commented but Sara had turned to look up at the sky. Chandra followed her gaze to see a white owl gliding toward them. She smiled and lifted her hand, knowing it had to be her old companion, Snow. Thorolf was looking between the two women and the sky, frowning. "What are you looking at?"

Chandra realized that Snow was a vision, but one that Sara could see as well. The bird appeared to land on her fist, but she couldn't feel the weight of it at all. It dropped something and Sara lifted her hand to catch it.

It was a red rock, just the size to rest on Sara's palm. The stone spun, looking like a globe, and Chandra was surprised to see the outline of the continents appear upon its surface, which had become very smooth. It rolled on Sara's hand and turned so that Australia was up. The continent glimmered, then a point of light lit in the middle.

"Uluru," Sara said. "We know that already."

But the stone cracked in half like an egg, splitting from the top to reveal a gold and red salamander trapped inside. He was missing one arm. His tongue flicked, his eyes flashed before a telephone rang close by. The salamander shimmered blue before he disappeared, then the rock vanished from Sara's hand.

Snow was gone as well.

Chandra blinked and met Sara's gaze. "Boris Vassily," Sara said. "The one without an arm."

"Where?" Thorolf demanded, looking around them. "What's up with you two staring at Sara's hand?"

"It was a vision," Chandra said. "Snow brought it."

"Snow was here?" Thorolf scanned the sky, just as the next contraction started. Chandra panted and hung on to Thorolf, then exhaled when the pain passed.

Eileen leaned out the door. "Niall just called Erik from Ohio. Rox had twins again."

Sara chuckled under her breath. "Better her than me."

"Exactly," Chandra said as Thorolf helped her toward the house. "One at a time is plenty."

"I don't think this one is going to linger," Sara said. "I'll call Sloane."

"He can't come soon enough for me," Chandra agreed, and it seemed, from the strength of her next contraction, that the baby agreed.

The thing Lee had missed most while in his brother Chen's captivity had been the sky. He'd always loved how it changed colors and moods, how clouds formed and dispersed, how the wind could be discerned in those clouds. He supposed he had that in common with his father.

He was glad that Chen had never guessed what he would have given for just one glimpse of the sky. His breath. His life. Every secret in his heart.

And now that he was freed, Lee was always watching the sky overhead. He liked Sloane's home, not just for its tranquil setting but also for its uninterrupted view of the sky. He slept outside when the weather was good, filling his mind with the sight of the sky.

When Chandra's labor began, he went outside, scanning the sky for a portent of what was to come. It was clear blue, and the wind was crisp with the scent of the ocean. It smelled of damp earth and new growth, of spring. On impulse, he went to the shop and gathered a collection of seeds, as well as a spade and a ball of twine. There was a part of Sloane's garden that was for annual plants, and Lee had already tilled it.

He wasn't going to plant tomatoes, though.

Zoë came to him several hours later, after Lee had marked out a curving trench in the soil. She watched him in silence as he finished the trench, measuring it again and pacing around his work to ensure that it was right.

Then he picked up the seeds and beckoned to her.

"Chandra's having her baby," she said, picking her way carefully to his side so she didn't disturb his work. There were times, like this one, when Lee thought Zoë seemed much older than her six years, when he could easily believe that she would become the Wyvern. "I'm supposed to find something to do."

"Should you be undefended?"

"I'm not undefended. I'm with you." She gave him a radiant smile that warmed Lee to his toes. "What are you doing?"

"I'm planting a garden."

"I thought gardens had rows."

"Not this one. This one is a spiral."

"Why?"

Lee turned the envelopes of seeds so Zoë could see the

pictures on their front. "What I like about spirals is that you see them in plants. See the spiral in the seeds of the sunflower head?" Lee traced it with his finger and Zoë nodded. "That happens in a whole family of flowers that include many little flowers in each bloom, like sunflowers and calendula."

"It's magic."

"Maybe it is. It's marvelous either way." Lee surveyed the trench. "I thought I'd plant a spiral of flowers that had spirals in them. I'm going to plant the calendula in the middle because they're smaller, then gradually work up to the tallest sunflowers around the outside edge."

"Why plant a garden like that?"

"Because it will be beautiful, and sometimes that's enough."

Zoë grinned. "Can I help?"

"Of course." Lee took her to the middle, then opened a package of calendula seeds, spilling some of them into her open palm.

"They look like dragon claws," she said and he started in realization that she was right.

"And these ones look like dragon eyes?" Lee suggested, showing her the sunflower seeds.

Zoë smiled at him, her green eyes dancing. "You're planting a dragon garden!"

"I guess we are," Lee agreed, then showed her how to space out the seeds and bury them in the soil. If this was a dragon garden, it couldn't hurt to have a Wyvern helping in its creation.

CHAPTER SEVENTEEN

Friday, April 3, 2015

fter two months, Ronnie felt both better and worse. Her voice had recovered and the casts were off her fingers. Six months into her pregnancy, she had an obvious baby bump, and a rhythm to her day in the isolation ward.

She'd used that laptop to advantage, first for getting her life back in order and then to do as much research as she could. She'd filed insurance claims online for the house and car, corresponded with Timmy's teachers about his school work, chatted by email with Joy Patterson about the boys, and been encouraged by Joy's stories of Drake's conquests at cooking class.

Joy thought she'd found a keeper, and Ronnie hoped it was true.

The fact that Drake was a dragon shape shifter was a detail she didn't want to share. She still had a ton of questions for Drake but Timmy had confided that Drake didn't use cellphones or email. Drake called Timmy at regular intervals, which pleased Ronnie, and Timmy had declared it was because Drake was deep undercover in a covert op.

She'd dug up all the references to dragons she could find online, particularly the recent stories about the *Pyr*. She developed a profound dislike of Maeve O'Neill, who seemed determined to twist everything about the *Pyr* to make them look bad. She'd watched the YouTube videos, including the new one of the night Drake had tried to rescue her. She could hardly watch the fight between him and Jorge, especially given the beating he'd taken.

Every time she heard her own urge to him to intervene, she wanted to weep at her stupidity and what it had cost Drake.

The way he hesitated instead of lunging right after Jorge told Ronnie that he had suspected what would happen.

But he'd followed her request.

She felt terrible about that and wished she could tell him so. She had to wonder whether it was important that she no longer had his scale and hoped he'd grown back another to replace it and complete his armor.

But there was no sign of Drake, only the reports of him talking to Timmy. Dr. Wilcox was increasingly agitated about having him come in for more tests, but Ronnie wasn't lying when she said she didn't know where he was. The infected nurse was still in isolation, as well, although they didn't tell Ronnie much about her condition.

She replayed Melissa Smith's specials a couple of times and wondered how much that reporter really did know about dragons. There was a kind of intimacy, a comfort, between her and the opal and gold dragon who appeared in her television specials. The woman's dismay had been clear when that same dragon had been injured on the air in October, and Ronnie wondered whether he'd healed.

The hospital had kept the media at bay until they lost interest, and Ronnie doubted that her testimony to the police had been much help in locating the perpetrators.

She was considering the merit of contacting Melissa Smith herself and maybe offering an exclusive interview about the dragons she'd seen up close and personal, but wanted to confer with Drake about it first. He must try to hide his true nature, and she didn't want to reveal anything he considered to be private.

She debated the merit of asking Timmy to ask Drake to call her, but surely the hospital was tracking all of her online activity. If not, they could. That was likely why Drake wasn't contacting her directly.

That morning in early April, Ronnie felt a new restlessness. She spun in the chair in her room, then wiped a bit of perspiration from her lip. It was warm, as if someone had turned up the furnace.

Maybe it was a particularly cold day.

When had she last even seen the outside world? Thanks to the curiosity of the media, the isolation ward had been set up in a windowless area of the hospital. Ronnie yearned to feel fresh air on her face again.

Was she going to die here? It was a horrible thought.

Would they decide at some point that she might remain asymptomatic and release her, maybe with periodic monitoring? Ronnie didn't want to infect anyone else, but she missed her freedom. Although they were good to her and the food was better, in a way it was just a different prison.

Maybe there'd be a cure for the virus.

Ronnie hoped for and dreamed of that, every moment of every day. She wanted to make a new life with Drake and Timmy, and to have a fresh start.

What were Drake's expectations, if she did survive? Ronnie didn't really know. She could understand his desire for a son after losing Theo, and she hoped she would deliver a healthy son to him. But even if the baby was fine, even if she was fine, how did Drake envision their lives together? She couldn't go back to the way she'd lived when Timmy was born, always waiting on Mark, always solving everything herself. Ronnie wanted far more this time around.

She'd changed.

She was surprised to realize just how much.

Where *was* Drake?

The airlock hissed, a sign of someone coming into the isolation ward. Undoubtedly it was time for her vitals to be checked. To Ronnie's surprise, it was Dr. Wilcox who came to take the readings.

"Slow day in the lab," she teased. "Or just looking for company?"

The doctor flicked a glance at her, one that was devoid of amusement. "Your temperature is up. It's increased a third of a degree on every reading for the past twenty-four hours. I thought I'd make sure there was no mistake." She offered a thermometer, and Ronnie held it in her mouth until it beeped. Dr. Wilcox frowned at the display, then held up so Ronnie could see.

Her heart sank at the displayed number.

She had a fever.

"I thought it was just a bit warm in here," she protested,

unsettled by Dr. Wilcox's steady regard.

"Your cheeks are flushed and your eyes are glittering. You haven't eaten much today."

"I'm not hungry." Ronnie frowned. "And my stomach is off." Fear awakened in her that the descent to the end had begun, far too soon for her taste. What would happen to her unborn son? What would happen to Timmy?

"You slept two hours longer last night than usual," Dr. Wilcox said gently. "Let's take some blood and see what's going on."

But Ronnie was afraid they both already knew.

Where was Drake?

"You're not going to let me see Timmy again, are you? Not even through the glass like last time?" she whispered, her tears rising. "You're going to send me to Atlanta, and I'll never see him again."

"It's too dangerous for your son to visit you..." the doctor began in her calming tone and Ronnie lost it.

"I don't mean to infect him!" she raged. "I'm not so stupid that I want him to die because of me!"

The doctor winced and turned away.

"I just want to see my son, and not on a computer screen. I want to give him one last hug. Can't you arrange that for me?" Ronnie heard her voice break. "Don't convicted criminals get a last wish before they die?"

"I don't think it would be responsible," the doctor said gently, and Ronnie, who wanted so much to be strong, broke down and wept.

The darkfire crackled in Marco's apartment.

It slid around the perimeter of the room, its blue-green light putting a static charge in the air along with its fitful light. Its activity was frenzied and grew steadily, as if it would do whatever was necessary to awaken Marco.

He felt it and opened one eye, wary of its presence. The months had passed in a haze of pain and near-delirium and he knew that he was severely weakened. It was all he could do to watch and wonder.

And yearn.

He'd missed the darkfire. He'd missed the way it fed his conviction of what should be, the confidence and the power it gave him. He watched it muster in one corner and knew he should never have turned away from it.

The darkfire knew the greater good and didn't care what had to be destroyed to make all come right. Maybe Rafferty had to be lost for the *Pyr* to survive the Dragon's Tail Wars. Maybe it wasn't his place to argue or to judge, because unlike the darkfire, Marco only knew part of the story.

The darkfire drew itself into a ball in that corner, burning brighter and making a larger orb of light with every passing moment. He wondered how much time was passing, whether his sense of time was accurate, then knew the darkfire was gathering its strength.

For something.

He chose to believe it was right.

He chose, once again, to believe.

The darkfire suddenly flared, like a bolt of blue-green lighting that arched across the room and struck him in the forehead. Marco's mind filled with blue-green light and heat surged through his body. He felt the power like a jolt to his heart. He shifted shape immediately without deciding to do so, his body responding to the stimulus of its own volition. He reared back in his dragon form and roared with new power, then chose to use the gift he'd been given.

He used the darkfire to spontaneously manifest elsewhere.

He chose to go to Jac, wherever she might be.

The darkfire was a part of him. It was his to command and his to follow. Distrusting it had been the mistake that had led to his entrapment, and Marco wasn't going to make that error again.

The night her fever built, Ronnie dreamed.

She dreamed of infernos, of flames and of Hell, of opportunity lost and love squandered. She tossed in her sleep, twisting up the sheets as she tried to escape the torment of her dreams. She dreamed of Timmy, growing up alone and felt tears on her own cheeks. She dreamed of her baby, of Drake's son, dying before he even came into the world, and tasted the salt of those tears. She dreamed of Drake, being injured because he'd ceded to her request, and being alone again.

Because she had compelled him to intervene.

It was going to end badly, Jorge was going to triumph after all, and it was her fault.

And then she dreamed of an amethyst and platinum dragon. He flew toward her from some distant point, his powerful form reflected in a dark lake as the star-filled sky arched overhead. He could have been a vision or a dream, a portent or a warning.

But Ronnie knew that he was the Dreamwalker.

He landed before her, shimmering blue and shifting shape to become a blond man as she watched.

"Niall," she whispered in recognition but he held a fingertip to his lips.

She felt him lean over her, as if he were truly there, and heard his whisper in her ear. His voice was low, though not as low as Drake's, and he spoke more quickly than Drake.

"I bring a message and a question," he said. "We *Pyr* think we have a cure."

Ronnie's eyes flew open, but he wasn't lying to her. She could see the sincerity in his eyes.

"It can't be administered here. It would have to be given to you in secret, by the Apothecary of our kind."

Drake. Ronnie mouthed his name soundlessly.

"Is the reason we found it," Niall confided and Ronnie realized that there *was* a reason he hadn't become infected that day. There was also a reason for his absence. The *Pyr* had done the research Dr. Wilcox had wanted to do. "Tomorrow, they're going to transfer you to Atlanta to watch the progression of the virus."

To watch her die and learn what they could. Bitterness rose in Ronnie.

"Drake wants your agreement to come with us instead."

Ronnie's heart leapt at the possibility, but she had to ask. *Timmy?*

"Will be defended as one of our own. Drake vows it will be so."

Ronnie felt relief. *How?*

Niall smiled and his eyes began to change to dragon eyes. "It doesn't matter. We'll come for you, if you agree. There's nothing else you need to do or to know." He held her gaze, willing her to trust the *Pyr*.

And Ronnie nodded, knowing this was her sole chance to survive.

The situation stunk.

Sam couldn't make peace with it. Once again, she'd given her all and failed. She sat up the night before Veronica Maitland was scheduled to be transferred and drank wine, even though she seldom did. The last time she'd drunk wine had been with Sloane.

And she'd done a lot of other things with him, too.

In fact, pretty much the only time she'd felt good about herself in recent years had been those glorious nights—and days—of sex with Sloane.

But what could she have said to Veronica Maitland? *Seeing you like this will haunt your son for the rest of his life?* The change in her appearance had been marked, and the virus was moving fast.

Sam ordered a large pizza and ate it, just because she never did and it seemed like the right choice when she was feeling sorry for herself.

It gave her indigestion, and she didn't care.

In fact, she wished she had a pack of cigarettes, even though she didn't smoke. Something, *some* substance that was less than good for her, had to take this pain away. This kind of frustration and disappointment made her wish she had bad habits, just so she could overindulge and wallow in her failure.

Veronica Maitland was going to die. And even as a scientist, Sam thought that dying in the isolation ward of a research hospital, unable to hug your son one last time and knowing that the baby you carried would die, if not along with you then shortly thereafter, had to be the worst possible way to go.

Plus she *liked* Veronica Maitland.

That she was going to die, and that Sam hadn't been able to help, totally stunk.

She knew Isaac had been trying to phone, but she really didn't want to talk to him. The arrangements would be made with or without her confirmation or agreement. It was protocol.

In fact, the only person she wanted to talk to was that Drake guy, the one who hadn't contracted the virus, who had just disappeared into the blue. Oddly enough, Veronica hadn't seemed to be troubled by his disappearance, even though he was the father of her unborn child. Did Veronica know more than she was telling? Sam couldn't believe it, not with her own life hanging in the balance.

No, the other woman just hadn't expected much of him. There was a sad commentary on modern relationships. Sam thought of her own relationship with Sloane and wished she had a cigarette to stub out. In this mood, she could have smoked her way through a whole pack. She'd fought him over emotional intimacy and had eventually shared some. Now, she wished she'd surrendered even more to Sloane. Maybe they could have built something that lasted longer than four months.

She wondered what Sloane was doing. She didn't even want to think about him finding someone else, or another woman making love to him. Sam would have given a lot for one of his hot slow kisses right about now, never mind feeling like a woman who'd been loved as thoroughly as she deserved.

Maybe that was the catch. Maybe she didn't deserve to be loved.

Sam wouldn't think about that.

She thought about work instead. She would have given a lot to have tested Drake. Not that there was anything saying that Sam would have figured out what had kept him from becoming infected. She just felt cheated that she hadn't even had the chance.

What kind of an asshole would disappear like that, when he was the one chance of the mother of his child being saved? Sam didn't think much of him, that was for sure. There was no way he could have missed her desire to test him. She'd even appealed in the media.

It was bizarre that the lab had destroyed the single sample of his blood that they'd had. It was infuriating that not a one of the staff working there could come up with a decent reason why they'd discarded procedure in this one critical instance.

It was bizarre and infuriating. Incompetent.

Maybe Drake would still turn up. Maybe there would be

another chance, a late one, like the cavalry riding to the rescue at the end of a movie.

Sam could only hope.

No, she could do more than hope for a better future. She could do something constructive instead of destructive. She thought of how hard it had been to talk about her feelings the first time with Sloane, then how easy it had become — and how much better she'd felt. She didn't feel that she could call Sloane.

But there was one conversation that was long overdue.

Before she could stop herself from following impulse, Sam turned on her phone and called Jac. The call went straight to voice mail and Sam winced in recollection of the email message Jac had sent her. Instead of hanging up at the tone, she decided to go with her gut and leave a message.

"It's me. Sorry I missed you because it would be great to talk right now." Sam swallowed. "Maybe I'll just talk anyway and you can listen later. Everything's gone to hell again, and that patient I was trying to save has progressed into the final stages of the virus. She has a son, Jac, and she's pregnant, too. I feel like such a failure, for the second time in rapid succession."

Her tears gathered and she shook her head. "I can hear you, even though you're not actually there, making some crack about coming to the source for advice, but that's not it. It's time to do something different." Sam swallowed. "It's time to talk about Nathaniel. I never thanked you for all you did for him, and you have to know that I don't blame you for what happened. He loved you so much. He told me once that he was the luckiest kid in the world because he had two moms, instead of the usual one." Her voice broke. "I miss him, Jac, I miss him so much. I would have given anything to save him, but giving everything I had wasn't enough."

She took a ragged breath. "I want to remember the good times as well as the bad ones. I want to remember all of it, and I want to talk about it, and that starts right now. Call me back when you can. I'm missing you, too." Sam broke the connection and stared at the phone in her hand. She felt raw inside, bruised and vulnerable.

But remarkably, she felt stronger and ready to fight that virus all over again. She'd had another setback, but that wasn't the same as defeat.

And the only real failure would be quitting.

Sam was still awake at five when her alarm went off. They'd decided to move Veronica early, before the media caught wind of what was going on. Sam showered and dressed, drank a whole pot of coffee to no discernible effect, and headed to the hospital. She suited up to help with the transfer and headed into Veronica's room when she heard the helicopter descending to the helipad.

"Change of scene for you today," she said, trying to sound cheerful.

Veronica didn't even try to smile. She was burning up with fever, and even though she couldn't have been dressed to go for long, the back of her shirt was wet with perspiration. She nodded, as if too tired to do otherwise, and let Sam hook up the oxygen. They were going to seal her inside a bubble on a stretcher that could then be lifted into the helicopter.

"Are you coming, too?" Veronica asked, her tone so bleak that Sam knew she expected otherwise.

"You bet," Sam said, changing her mind in that moment. That this woman who had been so strong for so long had finally lost hope broke her heart right in two.

They continued in silence, Sam pushing the gurney through the airlock, then removing her HazMat suit as the bubble was sprayed down. She took over from the orderlies—who looked as if they would have rather been anywhere else on the planet anyway—and pushed Veronica toward the waiting helicopter. The choppers were slowing and the two paramedics on board were watching her approach. The pilot was squinting up at the sky, but Sam didn't care about the weather conditions. It would be clear enough until they got on their way.

"One more with you today," she informed one pilot. "I've decided to come along."

He nodded. Veronica's eyes had widened and Sam leaned over her with concern.

"Are you okay?" she had time to ask, then four dragons dove out of the sky and attacked.

It had been too long.

Drake led the team, unable to restrain himself once he caught a glimpse of Veronica. She was strapped to a gurney, sealed inside some contraption, and he wanted to shred it. As planned, he flew straight for his mate and seized the entire gurney before flying high into the sky again.

"Drake!" Veronica gasped, but Drake concentrated on what had to be done. He could smell her pregnancy, the scent of child stronger than it had been. The doctor shouted something, and the men on the helicopter pad cried out. They might have taken flight in pursuit, but Kristofer ripped off one of the helicopter blades, casting it aside like a toothpick that had been in his way. The orderlies cried out and scattered as Kristofer and Arach breathed fire to keep them at distance.

Theo pursued Drake to high altitude. He ripped off the protective covering from Veronica, and slashed at the straps that held her to the gurney with his talons. Drake held tightly to his mate, ensuring she didn't fall, and Veronica clutched at him, obviously having the same concern.

"Good flight," Theo said in old-speak and gave Drake a steady look before flying the empty gurney to the ground.

"Thunder again," Veronica said, then scanned the sky. "Even though it's perfectly clear."

"That is not thunder but old-speak. It is too low for humans to understand."

Veronica nodded, clearly having heard the thunder of old-speak before. There were no *Slayers* in the vicinity, which was a great relief to Drake, and the weather was clear. Still he was glad he had brought a blanket and he wrapped Veronica in it with care.

When he was done, she sighed with relief and leaned her cheek against his chest. She was feverish and looked so sick that he feared he had come too late. "You were right about the baby after all," she said softly, her hand falling to the curve of her stomach.

"I will never lie to you."

She searched his gaze for a long moment. "I hardly believed it when Niall said you'd come. Do you really have a cure?"

"Sloane thinks so." Drake gathered her close, feeling cheated by the time she'd been lost to him. "How do you feel?"

"Hot and shivery at the same time," she admitted. "I definitely have a fever."

"Then haste must be made." Drake set his course and flew hard to the west. He was aware of Kristofer and Arach falling into formation behind him, while Theo flew ahead to ensure the way was clear. They were too high for humans to notice them, though he didn't doubt that someone had filmed Veronica's rescue.

She was running her fingertip over the scales on his chest, her touch returning repeatedly to one spot. "I had this one," she whispered. "But Jorge took it from me. Does that matter?"

Drake only knew that the mate could repair a scale, but little else. He saw, though, that she was worried about it and didn't wish to cause her any concern. "I doubt it."

"That's good. I was afraid I'd made a mistake or been tricked out of something important. It doesn't look as if one is growing back, though. Will you always have a gap in your armor?"

Her fear was clear and Drake tried to reassure her. "Scales grow slowly, especially when the *Pyr* in question is in less than good health."

"Is something wrong?"

"Only that I have given great quantities of my blood to Sloane, that he might find a cure." Drake shrugged. "My overall vigor would be affected by that."

"That's why you were gone."

"I could not risk being investigated by humans. They would have discovered many things about my nature that are better hidden." He tightened his grip upon her. "I did not stay away by choice, Veronica."

She nodded, evidently satisfied. "Where are we going?"

"California."

"How's Timmy?"

"He does very well. He is happy with the Pattersons and has been teaching me much of making a home." Drake frowned slightly, his normal equilibrium returning now that he had Veronica in his embrace. "I believe, however, that he may know the truth of my nature."

Veronica laughed a little. "He must be thrilled. He was obsessed with those videos of the *Pyr*."

"I would like to bring him to California, Veronica."

"You should call me Ronnie," she chided gently. "Everyone does."

Drake nodded as he settled into a steady rhythm of flight. "I find beauty in your full name, though. It means 'little truth' and you have shown me much of what is true in this world and of myself."

She smiled, though he didn't like how shallow her breathing had become. "Then you can call me Veronica. My grandmother did, too."

Her eyes were closing and Drake knew she would sleep soon. It would be best for her, although he yearned to learn everything she had seen and felt since they were parted. "I know you wish to see Timmy."

Veronica sighed, her hand rising to tangle in that string of pearls. "But the doctors are right. It wouldn't be safe for him to visit me. I wouldn't want him to get this, too." She coughed and the sound sent terror through Drake.

"When you tell me it's time, I'll get him. I pledge this to you."

Her smile was less joyous than once it had been and he saw that her color was fading. "And you keep your promises, don't you, Drake?"

"I try, with all that I have within me."

"It's all anyone can ask," Veronica whispered, then her eyes closed and she slept in his embrace.

As he flew steadily west, Drake hoped, more than ever, that his best would be enough.

Dragons!

Sam stood on the helipad and glared up at the sky as her patient was captured by dragons.

"She'll *die!*" she shouted after them in outrage, even though she didn't think they could hear her. They certainly didn't look back. Of course, Ronnie was going to die anyway, but this way, she'd probably infect a lot of other people first.

Dragons! How dare they meddle?

How dare they abduct a sick woman who was six month's

pregnant?

How dare these *Pyr* make so much trouble for the people she cared about? This was just more proof that all this nonsense about the *Pyr* defending humans as treasures of the earth was a lot of deceptive publicity. It was inexcusable that they'd seized Veronica Maitland in this state, and worse that they were responsible for her illness in the first place. The outbreak was going to get worse.

Sam flung herself back into the building. She wasn't looking forward to telling Isaac what had happened, but there wasn't much choice. If he learned from the news, there'd be hell to pay.

She pinched the bridge of her nose, debating her own choices. She'd still go to Atlanta, she decided, and continue searching for a cure. This had been going on so long that they had to catch a break soon.

Sam refused to think of all the other diseases and viruses that had never been cured and tried to focus on the positive.

She wouldn't think about Sloane and about the tranquility she'd found in California. No, this was her place in the world and hunting this cure was the best use of her talents. What else did she have in her life except work anyway?

That sounded pathetic and didn't help her forget the easy smile of one particular dark-haired man. She'd never see Sloane again, and she might as well get used to it.

The thought did just about nothing to improve her mood.

Talking to Isaac wasn't going to help either. Sam took a deep breath and punched in the number.

Timmy waited by the phone after he saw the video of his mom being rescued by dragons. He'd recognized the dark grey dragon in the group and he knew it was Drake.

Drake would call and tell him what was happening.

Timmy could hardly stand the wait. He tried to concentrate on his homework after school, his toes tapping all the while. He bolted his dinner, his gaze fixed on the clock. He groaned aloud when Mrs. Patterson got a phone call and settled in to chat with one of her friends about the crisis. He was consumed with impatience to hear Drake's plans.

Finally, Mrs. Patterson was done.

The phone rang again almost the second she placed it back in the cradle. Timmy held his breath while she answered, then exhaled in relief at her first words.

"Drake! I'm so glad to hear from you. We've had terrible news..." Mrs. Patterson fell silent. "You already know. I see. And Ronnie is safe. But how...?" She glanced up, her gaze landing on Timmy where he hovered on the stairs. "Yes, I think you're right. It would be best for you to talk to Timmy first."

She held out the phone to him.

Timmy leapt down the stairs and seized the phone, unable to contain his excitement. "Drake! I knew you'd call."

"I did not wish for you to worry, but I will not be around for a while."

"Another mission, Drake?"

"Something like that."

Mrs. Patterson went back to the kitchen, and Timmy waited until she was out of earshot. "I saw the video," he whispered. "And it was completely awesome. It was you, wasn't it? And Theo? Was that Arach and Kristofer, too?"

"I believe you know as much."

Timmy nodded with satisfaction. "You've taken her to a secret location to cure her."

"Something like that, yes. And she already improves with the antidote created by our Apothecary."

"How'd he do it? The Apothecary?"

"He realized that I had not contracted the virus when I was with your mother. He sought the answer to the riddle in my blood, and after much searching, he believed he had found it. He tested his antidote upon samples of the virus, improving its potency and effectiveness each time." Drake sighed. "He might have done more, but when your mother became ill, we had to act."

Timmy nodded vigorously. "And now?"

"And now she is resting. Her fever is breaking. She wishes to see you, but not until it is certain that she can't infect you."

"Will you come get me?"

"I will. You mother will call Mrs. Patterson when it is time."

Timmy bit his lip, knowing what he wanted more than anything but a bit afraid to ask. He decided to go for it. "I've been on an airplane, Drake, but never flown with a dragon."

Drake chuckled and the sound was deep, exactly how Timmy thought a dragon should chuckle. "Then we will have to remedy that."

Timmy sighed. "I wish I was a dragon shifter."

Drake's reply was firm and it surprised Timmy. "No, Timothy. You must never wish to be other than you are."

"But..."

Drake was resolute and the tone of his voice made Timmy sit straighter. "Each of us has strengths and weaknesses yet each of us face the same challenge: to be better versions of ourselves tomorrow than we were yesterday."

"I can't believe you have weaknesses." Timmy dropped his voice to a whisper. "Not when you're a dragon."

"Every one of us has weaknesses and makes mistakes, Timothy, and I am no different. The best men learn from their mistakes to keep from repeating them."

"And to be better versions of themselves tomorrow than yesterday."

"Indeed." Timmy could hear the smile in Drake's voice. "Your mother wishes to speak with you. She is better but still weak, so the call will be short today."

"Thanks, Drake," Timmy said quickly. "I'm glad you're taking care of my mom."

"She is my mate, my destiny and will be the mother of my son," Drake said softly. "I would give my life for her."

Timmy nodded to himself, liking the honor in Drake's words. Before he could ask about having a brother, his mom was on the phone, her voice softer than usual. She asked him about school and Dashiell, just like everything was normal, and Timmy hoped it soon would be. They spoke for a few minutes, and she explained he was going to have a brother. Then she told him that she loved him, and asked to speak to Mrs. Patterson. Timmy returned to his homework, both reassured and excited.

A brother. That was interesting and would be a change. He supposed they would be a family, and he liked the idea of Drake being his new dad.

But a dragon flight and soon! That was seriously going to rock. He hoped his mom got better fast, both so that she was better and so that he got his ride sooner.

One thing was for sure: if Drake needed any help, Timmy was going to give it to him.

Jac told herself that she was ready to face dragons.

She couldn't quite convince herself, which wasn't a good sign.

Although at first she'd been surprised that Jorge wasn't going to accompany her on her first journey to stalk dragons, in a way she was glad to have made the trip alone. He did give her the creeps. There were times when she found him watching her as if she'd make a nice light snack.

Jac shuddered and continued her unpacking. It was pretty awesome that he'd made all the travel arrangements and just showed up to hand her the tickets. She hadn't even known where she'd be going until then, although she'd known she was going somewhere for the lunar eclipse.

That made her feel a bit like a spy or a secret agent in a movie. She'd trained, she'd followed Jorge's instructions and tried to meet all of his physical challenges. She'd learned to throw a knife with pretty good accuracy and had taken to playing darts in the evenings at the corner bar. She wasn't happy that her apartment had been robbed and that Sigmund's book was the only thing missing, but she figured Marco had collected it. He'd given it to her in the first place and had known she was gone.

Jac had learned all she could from it, anyway.

The funny thing wasn't that she hadn't seen Marco at all, but that recently she'd a persistent sense he was around. She found herself turning around suddenly, expecting to find him just behind her. She'd been certain she'd caught the scent of his skin a hundred times and had spun around more often than that, convinced he'd be right there. She imagined often that she felt his breath under her ear in the night, but woke up every time to find herself alone. She'd seen a blue-green crackle of light in the periphery of her vision a number of times, then turned to find that it was a figment of her imagination.

Or that she hadn't turned fast enough.

There hadn't been any reply at his apartment after she came

home from California, and that hadn't changed. She'd gone looking for him when she'd discovered that Sigmund's book was gone, and had tried again repeatedly with no results. Still, she had that stubborn feeling.

Just a few nights ago when she'd won a dart game, she'd been sure Marco was leaning against the far wall, smiling a little as he watched her. She'd hurried to the spot, even stepped outside to look up and down the street, but there had been no sign of him. Was he following her? Or was she obsessed with a man who had long ago moved on to other conquests? He'd intrigued her, seduced her, then told her off and abandoned her. She should forget him.

But Jac couldn't.

This trip should straighten that out, because one thing was for sure: there was absolutely no chance of her running into Marco on the opposite side of the world. There was a depressing thought. She'd turned off her phone for the trip, and considered turning it on again, just in case he'd suddenly phoned her. That was crazy optimism, and a hope doomed to be disappointed. It wouldn't be worth the roaming charge to find out, so she left the phone off.

It was kind of good to be off the grid. It kept her focused.

Jac hung up the last of her shirts, stretched, and wondered if she'd ever manage to switch her body rhythm to local time. The only time she'd ever managed that in a hurry had been on Easter Island, and she knew that had been because of Marco.

Making love with him had been the perfect antidote to jet lag.

She couldn't deny her sense that it would be the perfect antidote to a lot of things.

Why couldn't he have just stayed the way he'd been at first?

Jorge had spared no expense in Jac's travel arrangements. She'd flown first class, because he'd insisted that she needed to be rested and ready to fight when she arrived. He'd arranged for a rental SUV with every possible feature, and her accommodation was a luxurious private cottage. It looked a bit like a tent, but was elevated with a flight of stairs from the ground and a glass window made up one full wall. Jac didn't even want to think about the room rate, but the view of Uluru was spectacular. The rock was turning red as the sun set and she could see it from the room. In fact, that window made it look as if the sky and Uluru were part of her room.

The place was romantic and made her aware she was alone.

Not that she would have wanted to share the room with Jorge, even though he was paying for it. She'd been relieved when he'd made his lack of physical interest in her clear. Given the way he'd been watching Maeve O'Neill in that restaurant on Easter Island, Jac had to guess that she wasn't his type.

She had to wonder where he got his money, though.

Jac watched the great rock turn redder as the sun set. She couldn't believe how hot it was. All day long she'd felt like she was standing in the middle of an inferno. Or maybe in the middle of the sun. She was melting, a steady trickle of perspiration running down her back and her mouth was dry. It seemed that each day was hotter, even though the temperature wasn't that high.

Maybe she'd been living in the Pacific Northwest too long.

No one else in Australia seemed to be affected in the same way, even the tourists.

The thermometer outside the cottage said it was seventy degrees Fahrenheit. Not chilly but not exactly blazing hot either. The room thermostat said that it was sixty-eight, which should have been comfortable.

All the same, Jac wiped the perspiration from her brow. She wondered if she were sick, which would be just her luck, right before her first "mission." Except from being really warm, though, she didn't feel ill. Just tired from the travel. A little jet-lagged maybe.

And aroused. That wasn't consistent with being sick, at least not in her experience. She couldn't help thinking of the way Marco had touched her, the way his eyes glowed when he studied her, the slow and sensual way he kissed, as if they had all the time in the world to explore each other.

He'd said that once, that he had all the time in the world.

He'd said it in that dark-chocolate voice of his, the one that melted her knees and made her want to rub herself against his hard strength and caress him from head to toe.

Once with Marco had definitely not been enough.

At least not for Jac.

Jac knew she wouldn't sleep that night. The strange heat simmered beneath her skin and awakened a tingle of desire where it counted. She could see the full moon rising behind Uluru and thought the sight was both primal and magical.

The strange thing was that insistent desire, which wasn't her usual reaction to the sight of a full moon or a large rock in the desert. Her fingers slid down her belly in an echo of the way Marco had touched her. As much as she liked the sensation of her own fingers trailing over her skin, she'd liked the warmth of Marco's hand on her much better. It was funny that months of his absence hadn't allowed his memory to fade.

Much less the recollection of what they'd done, and how awesome it had been. She just had time to think that she might as well try to solve it herself, since it wasn't likely any other volunteers would show up, when someone knocked on the door.

Jac sat bolt upright in bed. The cottages were individual and set apart from each other. She hadn't ordered room service, although she supposed that someone could have the wrong cottage. She was still dressed, so she swung off the bed and padded to the door in her bare feet. She looked through the peep hole and nearly had a heart attack.

Marco was standing on the other side of the door. His hair was a bit longer than it had been, which just made him look more sleepy and disheveled. Sexy. Her heart squeezed. He appeared to be tired and a bit frustrated, his expression prompting her to open the door even though she knew she shouldn't.

They stared at each other, and Jac found herself swallowing. She glanced over his small bag of gear and realized a little late that she should have expected to meet him here.

If this was where the dragons were going to be, he'd be hunting here, too.

CHAPTER EIGHTEEN

"ou have a gift," Marco said, even as his simmering gaze held hers.

"Do I?" Jac's voice sounded higher than it usually did and a little more breathless.

He almost smiled. "You're a complete mystery."

Jac found herself fighting an answering smile. "And that's a gift?"

"It is." He sighed and that smile widened. "And I can't resist an enigma."

"Funny," she said, her tone turning flirtatious. "You've done a pretty good job of denying temptation these past few months."

"How so?" He tried to look innocent and failed, which made Jac smile.

"You've stayed away."

Marco grinned and the expression made him look mischievous. He looked like trouble, actually. Sexy, unpredictable, haunting trouble. "Have I?"

"Were you really there the other night? I thought you might have been."

"I'll never tell," he said and his eyes twinkled. "I can't give away all of my secrets."

Jac knew there was one thing she had to say to him, even though the way he was looking at her made her long for more than conversation. "You were mad because I shot the dragon when you'd planned to do it yourself," she said quietly. "I'm sorry I stole your moment."

To her surprise, Marco's gaze darted away and his amusement faded. "Never mind that." His tone was rough and a bit dismissive.

Jac wasn't prepared to let it go. "I thought that was the problem."

Marco fixed her with a simmering look. "And you were wrong."

"Then what?"

"You shot the wrong dragon."

"I don't think there are any wrong dragons when it comes to killing them off."

Marco's gaze flickered, and she had the definite sense she'd made a mistake.

Jac leaned in the doorway, disappointed in the change in his attitude and wanting that sultry smile back. "Did you really come halfway around the world to argue with me?"

"No," he admitted. "But you do tend to have that effect on me."

"What effect?"

"You can make me angrier than anyone I've ever known," he admitted, then his gaze swept over her. "And at the same time, you manage to beguile me." It was a strange choice of word, one that reminded Jac of the entry on beguiling in Sigmund's book.

Before she could comment, Marco reached for her hand, lifting it in his and desire surged within Jac again. She forgot pretty much everything except the feel of his fingers on hers, and the memory of his hands sweeping over her. His eyes darkened, as if he was remembering the same thing, and Jac swallowed. When he touched his lips to her fingers, then met her gaze again, her throat tightened with need. His lips were so warm, so firm, and they moved so slowly. There didn't seem to be enough air left in the universe.

"That enigma again," she managed to say.

"Maybe the only one that matters," Marco breathed. He kissed her palm, not even blinking, then brushed his lips against the inside of her wrist. Jac shivered from head to toe and found her eyes closing in pleasure. "The only one that keeps me awake at night, and the one that fills my dreams in daylight."

His lips trailed a path down her arm and Jac found her lips parting. "We're making a scene," she whispered.

"No one to see," he said and nipped the inside of her elbow with his teeth. His eyes glittered when she looked at him.

Jac decided she couldn't be such a pushover as this. She

should make him work for it, even if they both knew what the end result would be. "You just need a place to stay," she accused and Marco laughed.

To his credit, he looked a bit embarrassed. "I had no idea so many people would want to see the blood moon from here."

"They said every room is booked."

"They did." Marco moved closer, trapping her between the doorframe and his body. There was nowhere else Jac wanted to be, and she couldn't regret that he had her cornered. He was tall and strong, muscular and hard. Her heart was leaping in anticipation of his kiss and she put her hands on his shoulders, wanting to feel him all over.

"I'm sorry," he whispered, his heart in his eyes. "I was wrong to say those things to you." His fingertips trailed down her cheek, leaving a line of fire. "The fault was mine, and I was angry with myself. I shouldn't have taken it out on you."

"That's a timely apology," Jac said, pretending she wasn't as affected as she was.

Marco smiled. "I was saving it for a good moment." He kissed her cheek, then her ear. His touch felt like heaven, and Jac heard herself sigh. "What if I threw myself at your mercy?" he murmured into her ear.

"I should leave you out there with the snakes and dingoes," she whispered back.

Marco nodded. "You should. I'd deserve it." His gaze swept over her, those impossibly long lashes hiding his eyes for a moment in a way that Jac found incredibly sensual. "But I thought it couldn't hurt to ask."

Jac bit her lip, noting how he watched her movement. Hungrily. She caught her breath, and his smile widened. "Seems we both have a problem," she whispered. "Maybe a little teamwork would straighten everything out."

He arched a brow, inviting her explanation.

Jac smiled. "I'm no good at making time changes. In fact, I was just thinking that the only time I ever managed to do it well was in Easter Island."

Marco's pleasure in that confession was clear. "Really?"

"Really."

"And what do you think the deciding factor was there?"

"You."

Marco lifted a hand to her cheek, and she saw him inhale sharply when his fingertips caressed her skin. She closed her eyes and savored his light caress. His fingers ended up beneath her ear, stroking that spot that was almost ticklish. Jac swallowed and opened her eyes to find him closer than he had been before. "Maybe you just need a little distraction," he whispered, and replaced his fingertips with his lips.

Jac sighed a little, his sweet kiss felt so very good. "Maybe I just need a little of you."

"Only a little?" he murmured, laughter underlying his words.

"Maybe a lot," Jac replied. "It's a big time change. I might just need all of you."

Marco pulled back slightly, his gaze so hot that she felt as sexy and alluring as a siren. "Is this the part where I say I'll work for accommodation?"

Jac wrinkled her nose. "I think it's the part where we stop talking and I haul you inside."

He grinned again. "I like assertive women."

"Even if they annoy you?"

"Especially if they do." Marco chuckled as she grabbed a fistful of his shirt to do just that. "Who's going to lock the door?" he asked, before Jac shut the door and flattened him against it. She ran her hands over his chest then crushed him against the door and kissed him thoroughly.

Marco didn't need a second invitation. He dropped his gear, grabbed her butt and lifted her against him, kissing her with a hunger that echoed her own. Jac found herself swung into his arms before he broke his kiss. He'd taken two steps but paused, looking down at her as if she was the most amazing prize in the world.

"You get the lock," he whispered and gave her a little toss. "I've got my hands full."

"And we don't want to be interrupted." Jac reached past him to shoot the deadbolt, then Marco was marching toward the bed with purpose. As far as she was concerned, he couldn't get there quickly enough.

Australia had been Jac's location, and Marco had to wonder why.

What was Jorge's scheme? Were there more eggs in Australia, ripening with *Slayers* inside them, destined to hatch when the moon was eclipsed? If so, Marco didn't want Jac to be fighting dragons. She'd be outnumbered, and he didn't doubt they'd be savage in finishing her off. Her scheme to kill dragons of any kind might be wrong, but he had to believe that once she knew the facts, she'd change her assessment of his kind. He couldn't just stand aside while she faced *Slayers* alone.

No one deserved that.

It had to be a sign that there was no room left at the resort once he'd realized where Jac was going. Not so much as a cot could be found, not on the night of the eclipse. Marco wanted to be as close as possible, not miles away in Alice Springs, and that meant the best choice was to be with Jac.

He wasn't at all sure she'd be glad to see him.

It was interesting to be aware of his own uncertainty when he'd knocked at her door. Doubts were new to Marco. He'd always believed in the darkfire and been completely convinced that his impulses were right and true. Now, he questioned his choices even as he tried to trust the darkfire.

He wondered whether the change was because he cared more about the results of his choices.

He'd decided even before coming to the cottage that he wouldn't beguile Jac. It was a matter of principle.

He was fiercely glad that Jac had let him in.

Never mind that she wanted him with a fervor that echoed his own.

The darkfire was delivering, putting what seemed impossible within his reach.

Marco didn't give it a chance to change the rules again.

He could feel the tingle of the pending eclipse already, like electricity in the air. It made him feel alive and volatile, as if he stood on the lip of a volcano about to erupt. As if he might dive in, just to see what it was like. He felt reckless and powerful, which was dangerous enough, never mind that it seemed in this moment that he could accomplish anything.

Even convince Jac to accept his hidden truth.

For the moment, though, there was only the overwhelming desire to be satisfied. Marco was glad that he wasn't the only one who had relived their intimacy on Easter Island, or to have dreamed of doing it again. Their need was hot and instant, their desire inescapable. Her hands ran over him, as if she wanted to remember every inch of him, and Marco wanted to caress her from head to toe as well.

Their kiss was enough to drive him insane, never mind that Jac seemed to be feeling the same urgency he was. He wanted her naked. He wanted her skin pressed against his. He wanted her heat wrapped around him, her breath in his ear, her breasts crushed against his chest. He wanted to make her scream with her release, then he wanted to torment her with pleasure all over again.

He wanted to feel utterly alive.

He had a feeling he'd never get enough of her. He felt engaged as he never had before, bound to one person and savoring one moment in time.

And he loved it.

Marco carried Jac to the bed and tumbled across the mattress with her in his arms. The bed was large and firm, and the view of Uluru was stupendous. The rock seemed to be aflame with the light of the setting sun, and the full moon rising behind it looked like a hole in the twilight sky.

Not that he had time to spare it much attention. Jac was tugging at his jacket, and he knew that their thoughts were as one. He kicked off his boots without breaking their kiss and the arch of her bare foot was immediately running up his leg.

He kissed Jac without hiding his need for her, loving how she responded in kind. She clutched a fistful of his hair, and he rolled her to her back, pinning her to the mattress as he feasted on her mouth. She moaned with satisfaction and writhed beneath him, driving him wild with a primal need to possess her. Marco was usually calm and in control but something about Jac—her passion, her vulnerability, her resolve—shook him to his core. He felt the need to treasure and protect her, to shelter her even as he helped her to reach her goals. Even as he drove her wild in bed. She smelled sweet and warm, her perfume and her enthusiasm making it impossible for Marco to think of anything else. The hunger in her touch took his own need to a fever pitch.

He lifted her shirt and impatiently tugged it over her head, discarded it, then freed her breasts from the lace of her bra. She was quick to peel out of her garments, her enthusiasm exciting in itself. Her nipples were taut and dark, irresistibly alluring, and he both caressed and kissed them. He ran the flat of his palm over her and she purred with pleasure. Jac arched her back beneath his touch, her dark hair strewn across the white linens and her eyes sparkling as she smiled at him. She crooked a finger at him and Marco stood to strip off his jeans. By the time he turned around, Jac had taken off hers as well, and he stared for a moment, savoring the sight of her nude on the bed. She was tanned and fit, her body taut and her breasts ripe. He wanted to remember this sight forever, to make it last.

She rose to her knees and Marco caught her nape in one hand, kissing her with possessive ease. Her tongue danced with his and her hands locked on his shoulders, her fingers digging into his skin as she pulled him down on top of her. Marco didn't give her time to catch her breath when he broke their kiss, but captured her thighs in his hands and bent to tease her with his tongue.

Jac twisted on the bed and gasped with pleasure, the power of her response feeding Marco's own. He took her to the brink of pleasure, feeling how her clitoris hardened with need, then pulled back, letting her slide away from the summit before he built her desire again. He wanted her to need his touch as much as he needed hers. He wanted this to be the most explosive mating of both their lives. Jac demanded release, she struggled against him, she whispered incoherently. Marco was glad to give her such pleasure, and her reaction making him want to possess her fully.

"Don't tease," she whispered when he drew back once again, but Marco did exactly that, bending to build the passion yet again.

He saw the flash of mischief in her eyes, then she moved so abruptly as to surprise him. She pushed him to his back with a determination he saw no reason to fight, then straddled him. Jac looked like a conquering warrior princess and Marco was content to have her claim him. She braced her hands on his shoulders and held him down, her hair in glorious disarray, then lowered herself over him. Marco moaned when she took him inside her in excruciating increments, tormenting them both with the slowness of her seduction.

"Now, who's teasing?" he demanded and she laughed, her pleasure making him smile.

As much as Marco was willing to let Jac have her way with him, he knew that this first time, he wouldn't be able to hold out. He was too consumed with her, his desire too hot, the pending eclipse making him simmer with the power of the dragon within. He was already close to release and if she teased him much more, he'd lose control.

He wanted to ensure that she was pleased, as well.

He gripped her waist as their gazes locked and pulled her down with steady force until he was buried inside her heat. They gasped in unison, and when she smiled at him, he felt that sense of power again.

"You look dangerous," she whispered, leaning over him. The temptation of her breasts was there, her disheveled hair and mysterious smile making him want to claim her forever.

If this was the power one human woman could have over him, what would it be like to experience a firestorm? Marco couldn't even imagine a union more potent than this one.

He didn't want to think about Jac not being his mate.

"I'm thinking you're the dangerous one," he mused, lifting her and drawing her down again. They both inhaled sharply, then Jac rolled her hips. Marco caught his breath at the seductive sensation. "See?" he growled and she laughed again.

"I have to get even for what you did with your tongue," she teased, swinging her hips and rubbing herself against him.

"Not this time," Marco said and eased his hand between them. Jac caught her breath and arched her back, her nipples taut as he teased her again. She rode him, her thighs locked around him, arching her back to display herself to him. She was beautiful, the sight of her as wild and powerful as that of the red rock in the distance. Marco felt that this moment was stolen out of time, that it was both endless and a mere instant of perfection.

Then Jac dropped to his chest and kissed him with hunger. He tangled his fingers in her hair, cupping her nape, and they nearly devoured each other as the rhythm of their lovemaking became faster and faster. He could smell her pleasure, he could feel the perspiration on their skin and the softness of her pressed against him. Her nails dug into his shoulders and he felt her heart racing.

She caught her breath suddenly and he felt the tumult ripple through her body, making her cry out as her heart skipped a beat. He heard himself cry out in his release and gathered her close, his body tightly around hers as his release seemed to stretch out to eternity.

He gasped and shuddered, closing his eyes in the aftermath. His hand swept over the silk of her skin as they dozed together, and he caressed her slender curves. Their legs were entangled and the red glow of the rock from the setting sun was fading as night fell. Marco could have remained there forever, even though he knew they had things to discuss.

Jac braced herself on one elbow and looked down at him. She brushed his hair out of his eyes, then kissed his forehead, the sweet press of her lips against his skin making his desire grow again.

"Wow," she whispered against his temple. "You are a force to be reckoned with."

Marco smiled and pressed a kiss to her shoulder. He felt filled with tenderness and the need to protect her from whatever would come in the night ahead. He wasn't sure where to start in asking her about Jorge's plans and didn't want to end the sweet mood of this moment.

But the eclipse would begin soon. A quick glance out the window revealed that it was only moments away. Jac framed his face in her hands, compelling him to look at her. "I won't compete with a rock," she teased. "Not matter how big it is."

Her kiss removed every thought from Marco's mind except for his conviction that he had to have her again. They rolled across the bed, kissing and caressing each other with newfound familiarity. When he finally found himself on his back again with Jac looking down at him with undisguised satisfaction, he tried to find the words. He reached to run a fingertip down her cheek, liking how she turned to kiss his palm.

And the first spark of the firestorm danced between his hand and her cheek, a brilliant orange flame that lit Jac's features with golden light. The spark sent both desire and confusion through Marco. He looked past Jac's shoulder to see the shadow of the earth just touching the circle of the full moon.

She was looking at her hand splayed on his chest, her dismay clear. Marco felt the circle of heat emanating from her touch and inhaled sharply at the caress of the firestorm's flames. The firestorm erupted at every point they touched, crackling with a heat that couldn't be denied, its flames burning yellow and orange. Marco was overwhelmed by both emotion and desire. He was astonished to not only have a firestorm but to feel its fire burn right after he and Jac had made love with such explosive power. His mouth went dry, his heart began to pound anew.

He felt his body match its rhythms to Jac's, the sensation of their hearts beating in time making him dizzy. He'd never imagined that any feeling could be so intense—or that he could feel such a surge of protectiveness to one specific human.

Jac pushed away and got to her feet, backing away from him. She tugged on her shirt and seized her jeans. The sparks leapt between them, the collision of each one against his skin making the heat in his veins grow even hotter.

"This is a firestorm," Jac whispered, her horror more than clear, and Marco wished a bit late that he'd never given her Sigmund's book. "Are you one of *them*?"

Marco wanted to reassure her. He wanted to explain. He wanted to dismiss her obvious dismay.

But he had no chance. The shadow moved across the moon, his firestorm burned hot with demand and he was unable to fight his body's need to change shape. He felt the shimmer of the shift rising deep within himself, he struggled against it and tried to control it, but Marco feared he would lose.

He did. The change rolled over him with explosive speed, surging through his veins and tearing through his body. He shouted as he shifted shape, and it seemed the pale blue shimmer of his change lit up the night.

Along with the golden light of the firestorm, he spied a spark of blue-green darkfire.

His becoming a dragon in the middle of the cottage did just about nothing to reassure Jac. By the time the change was complete, Marco was alone. He heard her footsteps on the metal stairs outside the cottage, he felt the darkfire ripple, and he knew that more than his firestorm had gone wrong. He could smell both *Pyr* and *Slayer*, which did just about nothing to reassure him. Filled with a new urgency to defend his mate at any price, Marco swung his tail hard. He took out the large glass wall with a single blow, then raged into the night in search of his mate.

He had to find her before it was too late.

Jac couldn't believe it.

But she knew what she'd seen. It had been just as the book had said. Marco had shimmered pale blue when he was on the cusp of change, then he had become a dragon. He was large and nearly black in his dragon form, sleek and powerful, his eyes seemingly lit with the heat of an inner fire.

He was one of them, one of the *Pyr*.

The flames that had lit between them could only have been the firestorm, a firestorm ignited at the same time as an eclipse of the moon. Jac was hyperventilating as she considered the import of that. She'd read the book. She knew. She was Marco's destined mate, the only human woman who could bear his son.

As much as she wanted kids, Jac didn't want to bear the son of a dragon.

So she ran.

She halfway feared she couldn't get far enough, that a dragon so much larger and more powerful than her would inevitably catch up. Still she had to try.

She was on the path to the main restaurant when she heard a cry that sent a shiver through her. She glanced back to see the dark dragon that was Marco fly high over the tents and hover in mid-air.

He'd be able to smell her and follow her scent, thanks to his keen senses.

Jac ran faster, her fear redoubling.

An SUV pulled across the road ahead of her and she was afraid she'd have to make an explanation that no one would believe. Instead, Jorge threw open the passenger door. She jumped in, more relieved to see him than she could have believed possible.

"I thought you wanted to kill dragons," he said with a calm Jac didn't share, then hit the gas. The truck shot forward, but it couldn't go fast enough for Jac.

"I didn't know Marco was one," she protested.

"You had a perfect opportunity," he chided. "You were alone together. No witnesses."

Jorge might have been right, but Jac couldn't imagine hurting Marco, even knowing the truth about him. She thought again of her good dragon vs. bad dragon list and had to hope that he was in the first camp.

"I should go back," she said.

"I don't think so," Jorge said with infuriating calm.

"Why not?" she demanded. "Don't you think I can do it?" Jac lurched to one side as Jorge drove off the road and headed straight toward Uluru. "What are you doing? Where are you going?"

Jorge chuckled. "To the hatching eggs, of course." He pointed through the windshield.

Jac saw five dragons in silhouette, fighting against the blood red of the eclipsed moon. Five of them! Plus Marco. She peered back and could see his dark figure flying after the vehicle with determination. Was he intent on saving her or destroying her? Jac rubbed her temples, confused. If all dragons were bad as Maeve O'Neill insisted, he'd be trying to kill her. If she was really his destined mate and all that stuff in the book was true, he'd protect her so she could bear his child.

It would have been nice to have had more than four seconds to decide. But there were six dragons in close proximity. This was more than she'd planned for and a heck of a way to test her ability to kill one.

"What are you going to do?" she demanded of Jorge, hoping that as a more experienced dragon hunter, he had a plan.

She really hoped it was a good one.

"Join the fight, naturally," Jorge said. "Not every dragon is going to survive this night."

Jac was a little bit more interested in the odds against the humans involved. She was going to ask Jorge, but the words died on her lips. She saw that his right hand had become the golden claw of a dragon, though it was still locked around the steering wheel. She scrabbled for the handle of the door, but Jorge turned to face her. His eyes flashed with fury.

They were dragon eyes.

Jac cried out in dismay.

There was a brilliant shimmer of blue and Jorge shifted shape, exploding through the roof of the vehicle as he did so. He flew overhead, breathing a plume of smoke that was brilliant orange against the night, just in case she'd failed to understand what he was. The truck jerked as it rolled over the rough ground, but was slowing without anyone pressing the accelerator.

Jac had a heartbeat to be relieved that the ground was relatively flat before she realized a terrifying truth: Jorge had become a topaz and gold dragon.

Exactly like the one that had spread the virus.

Jac looked up in horror only to find him watching her, as if waiting for her to realize the truth. He was enormous and his scales gleamed in the light of the eclipsed moon, his wings beating against the sky. She was back in that fateful moment when he'd suddenly appeared in Seattle. She could hear Nathaniel crying out with wonder that there was a dragon, then she saw again the arm dripping blood over the crowd as the dragon shredded it. She saw again the sores inside Nathaniel's mouth, where the infected blood had landed and burned.

"It was *you*," she whispered, and Jorge laughed aloud, his laugh much more menacing when it came from his dragon gullet.

"And you never guessed," he said with glee. "Go ahead," he invited amiably. "Show me how you intend to kill a dragon." He nodded at the approaching Marco. "The choice of which one is yours."

Jac looked between them. In running from Marco, she'd made a terrible mistake.

She only hoped she had the opportunity to fix it.

Brandon was impatient to begin. He and Thorolf were hidden in the bush at the park surrounding Uluru, along with Chandra and Liz. They'd lingered in the park after closing, hiding from the rangers, in order to be sure they were close when the action began. Their sons were all with Brandon's parents, far away from the Uluru, which they believed would be the location of the next phase of Jorge's plan.

Chandra had been trying to learn more from Myth, but she couldn't control her visions and couldn't journey there any longer. Still, she'd hoped that Snow might appear to her in a vision again to tell them more. Liz had felt the quickening in the dragon's eggs on Easter Island, so they hoped she would feel a similar sensation during the eclipse here.

The plan was for them to locate the hatchlings and capture one for Sloane.

He wished it didn't feel like such a long shot.

Chandra and Sara's vision of Snow had been discussed and dissected. Brandon couldn't see any more reasonable conclusion than that it was warning that the missing replica of Boris Vassily, the one who was missing an arm, would be here, as well. They hadn't been able to find him, but Brandon had to think he'd show up when the eggs hatched.

He'd been missing an arm, after all. Whether it had healed or was still regenerating, he'd need more Elixir. The hatchlings would be easy prey in their first moments out of their eggs.

Brandon was pumped and agitated, a combination of factors coming together to put him on the cusp of change. The eclipse was imminent. If all went as they expected, there would be an unknown number of *Slayers* appearing suddenly in their immediate vicinity. Liz was with him, and he knew he had to defend her. He couldn't have left her behind in safety, though, because her sense would direct them to the hatching stones. He paced, restless, wanting it to start and wanting it over.

"Too many questions," Thorolf muttered, his gaze on the sky. His fingers were tapping with similar agitation. "I wish we knew more."

"Too many rocks," Brandon agreed.

"You're going to wear a valley in the desert, the two of you," Liz teased, but her comment didn't make either of them relax.

"And there it goes," Chandra murmured, pointing to the moon. "The eclipse begins." They all looked up in unison, and Brandon saw the shadow appear on one side of the full moon. It looked as if someone had taken a bite out of it. He stared as the shadow grew larger and turned reddish brown. It was easy to remember his firestorm with Liz, and how incredible the sensation had been.

He felt the spark of a firestorm, not very far away. He glanced over his shoulder, wondering which of the *Pyr* was nearby, and caught Thorolf's frown.

He'd felt it, too.

"Who?" he asked but Thorolf's frown deepened.

Liz pivoted suddenly and looked up at Uluru. "There it is," she whispered, then shuddered from head to toe. She turned to a being of flame, all brilliant orange and red. Even though Brandon had suspected she would change form to increase her sensitivity, he was awed again by her powers as a Firedaughter.

Liz lifted a burning hand and pointed. She didn't need to say more. Brandon and Thorolf shifted shape immediately, seized their mates and launched into the air. Brandon took the lead, Liz securely in his grasp. She was like a beacon and even though the heat of her figure burned his talons, he knew he had to endure it until they identified the stones.

"Two," she whispered, even her voice crackling like a bonfire.

"Perfect," Thorolf murmured, then switched to old-speak to confer with Brandon. *"Remember that we have to take one alive."*

And that, Brandon couldn't help but think, would be the real challenge.

Darkfire crackled around the world, enclosing the planet in a flash of its blue-green light. Sloane felt it as well as saw it and rushed to check on Rafferty. The darkfire was flaring beneath the *Pyr*'s scales, and he groaned as if in pain. It was the first sound he'd uttered in months, and Sloane wished he could have known whether it was a good sign or a bad one.

"What's happening?" Melissa demanded, her fear clear. She'd been sitting beside Rafferty, taking her turn watching him.

"I don't know," Sloane admitted, watching the rhythm of the strange light, which rolled over Rafferty in waves. It was throwing blue-green sparks into the air, and it seemed to Sloane that it was getting brighter. The atmosphere in his house seemed to be crackling with energy and the shadows filled with strange shapes.

What was happening?

He looked into one corner and thought he could discern his father, sitting before the fireplace here as he had in that house in Ireland. Tynan lifted his head and smiled slightly at Sloane.

"It is the role of the Apothecary to heal, no matter the price to himself," Tynan said in old-speak, and Sloane remembered the day his father had first given him this warning. *"It is the role of the*

Apothecary to give, to choose where to give, to sometimes decide who will live and who will die. It is the task of the Apothecary to guide the dying to their release and summon the injured back to life. The task is not easy, but it must be done. You will be the Apothecary in dire times and you will be tested. Do not forget your abilities, my son."

Tynan nodded once. The darkfire illuminated his figure with a blue-green aura, then leapt to Sloane's tattoo. It slid over the lines of the caduceus, making the tattoo burn all over again, then winked out.

In the meantime, the room had filled with Sloane's guests. Rafferty seemed to be on fire, that blue-green light radiant beneath his scales. Which way should Sloane escort him? To death or to life? Eileen took one look and sent the girls back to bed. Erik was fully recovered and he, too, came directly to Rafferty. Drake was sealed into the isolation zone they'd created for Veronica, though Sloane could feel his attention.

Rafferty moaned again, a sound of pain that came from deep within him. Melissa fell to her knees beside him and put her hand upon him. "Is it burning hotter?" she demanded. "Is it hurting him?"

"He's fading," Erik said and shifted shape in a sudden flash. He breathed a stream of dragonsmoke and drove it beneath Rafferty's scales.

Sloane understood his tactic immediately. The *Slayers* used a conduit of dragonsmoke to steal energy from the *Pyr* in battle. Erik planned to use the same tactic to give strength to Rafferty.

Erik's dragonsmoke slid beneath Rafferty's scales and it glittered as Erik gave vitality to his old friend. The darkfire sparked more brightly and Rafferty twitched in agony.

It was only half of the solution.

"He's making it worse!" Melissa cried.

"No, the darkfire is stealing the power and using it," Sloane said. "We need to siphon it off and secure it." He needed to repeat Pwyll's feat of snaring the darkfire in the stone.

Even though he didn't know how to do it. He felt his father's hand on his shoulder, urging him on.

He had to try.

Sloane shifted shape in a brilliant shimmer of blue and seized the darkened crystal that had once held the darkfire. He had a terrible sense that Rafferty's fate would be decided during this eclipse.

He breathed another river of dragonsmoke, hoping he could save his comrade. It was difficult to breathe slowly and steadily, especially when he feared time was of the essence. The darkfire had crackled at the moment the eclipse had become total, and he knew this one would be of short duration. He suspected he had only about ten minutes to make a difference to Rafferty.

Rafferty's forebear Pwyll had been the Cantor of the *Pyr*, and the one to trap darkfire within the quartz crystals. Had he done it during a firestorm? Sloane didn't know. When his smoke finally touched Rafferty and swirled around that *Pyr*, Sloane tried to beckon to the darkfire with what he remembered of the Cantor's song.

He wasn't making much progress, but then there was a sudden crackle, as if electricity had swept through the room. The lights flickered and Sloane felt a shiver pass over his skin.

It was followed by a flush of distant heat. He inhaled sharply, knowing he was feeling the spark of a firestorm. It was far away, but tinged by darkfire.

Marco.

So, he hadn't turned to the *Slayer* side. Sloane's gaze flew to Erik, who was breathing steadily and slowly. The pressure of his father's hand on his shoulder increased and Sloane turned to look toward the kitchen.

He could discern a shady figure there, an older man he didn't know.

"This," the apparition whispered in old-speak. He began to chant a song that Sloane found both familiar and unpredictable. It was Pwyll's ghost!

Sloane echoed the chant, learning the tune and the sound of the words. He didn't understand the words themselves and guessed they were Welsh. He didn't know why Pwyll had appeared to him and not to Erik, but he didn't care.

He sang and Erik followed his lead.

The darkfire recognized the chant. From the first note, the blue-green light leapt and snapped, apparently in response to the summons. Erik closed his claw over Sloane's, making his own link to the crystal, and sang with vigor. Sloane and Erik continued together, compelled to keep the slow rhythm of the Cantor's chant. The darkfire glittered like a river of ice crystals, and it flowed toward the crystal, albeit at the speed of a glacier. Finally, Sloane saw its icy swirl inside the crystal itself.

The Cantor's chant was deep and low, as relentless as the movement of the earth's crust. Sloane and Erik sang together, holding the notes longer than Sloane could have believed possible, summoning the darkfire as best they were able. Sloane heard Drake add his voice to theirs and the walls of the house rumbled with their song. Quinn and Lee lent their voices to the chorus, too. The floor vibrated beneath them, as if the earth itself resonated, and the darkfire moved steadily into the stone.

The chant was filled with ancient power. The darkfire's hue brightened where Sloane's dragonsmoke touched Rafferty, creating a glow at those points. The chant seemed to be congealing the darkfire into a brilliant glowing orb of blue-green. Sloane could see the same effect in Erik's dragonsmoke. The darkfire had dimmed beneath Rafferty's scales at the most distant points from the dragonsmoke, as if extinguished there.

Encouraged, Sloane sang with greater vigor, well aware that the eclipse had passed its zenith. The shadow seemed to slide off the moon more quickly, or maybe he was just too aware of how much darkfire still lingered beneath Rafferty's scales.

Suddenly the shadowy outline of Pwyll disappeared.

The lights went out.

Before Sloane's eyes, the river of darkfire glowed as if it were phosphorescent. It danced and glimmered, and the dragonsmoke conduit sparkled along its length with the distinctive hue of darkfire. Sloane sang and the darkfire snapped, racing down the dragonsmoke to embed itself in the crystal.

The eclipse was over.

Rafferty's body was darker, now, touched only by stray glimmers of darkfire, like heat lightning after a storm.

Sloane broke the link between his dragonsmoke and Rafferty's body, creating a closed conduit with Erik's dragonsmoke instead. They both retreated, drawing the dragonsmoke with its snared darkfire away from Rafferty.

The quartz crystal flashed blue-green, as brilliant as a strobe light. The darkfire vanished from beneath Rafferty's scales and shone brilliantly within the crystal.

Rafferty gave a heartfelt sigh, a shudder rolling over his body.

His eyelids fluttered, then he began to hum the Cantor's song. Sloane and Erik exchanged a glance and sang with Rafferty. They sang until the eclipse was completed, then all three changed to their human forms in a brilliant flash of blue.

The darkfire burned in the stone, secured there.

The power came back on, the fridge humming to life in the kitchen.

Sloane heaved a sigh of relief and confided the news to Drake in old-speak. He was exhausted, but he didn't care. He'd given of himself to help Rafferty, and he would do it again, without hesitation. He felt his father squeeze his shoulder, then that precious weight was gone.

Rafferty rolled over and sighed. Melissa kissed his forehead and he smiled, enfolding her in his arms without opening his eyes. Even from across the room, Sloane knew it was a healing sleep, and that the older *Pyr* would awaken much recovered. He nodded to Erik, then returned to the lab.

One patient was recovering, but he had another yet to heal.

Even with his task incomplete, he was making progress and that lightened Sloane's step.

He was the Apothecary, and his role was to heal.

CHAPTER NINETEEN

orge reached out with a claw to snatch Jac from the vehicle, but she wasn't going to be captured as easily as that. She kicked at him and ducked lower. She felt his talons slide through her hair, but managed to crawl to the driver's side.

Her first dragon fight had her adrenaline pumping.

Jac jammed her foot down on the accelerator, then when the truck shot forward, managed to get in the seat. Jorge roared and spewed flame as she evaded his grasp, then he bore down on her. Jac could hear the beat of his wings and feel the heat of his dragonfire and doubted she'd get far.

There was no refuge, no place she could hide. The outback stretched in every direction, offering no sanctuary. Uluru was ahead of her and not much else. The tourist accommodation of Yulara was behind her, but she wasn't going to lead Jorge back to those people, not after she'd seen him in Seattle. She had the pedal to the floor, pushing the vehicle to go as quickly as it could. She was bounced around as it hit holes in the earth and ran through bush that obscured her vision, then snapped away. The wind rushed over her and she had a clear view of the stars and the eclipsed moon overhead.

She glanced back to find Jorge flying close behind her, his head bent low. His eyes were right behind the truck and she had the sense he was laughing at her. She couldn't even see Marco, which wasn't a good thing. Had he given up on her? Jorge opened his mouth and she knew what would come out.

"Come on!" she urged the truck, but it wouldn't go any faster.

She turned hard to the right, and the vehicle nearly rolled from the quick move. Dust spewed behind her, temporarily obscuring the sight of the dragon in pursuit, and Jac worked with that. She accelerated and slowed, turned right and left, drove in circles, and stirred up as much dust as possible. She heard Jorge roar in anger and then the crash of dragons colliding overhead.

A corona of flame erupted over her head and arms, as if her skin had suddenly erupted in fire. Jac stared in wonder at the sparks of the firestorm and remembered all too easily how it had felt to make love with Marco. Desire distracted her in a dangerous way, even though her heart was pounding.

Marco had come to save her!

The book *was* right.

There had to be an upside to being a dragon's mate. Jac pushed the accelerator to the floor again.

As she raced out of the cloud of dust, Jac saw that Jorge was locked in battle with the dark dragon that was Marco. They battled so savagely that she didn't want to look away from the fight. She had to do so, though, to steal glances at the ground ahead of her as she drove. She tried to think, despite her fear and the effect of the firestorm.

The two dragons were fighting, which meant that they were on opposite sides.

Or they were in competition for the prize — which was her.

She had the definite feeling that only one would fly away. They clashed overhead and roared, their tails whipping through the air. They were twined around each other, biting snapping, each grappling for advantage. Marco and Jorge raged dragonfire, lighting up the night with their battle.

They remained over her as they fought, following the path of the SUV. Jac guessed that Jorge wanted to snatch her up and Marco wanted to save her. She wished in hindsight that she hadn't run from him but it was too late to change that.

Jorge slashed at Marco and Marco retreated. He flew in a tight turn and dove at his opponent, so fast that Jorge was surprised. Marco slashed at Jorge's belly, who bellowed in pain as his flesh was torn open. Black blood dropped onto the leather upholstery of the passenger seat, its smell foul enough to turn Jac's stomach. She saw it burn through the seat and recognized that it had to be *Slayer* blood. Jorge breathed a torrent of fire at Marco and she smelled his scales being singed.

Jac tried to review everything she'd learned from Sigmund's book as she drove, heart thumping. These sparks were the sign of the firestorm. And that had to mean that Marco was *Pyr*, because only the *Pyr* had firestorms. Melissa Smith insisted that dragon shifters were of two kinds, *Pyr* and *Slayer*, and that the *Slayers* didn't count humans among the treasures of the earth.

It certainly would have been consistent with the beliefs of a *Slayer* for Jorge to have infected humans deliberately with an incurable virus.

So, Marco and Jorge were definitely on opposite sides.

What about the dragons who had hatched on Easter Island? What about the ones fighting over Uluru? Jac peered at the dragons locked in combat. No matter which side they each were on, their battles were pretty evenly matched. Jac had to figure that at least half of them were *Slayers*.

And she had no way to defend herself from the ones who wanted the world to be rid of her kind.

How exactly *did* humans kill dragons? Jac bit her lip and drove. Sigmund's book hadn't provided a lot of good advice for humans on the hunt, but before Marco had brought her the book, she'd been reading other sources. In medieval times, people had reportedly fed saltpeter to dragons, sometimes packed into cow carcasses, then ignited it to blow up the dragons. Sometimes the dragons had spontaneously combusted, the dragonfire inside them providing a spark to the explosive.

There was something very satisfactory about the prospect of making Jorge explode.

Jac reached over to the glove box and rummaged in it. To her relief, there were three flares there for roadside emergencies. She'd have preferred dynamite, but these just might do it. There was a waterproof can of matches, too. She decided she loved Australian car rental companies.

She'd just grabbed them when she heard a bellow from overhead.

Jorge was descending toward her, talons extended. His mouth was wide open and his expression triumphant. What had happened to Marco?

Jac swerved too hard in her fear and felt the SUV rock on two wheels. She accelerated, not having a lot of choice, and the vehicle started to roll. She heard sounds of battle from overhead, but was busy trying to right the vehicle. There was blood falling like rain, red and black mixed together. Even though she tried to correct it, the SUV was too top-heavy. It began to tumble to one side.

Jac screamed as flames lit all over her body. She had time to wonder how she could be on fire already, just as a dragon snatched her out of the vehicle. A hundred little fires were burning between her body and the dragon's claws, coaxed to burn brighter by his proximity. Marco! His talons were dark instead of gold, and his grip was protective instead of cruel. He soared into the sky with her captive in his grip as the SUV rolled over twice, then exploded into flames.

"Sorry. Wrong dragon," she said and heard him growl deep in his chest.

"You can be irritating," he muttered, but she hoped that was humor in his tone.

Jac had a heartbeat to hope that she was comparatively safe before Marco suddenly lunged forward and groaned. Even more alarmingly, the light of the firestorm dimmed. Jac saw the golden claws latched on to his wings and the blood flowing from Marco's wounds.

Jorge was attacking!

Dragonfire erupted all around them, Marco's body shielding Jac from the flames. She smelled his scales burning, though, and felt his shudder of pain. She shoved two of the flares into the top of her jeans, knowing what she had to do.

"Turn fast," she commanded, and Marco glanced down warily. His eyes lit when he realized what she had and he accelerated slightly. He pivoted suddenly and flew straight at Jorge, who opened his mouth to spew more flames.

Jac fought her fear, aimed and threw the flare right into Jorge's mouth. At such close proximity, she didn't figure she could miss, and she didn't. She saw it tumble down his throat, just before Marco spun and raced high into the sky. She knew he was trying to get them as far away from the result as possible.

There was an explosion behind him and a roar of pain loud enough to make the ground vibrate. Jac glanced back to see Jorge illuminated with the brilliant light of the flare, the bottom of his jaw half gone and his blood dripping. He fell toward the earth and she hoped he was dead.

Actually, she hoped he suffered a lot before he died.

"I have two more," Jac said and Marco nodded.

"I've got no argument with you annoying some different dragons for a change."

"No, I didn't think you would."

Despite his light tone, Marco was still bleeding badly from the roots of his wings. Ignoring his wounds, he flew straight at the other fighting dragons. She wondered whether the firestorm's heat helped or hindered him. She ran a hand over the scales on his chest and he seemed to shiver.

When he looked down at her, his eyes were bright and his expression so avid that she knew she wasn't the only one lost in desire. "That's a distraction I don't need right now," he murmured and she nodded.

"I wasn't sure if it would help."

She saw him grit his teeth. "It provokes a reaction, a primal need to defend you at any price."

"To satisfy the firestorm," she replied, and he nodded once.

Jac exhaled, recognizing the firestorm's influence on her. She hated dragon shifters. She wanted them all dead. She knew this with every fiber of her being. But the heat of the firestorm was confusing her, muddling her thoughts, feeding her desire and building her conviction that she should make an exception for Marco.

"Careful what you wish for," she whispered and his eyes narrowed in confusion. "That's what my father used to say. I always wanted to have kids." Jac grimaced. "Just not dragon babies." She heard a growl in Marco's throat.

"If you plan on denying the firestorm, you'll go beyond annoying me," he muttered and Jac almost laughed. He spared her a look that was hot with intent and all dragon, and she shivered in anticipation of him changing her mind.

"First things first," she whispered, pointing to the other dragons.

Marco nodded and flew more quickly toward them, as if determined to get this task done and return to the firestorm's allure. Jac gripped her next flare more tightly, knowing she'd have to be ready to take advantage of opportunity.

Was that the promise of the firestorm? An opportunity? Making love with Marco had been great before the firestorm. What would it feel like to be with him now?

Could the firestorm enchant her into forgetting her reservations?

Or was it revealing Marco's truth to her, the truth she should have recognized already?

Jac didn't know, but there wasn't time to think about it now.

His firestorm.

As much as he'd always hoped to have one, Marco had never expected it to be with a woman sworn to hunt and exterminate dragons. Not only that, but Jac had used the darkfire against Rafferty. She was responsible for injuring the *Pyr* he most wanted to see alive.

If that wasn't unpredictable, Marco didn't know what was.

Was the firestorm the reason why Jac had even been able to fire the crystal? Had the darkfire anticipated her role in his life?

And what would be her role in his life? She'd been quick to say she didn't want to bear his son. What would happen if their firestorm wasn't satisfied? What exactly was his responsibility to her? She was his mate and one of the treasures of the earth. Defending her was his responsibility and seducing her had been a pleasure already. Still, Marco couldn't forget her views about dragons and wonder at the wisdom of the firestorm.

Or was it darkfire, turning assumptions on their heads, just as it so often did? Once again, he had to wonder about the merit of trusting the unpredictable force that had governed so much of his life.

As Marco flew closer to the other dragons, he saw that three looked exactly like the ones that had hatched on Easter Island, their scales ruby and brass and their tails trailing long crimson plumes. They fought viciously against two other dragons, one with ebony scales edged in orange and the other as brilliant as diamonds edged in silver. He wasn't surprised that Brandon and Thorolf were here, because he'd sensed their presence earlier.

He had to assume that they knew of his presence, too.

"Which ones are *Slayers*?" Jac asked.

"The three who look the same, plus Jorge," Marco said, then roared flames at the closest one. That *Slayer* turned and they locked claws. Jac caught her breath as the two dragons collided with force and spiraled through the air with claws locked. To his relief, she held on tightly and didn't seem to be freaking out completely to have such a close view of a dragonfight.

"Nothing like a snack of fresh mate," the *Slayer* taunted. *"Just when I was feeling a little peckish."*

"She's all mine," Marco retorted, feeling a primal urge to claim and possess Jac.

"Not yet she isn't," the *Slayer* retorted. *"Oh, there's nothing like the heat of a firestorm. Give me a bite."*

The *Slayer's* eyes flashed as he lunged forward to snap at Marco's chest.

The firestorm burned brighter and hotter, blazing brilliantly as if echoing Marco's anger. He was livid that this *Slayer* meant to threaten Jac, but he had to trust her to seize the moment. They had to work as a team to defeat these foes.

The *Slayer's* teeth were enormous and sharp, and Jac had to have a good view of them as he opened his mouth wide to bite. She also had to be able to see down his throat. Marco held his position, willing her to hurry before he was injured. The *Slayer* was completely confident and even chuckled as he began to close his mouth.

Finally, Jac struck the match, lit the flare and flung it into his mouth. It fell end over end and disappeared down his gullet. Marco kicked his opponent in the teeth then and retreated quickly as the *Slayer* fell back. The *Slayer* laughed, obviously thinking that Marco was trying to escape the fight and gave chase.

Marco beat his wings hard against the night, although the *Slayer* was in hot pursuit. Marco knew Jac was watching over his shoulder, and he held her tightly in front of his chest. He knew the *Slayer* might breathe fire, and he'd be able to take its assault better than Jac.

"I think someone has indigestion," Jac said softly and Marco looked back. The *Slayer's* eyes had widened as he realized something was wrong. He glanced down just as his gut exploded in a very satisfying way. He bellowed with pain and black blood spewed into the air.

"Talk about heartburn," Jac said and Marco chuckled. He turned in a big arc over Uluru and saw that the moon was coming out of the eclipse.

The injured *Slayer* fell limply toward the earth, and he was rotating between forms.

To Marco's surprise, Thorolf ripped himself away from his fight and seized the falling *Slayer*. He flew off quickly with the injured dragon, leaving Brandon to fight the last two identical *Slayers*.

They had turned on Brandon, who battled valiantly even though he was outnumbered. Marco had to guess that Chandra and Liz were in the vicinity and knew his fellow *Pyr* would want to defend their mates. As he raced closer, one *Slayer* locked all four claws with Brandon. The pair snapped and bit at each other, their tails thrashing with fearsome strength. The other *Slayer* turned on Marco, his eyes gleaming with malice. When he lunged toward them, Jac lit the flare and threw it.

Marco saw immediately that her enthusiasm had failed her and she'd moved too quickly. The *Slayer* dodged the flare and it dropped toward Uluru like a shooting star.

The *Slayer* laughed and lunged at Marco.

His partner shredded Brandon's gut, who faltered in flight. The *Slayer* beat at Brandon with his tail, but the *Pyr* rallied. Marco saw the gleam of purpose in his eyes before he attacked the *Slayer* with newfound strength.

Meanwhile, the closest *Slayer* and Marco locked claws and battled with savage force. The blows they gave each other sent first one and then the other plummeting toward the earth. Marco had never fought so hard, but the firestorm made victory imperative. He slashed the *Slayer*'s face so that black blood dripped, then flung his opponent across the sky. The *Slayer* flailed, then regained control. He soared back toward Marco, dragonfire blazing and talons extended. He attacked Marco with even greater vigor than before. Marco breathed fire and swung his tail, defending himself and Jac, then took a blow to the head that left him dizzy.

The *Slayer* ripped Marco's gut open while he was disoriented, and he felt Jac's heart skip a beat in fear. Marco's blood was flowing even before the *Slayer* snatched at Marco's wings. The *Slayer* made the wound bigger and it bled more profusely. He breathed fire at Marco then, and Marco turned, taking the heat of the flame on his injured back to defend Jac.

When he spun in mid-air, Marco discovered that Jorge was hovering in the air behind him. The *Slayer* must have flown silently in pursuit. His jaw hung by a tendon, blood running from his wound. Marco recoiled slightly, then stiffened at the new assault of dragonfire. He wrapped his claws around Jac, even as he took fire on all sides. His scales burned and the pain was excruciating. He wanted to tip back his head to scream, but that would have exposed Jac, so he bent over her, shaking in agony.

He realized he could die here, before satisfying his firestorm.

Jorge's eyes narrowed slightly and when he spoke, his words were hard to distinguish. *"Let me help,"* he offered in old-speak, as oily as ever, and he reached out to pluck Jac from Marco's grasp. Marco tried to grip her more tightly. Jac kicked and struggled, but the *Slayer*'s claw closed over her so tightly that she could barely squirm. She spat at him, having no shortage of spirit, and Marco was proud of her. He hung on to her to the best of his abilities, and she gripped his talons as the firestorm burned hot.

Jorge breathed slowly then, sending a stream of dragonsmoke at Marco.

"Dragonsmoke," Jac whispered and Jorge nodded with satisfaction.

Marco couldn't make a sound other than gasping at the pain. His scales burned and smoked, and then they curled so that his skin was exposed. He'd never been so pounded before. The dragonsmoke slipped beneath his scales, setting his flesh on fire. He was too injured to use the darkfire to manifest elsewhere, even though he tried.

Jorge reached out and ripped one of Marco's scales free, and Marco winced at the wrenching pain. He felt his blood flow from that new wound, warm on the skin so suddenly exposed. Jorge exhaled with a vengeance and the skin felt as if it had been burned by acid. Marco couldn't bear much more.

Only a feint would give him a chance to survive. Otherwise, he'd die here and now, and he owed Jac better than that.

He had to convince Jorge to snatch them both and take them

both to his lair.

There was only one way to tempt the *Slayer* to do that.

Marco groaned, twitched and flailed. He let his body go limp and fall toward the earth, well aware that Jorge watched him with satisfaction. Jac was panicking and Jorge was flying in pursuit, clearly intent on snatching her away as soon as Marco's grip loosened.

Marco whispered in old-speak, sending the ultimate temptation to Jorge. *"The Elixir,"* he whispered. *"Please give me the Elixir!"*

He felt Jorge's shock.

Then the *Slayer*'s delight.

A heartbeat later, he was snatched out of the air. He smelled that Jorge had seized the wounded *Slayer*, then they were all caught in a ferocious windstorm.

Marco sighed with relief, because his ploy had worked.

His firestorm was burning and he wasn't dead yet.

Brandon couldn't believe what he'd heard.

Thorolf had carried off the one newly hatched Boris Vassily, that *Slayer* seriously wounded and unconscious but not dead. He didn't doubt that Thorolf would have to thump the *Slayer* en route a couple of times to keep him in that state, because the Elixir would repair his body quickly. Ideally, Brandon would have gone with Thorolf, but he didn't dare leave Chandra and Liz undefended.

To his relief, Jorge snatched up the second hatchling, who was also wounded, and disappeared in a flash of light along with Marco and his mate.

The third *Slayer* hesitated, as if indecisive. Could he follow Jorge? Or did he have doubts about the wisdom of doing so? This *Slayer* had to be one of the ones who had hatched at Easter Island.

He circled with Brandon, preparing to fight instead of following Jorge. Brandon was ready to thump him, when the *Slayer* was jumped from behind by a version of Boris Vassily that appeared abruptly. That one had only a stub of an arm, but that didn't keep him from seizing the uncertain *Slayer* and ripping his throat open. His prey had time to gasp, then they both disappeared as if they'd never been there.

There was nothing saying this armless one wouldn't stash his prize and return. Brandon patrolled the area, then returned to Liz and Chandra, disgruntled. "I wish I could spontaneously manifest elsewhere," he muttered when he'd shifted back to human form and Liz gave him a hug.

"You have other skills," she said with a wink. She was clearly in a better mood than he was and gestured to the sky. "Did you see what she did with the flares? I love a mate who thinks quickly."

"I don't think the news is as good as that," Brandon growled.

"What do you mean?" Chandra asked.

"I heard their old-speak at the end," he admitted, sparing another glance at the sky. He couldn't smell *Pyr* or *Slayer* but he didn't trust any of the *Slayers* to stay wherever they had gone. It would be sweet to see the end of the Dragon's Tail Wars and be rid of *Slayers* for good.

Even if this night's events meant there would be one more.

"Weren't they just exchanging taunts?" Liz asked.

"It always just sounds like thunder," Chandra agreed.

The two women faced him expectantly, both of them so pleased that Marco had had his firestorm that Brandon didn't want to be the bearer of bad news. "I'm afraid Erik is right," he said. "I don't think we can count on Marco anymore."

"I don't believe it," Liz said. "He loaned me the darkfire crystal during our firestorm, and that was the only reason I was able to defend myself against Chen."

"And he helped Lee during our firestorm," Chandra said. "Just because he's mysterious doesn't mean he's bad."

Brandon sighed, knowing he had to tell them the worst and destroy their optimism. "After he was injured, Marco asked Jorge for the Elixir. That can only mean one thing."

Liz caught her breath.

"He's turning *Slayer* after his firestorm," Brandon said, knowing it had to be stated aloud.

"I don't believe it," Liz said. "He could have been trying to trick Jorge." She shook her head vehemently. "I'm going to need more proof than that."

"Where did they come from?" Chandra said. "They must have been staying in the vicinity to arrive so close to the eclipse."

"There's really only Yulara," Brandon said. "Let me see if I can find their scent."

Jac wished she could understand old-speak. Marco and Jorge had clearly communicated that way before Jorge had snatched them, and she wished she knew what Marco had said. He was folded protectively around her in his dragon form and she could smell the damage to his scales. His thigh was bleeding where Jorge had ripped that scale free and the skin there was blistered with a burn. He was also out cold, which meant she couldn't ask him what was going on.

It was a little bit disconcerting to discover that her dragon was vulnerable.

They landed hard. Jac felt as if she'd been plucked out of a maelstrom and flung down by an invisible hand. That wind swirled around her for a moment and she kept her eyes closed against the assault.

When the air stilled, she looked.

She was in a room that looked like a great library, with Marco lying on the carpeted floor beside her. His scales were still smoking and his blood flowed onto the rug. His tail stretched almost the full width of the room, and he was clearly unconscious.

At least he wasn't dead.

The weird thing was that they were alone together. Where had Jorge and the *Slayer* gone?

Jac looked around, searching for an escape. The room was lined with built-in book cases that had glass doors, so she could see that the books inside had gilt on their spines. They appeared to be leather-bound volumes, and Jac could see a couple with gems mounted on the spines. Each pair of doors locked, and even the locks were incredibly beautiful and intricate in their design.

The doors on the cabinets were ornate, elaborately carved and adorned with gold as if they'd been transported from Versailles. Candles were lit in sconces mounted on the walls, which were placed at regular intervals between the bookshelves.

The ceiling was fancy, as well, with detailed moldings at the tops of the walls and a large plaster medallion in the middle of the ceiling. A glittering gold chandelier thick with crystals and aflame with lit candles hung from it, but the ceiling was so high that it seemed too far away. There was a massive carved stone fireplace on one wall and a fire blazed on its hearth, heating the room. The carpets were thick underfoot, but there were no windows.

And there wasn't a door.

A pair of chairs upholstered in red leather were placed before the fire, the brass studs gleaming in the upholstery. The wooden legs of the chairs were carved, and each one had four feet. Jac supposed she shouldn't have been surprised that each one was a claw holding a ball, like a griffin's claw.

Or a dragon's.

Despite all the candles and the fire, the air seemed damp, and Jac shivered in the chill. She eyed the chandelier and wondered how the candles had been lit. There wasn't a ladder in sight. Then she considered the dimensions of the room and guessed.

This was Jorge's lair. In his absence, she should seize the opportunity to learn a little bit more about him. The treasures in his hoard should offer some insight, if she could find them.

On the wall opposite the hearth, there was a reading table, high enough that a person could stand to examine a book. It wasn't empty, so Jac went to look at what her host was reading.

She gasped when she saw that Sigmund's book, the volume that had been hidden in her closet, was open on the table. So, Marco hadn't retrieved it, after all. She should have known it would have been Jorge—on the other hand, she hadn't understood his true nature then.

The book was open to a page on darkfire.

Darkfire. Was that what was governing her firestorm with Marco? He'd had the crystal, which had contained the darkfire. She'd seen its blue-green spark a couple of times in his presence, and the verse had mentioned it. Darkfire was supposed to cause inversions, to challenge expectation, and to make unpredictable events happen. She ran her finger over the entry and recalled the verse.

> *Three blood moons mark the debt come due*
> *Will the* Pyr *triumph or be hunted anew?*
> *Three eclipses will awaken the spark*

In thirteen monsters breeding in dark.
Three times the firestorm will spark
Before darkfire fades into the dark.
Firestorm, mate or blood sacrifice
None or all can be the darkfire's price.
When the Dragon's Tail has turned its bore
And darkfire dies forevermore
Will the Pyr *be left to rule with might*
Or disappear into past's twilight?

Firestorm, mate or blood sacrifice. She didn't like the idea of the darkfire having a price like that, particularly not now that she was a mate. She glanced at Marco and didn't like the idea of him being a blood sacrifice much better.

Beside the book was a stoppered glass vial, like something from a laboratory. It was empty but Jac could see a tiny bit of dried red residue in it. Blood. She grimaced, not wanting to touch it.

Alongside that was a scale that had to have come from a dragon. It was larger than her outspread hand, closer to the size of a dinner plate. The scale was hard, like a seashell, but it was many hues of charcoal grey, like a dark pearl. It tapered to a point, which had a number of protrusions, like thorns. It looked like a magical thing and Jac couldn't resist the urge to run her fingertips over it.

She eyed Marco and recalled how his scales had seemed to be lit with inner fire before he'd been injured. His scales didn't have these protrusions and were a different hue of grey. There was a glow between them of faint golden light and she wasn't sure whether the firestorm would help him or hinder him.

Jorge didn't seem to have any ointment for burns, unfortunately.

There was also a stone displayed on the table. It was about the size of an olive and similar in shape. It was green with red lines on its surface that almost looked like veins. It was set in pewter, in a setting that looked like a tiny egg cup — except that it was sculpted to look like dragon talons. What was it? Jac reached out a finger to touch it, but the air shifted suddenly in the room and the pressure changed.

Her ears plugged then popped, and she spun around, recognizing that she had company, or soon would.

A ruby and brass dragon with bleeding wounds was flung down on the carpet under the chandelier, landing heavily beside Marco. Neither of them stirred or opened their eyes. Jac thought maybe the *Slayer* emitted a low moan. Black blood was running from his open wounds and she could see it burning the rug. It had to be the *Slayer* she'd injured with the third flare.

But now he had a chunk torn out of his gut. Had he revived enough to fight Jorge? Jac had to think so. He seemed to be hanging to life by a thread now. That worked for Jac in a big way.

The *Slayer* shimmered, then changed shape to a man. He looked like a gentleman you'd pass on the street somewhere in Europe, his hair fair and his figure trim. It was the shoes that made him look European, Jac decided. They were dress shoes, worn on the soles from extensive walking but polished to a gleam. He was also dressed more formally, and she guessed he often wore trousers and a tweed jacket like this.

In the blink of an eye, he changed back to a ruby and brass dragon, flicking between the forms until he abruptly remained in his dragon form.

There was a flash of light, then a golden salamander appeared on the floor of the cavern, not twenty feet away. Its body glinted like it was made of gems, and it ran around the fallen *Slayer* as if checking on him.

Or confirming that he had arrived in one piece. The salamander then shimmered in that familiar pale blue hue. Jac narrowed her eyes against the light and just barely discerned the silhouette as the salamander became a dragon of topaz and gold. His bottom jaw was gone, and his black blood flowed from the mess of torn flesh that remained.

Jorge.

Jac took a step back, doubting that he'd thank her for the injury she'd inflicted on him.

The library's dimensions didn't seem generous enough, not with three dragons in residence. Jorge bent and Jac saw his tongue slide into the fallen *Slayer*'s gut, then Jorge sucked. The sound was disgusting, but Jac couldn't look away. Jorge feasted on his former ally, tearing into the corpse with his upper fangs, then using his tongue to slurp up the black blood.

Was that a glint beneath Marco's eyelid?

Was he awake?

Jac turned her back on them both, revolted by Jorge but not wanting to give Marco away. Her heart was racing and she suspected the *Slayer* could sense it. Their senses were supposed to be very keen. Maybe the smell of her fear would cover her reaction to that glimpse of Marco's eye. The firestorm seemed to be burning a little bit brighter, and Jac hoped Marco didn't notice that either. Marco was still badly hurt, so every minute she could give him to recover had to help his condition improve.

He might be a dragon, but if she had to choose a champion between Marco and Jorge, the choice was a gimme. One had made sweet love to her. One had killed her nephew. Easy choice.

Jac pretended to study the spines of the books—which weren't in any language she could read—and fought the urge to look over her shoulder to see what Jorge was doing. She eventually turned, catching another glimpse of Marco's eye.

Okay. She and Marco were in this together. She had to distract Jorge and find out all that she could. There was no telling how much Marco knew, but she might be able to help.

Finally, Jorge straightened and surveyed her, his eyes gleaming. To Jac's amazement, his lower jaw had already partially grown back. He could chew, although his teeth weren't all formed on his lower jaw yet. This was the Elixir in action. The Elixir conferred a kind of immortality, Jac remembered, allowing those who had drunk it to heal rapidly. Jac was impressed. She thought of newts growing new tails and wondered whether this skill worked for all parts of his body.

When his eyes narrowed, she decided not to ask. Jac had to wonder whether she looked appetizing and fought the urge to retreat. It was easy to think of other large predators and how flight only prompted their instinct to hunt—by running, the observer became prey. She held her ground, just barely, her heart thumping with terror.

It helped, actually, that Marco was in the room. Jac felt as if she were putting on a display of bravery, just for him. Like she was performing in a play, not really at risk of losing her life.

"Multiple forms," she said to Jorge, trying to sound confident and unafraid. "A characteristic of the Wyvern or of a *Slayer* who has drunk the Dragon's Blood Elixir. What other forms can you take?"

Jorge shifted shape again, taking his human form. He strolled toward her, his one fist clenching and unclenching, and she couldn't decide whether he was more menacing as a fire-breathing dragon or as a man with ice-cold eyes. His wounded jaw, the flesh raw but the bones regrown as she watched, made him look even worse.

Like a zombie.

He paused to kick Marco, but the *Pyr* didn't respond. "I'm not going to force-feed you," he muttered, his speech still labored, then turned on Jac again.

"He has to get his own Elixir?" Jac asked. "No table service?" Jorge snorted at the idea. "What if Marco doesn't want it?"

"Then he shouldn't have asked for it," Jorge snapped. "I would have left him behind."

That had been the old-speak Jac had heard then. It had been Marco asking for the Elixir, probably because he'd guessed that Jorge would bring him along to this lair. He had to be playing dead because he didn't intend to really consume it.

Jac couldn't blame him for that, although his injuries looked painful. Marco bled red, though, which meant he was *Pyr*, and she guessed he meant to stay that way.

There really were good dragons and bad ones, and she had the rotten luck to be snared by the worst one of all.

"You showed some initiative in the fight," Jorge said, his hand rising to his healing jaw. It was strangely fascinating to watch it rejuvenate and to hear his speech become clearer each time he spoke.

Jac decided to disguise her fear as well as she could. "Too bad the effect didn't last longer."

"Nothing will, not when a *Slayer* has drunk the Elixir."

"Where does it come from?" she asked. "I thought those who had drunk the Elixir always needed more."

Jorge's eyes narrowed. "You've been doing your homework," he said softly.

"I was, at least until someone stole my research book."

Jorge glanced back at the fallen *Slayer* then at Jac, raising a brow. "I feel so much better since that snack."

Jac couldn't hide her horror as she realized what he meant.

"He'd drunk the Elixir, as well." She eyed the pair of dragons, one dead with his guts ripped open and one still smoking after the battle. "Are you saving the rest of the carcass for later?"

"I'll give Marco a chance to share." He nudged the fallen *Pyr* with his foot again to no result. Jac saw a spark brighten on the end of her fingertip and put her hands behind her back to hide it. Marco must be waking up.

"So, now you know what I am," Jorge mused.

Jac nodded and swallowed. It wasn't good news to be trapped in a sealed room with a *Slayer* who was as close to immortal as a dragon shifter could get.

"And you know about Marco now, too." Jorge smiled. "A night of revelations."

"And questions, too."

Jorge lifted a brow in silent query.

"Why bring me here? I'm a mate, evidently, but the firestorm isn't satisfied."

"Exactly." Jorge's sudden smile did just about nothing to build Jac's confidence. "The firestorm makes you particularly useful."

"Because the firestorm draws *Pyr* like moths to the flame," Jac remembered, trying to sound as if she wasn't terrified. "You're going to use me as bait."

A smile lifted the corner of Jorge's mouth. "How badly do you want to live?"

"As badly as you do, I'll guess."

Jorge smiled as he approached the display of his treasures. His manner gave Jac the definite sense that he knew something she didn't. He fanned through the pages of the book, then turned to offer it to Jac. "Yours, I believe."

Jac eyed it with skepticism. "You don't strike me as someone with a giving nature."

Jorge's smile widened. "I've no need of this volume any more."

"Did you read it already?"

"Of course. But it wasn't as interesting as I'd expected."

"How so?"

"It's out of date." Jorge bit off the words.

"What were you hoping to learn from it?"

Jorge glanced toward the fallen *Slayer* then seemed to change the subject. "Notice anything strange about my fellow *Slayers*, the ones who have been hatched?"

"They're identical, like twins."

"They're clones," Jorge confirmed.

Jac recalled the reference in the verse on Marco's wall to thirteen monsters bred in the dark, awakened by the blood moon. "Clones of who?"

"A *Slayer* named Boris Vassily, who died several years ago." Jorge strolled back to his supposed ally, and Jac didn't trust that he was telling her so much. Was he telling her the truth? Or lies that would mislead her? "He was the leader of the *Slayers* after his father. He was cloned by Sigmund Guthrie before he died, although Sigmund himself died before completing his experiment."

"You were hoping for notes on making more."

Jorge's quick glance was cold enough to freeze Jac's marrow.

There was a rumble then and the floor vibrated. Jac looked up to see the chandelier shaking, the flames dancing on the candles.

Was it an earthquake?

Would she die in this place even before Jorge attacked?

CHAPTER TWENTY

he rumbling faded just the way it had grown in volume. Jac thought she heard a whistle then realized that Jorge was smiling as he watched her.

"Was that old-speak?" Jac asked and he laughed.

"No other dragon shifter knows of this place."

"Then thunder?"

"So far underground? I think not."

"An earthquake, then."

Jorge's smile broadened. His face was healed, now, just a bit of skin missing on his cheeks. "A train," he whispered. "A subway train, about two hundred feet above us."

Then there were people close by. Jac felt her mouth drop open as she looked up at the ceiling.

"So close and yet a world away," Jorge murmured. "They're all oblivious. This place has been secure for hundreds of years. They've never even found the ventilation shafts, which truly is a sign of the inferiority of humans."

"Where *are* we?"

"In the lost library of Ivan the Terrible."

Jac had heard of that library and its treasures. "Isn't it supposed to be under the Kremlin?"

"It is," Jorge agreed. "Far beneath both the documented and the undocumented subway systems. Though its existence is rumored, no one knows where it is." He leaned closer. "Even the *Pyr* don't know this place is here, much less that the greatest prize of all has been safely kept within it."

Jac glanced to the display of treasures and her gaze was drawn to that green stone. "The stone," she said. "Was it here?"

"An aristocrat's prize," Jorge said, picking it up with obvious admiration. "A Dracontias. Perhaps *the* Dracontias."

Jac had read about the Dracontias but neither she nor the sources had believed it was real. "I thought that stone was a myth."

Jorge gestured to himself. "You stand in the company of a myth come to life."

That was true enough. Jac's gaze lingered on his jaw, which looked exactly as it had before. "There was supposed to have been a Dracontias cut from the brow of a fallen dragon in the Middle Ages."

"Chevalier de Gonzo, Grand Master of the Order of St. John of Jerusalem, slew a dragon on the island of Rhodes, successfully extracting the Dracontias from its brow before it died."

Jac recalled all of the story now. It was in Sigmund's book. "But the dragon had lost his ability to taint the power of the stone at the point of his death, presumably because the knight had enchanted him."

"Beguiled, I would guess."

"I didn't think humans could beguile dragons," Jac said. "I thought it only worked the other way around."

"Perhaps the knight learned a new trick." Jac sensed that Jorge knew more of this than he was telling and wondered why he'd told her anything at all.

Was he just bragging about his treasure?

Meanwhile Jorge turned the stone in his hand. "The gem became a family heirloom."

"And was used to both cure illness and to detect illness."

"Put the Dracontias in water and it will cause the water to boil. When the water cools and the stone is removed, the antidote to any illness is in the cup." Jorge put the stone back down on the table with elaborate care. "Although I'm somewhat skeptical that there truly is a universal cure. The second version of the tale, that putting the Dracontias into a cup of poison will turn that poison to water, is more compelling to me."

"Why are you telling me this?"

"Because I want something that you may be able to get."

"And if I do get it for you, you'll let me live."

Jorge inclined his head in agreement.

"Why don't I believe that?" Jac asked and he smiled.

"Maybe we share a certain skepticism of the claims of others."

"What's that supposed to mean?"

"Marco said he wanted the Elixir. He indicated that he wished to turn *Slayer*." Jorge gestured toward the fallen *Pyr* and Jac tried to appear indifferent to Marco's fate. "But *Pyr* don't change their alliances that readily." Jorge shook his head. "I'm afraid he meant to trick me."

And what would Jorge do about that? It was easy to see that the *Slayer* was quickly recovering from his wounds, while Marco was still badly hurt. Jac was sure Marco would lose any dragon fight started now.

"Maybe now that he's had his firestorm, he sees the appeal of turning *Slayer*. Of being immortal with the Elixir."

"Maybe." Jorge reached into his shirt and removed something that made Jac's heart still. It was a scale, a dragon scale, of deepest black that looked as if it had been lit by an inner fire. He placed it on the table, and Jac knew whose scale it was even before the firestorm sparks lit between it and her. "But I think he lied to me," Jorge said softly. "I think Marco said he wanted the Elixir so that I'd bring him here with you."

Jac didn't know what to say to that. Had Marco known that Jorge would take her to a sealed lair? Could any of the *Pyr* spontaneously manifest in other places, like these *Slayers*? Or had this ploy been the only way to ensure he knew where she was and could defend her? She felt keenly aware of her vulnerability.

Marco didn't even seem to be breathing.

Jac had to hope that was because he was paying close attention. "You're pretty suspicious of someone who wants to join forces with you," she managed to say.

"I am," Jorge admitted. "It's a learned response." His eyes lit with inner fire and he placed the scale alongside the other one on the table with a reverence that made Jac wonder why it was important. She couldn't remember reading anything about that in the book, just that the Smith repaired the armor of the *Pyr*.

"Is this the part where you make me an offer I can't refuse?"

"Not you," Jorge murmured, his eyes glowing. "Not you." Before her eyes, his right hand shimmered blue then changed to a massive dragon claw. His talons glinted as he made a fist, then he smashed Marco's lost scale so hard that the table cracked in the middle.

The scale broke into pieces as Jac jumped back, and Marco howled in pain.

"Sorry to disturb your slumber," Jorge had time to laugh, then Marco reared back and breathed a plume of dragonfire. His eyes blazed and the firestorm brightened to a blinding light.

In a heartbeat, Jorge had changed shape and the two of them had locked claws. Marco lunged toward Jorge and slammed the *Slayer* into the wall, showing a fortitude Jac hadn't expected, given his injuries. The firestorm blazed with brilliant light, which maybe gave him new strength.

She guessed then that he meant to use what power he had to get her out of this prison.

Just in case, she grabbed the book that Jorge had given back to her. Then she snatched up the Dracontias. As Jorge and Marco collided with the opposite wall, cracking glass panels and making books fall to the floor, Jac closed her grip over the stone and hoped for the best.

Surviving this day was a long shot, no matter how she looked at it.

"I've got one."

Sloane looked up at the sound of Thorolf's old-speak, understanding what he meant. They'd captured one of the identical versions of Boris Vassily. Sloane felt both excitement and trepidation. *"Alive?"*

"He was barely so. But the Elixir is working fast."

He was going to have a live *Slayer* captive in his home. Even though Sloane had made preparations, the prospect still frightened him. He guessed that refrigerating the *Slayer* would slow his metabolic processes, including the regenerative power of the Elixir, but he had no idea how quickly the *Slayer* would recover.

Although he could guess what would happen when the *Slayer* could spontaneously manifest elsewhere again.

The logistical realities were no less daunting. It was the middle of the day and there were customers arriving at the shop, not to mention the ones on the road outside. Lee had taken charge of the store while Sloane worked in his lab. If Thorolf landed in dragon form, carrying a wounded dragon, lots of people would notice. Fortunately, the other *Pyr* were still at his home.

"I'll meet you," Erik interjected. He'd obviously heard Thorolf's old-speak and Sloane was glad.

"We'll take the truck and trailer," Quinn added. *"That way, it doesn't matter what shape he takes."*

"He's in human form now," Thorolf said. *"Thank the Great Wyvern."*

"Thorolf has to be exhausted," Sloane said aloud.

"Thorolf is coming?" Eileen asked, having lifted her head at the sound of old-speak. When Erik nodded, she now stood up with purpose. "I'll cook," she said and stepped into the kitchen. "He'll be starving."

"He'll want to go back for Chandra," Sara contributed.

"He'll need to eat first," Eileen countered.

"We need to meet somewhere remote," Quinn said.

"But not too far," Erik added and Sloane nodded agreement.

"Lassen Volcanic National Park," he suggested. "It's closed to visitors this time of year."

"We'll park at the perimeter and fly in," Erik said with a nod, and Sloane gave Thorolf directions in old-speak.

"It's farther inland for him to fly," Eileen said with concern. "He must be exhausted."

"He is stronger than he knows," Erik said. "The son of champions."

"We'll pick up some roast chickens and a couple of pies to hold him until your meal is done," Quinn said with a wink. "Let's go, before that *Slayer* recovers enough to fight. Thorolf won't be in any state to subdue him again."

"What are you going to do with him?" Eileen asked worriedly.

"Won't the Elixir allow him to recover?" Sara asked.

Sloane was well aware of Drake listening to their conversation. "There's a balance to be struck. If he dies and is exposed to the four elements, he'll disintegrate to dust and I need his blood. If he's kept under normal conditions, the Elixir will ensure that he heals and can escape."

"So?" Eileen asked.

Sloane smiled. "I'm going to refrigerate him. It'll slow down his metabolism but not kill him."

"We'll save that task for later," Erik said grimly.

"After we've learned all we can from him," Quinn agreed, and Erik lifted a finger.

"I would remind you that Boris Vassily and I have exchanged challenge coins. No matter how many of him there are, the pleasure of exterminating this one will be all mine."

Ronnie awakened, feeling less sick than she had in the hospital. She touched her own forehead and it was cooler than it had been. She had no idea how long she'd slept and braced herself on her elbows to look around.

She didn't remember much of the flight with Drake. She knew he'd rescued her from the hospital but as soon as she'd been safely in his embrace, she'd fallen asleep. She'd awakened when they arrived wherever they were, but her fever had been building. She had a vague recollection of an intense dark-haired man giving her an injection, then of Drake helping her into bed. She remembered telling Timmy that she loved him.

After that, there was only the blissful oblivion of sleep.

It turned out she was in a solarium that was lush with plants. The sun was shining through the shades on the glass ceiling and water splashed somewhere close by. She could smell the humid peaty scent of damp earth and the perfume of more than one flower. She was lying on a normal bed in a regular nightgown, which was a welcome change from the hospital. It was as if she'd slept in an enchanted garden. She felt refreshed and a little bit hungry.

She heard a step and saw Drake coming toward her, carrying a tray. She smelled coffee and her stomach growled in demand.

"There is a good sign," Drake said and set down the tray on a table beside the pool and fountain. He came to her and knelt in front of her, sliding sandals on to her bare feet.

"I can do that," she protested, but Drake gave her a look.

"Sloane says you have need of rest and relaxation to recuperate. I am to take your temperature." He produced a thermometer, and Ronnie slipped the end under her tongue.

Drake stood with folded arms, watching her, like a guardian angel. "It has been forty-eight hours since he gave you the antidote. Tomorrow, he wishes to take a blood sample to monitor your progress. Sloane has midwifery skills and would like to check on the baby, as well." Ronnie nodded agreement, relieved to have her concerns about the baby's arrival so easily addressed. When the thermometer beeped, she gave it to Drake who nodded crisp approval. "Much diminished. And your hunger is, as I said, a good sign."

"I had no idea you were a nursemaid," Ronnie teased.

"I learn new skills each day," he replied, and she saw the twinkle in his eye.

"Is his cure working then? I feel better."

"He is optimistic for the first time in a long while. If his antidote does work, Sloane will be glad to share it to ensure that humans are healed, too."

"So, I'm the test group?"

"A volunteer," Drake said with a smile. "I am glad that you agreed, and that the results are so good already."

The way he looked at her made Ronnie feel cherished, which was a wonderful sensation. She gestured to her rounded stomach. "I should have believed you."

Drake sobered. "I should not have been so determined to have privacy. I underestimated the power of the *Slayers*, and you suffered as a result of my error. I am sorry, Veronica."

"Should I demand that you make it up to me?" She used a teasing tone because he looked so contrite.

A gleam of determination lit Drake's eye. "I intend to do just that."

He put his hand beneath her elbow and helped her to rise to her feet. Ronnie was weaker than she'd realized and was glad of Drake's support as he escorted her to the table. It was pure heaven to feel the skin of another against her own again. Drake's hand was warm, his touch both gentle and strong, and she leaned on him with gratitude.

The table was set in a golden sunbeam, and even though the sunlight came through the glass overhead, its warmth was more than welcome. She closed her eyes as she sat down, feeling profoundly grateful to both be in this place and with Drake, then opened her eyes to find him watching her.

His smile made her heart leap.

He nodded at the tray. "Your meal grows cold," he said softly.

The food smelled delicious. There was a fluffy omelet with spinach and feta tucked inside, sliced tomatoes alongside it and whole wheat toast. One of those pink vitamins sat in a cup alongside her coffee, and Veronica began to eat with pleasure. She had a sense of wellbeing as she sat with Drake in the sunshine eating this meal, and she remembered how she'd enjoyed her third trimester when she was carrying Timmy.

Maybe the challenges were behind them.

Maybe it was time to make sure.

If nothing else, Drake was direct. Ronnie fully expected him to explain his plans in short order. She had no issues with asking for clarification if necessary.

Drake gestured to the solarium when she glanced up at him. "Although this looks quite different, it is much like the hospital isolation ward. Sloane prepared it for your arrival, and only he and I will enter it."

"Because you can't catch the virus."

Drake nodded and she noticed again how haggard he looked.

"That's why you stayed away from the hospital," she guessed and he nodded again.

Drake leaned closer. "If they had looked more closely at my blood, they would have found many anomalies that indicate what I am. Because I hope to remain with you, my mate, and because you have made a home in that city, I did not wish to compromise our future so simply as that. I let them take the sample, but beguiled them into destroying it. I let them keep me in isolation, too, but then I had to disappear to ensure our future."

Ronnie watched him, liking the implication of his words. "So you came here instead."

"This is the home of Sloane, the Apothecary of our kind. He found an antibody in my blood and managed to isolate it. I understand little of this science, but he created a means of sharing that antibody with you. His hope was that your body, equipped with this tool, would multiply it and dispatch it in battle against the virus."

"I guess it is like a war," Ronnie said, then sipped her coffee. It tasted heavenly, hot and rich, just the way she liked it.

"Or perhaps I can only understand it that way," Drake acknowledged. He was watching her closely, and Ronnie smiled for him.

"You look tired."

"I have feared for you, every day and every night." He ran a hand over his cropped hair, his expression so concerned that Ronnie's heart clenched. "I erred and you paid the price. It was irresponsible and unforgiveable..."

She reached out and caught his hand beneath hers. "I made a mistake, too."

"I erred first."

"And I forgive you."

His gaze lifted to hers and he smiled, his expression rueful. He turned his hand over and interlaced their fingers. "You give me more than I deserve."

"I don't think so."

"I do, and I mean to earn the faith you grant so readily." Drake frowned as she watched and he moved his other hand to caress her captive one. "I have made mistakes in my time, Veronica. One of those errors has been confessing little of my truth, my past or my feelings to others." He nodded toward the door that connected the solarium to the rest of the house. "I watch these modern *Pyr* and I see the partnerships they make with their mates and I am envious of that bond. I would build such a partnership with you, if you will have me, even though it means I must break my habit of silence."

This sounded like the reassurance she had wanted from him. Ronnie swallowed and dared to speak her mind. "I've been a warrior's wife before, Drake. I've been the anchor and the homemaker, the one who kept hearth and home, the one who sacrificed needs and opportunities for my husband's career and its demands. I don't want to do that again. I don't think I can."

"I would not ask it of you. I expected it of Cassandra, it is true, but times were different. I'm not sure she would have expected otherwise."

"You talk about her as if she lived a thousand years ago!" Ronnie protested.

Drake studied her hand and lifted a brow. "It was more like

three thousand years," he admitted softly, then lifted his gaze to hers. "And this is where my confession must begin."

"I don't understand."

"And I will begin to explain, though I have little talent with such tasks."

"You might improve with practice."

"Indeed, I might." Drake's smile was banished. "The firestorm is a gift," he said slowly, as if choosing his words with care. He sat down opposite her, watchful but not hovering. Ronnie poured him a cup of coffee from the carafe, then one for herself, and smiled at him.

"A wonderful gift in the view of the *Pyr*, at least from what I've read."

Drake nodded. "And to be given a second one is no small thing. I was honored and almost overwhelmed to have the opportunity. That it should be with you..." He shook his head and Ronnie was surprised to see that he didn't appear to know what to say. When he continued, his voice was husky. "It was good fortune unexpected."

Ronnie was flattered, but she needed to hear more. "Why?"

Drake impaled her with a glance. "Because you were the one who gave me hope. You were the one who restored my reason to continue when I saw no point in life. You were the one who showed me the merit of what we could do." He raised his fist to his heart. "I have treasured the memory of my short time with you. I have called upon my recollection of your strength to feed my own." He smiled a little. "To be given a firestorm with a woman I so admired already was beyond belief."

Ronnie basked in his admiration, unable to doubt his sincerity. She forgot all about her breakfast when her gaze locked with his, the heat in his eyes making her think only of how they *had* satisfied the firestorm that night.

Before she could speak, Drake continued in a more grim tone. "But I failed the promise of the firestorm. I failed to give my all to you from the outset."

"There wasn't much time to give more than you did, not before the *Slayers* attacked," Ronnie protested, wanting to defend him from his own criticism.

Drake shook his head. "I take the blame. You cannot change

that, Veronica. I believe that the Great Wyvern judged my commitment to the firestorm and found me lacking." He heaved a sigh. "And so I resolved to change."

Ronnie blinked. "How?"

"I have been rootless all these years. I have made no home and no firm associations with human society. I have remained a warrior, always traveling to the next battle. I do not confide readily in others, and I rely only upon the men sworn to my command. This is the way of a solitary *Pyr*, not that of one committed to his mate."

"I'm glad you spent time with Timmy. I really appreciate it."

"He will be a fine man. I like him a great deal, and it was no burden to share some of my experience with him."

"He's missed Mark terribly."

"He told me of his father." Drake glanced up. "And of his nightmares. I am told that he has not had them this year, but then, he is older than he was."

"And he had you," Ronnie pointed out. She had heard the difference in her son even over the phone. He was more confident and outgoing, and Joy had said that both boys had done better at their sports with Drake coaching.

"He did." Drake nodded. "I resolved that I must put time to good use. When you were hidden from me, I determined to learn more so that I might make a better partner to you. Timmy taught me much of making a home and of expectations of men in these times. I strove to better myself."

Ronnie couldn't help but tease him. "Joy said you took a cooking class."

Drake glanced up at her with a twinkle in his eyes. "In my day, a man would not have survived an attempt to invade the vicinity of the hearth, but I enjoyed it."

In his day? Just how old was Drake? Nothing she had read online mentioned the life span of the *Pyr*. She recalled his claim that Cassandra had lived three thousand years before? Were the *Pyr* immortal?

Drake raised a finger. "But the true challenge for me lies ahead, and I must address it while we can."

Ronnie chilled. "What's that?"

"I must confide in you, Veronica." Drake ran a hand over his brow with such obvious consternation at the prospect that Ronnie almost smiled. "I must tell you of my past, of my feelings, of my thoughts." He gritted his teeth and visibly shuddered. "I must prove myself to be a worthy partner so that the Great Wyvern does not deprive us of the blessing She has granted." He spared her a wry glance. "You will heal and I will talk. We both shall find our challenges in this path ahead."

"And maybe our reward?" Ronnie dared to suggest and Drake smiled.

His eyes glowed as he watched her. "I like to think our shared future more probable than that."

Marco flung himself at Jorge, trying to use the firestorm to buttress his own strength. The pain when Jorge shattered his scale had been white hot, but he had to save Jac from this *Slayer*. His need to protect her was almost overwhelming, his passion for the firestorm giving him a power beyond any he'd had before. He was keenly aware of the scent of her skin and the tinge of her fear.

There was something strange about this compulsion to save a dragon hunter, never mind the one who had injured the only *Pyr* he cared about, but the firestorm allowed no argument. Marco's need for Jac was so powerful that it blotted every other thought from his mind.

She was his mate.

She could bear his child.

The darkfire had brought him the most unlikely mate possible, and theirs would be a union to change the world. Marco felt the darkfire crackle and knew that Jorge was the obstacle to his destiny.

He refused to accept defeat.

Once he could have seized Jac and manifested elsewhere, but his injuries were such that he feared he didn't have the strength. It cost him mightily to manifest elsewhere, and he knew Jorge would simply follow him. Although his state wasn't the best, it would only be worse after manifesting. His best chance to eliminate the *Slayer* was here and now.

Marco roared and slammed Jorge into a wall of bookcases, and the doors broke in unison. Glass fell to the carpet and books tumbled forth only to be trampled beneath the battling dragons. The entire room shook and not from a train. Marco squeezed the *Slayer*, letting his talons dig deep into his opponent's flesh. Black blood spurted beneath the points of Marco's claws but he ignored both it and its corrosive burn. He was burned from nose to tail already. Jorge had to die. Marco slammed him into the wall again, bashing Jorge's head hard against the cabinetry and breaking a lot of it.

Jorge bellowed and swung his tail. Marco moved and Jorge's tail crashed into the broken bookcases. Dozens of slashes appeared on his tail where the glass cut him. Jorge breathed fire, setting the carpets alight, and swept a pile of books across the room. A number of them were flung into the fireplace and the fire began to burn with greater vigor.

He fell on Marco then, snatching and biting. Marco found himself on his back, but he abruptly pushed himself off the floor and hauled Jorge upward. He slammed Jorge's head into the ceiling, then forced his face into the chandelier. The candles burned Jorge's face, making the *Slayer* writhe in pain and bellow. The grappling pair fell to the floor again, and tripped over the carcass of the dead *Slayer*. The scent of his corpse was enough to sicken Marco, and he rammed Jorge into a corner, then bashed the *Slayer*'s head against the wall.

He saw Jorge inhale and guessed that the *Slayer* would breathe smoke.

Marco kicked Jorge in the chest, making him choke on his own smoke. His eyes glinting with malice, Jorge rolled beneath Marco. The room was filling with smoke as the carpets burned. Jorge twisted and snatched for Jac. She kicked him in the snout in one of her best kickboxer moves, and Jorge flinched. She then ran toward Marco. He snatched her up, hoping he could manifest elsewhere, and she seized a candle from a sconce.

Jorge snapped at them, but Jac shoved the burning candle into his eye. He roared with pain and fell back, even as Marco tried to summon the strength to manifest elsewhere. He had to get Jac out of the burning library before it was too late.

He shimmered but the shimmer faded too soon. Jorge was getting up, his eyes red with rage, and Marco tried again to manifest in another place.

Any other place.

The blue glimmer of light was far less than it needed to be, and he feared his exhaustion would condemn them both. Jorge guessed his trouble and laughed, then reared back to leap toward him.

"Open wide," Jac whispered and Marco stared at her. She held up the green Dracontias stone between finger and thumb. "An antidote to every ill," she reminded him.

Would it really heal him?

It couldn't hurt to try—and it might foil Jorge's plans to take the stone. Marco opened his mouth and Jac cast the small stone down his throat. It was cold, and he felt its passage as if he'd swallowed an ice cube.

To his amazement, Marco felt the difference immediately. The stone seemed to radiate from deep inside him and he could feel the burns on his skin becoming less angry.

"It's working," Jac said, running her hands over his scales. The firestorm's caress didn't hurt either, her touch sending vigor through his body.

Marco needed more, and he needed it fast. Now that he could think clearly, he knew where to get it. As the haze of pain faded, he knew what to do.

Marco summoned his own dragonsmoke and breathed it at Jorge in savage fury. The *Slayer* was clearly caught off guard by the speed with which Marco breathed the smoke, and he fell back, flinching as it pursued him.

Jorge backed into a corner, but there was no escaping Marco's wrath. He breathed a thick cord of smoke and tightened it around Jorge's neck like a noose, then drew on it. It was like sucking a straw and he felt the jolt of Jorge's energy passed to him through the dragonsmoke conduit. He felt bright and bigger, stronger and more radiant. He inhaled as Jorge screamed, but didn't stop, pulling every morsel of strength from the *Slayer* without remorse.

"Finish him," Jac said. "Suck him dry."

Marco took and took until he was sure he could take no more. He sensed the black heart of Jorge and tasted the *Slayer*'s rage. He felt the *Slayer* trying to turn the direction of the conduit and snapped it with a thrash of his tail. Then he pulled down the rest of the cabinets and books, breathed fire on the wreckage so the flames burned high, and wished himself and Jac out of there.

Ronnie walked around the solarium with Drake, glad to be in a new environment. It was wonderful to be surrounded by the healthy collection of plants, to feel the sun and to listen to the fountain splashing in the pond. The solarium was beautifully designed, like a little oasis or a corner of paradise. When she tired, they sat together on the rocks beside the pool, their hands entwined. Ronnie watched the goldfish in the depths of the pond then Drake brought her hand to his lips.

She looked up to meet his gaze and smiled at the heat in his eyes. It said something for this man's effect on her that he could make her feel desirable when she was six month's pregnant. "Will you tell me about Cassandra? And Theo?"

Drake nodded, tracing a line on her hand with his fingertip. "But first, I will tell you of Cadmus, and of the company that became known as the Dragon's Tooth Warriors."

"Your company," Ronnie guessed. She reached a fingertip to his upper arm, where she'd seen his tattoo of a dragon rampant.

"They were my command," Drake said. His hand rose to cover hers. "This is the mark of the Dragon Legion, and though there are connections between the two, they are not the same. I must begin at the beginning."

"With the Dragon's Tooth Warriors."

"We were an elite corps, specialists in the elimination of a particular type of evil."

When he paused, Ronnie dared to guess, remembering her research. "*Slayers?*"

Drake shook his head. "I am older than that, Veronica. In my time, there were no *Slayers*. There is, however, good and bad in every kind, as they say, and there was evil in dragon shifters even then. We called them worms or vipers. Instead of defending mankind as one of the treasures of the earth, they turned men's thoughts to evil and fostered wickedness in their minds and in their intentions."

"How?"

"With their songs. These were chants, so low that men did not realize they discerned them, and certainly deep enough that the words of the spells they cast were impossible to identify clearly. They feasted upon the malice they created and reveled in the crimes that resulted from their influence."

Ronnie shivered. "I'm not sure they're gone from the world."

He gave her an intent look, but didn't reassure her. "We hunted vipers and we slaughtered them in their dens. We believed that our mission was of great import, greater import than remaining home with our loved ones."

"No one can fault such a noble impulse," Ronnie said.

"But I do fault my failure to realize that each time I left, I might not return." He shook his head. "I never told Cassandra anything of my fears or my hopes. I told her little of my history. I never told my son that I loved him. I was sure he knew."

Ronnie stroked a fingertip over his hand, her understanding dawning. "But one day you didn't come home."

Drake sat back and took a deep breath, and his body language showed Ronnie that he wasn't finding it easy to bare his soul. That he was determined to do it made her admire him more. "Let me tell you of the great worm, Cadmus. He was old and powerful even in my time, and his song had led many men to their doom. He is the bond between you and me, for he was the one who fed the wickedness that led to your husband's death. He was only able to do as much because I—we—failed to kill him, that first time."

Ronnie glanced up, struck by the bleakness of his tone.

Drake didn't blink. "Over two thousand years ago."

"Are *Pyr* immortal?" she whispered and he shook his head.

"We live long, it is true, although my survival for so many centuries is uncommon. You will hear why." He reached up and brushed the silver in his short hair. "It is said that we grow to manhood, then age very slowly until our firestorm sparks. Grey in the hair of a *Pyr* often indicates that he has had a firestorm. There are those who insist that those of us who remain with our mates match our rhythms to those of the lady in question so that we age in harmony from that point forward."

Aging in harmony. Ronnie liked the sound of that. "But how is it that you lived so long after your first firestorm?"

"Cadmus enchanted us and took us out of time. He cast his spell and he snared us." Drake shook his head. "He had the power to add his victims to his own great maw. He defeated us, ensorcelled us, and turned us into teeth."

The Dragon's Tooth Warriors. Ronnie blinked as the meaning became clear to her.

"We were trapped in that form for centuries, unable to affect our own fate and unaware of the passage of time." Drake was making a swirl on his own thigh with his fingertip. "The strange thing is that a tale of such an enchanted army survived in human stories, so these modern *Pyr* guessed what to do with the teeth when they were discovered."

"Like our kinds need each other."

Drake spared her a smile. "Indeed. They planted them in the soil, and we sprang forth like the Spartans in the tale humans tell, an army prepared to fight once more. But by the time the spell was broken and we were released, the world had utterly changed. The foes we had fought before were gone."

"As were Cassandra and Theo," Ronnie guessed, her chest tight with sympathy when Drake nodded.

"Lost to me forever," he agreed softly, then frowned. Ronnie stayed silent, guessing that he still grieved their loss.

She hoped that he could love again, and that his heart hadn't been lost forever with Cassandra. It was odd, because she had believed she would never love again after losing Mark, but she could feel herself losing her heart to Drake.

He leaned down, his voice a low rumble as he continued his tale. "I said that our old foes were all gone when we awakened, but that was not quite true. Cadmus remained alive, spreading his toxin into the world. That viper had dug his way deep into the earth so that even I could not discern his chant. It was when Timmy asked me to find your husband and we followed the scent of Mark that I realized Cadmus was still alive. I gathered my company, we followed the chant, and we did what we always did best. He was old and withered, unprepared for our assault, yet he fought with vigor. He used all the men within earshot to aid his cause, and I lost good men."

"But you killed him."

Drake lifted his gaze to hers. "I did." His voice softened. "It was near his lair that we found Mark."

Ronnie nodded. The details Drake was confiding in her filled in the gaps she'd wondered about, and they made perfect sense. She was honored that he trusted her with such a detailed account, because the *Pyr*, from all she'd read, valued their privacy and their secrets.

He really was trying to change his habits, and he was doing it for her. He offered his hand and they stood together, then walked around the garden again. It was as if he could guess her thoughts and desires, or anticipate them.

As if they built an understanding of each other.

"I could not tell the authorities the truth, and so we arranged for his remains to be delivered to the embassy. I knew that you and Timothy had to know his end and that it had been honorable." Drake took a deep breath. "And that was the first I realized not only the good we could do in the world, but the disservice I had done Cassandra."

"It wasn't your fault that you were enchanted!"

"No, but it was my error to never tell her what was in my heart. I loved her, though we never spoke of such things. I admired her valor and her resolve, her laughter and her practicality. I liked that she believed she could conquer any foe, and I believe she would even have confronted Cadmus, given the choice. She was self-reliant and strong, and it never occurred to me that she was troubled overmuch by my absence. She was glad of my return, of course, and welcomed me, but I wonder now how much I truly knew of her."

"I wish I could have met her."

Drake smiled. "You remind me of her, in a way, but not in others." He studied her as if she were a marvel, although Ronnie felt she was at less than her best. "You are strong, as well, and fearless when something is of import to you. But you are softer, more ready to confess your needs and your desires. It takes tremendous strength to allow vulnerability to show, and I can only learn from your example." His voice turned hoarse. "I find myself enchanted again, Veronica, but by a spell I have no desire to escape."

Ronnie's heart skipped a beat, and then another. Drake surveyed her, as if fearing she would reject him, then bent slowly to kiss her. Ronnie found herself rising to her toes to meet his embrace, yearning for his touch.

It was a sweet kiss but a potent one as well, a kiss as welcome as any touch could be. Ronnie twined her arms around his neck and Drake lifted her closer, gentleness and power in his touch.

"I would build a future with you, Veronica," he confessed when they parted. A smile lifted the corner of his mouth. "I have learned much of building a home from Timothy, but I believe we could do better together."

"I think you're right," Veronica confessed, and Drake kissed her. She found her concerns about his intentions melting away and her own desire for a future with him redoubling.

Could Drake be all she desired in a partner?

Could she have the opportunity to see her every dream come true?

She kissed Drake and hoped with all her heart that this virus could be banished and the promise of the firestorm could be theirs.

CHAPTER TWENTY-ONE

ac figured she was never going to get used to being hurled through space and slammed down somewhere new. It seemed to be a hazard of hanging out with dragon shifters, or with Marco. Good sense decreed that she should just walk away from him as soon as she had the chance, but Jac guessed that the firestorm wasn't going to be easily ignored.

Marco, even without a firestorm, had been hard to forget.

This time, she landed with similar force, but against a softer surface. She opened her eyes after the wind had died to find herself in a hotel room, decorated in shades of tasteful beige. The carpeting was thick and plush beneath her hands, and the sky outside the windows was a brilliant clear blue. They could have been anywhere in the world.

Marco was in his human form, cast against the far wall. There was blood on the thigh of his jeans, in the place where Jorge had ripped away a scale. Jac remembered that injuries were consistent between forms for the dragon shifters. That had been in Sigmund's book. Marco didn't look burned anymore, although he was dirty from all the fighting. Jac supposed she was a mess, too. Marco's eyes were open and he was watching her in that sleepy way that made her crazy.

Sigmund's book was on the floor beside her and looked as if she'd dropped it. It was open, though she couldn't read the text from where she sat. She didn't much care about the book, not when Marco was looking at her as if he'd have her for breakfast. The firestorm's glow lit the room with a golden glow, one that made Jac feel languid and sexy.

"Hi," she said, and her voice was husky.

Marco smiled and gave a quick wave. He lifted one hand to his mouth and took out the Dracontias. He pushed to his feet, then went into the bathroom, returning with a glass and a small bottle of mouthwash from the supplied toiletries. The Dracontias was in the glass and he poured the mouthwash over it, then set the glass on the vanity.

The mouthwash had been minty green but it turned clear.

Marco either didn't notice or didn't care. He ran a hand through his hair and surveyed the room. His eyes narrowed as he glanced out the window, then he went to the desk beside the television. He opened the guest services binder and nodded once.

He glanced over his shoulder. "Know anyone in Virginia?" He named the town where Sam had moved to fight the Seattle virus.

"My sister lives there now. Why?"

Marco indicated the binder, then put it back down. "Welcome to the Holiday Inn." He put his hands on his hips and surveyed the room. "At 3:42 in the afternoon."

"That's an incredible coincidence, that we should end up where Sam is," Jac said. "Did you plan it that way?"

Marco shook his head just as blue-green light flashed around the perimeter of the room. She saw that Marco was watching it as well, and when it disappeared, their gazes met. She had about a million questions, but decided to start with the most obvious.

"So," he mused. "I didn't imagine your effect upon the darkfire." He fixed her with an intent look. "And now it's taking direction from you."

"I didn't direct anything."

"Not consciously maybe."

"Is that how we got here?"

"I didn't choose this place." His eyes twinkled unexpectedly. "If I was going to recover in a hotel and possibly seduce you, I'd choose a more upscale place. Maybe with a great view, like that cabin in Australia." He moved to the window. "We're in a three-star hotel, at best, in a suburban business park." Marco's expression made his view of that clear.

"How can you spontaneously manifest elsewhere? You're not the Wyvern or a *Slayer* who's drunk the Elixir."

"Darkfire," he said, as if that single word answered everything, and headed into the washroom. By the time Jac had scrambled to her feet and followed him, Marco had peeled off his jacket and shirt. He was checking out the burns on his own back in the mirror.

Jac inhaled, knowing she'd never been with a guy who looked so good naked. He was all muscle, tanned and toned, perfectly proportioned with broad shoulders and narrow hips. There was just a little bit of dark hair on his chest, and she caught herself ogling his physique instead of his wounds.

"Your skin doesn't look too bad," Jac said, refraining from suggesting that he drop his jeans so she could do a thorough survey. "I thought you would have worse burns."

"I think I did. You were right about the Dracontias." He gave her a slow smile. "Good thinking."

Jac felt herself blush. "Thanks."

"You're pretty resourceful with this dragon hunting."

"How so?" Jac was fishing and she didn't care.

"The flares were a stroke of brilliance. The candle in Jorge's eye was a good tactical choice, as was milking him for information beforehand. And making me swallow the Dracontias probably saved my life."

"And mine."

"Ah, I knew there had to be a reason." Marco was watching her in the mirror, amusement in his gaze. "Are you just lulling me into complacency so you can finish me off later, when my guard is down?"

Jac frowned. She had a definite sense he was teasing her and couldn't figure out why. "I said I didn't plan to kill you."

"Which isn't quite the same as saying you *won't* kill me."

Jac folded her arms across her chest and studied him. "You're in a really good mood for a man talking about his own demise."

"Am I?"

"You are. What's changed?"

Marco was rummaging in the basket of toiletries on the vanity. He chose a disposable razor and opened a package of soap, then turned on the tap. "Why shouldn't I be in a good mood? I just rescued my mate from peril, was healed by her intervention, and thumped a *Slayer* hard enough that he'll be down and out for a while." He winked at her in the mirror. "Plus I'm enjoying the once-in-a-lifetime opportunity of having a firestorm." He began to shave as she watched.

"I thought I annoyed you."

"And you intrigue me." He wagged the razor at her. "Don't forget that part."

Jac knew her eyes were narrowed in suspicion. "Still, you seem pleased with yourself."

Marco spun and came to her, looking down at her with undeniable pride. His right cheek was still lathered with soap, but the gleam in his eyes and the proximity of his bare chest ensured that Jac couldn't find him anything but impossibly sexy.

"You saved my life," he said softly.

Jac saw where this was going. "Because I had to, in order to save my own life."

"Is that all?" Marco returned to his shaving, apparently not expecting an answer. "Only a *Slayer* who had drunk the Elixir or one of two *Pyr* could have gotten you out of that room."

Jac sat on the vanity. "Two *Pyr?*"

"Me or Rafferty. We're the only ones who can spontaneously manifest elsewhere. For me, it's a darkfire thing. I'm not sure with Rafferty."

"Looks like you were my only shot, since I don't know Rafferty."

"Sure you do. You shot him at Easter Island." Marco spoke with such nonchalance that she knew it was important.

"Is that one of the reasons I tick you off?"

"Oh yeah." He nodded easy acknowledgment, and she saw a familiar glitter in his eyes. "It's a gift."

"You know Rafferty then?"

"He would be the only *Pyr* to whom I owe anything," Marco said. "He was my guardian and my defender. He's the grandson of the *Pyr* who saved my life and hid me from *Slayers*. He awakened me and it's entirely possible that he loves me like a son." Marco met her gaze in the mirror again and his eyes were very dark. "I certainly love him like a father."

Ouch.

"Sorry," Jac said, meaning it. "This whole good-dragon-bad-dragon thing is a bit new to me." Marco didn't say anything. "What happened to him?"

"He's in a coma, near death." Marco's voice hardened. "And

it's my fault."

"But I did it."

"You only had the chance because I underestimated you."

Again, his tone was a clue to his thoughts. He spoke more softly than she might have expected. "How so?"

"You shouldn't have been able to shoot the darkfire crystal. Only one other human has ever done it, and she's a Firedaughter."

"A what?"

"An Elemental Witch. All flames respond to the call of a Firedaughter."

Jac folded her arms across her chest. She was watching the dancing flames of the firestorm on her own skin, enjoying the heat they kindled in her body and the sense of intimacy she felt with Marco. It made her feel alive. Tingly. Filled with temptation and possibility. "I'm not a Firedaughter."

"I know."

"So, how could I fire the crystal?"

"I don't know." Marco had finished shaving. He rinsed his face and wiped it off, running a hand over his chin to check his job. "I'll put that in the intriguing column."

"But the fact that I did it in the annoying column."

"Pretty much. I don't think anyone or anything has ever made me so angry."

Jac swallowed. At least he hadn't slaughtered her for that. Her gaze slid to the Dracontias and hope flared in her heart. "Maybe we can make it right," she said. "We could take the Dracontias to Rafferty. It would heal him."

Marco considered the idea for a long moment, then shook his head. "No. We have to trust the darkfire."

"What does that mean?"

"It brought us here. If Rafferty needed the Dracontias, the darkfire would have taken us to him. He's not in Virginia."

"But my sister is!" Jac said with rising excitement. "And she's looking for a cure for the Seattle virus, the one that Jorge spread."

Marco nodded with satisfaction. "Then the stone is for her. That's why the darkfire brought us here. It's probably the key to finding the antidote that will undo some of the damage."

"Because the *Pyr* defend the treasures of the earth, including humans," Jac recalled from the book.

"Exactly." Marco met her gaze in the mirror, and Jac felt the simmer between them grow hotter. It was impossible not to think about sex.

And the inevitable result of satisfying a firestorm.

"Why would you want me to have your son anyway? I might raise him with a conflicted view of himself."

Marco gave her a hard look. "*Pyr* don't have conflicted views of themselves."

"Your kind might not even survive the year."

"Not if you have anything to say about it, you mean?"

"Well, not necessarily."

He smiled quickly, but not so quickly that Jac didn't see his triumphant expression.

"Jorge could finish you off," she insisted. "Or some other force of nature."

"Which just implies that opportunity shouldn't be wasted."

"We're *not* satisfying the firestorm." Jac didn't feel nearly as certain of that as she hoped she sounded.

"That's your opinion, I know." He was maddeningly, infuriatingly calm.

"You know, I'm not the only one who both irritates and intrigues."

Marco actually laughed. Jac didn't think she'd ever heard him laugh out loud like that before, and she liked it. "Good. It means the darkfire is working for and against us."

"What's that supposed to mean?"

"That darkfire has governed my life and darkfire has its sparks in my firestorm, too. Think about it: you're the least likely candidate to be the destined mate of a *Pyr*. What are the odds of my having a firestorm with the one mortal woman on the planet sworn to wipe my kind from the face of the earth?"

"Pretty long, I'd think."

"More than long. It's completely improbable. It defies expectation and challenges assumptions, both yours and mine." He seemed to find this reassuring.

"Like darkfire does," Jac said and Marco nodded.

"Darkfire pushes and pulls, inverts situations and challenges us to see things in new ways. Like the way you fought Jorge and the *Slayers*. Like the way we both excite and get at each other.

Darkfire is lighting our firestorm and making both of us reconsider what we believe to be true."

"But that doesn't change everything. I'm still not going to have your son."

Marco smiled the smile of a man accepting a challenge. He turned a glittering glance on Jac, one that reminded her of what he was and also what they'd done before, one that dissolved her resistance and put her body on his side. The flames of the firestorm seemed to sizzle with greater heat.

"Which only means that I'm going to have to change your mind," he murmured and Jac knew it wasn't going to be as hard for him to succeed as she might have hoped.

She could be pregnant in moments.

She could be alone with a son on the way in six months, if the *Pyr* faced their final challenge and lost.

Or would he die, too? "Wait. If only *Slayers* survive the final battle, what happens to the sons of the *Pyr*?"

Marco paused. "No one knows. This has never happened before."

"But if the *Pyr* lose..."

Marco was grim. "I'd rather think about us winning."

"But if the *Pyr* lose, any son of a *Pyr* would have to either die, become *Slayer* or become fully human. Which would it be?"

He frowned and stared at the floor, considering. "I don't think it's possible to become *Slayer* without making a conscious choice to do so," was what he finally said.

That still left two crappy options for any surviving child.

At least that was what Jac thought. Marco, however, thought of a third.

"They probably won't have a chance to reach puberty, not if the *Slayers* triumph and eliminate all of us *Pyr*," he said softly. "Slayers like Jorge would hunt down the survivors to ensure there was no chance of them ever becoming *Pyr*, much less trying to avenge the death of their fathers."

"So, I'm supposed to conceive a son who will have a future like that?"

Marco's eyes narrowed. "We're going to win."

Jac wasn't so sure. She panicked and said the first thing that came to mind. "And you *have* to change my mind, right? Because the firestorm has to be satisfied, regardless of what I might think of it all?"

Marco eyed her with new wariness. "What do you mean?"

"I mean that I'm sick of being useful," Jac said, surprised by the heat in her own tone. "I mean that I expected better of a *destined* partnership." She folded her arms across her chest, feeling as if she'd bared her soul to him on a whim. Her voice dropped low. "I mean that when I have a child, I want it to be with a man who loves me for who I am and wants to be partners for the duration. I want that child to be an expression of love, not for me to be a means to an end."

Marco looked away, and Jac feared he'd walk out and leave her behind. She had time to wonder whether she'd said too much.

But Marco nodded with resolve, then faced her, his eyes dark with intent. "Then I have work to do," he murmured, a smile curving his lips. "I'd better get started."

Their gazes locked and the firestorm flared. Jac guessed that between him and the firestorm, she really didn't have a chance.

Brandon didn't like leaving the kids alone any longer than necessary, but Liz was so agitated that this search had to be necessary. He flew her and Chandra back over Marco's path to Uluru, following it by scent.

"No surprise that he was staying at Yulara," Liz said under her breath. "It's pretty much the only place to stay that's close."

"But it is a surprise that he stayed high-end," Brandon said, landing outside the private cottage that was the terminus of Marco's trail. He didn't know Marco well but thought him a *Pyr* disinterested in physical comforts. It was his firestorm, but he couldn't have known of it enough in advance to book this place for this night.

Or had Marco known? Brandon wasn't sure how much the darkfire twisted things around. He felt alert, aware of the mate's presence as well as the lingering heat of their firestorm. His body was remembering his own firestorm.

"Nice," Chandra said and took the stairs two at a time. The door was unlocked and they stopped as one in the small foyer. The cottage was luxuriously appointed and the view of Uluru was amazing.

"Wow, firestorm satisfaction in style," Liz murmured, but Brandon was scanning the cottage for details. Marco and the woman had been intimate, he could smell that, but he could still feel the firestorm's heat. They must have been together *before* it had sparked.

Interesting. Did the darkfire give Marco foresight?

Liz was in the closet. "There's one piece of luggage, and it's tagged for Jacelyn Wilcox." She rummaged through the clothes. "Nothing special here."

"Nor here," Chandra said from the bathroom.

Brandon followed his nose to the far side of the bed. He reached under the mattress and withdrew a notebook. It was redolent of the scent of a human, and he filled his nostrils with her smell as he cracked open the book. The scent was that of Jacelyn, Marco's mate.

Dragon hunter.

The interior pages were filled with pictures of *Pyr* and *Slayers*, printed out from a computer. They were organized with images of any given dragon shifter on the left hand page and notes about him on the right. The book was divided into three sections, although Brandon didn't understand how any *Pyr* ended up where he did. Brandon's scalp prickled when he found his father's image, from the time Brandt had closed the Thames Barrier with Erik and Sloane.

The page for Rafferty noted that he had a bond with Melissa Smith, that he appeared in her broadcasts, that he might live in London or Washington D.C. There was a big red X through the main picture of Rafferty along with a date.

October 20, 2014.

Liz came to look over his shoulder, his silence having drawn her attention. "The day he was shot down," she murmured and Brandon nodded. "Wasn't Marco there?"

Brandon nodded again.

"Melissa said he was shot by a woman," Chandra said, coming to their side.

This woman?

Marco's mate? That didn't ally with anything Brandon knew

to be right. He fanned through the book, finding more images of Erik, his father, Lorenzo, Sloane, Thorolf and Jorge. His anger rose that this woman dared to compile this data on them, to hunt them, to target them, then he turned the last page.

Liz tilted her head to read the verse. "It's a prophecy, like the ones the *Pyr* usually have for firestorms."

"But why does *she* have it?" Chandra asked. "It wouldn't have been given to her."

Brandon had a terrible feeling he knew. "What if it was given to Marco?"

Liz frowned. "Wouldn't he have given it to Erik?"

Chandra inhaled sharply. "Not if Erik's right and Marco is changing sides."

"What if he knew about his firestorm?" Brandon asked softly, then confided what he'd learned. "He was here with her before the firestorm sparked, before the eclipse. It hasn't been satisfied."

"You think she's the one who shot Rafferty?" Chandra asked.

"I'm wondering if they were together even then," Brandon said.

"But Marco brought Rafferty to Sloane," Liz protested.

"Maybe things didn't go exactly as he'd planned," Brandon suggested. "Maybe Rafferty's appearance was a surprise. He is probably closest to Rafferty of all of us." He looked up. "Maybe if it had been another one of us, he wouldn't have intervened."

"You think he's changing sides, too," Liz whispered, looking as dismayed as Brandon felt.

"He told Jorge he wanted the Elixir."

"I still think it could have been a ruse," Liz insisted, though she was less confident than before.

"Either way, we need to get this to Erik," Brandon said and they nodded in agreement.

"Let's scan it and email it to him," Liz said briskly.

Chandra nodded. "We need to stick together and there are too many of us for you to carry." She met Brandon's gaze, anticipating his suggestion. "We should be with the boys, and wait for Thorolf there."

"Erik might want us to stay put," Brandon said, but Liz shook her head.

"The next eclipse will be seen best from North and South

America," she said briskly. "Chandra and I found these eggs, but not quickly enough. Maybe we can find the next batch sooner."

"Are you sure there will be another batch?" Brandon asked, suspecting he knew the answer but hoping to be wrong.

Chandra tapped the verse in the book. "Thirteen monsters," she read, then met his gaze. "So far, I've only counted seven."

"And there's another blood moon in October," Liz said. "The last eclipse of the Dragon's Tail."

She was right. This battle wasn't finished yet.

Veronica was tired, both from her pregnancy and her illness, but Drake was content to simply be in her presence. She seemed to be glad to have him beside her as well, and he savored the opportunity to help her bathe that afternoon. They shared a light meal and then her eyelids drooped again. She refused to go to bed, which Drake took to be either a sign of stubbornness or of improvement—both of which he respected—and laid down on a settee at the far end of the garden. Drake sat opposite her and breathed dragonsmoke, piling it higher and deeper around the greenhouse, around Sloane's home, around the property itself.

Evening fell and the lights in the greenhouse garden came on. There were dozens of them tucked in between the plants, all powered by solar batteries, and they created an intimate golden light. Sloane rapped on the glass barrier and Drake went to speak to him, the pair deciding that Veronica would probably awaken soon and be ready to eat. Sloane was much encouraged by the progress in her condition and gave Drake a thumbs-up.

Drake returned to find Veronica stirring from sleep.

She smiled as he placed a hand upon her forehead. "Cooler yet," he said with a smile, and she stretched luxuriously.

"I feel much better." She glanced around the greenhouse, her eyes shining with pleasure. "It looks like a fairyland."

Drake shrugged, not really understanding the reference. "I find it romantic," he admitted, hoping that was similar, and was relieved when she smiled again.

"So do I." They walked around the gardens again and she used the washroom. Drake went through the airlock to the halfway point to get their meal then lit candles on the table while he waited for Veronica. She had twisted up her hair when she appeared again, and looked so beautiful that his throat tightened.

Drake had to press on with his confessions. He had to ensure that the Great Wyvern's pleasure was won. There was pasta with vegetables and grilled chicken, as well as a salad and sparkling water. Veronica ate with an enthusiasm that reassured Drake.

She pointed at him with her fork. "Don't I get another story?" she teased and he smiled before leaning closer to begin. He knew just the one.

"The first of my men to be freed from the spell was Nikolas of Thebes, a valiant warrior of great honor. I cannot share his tale and the lesson it granted to me without telling you more of our kind. We *Pyr* are all male and we bear sons, always."

"That's how you knew the baby would be a boy," Veronica said. "I learned that in my research."

"But at any given moment, there is one female in our kind. She is called the Wyvern and has the power of prophecy, among other gifts. In our time, she was elusive. We knew of her, but it was considered miraculous indeed to ever see her. I don't know that I ever knew a *Pyr* who had seen the Wyvern, not until I awakened in this era." He gestured broadly. "The Wyvern when the spell upon us was broken was a beauty named Sophie, and she engaged actively in the affairs of the *Pyr*."

Veronica looked up with curiosity. "Why the change?"

"We are engaged in a war, a battle called the Dragon's Tail Wars, a war that will end this October."

"Six months from now?" she demanded. "What kind of war?"

"A war that only we or the *Slayers* will survive."

Veronica put down her fork. "You could all be dead?"

Drake held her gaze, knowing she would not like this part of his truth. "It is prophesied that only *Pyr* or *Slayers* will survive when the moon's node changes to the Dragon's Head. We will triumph or we will die. The Wyvern, I believe, revealed herself in the hope that her influence would turn the tide."

Veronica was clearly dismayed. "I don't like the sound of that."

"Nor do I," Drake said. "I assure you, Veronica, that I do not mean to die so soon as this."

"I wonder what the Wyvern saw in the future," she murmured. "Maybe the view was enough to convince her to become involved."

"It might be so. I have to think that her choices made a difference."

"Why?"

"First a bit more about Nikolas of Thebes." Drake smiled a little and saw that she was encouraged. "Nikolas took one look at Sophie and lost his heart forever. Sophie, I believe, felt the same way, but an amorous bond between the Wyvern and a *Pyr* is unthinkable." He met her gaze. "We mate with humans, not each other. Such a love was not only forbidden, but a violation of everything we know to be true."

"And they knew it?"

"Of course. That is why I believe they chose to sacrifice themselves to save our kind." He swallowed, remembering the sight in Magnus' hidden Academy all too well. "I was there when they chose to die in order to save others. It did not have to be that way."

"But they chose for the greater good." Veronica was guessing, her gaze fixed on Drake.

"They did. I was there when they clutched talons for the last time. I saw the spell that they wove with their devotion and their passion, and I saw them die."

"Did their choice save others?"

"With their sacrifice, they destroyed the Academy, a place of great wickedness where *Pyr* dead and alive were enslaved."

"Another viper," she said and Drake was startled.

"You are right. Magnus was called a *Slayer*, but he had much in common with the vipers and worms I knew."

"And you saw it because you were hunting again." She smiled.

Drake nodded. "It is what I do."

Veronica put down her fork again. "You're using the past tense. Is that part of your life over?"

Drake raised a finger to continue his tale. "Their deaths were tragic, but the remarkable thing to me was that they loved with such vigor that they could not imagine life without each other. I had never seen such a commitment between two beings, and I wished then to feel such passion once in my life." He met her gaze steadily. "When I met you, Veronica, I knew that I could love you with such power that my own survival would be an easy price to pay to ensure your own."

She looked to be astonished, then spoke with quiet heat. "You gave your blood for the antidote," she said, her voice husky. "And you nearly died twice defending me from *Slayers*." She shook her head. "That means you've almost died for me three times, Drake," she whispered then smiled tremulously. "I think you can stop now."

"I will never stop defending you," he vowed and meant it. "I do intend, though, to stop hunting vipers."

Veronica shook her head, her vehemence surprising him. "No, not yet. Spend the next six months exterminating every *Slayer* and viper you can find and make the world a place where there are *Pyr* not *Slayers*." She arched a brow, her mischievous smile making his heart pound. "Then you're all mine."

It was an offer Drake could not refuse.

"There is an agreement to seal with a kiss," he murmured, rising from his place at the table.

Veronica stood to step into his arms, lifting her face for his kiss. "I'm hoping we can do a little better than one kiss," she whispered with a smile that heated his blood, then he kissed her and forgot all in the world but the allure of his mate.

Marco knew from the change in Jac's tone that he'd made a mistake.

There was more than the firestorm between them. In fact, he wondered if it burned hotter because of the attraction that already existed between them. The darkfire's spark was at work, as well. Jac had changed her mind at least a little bit about dragon shifters, because she'd chosen to save him. He'd thought that put him and the firestorm on safe ground, but clearly things weren't resolved yet.

The remarkable thing was how much he cared. Marco didn't remember the first centuries of his life because he'd been enchanted and had slept through most of them. Since being awakened by Rafferty, he felt apart from the world around him. He participated in the battles and he tried to help the *Pyr*, but none of it really touched him.

Until Jac had injured Rafferty. That had infuriated him beyond all expectation. He hadn't known what to do with so much anger and passion. He hadn't been certain whether to kill her or seduce her. It had been almost overwhelming and more than a little confusing.

Had it been the darkfire? The pending firestorm? Or just Jac's influence upon him? Marco didn't know, but he recognized that her disappointment bothered him more than anything any other human had ever said to him. She'd truly awakened him and then she'd helped him to survive Jorge's assault.

He had to make this right.

Jac was standing on the far side of the room, her arms wrapped around herself as she stared out the window. Her body language was far from welcoming, and he felt the rapid pulse of her heart. The firestorm glowed between them, so golden and inviting that Marco knew it was trying to urge him to close the distance.

He sensed that would be the wrong move. He could overwhelm her with his touch, especially with the firestorm on his side, but he wanted her to come willingly to him.

It appeared that he would choose his mate's favor over the firestorm's demand.

Marco had to acknowledge that she'd experienced a lot since meeting him and a great deal since the spark of the eclipse. Was the firestorm changing her as well? If he had to choose between the darkfire and the firestorm, which would he pick?

"Do you want to have a shower?" he asked.

She spared him a glance. "Alone or with assistance?" she asked, and he understood her expectation.

He folded his own arms across his chest and leaned in the doorway of the bathroom. "I'm not going to use the firestorm against you," he said quietly. "If it's satisfied, it'll be because you've decided it should be."

"Why would I decide that?" Jac shrugged. "If you leave it up to logic, there's no reason to go there. That must be why it's such a powerful force, so women *don't* think about it."

"What do you mean?"

"I mean that conceiving and carrying a child is a big

obligation. It's life-changing stuff. It's a path that should be chosen for a better reason than just making more."

"Don't you want kids?"

"I've always wanted kids," she admitted, a yearning in her voice that touched his heart. "But I've never wanted to raise them alone, and I've never wanted a child who felt like an accessory."

"I don't understand."

Jac sighed. She pivoted and marched to the couch, then sat down on the edge of it, facing him. "My sister is goal-oriented. Her life is all about setting objectives and achieving them, so when she got married, I wasn't surprised that they not only had a kid but had a boy."

"Why?" Marco sat on the chair opposite Jac. He echoed her pose, sitting on the edge of the chair, but leaned forward, bracing his elbows on his knees. They were closer this way, which had been his motivation, but when the firestorm flared to new power between them, he saw that Jac thought he was breaking his word. "Sorry." He stood up and paced the floor behind the chair. He grimaced. "I forgot for a minute."

Jac watched him, then nodded, as if she accepted his explanation. "Having the eldest be a boy is a traditional choice, I guess, and satisfies people who still prefer to have a male heir."

"People?"

"My father. Oh, he was really proud of Sam, then." Jac sighed. "But the thing was that kid was like an accessory. He could have been the right kind of car or a house in the right neighborhood. They both continued working as much as ever—which was too much—and I don't even think they noticed how lonely Nathaniel was." She shook her head and Marco saw the glitter of her tears. "Maybe they didn't know how amazing he was."

"Tell me about him."

She smiled then. "Oh, he was totally a science geek. He wanted to be an astronaut and establish colonies in space. I don't know how many space stations we made out of Lego. He'd finish up the one illustrated on the box, then take it apart and make a bigger and better one. He was a sweet, smart, lovable kid." She shrugged. "We bought two sets of sticky fluorescent stars at a museum one time, one for his room and one for my apartment, because he insisted we should always be looking at the same stars at night. He organized them with a map of the solar system, and it took us a whole day to get them just right in both rooms." She sighed. "We celebrated with ice cream sundaes."

"Sounds like you loved him."

"I adored him." Jac shook her head. "I would have chosen to be with him in a heartbeat. But it seemed that it only happened because to them I was *useful*. They were working all the time, after all."

Marco looked down at the carpet. "There's that word useful again."

"That's how my family saw me. *Useful*. Jac doesn't have a plan for her life, so we can use her as a cheap resource." She lifted her gaze to his. "The thing is that none of them ever valued the tasks they expected me to do, so none of them ever saw the value in my doing them. I chose to be with my mom at the end, because I wanted every minute possible with her. It wasn't easy to be her caregiver as she died, and there were times that it just broke my heart to see her slipping away, but there were sweet moments, too. I wouldn't trade those or lose them for the world."

"Tell me one," Marco encouraged.

Jac took a breath, as if composing herself. "Mom loved her garden and had always tended it herself. When she couldn't, I did it. We went outside in the afternoons, when the weather was good, and she told me what to do. She knew that garden and its seasons better than anything else in her world. She remembered the Latin names for every single plant and also the useful traits of the herbs, so we played a game. I'd bring her flowers, one at a time, and she'd tell me about each one. Every day that we were in the garden, we built a little bouquet that way, then I'd put it on her nightstand when we went inside. She always studied it in the evening, whispering the names of the plants. It seemed to both anchor her in the world and distract her from the pain."

She swallowed as Marco watched. "In time, she didn't talk as much and she wasn't as physically capable as she'd been. I had to practically carry her outside, but I knew she loved it so I did." He watched her blink back her tears. "She was pretty light by then. When I brought her flowers, her lips would work but no sound came out. I told her what I remembered of what she'd told me, and she'd nod."

Marco said nothing, but put his hand over Jac's. He had no recollection of having any family, not except a brief memory of Pwyll. He supposed that the *Pyr* were his family and wished he knew them better.

Jac cleared her throat. "Near the end, her favorite rose bloomed. It was June and I knew it would bloom soon, but she was slipping away and I wasn't sure there would be a flower in time for her. There was, although she was in a lot of pain and staying in her bed by then. I put the flower under her nose and she inhaled the scent, then gave me the sweetest smile in the world. She whispered its name. I wrapped its stem in a damp paper towel and wrapped her fingers around it, so she wouldn't have to move to smell its perfume."

She took a shaking breath. "I believe it put her back in her garden, in her mind at least, and that she died in her favorite place in the world. I'll never forget the serenity of her expression or my conviction that her pain was finally gone." Jac cleared her throat. "I couldn't care about much of anything for a long time after that."

"Your family must have appreciated that you were there."

Jac shrugged. "I guess so. The thing is that they didn't think I had anything else to do. Sam had to fly in from grad school and she almost arrived too late to say goodbye. My father had been working like a fiend, as if he had to find a reason not to be home, so even he nearly missed her passing. They were there for the funeral, of course, and my father gave me money for helping out. He sold the house right away and the new owner backhoed the garden to put in a swimming pool." She exhaled. "It's funny, but that's the incident that sticks in my craw, even though it wasn't his fault. I couldn't bear that her garden was gone, and that I didn't even have the chance to dig up that rose. It probably wouldn't have survived a transplant, anyway, it was that old, but still."

"You could plant one of the same variety beside her grave," Marco suggested, more than ready to help with that task.

Jac glanced up at him with surprise. "I did, although I'm the only one who ever goes there." She shook her head. "I'm not even sure my father even knew that I did it. I'm sure Sam doesn't."

Marco leaned on the back of the chair and held her gaze. "Did Nathaniel know?"

Her smile sent a pang through his heart. "Yes. We always went there together and took care of the rose. Mom died before he was born, of course, so I felt like she needed to get to know him a bit."

Marco nodded, understanding her impulse very well even though he'd never had a similar experience. He knew that he had to tell her as much.

He had to share a bit of his past to put them on even footing.

He was surprised by how instinctively right the choice felt, and by how much he wanted to do it.

CHAPTER TWENTY-TWO

 never knew my parents," Marco admitted quietly and felt Jac's heart leap as she watched him. "My father was killed by a *Slayer* right after the consummation of his firestorm. He died without revealing my mother's identity, in order to protect her."

Jac's lips parted in surprise.

"I always thought that said a good thing about his character."

"Was he tormented?"

"Probably. He was killed and incinerated."

She paled. "And your mom?"

"She died in childbirth or shortly thereafter." Marco frowned, knowing the story but not actually remembering it. "I'd been rescued by another *Pyr* who realized what the *Slayer* had done. He knew my father and wanted to help my mother. He managed to get my mother to a sanctuary where she could have me."

"Is there a sanctuary from *Slayers*?"

"There was then, at least for a while. There wasn't any Elixir so they couldn't spontaneously manifest elsewhere. In those days, only the Wyvern could do that. My mother was taken to the lair of another *Pyr*. His name was Pwyll and he was the grandfather of Rafferty, the *Pyr* who saved my mother from the *Slayer*." He fell silent then, thinking of Pwyll.

"The same Rafferty I shot?" Jac whispered.

Marco nodded.

She exhaled. "I'm sorry. Did he die?"

"Not yet."

She winced. "Is he okay?"

"Not yet." Marco didn't actually know Rafferty's state, but he feared it was bad.

They sat in silence for a moment, their hands clasped. "What happened after Pwyll took your mom in?" Jac asked softly.

"She had me." Marco frowned. "Just as all *Pyr* and *Slayers* feel the spark of a firestorm, they sense the birth of a new *Pyr*, no matter where it happens in the world. We say we hear the child's first cry, but really, it's the beat of his heart. We feel it, like he's our son in a way."

"And the *Slayer* felt your birth," Jac whispered.

Marco nodded. "But Pwyll hid me. He tricked the *Slayer* and raised me in secret."

"You must have loved him."

"I did because I owed him that debt, but I didn't know him very well."

"I don't understand."

"Pwyll was the Cantor of our kind. He sang the songs of the earth as well as the hymn of darkfire. He saw that I could only survive if he could *really* hide me."

"Because dragon shifters have such keen senses."

"And so he enchanted me to sleep until it was safe for me to awaken." He swallowed. "I was cursed to sleep until the darkfire burned."

"Hasn't the darkfire always burned?"

"Pwyll trapped it in three crystals. It wasn't until the first crystal was broken and the darkfire released that the spell was broken."

"When was that?"

"December 2010."

"How long were you asleep?"

"Fourteen or fifteen hundred years."

Jac's mouth opened, then it closed. "Is there any way to find out whether Rafferty is going to be all right?"

"Want to come with me and see?"

Jac looked around the room then shook her head. "Wouldn't it be dangerous for us to stay together? Doesn't the heat of the unsatisfied firestorm draw *Pyr* and *Slayers* like moths to the flame?"

"It does, and that's one good argument for satisfying it."

"That didn't make a lot of difference to your mom."

"No, it didn't." Marco straightened. "That's why I want to retrieve the darkfire crystal from Sloane's house and give it to you."

"Who's Sloane?"

"The Apothecary of the *Pyr*. I took Rafferty to him and left the crystal there." Marco squeezed her hand. "You can fire it, so you'll be able to defend yourself."

He could see by the way her eyes lit that the prospect pleased her but she protested anyway. "That has to be against someone's rules."

"It's not against my rules, and when we're talking darkfire, my rules trump all the others."

Jac's smile lit the room. "You're just trying to have your way with me."

"I'm just trying to take care of you the way you've taken care of people in your life. Rafferty believes that the firestorm is an opportunity for us to become stronger, that the Great Wyvern chooses a mate for each *Pyr* who can both compound his strengths and compensate for his weaknesses."

"You can't expect me to seriously believe that dragon shifters have weaknesses."

"I've slept my entire life away. Rafferty awakened me from the spell, but I could have been sleepwalking after that. It's all been like a dream, and I never thought that anything could touch me." Marco pointed a finger at her. "Until you shot him, and then everything changed."

"You said you'd never been so angry."

"I'd never been so alive or engaged. I think that he disturbed my slumber, but that you really woke me up."

"With a kiss?" she asked, a sparkle in her eye again.

Marco smiled, liking that she liked the idea. "Maybe. Anytime you want to confirm your effect on me, you know where I am."

Jac raised her hand and the firestorm flared from her fingertips. A brilliant orange spark leapt from the tip of her hand and soared through the air, landing with a sizzle upon Marco's chest. He caught his breath as the heat of desire raged through his body and felt himself shimmer on the cusp of change. His heart was pounding and he felt Jac's pulse race as well. He closed his eyes as his heart matched its rhythm to hers, the sensation leaving him dizzy. He had never felt so vital or aware of his own body.

And it was because of his mate.

"The way I see it," Marco continued softly. "You'll always take care of everyone else in your life. I'm going to prove myself to you by being the one to take care of you."

"I don't need anyone to take care of me."

"Everyone needs someone to take care of them." Marco nodded. "To watch their back and give them a hand when they need it. I've learned that from the *Pyr*."

Jac considered that, her gaze sliding from his to the window, then to the green stone in the glass of mouthwash. He waited, knowing that the decision of what happened next was hers. She went to the window and dug in her pocket, pulling out her phone as if she'd just remembered it was there. He waited while she checked her messages, guessing that she was stalling while she made her choice, and deliberately didn't eavesdrop.

Marco was surprised when she turned to face him, tears on her cheeks. "What's wrong?" he asked, standing up quickly.

Jac smiled through her tears. "Not wrong but right. Does your darkfire work on humans? Making the improbable happen?"

"I don't understand."

She waved her phone. "My perfect sister is becoming human." She pointed to the stone. "We have to take her that. The darkfire is right."

Marco was glad she agreed about that, but was still waiting for her decision about the firestorm.

She crossed the room abruptly, untucking her shirt and kicking off her boots. "I want a shower," she said with resolve, and Marco thought she was going to ask him to leave. To his surprise, she looked him right in the eye. "If the firestorm draws *Pyr* and *Slayers*, you need to stay to defend me." Jac smiled a little. "I understand what you want, but I'm not convinced I should have a son."

"What would change your mind?" Marco watched her gaze slide over him and saw her catch her breath. His heart was matching the pace of hers again, and with such close proximity, the firestorm was blazing bright enough to steal his breath away.

"I'm playing with fire," Jac said as she flung her shirt aside.

"But I might have to get used to that." She strode toward him, as purposeful as a warrior and as alluring as a princess. "I need to know a lot more before I commit to having your son."

"Fair enough."

"Would you stick around afterward?" she asked, her uncertainty in her eyes.

"Yes," Marco said because he knew it was true. "Rafferty taught me that the firestorm is forever." He raised a hand to her chin and they both inhaled sharply at the firestorm's power. It *was* getting stronger. "Although I never really believed it until I met you."

"You're one persuasive dragon," Jac whispered as she took a step closer. "But I'll never forgive you if you use the firestorm to argue your case." She shook herself and stepped back, clearly against her own desire. "Or if you beguile me."

"Then what do you suggest?"

"Prove your intentions are good," Jac said. She reached out, as if unable to stop herself, and brushed her fingertips over his skin. The assault of the firestorm's sparks made Marco close his eyes against an inferno of desire. "And survive that last eclipse of the moon's node," she said softly. "Then we'll talk."

Marco wasn't sure he could survive this test, but he knew he had to earn his mate's trust. It would either kill him or make him stronger, and he couldn't think of a better way to go.

Jorge was broken, burned and bruised. He'd put all the energy of the Elixir into healing his jaw and after the fight with Marco, he was spent. He changed to salamander form in the ruined library and panted. The room was a disaster, the ceiling fallen in, the books in piles everywhere, fire burning at a dozen points other than in the hearth. There was a lot of dust in the air, but the strange thing was that Jorge couldn't find the half-consumed dead *Slayer* that he knew had to be there. He sought the corpse in as much of a frenzy as he could manage, feeling his power ebb with the effort.

His strength would rebuild and his body would heal, thanks to the residue of Elixir within him, but he knew he'd over-extended himself. It would take time, precious time, time he didn't have.

What he needed was more Elixir, and he wanted it now.

He closed his eyes, stifling the urge to moan, and the taunt came. It was low and fast, slithering into his mind to merge with his own thoughts. It was old-speak uttered by a master, and it definitely caught his attention.

"Thirsty?" The oily voice was familiar in a way that raised Jorge's hackles. How like Boris Vassily — or one of his clones — to kick a *Slayer* when he was down. Jorge snarled instead of replying.

"What you need is some Elixir," Boris continued with a confidence that made Jorge long to tear him limb from limb. *"Lucky for you, I have too much."*

Jorge's head snapped up. His prize had been stolen! That was why he couldn't find the corpse.

"Okhotny Ryad station," Boris said. *"A couple of hundred meters straight up. Surely you can manage that, if the stakes are survival."* He chuckled. *"If not, I'll eat well today."*

Jorge wanted to roar but he saved his strength. He latched on to the *Pyr* scale remaining on his table of hoard, closed his eyes and flung himself in pursuit of Boris.

And his stolen treasure.

Jorge and the clone who called himself Boris IV met in the middle of the three tunnels in the subway station. Both were in dragon form and both were snarling. The half-devoured dead clone was cast on the checkerboard tile of the station floor, his head resting against the system map in the very middle of the area. A black pool of blood had gathered beneath his body, just the sight of it making Jorge want to lick the floor.

But between him and the prize was the other Boris.

Fresh. Uninjured. His eyes glinting with malice and his tail thrashing. His one arm was paler than the other, which revealed his identity to Jorge. It had regrown, though, and healed. Jorge didn't doubt that it was strong.

Because this Boris had taken and eaten the other hatchling from Uluru.

To the left and to the right were the adjacent narrower tunnels, each with a platform for passengers and track for the trains. The entire station was tiled in silvery grey marble, and this central tunnel was illuminated by spherical lights down the middle of the heavily carved ceiling.

Jorge couldn't have cared less about the decor. He roared and flung himself at Boris.

He wanted that corpse.

He needed that blood.

He took Boris by surprise with the vigor of his attack and made the most of his advantage. It would probably be fleeting, after all. He slammed the other *Slayer* hard into the carved ceiling, the force of impact hard enough to break some of the plaster free. The spherical light fixtures swung and the closest one smashed, that light going out.

Boris roared and dug his talons into one of Jorge's eyes. Jorge's grip loosened as he screamed, and Boris kicked him hard in the gut. Jorge felt his strength fading fast. He breathed smoke, desperately trying to latch it onto Boris in time. The *Slayer* slashed through it, ignoring the way the dragonsmoke left his claw smoking, then exhaled a plume of fire on Jorge.

He'd be killed in this subway station, killed like common vermin. Jorge should never have accepted the taunt. He should have let his strength rebuild.

But he wasn't going to die over a miscalculation.

Jorge fell back, pretending to be more hurt than he was, and stumbled into the side tunnel with its empty platform. Once out of the view of his opponent, he made a remarkable recovery. He flew down the length of track and ducked back into the central corridor behind Boris.

Jorge leapt on the dead *Slayer* and managed three greedy bites before the live Boris spun to attack. Boris's claws were raised, but Jorge was sufficiently restored to escape. He couldn't take his prize, unfortunately, but he could get away.

He blew fire at Boris, then launched a serpent of dragonsmoke when the other *Slayer* fell back, his feathers scorched. The dragonsmoke latched on to Boris's tail and Jorge drew deeply on it, needing all the power he could get.

Where would he go? He had no lair, not any more, and there were no other *Slayers* he could trust. The *Pyr* were probably watching all the lairs he'd used recently, so he couldn't risk a return to any of those places.

Not when he had to lie low and recover for a while. Regenerate. He needed a sanctuary and a cover story, a safe haven.

He sucked deeply on the dragonsmoke, savored the surge of stolen power, and eyed its glittering length. It looked like a serpent of frost.

It reminded him of cigarette smoke, in a pizzeria on Easter Island.

Jorge smiled at the inspiration. Boris roared and tore free of the dragonsmoke, then lunged at Jorge. He let himself shimmer blue, changed form to a salamander so he could get as far as possible, and filled his mind with the scent of French cigarettes, Chanel Number Five, and one particular woman.

Sam was packing up her gear. She was just finishing up, and planned to move to Atlanta the next day. There was no reason for her to remain in Virginia now that her patient was gone. The infected nurse remained in the latent phase and had been moved to Atlanta. There wasn't much for Sam to do here, but she didn't look forward to returning to Atlanta.

It would be like the past two years of her life hadn't even happened.

By four, she'd run out of things to do and decided to treat herself to an early dinner. Once she got back to the main labs, she'd probably return to her routine of working all the time. People were still dying. It was up to her to find a cure.

Even if she was infuriated by the intervention of dragons. She really hoped that Veronica Maitland was okay, but wasn't particularly optimistic. A characteristic trajectory would have that woman quite seriously ill by this point. How many more had been infected by now?

Sam was so lost in her thoughts that she didn't even notice the woman leaning against her car until she was reaching for the door handle. "Jac!" she said, jumping a little in her surprise. "What are you doing here?"

"Nice to see you, too," Jac said, her eyes twinkling.

Jac looked good. Happy. Radiant.

In fact, she seemed to be glowing.

"Are you pregnant?" Sam asked, unable to think of another explanation.

Jac laughed as if surprised. "Not yet."

Sam hugged her sister, guessing what had made her sister so happy. Another guy. More great sex. Whether it was a fling or something more permanent, Sam felt an unwelcome stab of jealousy.

It made Sam feel even more alone.

"I called you," she said.

"I know. Awesome message. I thought an alien had stolen my sister again."

"Where were you?"

"You wouldn't believe me if I told you."

Sam surveyed her sister and Jac blushed a bit. "Does he have a name?"

"Marco."

"Just Marco?"

"Just Marco. Marcus, actually, but he prefers to be called Marco."

"Okay. Is he treating you well?"

"Slaying all my dragons," Jac said and Sam froze.

"That's not funny."

"It's not supposed to be. It's true."

"Don't even go there..."

"Don't worry about Marco, Sam. I just had to bring you something."

To Sam's surprise, her sister pressed something cold into her hand. It looked almost like an olive and was pretty much the same color. It was stone, though, and had red lines on its surface. Jac's manner was so expectant that Sam was confused. "Should I know what it is?"

"It's a Dracontias," Jac said, as if that was perfectly obvious. "A stone harvested from the brow of a dying dragon."

Sam had to wonder whether her sister had lost touch with reality. "Be serious."

Jac nodded. "A Dracontias is a stone that medieval people believed would cure anything."

"Okay," Sam said slowly, turning the stone in her hand as she chose a place to begin. "Where'd you get it?"

"From the lost library of Ivan the Terrible. It really is below the Kremlin and I was there and this stone was in the treasury."

Sam blinked. Her sister had been in Russia? Jac looked completely confident of her story, though, and she *was* a lousy liar. "And they just gave it to you?"

Jac shook her head and dropped her voice. "I *stole* it." The way her eyes were sparkling made Sam wonder whether her sister was putting her on.

Sam fingered the stone, at a complete loss for words.

Jac didn't seem to have the same problem. "It's referenced in old manuscripts. It was harvested in the fourteenth century and kept as a treasure by an aristocratic family," she enthused. "There are a couple of ways to use it, but I like this one: you just put it in a glass of any poison and it will turn the liquid into an antidote."

Sam looked at her sister, incredulous.

"It cures, Sam! I've seen it."

"Really."

"Really. It healed Marco."

"From?"

"Extensive burns. We were fighting a dragon and he took the brunt of the dragonfire to defend me." She winced. "He was a mess."

Sam's eyes narrowed. "How did you put this stone *in* a burn?"

Jac grinned. "I put it *in* Marco. Don't worry, we sterilized it afterward."

Sam tried to give the stone back, but Jac closed her fingers over it insistently.

"No, you have to keep it," her sister said. "You have to *use* it to find an antidote to the Seattle virus." Jac squeezed Sam's hand, her enthusiasm clear. "That's the whole point. The Dracontias is the key to your dreams, Sam, and the magical thing is that it came to me, so I could give it to you. Use it to become the great Dr. Wilcox who cured the Seattle virus. Make your mark, just like Dad wanted. The third time will be the charm!"

Sam averted her gaze and composed her argument. As much as she didn't want to hurt Jac's feelings, this was nonsense and she had to say so.

She took a deep breath, then looked her sister in the eye.

"You're kidding me, right? There's no magic, Jac. There are no stones that cure all poisons or create antidotes to *everything*. There is no *alakazam* or *abracadabra* in the real world. We don't do mumbo-jumbo or voodoo at the CDC. We're *scientists*."

"But..."

"The Seattle virus is a biological organism, Jac. It kills people. It's insidious, infectious and constantly mutating. It's also—so far—impossible to stop. It's relentless and it's merciless and I just lost another patient to it this week, which is just about the worst news possible." She thunked the stone back in Jac's hand. "If this is a joke, it's a badly timed one. This isn't funny."

"It's not a joke. Sam! I'm serious."

"Then you shouldn't be," Sam replied. Her sister took a step back, the spark in her eyes fading away.

"You think you know everything, don't you?" Jac asked softly. "But there are lots of things in this world that you don't understand, that none of us understand."

"And there are things I don't want to know."

"You could try!"

"To believe in a magic stone? I don't need to become a joke in my workplace!"

"You're supposed to think outside the box."

Sam nodded at the stone. "This is so far outside the box that it's in another universe."

"It couldn't hurt to try."

To Sam's amazement, she was almost tempted.

Was she losing her mind?

Or just tired?

"It's time to heal, Sam. We agreed on that. It's time to move forward," Jac insisted. "If not now, then when? We're not going to live forever." She grabbed Sam's hand and pushed the stone into her palm again. "If nothing else, Nathaniel's death should have taught you that there are no guarantees that tomorrow will come."

Sam held up the stone between her finger and thumb. "And you're saying I'd be moving forward by indulging your idea about this stone." She couldn't keep her tone from being tart, even though she knew there was truth in Jac's words.

Just not in this stone.

Jac's eyes narrowed. "You'd do that by taking a chance on

being wrong once in a while."

Sam winced at the accuracy of that barb, but Jac had already turned away. "We were getting along okay until you decided to talk about dragons and their magic stones," she said, suddenly feeling even more exhausted than she had before.

"You mean we were getting along okay until I challenged your assumptions," Jac replied. "The problem is that I think it's healthy for everyone to have their world shaken up once in a while, even you."

"What's that supposed to mean?" Sam demanded, but her sister was marching away. Jac didn't even glance back.

No, she was off to Marco, superman lover and dragon fighter.

Sam flung herself into the car, her guts in turmoil, then started the engine. It was only when she fastened her seatbelt that she realized she still had the stone in one hand.

The Dracontias. Sam shook her head. Honestly, the nonsense that Jac came up with. She sounded like a little kid.

Maybe that was what falling in love did to you.

Still, it might be nice to fall in love again, to believe that tomorrow would come and that it would be worth the wait. It had been good to see Jac so happy and excited.

Sam closed her eyes and saw Sloane Forbes, his chest bare, that stupid dragon tattoo on his arm, a smile curving his lips and sensual promise in his eyes. Her mouth went dry. She felt a little hum inside, but she needed more than sexual satisfaction.

She wasn't likely to get either anytime soon.

She eyed the stone. She turned it in her hand.

She wondered what it would hurt to give it a try, to risk being wrong.

Then she shook her head and shoved the stone into her purse, impatient with the very idea. No, there was unconventional thinking and there was insanity, and Sam Wilcox still knew the difference.

Ronnie awakened as the sun was rising, painting the windows in shades of pink and pale orange. It was humid in the greenhouse and lush, several new flowers opening on the red hibiscus bush beside her bed. She was wearing only her pearls. She was entangled with Drake, his body warm and solid against her own, and she felt better than she had in months.

Well, since they'd satisfied the firestorm. They'd loved sweetly and slowly the night before, and though they hadn't had intercourse, Drake had taken care to pleasure her without disturbing the baby. Ronnie had to think that the boy would believe he'd been in an earthquake, and that made her smile

She ran her hand over Drake's bare chest and smiled at him, then traced the dragon on his arm with a fingertip. "And how is the Dragon Legion different from the Dragon's Tooth Warriors?" she asked.

Drake kissed her thoroughly before he answered and tucked the blankets over both of them. Ronnie nestled against him with satisfaction, liking the rumble of his voice beneath her ear. "There is a force known to the *Pyr* as darkfire. It burns blue-green and challenges expectation wherever it appears. I never knew of it in my time, but during the Dragon's Tail Wars, three crystals were revealed, each holding a spark of darkfire snared within it. Two have been broken, loosing the darkfire into the world, but the one granted to me remains intact. Its spark, however, died."

"Why?"

"Because its power was expended. The Dragon's Tooth Warriors were beckoned by the gem and I claimed it, as it commanded me to do. Once I held it in my possession, each time the darkfire brightened in the stone, my company was cast through time and space. At each place, at least one of our members would be left behind."

"How horrible!"

"It was a wearisome journey and an ordeal, and when it was done, I alone was returned to this time with the stone, and its heart had gone dark. I thought I had lost my entire company and I was certain that my solitude was a mark of failure of the worst kind."

Ronnie stretched up and kissed his cheek.

"We had suspected on the journey that some of the men were being taken to the time and place of their firestorms. It subsequently turned out that all of the men in my company were taken to their mates. Because we had been enchanted for so long, I suppose we had missed our opportunities, and the darkfire made it come right."

"Oh! That's a wonderful story."

"More than that," Drake said with satisfaction. "They had their firestorms."

Ronnie felt her mouth fall open. "They had *sons*."

"And their sons had sons. Because of our travel through time, history was changed. Suddenly there were generations and generations of *Pyr* that had not existed before our departure. They all have this tattoo. I was urged to get one in honor of my role in their creation."

"The quest you thought a failure was a tremendous success."

"We have a better chance in the Dragon's Tail Wars because of our mission and the darkfire crystal. The men I asked to guard Timothy are of the Dragon Legion. Their leader is named Theo."

"Just like your son."

"He is descended from my son, so he is both comrade and blood kin."

"But you weren't taken back to Cassandra," Ronnie said, wondering whether Drake regretted this situation.

He gazed down at her with a satisfaction that made her heart thunder. "No. I was brought to my own firestorm that I might fulfill the promise of the future." They kissed again, lingeringly, and Ronnie knew her last doubt was banished. She was breathless when Drake lifted his head, the glow in his eyes making her want to preen.

"You must eat to build your strength," he murmured, stealing kisses between his words. "And today, Sloane will wish to check upon our son."

"No more stories?" she teased and Drake grinned.

"One more," he said. "You will tell me of these pearls." He kissed her temple. "There is a reason you do not take them off."

"They were my grandmother's and are the only thing I have from her."

"Except your memories."

Ronnie smiled. "She was wonderful, both practical and elegant. She made everything look easy and did it with style."

"Ah, so you have much in common with her," Drake murmured, rolling over to kiss Ronnie again.

"We agreed about Mark, if nothing else," she admitted without having meant to do so. He froze and considered her, his expression confused. "My parents didn't want me to marry Mark." She forced a smile. "They thought I'd be unhappy as a military wife and that I could marry better."

He studied her solemnly. "But you followed your heart."

"And they disinherited me." She shrugged, trying to hide the sting of that memory even though Drake's avid gaze made her feel that he could read her thoughts. "My grandmother died shortly after we were married, but she was the only family member from my side who attended the service. She gave me these pearls that day, along with her blessing." Ronnie's fingers found the pearls and held fast to them. "It was all I needed, and so much more."

Drake might have said something, but he lifted his head and stared at the glass partition that divided the house. His eyes narrowed as Ronnie watched and she saw him inhale deeply. She couldn't hear anything, but she already understood that he perceived more than she did. "What do you hear?"

"An intruder," he murmured, then got smoothly to his feet. There was a blue shimmer around his body, like an aura of light, and Ronnie felt that something bad was going to happen.

How could there be an intruder in a dragon shifter's home? Who would dare?

Someone knocked on the door of Maeve O'Neill's Manhattan brownstone. Her home was located on the Upper East Side, on a fashionable but quiet street. The hour was late, but the knock was demanding. Expectant. Maeve frowned. She wasn't expecting any guests much less any appeals for her assistance.

Of course, the most interesting requests were the unanticipated ones. They came from those individuals with the most to lose. Maeve's curiosity pricked.

The visitor knocked again, harder and longer.

Maeve went to the window. There was no car or taxi in the street, no one walking by, no fading taillights. From this window, she couldn't see her front step, although clearly someone stood there.

Fortunately, Maeve had other resources at her disposal. She

turned her wrist, conjuring a sphere of light in the palm of her left hand. It was like a glass snowball, albeit with a more golden light, and might have been a living model of her front step. She peered into it, studying the scene.

A man stood before her door, impatience in every line of his body.

He was tall and blond, as fit as a commando. His hands were propped on his hips and he was glaring at the door as if she defied his will by not opening it. How could he be so sure she was home? He rose his hand to knock again just as Maeve recognized him.

The dragon hunter from Easter Island.

The one who wasn't human. Maeve hadn't been sure initially just what or who he was, but she'd have bet her last spell even at the outset that he wasn't human. During their conversation, she'd realized that he was a dragon shifter, another half-breed, and had cast some amorous vibes his way, just to entertain herself.

Evidently one of them had belatedly taken root. There was little more satisfying than encouraging a love spell and snapping it tight. Maeve liked when men capitulated to her and were snared by her wiles.

How like a dragon to wait for his moment. Their patience was legendary, as was their romantic prowess. This one was tasty and likely had good stamina. As much as she despised both *Pyr* and *Slayers* for their nature, she'd been content to let them take each other out in their private war. She eyed the dragon shifter on her doorstep and wondered whether this might be a good moment to intervene.

He was the last *Slayer*, unless she missed her guess, and he was wounded. Those *Slayers* hatching from eggs seemed fixed on eliminating the *Pyr*, and she was sure she hadn't seen the last of them. Let the *Pyr* battle the hatchlings.

By taking down this *Slayer*, she could tip the balance in favor of eliminating them all.

The world would be contaminated by one less half-breed species.

And she hadn't had a dragon in a good long while.

It was hours until morning anyway and she never slept. She liked the idea of changing the odds in one night, putting the pieces in motion to make the world as it should be, according to her.

Maeve tugged on a silk robe and put on a pair of satin mules. She wasn't wearing anything else—other than her perfume—and her ebony hair hung loose over her shoulders. She took her time descending the stairs, ensuring that her heels clicked loudly on the marble floor. He'd hear them, she was sure. She drew another deep breath in the foyer, nodding to herself as she verified her impressions. He had a whiff of immortality about him, contrary to her expectations.

Which only made him more interesting.

Indeed, she was all a-tingle at the possibilities.

Maeve opened the door, forgetting that a human woman would have been more cautious in a big city in the middle of the night. His blue eyes narrowed and she knew he'd noticed her mistake. She exhaled, sending an aura of desire his way and saw him forget his observation. It was almost too easy.

His gaze flicked over her, and his throat worked. "Maeve, I need your help." His voice was tight, and Maeve guessed he hadn't asked for help in a very long time.

Desperation suited him.

Or maybe it just suited her. "How did you find me?"

"You gave me your address. When we met at that little restaurant."

Maeve smiled. "I never give anyone my address. A woman can't be too careful in these times."

He held her gaze, so confident that she wondered whether he had forgotten her oversight. Or had he guessed something about *her* nature? She found herself even more intrigued—and excited by the prospect of a challenge.

"You must have," he insisted. "How else could I have found you?"

Maeve leaned in the doorframe. "Maybe you have superhuman powers," she suggested, letting her voice turn sultry.

He smiled then, casting a glance down the street before he leaned against the door frame, too. His face was just inches from hers.

She saw the glitter in his eyes and it confirmed his nature. She hadn't had dragon in a while. She let her smile widen.

"Maybe you'd like to find out for sure," he said, his voice lower and his eyes warmer.

"An offer I can't refuse?"

"An opportunity you'd be crazy to miss." Again, his gaze swept over her, but this time, it lingered on the curve of her breast, the indent of her waist, the arch of her foot. When he met her gaze again, his own eyes were blazing with a desire that made Maeve lick her lips. "You may be many things, Maeve O'Neill, but I doubt you're crazy."

He smiled hungrily and reached into his shirt. Maeve felt her eyes narrow, but he pulled out a large dark disk.

Actually, it was a dragon scale. She wondered whether it was one of his own, whether he was going to make some sappy claim that he'd lost it due to his love for her, but the way he looked at it made her suspect otherwise. It was a prize to him. A trophy. The scale was as dark as a black pearl, and its surface was slightly opalescent. It had thorns on the lower edge and somehow gave the impression of being very primitive.

"Is that what I think it is?" she asked.

"A dragon scale," Jorge said. "This one's old."

"Where did you get it?"

"From the *Pyr* who grew it." A nasty glint lit his eyes. "Let's see if he's paying attention."

"I don't understand."

"It's an old spell. I learned it from another dragon hunter. It should cause excruciating pain to the *Pyr* who lost this scale, if it works."

"Anything that weakens the *Pyr* is fine by me."

Jorge smiled. "I knew we had something in common."

"More than good looks, you mean?" Maeve flirted a little, satisfied when his gaze heated even more.

"More than that," he murmured, again making her wonder how much of her truth he saw. "Much more than that." He claimed her mouth in a hungry kiss, one that made Maeve's heart leap with the possibilities. All too soon, he ended the embrace, holding the scale between them. "First things first," he murmured. Jorge's mouth drew to a thin line as he cracked the scale in half.

Maeve heard the other dragon's scream of pain. It was distant but distinct. Despite her determination to hide her nature—and her skill at doing so—she was sufficiently surprised that her eyes widened.

And Jorge noticed. His smile was predatory. "You heard it, too," he murmured, then broke the scale again and again, and Maeve liked the glee in his expression. He was destructive, vengeful, vicious, heartless.

They did have more in common than good looks.

What if she showed him her truth? Would it drive him mad?

Or capture his heart? Maeve smiled at the prospect of giving this *Slayer* a similar weakness to his victim. She tried to veil her excitement, reminding herself that he was watching her closely and that his senses were keen.

"You're sensitive, then," Jorge said. "Maybe sensitive enough to be a dragon slayer yourself."

"I don't like to get my hands dirty."

"Trust me—I'd do all the dirty work for you."

"We could make quite a team," Maeve replied, letting Jorge make his own assumptions before she grabbed his collar and hauled him into her foyer. She slammed the door and turned the deadbolt, then pushed him into the wall. He smiled down at her, so clearly satisfied with his victory that Maeve wondered how she'd ever doubted his nature.

There was something dragon-like in that smile, to be sure.

She wondered how many times he'd manage, and how rapid the succession. She couldn't wait to find out.

"Good thing I don't like shy women," he said and Maeve laughed.

"I've never had any interest in being a demure maiden."

"And I've never found such women interesting." He looked at her again, and she thought she saw his nostrils flare.

This was fun. Why exactly *hadn't* she indulged in dragon in recent centuries?

"Jorge, wasn't it?"

"Jorge." He nodded.

"So, how do you see this partnership working, Jorge?" she murmured, leaning against him as she kissed his ear. He didn't need to know that she knew his real nature.

He made a growl deep in his throat and his hands locked around her waist. He grazed her throat with his teeth, a move that was both erotic and dangerous, given his nature. Maeve shivered at the deliciousness of it all, then Jorge whispered in her ear. "First, I need a little break from the dirty business of hunting the *Pyr*." He pulled back slightly. "Some R&R."

"And what constitutes rest and relaxation for a dragon slayer?"

Jorge's smile was immediate and hungry, the look in his eyes answering Maeve's question more clearly than words ever could. She locked her hands around his head, pulling him closer as he bent to kiss her, and savored how he nearly devoured her mouth in his passion. He definitely had promise with such passion as this, if not a polished technique.

Maeve would have her fill of him before she orchestrated his destruction.

She had to wonder whether Jorge would even realize his mistake. He certainly wouldn't be able to correct it in time. He was in her lair already.

His fate was sealed.

CHAPTER TWENTY-THREE

 arco left Jac alone reluctantly and went to collect the only thing that could protect her. He manifested in Sloane's home, right beside the opal and gold dragon in the great room. The house was hushed and he knew that it was early in the morning. He heard humans sleeping and *Pyr* breathing smoke and refused to count how many were in residence. He heard the murmur of low conversation coming from a room ahead, the talkers out of sight and apparently behind a glass partition. None of it was important.

The only thing that mattered here was Rafferty's state. That *Pyr* was sleeping deeply, and the darkfire crystal was clutched in his golden talons. When Marco narrowed his eyes, he could just barely discern a crackle of darkfire deep in the stone.

He quickly considered his options. Was the stone keeping Rafferty alive? If so, what right did he have to take it? Would that condemn his oldest friend and the *Pyr* to whom he owed the most? Marco didn't want to even think about causing further injury to this dragon who had done nothing to deserve it.

On the other hand, Jac needed to be able to defend herself. As long as the firestorm burned, it would blaze when Marco was near her and attract the attention of *Pyr* and *Slayers*. If he stayed away from her to dampen the flames, he wouldn't be able to defend her himself. He also knew that by giving her this gift, by empowering her at the same time that he acknowledged her ability to take care of herself, he'd bring the firestorm closer to fruition.

Marco had a feeling he could guess what Rafferty would say. This *Pyr* had always been the one to argue in favor of the firestorm. Marco had to hope that if he chose the firestorm, the darkfire would defend his back and see to Rafferty's survival.

He had to trust the darkfire, as completely as he once had.

He wished he could ask Rafferty for advice, but any other *Pyr* within proximity would hear his old-speak, never mind anything spoken aloud. He had to think that Rafferty wouldn't reply, or would answer enigmatically, compelling Marco to make the choice in his own heart.

He mouthed a request for Pwyll to forgive him, then reached for the darkfire crystal. As soon as his fingers touched it, the darkfire flashed, the brilliant blue-green light erupting between his fingers. Marco closed his eyes against the light and felt the air move. When he opened his eyes, Rafferty had shifted to his salamander form. His eyes were open and he was watching Marco, as if to encourage him to act.

To act in favor of the firestorm.

The darkfire was supporting his choice and so was Rafferty. Marco lifted Rafferty with care and tucked the opal and gold salamander into his shirt pocket. He felt the slight weight settle into the bottom of his pocket, and the pressure of Rafferty resting against his heart. He thought he heard the *Pyr* sigh with contentment.

He knew he heard Rafferty murmur in old-speak. *"The firestorm."*

The darkfire flashed. Marco stood and chose to return to Jac.

He heard a slight sound just as the darkfire surrounded him and spun to find Melissa watching him from the doorway, her hands raised to her mouth. She opened her mouth to scream, but Marco was gone by the time the sound passed her lips.

Sloane was in his lab when he felt the prickle of another *Pyr*'s arrival in his home. He didn't rush to find out who it was, because the last thing he needed was another guest.

Especially a wounded one.

His sense of triumph had faded, only to be replaced by the sense that he was, once more, falling short. Rafferty had stabilized, but hadn't healed. He hadn't even opened his eyes, although at least the darkfire had moved back into the crystal. Veronica had improved, but the virus—as far as Sloane could tell—had returned to the latent phase. He'd hoped to eradicate it completely from her system, but his antidote had failed to do that. He wished he had Sam's expertise or her assistance, but that would mean telling her the truth of his nature and he could guess how she'd respond to that.

Quinn and Sara had taken the boys to town earlier in the day to do some shopping. There was nothing like a houseful of dragons—almost two housefuls, actually—to clean out provisions. Sloane was glad that Lee was running the store. Eileen and Lee were taking turns with the cooking, too. Erik was pacing troughs in the floor of the house, sufficiently recovered that Sloane wished he'd go back to Chicago. Thorolf hadn't lingered when he'd brought the Boris Vassily clone, but Sloane hadn't had time to do much more than stuff the body into a refrigerator with a lock.

And hope for the best. It was only a matter of time until the *Slayer* regained his strength sufficiently to manifest outside the fridge. The Elixir would work steadily, although the *Slayer*'s healing would be slowed by the cold. Thorolf had said that the *Slayer*'s gut had been blown open in the battle, but even in the course of the flight to California, that wound had closed.

Sloane felt the need for time he didn't have. He should be testing the *Slayer*, exploring his nature, but trying to cure Ronnie was taking all his time.

Because the antidote hadn't worked as well as he'd planned. Sloane reviewed all his research and his tests, repeating many of them in the lab, seeking the detail he'd missed. He wasn't finding it, but exhaustion didn't help.

There had been a firestorm sparked in Australia, and Erik was growling about new videos of the dragonfight appearing online. Sloane couldn't have cared less. Melissa had plenty to say about her competition, that reporter Maeve O'Neill, the one determined to paint dragons in a bad light. Sloane wasn't quite at the point of agreeing with her, but he was less enamored of his fellows in this moment than was usually the case.

He wanted Sam, but she was gone.

He had no right to want her, not when she wasn't his mate.

He'd ground his teeth in frustration just as Melissa screamed from the great room. Sloane swore, abandoning his test in a fury. It was impossible to achieve anything under such conditions! He raged through the containment barriers, wanting his house back.

"He abducted Rafferty!" Erik roared.

Sloane took a breath as he strode into the great room and discerned Marco's scent, then guessed what had happened. The dragonsmoke barrier around the house hadn't been disturbed and for the first time in a while, there was no blue-green glimmer of darkfire. The crystal was gone, as well as Rafferty.

"It was Marco," Melissa said. She was standing where Rafferty had been and Isabelle was hugging her tightly. "I saw him. He was standing right here, and he reached for the crystal. As soon as he touched it, Rafferty changed to a salamander. Marco took both and disappeared."

Sloane took another deep breath, discerning a heat in the residue from Marco's appearance. "It *is* his firestorm."

"And he hasn't satisfied it," Erik snapped. He paced the room with agitation, then flung out a hand. "His mate wasn't with him, which means he's left her undefended when there are *Slayers* on the hunt! Maybe he can't satisfy it because he's turned *Slayer*."

"Wouldn't the firestorm extinguish itself then?" Sloane asked.

"I don't know!" Erik said and paced in his frustration.

"Jorge might have her," Eileen said. "The video showed both of them being snatched by Jorge."

Erik grimaced at that. "The notion that he's free of Jorge but left her trapped isn't very reassuring." He ran a hand over his hair. "He asked for the Elixir in old-speak."

"He could have erred," Drake contributed in old-speak, evidence that he was listening, as well. The *Pyr* exchanged glances, and Sloane knew that Drake wouldn't welcome any discussion of mates kept captive by Jorge.

"Why would Marco take the crystal?" Erik demanded of no one in particular.

"Maybe he knows more than we do," Sloane said. "Maybe he needed the crystal as much as Rafferty did."

Erik grimaced. "I'm having a hard time believing in his good will."

"Because you didn't see him that day," Sloane retorted. "Marco was devastated that Rafferty had been injured. I'm glad he isn't denying the darkfire any longer."

"Even though his mate is the one who injured Rafferty?" Melissa asked.

"What's this?" Sloane asked, and saw that the features of the others were set.

"Brandon emailed pictures of the notebook they found in the mate's hotel room," Eileen contributed. Erik went to his computer and pulled up the files, then displayed them on the large television screen on the wall.

Sloane felt cold at the pictures of *Pyr* in action, clearly taken from different videos. They were organized into pages, with images of the same *Pyr* grouped together, and notes made alongside. His heart leapt at the sight of his own page.

Then it stopped cold at the red X through Rafferty's image.

"She's a dragon hunter," Erik said with quiet heat. "It's happening again, just the way it did before. People are turning on us. Humans shouldn't be able to defeat us, but with one of our own helping a dragon hunter, there's no telling what she can accomplish. Thorolf said *she* took down that *Slayer* in your fridge, with a road flare." He sighed. "We can't risk her survival."

Sloane was horrified by the suggestion. "Wait a minute! Humans are the treasures of the earth! We can't hunt one down, especially one who's the mate of a *Pyr*."

"We don't know that Marco will stay *Pyr*."

"We don't know that any of us will stay *Pyr*, although we hope as much," Sloane argued.

"He's having a firestorm," Quinn pointed out. "*Slayers* don't have them."

"That only means he hadn't turned *Slayer* when the firestorm sparked," Erik said. "I don't think we can make any assumptions."

Sloane shook his head. "I'm not abandoning my trust in the firestorm."

"It's not the firestorm I distrust," Erik argued. "It's Marco. The darkfire is known to invert everything. Why couldn't it invert the goodness of the firestorm?"

"I don't believe it," Sloane said, seeing that Quinn's eyes had narrowed in consideration of this idea. "The firestorm heals. I won't accept that it could ever wound."

"Could the darkfire change the rules so that *Slayers* could have a firestorm?" Quinn asked.

Sloane shook his head, but Erik seemed to be considering the possibility. "There's no way to be sure," Erik said, then frowned. "I must ask you all to abandon Marco's firestorm, at least until we know his intentions toward the rest of us."

"You're kidding me," Sloane protested. "He's *Pyr*! He's having a firestorm!"

"He injured Rafferty. His mate aspires to kill dragons. Marco abducted Rafferty. He stole the darkfire crystal," Erik retorted. "Until we know we can trust him, we don't dare go to his firestorm."

"He might use its power as a lure," Quinn said, doubt in his tone.

Sloane shook his head, incredulous that his fellows could even doubt the power of the firestorm that much. "Rafferty might have chosen to go with him," he suggested. "You know how he feels about firestorms."

Melissa bit her lip but Erik flipped through the images of the mate's book, ignoring Sloane's words. "There was a prophecy in her notebook, as well."

"Is it legitimate?" Eileen asked.

"That depends upon its source," Erik said.

Sara stepped forward and read the verse aloud when it was displayed on the screen.

> *"Three blood moons mark the debt come due*
> *Will the* Pyr *triumph or be hunted anew?*
> *Three eclipses will awaken the spark*
> *In thirteen monsters breeding in dark.*
> *Three times the firestorm will spark*
> *Before darkfire fades into the dark.*
> *Firestorm, mate or blood sacrifice*
> *None or all can be the darkfire's price.*
> *When the Dragon's Tail has turned its bore*
> *And darkfire dies forevermore*
> *Will the* Pyr *be left to rule with might*
> *Or disappear into past's twilight?"*

"It certainly sounds like a *Pyr* prophecy," she said.

"But where would she have gotten it?" Quinn asked.

"Maybe she's a Seer, too," Sara said.

"No." Erik shook his head. "It must be fake or stolen."

"Marco could have given it to her to help in the hunt," Melissa said.

Sloane ignored the skepticism of his guests and read the verse again, seeking meaning in its cryptic words. "There must be thirteen of these *Slayers* who look like Boris in total," he said. "Which leaves six more to be hatched on the third eclipse."

"Wherever it's going to be," Eileen said.

"The darkfire's going to be extinguished," Sloane said. "But it has a price first."

"Firestorm, mate or blood sacrifice," Drake repeated from the other room. He continued in old-speak, probably to project his words farther. *"It could be said that the mate was the price in my firestorm."*

So, Drake knew that Ronnie's cure wasn't complete. Sloane closed his eyes in relief, glad he didn't have to tell Drake that truth. He could hear the undercurrent of despair in Drake's tone, though, and his determination to save Ronnie redoubled.

"Was Rafferty supposed to be the blood sacrifice?" Melissa asked in a small voice and Eileen took her hand.

"Maybe Marco is sacrificing his firestorm," Sara said.

"Given the options, it might be tempting to try," Quinn said.

"There's nothing saying the blood sacrifice has to be the *Pyr* or mate in question," Erik said firmly. "I don't think we should trust Marco or his mate until he provides an accounting of his choices. We need to find Rafferty before it's too late. I'll have Donovan help us to hunt down Marco, wherever he's gone..."

"I think we have to trust Marco," Sloane interjected. "I think that the darkfire is testing us."

Erik pivoted slowly to face him, his opinion of Sloane's dissent clear. "I am the leader of the *Pyr*," he said softly.

"And I am the Apothecary. I'm starting to think it's my task to heal the world, and you're not helping."

"Trusting Marco could be dangerous!"

"Not trusting him could be more so." Sloane gestured to his fellows. "Maybe this lack of faith in what we should know to be true is what will shape the future of the *Pyr*. Maybe we need to heal our own doubts to save our kind."

"Maybe the darkfire is twisting your thoughts," Erik countered.

Was the darkfire causing dissent between the *Pyr*? Was his desire to challenge Erik another manifestation of that unpredictable force? Or was the darkfire demanding that Sloane discard his preconceptions to fulfill his destined role? Sloane knew with sudden conviction what he had to do.

"Then we agree to disagree," Erik said quietly. His eyes were glittering with determination, but Sloane was sure he was wrong.

"We're going to disagree more," Sloane said, his decision made. "I need help to complete Ronnie's cure."

"We're all willing to assist however we can," Erik began, but Sloane shook his head.

"I need a scientist to help me, someone who knows more about human physiology and immune systems than I do." He held Erik's gaze. "I know the exact one, but soliciting her help means revealing the truth of my nature to her."

Erik inhaled sharply. "You have sworn the Covenant and I forbid..."

"I will reveal myself, and per the terms of the Covenant, I'm informing you of my intention," Sloane said with resolve.

Erik was hovering on the cusp of change, his displeasure clear. "You will *not* betray the rest of us."

Sloane shook his head. "No, not if you leave." He shrugged, not flinching from Erik's reaction. "If you're here when she arrives and she sees you, you'll be revealing yourself."

There was a long silence, as Sloane and Erik stared unblinkingly at each other. The air was charged with tension, then Quinn took a minute step toward Erik.

"I will remain," Drake said. "My future is bonded to that of the Apothecary."

"We'll head north in the morning," Quinn said. "It's time for the boys to be home again."

"Lorenzo has requested my counsel," Erik said stiffly. "We, too, will leave in the morning."

And it was done. The price would be higher than their departure and Sloane knew it. He didn't doubt that it would take him time to regain Erik's trust. On the other hand, he was encouraged that his home would be his own again. Not much had changed, but his mood was vastly better.

Because he'd see Sam soon. He could only hope she accepted his invitation and could then accept his nature.

Sloane had a definite sense the darkfire was on his side.

He didn't know how to contact Sam, except through her lawyer, but fortunately he had other resources at the tips of his talons.

He was pulling out his phone when Drake bellowed in pain.

Jac went back to Seattle and her empty apartment, for lack of any better choices. She figured there was no reason to hide—in fact, it probably wasn't even possible to hide from *Slayers* during the firestorm. There was a faint sensation of heat at the ends of her fingertips, even though Marco wasn't in the vicinity, and Jac was pretty sure that *Slayers* and *Pyr* would be even more keenly aware of it than she was.

It wasn't the most reassuring feeling in the world.

She was angry with Sam, too, although in hindsight, she shouldn't have expected anything different. Sam never wanted to take a chance on looking foolish, much less on being wrong. Jac wished a little too late that she'd kept the Dracontias.

What was going to happen now?

She went through Sigmund's book again, but couldn't find anything about *not* satisfying the firestorm. Surrendering to its power didn't seem to be optional, and Jac could understand that. It was an overwhelming power in itself, and a *Pyr* with the firestorm on his side in a seductive mood might not be possible to resist. Jac knew she was only thinking straight because Marco was at a distance.

She wondered where he'd gone and what he was going to do. She had no doubt he'd be back. She guessed that he was doing something that he believed would convince her to satisfy the firestorm. As much as she appreciated that he wasn't using physical sensation to undermine her decision, she missed him and his presence.

It seemed the firestorm could do its work even without a *Pyr* in the vicinity.

As she always did when faced with a decision, Jac made a chart. The first column was satisfying the firestorm, and she divided it in two. In the plus section, she noted that she'd know how it felt, and that there would probably be tremendous pleasure. In the negative section, she noted that she would conceive Marco's son according to the *Pyr*'s stories and that son would become a dragon shifter at puberty. She added to the positive part Marco's resolve to stay with her after the firestorm was satisfied, then added to the negative part that his kind might be exterminated in six months.

If the *Pyr* lost the war, then the *Slayers* would be the survivors. Jac added an item to the negative section that she'd be carrying a *Pyr* son in a world with only *Slayers*. She wondered how that would work: would her son be simply human, or would *Slayers* destroy him before he had a chance to grow up? She suspected the second option, and knew that she'd let herself be killed in her child's defense.

She thought of Sam and didn't want to have that kind of loss in common with her sister.

The second column was not surrendering to the firestorm. Some of the entries were easy, because they were the opposite of the ones in the first column. She wouldn't conceive a son who was *Pyr*. She wouldn't face the possibility of being left alone to defend herself and that son against *Slayers*. She wouldn't know the pleasure of the firestorm.

Jac considered the list and added a negative to the second column. It might not even be possible to resist the firestorm forever. Would it burn until the next eclipse, or for the rest of her life? Or for the rest of Marco's life? Jac didn't know.

She put her list on the fridge with some magnets and kept circling back to it. In an ideal universe, she would have denied the firestorm until the eclipse in September, until she knew for sure whether Marco and the *Pyr* would triumph and survive. Then, maybe, if she came to know and trust him, maybe even to love him, she'd agree to satisfy the firestorm.

The problem was that Jac had never been good at resisting temptation, and six months was a long time. If Marco was near her, the firestorm would feed her desire and practically drive her crazy with need. She didn't even know where he was and she couldn't sleep. If he stayed away from her, he couldn't defend her from *Slayers*, which was far from ideal. In terms of her personal security, satisfying the firestorm might make the most sense.

But the baby. Jac couldn't willingly conceive a son who might not ever know his father.

Never mind one destined to die young at the talons of *Slayers* if his father was gone.

It was two days after Jac made her list that she had an idea. She was in bed, on her back, staring at the star stickers she'd brought from Atlanta and put on the ceiling here. A couple of them were dangling from a point or two, their adhesive having been compromised in the move. Sigmund's book was on her belly.

Sigmund said that the firestorm's heat drew *Pyr* and *Slayers* like moths to the flame. What if she and Marco used the firestorm to change the prospects of the *Pyr*'s victory? What if they deliberately attracted *Slayers*, so Marco could take them out? What if they created the future Jac wanted for their son?

She gasped at the perfection of the idea and sat straight up in bed, just as golden heat suffused her body. She caught her breath as sparks emanated from her skin and nearly moaned at her need for Marco's touch. She closed her eyes and swallowed, knowing that he was close, then swung her legs out of bed. She was wearing just a short cotton nightgown and wanted to peel it off, but was glad she didn't.

Marco appeared in a flash of blue-green light at the foot of her bed. He smiled at her, giving her an appreciative glance, then held out his hand. The darkfire crystal sat on his palm, the flame so bright inside it that the room was illuminated with its blue-green light. Jac reached for it, then stopped.

"It has a setting now," she said, studying the opal and gold salamander that was wrapped around it.

"It has a passenger," Marco said. He ran a fingertip over the salamander's back and Jac saw it shiver a little.

"It's alive?"

"It's Rafferty. You need the crystal to defend yourself against *Slayers*, but he needs the power of the darkfire to survive."

"You brought me this? As a gift?" Jac was awed that he would do this, especially after she'd injured his friend.

Marco's smile widened. "It's part of my plan to prove myself to you."

He offered the two to her and the firestorm flared brilliantly at their closer proximity. The crystal seemed to be snared in an orb of glowing golden light, its distinctive light crackling like a trapped bolt of lightning. There was a vestige of a blue-green shimmer around the scales of the salamander but as Jac watched, it seemed to move from him into the crystal.

"What's happening?" she whispered.

Marco was watching the salamander closely. "The firestorm might be healing him," he said quietly, his low voice sending a thrill through Jac.

"We should find out," she said, hoping she could fix her mistake.

At his gesture, she took the crystal, cupping her hands together so the crystal and salamander were framed in the bowl of her grasp. Marco folded his hands around hers, making another bowl around hers. He was so close that she could have drowned in his eyes.

The firestorm burned brilliant orange, then heated to gold. Jac could feel her nipples beading and her desire for Marco burning through her veins. There was a bead of perspiration on her upper lip and another one sliding down her back. She licked her lips, well aware of how avidly Marco watched her. His eyes were glittering as he leaned closer, studied her, then bent to brush his lips across her own.

Lust fired through Jac's body and she wanted him more than she ever had before. He kissed her with deliberation, making the embrace last, coaxing her desire from a simmer to a boil.

Jac closed her eyes against the radiant yellow light of the firestorm and kissed Marco back. Their hands were heating and she could hear the darkfire sizzling in the stone. She could taste Marco's kiss and smell his skin. She wanted to press herself against him. She wanted to drag him into the shower and have him against the wall, the water flowing over them as they pleasured each other. She wanted to drag him into her bed and claim him as her own.

Their kiss became frenzied with need, more potent and passionate, and the firestorm blazed white hot between them. Jac heard herself moan and opened her eyes in time to see Marco inhale sharply. Then he broke the kiss, leaving her desperate for more.

He looked down and smiled.

Jac followed his gaze and saw that the salamander was watching them. Their hands were golden, burning with heat, but the darkfire crystal was as cool as ice. The salamander lashed its tail, showing more energy than Jac expected.

"I thought he was hurt," she whispered.

"The firestorm heals," the salamander said with satisfaction. "The firestorm burns away secrets and fears. It banishes injuries and cauterizes wounds." Rafferty tipped back his head to look into Jac's eyes. He seemed to be basking in the brilliant white light. "The firestorm saves and I thank you for saving me with yours."

Before Jac could reply, the salamander shimmered blue and disappeared.

She glanced up at Marco to find him grinning with relief. "I should have thought of it sooner," he said. "I should have known. It's Rafferty who always lists the benefits of the firestorm. It's Rafferty who believes most in its promise."

"Not you?" Jac couldn't help but tease.

Marco laughed. "I do now." His eyes were shining, and he'd never looked so enticing to Jac. He'd brought her a gift, and they'd used their firestorm for good. His gaze dropped, his appreciation clear as he surveyed her.

"I have an idea," she said, because she could see the direction of his thoughts clearly enough.

"So do I," he murmured with a smile.

"We need to use the firestorm for good," she said hastily, knowing that if Marco kissed her again, she would drag him into the shower and have her way with him. "We need to use it to change the future."

"How so?"

Jac took a deep breath, guessing he might not approve of her plan. "We need to deliberately attract *Slayers* with it, so you can destroy them. The fewer of them there are, the better the chance that the *Pyr* will triumph."

"And you want dragons to win?"

"If I'm going to conceive a son, I want him to have a dad."

And a future.

Marco exhaled and scanned the room, as if he couldn't believe what she'd said. "You think we can resist this for six months?" He was so incredulous that Jac found herself smiling.

"I don't know. But the more *Slayers* we can take out before we succumb, the better your odds of surviving."

He smiled at her then, a smile that heated her so that her skin practically sizzled. "Well, that is progress," he said, his words low and silky. "You now want me to survive." Jac couldn't deny that. Marco bent down, his intentions clear, then inhaled sharply and spun away from her. "Looks like your wish is coming true quickly."

"What do you mean?"

He spun to face her, that familiar blue aura shimmering around his body. "I smell *Slayer*," he whispered, just before the air rippled and something — or someone — roared in the living room.

Donovan was so restless that the sparks were practically flying off him. Niall knew the Warrior of the *Pyr* wasn't happy to have been assigned by Erik to guard them all at Delaney's farm. He'd made it clear that he felt he was left out of the action, and Niall couldn't blame him for that. Still, with infant twin boys, Niall was glad to have his family with other *Pyr* and knew that Sloane couldn't have everyone at his place, not if he intended to get any work done. It made sense for the *Pyr* to be in groups, even if the inactivity of waiting chafed at Donovan.

"You'll have plenty to do at the final eclipse," he reminded the other *Pyr*, whose lips set in a grim line as he paced the floor.

"You're looking more like Erik all the time," Delaney teased. "Maybe you'll be the next leader of the *Pyr*."

"The one we have is just fine," Donovan retorted.

"I could use some help with the milking," Ginger interjected cheerfully, then hauled on her boots and headed for the barn. Delaney followed her but Donovan continued to pace, his mood clear.

Alex lifted one of the twins from Rox's arms and blew him a kiss. "They're so adorable at this age."

"No more," Donovan advised his mate and she smiled at him.

"But they never do anything at the same time," Rox said, then yawned. "Especially sleep."

Ahern proved that by giving a mighty yell, increasing the volume of his bellow despite the way that Alex cooed to him. His brother, Ruark, nuzzled Rox's breast, clearly hoping for a snack.

"I'd take him but that's beyond my abilities," Niall teased and Rox smiled at him.

"You're welcome to do the honors of burping him afterward," she said, and Niall nodded agreement.

"Deal." While he waited, Niall reviewed the videos of the dragonfight in Australia for the hundredth time, trying to identify the dragons involved from the footage. The lighting wasn't very good, with the only light on the scene from the eclipsed moon, but as far as Niall could determine, Thorolf and Brandon had fought two new versions of Boris Vassily and one of the earlier hatchlings had joined the fight. Jorge had seized a hatchling and a *Pyr* — and the glow of light around that *Pyr* indicated that he was having his firestorm.

"Two more," Donovan said. "That brings us to seven."

"But not many survivors, so far," Niall noted.

"I have to wonder how many of them there will be in total," Donovan said and paced the room again.

It was Marco having his firestorm, unless Niall missed his guess, and he could glimpse the mate in the brilliant light of the firestorm.

She had to be the one throwing flares at *Slayers*.

"Some mate," Alex said, watching over his shoulder. "She's kicking *Slayer* butt."

"Works for me," Rox agreed. "I like her already."

"But when the *Slayers* disappeared, where did they go?" Alex asked.

Niall was more worried by the soundtrack. Had he really heard Marco ask Jorge for the Elixir just before they disappeared?

No matter how many times he watched and listened, Niall couldn't be sure.

"You're worried," Rox noted, as observant as ever, but Niall didn't reply.

"Does it sound to you like he's asking for the Elixir?" Donovan said in old-speak and Niall winced before he met the

other *Pyr*'s gaze. That Donovan thought the same wasn't reassuring.

"Old-speak!" Alex and Rox cried together. "No fair." The *Pyr* exchanged rueful glances.

"Maybe Sloane knows," Niall said.

"Knows what?" Alex demanded.

"What aren't you telling us?" Rox asked.

"Maybe Sloane is too busy to answer questions," Donovan noted.

Alex came to stand right in front of him, her stance determined, as Ahern roared. "Spill it," she insisted, and Donovan sat down with the two women.

"It sounds like Marco is asking Jorge for the Elixir, right before they disappear," he admitted. Alex and Rox were horrified by that and began to ask questions. "The sound isn't very clear, so we can't be sure."

Niall didn't want to interrupt whatever was happening at Sloane's place, but he couldn't stand the suspense. He'd just decided to call and ask for more details when his phone rang.

The caller was Sloane. Niall grabbed the phone, held up a hand for quiet, and answered. "Was it Marco's firestorm?" he demanded by way of greeting. The others watched him intently and he knew Donovan would hear both sides of the conversation. "Did he really ask Jorge for the Elixir? What happened to the *Slayers* who look like Boris Vassily? Are Brandon and Thorolf okay? Where were their mates?"

"I don't have time for this," Sloane said tersely. "Drake's mate is here in quarantine, and now Drake is hurt, too."

"You've got to tell me something!"

Sloane sighed and updated Niall in a hurry. Even though he spoke quickly, there was a lot to tell and Niall sank to a chair in surprise. He didn't know Marco very well, and he could see why Erik had his doubts, but it was hard to believe that even the darkfire could be strong enough to convince a reluctant *Pyr* to turn *Slayer*. He also couldn't believe that Marco would hurt Rafferty. He said as much to Sloane.

"That's my thinking. Plus the firestorm heals. Even if he had any inclination to change his perspective, the spark of the firestorm should have brought him back to our view."

"Just the way it did with Delaney," Niall agreed.

"Exactly. Erik's rattled, though. I wonder whether he knows more than he's telling us."

Donovan frowned and got up to look out the window.

Niall recalled Erik's gift of foresight. In his experience, Sloane had a good measure of it, too. "That's not why you called, though, is it?" he said, remembering the Apothecary's earlier agitation.

"No. I need your help."

"You said Drake was hurt."

"He's lost a scale and the pain is emanating from that point."

Donovan spun to face Niall and their gazes met. The women looked between them. "That's what happened to Brandon when Chen took his scales and broke them."

"Right, but Chen's dead. I'm wondering whether Jorge learned how to do this from him. Lee is trying to undo it, because I don't know where to start."

"How about Ronnie? Did your antidote work?"

"It helped, but it didn't cure her." That frustration was back in Sloane's tone. "The thing is that I don't know enough about human physiology. The antidote should have worked, but it just pushed the virus back to its latent phase."

"Is that possible?"

"I wouldn't have thought so, but maybe the darkfire is affecting that, too."

"Is she going to die?' Niall asked with concern. Rox's eyes widened when she overheard his question. The silence that followed was a little bit too long to reassure Niall. Donovan looked, if anything, even more grim than he had.

Sloane sighed again. "She might if I don't get help. If it gets worse again, I'm afraid it'll progress more quickly the second time."

"Tell me what I can do."

"I need you to dreamwalk to someone."

"Deal. Tell me who and I'm on it."

Sloane made a growl in his throat. "You should know that Erik doesn't approve of my plan, but it's the only way I can see to solve this. I need to ask for help, and that means I need to reveal my nature to someone who doesn't know what I am."

And it was someone who wasn't Sloane's mate or could

otherwise be expected to keep his secret. Niall frowned. Erik wouldn't like a deliberate breach of the Covenant, though he could appreciate that Sloane wanted to save Ronnie. "But who is it? Do we know her at all?"

"I do," Sloane admitted. "There's a doctor in the news casts. She's the one pushing the gurney in the footage of Drake's rescue of Ronnie."

"Dr. Samantha Wilcox. They've posted an interview with her about Ronnie..."

"That's her," Sloane said, interrupting Niall with uncharacteristic terseness. "Can you walk her dreams? Will you?"

Niall understood that Sloane was warning him about Erik's reaction. "Do you know where she is?"

"Not exactly. She might still be in Virginia, or she might have gone back to Atlanta by now."

"Any idea what or who she dreams about?"

Sloane made a sound of exasperation. "I'd like to think it was me, but I doubt that." Niall straightened, wondering just how well Sloane knew Dr. Wilcox. "I'll guess that she dreams of her dead son. He was the first victim of the Seattle virus." Donovan blinked, then sat down with care.

"What?" Alex mouthed, seizing his hand. Donovan shook his head, his eyes glittering as he listened.

Niall had caught his breath. "What's she going to do when she finds out you're a dragon shifter?"

"I don't know. I don't actually care, not if she comes and helps Ronnie."

Niall doubted that was true. It sounded as if Sloane cared a lot about the doctor's reaction.

Sloane continued with resolve when Niall was silent. "Look, if we can heal Ronnie, and Sam can replicate the antidote and save all the humans Jorge infected, we'd be doing what we were born to do. We'd be defending humans as a treasure of the earth." His voice hardened. "Even if the price is spilling my secret. That might be the price of the cure."

"But Erik doesn't agree?"

"You know how he is about the Covenant. I know what I know about being Apothecary, though." Sloane sounded exhausted. "So, can you do it? Will you do it?"

"I will. I'll try." Niall had to believe that the doctor's dreams of her son would be vivid and emotional. "If I could dreamwalk to her, what would I say?"

"You don't have to say anything. Just find a way to provoke her memory of Ronnie."

"I doubt she's thinking of anything else. She sounded pretty angry in that interview." Niall didn't add that the good doctor was furious with dragons and dragon shifters, much less that she had refused to accept a distinction between *Pyr* and *Slayers* when prompted by the interviewer.

"And show her my tattoo," Sloane said, as if Niall hadn't spoken.

"The caduceus that Rox did?"

"That's the one."

"But..." Niall started to protest, only to be interrupted by Sloane.

"Tell Donovan to call Erik. He wants him to find Marco," he said, then terminated the call without waiting for a response.

"He really is getting grumpy," Niall muttered, then spoke to Rox, who was still feeding Ruark. "Do have any pictures of the tattoo you did for Sloane?"

"Sure. Preliminary drawings, final sketch and pictures of the finished tattoo. I've got the full documentation of that one, even on my phone." Donovan retrieved Rox's purse, and Alex followed him, rocking Ahern as she demanded to know what he'd learned. Their voices dropped to a murmur. Donovan pulled out his phone to call Erik.

Rox smiled at Niall over their son's head. "It's one of my favorites."

"Don't let my Phoenix hear that," Niall said, referring to the splendid back piece Rox had done for him.

Rox's eyes shone. "Your Phoenix knows she has pride of place in your hoard." They smiled at each other for a moment, and Niall doubted he was the only one remembering the prophecy of the Phoenix and the Dragon from their firestorm.

Then Alex returned with Rox's purse, and Rox scrolled through the images she had saved on her phone. Niall replayed the news. He'd never met the doctor, didn't know her scent or her location, but this was a matter of life and death. He found the footage of her son being exposed to the virus by Jorge and watched it closely. It didn't look like the woman holding the boy's hand was her. He went back to the interview, concentrating on her features and the sound of her voice.

He had to find a way to dreamwalk to Dr. Wilcox, for the sake of Drake's mate.

"Can you do it?" Alex asked.

"I have to," Niall replied. Sloane's concerns made it clear that he had to succeed and do it soon.

Donovan returned, his stride filled with purpose. "And I have to find Marco. Wherever he's gone."

CHAPTER TWENTY-FOUR

am sat straight up in bed. She'd had a dream, a dream of a man talking to her, but as soon as she tried to recall it, the dream broke into shards. They faded like mist, but in their place, a network of associations formed in her thoughts. She could remember only the last image the man had shown her.

It was Sloane's tattoo. A caduceus with dragons instead of snakes.

Veronica Maitland had been abducted by dragons.

A dragon had spread the Seattle virus.

The big blond guy helping out in Sloane's shop had a dragon tattoo.

The trailer on the black truck in Sloane's driveway said 'Here Be Dragons'.

Sloane's father had been called the Apothecary and that Asian man had called Sloane by the same title.

Sloane had gone to Chicago and then New York, in rapid succession. Sam threw herself out of bed and turned on her computer, navigating straight to the videos that had been uploaded recently featuring dragons. Six months before, there'd been a dragon fight in Chicago, then one immediately afterward in New York, both of which had left dragons badly injured.

The dates matched Sloane's sudden departures from California.

After her dream, Sam could guess why. Sloane was a very specific kind of Apothecary, one who treated dragon shifters.

Having injured dragon shifters drop by without notice would explain why Sloane was so private.

She didn't understand why it should be so, but her dream meant that dragons had taken Veronica to Sloane. Once she would have scoffed at this conclusion, but Sam trusted her intuition more than she had. As soon as she connected the dots, she knew it was true. No doubt, Sloane was going to try to heal Veronica Maitland but even with his extensive reading, his treatment might make her worse. Maybe he wasn't even doing it by choice. Maybe the dragons were making him do it.

But Veronica Maitland was Sam's patient and Sam's responsibility. Sam wasn't going to just step aside and let dragons do whatever they wanted to that woman.

Sam called the airline on her way to pack. She needed a flight to San Francisco and she needed it now. Sloane Forbes had been less than honest with her, and it was past time he explained himself.

Sam refused to consider the tingle of excitement she felt at the prospect of seeing him again.

This was *business*.

Marco needed a plan.

Preferably, it would be one that didn't feature him or Jac dying during their firestorm.

He was a bit spooked by how readily his body shifted shape as soon as he discerned a threat, and how the firestorm made him feel less in control of his own body. His need to protect Jac was strong but the firestorm made it all-consuming. He couldn't think of anything else, not when there was a *Slayer* in close proximity.

He was in the living room without realizing he'd gone there, in dragon form, confronting a *Slayer* who had drunk the Elixir. The intruder was in human form and stood by the sofa, as if waiting for an invitation to sit down. He smiled at Marco, something glittering in his eyes that might have been envy, then sat down with care. *"Ah, the heat of the firestorm,"* he said in old-speak. He smiled coldly. *"Is she worth it?"*

A *Slayer* had come to talk to a *Pyr* during his firestorm. Who said the darkfire was fading? Marco couldn't think of another incident that would be less likely.

And that intrigued him.

If the *Slayer* wanted help from him, he might be able to create a strategy that protected Jac.

Marco shifted shape, returning deliberately to his human form. The golden heat that revealed Jac's presence warmed his back. "You're one of the hatchlings." He spoke aloud, wanting Jac to be able to hear the conversation. He hoped she stayed in the bedroom but doubted she would stay out of view. In another time and place, her fearlessness might have made him smile.

Now it made his pulse leap with trepidation.

The *Slayer* winced slightly, apparently thinking that Marco smiled at his expense. He then nodded. "I'm Boris Vassily. I know I died, and I remember everything since then."

"Since dying?" Jac asked from the doorway.

Boris surveyed her with a hunger that made Marco want to injure him. Then he averted his gaze and seemed to compose himself, taking a light tone. "It's been most interesting." He appeared to spot Sigmund's book on the coffee table and smiled, reaching to flip it open. "So, this is where it ended up. No wonder your mate knows so much about us."

Jac and Marco kept silent. Marco wished he had a way to communicate with her without Boris being able to hear. He continued into the room then sat in the nearest chair, sparing her a glance.

Jac understood and came to his side.

Boris wasn't reading the book, just turning the pages idly. "It was Sigmund's idea, you know. Well, my idea, but he acted upon it."

"What do you mean?" Jac asked. Marco decided to let her do the talking. If he said little and appeared enigmatic — or undecided — he might be able to trick the *Slayer*.

"During the firestorm of the Smith, we were stretched thin. I commented to Sigmund that it would be useful if he could clone me." Boris lifted his gaze to Marco. "To my astonishment, he did."

"But isn't Sigmund dead?" Jac asked.

"Of course. He died before seeing his experiment completed, just as I died before knowing what he had done. But the pieces were in place and the experiment set in motion. It simply needed time and the exposure to the right influences to come to fruition."

"The light of the blood moon," Jac said.

Boris smiled then glanced at Marco. "How interesting for you to have a mate so schooled in our lore. Is that a coincidence?"

"It's darkfire," Marco said flatly. "Turning all assumptions on their heads."

Jac revealed that she held the crystal Marco had brought to her, and the darkfire spark leapt inside the stone.

Boris's eyes narrowed as he studied Jac and the crystal. "She was quite intrepid in Australia at the eclipse." He leaned forward. "Who fired the crystal at Easter Island?"

"I did," Jac said, taking credit for what she'd done so quickly that her honesty couldn't be doubted. "We went there to hunt dragons, after all."

Boris closed the book. "My own father turned *Slayer* after having his firestorm."

"Obviously," Jac said.

Boris chuckled. "Yes, I suppose it is obvious, given my existence." He stood up and brushed some invisible lint from his sleeve, obviously choosing his words with care. Marco watched the *Slayer* closely. What did he want? Why had he come? They could have been locked in battle already, but the *Slayer* must have an alternative plan.

Marco guessed that Boris was working up to sharing it and chose not to interrupt. Jac came to sit on the arm of his chair, holding the crystal on her lap. He almost smiled when he noted that she sat on his right, so that his dominant left hand was unobstructed. He liked that she was asking the questions.

It would give them more choices.

Again, they were working as a team. That realization combined with the firestorm to make him feel optimistic about their future.

"My father, however, could be said to have been not just the first leader of the *Slayers* but the most effective," Boris continued. He began to stroll around the room, pausing to look at items as he went. Jac bristled but didn't move. Marco put his hand on the small of her back, savoring the flurry of sparks that erupted from the point of contact.

"At the next blood moon, there will be six more clones hatched," Boris said. "Creating an elite corps of fighting *Slayers*, each one with my skills, training and memories. Each one carrying the Dragon's Blood Elixir in his veins. Each one my own mirror image." He turned to confront Marco. "I never had siblings. I never had to compete for anything within my family and I don't intend to start now. The way I see it, I have the opportunity to assert myself as the leader of choice within this band of brothers."

"You want to kill Jorge," Jac guessed.

Boris smiled and shook his head. "I want to enlist him as one of my troops. Even that won't win the respect of the other clones. There's only one way to do that, and if you help me, I'll ensure that you're rewarded."

"How?" Jac asked.

"Marco and I could rule the *Slayers* together, after the *Pyr* are defeated and exterminated. In doing that, we'll rule the world. We'll be immortal, with Elixir coursing through our veins, and we'll make this earth a paradise for our kind. With two of us, we can watch each other's backs and control whatever other *Slayers* survive."

"How?" Jac asked again.

"By deciding who gets a sip of the Elixir, of course. Once the *Pyr* are gone, we'll be able to reduce the other *Slayers* to groveling slaves, even Jorge. We'll replicate Sigmund's feat and make more, entire armies who look just like me. We'll sacrifice one at intervals, giving the others a small sip of Elixir, just enough to ensure that they survive. We'll pour all of our resources into creating the Elixir's source again, then keep it for ourselves." Boris lifted a photograph of Jac's parents from the mantle, then replaced it after the barest glance. He turned on Marco with gleaming eyes. "Did you know Cinnabar?"

Marco shook his head.

"I thought you might have been contemporaries. Your uncle took him in from the streets of Rome."

"Your uncle?" Jac asked, turning to Marco with a question in her eyes.

"Magnus Montmorency," Boris provided. "A *Slayer* of uncommon resource and knowledge, and my successor as leader of the *Slayers*. Your dragon has a strong *Slayer* legacy, which is why I'm here."

"Cinnabar," Jac said and reached for the book. "I don't

remember a mention of him."

"You might find him under Sahir, which was his original name, or under Sylvanus Segundo, which was the name Magnus gave him." Boris cleared his throat. "But I doubt, actually, that Sigmund recorded those details, even if he knew them. Cinnabar, you see, was the most recent source of the Dragon's Blood Elixir, as concocted by Magnus. It was too great a secret for Sigmund to reveal."

"But the source of the Elixir was destroyed," Marco said.

"One of the first epic losses of the Dragon's Tail Wars," Boris mused, then eyed Sigmund's book. "I think that a dragon of your lineage might best be able to replicate your uncle's feat." He looked up, eyes shining. "Magnus, after all, had also learned the songs of the Cantor."

So this was what Boris wanted. More Elixir, concocted by Marco. For once, Marco was glad that Pwyll had been so secretive about the songs of the Cantor.

There were only two *Pyr* surviving who knew any of them, and Marco knew more of them than Rafferty.

"And what's in it for me?" Marco asked, keeping his tone defiant.

"Shared leadership. Survival. Satisfaction." Boris glanced over Jac. "The opportunity to see your son born and grow up." He shook his head. "If you remain *Pyr*, you'll be dead in a matter of months. The *Slayers* are going to triumph in the Dragon's Tail Wars. We're immortal. We're almost impossible to kill. And there will be *six* more of us on the blood moon, thanks to my suggestion and Sigmund's skill."

Boris needed him.

Marco shrugged. "What makes you think I want to share with you?" he asked and Boris couldn't hide either his pleasure or his surprise.

"Destiny *is* bred in the bone, then," he murmured. "You've begun?"

"I've snared Rafferty," Marco lied. "Another excellent candidate to be the source, since the last Cantor was his forebear. He's trapped and being exposed to mercury right now."

Boris leaned forward, shimmering a little in his anticipation. "When do you think the Elixir will be ready?"

"It'll take a few years to brew," Marco said. "And frankly, I have my doubts about Rafferty as a good source, given that he's resolutely *Pyr*."

"Jorge," Boris whispered with excitement. "Jorge would be ideal."

"Jorge will hardly volunteer."

"But using him could jumpstart the brewing," Boris said. "Given the amount of Elixir he's already consumed."

Marco considered this, well aware that Jac was watching him. "You're right, of course. That *could* make a difference. The *Pyr*, though, are still an obstacle, and your leadership of the *Slayers* is hardly assured. It might be better for me strategically to stay in the shadows, work on the Elixir, then negotiate after the last eclipse."

"No," Boris said with surprising finality. "Strategically the best plan is for you to help me ensure my position as leader."

"How will you do that? They aren't even hatched yet."

"But when they are, they will all burn to complete one deed." Boris held up a finger. "One mission that was unsatisfied when I died. If I've completed it already, I'll be established as first among them, without question."

"What deed?" Jac asked.

"Killing Erik Sorensson," Boris said. "We exchanged challenge coins years ago. I would eliminate the leader of the *Pyr*, for once and for all, and that would secure my claim to leadership of the *Slayers*."

Marco's thoughts flew like quicksilver. He recalled that two of the clones had already attacked Erik, after the eclipse in October, and they'd injured him badly. He'd been outnumbered, but saved by the intervention of other *Pyr*. That indicated that Boris was telling the truth about the memory and the desire of the clones.

If this clone of Boris plus the remaining six attacked, Erik might be killed—and the *Pyr* might lose focus without a leader. They might lose the final battle as a result.

"You should do it soon then," Marco said.

"*We* should do it soon," Boris corrected and extended a hand to shake on their agreement. His thumb changed to a dragon talon, then back to a human thumb, and he smiled, showing all his teeth. It wasn't hard to believe that he was a dragon shifter.

Nor was it hard to remember that his interest was solely in

himself.

"You'll have to swear to never injure my mate or my son," Marco said.

"You don't have a son yet."

"Like you, my mate wants to ensure I survive the war."

"So you won't fully turn *Slayer* until your firestorm is satisfied," Boris mused. "You might be the first *Slayer* to have a son delivered."

"That would be the mark of the darkfire."

"The force that colors your life." Boris watched the blue-green spark. His smile widened and he extended his hand a little further. "Then of course I will defend her, prize that she is. She might even use her skills for our side."

"If taking Jorge down is part of your plan, I'm in," Jac said with such gusto that Boris laughed aloud.

"It will do my old bones good to feel the heat of a firestorm for a while," he said, and Marco shook his hand.

A *Slayer*'s pledge was worthless, but Boris seemed to believe that their contract was sealed. Marco had no intention of keeping his apparent agreement for one moment longer than was useful.

Boris had already told him a great deal, and he'd admit more before he died.

Marco would make sure of it.

He would also guarantee that Erik survived. The darkfire was giving him the chance to influence the outcome of the war.

Jorge couldn't figure out Maeve O'Neill.

He wasn't in a hurry to do so. He lounged in her bed, listening to her in the shower in the adjacent bath. They'd already had sex three times, and she'd disappeared into the bathroom after each coupling. Each time, he thought she'd return to sleep but each time, she'd reappeared in different lingerie and revealed her plan to seduce him again. It was the middle of the night, but he suspected she'd soon be back for more. Jorge had to rest while he could.

He'd looked for a sanctuary and found a slice of heaven.

Seeking haven with Maeve had been a brilliant choice on his part. Jorge couldn't sense any *Pyr* in his vicinity at all. His body was healing with its usual speed. Maeve's home was secure and luxurious, and the sex was phenomenal. She was insatiable, which he liked enough to have been distracted by her powerful influence on his senses. She wore a lot of perfume and it muddied his thinking in a way that was unusual.

Was he just unaccustomed to perfume?

Or was there something more in the mix?

His eyes opened suddenly. Why *exactly* couldn't he smell her mortality? She was human, after all. There should have been a whiff of decay about her, one perceptible with careful study. Jorge inhaled slowly, filling his lungs with Maeve's scent, but could identify only perfume, the scent of her desire, and something that made him dizzy.

"All rested up?" she asked from the doorway to the bathroom. Her dark hair was coiled up this time, revealing the pale soft length of her neck and shoulders. She was wearing a sheer red nightgown that swirled around her knees in a froth of lace. The fabric cupped her breasts, as if displaying them for his pleasure, and the light from the room behind shone through the sheer fabric to silhouette her figure.

Jorge sat up, more than ready for another interval with Maeve. Her lips were painted a glossy red this time, as were her nails, and she strolled into the room in lacquer red heels. Jorge thought of blood and death, which was an unexpected association with an alluring temptress.

Maeve smiled, as if she'd read his thoughts.

"What are you?" he asked and her smile broadened.

"A hunter, just like you." She crooked a finger, beckoning to him then strolled across the bedroom, leaving him behind. Her hips swayed in invitation, and Jorge realized he would have followed her anywhere.

He should have been concerned about that.

Instead, he pursued her. Maeve made her way up the stairs of the townhouse to the top floor. Jorge was transfixed by the movement of her legs and the flex of her muscles, as well as addled by that perfume. When she reached the summit, he realized he wasn't even aware of having walked up the stairs.

He frowned. He had assumed there was only an attic below the roof of the house, but Maeve produced a golden key and turned it in the lock of the door there. It was a heavily studded wooden door, as if she admitted him to a fortress. She cast him a playful glance, then flung open the door, gesturing for him to precede her.

Jorge felt his body prickle on the cusp of change. He sensed danger and saw the pale blue halo of light emanating from his body. He was fully alert, but curious, too. What could she do to him? He boldly stepped past Maeve into the attic as she flicked the light switch.

On the far wall was a book case with glass doors, but there were no books within it. The contents of each section were composed. He thought immediately that it was a shrine.

His gaze fell first on a mirror and comb. They looked to be made of silver, and something about their shape reminded him of seaweed. In a jar beside them was secured a green scale, about the size of his thumb, floating in some liquid.

"A scale from the tail of the last mermaid," Maeve said behind him, her voice reverent. "And her favorite mirror and comb, just because."

In the section of the case to the right was a long twisted shell with a pearly finish. It was only on closer inspection that Jorge realized it was a horn. A trio of long fair hairs were braided together to make a long cord, one that was twined around the horn with a pair of dried daisies.

"The horn and harness of the last unicorn," Maeve said. "I wish I could have taken more, but he disintegrated into stardust so quickly at the end." She sighed.

Jorge realized he was in a trophy room.

The next held a golden harp and the grisly memento of a pair of pointed ears. They looked as if they'd been cut from the victim's body and had twisted a little as they dried.

"Last elf," Maeve supplied. Jorge glanced back in time to see her shudder. "Horrific creatures. Always singing and *lilting*. The world is better without them."

Jorge turned back to the display of prizes, barely able to identify the meanings of them all in his excitement. "You hunt immortals," he managed to say.

"No." Maeve came to stand beside him, and he noticed how resolute her tone was. She folded her arms across her chest, pushing her breasts to fascinating prominence. He almost missed the fury that lit her eyes, he was so distracted. "I eliminate the unnatural creatures from the world. Their end times can't come soon enough for me. I consider it to be a clean-up operation."

Jorge had a hard time believing that the beautiful woman beside him was so effective a huntress. He recalled her picking her way across the uneven soil on Easter Island in her high heels, every hair in place, and couldn't reconcile what he knew of her with this confession. "*You* hunted mermaids, elves and unicorns to extinction?"

"Of course. And more besides." She gestured to the cabinet. "Centaurs, giants, dwarves, and so many more." She winced at a pile of particularly lustrous feathers in one section. "Fallen angels are like cockroaches. Just when you think you've found the last one, there's another." Maeve smiled, and there was a familiar hunger in her eyes that Jorge found reassuring. "Still it adds to the sport. Call this my hobby."

Jorge's pulse quickened. "What about the *Pyr*?"

"I have a larger section reserved for them down here." She gestured to the lower right corner of the case, where a section was empty. "I should dust it out and get it ready, don't you think?"

Jorge couldn't completely stop his smile. The idea of this woman, who was admittedly delectable, destroying and eliminating dragons was difficult for him to believe. "How do you expect to slay dragons?" he asked, unable to keep a slight edge of scorn from his tone.

"I have you to help," she said with such confidence that Jorge wondered what he was missing. "Didn't I say we'd make a great team?"

"But why would I let you take the trophy, when I'll be doing the work?"

"Because I'll reward you, of course," Maeve whispered, her eyes lighting with an amorous intent that made Jorge's thoughts spin.

"You don't have anything I need..."

"Not even immortality?"

Jorge fell silent at that.

"Oh yes," Maeve said with a smile. "Did I forget to mention that I'm an immortal queen?" He might have doubted her claim, but Maeve drew a door on the exterior wall of the attic, using a pen she'd obviously brought with her. Jorge didn't know what kind of a pen it was, but it left a sparkling trail after it. He saw the outline of the door, then she drew a knob, then a keyhole. She inserted the end of the pen into the keyhole and a bright light emanated from the lock. It swept around the perimeter of the drawn door, then with a sigh, the portal opened.

Instead of a patch of sky, or the neighboring rooftops, another reality was revealed.

Jorge kept his dragon in check only with a great effort. His eyes widened as a great hall was revealed, one that extended far beyond the confines of the attic. It was filled with beautiful courtiers dancing and drinking red liquid from golden cups, wondrous music that made Jorge yearn to dance, and laughter filling the air.

"Queen Mab!" they cried in delighted recognition and fell to their knees in homage.

Jorge glanced at Maeve to see that her appearance had changed. She was dressed in tremendous finery, but all in the same bloody hue of red. There were rubies on her fingers and a sparkling crown on her head with more. The hem of her red velvet gown was sewn with jewels, and her train stretched across the attic floor. She was also radiating sexual allure, her lips red, her breasts spilling forth, her gaze knowing.

Jorge felt that strange disorientation again, that muddying of all he knew to be true. There was only gorgeous Maeve, her beauty, and his desire for her.

"Another dimension?" he asked, unable to keep the wonder from his tone.

"An eternal one." Maeve watched his reaction with a knowing smile. She caressed his arm possessively and Jorge's lust only increased. He had a strange sense that only Maeve would satisfy him from this point forward.

Because they were two of a kind.

The thought wasn't his, but it resonated within him with the power of truth.

"The Elixir is a pale substitute for what I can give my partner, consort and co-regent," Maeve whispered, her words sparking a greed within Jorge. It burned like a flame in his heart, a complete conviction that they would be stronger together.

As well as more successful.

He knew he could finish the *Pyr* himself, but there would soon be no more Elixir. What Maeve offered was far simpler than trying to concoct the Elixir's source again. No *Pyr* and himself immortal! It sounded like heaven on earth, even without Maeve's charms to be savored.

"All I have to do is eliminate the *Pyr*," Jorge said, wanting the terms to be clear.

"And love me as your queen, of course," Maeve murmured with a seductive smile.

A heartless, insatiable queen who could give him immortality would be easy for Jorge to love.

"The key to a portal," Maeve said softly, tapping the pen on her opposite palm. "Wherever when you need it." She smiled and handed Jorge the pen. "Just in case you ever do."

Jorge accepted the pen, although it looked like a small wand. It was cold enough to send shivers over him and so clear that he wondered whether it was made of ice. Then Maeve's disorienting perfume swirled around him, and she drew his head down for a kiss that lit a fire deep within him. The company cheered their approval. Jorge thought he saw a glimmer of blue-green light at the periphery of his vision just before he closed his eyes. He felt a shudder slide over his skin, but then Maeve's mouth was locked on his, her kiss as demanding as if he hadn't pleasured her repeatedly already this night.

He was lost in her kiss in a heartbeat, so captivated by her spell that he didn't even feel the scale loose itself from his hide.

He certainly wasn't aware of the minion who seized that prize and hid it safely away. There was only Maeve, her rapacious need to conquer, her insatiable lust, and the gift of immortality she could bestow upon him.

That was more than enough for Jorge.

Lee knew the *Pyr* expected him to heal Drake, because Jorge had learned how to injure other dragon shifters remotely from Chen. The problem was that Lee didn't have time to put all the pieces in place, as Chen had done in concocting his spell. He had to help Drake quickly.

He felt a kinship with this *Pyr*, though their backgrounds were vastly different, because both of them had been enchanted and snared for centuries. Both of them had left the times and the souls they knew behind. Both of them had begun again. Lee was encouraged that Drake had been granted a second firestorm and dared to hope for his own future.

But it would be wrong for Drake to be sacrificed when all gifts came to his talons.

Lee had to make this right.

He shifted shape beside Drake, savoring the power of the transition and the way it made him feel invincible. His scales were brilliant gold again, his nails and horns a vivid scarlet. Each scale was touched with red on its tip and his belly shone metallic red. Just as he was the opposite in nature to his younger brother, Chen, he was the opposite in color, too. He leaned over Drake, listening to his breath, which was too shallow. He could feel the tremor of pain deep within Drake, even when the *Pyr* was in his human form.

Chen had twisted their father's ancient magic, perverting it into a force of ill will and injury. He had used the mystical spiral and placed his victim's scales at the compass points, considering also the power of the elements. His spell had taken a long time to bring to fruition, and Lee sensed that Jorge had managed to harness that wickedness before its fury was spent.

The trick would be invoking a similar spell, without drawing that foul power.

Lee thought of the healing powers of the earth, remembered his impulse and that Zoë had helped him with the work, and knew what he had to do.

"Can you help him?" Ronnie whispered.

He nodded and lifted Drake with new purpose. When his wings began to flap, Sloane pointed to a glass panel in the far corner of the solarium. Lee took flight and burst through the ceiling, then carried the injured *Pyr* to the spiral he'd planted with Zoë. The plants were about a foot tall, but only the calendula in the middle had bloomed. The flowers made a brilliant cluster of yellow and orange, much like the heart of the sun. Lee landed in the very center and knew immediately that it was the right choice.

He could feel the spiral as a protective force.

But what spell to sing? He recalled all the ones Chen could have invoked to do injury and feared to even think their words, lest he make Drake's condition worse. He thought of Chandra's dream of twin brothers, one who had snakes leap from his mouth when he spoke and the other who loosed pearls when he spoke. Good and bad. White and black. He and Chen had been such opposites, yet like two sides of the same coin, derived from the same source but each distinct from the other.

Lee thought of his father, so wise and ancient, the father of them both. He looked up at the clouds gathering overhead and wondered whether it was his father's claw at work. His father had been a storm-gatherer of remarkable power, much venerated by the people who relied upon his skills to bring rain. In the rumble of distant thunder, Lee heard his father's voice.

It matters less what words are spoken than the intent of the one who utters them.

Of course.

Lee spread his wings high, creating a protective canopy over Drake, and began his father's favorite chant. He felt the wind blow and the first drops of rain fall on his wings, but he chanted on. He kept his gaze fixed on his patient, though he heard the other *Pyr* gather around the perimeter of the spiral. Sloane's voice was the first to take up the chant, the first *Pyr* to lend his power to the ancient song. Lee smiled at the Apothecary's power, feeling that the tremor of pain within Drake was diminishing. Erik and Quinn lent their voices, as well, and Lee heard a fifth voice, one he couldn't identify. Who else aided their quest? It didn't matter—they would all help Drake.

The *Pyr* sang together and time became difficult to measure. Lee's father's chant blurred the minutes and seconds, even the hours. It was only when Drake stirred and opened his eyes that Lee realized pearls had been falling from his lips all the while.

Drake looked about himself with wonder, scooping up a handful of the lustrous gems, and they shimmered as they slipped through his fingers. They turned to drops of rain and rolled into the garden around them, disappearing into the soil to nourish the plants.

Lee smiled at this gift.

The other *Pyr* shifted back to their human forms and Sloane applauded Lee's efforts. "Wow," he said. "I'd love to learn more of that chant."

"It'll be my honor to teach you," Lee said.

"Thank you," Drake said, then exhaled in a shuddering breath. "I have to tell Veronica that all is well." He shook Lee's claw and held his gaze. "Thank you," he said again, his words heartfelt, then strode back toward the house. Lee smiled to note that Drake stepped over the young plants with care.

He considered the spiral of flowers, pleased with what he had done. That was when Lee saw the opal and gold salamander, watching from between the plants. If a salamander could smile, this one did.

Then he shifted shape in a shimmer of pale blue, and Rafferty appeared in his human form. Lee shifted, as well, so the two of them stood in the middle of the floral spiral as fat drops of rain fell around them.

"Well done," Rafferty said with satisfaction and shook Lee's hand heartily.

While the other *Pyr* welcomed Rafferty's return and expressed their relief, Lee looked down and saw the strange ring that Rafferty wore. It looked like it was made of spun glass, of black and white swirled together, and it seemed to spin on the other *Pyr*'s finger as he eyed it. He lifted his gaze to find Rafferty watching him and felt a commonality with the *Pyr* beyond anything he'd felt before.

He'd lost his blood kin, but Lee had found a new family with the *Pyr*.

His father would have advised him to do whatever was necessary to defend this unexpected prize, and Lee would do just that.

The *Pyr* conferred quickly, for Erik and Quinn were both determined to leave as soon as possible. Erik had doubts about Lorenzo's intentions and seemed to think he could stop that *Pyr* from doing something foolish.

Sloane doubted that anyone could stop Lorenzo from doing anything once that dragon made up his mind, except maybe Cassie.

He didn't want to argue with Erik again, though.

Rafferty insisted that Marco wasn't turning *Slayer*, although Erik was unconvinced. Quinn suggested that the Sleeper might simply want to savor his firestorm in private, a notion that Erik didn't find compelling but one that made Sloane recall that Quinn had once felt the same way.

The mood was far from harmonious between them all when they parted ways, but Sloane was simply glad they were finally leaving. Maybe they'd been in close quarters too long.

Besides, he had work to do. He had to get his conservatory repaired, and he still hadn't had five minutes to himself to examine that *Slayer*. He'd been working too hard and sleeping too little, and he was unhappy about his lack of triumph. Lee suggested he'd take care of the broken glass, and Sloane dispatched Drake to sleep in Veronica's company, then headed back to his lab.

He didn't even wave farewell to all his departing guests.

Sam couldn't arrive soon enough.

Samantha Wilcox returned to California with all the fury of a tropical storm. She raged through the airport and seized the keys from the car rental clerk. She squealed the tires as she backed the rental out of its spot, then made at least six traffic violations in her haste to get to Sloane's residence. She turned into his driveway and gunned the engine, zooming up the driveway far too quickly. She braked to a halt so hard that plumes of dust rose behind her.

The car was parked crooked and blocking the drive, but Sam didn't care. She flung herself out of it, left the door open and marched up to Sloane's front door. She was going to lean on the bell, but didn't have a chance.

The door was hauled open, as if someone had been watching for her. Sloane stood there, looking haggard and sexy as hell. "What took you so long?" he demanded before she could say anything, then pivoted and strode into the house, leaving the door open behind him.

If she'd been in a less murderous mood, Sam might have laughed. All those times she'd wanted to see into his home and he'd avoided the situation. Now he left the door standing open for anyone who cared to come in.

Even her.

"Where's Veronica Maitland?" she demanded, even as she followed him. "What did they do with her?" Her gaze flew over the comfortable interior, then she caught her breath at the light spilling into the space beyond the kitchen. There was a greenhouse back there, and Sloane gestured to it with one hand.

Veronica was there. She was dressed in street clothes, a casual dress and sandals, and sitting on the rocks that edged a pool and fountain. A man with salt-and-pepper hair cut very short sat with her, and they were deep in conversation.

Sam turned on Sloane with outrage. "What the hell are you doing? This is a violation of every possible safety protocol, not to mention a public health hazard..."

"I don't see a lot of public around here," Sloane said tightly.

"But *him*! He's with her without any protection. She's *infectious*!"

Sloane shook his head with resolve. "Not to him."

Sam felt her mouth drop open, then she understood. She looked at the couple again and noted Veronica's smile. The other woman's hand curved over her belly as the man clearly tried to make her laugh.

And succeeded.

"That's the elusive Drake," Sam whispered.

"Yes, it is. You want something to eat?"

The question restored Sam's anger. "Eat? Are you crazy? She's getting to the end of the progression. We can't just sit back while she dies right in front of us."

"Dies?" Sloane echoed. He arched a dark brow, then looked pointedly toward the greenhouse.

Wait a minute. "The progression from the first spike of the fever to death takes a week," Sam murmured. She knew the symptoms by heart. "If she's alive, she should be in the second phase."

"The third one, actually, if you count the latent phase."

"She should be confused. There should be red lesions on her body," Sam murmured, unable to account for her former patient's apparent good health. She walked closer to the glass barrier, amazed by the evidence before her own eyes. "She should have diarrhea."

"But she doesn't," Sloane observed.

"Dr. Wilcox!" Veronica said, obviously noticing her presence. She stood up and Drake supported her elbow as she came to the glass wall. She was clearly weakened by her illness, but recovering. Her color was excellent and her spirits obviously good. Her partner was more somber, and Sam wondered what he knew.

Probably Sloane had confided in Drake.

Veronica waved but made no effort to open the barrier. She was still too thin but there was a sparkle in her eye and a slight flush to her cheeks.

"You look well," Sam said, astonished by the truth of it. "I'm so glad."

"I feel so much better," Veronica confessed. She laid her hand against the glass. "I'm sorry I had to deceive you. I knew what was going to happen, but I was afraid you wouldn't agree."

"I wouldn't have," Sam admitted. "But it's wonderful to see you recovering."

Drake bent to murmur to Veronica and she nodded, holding his elbow as he took her back to sit in the sun.

Sam watched, then sat down hard in Sloane's kitchen. "What did you do to her?"

"I gave her an antidote," Sloane admitted, putting a cup of hot tea in front of her. Sam hadn't even realized that he'd brewed it. He poured another cup and sat down beside her at the breakfast bar, his arm almost brushing against hers. She could see the bottom of the caduceus tattoo protruding from beneath the hem of the sleeve of his T-shirt, just the point of the staff and the two coiled dragon tails.

Sam recoiled from the reminder of that quote about necromancers. On the other hand, he effectively had brought Veronica back from the dead. "And you tested it on her? Like she was a guinea pig?"

"I had a sample and tested it first. She agreed to give it a try," Sloane replied, a slight edge in his tone. "She volunteered, for the sake of medical research." He touched his mug to hers and took a sip of tea.

"How did she volunteer? When?" Sam demanded. "When? I was her primary caregiver. I saw all of her correspondence and her visitors."

"I guess you missed one," Sloane said, his voice hard.

Sam thought of that little smile of anticipation that had curved Veronica's lips when she'd been pushing the gurney. She'd known. "But how did you do it?"

"I guess we have a few resources at our disposal that can't be easily explained."

Sam thought of Jac's stone and frowned, shaking her head. "How did you find an antidote? We've had no real success."

"I found it the same way you would have, if you'd had the chance. I identified and isolated a component in Drake's blood that countered the virus."

"Because he didn't contract it." Sam drummed her fingers on the counter. "He didn't respond to my appeal and I thought that was because he didn't care. The truth, I'll guess, is that he had a secret to keep, one that we'd uncover with more tests."

"He's *Pyr*."

Sam had already guessed that. He was probably one of the dragons who had abducted Veronica. "And that's why he didn't get infected."

"No," Sloane said and Sam looked at him.

"No?"

"Drake has been exposed to this virus before."

"He had antibodies," Sam repeated, then shook her head. "But what is the virus? Why can't we identify it now, if he's been exposed to it before? Where was he exposed? It should be documented."

"It was." Sloane crossed the room and picked up a book, cracking it open in front of Sam. It was *The Peloponnesian War* by Thucydides. "'The plague originated, so they say, in Ethiopia in upper Egypt and spread from there into Egypt itself and Libya and much of the territory of the King of Persia.' Thucydides goes on to describe its symptoms and development, and how it killed so many in Athens."

Sam stared at the book. "But that was over thousands of years ago."

"Drake is thousands of years old." Sloane held her gaze when she stared at him in astonishment. "This virus is an ancient scourge, but Drake was alive when it struck before. Jorge brought that arm into our time from an infected individual in the past, from roughly the same era as Drake."

Sam opened her mouth and closed it again. She deliberately chose to ignore Drake's age and its apparent impossibility. She'd thought until recently that it was impossible for a man to change shape and become a dragon, too. Her gaze trailed to Sloane's tattoo as she wondered just what other supposed impossibilities were realities.

Jac's stone.

Sam shook her head. She stuck to the science. "But viruses mutate over time. Even if Drake was exposed several thousand years ago, over that time period, the virus would have mutated. He might not be immune to it any more—just as humans aren't immune to each new strain of influenza, even if they've had flu before."

"It didn't have time to mutate," Sloane said. "The infected arm and the topaz yellow dragon that is Jorge traveled through time, passing centuries in the blink of an eye." He spoke with confidence, as if such a feat were completely reasonable. Sam decided to use the descriptor "impossible" less readily. "Drake was enchanted for the better part of those centuries, so he essentially was frozen as time passed. Neither he nor the virus had a chance to mutate."

Sam took a gulp of hot tea. "Next you're going to tell me about the healing power of the Dracontias."

Sloane snorted. "That's a myth," he said with a disparagement that relieved Sam. "*Pyr* don't have healing stones in their foreheads. If they did, my job would be a lot easier."

"Why do you help them?" she asked, not bothering to hide her bitterness. "Why do you serve them and tend them, helping them to heal? They're abominations..."

"Why do you *think* I do?" Sloane said, interrupting her with a severity she knew was out of character. His eyes were very dark and he seemed to be glittering right in front of her.

Sam put her mug down and stood up, suddenly understanding even more.

The answer was a lot more than she wanted to know—but it explained everything.

CHAPTER TWENTY-FIVE

ou're one of them, aren't you? It's not them, it's *we*."
Sam wanted Sloane to deny her conclusion, but he
held her gaze steadily.

Daring her to believe another impossible thing in
rapid succession.

Sam had to turn her back on him, she was so agitated. He and
the dragon that had infected Nathaniel were two of a kind. It was
appalling to think that she'd been having sex with a dragon shape
shifter, with one of the species responsible for the loss of her son.
Never mind that she'd even been hoping for more from him.

The realization made Sam want to hurl in the sink.

Or hurt something.

Preferably Sloane.

She spun back to face him, wanting to find some hint that it
wasn't true, but Sloane just looked resolute.

"Of course I am," he snapped. "I heal my own kind."

"That's just wrong," Sam muttered.

"Is it? What you don't seem to understand is that we are
divided, into *Pyr* who defend the treasure that is the human race,
and *Slayers* who would exterminate both *Pyr* and humans from the
face of the earth."

"Which are you?" She shivered at the coldness that filled his
gaze.

"You have to ask?" Sloane's disgust was clear. "I am the
Apothecary of the *Pyr*," he said with some pride. "I heal my kind. I
protect humans and heal them when I can. When I can't, I ask for
help." His gaze bored into hers and Sam found it very easy to
believe in that moment that Sloane could become a fire-breathing

dragon. "Why do you think I invited you here?"

"You didn't invite me. I had that dream..." Sam's voice faded to nothing as she gaped at him. "That's how you communicated with Veronica, too, isn't it? You infected her dreams!"

"Her dreams weren't *infected*. Dreams can be a good way to communicate with people, without leaving any discernible signs."

"This is all about hidden power, isn't it? It's all about subversion and conspiracy..."

Sloane's eyes flashed and he jabbed a finger toward Veronica. "Does that look like subversion to you? You said yourself that she was healing! How can you look at Ronnie and doubt my intentions?"

There was that. He had helped her. Sam bit her lip, sat down, and forced herself to take a soothing sip of tea. That gold dragon wouldn't have helped, which implied that maybe there *were* two kinds of dragon shifters. "Why did you invite me? You said Veronica had your antidote."

"It didn't heal her." Sloane showed a frustration that again Sam could understand. "It pushed the disease back into its latent phase, but didn't eradicate it. That's why I'm asking for your help, so that together, we can ensure she survives."

"Why? Because she's bearing the son of a dragon?" Sam couldn't hide her disgust at the thought. "You need her to breed more of your kind, like some kind of surrogate..."

Sloane seized her wrist and pulled her closer. There was a shimmering blue light around his body and his eyes were glittering. For the first time, she feared him. "Because no one else needs to die, that's why," he said, his voice hard.

"Why should I help you?"

"I thought healing was what you did." There was a challenge in his tone. "I thought we had that in common. I thought you wanted to find a cure."

Sam swallowed and couldn't avert her gaze. She felt pinned to the spot, and her pulse was racing. "You're right," she admitted. "I do. I'm just not sure that you do."

Sloane granted her a look so skeptical that she was chastened. "Look at my house. Look at how much money has been expended to create a refuge for her. No expense has been spared, because this ancient scourge has to be eliminated and anything I can do, I will."

She couldn't argue with that evidence. What he had done to his house defied belief.

Sam squared her shoulders. "Okay. What can I do?"

"I missed something," Sloane confessed and she again felt a commonality with him. "I must have overlooked some detail." Partial victories were the worst, although they always brought the solution closer. "Maybe I don't know enough about human physiology to see the nuance." He met her gaze again. "You do."

Sam was keenly aware of the heat of Sloane's body, of his muscled strength so close to her own. It was easy to remember how good it had been with him...

She frowned, trying to force herself to think of practicalities instead of the appeal of more sex with Sloane. "Have I been infected already by coming into your house?"

"Don't be ridiculous. The greenhouse was converted to an isolation chamber with airlocks and negative pressure before Veronica arrived. Only Drake goes in there without a suit, and frankly, I don't think anyone could keep him out."

Sam blinked. "But you can't just isolate a virus or an antivirus in the kitchen. We'll need equipment and..."

Sloane stepped back and gestured with impatience. Sam preceded him to the far side of the kitchen. The airlock was there, and she saw that a whole section of the house was sealed off, along with the greenhouse. Once again, she'd underestimated him. Or once again, he'd gone so far beyond expectation that his choices couldn't have been anticipated. "There's a full lab behind that door. It's down a few steps then built into the hill behind the house. You'll have to suit up to check it out."

Sam was awed. "This is why you wouldn't let me into your house."

"You're the one person who might have guessed the truth."

Sam nodded as she took it all in. "I'm sorry. I made assumptions again."

"You did," Sloane said, his voice tight. "But they weren't unreasonable ones."

She studied him once more, guessing that he'd been pushing himself hard in this quest for a cure, and her heart squeezed. "You realize that if you *have* found a cure, it would be a huge discovery."

"I only found the first part of the puzzle. I need your help to solve the rest." Sloane eyed her. "I don't want credit for this, or really, even to be named as being involved. It can be your discovery."

Sam was astonished. "Sloane! This is the kind of thing that puts scientists in history books. Everyone dreams of it. You can't just give it away."

"I can and I will." When he spoke with such determination, she couldn't doubt that he was telling her the truth. "If that's the price of your help, it's an easy one for me to pay. Fame isn't in my cards."

"You work in secret," Sam guessed.

"To protect my kind."

Sam held his gaze, understanding what a huge sacrifice he was prepared to make. A discovery like this, and the chance to refine it, was everything she'd always told herself that she wanted. The funny thing was now that it was within her grasp, it felt inadequate.

She would have been a lot happier if Sloane had been glad to see her.

And happier yet if he wasn't what he said he was.

Sam shook her head. She just needed more sleep to have a better perspective, but it didn't seem likely that she'd get it soon. The fact was that the virus was still spreading, people were still falling ill and dying. She'd be crazy to decline this opportunity to make a difference.

She had to make sure she didn't make a mistake, though.

"I'll do it for my kind," she said. "Not to help dragons in any way."

"Understood," Sloane said tersely.

"And this is purely a working relationship," she added, not knowing how she'd keep her thoughts straight if he touched her.

Anger flashed in Sloane's eyes. "Right. No cross-species contact."

"That's not what I meant."

"It's exactly what you meant." Sloane lifted five huge binders off the shelf and offered them to her. "All my notes. You can find me in the lab when you're up to speed."

It was outrageous.

Sam was determined to think the worst of him. Sloane didn't have to be a tarot card reader to pick up on her impressions. Her eyes showed her thoughts so clearly.

It had been weird initially that she'd wanted him for one thing only—or insisted as much—but he hadn't been able to really hold that against her.

After all, he had little to offer her in the long term.

Besides, Sloane knew that touch and pleasure could heal. He'd known that Sam was making progress.

The fact that she could think so little of him now, that after all the lovemaking they'd experienced, the dinners they'd shared and the conversations they'd had, that she could assume that he was some evil *Slayer* like Jorge infuriated him as little else could have done.

That he needed her help was salt in the proverbial wound.

Sloane wanted more, much more, but without being able to promise Sam a future, without being sure when his own firestorm would spark, he knew it would be wrong to return even to their earlier relationship. They'd be co-workers.

That Sam apparently didn't even want simple sex—or him—now that she knew his truth only made him more infuriated with the injustice of it all. He could have loved her with all his heart, but he didn't have the right to do so, and she didn't want him.

Once they solved this mystery and ensured Ronnie's welfare, they'd part forever.

Sloane realized that the price of healing the world might be higher for him personally than he'd ever dreamed. His father had warned him that it might be this way, but Sloane couldn't turn away from the search for an antidote.

Whatever the price to himself, he would pay it willingly.

"He's expecting you," Cassie said when she answered the door to Erik.

The words gave Erik a bad feeling. The last time he'd visited and Lorenzo had been expecting him, he'd walked into an illusion. He forced a smile, dismissed his foreboding and ushered Eileen and Zoë into the foyer ahead of him. The women greeted each other and kissed cheeks, then Cassie exclaimed over Zoë.

Erik took the opportunity to look around. The house was like Lorenzo's previous abode in Nevada in that it was luxuriously appointed, defended on all sides and remote from the city. It was unlike the previous house in that everything was an order of magnitude bigger, shinier and more expensive.

Plus Cassie and the boys were there.

Erik was aware of the prickle of dragonsmoke as he entered the palatial foyer and understood that Lorenzo was determined to defend the prizes of his hoard. He couldn't have missed Zoë's awe at her surroundings, mostly because his daughter was silent. He looked back to see how wide her eyes were. Eileen held fast to Zoë's hand, not hiding her own astonishment much better.

"Is he at the theatre?" Erik asked, guessing that Lorenzo was making preparations for his new show.

"No. He's by the pool with the boys." Cassie invited them down a corridor that led to the right and toward the back of the house. There was an indoor pool there, one long glassed wall giving a view of the property and an adjoining pool that sparkled outside in the sunshine. The landscaping ensured that the area was completely private and hidden from casual view. Lorenzo was on the phone, insisting to a contractor that he *did* want the more expensive seats in the theatre, despite the contractor's opinion that the extra cost was unnecessary. A young boy with Lorenzo's dark coloring played on the marble floor with building blocks, while a younger boy with more fair coloring slept in a cradle.

Evidently they were accustomed to the sound of their father's voice.

Lorenzo turned and raised a hand. He looked well, to Erik's eye, as tanned and fit as ever but somewhat more relaxed than he had been. His eyes were bright with the challenge of bringing his new show to life, and Erik wondered how well his fellow *Pyr* had done with retirement.

He could guess.

Lorenzo ended his call and came to greet them. The satisfaction that Erik thought he'd detected over the phone was obvious now that they stood face to face.

"What are you scheming?" Erik demanded.

Lorenzo smiled. "Scheming?" He turned to Cassie. "Do I scheme?"

"Of course you do," she said with a roll of her eyes. "It might be your best trick."

"How so?"

"Because you usually anticipate everything."

Lorenzo's eyes lit with delight at that response.

Cassie then addressed Eileen. "Coffee? Iced tea? What can I get you?" The two women walked together, Zoë following, and Eileen admired the boys and the house.

"What then?" Erik asked in old-speak.

"You won't like it. You never approve of anything truly audacious."

Erik's sense of foreboding grew. "While you never seem to understand the merit of restraint."

"When we're fighting for our survival and that of our sons?" Lorenzo's eyes glittered. "Restraint has no part in that battle."

"And that's why you're back?"

"I'm back to do my part," Lorenzo said flatly.

"But on your own terms," Erik guessed.

Lorenzo smiled. He pulled a business card from his pocket and flicked the corner of it before handing it to Erik. "I'm giving an exclusive interview tomorrow. You might have heard of the journalist in question."

"Maeve O'Neill?" Erik was appalled. "She's determined to show us in bad light and turn public opinion against us..."

"Which is why she needs to change her mind." Lorenzo opened his eyes wide, feigning innocence. "I thought I could help."

Erik sat down hard, once again having the sense that matters were spinning out of his control in Lorenzo's presence. "Wait a minute. What am I missing? Why is she interviewing you?"

Lorenzo sat down beside him. "Because Cassie offered to get her an exclusive interview with the *Pyr* she photographed in the desert while he shifted shape."

Erik couldn't summon a word for a moment. "But that was you!"

Lorenzo waved a hand. "Ergo, my interview with Maeve."

"But how are you going to do it? In which form?" Erik pushed to his feet again, guessing the answer. "Are you going to break the Covenant and reveal your human identity to her? In front of a camera?"

"Yes," Lorenzo said easily. He laughed at Erik's shock. "I had to offer something juicy for her to even show up."

"But this is outrageous and a violation of every...." Erik began to roar. Cassie and Eileen looked back at the two *Pyr*.

"I'm going to beguile her," Lorenzo said, interrupting Erik flatly. "I'm not that careless."

"How do you know that you can?"

Lorenzo scoffed. "Because I'm the best."

Erik exhaled, glared across the pool then back at Lorenzo, who smiled at him with a serenity Erik didn't share. "It's risky."

"That's what I like about this plan."

"You could reveal us all!"

"But I won't." Lorenzo shrugged. "Maybe we should have prosecco with lunch. Cassie? What do you think?"

Erik shook the business card under Lorenzo's nose. "Don't you smell *Slayer* on this? Don't you smell Jorge? If she's in alliance with him, this could be a trap."

"I hope it is," Lorenzo replied with a confidence Erik didn't share. "I'd like nothing better than to go talon to talon with Jorge." His eyes glimmered. "Just think. I could be the one to wipe the last *Slayer* from the face of the planet. It would look good in lights, don't you think?"

With that, Erik knew he wouldn't change Lorenzo's mind.

Lorenzo meanwhile popped the cork and poured four glasses of prosecco. He held his up so the bubbles caught the sunlight and saluted them all with characteristic confidence. "To our health, our triumph, and our future as guardians of the earth," he said, lifting the glass with a flourish.

Erik drank the toast, hoping it wasn't the last drink he ever shared with this infuriating *Pyr*.

He knew better than to expect that Lorenzo would ever change.

Sloane and Sam worked together in charged silence, day after day.

She could feel his controlled fury, but didn't really know what else he expected of her. A dragon shifter had infected her only son with a virus that had ended his life too soon, a virus that was ending lives all over the world. Sam had no kindness in her heart for dragon shifters, no matter what label they gave themselves.

Maybe Sloane had no expectations.

Or maybe he didn't have any expectations of *her* any more.

The thing was that she had lots of feelings for Sloane. Sam found herself slanting glances at him as they worked side by side in his lab, and hated that even in protective gear, he was the sexiest man she'd ever known. When he cast her a simmering glance, or asked for help in that measured tone, she couldn't believe how powerful his effect upon her still was.

She wanted Sloane, in every possible way.

It was crazy, but it was true. Even knowing what he was, she wanted to be with him. She was really glad to be back in California and at least to see him daily, even though their conversations were terse and focused on the research. She could have revealed him and shared his secret, and he hadn't demanded her silence, but she couldn't expose him. Her reaction was illogical and conflicted, even though Sam had never been illogical in her life.

That she wanted to be more illogical and jump his bones until he begged for mercy might just be a sign that she was losing it. She was pretty sure she wouldn't feel conflicted about doing that.

Maybe that was the danger.

They worked together for the first third of the day, comparing notes, analyzing results and making plans for new strategies. Then they worked in shifts, each alone in the lab for a third of the day while the other slept, ate, and revived a little. They were long days, but there was little choice. Sam read the account in Thucydides over and over again, then researched that plague online. Medical scholars were divided as to what it had been. A variant of plague, but without buboes? A kind of typhus with different lesions? Perhaps the scholars who said it had mutated itself out of existence were right—except that it was back and killing again.

No wonder humans had no antibodies or resistance to it. It might as well have come from Mars.

Sam found herself consulting the various books in Sloane's extensive library, reading in bed, eating very little. There had been a lot of speculation about the disease documented in Thucydides' book, but there was no clear conclusion. She spoke to Drake about it, but he hadn't actually developed the illness. He'd seen it but the symptoms he reported were similar to those in the book.

Lee, the man she'd met on the road and offered a ride, was also staying at the house. He had taken charge of the kitchen. Sam felt a little bit guilty that she forgot to eat regularly, as was typical when she was trying to solve a riddle, and often reheated his beautifully prepared meals in the microwave. He wasn't much for talking, but the house was always filled with the sounds of his work. Was he another dragon shifter? Sam didn't know and didn't want to. His wholesome cooking was helping Veronica to heal and that was a good thing.

Were they *all* dragon shifters?

When Sam did lie awake, she thought about dragon shifters, good and bad, and had to admit that there was merit in Sloane's argument. She often woke up in bed in the spare room that she was using, even though she'd fallen asleep on the couch, or found a meal left for her in the kitchen.

It was Drake who finally broke the tension between herself and Sloane.

"You are vexed with him," Drake said softly. He was leaning on the glass divider between the house and the conservatory when Sam entered the kitchen one morning.

If he was going to be blunt, Sam could play that game. "He didn't tell me the truth."

"You did not confess all of yours, either," the other man observed, no accusation in his tone.

"That's different," Sam said and took a sip of coffee.

Drake watched her steadily. "There is much you do not understand about our kind."

"And I hope I never know it. As soon as she's healed, I'm out of here."

Drake shook his head. "There is too much heat in your words for that to be true." Sam might have protested, but he held up a hand. "You speak like a woman spurned, not one who has been told less than the whole story."

Sam had to admit that there was truth in that, but she wouldn't admit it aloud. Instead she sipped her coffee and waited.

"I will guess that Sloane offered both more than you desired and less," the older man continued. "As is often the way of our kind. The issue is that there is no firestorm between the two of you, and that restricts his choices." Drake shrugged. "At least, it restricts the choices of a man with any honor in his soul."

While Sam liked that character reference, she was confused. "I don't understand."

"No, but you will. Let me tell you about the firestorm." Drake gestured and Sam pulled out a stool, guessing that this might take a while. She leaned against the glass on her side, while Drake was close on the other.

Lee had made croissants fresh that morning, and just this once, Sam treated herself to two as she listened to Drake.

Chandra dreamed.

She dreamed that she became Snow, that she flew through mist with the bird's agility and confidence. She saw jagged green peaks snared in fog and heard the sound of dripping water. She smelled lush vegetation and heard the screams of parrots just before the mist suddenly cleared.

The parrots flew past in a massive flock, an explosion of color against the green of the jungle. She soared high, then dipped between mountain peaks, coasting over a city made of fitted stone. It was perched in the mountains and moonlight fell upon the stones.

Chandra awakened abruptly, finding herself jostled against Thorolf in a rental van. She could taste blood and chocolate and was a bit disoriented to find herself back in her own form again. Raynor slept contently in a car seat beside her, already showing an ease with travel that impressed her.

They were hunting dragon eggs in the area that the next eclipse would be visible. They'd started in Chile, thinking there might be a connection with the Easter Island site and had been driving northward with no clues and no luck.

Until now.

Brandon and Liz were on a boat, doing the same thing but starting at Easter Island.

"They're at a ruin in the jungle," Chandra said. "Like a hidden city. Snow just showed me."

"What kind of jungle? What kind of city?" Thorolf asked with excitement. "Could you draw it?"

He pulled over and Chandra drew the sight from her dream as well as she could. "It was misty and very lush. I could hear water dripping, and a river too."

"Wait a minute," Thorolf said, snapping his fingers. "Didn't this all start at Machu Picchu?"

Chandra looked up, confused. "What do you mean?"

"The Dragon Tail Wars," he said with visible excitement. "Quinn's firestorm was first, after the moon changed nodes. I remember he said that Ambrose—"

"Who?"

"Dead *Slayer*." Thorolf said dismissively, then continued. "Ambrose had targeted Sara and her parents while they were on vacation, right after the node changed. They had a car accident on their way to Machu Picchu and were burned to death."

"And Sara?"

"She'd cancelled at the last minute so they went without her. He was targeting her, trying to stop the Smith's firestorm before it began." Thorolf tapped at his phone, and against all expectation, there was an internet connection. "Is that it?" He showed her an image of Machu Picchu and Chandra caught her breath.

"Yes."

"Then we have a destination." He handed her the phone. "Can you call Erik? We've got a lot of driving to do, and we might as well take advantage of the connection. It probably won't last."

One opportunity to conceive a child.

One destined mate, even though the *Pyr* could live for centuries or even millennia.

It was incredible. Sam stared into her coffee, thinking about Drake's confession. She couldn't imagine how someone would wait for the firestorm, given that the *Pyr* could live for so long.

On the other hand, she had to think that it would be great to have such a clear signal as the sparks of a firestorm. She wanted to see one, just to observe its effects. She wanted to feel one.

But at the end of it all, she respected what Drake was telling her about Sloane. The good *Pyr* made permanent relationships with their destined mates, after those mates were identified by the firestorm. They ensured that their sons had solid homes and that their mates were defended from harm.

This explained Drake's devotion to Veronica: she was his destined mate, and they'd had a firestorm. They'd satisfied it and she was carrying his child. He'd known the result from the sight of the first spark and had known that the baby would be a boy.

Also that the boy would develop *Pyr* traits at puberty.

Drake intended to stick around for the duration, which Sam admired.

But Sloane hadn't had a firestorm.

And when he did, he would choose as Drake had chosen. He would commit to his destined mate and to his son. His firestorm could spark in a week or in a century, but when it did, its importance would trump any relationship he had at the time.

But Drake had said that there was a prophecy that only *Pyr* or *Slayers* would survive the last blood moon in the Dragon's Tail of the moon's node. Sloane had to be hoping that his firestorm would spark in the next few months.

Otherwise, it might not spark at all.

He might not even survive.

None of them might survive. The prospect made Sam feel a bit sick. What if Veronica survived all of this only to lose the man she loved and the son she was carrying? What if Sloane was killed? Whether or not he was with Sam, she wished him well.

She wanted him to be alive and well somewhere in the world.

The truth was that his dragon nature was less important to her than she'd believed.

Sloane wasn't promising what he couldn't deliver, and Sam had to respect that.

On the day that they'd parted, she'd hoped he might leave an opening for them to get together again. When he hadn't, she assumed her feelings weren't reciprocated.

But that wasn't it. Not necessarily.

It was honorable of Sloane to decline to deepen the relationship if he feared he couldn't see it through. She admired him for his restraint and wished she hadn't spoken to him so harshly. He had helped her to heal, to begin her life again after her complete meltdown, and she owed him more than she'd given him.

Even if they had no real future.

Drake had suggested she watch the video footage of the eclipse over Australia, because he said it showed a *Pyr* experiencing his firestorm. The golden light that burned between the dark dragon and the woman he snatched from the talons of the other dragon was amazing. The image was blurry and taken in poor lighting from a distance. The woman's features were impossible to see, and Sam wondered whether she might have walked past her in the street.

But the topaz and gold dragon was more than familiar.

As was his ferocity.

Sam watched it repeatedly, unable to deny that the fighting dragons were clearly on two sides. Did she dare to believe that Sloane and his allies, the *Pyr*, hated this gold dragon as much as she did?

Could she and Sloane defeat the plan this dragon had put in motion if they worked more closely together?

It was more than worth a try.

Sam felt Sloane come into the kitchen, his presence as evident to her as a crackle of electricity. If this was just sexual attraction to a dragon shifter, the firestorm must be an incredible feeling.

"Planning to get any work done today?" he asked, a thread of impatience in his tone.

She spun to face him, letting him see what was on her laptop screen. "Drake told me about the firestorm."

Sloane's lips tightened in disapproval. "Did he?"

Sam knew she deserved his tone, but she wanted to start fresh. "What do you think it's like?"

"I expect it's amazing. I've only felt it second-hand, and even that's electrifying."

Sam watched him pour a cup of coffee. "What will happen to

the *Pyr*'s children, if you don't win?"

Sloane looked bleak. "I'm not sure. The oldest of this generation just turned seven. I doubt he'll have the chance to come into his powers at puberty, not if all the adult *Pyr* are gone. No *Slayer* would allow that."

His exhaustion touched her heart. "How old are you?"

Sloane took a slow breath and exhaled, his gaze darting over the kitchen then back to her. "I was born in 1655. My father, unlike many of the *Pyr*, kept precise records." He lifted a brow. "I'm a Scorpio."

Sam swallowed a smile. "Life and death, mystery, healing, secrets. I think even I might have guessed that," she teased and was rewarded with the brief flash of his smile. She sobered as she watched him stir his coffee. "What's it like, waiting for a firestorm?"

"Lonely," Sloane said. He lifted his gaze to hers. "What's it like, being unable to help your son survive?"

Sam's throat tightened so much that she could scarcely take a breath. "It's hell," she admitted. "It casts everything into doubt and leaves you second-guessing every decision." She turned her mug on the counter. "Did you know about Nathaniel from the very start?"

Sloane leaned his hip against the counter. "I knew you were hurting. When I found the picture, I recognized him. That smile could light the universe."

"Yes," Sam agreed. "It lit mine."

Sloane's voice softened in a way that made her want to fling herself into his arms. "I'm sorry, Sam. No parent should have to go through that."

"No, they shouldn't."

They stood there for a long moment, and Sam found it hard to take a breath. She ached for the loss of Nathaniel all over again, and for all the other failures of her life. "Wish you were here," she said, quoting the last note from her son. Her fingers were tangling in the chain of the necklace. "I'm never there, you know."

"I suspect every working mom says that."

"No, I'm never there," Sam corrected, her anger turned on herself now, where it belonged. "I always think I'm making the right choice, and it never quite works out. I'm always sure of how things are, then find out that I'm wrong. I know things are impossible, but then they happen." She lifted her head to find Sloane watching her closely. "I thought my mom would always be there, and even when she died, I thought my father would always be there. That's stupid."

"That's optimism and trust."

"It's illogical." Sam shook her head with frustration. "It's about assumptions. I assumed marriage was forever. I assumed people would see their grandchildren born. I assumed children survived their parents. I was wrong."

"You're not the only one who has believed in the future and been disappointed."

"I took things for granted. I took *people* for granted. I thought they'd always be there, waiting for me to finish what I was doing." Sam lifted her gaze. "But they aren't. It's not always their fault, but that doesn't change the fact that everything can be snatched away in a heartbeat."

Like Sloane.

Sam caught her breath, realizing that he could be snatched away within months.

She didn't want to even think about it.

She needed to change, and to change right now.

"It isn't usually," Sloane said. He pursed his lips, considering her words, and she liked that the anger was gone from his expression. He was giving her a second chance, just because she was trying again. He really did understand intuitively how to heal, both people and situations, and her heart swelled with something more than admiration.

"I've said crappy things to you," she said. "I've made assumptions. I'm sorry."

"You were hurting."

"Still." She swallowed. "I was wrong."

"Even though I'm a dragon shifter?"

Sam nodded. "Thank you for helping me."

Sloane held her gaze, that little hum of electricity between them becoming stronger. "I think there's a balance to be struck, between taking care of what and who you love, and trusting in the future. Taking care of what matters today, so that if tomorrow doesn't come, you don't have regrets."

"Do you know how to do that?"

His smile was rueful. "No, but I keep trying." Their gazes locked and held for a potent moment.

"What do you regret?" Sam asked on impulse. "Is there anything?"

"Lots of things. I've had some time to mess up."

Sam smiled because she knew he expected it.

"Bad partings. Blunt speech when it was more cruel than honest."

"Oh good, I'm not the only one."

Sloane shrugged. "Things I never said aloud to my father. I hope he knew how much I admired him." He considered his coffee as if it were fascinating. "I was young when he died. We were in the midst of arguing about my future plans."

"Whether you'd become the Apothecary or not."

"How I'd become the Apothecary," Sloane corrected. "The role and the responsibility was mine, but I wanted to do it differently. My father always argued for the power of tradition."

"You wanted to go to med school, such as it was then."

"I see now that he was afraid for me. He feared that I'd be revealed."

"Probably not then, but now you would. Drake's blood is seriously awesome, and in med school, we did use our own blood for various tests. Now you'd be outed immediately."

"My father only saw the risk." Sloane studied the floor. "There was a time when our kind were nearly hunted to extinction by humans. It was before I was born, but my father remembered the hunts, as does Erik, our leader. It left a scar upon the surviving *Pyr*, an inability to trust the human race as much as they might want to."

"I'll guess even you can't treat that."

"No. There are injuries that we carry with us to our graves. That's something that *Pyr* and humans have in common." His gaze was steady and warmed her. "Maybe those are the injuries that we can only try to move past ourselves, with the power of our minds."

"Physician, heal thyself?" Sam asked, her tone teasing.

Sloane almost smiled. "Or Apothecary, as the case might be."

Could she heal her own wounds? Since meeting Sloane, Sam was starting to believe it possible. She stood in his kitchen, which was filled with the scents of warm butter and hot coffee. She watched him, feeling more alive than she had in years even as he was utterly still. The moment could have been frozen in time, potent with possibilities. She sensed the opportunities ahead of her and a vitality that she'd nearly forgotten could exist. She could shape her life. She could change her choices. She could try to heal her own wounds. She could choose differently, change herself, reshape the world.

She was glad that she'd decided to wear Nathaniel's gift and knew she'd only done it because of Sloane's gentle persistence.

Her fingers rose to it and tangled in the chain. "My sister adored Nathaniel, you know. He might have been her own son. She always wanted kids, lots of them, and she'd be an awesome mom. She just never seems to meet the right guy. In a way, I felt that I was giving her the chance to live vicariously, to have Nathaniel all to herself." Sam bit her lip. "Of course, she saw it differently. She thought I was just handing him off because he was inconvenient."

"That's hard."

"We've said a lot of hard things to each other over the years. We said more when Nathaniel was infected. I think we both blamed ourselves for his condition, but out loud, we blamed each other. We weren't even speaking during his illness, although we both visited him." Sam shook her head at her own pride and stubbornness. "We ensured that we visited at different times. But I didn't visit nearly enough. It broke my heart to see my son like that, to know that I'd failed him and that I was still failing him, that taking time to visit him was time away from the lab and a possible cure."

"You must have been exhausted," Sloane said quietly. "No wonder you burned out."

"Spun out, burned out, imploded." Sam grimaced. "All of the above and more. Jac gave me the gift box at the funeral. I guess she'd tried to do it sooner, but I rebuffed her. That note." She swallowed. "That note just finished me."

"It would," Sloane agreed. "Although Nathaniel couldn't have known the power his words would have, not when he wrote them."

"Of course not, but right then and right there, it was the straw that broke the camel's back. My back. I walked away from all of it, without a backward glance, bought the house in California and wept for a week after I moved in."

Sloane smiled gently at her. "That was when you decided to read tarot cards?"

"Illogical!" Sam admitted. "Insane maybe. But Jac had said I needed to get in touch with my own feelings and her accusation hit a nerve. All that intuition, emotion and touchy-feely stuff had never been my department. It was hers. I was drawn to the cards in a shop, and for once, I decided to follow my impulse. I thought it would be easy to learn to interpret them."

"You thought you would apply logic to it and memorize the system."

"I guess I did." Sam dared to look at him and liked that he didn't seem to have judged her and found her wanting. "But there isn't a system. It's like they have a life of their own, and their meanings change depending upon who asks the question and when."

"Isn't that impossible?" Sloane asked with a smile.

Sam smiled back at him. "Once I would have said that it was, but I've learned that a lot of apparently impossible things are real."

Sloane chuckled and topped up their coffees. "Maybe the cards called to you, because they knew you needed them."

Sam shook her head. "No. It was a dark-haired stranger, a Knight of Cups, who came to my door bearing wine who did that."

Sloane averted his gaze, reminding Sam of what Drake had told her about the firestorm. He wouldn't promise what he couldn't deliver. She respected that. It was a sign of a moral code that she admired.

"What if you never have a firestorm?" she asked softly.

"I will," he replied, with a confidence Sam wished she shared.

Sam swallowed, then admitted something she never would have expected herself to say aloud. "The world is in flux all around me now, for the first time." It was terrifying to make such a confession, but it also felt right. "It's unfamiliar and unpredictable, and I feel a bit lost."

"You'll find your stride. We all do."

"Probably. But in a way, I'm jealous of your firestorm. It would be nice to know that *something* was absolutely true and unassailable."

Sam found Sloane in front of her then, though she hadn't seen him move. His fingers were under her chin and he bent to kiss away a tear she didn't even know she'd shed. He felt so good and she couldn't keep herself from leaning against his warmth and strength.

"Here's a truth," he murmured. "You did more for Nathaniel than anyone could have done. You gave your all."

"It wasn't enough." Sam heard again her father's expectation that she could always do more and always give more.

"That doesn't mean there was no point." Sloane was holding her shoulders in his hands, and Sam welcomed the weight of his grasp as much as his reassurance. "You know that success comes in stages when combating viruses. You know that there's no instant or easy answer."

"He was my son," Sam whispered. "I wasn't even there when he died!"

Sloane shook his head. "You were in his mind, in his memories and in his heart. We should all be so lucky to have someone fighting with such diligence on our behalf." He seemed to believe what he said.

Sam knew she wanted to believe it more than anything she'd ever heard.

"Nathaniel *was* your son," Sloane whispered. "He had to love you for everything you are." He bent to touch his lips to her forehead, and Sam felt her eyes close in gratitude as his arms closed around her.

"I don't deserve your solace," she whispered and heard Sloane chuckle. "I'm not your mate and this isn't your firestorm."

"You're stuck with this kiss anyway."

But not more than that.

But then, that meant she had little to lose by telling him the truth in her heart.

Sam tipped her head back to meet Sloane's gaze. "I've missed you," she admitted.

His eyes darkened and he backed her into the counter, his gaze sweeping over her before he bent to capture her mouth with his. His kiss was potent and gentle, as if he feared she'd reject him, and Sam couldn't bear that she'd put any such doubt in his mind. She wrapped her arms around his neck and pulled him closer, surrendering all she had to his kiss.

When Sloane deepened his kiss and locked her in his embrace, Sam didn't care who or what he was.

She just wanted more of his touch.

No matter what he was.

CHAPTER TWENTY-SIX

here was a better rapport between Sam and Sloane, thanks to Drake's intervention. They worked together in the lab after that, comparing notes and observations, and Sam dared to believe that their progress was better.

Faster.

Drake's blood was amazing. Sam knew she'd never tire of studying it. The cells within it were sufficiently similar to human cells that she could identify them, but their actions were so different. White cells, for example, always defended the body from infection, but Drake's white cells rode for war with a vigor and speed that astonished Sam. Not only did they isolate and surround any virus she injected into the sample, but they multiplied at a phenomenal rate. They were apparently driven to contain and destroy any intruding cells and to do so with incredible speed. Sam was blown away by it.

"Do you *Pyr* ever get sick?" she asked Sloane one day.

"We tend to be wounded more often," he replied, his tone revealing that he was giving all his attention to the sample he was studying.

"Did any of you get this virus?"

Sloane shook his head. "We haven't been taking any chances."

"So, as Apothecary, you mostly tend battle wounds. Unless there are specific diseases that only *Pyr* get."

He nodded once, then frowned. "There is one thing you could call an illness specific to us, one that might as well be fatal. When *Pyr* turn *Slayer*, it's a choice that manifests physiologically."

"How so?"

"*Slayers* have blood that's both black and corrosive."

Sam looked up at that. "What makes it black? Extra hemoglobin?"

"Their decision to turn away from the Great Wyvern and her wisdom," he said. She saw that he was completely serious, even though he sounded like Jac. "Their decision to be selfish and to decline the quest of the *Pyr* to defend the earth and its treasures means that the divine spark dies within them. *Slayers* aren't dead, but they might as well be." Sloane shrugged. "The world would be a better place if they were dead."

They didn't talk about the reckoning that was pending.

"Good dragons and bad dragons?" Sam kept her tone light, but Sloane straightened.

"The last living *Slayer* was Jorge, who is topaz with gold," he said. "You might remember his appearance in Seattle."

Sam flinched, hiding her reaction by looking into the microscope again.

"Since then, there have been new *Slayers* appearing."

"Like the ones in the video from Australia?"

Sloane nodded. "Groups of them, hatching at each eclipse." He shook his head. "We've never seen anything like it before. I think they might be clones of a dead *Slayer*."

Sam shuddered. Then she realized something and looked up. "Wait a minute. Jorge wasn't infected with the virus."

"Possibly because he's consumed the Elixir, and it ensured that he recovered quickly from any infection."

"The Elixir?"

Sloane turned an intent look upon her. "There's a substance called the Dragon's Blood Elixir. It confers a kind of immortality upon any *Pyr* who consumes it. He'll heal quickly after taking it, but always needs more."

"Like a drug, then," Sam mused.

"It's a toxin," Sloane corrected. "Only *Slayers* have ever consumed it, so it makes them both more violent and harder to kill. I'll guess that Jorge healed from the exposure to the virus, because of the Elixir."

"But Drake wasn't infected with the virus, either, and I'm guessing he hasn't had the Elixir?"

"No. His immunity is probably because he had antibodies as

old as the virus itself, also unmutated."

Sam spun on her stool to face him. "But what if *Pyr* can't get this infection at all? What if it's not the Elixir and not Drake's age but something fundamental in your physiology that ensures you can't get it?"

Sloane turned to stare at her and she knew she had his attention.

"Do you know *any Pyr* who've been infected with the Seattle virus?" Sam asked.

"No," Sloane said, shaking his head. "No! Not one. That's brilliant. I was assuming they hadn't been exposed, but you're right. They must have been, given how widely it's spread. Plus Theo and Kristofer helped Drake recover Ronnie from Jorge—they were exposed and they never got it."

Sam shrugged. "It might be simply that they failed to have an exchange of body fluids with her..."

Before Sam could finish, Sloane peeled off the hood of his HazMat suit and chucked it aside, then shed his heavy gloves. "There's one way to find out." He unzipped the top of his suit and shrugged out of it, revealing the T-shirt he wore beneath and his muscled build. He grabbed a wide elastic band and wrapped it around his upper arm, then gestured to the syringes. "We'll take a before and an after sample," he instructed Sam. "And compare the differences."

"Before and after what?" Sam asked, even though she was afraid she could guess what he was going to do.

"We're going to test *Pyr* immunity to the Seattle virus, right here and right now." His eyes were shining with resolve.

"No! You aren't going to inject yourself with it! That's not protocol," Sam protested. "We need to do this in a controlled process..."

Sloane interrupted her flatly. "We don't have time for protocol."

"We'll take a sample of your blood and infect it first..."

"And we won't learn nearly enough about the way my immune system responds," Sloane said, interrupting her again. "I'm going to infect myself and you're going to study the results. You're going to compare my body's reaction to Ronnie's, then try to isolate the variable that makes the difference." He shrugged.

"Assuming that there is one that does."

"You can't do this. It's irresponsible. Put your hood back on to protect yourself..."

Sloane seized Sam's hand and his gaze bored into hers. "It's my responsibility to defend the treasures of the earth, which include humans. I *can* do this, and I will." His intensity made her mouth go dry. "You can help me or I can do it alone."

Sam wanted to insist on protocol. She wanted to keep Sloane safe.

"My father warned me, Sam, that sometimes the Apothecary has to sacrifice his own welfare to serve the greater good," he said softly. "My destined role is to heal, regardless of the price."

She saw a determination in his dark eyes that told her she would lose the argument. And he was right: every moment counted.

His choice made her heart squeeze tight. She tied the tourniquet around his arm and took a syringe, turning his arm to find a vein. There was no denying the raw power of his body or his sheer good health. Sam's mouth went dry, though, because it was easy to remember how gently he had touched her.

But there wouldn't be any more of that. He'd have to go into isolation until they knew whether he was infected, if he exposed himself to the virus.

Sam didn't want to think about it. "Tell me about this treasures-of-the-earth thing that Drake mentioned," she invited, then eased the needle into his vein to take a blood sample.

"In the beginning, there was the fire," Sloane said quietly. His voice was low and melodic and it awakened her desire all over again. "And the fire burned hot because it was cradled by the earth. The fire burned bright because it was nurtured by the air. The fire burned lower only when it was quenched by the water. And these were the four elements of divine design, of which all would be built and with which all would be destroyed. And the elements were placed at the cornerstones of the material world and it was good.

"But the elements were alone and undefended, incapable of communicating with each other, snared within the matter that was theirs to control. And so, out of the endless void was created a race of guardians whose appointed task was to protect and defend the integrity of the four sacred elements. They were given powers, the better to fulfill their responsibilities; they were given strength and cunning and longevity to safeguard the treasures surrendered to their stewardship. To them alone would the elements respond. These guardians were—and are—the *Pyr*."

Sam set the filled vials aside, withdrew the needle and pressed a cotton ball into the puncture. "That's a very powerful verse. Did you just make it up?"

Sloane shook his head. "It's our story of who we are, of why we are." He took a clean syringe, then a vial of Ronnie's infected blood. He loaded the syringe and didn't hesitate before injecting it into himself. Sam watched, speechless, thinking it was the most heroic thing she'd ever seen.

"You really shouldn't have done that," she whispered.

"But I did," Sloane said, apparently without regret. "I'll join Ronnie and Drake in isolation until we're sure of the results." He pivoted then and might have left the lab, but suddenly turned back. "By the way, if I do get sick..."

Sam folded her arms around herself and waited.

Sloane pointed to the line of refrigerators. "Those *Slayer* clones I told you about? There's one in that fridge. Do not open the door."

Sam's mouth fell open. "He's not dead."

"He'd disintegrate if he was, and I'd have nothing left to test."

She turned to look at the fridge in question and couldn't stifle her shudder. There was a not-dead evil dragon that close? By the time she turned around again, Sloane was saluting her with two fingers and walking away.

What Sam really wanted was a kiss.

But he couldn't kiss her. Not now.

She spun to face the bench, feeling a bit sick. Sloane could contract the virus. In fact, given everything Sam had seen, chances were pretty good that he would—unless they were right about *Pyr* blood. In a way, she wished she hadn't speculated aloud. If Sloane did contract the virus, he might die, unless she managed to create an antidote.

And if she did manage to do that, it would be all because of Sloane and his choices.

He would even let her take all the credit.

But the prospect of losing him, even of him not being in the world any longer, was enough to shake the foundations of Sam's universe. She bit her lip and stared at the bench, filling with the certainty that she loved him.

Then she turned back to her work, knowing that it was up to her to ensure that Sloane survived his heroic choice.

Her gaze rose more than once to that fridge. She thought of the quote that reminded him of his father, of the caduceus and wondered if the *Slayer* might hold a key to the *Pyr*'s future.

First she had to work on ensuring that Sloane had a future.

Jac was excited and frightened. She knew exactly what Marco was intending to do, without him saying a word. She'd seen his devastation at Rafferty's injury and felt the power of the firestorm. He was *Pyr*, right to his marrow. There was no way he'd ally with the clone of Boris Vassily, not for any price.

He was going to trick the *Slayer*.

And she was going to help.

They waited in her apartment for Boris's instructions, keeping their distance from each other to try to manage the firestorm's insistence. Jac was pretty sure she wasn't the only one losing the battle. All she could think about was Marco, the way he'd touched her, the way he kissed, the way his body felt when he was crushed against her. She loved the way he took his time when seducing her and how thoroughly he satisfied her. She was dying of curiosity to know how much better the firestorm might make their lovemaking, and pretty certain she wouldn't last until September. Every time she glanced his way, it seemed she found his gaze upon her, his eyes dark and his expression sensual.

He looked like he could eat her alive.

She really wanted him to go for it.

"Will it kill us?" Marco asked on the second night that they were sleepless. The apartment seemed to be filled with a simmering heat, even though it was chilly and raining outside. Jac listened to the rain pattering on the window, sure there was no sexier sound on the planet.

Actually, all sounds were sexy to her now. The sound of water running in the bathroom meant that Marco was naked in the shower. The sound of cloth sliding over skin meant that Marco was getting undressed. The sound of a bare foot on the hardwood floor meant that Marco was close, maybe behind her, definitely watching. All or any of them were enough to make Jac tingle.

The sleepy sound of his voice made her catch her breath.

She rolled over to find him sitting on the floor in the doorway of her bedroom, keeping watch over her. The light from the firestorm's glow burnished his features, making him look both enigmatic and alluring.

"It might," she whispered. "Any *Pyr* reports of death by firestorm?"

Marco shook his head, a smile curving his lips slowly. Jac wanted to trace its path with her fingertip. "Not one."

"How about by spontaneous combustion?"

His smile flashed. "I think that only happens when a mate throws a road flare down a *Slayer*'s throat."

Jac rested her chin on her hands. "It was pretty satisfying."

"You're probably single-handedly responsible for how quiet it is."

"How so?"

"Fewer *Slayers* and Jorge has got to be hurting."

"Won't he recover?"

"The more serious the injury, the longer it takes, from what I understand."

"What about Boris?"

Marco flicked a glance her way in warning, and Jac remembered about the sharp senses of dragon shifters. "He'll be back," he said casually. "Once he figures out the best place to attack."

"Which just leaves us with time on our hands."

Marco shrugged. "He probably wouldn't mind if we satisfied the firestorm. We'd be less likely to draw the attention of the *Pyr* then."

"We should wait until after the fight, at least," Jac said and Marco arched a brow. "It says in the book that the firestorm can heal a *Pyr*'s injury."

His smile was slow and warm. "Sounds like you're thinking of keeping me around."

"Sounds like I am."

They eyed each other for a long hot moment, one that seemed to stretch through forever. The rain pattered on the windows, and Jac fought the urge to wriggle on the bed. She was burning with desire for Marco and couldn't resist him. Something about being alone together on a rainy night did it for her, and the firestorm was working with it. She swung her legs around and got out of bed. She peeled off her nightgown and cast it aside, seeing how he caught his breath as he watched. He seemed to have frozen in place, neither blinking nor breathing.

Just watching.

"There you go, playing with fire again," he murmured.

Jac laughed a little, then took measured steps toward him. It was amazing to watch the firestorm's sparks grow in power with every step and to see its glow brighten from orange to yellow to blinding white. Jac got hotter with every step, and she licked the salt from her own lip. She felt her nipples bead and let her hips sway, feeling like she was the hottest seductress on the planet.

When she had almost reached him, Marco eased to his feet. He had the effortless grace of an athlete and the body to match. He was wearing only his jeans, his T-shirt already discarded. He waited for her, that dragon confidence in his smile, and Jac took another step, bringing them toe to toe. They inhaled as one as a flurry of white sparks erupted between them, the flames dancing between them in a frenzy.

"It's like being struck by lightning," she whispered, then placed her hand on his shoulder.

"And wanting to have it happen again," Marco agreed. "There is an upside to not satisfying the firestorm, that's for sure."

"Have you ever been so hot?"

"Never. You?"

"Never." Jac eased closer. "Could it possibly be good enough to make it worth giving this up?"

"Only one way to find out," Marco murmured and slid his arm around her waist. He pulled Jac hard against him and the resulting flash nearly gave her heart failure. Then his mouth locked over hers, his kiss as demanding as she wanted it to be, and Jac drew him even closer. She dug her nails into his shoulders, wanting all he had, so snared in the firestorm in this moment that she couldn't have cared less about the future. Marco slanted his mouth over hers and deepened his kiss, turning around so that he had her pinned against the wall. Jac ran one foot up his leg, then locked her leg around his thigh. Marco speared his fingers into her hair, then rocked his hips against hers, giving her a teasing sample of his response to her.

"And you had to be a dragon shifter," Jac muttered when he lifted his head. "You couldn't just be a hot guy meant for me."

Marco grinned. "I am meant for you, and being a dragon shifter is what makes this so hot."

Jac couldn't argue with that. She wouldn't have argued, at least, if she'd had a chance to say anything.

In that moment, Boris manifested in the living room in a shimmer of blue.

"You could call ahead," Marco growled, even as he hid Jac's nudity from the *Slayer*'s view.

"I like surprises," Boris said mildly, though Jac peeked and didn't like the way his whole body seemed to glitter. Marco carried her back into the bedroom, his gaze locked with hers and she knew without a doubt that he intended to give Boris a surprise that *Slayer* wouldn't forget.

"Bring the crystal," he murmured in her ear. "We might need it." Marco then turned back to their guest, who surely had overheard his whispered words.

He meant, Jac knew, that she might need it to defend herself.

She was frightened then, frightened that Marco might not survive Boris's plan and that she wouldn't even have a chance to conceive Marco's son. As she dressed quickly, Jac acknowledged the truth. Marco was unlike any man she'd ever met, but in ways that were more important than his being a dragon shifter. He was honorable and noble. He kept his word and stood by his friends. He defended her and gave her the means to defend herself. If he died without their satisfying the firestorm, without an echo of him left in the world, it would be a tragedy.

That's when Jac knew exactly what she'd do if Marco survived. She'd accept the firestorm's challenge and face the future fearlessly, whatever it might bring.

"I have a bad feeling," Erik murmured for the umpteenth time.

"You're not alone in that. We should have left earlier," Eileen said.

It was late morning and they were driving across the desert. Their departure had been delayed and Eileen had a bad feeling of her own. Even though the air conditioning in the car was on full blast, it was getting hot. The sky was clear blue and the sunlight was blindingly bright. They still had a long drive to the next potential rest stop, and she didn't like that they'd be in a rental car under the midday sun.

"I had to speak to Lorenzo again," Erik said.

They'd circled this argument a dozen times already and Eileen's temper was fraying. Her only child was in this car and looked as if she were wilting. Eileen wasn't feeling so great herself. "We should have stayed another day," she said tersely.

"You're the one who wanted to get home."

"You're the one who forgets that not everyone has the longevity and strength of a dragon," Eileen snapped.

Erik turned to give her a look. "I don't forget. I *never* forget. I'm trying to balance a hundred concerns, including your desire to get home, but nothing is going right..."

"Just because Lorenzo isn't doing what you want him to do, you shouldn't take it out on us."

"I'm not!"

"Lorenzo *never* does what you want. Lorenzo never does what *anyone* wants." Eileen wiped her brow. "Except maybe Cassie, but we don't all have the power of the firestorm on our side."

To her surprise, that made Erik smile and relax a little. "You do," he said quietly, then reached to close his hand over hers. "I'm sorry. I want everything to end well."

"And you think I don't?"

"I know you do."

"I think you worry too much. You think there's only one *Slayer* left from those eggs, not counting the one in Sloane's lab, and that's assuming they really did die. Then there's Jorge, who is quiet..."

"And her card smelled like him," Erik admitted in a terse undertone.

Eileen turned to stare at him. "That journalist? The one who was going to interview Lorenzo?" She watched in horror as Erik nodded. "You're seriously telling me that Maeve O'Neill knows Jorge?"

"His scent was on her card. It was subtle, but it was there. That's why I lingered. I wanted to try to convince Lorenzo that he was being too confident."

That wasn't a stretch, to Eileen's thinking. Although none of the *Pyr* were insecure, Lorenzo had enough confidence for all of the *Pyr* together, with at least as much left over. "So, why did we leave at all, then?"

Erik frowned. "Lorenzo told me to."

"Since when do you do what he tells you to do?"

"Since he told me that he's going to beguile her and doesn't want any distractions." Erik scowled at the road. "He made it clear that he wanted to handle the interview alone, and I was frustrated enough to leave him to it."

"But now you have a bad feeling."

Erik inhaled slowly and his eyes narrowed, but not before Eileen saw how they were glittering. "Well, well," he murmured. "My foresight *isn't* gone." He pulled over the car and reached for the door. "Time for you to drive," he said softly, his gaze intent. "Just keep on toward our destination."

"What's going on?" Eileen asked as she slid behind the wheel.

"I feel a firestorm, and it's approaching fast."

How could that be? Whose firestorm was it? Eileen had no time to ask questions because Erik got out of the car. There was a shimmer of blue light around his body, and she knew he was hovering on the cusp of change.

"Mom?" Zoë asked from the backseat.

"Crawl over the seat and buckle up," Eileen said as she put the car into gear. She didn't like leaving Erik behind but she knew that their presence might only impede his ability to fight. Her heart was hammering and her mouth went dry. Zoë looked back as dust swirled behind them, and Eileen realized her knuckles were white on the steering wheel.

That was even before the woman dropped on the hood of the car. She seemed to have appeared out of thin air. She fell against the windshield, blocking the view. Eileen hit the brakes and the woman slid forward, then leapt to land on her feet in front of the car. She'd come around the car and was trying the passenger side door before Eileen could blink.

It was locked, of course.

"Open up!" the dark-haired woman demanded. "I'm a mate!"

She gestured to the road behind them, and Eileen saw the brilliant gold spark of a firestorm jump from the woman's hand. She still might have declined, but Zoë unlocked the door and slid across the bench seat to press against her mother. The woman threw herself into the car and leaned over the seat, watching whatever was happening behind them.

She held the darkfire crystal in her right hand and the spark within the stone was burning vigorously.

"I'm Jacelyn," she said. "You'd better hit it so I don't have to use this. I think it only carries one shot and we might need it later."

Eileen looked in the rearview mirror and saw that Erik was no longer alone. He was in his dragon form, his pewter and ebony scales gleaming under the midday sun. A familiar *Slayer* of ruby and gold was fighting him and another dragon of darkest anthracite was hovering in the air alongside the battling pair.

"That's Boris Vassily!" Eileen said, unable to believe her eyes.

"The third clone of him, actually." Jac said. "He calls himself Boris IV. There are six more hatching at the next eclipse, by the way, bringing the total to a tidy thirteen."

Eileen turned to stare at this woman, who was matter-of-fact about something so horrific. "You have to be kidding me."

Jac shook her head with such confidence that Eileen believed her. "Nope. Let's get out of here."

Eileen didn't share her casual acceptance of the situation. If Erik was going to need to fight to the death seven more times in the next six months, she wasn't letting him out of her sight for this fight. She turned the wheel hard, sending up a huge cloud of dust. They went off the road to make the turn and bounced over a few holes before reaching the pavement again.

"What are you doing?" Jac demanded.

"They've exchanged challenge coins," Eileen retorted. "I won't leave him behind." She gripped the steering wheel and pointed the car directly toward the dragonfight. She didn't know what exactly she could do, but she wouldn't just run away.

She heard Jac inhale and saw the firestorm's glow brighten

with proximity.

"Who's your *Pyr*?" she demanded.

"Marco."

Eileen frowned. The dragon Erik believed a traitor to the *Pyr* had appeared with Boris. That couldn't be a good sign. Was Marco turning *Slayer*, as Erik feared?

On the other hand, his mate was in Eileen's car, with the darkfire crystal. She looked as if she knew how to use it.

Maybe things weren't as bad as they looked.

Eileen crossed her fingers on the steering wheel and drove.

Boris materialized out of thin air.

Just as Erik had envisioned. He was in his dragon form, talons raised when Boris appeared before him. They both were in flight, circling and assessing each other's strengths. Boris smelled like *Slayer*, but had a vitality about him that didn't bode well for Erik. His ruby and gold scales glittered in the sunlight, and he looked like a treasure come to life. Erik was well aware that this version of Boris was in perfect health, while he could still feel the wounds he'd sustained in his battle against the other two versions of Boris in the fall.

At least Eileen was driving away.

He lifted his claws, ready to fight to the last. He wasn't going to think about the blood sacrifice in the prophecy.

Much less the other monsters said to be coming. How many times would he have to fight this duel to the death?

Could he win every time?

Boris surveyed Erik, his eyes shining as if he could discern Erik's doubts. *"We have unfinished business,"* he said in old-speak, then lunged at Erik with his claws extended. They locked talons, the force of the collision sending Erik backward.

Erik's thoughts flew as he strategized. The *Slayer* was stronger than he had expected, as strong as a much younger dragon. That had to be the result of the Elixir: Boris was younger than Erik but not by that much.

And he should be dead.

Erik had to defeat his opponent quickly to have any chance of winning. He rolled into a reverse somersault in the air, gripping Boris tightly, then flinging him across the sky. He flew after him and batted the *Slayer* hard with his tail, sending him soaring over the desert. Boris flailed as he tried to slow his own flight and Erik enjoyed the sight of his helplessness.

It wouldn't last.

That was the moment that Erik noticed Boris hadn't arrived alone. A very familiar *Pyr* hovered in the air behind Erik, his dark scales reflecting the light like mirrored sunglasses. Marco. He still smelled *Pyr* and the glow of the firestorm was on the tips of his talons, but Erik found the motionless Sleeper as inscrutable as ever. They stared at each other for a long moment, and Erik waited for Marco to declare himself.

The other *Pyr* just watched, which enraged Erik.

"Checking the fit before you finally turn Slayer?*"* Erik demanded in old-speak. *"Or have you just come to take me down, like you did Rafferty?"*

Marco seemed to smile. As he so often had done, he kept his opinions to himself.

Erik distrusted that trait as much as his presence.

Boris roared in that moment and Erik pivoted to find the *Slayer* raging back toward him, breathing fire. Erik exhaled a barrier of dragonsmoke, hating that he'd lost time by confronting Marco. It was almost as if the other *Pyr* had deliberately distracted him, compromising him even more. He was aware of Eileen driving closer and irritation that she hadn't done as he'd instructed was enough to break the flow of his dragonsmoke.

Boris found the gap, of course, and slipped through it. Erik blinked as his opponent shifted to the shape of a salamander to fling himself through the small space, then back to dragon form before he lost altitude. Boris laughed at Erik's surprise and loosed another torrent of dragonfire as he roared closer.

Erik hovered in place, waiting, then slipped aside quickly. He felt like a matador when Boris flew past him, but blew hot dragonfire on the *Slayer*'s tail. Those trailing feathers were incinerated, which gave Erik some satisfaction.

He was also pleased to have both of his opponents on the same side.

He felt his eyes widen in surprise at the golden glow that

surrounded Marco. His mate was close, then. Erik glanced toward the car and saw that there was another woman in the passenger seat beside Eileen.

If Marco was turning *Slayer*, what did his mate want with Eileen?

Never mind Zoë.

Erik lunged at Boris, moving so quickly that he tore open the *Slayer*'s chest. Black blood dripped to the desert far below, but Boris bellowed and bit at Erik's shoulder. The pair locked talons, and Erik dug his claws deeply into those of his opponent, again drawing blood. Boris snapped suddenly at Erik, his teeth ripping open Erik's face.

It seemed that Boris meant to end this quickly, too. Erik was well aware of Marco just watching.

Probably waiting for him to weaken.

Probably intending to step in if Boris were injured.

The very idea infuriated Erik and gave him new strength. He battled against his opponent, countering blows and inflicting as much damage as he could. There were no *Pyr* within range to come to his aid. Quinn was miles ahead, because he hadn't stopped to meet with Lorenzo. Lorenzo was meeting with Maeve. Rafferty was the only one who could spontaneously manifest elsewhere, but he had to be recovering from his injuries still.

Erik was on his own.

He and Boris were locked together, thrashing and ripping at each other. Boris bit again at Erik's chest, tearing the flesh open with gusto. The pain was excruciating and Erik faltered a little in his assault as his blood flowed over his scales. He spun Boris around, then snatched at the *Slayer*'s wings, damaging one but not ripping it free. Boris twisted like a serpent, clawing into Erik's guts, then burying his talons in the wound to tear at Erik's entrails. Erik moaned in agony and thrashed with new vigor.

He would not be murdered in front of his mate and child.

Erik locked his tail around that of the *Slayer*, then dropped hard toward the ground. Boris struggled but Erik held him tightly, knowing this might be his last chance. He slammed Boris into the road, ensuring that his head cracked against the asphalt. He smacked him down again, then breathed fire right into Boris's face. The *Slayer* had always been vain, and it seemed just to burn him to a crisp, starting with his face. Erik was aware of car tires squealing, but he didn't dare avert his attention from the *Slayer*.

Not until Boris was dead.

Boris snarled and twisted. He writhed and wriggled. He struggled for his life even as the smell of his burning scales filled Erik's nostrils. Erik stopped only to inhale another deep breath, but Boris took advantage of that moment. He reversed their positions with astonishing speed and held Erik down, one back claw digging into Erik's guts. He locked his front claws around Erik's neck and squeezed tightly, the sight of his laughing maw filling Erik's vision.

"Looks like I win," Boris said, clearly pleased with his triumph.

Marco applauded from some distance away, the sound sending fury through the leader of the *Pyr*.

Erik wasn't dead yet. He exhaled smoke as quickly as he could, driving it into Boris's chest wound. He felt a jolt as soon as the conduit was established and began to suck strength from it. It was sweet to weaken Boris this way, as he'd learned the trick from Boris the first time they'd fought to the death.

Boris's grip faltered and Erik breathed more deliberately. He sucked harder on the conduit, drawing the power of his opponent and using every bit of it.

"What if it turns you Slayer*?"* Boris whispered in old-speak. *"What if using my strength puts the Elixir in your body?"*

The idea was so disgusting that Erik hesitated, just for a heartbeat. In that instant, Boris turned the direction of the dragonsmoke conduit. He began to draw power from Erik with fearsome speed, and Erik panicked that his opportunity had been lost. He fought against his body's inclination to shift shape, knowing that it would be seen by the *Slayer* as an indication of pending triumph.

He felt a shadow fall over them and opened his eyes to find Marco descending. The other *Pyr* was silhouetted against the brilliant blue of the sky, and Erik feared the worst. *"You are an abomination,"* he said to Marco but Boris laughed.

"He is a convert, because he wants to survive."

It was a horrific notion, that the *Pyr* should be eliminated and the *Slayers* should win the Dragon's Tail Wars. The very possibility compelled Erik to fight with all his might. He struggled against Boris, determined to survive, then the *Slayer*'s weight was abruptly ripped away from him. Erik lay gasping at the realization that Marco had attacked Boris.

He wasn't a traitor, after all. Boris and Marco locked in combat overhead, battling against each other with fearsome power. Erik saw that Marco's blood was running brilliant red, as sure a sign of his true allegiance as there could be. The firestorm illuminated the pair with golden light. The *Slayer* was fortified with Erik's own strength, but Erik could change that.

He rolled over and breathed a new conduit of dragonsmoke, dispatching it toward Boris like a cobra on the hunt. Erik breathed smoke more quickly than he ever had, and watched its glittering path across the desert floor. He launched it toward Boris and drove it deeply into the *Slayer*'s wounds. He wound the dragonsmoke into Boris's innards, wrapping it around his bones and tendons, ensuring that it couldn't be easily dislodged, and then he drew upon it with all his might.

Boris visibly faltered under this assault. He roared at Marco and bit with new vigor, as if sensing that he didn't have much time to save his near-victory. He breathed dragonfire, but Marco simply hovered in the air, as if to taunt him.

"*Liar!*" Boris bellowed then lunged at Marco, who didn't move.

Erik saw the sudden flash of darkfire. It came from behind him, a blue-green bolt of lightning that shot right over him and struck Boris in the heart. The *Slayer* twitched in pain and shouted loud enough to make the ground vibrate. The crackle of darkfire didn't stop, just burned and burned, a conduit of brilliant light.

The *Slayer* exploded before Erik's eyes, burned to a crisp by the darkfire.

There was only black ash left to fall to the desert floor.

Ash, pain, and the weight of Eileen's hand upon his claw. Erik closed his eyes and let himself shift back to his human form as the pain of his injuries swept over him. "Water," he whispered. "We need to expose his remains to water." He heard the splash of liquid and didn't care what it was, only that it had been done.

Then, for the moment, Erik knew no more.

Jac was getting used to dragon fights, evidently.

She wasn't sure she'd ever be completely at ease with them, but this one had been a bit less terrifying. Her heart was hammering but didn't feel like it would leap out of her chest and make a run for it.

She'd thought that Marco was never going to give her the signal, and that the ebony and pewter dragon would be killed first, but he'd chosen his moment well. They had to have been exchanging taunts in old-speak, because she'd heard the rumbling. And they must have been breathing dragonsmoke, then using it to steal power from each other. She couldn't see the dragonsmoke but she'd seen the reactions of the two warriors.

She was well aware that Erik's mate Eileen hadn't trusted her and didn't blame her for that. As soon as the Boris clone was fried to nothing, though, Eileen gave her a tight hug. Then she dropped to her knees beside her fallen *Pyr*.

It had been the little girl who had dumped the bottle of water from the car over the pile of ashes that had once been the *Slayer*. Jac would have to think about her presence later. She knew the *Pyr* only had sons, except for the Wyvern. Was this little girl the product of another marriage? She looked so much like her father that Jac doubted it.

Could she be the Wyvern?

Marco landed beside Jac in his dragon form, but didn't shift. "Awesome job," he said to her, his claw closing around her hand. "You chose the moment just right."

"You gave me the signal," she admitted, liking that they'd worked together. Marco gave her a look that would have warmed her to her toes, even without the dazzling power of the firestorm.

"You had this planned?" Eileen demanded. Erik had shifted to his human form after falling to the ground, and Jac guessed it had been an involuntary shift, the kind the *Pyr* made when they were seriously injured. At least he wasn't rotating between forms. "You meant for me to turn around?" She'd bound Erik's torso as well as she could, but he was bleeding steadily and her fear for him was clear.

"I guessed you would when you saw the fight."

Marco gave Jac a steady look and she explained, speaking quickly. The information would help Eileen decide what was best for Erik. "The new dragons are clones of Boris Vassily. There will be thirteen of them all together, six more coming at the next eclipse."

"The blood moon will ripen the eggs," Eileen murmured. "Do you know where they are?"

"No, but Boris has exchanged challenge coins with Erik—"

"I remember that part," Eileen interjected.

"—so, each and every one of them has a burning desire to kill him. This one was the last survivor of the first two batches. He was determined to take out Erik to establish himself as the leader of the clones."

"He'd have accomplished their objective before they hatched, making himself ascendant," Eileen said with a nod. Her gaze never left Erik, who was unconscious and bleeding. "But now he's gone, thanks to you. How many *Slayers* are left?"

"Just Jorge, but he's badly hurt after his fight."

"So, there's time." Eileen nodded, her decision made. "Will you help me take him back to Sloane? If we drive, I'm afraid the journey will take too long."

"I'll do better," Marco said. He drew Jac against his side, making the firestorm blaze brilliantly between them. Eileen shaded her eyes. "Erik can use fire to heal himself. We'll heal him with the firestorm."

Jac was awed by his choice. Eileen was clearly pleased. She nudged Erik and whispered to him, and he stirred. His eyes opened as he watched the sparks of the firestorm and Jac felt his wonder.

She felt a good bit of that wonder herself. She liked that Marco was offering this to heal the leader of the *Pyr* and that she could be a part of helping the good dragons to win.

"You bleed red," Erik whispered. "I should have asked instead of guessing your intentions."

"It looked bad," Marco admitted. "I don't blame you. I had to trick you to deceive him. But let's see you healed before we talk more."

Erik shifted to his dragon form in a shimmer of blue then Marco reached out to him. They locked claws and Marco held her more tightly. The firestorm heated to a brilliant white radiance and

Erik tipped back his head, baring his teeth as the firestorm seared his wounds. He drew Eileen against his one side and she beckoned to Zoë. The five of them were in a tight circle, the firestorm blinding in its radiance.

Then Zoë reached out and touched the darkfire crystal still in Jac's hand. The light in the stone flared brilliantly, illuminating them all with blue-green light, and Jac saw Erik's wound close completely. He gasped, then sighed as Eileen shed a tear of gratitude.

That was when Jac saw the scale on Marco's chest loosen, seemingly of its own volition. It worked itself free of his armor and began to fall.

Jac caught it, smiling with the certainty of what it meant.

"I love you, too," she said to him, not caring who heard her confession.

Erik cleared his throat and there was a gleam of humor in his eyes. "I think you two need a little privacy now," he said, his voice a deep rumble in his dragon form. Eileen smiled and caressed her daughter's head and Jac felt her heart thunder in anticipation.

"Yes, we do," she said to Marco. He laughed, then she was in his arms and the darkfire crackled. She didn't care where they went.

She just wanted to be with him.

Forever.

CHAPTER TWENTY-SEVEN

arco manifested in Jac's apartment, his mate crushed in his arms. They were hot and covered with dust from the desert, and he could feel the dried blood on his wounds. He was also filled with the aftermath of victory, the need to celebrate his survival in the most fundamental way. His blood was pumping and his firestorm was burning brighter and hotter than ever. That Jac had made such a noble choice had stolen his heart away for good.

That she loved him was the best news he'd ever heard.

Marco supposed it was no surprise that he'd manifested in her bedroom, in the place most indicative of what he wanted to do. The apartment was filled with the pewter light of late afternoon and the coolness that accompanied a day of steady rain. The firestorm illuminated the bedroom like a thousand candles.

Jac smiled up at him and lifted her hands away from her chest. His scale was in her grasp, held against her like a breastplate. He wished he could protect her from head to toe in similar armor, but had no chance to say as much. She pulled his head down and kissed him with a hunger he recognized as equal to his own.

Just as her power and passion was equal to his own.

She was the perfect mate for him.

There was no need for conversation.

The firestorm lit to a brilliant white light between them, and Marco felt as if he'd stepped into the center of the sun. He was sizzling with desire and overflowing with love, and Jac's kiss told him that she felt the same way.

"The shower," she whispered when he gave her the opportunity to catch her breath, and he couldn't think of a better place. He carried her into the bathroom and started the water running, then tugged off his T-shirt as he turned to face her. Jac had peeled off her own shirt and discarded it. There was a smudge of dirt on her white bra and another on her cheek, but she was smiling at him with delight. She wriggled out of her jeans and he kicked off his own, then their underwear was cast out of the small bathroom, too. Her fingertips landed on the cut on his shoulder, but Marco could hardly feel it.

There was only Jac and the firestorm. He kissed her, silencing the question she would have asked, then carried her into the shower. They washed each other slowly and thoroughly, coaxing their mutual desire to a fever-pitch, even as the firestorm made their blood boil. He caressed her with his fingertips, wanting her to find her pleasure, but she stopped him with a touch.

"All of you," she demanded. "Right now and right here. I can't possibly wait any longer."

"We should make it last."

"We can't make it last any more, at least I can't." Jac smiled and brushed her lips across his, her eyes dancing. "And I think it can only be a good thing to conceive a *Pyr* while celebrating a victory. He'll have triumph in his veins."

Marco smiled down at her. "A good sign for the future."

"The very best." Jac trailed her hands over him, her touch making him catch his breath. "Now," she whispered again. "Let's see if a *Pyr* and his mate can spontaneously combust in satisfying their firestorm."

Maeve had her driver leave her outside the construction site in Las Vegas. A sign proclaimed that this would be the location for the new spectacular of master illusionist, Lorenzo, *Rising from the Grave*. Maeve smiled, liking the title of the show a lot. Maybe she'd stop by in December to see Lorenzo in action.

Assuming his kind were the survivors of the Dragon's Tail Wars. Jorge had told her a lot about the *Pyr* and the *Slayers*, but not nearly enough. Maeve liked to have as much information as possible. She'd wanted to hear the *Pyr* side.

Then Cassie Redmond had contacted her.

Kismet.

The interview had seemed too good to be true, but then Maeve realized this *Pyr*—whose identity she still didn't know for certain—wanted something in return from her. He wasn't offering an exclusive interview for nothing. It was a wager. An exchange.

With Maeve O'Neill, internationally famous reporter.

When Maeve saw the billboards, she guessed that Lorenzo himself was the *Pyr* who would interview her. She liked his audacity a lot. Scheduling the interview at the construction site of his new theater was bold, a taunt to her to draw the obvious conclusion, a dare for her to do something about it. He thought he was baiting the hook with a big story.

Unfortunately for Lorenzo, he didn't realize he was negotiating with Maeve the Black Queen, who was far more influential in worlds both seen and unseen than any mere reporter could be. She'd take what she wanted from him, which was every morsel of information he knew about the *Pyr*, and give nothing in return.

Except maybe clemency, if she thought he was worth it.

She picked her way to the entrance, stepping carefully through the construction debris so she didn't mar her new Christian Louboutin shoes. She knew she was being watched and she guessed who observed her. When a gorgeous Italian man stepped out of the building and called a greeting, Maeve felt a thrill at how perfectly tasty he was. She could smell the dragon on him and wondered how humans missed such obvious clues. Lorenzo's dark eyes gleamed with intent and intelligence and a bit of mischief. He had a scheme of his own, and she knew he wouldn't be easy to overwhelm.

Her heart skipped in anticipation as he kissed the back of her hand. He glanced up at her, and she saw the flames dancing in the depths of his eyes, a feat that should have been impossible.

Maybe it was an illusion.

Maybe it was a trap. Maeve held his gaze and realized what he was trying to do. Even she felt a tentative response to the spell he would cast, and she admired his skill.

It had been so long since she'd faced a truly worthy adversary.

But that would only make victory all the sweeter.

For the better part of two weeks, Sam battled the riddle.

Sloane had already isolated the antibody in Drake's blood that had kept him from getting the virus. Sam had a variety of samples to compare and it took time, even with the equipment in Sloane's lab. She had her own uninfected human blood, Veronica's blood after infection and after the virus had been pushed back to its latent phase. She had Drake's blood, which resisted the invasion of the virus, and she had Sloane's blood, both before and after his exposure to the virus.

To her relief, he hadn't become infected even though he didn't share Drake's antibodies. His white blood cells had staged the same kind of vigorous defense, and had eliminated the invading virus with impressive speed.

He insisted on being contaminated again, to see if it was repeatable, and it was. His body's reaction wasn't affected by the fact that it had recently defended itself.

But he began to make antibodies himself.

They were slightly different from the ones Drake carried and different again from the ones Veronica's body had made after her exposure to Drake's blood. Somewhere, there was a key as to why the virus was banished in the *Pyr* but returned to the latent phase in Veronica. Sam began a detailed comparison of each kind of cell in each situation, seeking the critical difference.

It could take years to isolate the differences and determine their importance, and Sam knew it. She barely slept, working around the clock, pausing only to eat when she felt a bit faint. It was when she awakened that morning two weeks after Sloane's infection that she recalled Jac's stone.

Why *shouldn't* the Dracontias be able to heal?

Why shouldn't this impossible thing be as true as all the other impossible things she'd come to believe were true?

Sam leapt out of the shower and dressed in haste. She found the stone in her purse and hurried downstairs to sterilize it again. She suited up, not even bothering with breakfast, and charged back into the lab.

Once there, she put a sample of Veronica's blood in a slender glass beaker. Then she put the Dracontias into it.

To her astonishment, the blood turned very dark and began to swirl in the beaker. It had been perfectly still before, but the stone was creating some kind of vortex. The stone was obscured from view for a moment as the blood spun all around it. Sam watched, transfixed.

Then the motion stopped and the blood returned to its lighter color. The stone floated to the surface. Sam followed her impulse and removed it from the sample, placing it in another beaker to be cleaned. She had a whole suite of tests to perform but she had a feeling already of what the results would be.

She was going to have to eat some crow if she had to tell Jac that she'd been right about the Dracontias, but Sam didn't mind that in the least.

In fact, she was looking forward to it.

Lorenzo awakened suddenly, as if a cold hand had given him a shake.

It was dark, wherever he was, only an Exit sign glowing red in the distance. He was chilled and stiff, and had a crick in his neck as a reward for sleeping in a straight chair. He scanned his surroundings, then stood up warily, feeling relief as he recognized his location.

But what on earth was he doing in his partly constructed theater? Why was it so dark? Where were all the work crews? He glanced at his watch and was shocked to discover that it was after three in the morning.

It was incredible that he'd dozed off and lost track of the time, but that seemed to be what had happened. Lorenzo frowned. He had been working all out and hadn't slept much lately, but that didn't usually trouble him. He checked the date on his watch, recalling that he had come to the construction site to do an interview with Maeve O'Neill. That had been first thing the previous morning.

He remembered arriving at the site.

He remembered clearing the crews from the site, giving them a paid day off so he and Maeve could chat in private. So he could show her what he was and beguile her to report what he desired, and do so without witnesses.

Had she even arrived?

Lorenzo couldn't recall.

He knew he had waited at the door, watching for her. He had a vague memory of a limousine pulling to a halt outside, but even as he thought of it, the scene faded from his mind.

As if it had never happened.

When had he come back into the theater? Why? And why had he chosen to fall asleep here, instead of returning home? Why hadn't anyone called him? Lorenzo pulled out his cell phone, only to discover that it was turned off.

He frowned. He never turned it off.

He turned it on and the display was instantly flooded with messages from Cassie, as well as some from the foreman. There was one from Maeve, forwarded from Cassie, regretting that she had to cancel their interview.

Had she really not arrived? Lorenzo was sure he could smell a strangely troubling perfume, one that hadn't been in the building when he arrived in the morning. He had an odd sense, too, that he was forgetting something, although he couldn't have said what it was.

Was this what it felt like to be beguiled?

The idea was chilling.

But how could a human have beguiled him? And why? It was ridiculous, even though Lorenzo couldn't entirely shake his unease. His phone rang then, the sudden sound making him jump, and he answered it immediately.

"Where are you?" Cassie demanded, her concern clear. "Are you all right? Where did you go after Maeve canceled?"

"I stayed here, at the theater," Lorenzo admitted, the truth sounding more plausible as he gave it voice. "I fell asleep."

"And lost track of time," Cassie said. "While I've been losing my mind with worry." He heard Bart give a bellow in the background, and Cassie audibly soothed the boy. "I guess I would have been awake anyway with this tooth coming in," she said. The sound of her exhaustion filled him with guilt, and a determination to make it up to her.

"I'm sorry," he said, and meant it. "I don't know what happened."

"You're probably just worn out."

"I'll be home in a few minutes," Lorenzo said. "And you can sleep all day tomorrow. I'll take the boys so you can have a break."

"But you're okay?"

"I'm fine," he insisted and almost believed it. "I'll be home as quickly as I can."

Lorenzo strode through the construction site, that perfume making him see things he knew weren't there.

Black shoes with stiletto heels and red soles.

An unexpected kiss chilling him to his marrow.

Secrets spilling forth, secrets he had no right to share.

He shook his head. It must have been a bad dream. A nightmare. Nerves, due to the pending re-launch of his career and the final battle of the *Pyr*. Erik sending him disapproving looks.

Maeve, after all, hadn't shown up.

Sloane looked through the microscope at the blood sample as Sam practically bounced with anticipation beside him. He was careful and confirmed the results in multiple samples, even as relief nearly took him to his knees. "You're right. It's gone," he said to Sam, and she let out a whoop of joy.

She threw herself at him and he hugged her tightly, more than ready for her HazMat suit to be unnecessary. Her eyes were shining with triumph, and he smiled down at her. "You did it."

"*We* did it." Sam exhaled happily. "I could never have solved the riddle without the *Pyr* and without the Dracontias."

"So, you have your cure."

"And a lot of work to do." She stepped out of his embrace, and he could practically see her thoughts flying. "There will have to be clinical tests, of course, and I'll have to go back to Atlanta to manage them. We could start with volunteers..."

"The nurse who tended Ronnie on her admission to the hospital might volunteer."

"You're right. She was still in the latent phase when I left, and they'd moved her to Atlanta. And there will be others, I'm sure. Once word gets out, we'll have people clamoring at the door. The challenge will lie in manufacturing enough antidote quickly enough, if it does succeed in the trials."

Sloane smiled at her omission, which he thought was telling. He folded his arms across his chest and leaned on the bench. "Not in convincing the CDC to use an antidote concocted from *Pyr* blood and the Dracontias?"

Sam winced. "You're right, of course. I'll have to think of a better story." There was a glimmer of humor in her eyes. "No one will believe the truth."

"I'm surprised you do," Sloane noted.

Sam sighed and blushed a little bit. She looked younger and unexpectedly uncertain, so her words surprised him. "Well, sometimes you have to abandon pre-conceptions in order to move forward. Sometimes you have to admit you're wrong to even be able to see the truth." She lifted her gaze to his and her voice turned husky. "Sometimes you're lucky enough to have help with that, maybe even help you don't deserve."

Their gazes clung for a hot moment. "No regrets," Sloane murmured.

"None," Sam agreed. "Except for what comes next." She sighed. "I'll be leaving. Again."

Sloane didn't want to dwell on her departure. "And your name will go down in the history books as the doctor who cured the Seattle virus. Maybe they'll name the antidote after you." He was sure this was what she wanted, a kind of immortality based on her medical achievements, but Sam didn't seem very excited.

"I guess it will," she mused. "I'll probably get a chair at a university, or a research position for the duration, and my career will be secure. My job will be less demanding."

Sloane was confused by her temperate reaction. "Isn't this the fulfillment of the dream?"

Sam frowned. "A year ago, I would have said that it was, but now it feels lacking." She considered him. "Empty, because I won't have anyone to share it with."

This was the conversation Sloane had been dreading ever since Sam had learned about the firestorm.

"You'll find someone. Another scientist probably."

"I've tried that before. I'm thinking that differences add spice. I like how you've challenged my assumptions and shown me that more is possible than I'd believed." She swallowed. "I haven't just found pleasure with you, Sloane, or even just healing. I've learned a lot from you." She fell silent, then continued. "That must be why I've fallen in love with you."

Sloane had to avert his gaze from temptation. He knew he could lie to Sam about the future by making promises he might not be able to keep. Honesty was in his nature, though, and he had discovered that he was as romantic as his father. "I know what you want me to say," he said. "But I won't make a promise I can't keep. I think it's for the best if we part now."

Sam's lips tightened, but she wasn't surprised. "Because you don't know when you'll have a firestorm."

"No. But when I do, it will be more important than anything else in my life from that point onward. I don't want to ever hurt you, Sam." He cleared his throat. "And I also think that having another child might be part of your healing process. I can't give you that child."

"People adopt."

"It's the same thing, though. I could have to leave, suddenly."

Sam's eyes narrowed as she watched him and her voice was husky when she continued. "What makes you think you'll have your firestorm before I die?"

Sloane surveyed the bench, not really seeing the samples and syringes there, then gave voice to his deepest fear. "Something is going to change for us when the node of the moon changes in September, after the end of the Dragon's Tail Wars. There might not be any more *Pyr*, because the prophecy declares that only *Pyr* or *Slayers* will survive."

"But don't the other *Pyr* have children? Children are the future."

"If we lose, they'll either die with us or be hunted to extinction."

Sam shuddered and he knew she was thinking of Jorge. "Aren't the *Slayers* diminished in number?"

Sloane nodded. "Although they seem to have figured out how to create more. It's not obvious that we'll win."

"And if you do, you'll still wait for your firestorm." Sam didn't even question his speculation, much less challenge his belief in a prophecy. Sloane knew that showed the change in her perspective and her trust in him. She considered what he'd told her, then looked him in the eye, as decisive as ever. "I have to say that I don't like the idea of you being killed in September."

"Thanks. It doesn't work for me either."

"I also don't like that you as the Apothecary are always surrendering yourself for the greater good."

"It's my role," he said with some weariness.

"I hope you *Pyr* have a plan for the fall."

"We're working on it."

"I hope you win."

"Me, too," Sloane admitted.

Sam bit her lip. "Walking away from you to administer this clinical test, knowing that it might be the last time I ever see you, will be the hardest thing I've ever done."

Sloane couldn't resist her then. He pulled her into his embrace and she came readily. She felt so good in his arms that he didn't want to let her go.

Sam rested her hood against him. "How about this: you go and tell Drake and Ronnie the good news. I'll clean up and meet you upstairs." She tipped back her head to meet his gaze. "I've heard how you *Pyr* like to celebrate and I'm thinking this is a victory worth a celebration. Let's say goodbye with style."

"I'll bring wine," Sloane promised.

"No, I have to get to work right afterward." Sam's smile turned mischievous. "Just be naked and don't be late."

Sam was feeling both serene and excited. She and Sloane had made love slowly and thoroughly, and it had been wonderful. She didn't want to leave him, but she did want to get this antidote into production. She knew what she had to do.

The CDC was sending a helicopter to pick her up at the airport, a condition she'd made to keep Sloane's location hidden. She didn't think her cover story about finding the cure was very compelling, because she was a lousy liar, but Isaac was so relieved to have progress that he wasn't asking many questions. They'd almost certainly come later. She was packing antidote, samples and serums with care in HazMat containers in Sloane's lab. She'd have to make a case and her results would have to be replicated before the testing could begin, but she was optimistic.

The *Pyr* had made the solution possible, which meant that there *were* good dragons and bad dragons.

Sam had a definite favorite in the herd.

She could hear Sloane talking to Ronnie, although she couldn't discern his words. Drake had gone to pick up Timmy, and Sam halfway wished she could witness the happy reunion between mother and son.

It would be better, though, to head out and save more sons sooner.

She thought of all the obstacles facing Sloane and his kind and knew she wasn't the only one who felt the odds were too long. What if she could do something to help ensure the survival of the *Pyr*?

The Magician created new realities.

The Magician changed the world.

Could she save Sloane? She sure wanted to do whatever she could.

Sam's gaze slid to the last refrigerator in the lab. It was one at the end with a stainless door and a lock. There was a key on a shelf at the opposite end of the lab and since nothing else had a lock, Sam had guessed which lock it opened.

It was easy to recall Sloane's confession. The *Slayers* were being replicated or even cloned and he had one of them here in the lab. What determined that a dragon shifter was *Slayer*? It had a physiological manifestation in that black corrosive blood.

The Dracontias was perched on the bench.

Sam wondered just how much it could cure.

It was an impulsive, impetuous, intuitive thought, but once she had it, Sam acted upon it. She trusted her instinct in this, as she never had before.

"Sloane!" she called as she picked up the stone. "Sloane! I have an idea. Come quickly!" Too impatient to wait, Sam marched down the lab to get the key.

"What is it?" he called. He was up in the house, but his voice carried to her from the distance.

She shouted again, to make sure he heard from the other side of the airlock, but couldn't wait. This idea was too exciting. Sam opened the fridge, then stepped back in shock, even though she'd anticipated its contents.

Sloane had said that the *Slayer* wasn't dead, but this man clearly was. Maybe he'd died in the fridge. He had fair hair and was dressed conservatively in a jacket and trousers, although he wore no necktie. There were icicles hanging from his nose, chin and earlobes, and his skin was faintly blue from the cold. There was dried blood on his shirt and it looked as if the fabric had stuck in a wound across his chest.

It was a deep gash, like the kind Sam imagined would be made by a dragon's talon. It hadn't healed, which hinted that the Elixir hadn't been able to repair this injury.

Did the *Pyr* and *Slayers* solve all disputes with violence? She couldn't reconcile that with Sloane's nature. Did the *Pyr* have courts or a justice system? Sam was suddenly aware of how little she knew about Sloane and his kind.

The warmer air of the lab was wafting into the fridge, but this corpse wasn't going anywhere anytime soon. Sam leaned forward to look more closely, curious.

Sloane must have been with Drake and Ronnie, because it was taking him ages to get to the lab. She reached to tug the fabric away from the *Slayer*'s wound, wanting to see the injury.

Sam gasped when the *Slayer*'s eyes opened. They were a clear blue. She might have thought it just a delayed physical reaction of some kind—like corpses having erections—but he blinked, then smiled. His eyes lit and he snatched for her. He shimmered blue as his thumb became a dragon talon of brilliant gold.

That was when Sam screamed.

Sloane raged out of the greenhouse when Sam screamed, shifting shape en route. He crashed through the airlocks to the lab and leapt toward the *Slayer* emerging from the fridge. This version of Boris Vassily snarled as his body warmed and he shimmered blue around his perimeter. In a heartbeat, he'd shift shape completely.

Sloane rammed him into the wall first, pummeling him hard to keep him from changing shape. In dragon form, the clone wouldn't fit in the fridge. He slashed at Boris, giving him enough new injuries to keep the Elixir busy for a while, then jammed him back into the fridge and slammed the door.

He pivoted to find Sam backed against the far wall, her eyes wide.

She held out the key with shaking hands. He could see that the Dracontias was clutched in her other hand.

Sloane waited for her.

She took a deep breath, more valiant than he'd expected, then crossed the floor with a little bit of trepidation. "Sorry again. I should have listened, especially the bit about him not being quite dead." Her eyes widened as she surveyed him, and Sloane recalled that she'd never seen him in his dragon form. "It is you, right?"

He nodded slowly, then pointed at the lock. Sam came to stand beside him, her terror clear in her scent, and locked the fridge quickly. Sloane could hear Boris whimpering, then the *Slayer*'s breathing changed as he passed out again.

Sloane released the breath he'd been holding and gestured to Sam to look away.

"Oh, I want to see this," she said, evidently guessing the reason for the blue shimmer of light around his body. She folded her arms across her chest, determination in her gaze.

Sloane knew better than to argue with her. She was stubborn. He summoned the change and tipped his head back as it ripped through his body, then opened his eyes to find her watching him closely.

"Your eyes changed last," she said and Sloane was surprised. He'd hadn't known that. She looked at the fridge. "Will he stay there?"

"Only until his injuries heal. He's consumed the Elixir."

"Which means he always heals and is practically immortal." Sam nodded understanding. "That's why you hurt him more. The refrigeration must be slowing his metabolic rate, but he'll still heal in time." She glanced up. "Have you had time to do any tests on him?"

Sloane shook his head. "There hasn't been time." He couldn't think of a way to explain it. "He's not normal, not for our kind. He and multiple others appeared at the same time. They look identical to a *Slayer* who is long dead. That's why I think they're clones."

Sam grimaced. "If there are more of them, they could outnumber the *Pyr*, or at least turn the tide of the war."

Sloane nodded.

"How many more?"

"There have been seven so far. One's here. It's tough to say for sure how many of the others have survived. When they're injured, the other *Slayers* collect them."

"So the Elixir has time to heal them?"

"Maybe." Sloane watched her. "Maybe to eat them to harvest more Elixir. The source is gone."

She shuddered with revulsion and retreated a step, her move expressing her opinion about dragon shifters. She glanced over the wreckage of the lab and he guessed that she was avoiding his gaze. "It's trashed."

"I'll clean it up." He was glad that she was in her HazMat suit, and that there were no other humans in the vicinity.

"The blood samples with the virus are locked away, but your control of the lab environment is compromised," Sam noted.

"I'll burn it all." Sloane nodded at her surprise. "Dragonfire purifies."

She smiled, but only a little. He feared that seeing his truth had changed everything. That filled him with both anger and sadness, a frustration that he'd been cheated by fate of the one woman he desired, along with a bittersweet regret that things couldn't have been different.

Or maybe that he hadn't managed to change them.

It felt to him that this time, the price to the Apothecary was too high.

"You should go," he said quietly. "You don't want to be late for your connection and you'll need to scrub up."

"No, I don't want to miss the flight." Sam took a breath then stepped toward him. She took his hand in hers, then placed the Dracontias in his palm. "I had an idea that this could eliminate *Slayers* from the world forever, leaving the *Pyr* to survive the Dragon's Tail Wars," she said quietly. She closed his fingers over the stone. "I don't know if it will work. I didn't have time to try it, but that's the way I want this story to end."

"I don't want the story to end at all," Sloane murmured.

Sam smiled and bowed her head, her hands wrapped around his for a sweet moment. Even with the barrier of her gloves, he savored the pressure of her grip. Then she turned and walked across the lab, then paused to glance back at him. There was admiration in her eyes. "Your dragon form is beautiful, you know. So majestic and powerful." She swallowed, then smiled at him. "I can see why damsels in distress lost their hearts so easily."

Hope was a tightness in Sloane's throat, but then Sam was gone.

In the greenhouse that had been part of the isolation room, Ronnie bent and picked up something from the stone floor. It was a scale, a dragon scale, one that gleamed with the hues of tourmaline and was edged with gold. She'd seen it fall when Dr. Wilcox had screamed and she knew what it meant.

The Apothecary was in love.

Ronnie smiled and caressed the scale with her fingertips.

Then she left the rooms where she had been living, intent upon meeting Dr. Wilcox in the foyer. She'd say farewell and thank the other woman.

Plus give her this very precious souvenir of Sloane. Ronnie couldn't think of a safer place for such a treasure to be.

Timmy couldn't sit still. He certainly couldn't eat his dinner, even though it was hamburgers and fries, his very favorite. Mrs. Patterson had told him that Drake was coming to pick him up and take him to see his mom, and Timmy knew what that meant.

A dragonflight.

He couldn't wait. He didn't care where they were going or how long it took. He was going to love every minute of it. He wanted to see his mom, too, because talking to her on the phone wasn't like being with her. He had a hundred things to tell her.

Dashiell was excited for him, too, even though Timmy hadn't shared Drake's secret. That was how it had to be. He wasn't authorized to share information, although he was going to ask for permission. His stuff was all packed, because he knew he'd be moving now that his mom was better.

"Don't be sad, Dashiell," Mrs. Patterson said. "Timmy will be back in a week or so."

"And then he'll need your help moving," Mr. Patterson added. "It'll be great to have you all as neighbors."

Drake had bought a house just down the street from the Patterson's, having located it with Mrs. Patterson's help and Timmy's mom's suggestions. Kristofer and Theo had taken Timmy and Dashiell past it the other day. It looked awesome, with a backyard that led to the creek they'd been wanting to explore, but the best part was that he and Dashiell would be living so close to each other.

Well, the best part was that he'd be secretly hanging out with the *Pyr*. He hoped they let him tell Dashiell soon.

"And then the baby will be coming," Mrs. Patterson said. "There are going to be a lot of changes for you, Timmy."

"All good ones," he said happily. "I knew Drake would make everything right."

Dashiell's parents exchanged a smile, then the doorbell rang.

Timmy excused himself and ran to the door, Dashiell right behind him. Drake was there, smiling as he crouched down before Timmy. He hadn't changed a bit. "Are you ready?"

"Absolutely," Timmy said. He might have lunged out the door in his excitement, but Drake raised a brow in silent reminder. He stood, waiting, and Timmy pivoted to thank the Patterson's for hosting him.

The adults all shook hands and wished each other well, and Drake told Mrs. Patterson when to expect them back. He confirmed that Timmy's mom was healing well and that the pregnancy was proceeding as anticipated, his confidence obviously reassuring them. Drake took Timmy's bag and they strode into the evening together, Timmy fighting his urge to run.

"The house is empty," Drake said quietly. "Because it's ours now. We'll have a quick look at it now, to confirm that everything is as it should be, then go into the backyard."

"That's why you chose one with a big yard," Timmy guessed. "And one that leads into the forest."

"Privacy must be defended, Timothy, for your safety and that of your mother. You have done well with this secret, but you must keep it forever."

"I know. I'm on it." He flicked a glance at Drake. "I'd like if Dashiell could know, too."

Drake nodded slowly. "There may be a way for that to be possible, but not before the eclipse in the fall."

Timmy nodded agreement, more excited than he'd been in his life.

It seemed to take a million years for them to get to the house and for Drake to walk through it, checking doors and windows. Timmy was going to be able to pick his room, but for the moment, he didn't really care. He was impatient for his dragonflight. Drake smiled at him, as if understanding his reaction, then led him into the backyard. They walked to the end of the lot, where the forest began, then into the shadows under the trees. Timmy could hear the water in the creek as it flowed over stones and he watched as Drake surveyed the distant houses.

"Better than I had hoped," he murmured, and Timmy noticed that no windows faced them. Then Drake began to shimmer, just like the dragons in the videos. A pale blue light radiated from his body as Timmy watched, then suddenly grew so bright that Timmy had to close his eyes. When he opened them, he knew what he would see.

Drake was a massive dark dragon, as black as the shadows in the forest, with teeth and claws and a long tail. He was obviously strong and his wings were leathery. He waited, watching with the same stillness Timmy associated with Drake. Timmy raised a hand and touched Drake's scales, feeling how hard they were and how they overlapped.

Like armor. They even had points on them, like thorns, and were cool to the touch.

There was one missing on Drake's chest and Timmy's hand rose to the spot.

"It will be repaired soon, at your mother's request." He sounded like Drake, too, although his voice was deeper.

"Do you always lose scales?"

The dragon that was Drake seemed to smile. "A *Pyr* only loses a scale when he loses his heart. It is because I love your mother that my scale is gone."

"And she's going to help you fix it because she loves you."

Drake inclined his head in agreement and offered Timmy a

claw. "Shall we go to her?"

"Is she really having a baby?"

"She is. It will be a boy."

"Will he be a dragon, too?"

"One day, if all is right, he will develop his *Pyr* abilities. He will be your brother from the outset, though."

"I always thought it would be cool to have a brother," Timmy admitted. "Having a dragon brother will be even better." He grinned up at Drake. "But not as good as having a dragon dad." He took Drake's claw, amazed at the size of his talons. "Let's do this thing."

"Indeed," Drake said as he picked Timmy up. His wings flapped and he seemed to leap into the sky with a single bound, clearing the tops of the trees so fast that Timmy couldn't believe it. Then he was soaring high over the town, his wings beating hard against the air and his claw holding Timmy safely against his chest.

Timmy hung on, not even wanting to blink in case he missed something. He saw Dashiell's house and their school, the soccer field where Drake had couched them, and the mall. He saw the town get smaller beneath them and fade from view. The stars seemed close enough to touch and the wind was cool against his skin. He felt Drake look down at him, checking on him, protective as a dragon should be, and Timmy knew that everything had come right.

He'd never forget his father, but he was glad to have a new dad.

And new dads didn't get any better than Drake.

CHAPTER TWENTY-EIGHT

t was July when the *Pyr* gathered behind Sloane's house in the forest. The moon was full and its light was brilliant. The air was remarkably cool and the stars seemed very bright. In Ronnie's opinion, it was the kind of night that you'd expect something magical to happen. She held tightly to Timmy's hand, her heart thumping in anticipation.

The film crew was set up, but Melissa was determined they not be able to even see any of the *Pyr* shift shape let alone film them. The *Pyr* would arrive in dragon form, a compromise that mollified Erik. He had also decreed that the ceremony must be done at night, much to the grumbling of the film crew, who wanted better light. The children and the other mates stood back in the shadows and the crew was to hide their identities. Ronnie herself was wearing a domino mask, to protect the privacy of Drake and of Timmy.

She was ridiculously happy and madly in love. She was surrounded by a group of strong women, women who had already made the choice she was making, and she already felt as if she'd been welcomed into a large and protective family. She knew she'd tested their approval by insisting upon this, but she wanted the world to know that the *Pyr* were good.

They were a fertile family, too. Sara, the Seer of the *Pyr,* stood to her left with her own infant son in her arms and her young sons standing around her. Eileen was to Ronnie's right, with her daughter Zoë close by. Chandra rocked her infant son, and Melissa's daughter Isabelle stuck close to Eileen.

Quinn's forge was in place and Ronnie stood beside it, as nervous as she had been the first time she'd exchanged marriage vows. It was different this time, though, not just because Drake was more than a man. She knew what she was getting into better than she had that first time, plus she had already borne Drake's son. She nestled her baby close.

"He's awake," Timmy said, peeking at his younger brother. "It's like he knows this is important."

"They do have sharper senses than we do."

Timmy made a face. "I wish I was a dragon, Mom."

She bent and kissed him. "I think it's just as good to have a dragon for a dad." He smiled at her, his adoration of Drake clear, and Ronnie felt confidence in their shared future. "Besides," she added in a whisper. "You're the oldest of all these boys, like their new cousin." Timmy beamed at that thought.

Ronnie stepped forward at Melissa's direction and entrusted her infant son to Eileen, who cuddled him close.

"I'm Melissa Smith," Melissa said to the camera. "And we have the honor tonight of witnessing and recording a ceremony of the *Pyr* dragon shifters. I've been invited to a gathering of the *Pyr*, where they intend to heal the scales of one of their fellows. With me are a number of women who have pledged themselves to these men, although their identities have been disguised to protect their privacy." She gestured to Ronnie. "This woman will see her partner's armor repaired in this forest tonight. Welcome."

Ronnie stepped forward and lifted her chin. "Thanks for coming, Melissa."

"Why did you suggest the filming of this ritual?"

"I love a man who is *Pyr*. I am awed by his honor and his sense of duty and his loyalty to those he perceives to be under his care. He is a warrior and a valiant one, and I want the world to see his merit."

"Maybe you can tell our audience what we're going to see tonight."

Ronnie nodded. "This will be a ceremony to repair or replace a missing scale. When a *Pyr* meets his destined mate—that is, the only woman who can bear his child—he and she experience what is called a firestorm. Heat flares between them and sparks fly, a sign of the promise of their union. It is a magical and powerful sensation, and one that fades once the *Pyr*'s son has been conceived."

"So, you've had a firestorm."

"I have. I knew him before and admired him before I knew the truth of his nature."

"And the scale?"

Ronnie smiled. "The *Pyr* are fiercely protective of their families, their partners and their children, and to see them fight is impressive. But when a *Pyr* loves another person, as he often comes to love his mate, there's a physical manifestation of his vulnerability."

"Meaning?"

"He loses a scale from his coat of armor, usually in a location where a blow on that unprotected skin can kill him. Love makes him both stronger and more vulnerable."

"But surely the scales grow back?"

Ronnie shook her head. "Not one lost for love. It has to be repaired, and it can only be repaired with a gift made out of love by the *Pyr*'s mate. In a way, this ceremony is the *Pyr* equivalent of the exchange of wedding vows." She showed the string of pearls coiled on her palm. "The *Pyr* have a bond to the natural world—"

"As defenders of the four elements," Melissa interjected.

Ronnie nodded. "So, the best gift is one that not only comes from the natural world, but also reflects the affinities in their partnership."

"Affinities?" Melissa asked, prompting Ronnie even though she obviously already knew the answer. "What does that mean?"

"Each *Pyr* has an affinity or a connection to two of the four elements. This affinity colors his nature and even his personality. It's the mark of the firestorm for a *Pyr* to be mated with a woman who has affinities to the other two elements. That means that their union brings all four elements together in harmony."

"Making their partnership greater than the sum of the parts."

Ronnie nodded, then smiled. "My *Pyr* is governed by earth and fire. He's passionate, loyal, steadfast and practical. I am governed by air and water. I'm empathic and a little more emotionally sensitive. I also have an affinity for ideas and dreams, which explains my bond to these pearls. Pearls are from the sea, which echoes the water of my affinities, but these were left to me by my grandmother. She inspired me and because of that, they're the most precious thing I own."

"And you're offering them to your *Pyr*, to see him healed."

"I am."

"Will they fill the space left by the lost scale?"

"No. Unfortunately, the scale was lost, so it has to be replicated." Ronnie picked up the cold piece of steel from the forge. "The Smith of the *Pyr* has made a new scale for my *Pyr*, and you can see that he's already shaped it to hold the pearls in place. The combination of elements has to be done during the ceremony."

"And we're here to witness that. Thank you so much for sharing both your knowledge and this moment, which must be a very special one for you."

"Thank you for giving me the chance to show the world how wonderful the *Pyr* are."

"We'll be silent observers now," Melissa informed one camera. "If you hear a deep rumble, like thunder, it's just the *Pyr* talking to each other in old-speak. There will be no rain tonight. Let's watch."

Ronnie took a deep breath, looking skyward as the first of the *Pyr* came over the tops of the trees. It was Rafferty, his opal and gold scales gleaming in the night as he gracefully descended to the clearing. He landed beside Melissa, fixed the camera with a steady glance, then folded his wings with an elegance that made Ronnie smile.

Sloane was next, his scales shining tourmaline and gold. Ronnie was awed by the way his scales shaded from green to purple and back again over the length of his body. He landed beside the forge, then looked up in anticipation.

Quinn landed next, his build even in dragon form more muscular from his time at the forge. He was sapphire and steel, his scales blindingly bright and the way he placed a talon on the forge revealed that it was his. He breathed fire and lit the forge, his eyes gleaming as he coaxed the fire to burn hot for his repair. One cameraman focused on him exclusively, filming the way that Quinn heated the scale in the forge, using his talons as tools.

Erik appeared next, Thorolf right beside him. Erik was ebony and pewter and still not fully recovered from Boris's assault, although he insisted otherwise. Thorolf glittered like a gem in the night, all diamond and platinum, like a dragon made of moonlight. The *Pyr* formed a circle around Ronnie, then all tipped their heads back to watch the sky. She heard the thunder of their old-speak and smiled when Quinn's son, Garrett, tried to respond in kind.

Drake and Theo were the last to join the group, Drake's scales so dark against the night sky that it was easier to see his location by noting where the stars were blocked. Theo was carnelian and gold, like a shard of sunlight. He landed first, completing the circle of *Pyr,* and Ronnie was sure she felt a crackle of energy slip around the ring of dragons.

Then there was only Drake for Ronnie. She stood and awaited him, knowing the moment his gaze locked upon her. She watched how widely his wings spread, how he flew with elegant economy, and her heart thundered in welcome. He descended in complete silence, like the covert warrior he was, then landed beside her with easy grace. He swept his tail around them both, the gesture filled with the protectiveness and power that she associated with him.

He bent to touch his brow to hers and she was sure he was smiling at her. He inhaled deeply and she wondered if he was feeling their hearts beat as one, the way he'd told her they did. His eyes were dark but seemed to be filled with stars, and the way he offered his talon to her made her ferociously proud to be his mate.

Quinn blew into the forge and the fire burned hot. The flames leapt high, shooting white sparks into the night sky. The scale he'd made for Drake was heating steadily, now as bright as a strangely shaped coal of glowing yellow. He blew on the flames again, his eyes glinting with the intensity of his attention, and the scale turned white hot. He flicked a glance at Ronnie, and she understood. She stepped closer to the fire and offered the pearls.

Again she was struck by the gentleness these dragons could show. Quinn lifted the string of pearls from her hand with a kind of reverence. He heated the scale again, breathing directly on it this time, and the flames of his dragonfire licked its surface. It was lost to view for a moment in the torrent of fire, then Ronnie saw Quinn drop the pearls into the flame. He smiled a little, his satisfaction clear even in his dragon form, then blew fire on the scale again.

When he lifted it, the scale was brilliant silver, the pearls gleaming upon its surface. Quinn stepped forward and pressed the hot scale into the gap in Drake's armor. Ronnie felt his heart jump at the pain. He tipped his head back and roared a plume of flame that shot into the night sky like a geyser.

"Fire," the *Pyr* said in unison, their voices a low rumble in which no individual voice could be clearly discerned.

"Air," Ronnie said, knowing her part. She pursed her lips and blew on the repaired scale with all her might.

"Earth," the *Pyr* said in unison again, referring to the steel used to make the scale.

"Water," Ronnie whispered, tracing the circle of pearls that now glowed on Drake's chest. He ducked his head to look at her, and she saw the tear he had shed in his pain. She lifted it from his jowl and placed it on the cooling scale. Even though the repaired scale was already silver, the tear sizzled on impact.

Drake considered Ronnie and she placed her hands flat over the pounding of his heart. "Let's celebrate," she whispered and he laughed aloud. He swept her up then and lunged into the sky, taking flight with a bound, then circling once over the group of *Pyr* in the clearing. He breathed a stream of dragonfire that could only be interpreted as joyous, then flew high into the night with Ronnie clasped against his chest. She heard Timmy shout in approval, his cry taken up by the other boys, and smiled.

It didn't get any better than this.

Although, actually, it could. She reached up to whisper to Drake, though she knew he'd hear her no matter how quietly she spoke. "I thought dragons celebrated by enjoying the pleasures of the physical realm," she said and Drake smiled down at her.

"I seldom drink," he murmured. "And I am not hungry."

"Good," Ronnie said. "Because I had a different kind of celebration in mind."

He laughed and she realized she hadn't heard him laugh before. She would make her *Pyr* laugh often, Ronnie decided in that moment.

And she might just give him another son.

Sam was back in Atlanta, rolling out the clinical tests for the new antiviral. The nurse who had tended Ronnie had been the first to get it, and the first success story. The results were excellent and between managing the manufacture of the antidote, overseeing its distribution and speaking to the media, she'd been working long hours. She was back at her hotel for some much-overdue rest, wishing she wasn't doing it alone. It was the kind of night that she would have liked to have shared with someone.

It was a triumph she wanted to share with Sloane. The antidote was more than half his doing, after all, and wouldn't have been possible without the aid of the *Pyr*. That wasn't the only reason she wanted to celebrate with him, though. She wasn't feeling nearly so greedy about having him to herself forever either. Right now, just one night would work.

This night.

But that wasn't going to happen. Sam sighed and took out the scale that Ronnie had given to her. She kept it hidden inside her emptied suitcase, sealed into the secret pocket in the interior, and invariably pulled it out in the evening. Just looking at the scale reminded her of the splendor of Sloane in his dragon form and made her mouth go dry in recollection of the way he'd raced to her rescue.

No obstacle could have stopped him. The scale reminded Sam that she didn't understand everything in the world, that there were truths hidden from human perception and mysteries that remained unsolved. She thought of the *Slayer* in the fridge and hoped he hadn't healed enough to injure Sloane.

She'd done a little research, trying to learn more about the *Slayers* hatched at Easter Island or Uluru. In the human world, details were few. Sloane had told her more than most people knew. She'd dug into the research that existed on cloning, but didn't know enough about *Pyr* physiology to make any suggestions that might have been of help to Sloane. She guessed that the Elixir was one of the reasons that duplicating *Slayers* had been possible.

How many more of them would there be? It was impossible to say. Anyone with any sense would have done a test hatching, or two, before unleashing a major force. Would there be hundreds of *Slayers* hatched on the next eclipse? Sam didn't even want to think about that.

What more could she do to improve the chances of her favorite *Pyr* surviving the Dragon's Tail Wars? That final eclipse and the turning of the moon's node was too close for Sam's taste, only months away.

But she couldn't think of a thing to do to help.

Sam rubbed her brow in exhaustion and put the scale back in its hiding spot. She turned on the television, only to find Melissa Smith broadcasting another special about the *Pyr*.

In California.

Sam couldn't turn away from the screen. She perched on the end of the bed, her exhaustion forgotten, and watched the *Pyr* heal Drake's scale. It was magical and awe-inspiring and made her believe that everything was possible. The night setting in the forest was perfect. She knew exactly where this was being filmed, behind Sloane's house, and could practically smell the fields of his herbs.

She tried to identify the various *Pyr* in attendance. The one with the missing scale had to be Drake, and she recognized Ronnie. The Smith who was doing the repair? Sam bit her lip. That had to be the guy with the artisan blacksmith business. Quinn. *Here Be Dragons*, indeed. There was something about the diamond and silver one, maybe his sheer size, which made her think of the blond guy with the dragon tattoos.

Once she spotted Sloane—tourmaline and gold, shading from green to purple and back again over his length—she wanted the camera to focus on him exclusively. Of course, it didn't, but she greedily watched for glimpses of him. The show ended all too soon, the camera showing the starlit night sky as Melissa made her concluding remarks about the *Pyr* and their legacy for humankind.

Sam was left hungry for something she couldn't have. She'd been talking to Jac regularly, which was wonderful, although her sister's happy romantic relationship made Sam more aware of her solitude. She was happy for Jac, though, and couldn't wait to meet this Marco.

She showered and ordered some room service, picking at her meal before she put the tray back outside the door. It was funny that she felt so exhausted, yet was tingling with desire and anticipation. She turned out the lights and went to the window, thinking how the same stars that shone over California were shining here. The broadcast had been live, and she wondered what Sloane was doing now. His house was probably full of *Pyr* in celebratory moods, eating, drinking, and laughing. In a way, she envied him the camaraderie of his kind. He might be lonely waiting for his firestorm, but he'd never be as alone as she was.

She stood at the window and watched the stars slowly move,

not wanting to go to bed. The lights of the city gradually went out, buildings fading into darkness and shadows growing deeper. That only made the stars look brighter and closer.

Sam felt as if she were waiting for something, but she didn't know what it was.

It was almost dawn when she found out. She saw the silhouette of a dragon as he flew past the moon. The moon was in its last quarter and brilliant white in the clear sky. She thought for a second she'd imagined the sight, but then she spied the dragon's silhouette against the night sky.

Her heart leapt to her throat with a conviction of who the dragon was.

He flew directly toward the hotel, coming steadily closer, and Sam watched him as anticipation grew within her. He was powerful and graceful, and she craned her neck as he flew directly over the hotel. The windows didn't open, of course, and she was annoyed that she could only see in the one direction. She wondered whether she'd be able to see him from the roof of the building, if there was an exit she could use without setting off an alarm, if her room key would allow her to re-enter the building. She'd taken three steps toward the door, determined to find out, when someone knocked on it.

Sam froze. She swallowed.

Then she ran to the door and hauled it open.

Sloane stood there, smiling at her, a question in his eyes that melted her knees. That he could even doubt she wanted to see him made her want to kiss him senseless.

"How did you find me? I never gave you an address."

He touched the side of his nose and she remembered what she'd been told about the keen senses of the *Pyr*.

"I saw the show."

His smile widened. "Was it good?"

Sam nodded, feeling suddenly awkward. "I thought you'd have a houseful of guests after that."

Sloane shook his head, a little bit rueful. "I do. There won't be a crumb left in the place by the morning and probably a few sons born in nine months or so."

"Why?"

"Because we celebrate by savoring earthly pleasures," he

murmured, his gaze dropping to her lips. He lowered his voice to a whisper and lifted one hand to brush his warm fingertips gently across her mouth. "That's why I wanted to be with you."

There was nothing to say then, nothing to do but draw Sloane into her room, lock the door, and surrender to his touch.

Sloane had sought out Sam on impulse, following his heart, and he was glad of it. They awakened together in the morning, their legs entangled and the sunlight streaming through the window. Sam nestled close to him, then kissed his shoulder. "I wish I didn't have to go to work."

"I have to head back anyway," Sloane admitted, then bent to kiss her. He was never going to get enough of this woman and couldn't imagine how even a firestorm could compete with this.

"Dragons to slay?" Sam teased and Sloane chuckled.

"Something like that."

"I was thinking about the *Slayer* in the fridge."

"I try not to think about him."

Sam twisted to look at him. "What happened when you put the Dracontias into his blood? Did it purify his blood of the Elixir."

Sloane frowned. "Theoretically, it wouldn't make him *Pyr* again, because that's a choice. The Elixir, though, does cause a physiological change." Sloane realized that Sam was watching him closely.

"Theoretically?" she echoed, her disappointment clear.

"I've wanted to try out your idea, but I haven't been able to work with his blood at all," he admitted. "It's so corrosive that it burns through everything. There are holes in the bench now, and in the floor. They might have burned right into the earth below."

Sam nodded. "The only thing that can contain it then is a *Slayer*'s own body. Interesting. Okay, I see two options. One of the guys I know from school works at NASA. They might have developed something to contain highly corrosive substances. I could ask for a little help."

Sloane instinctively disliked the idea of bringing another person into the circle of those who knew any of the *Pyr*'s secrets. "What's the other idea?"

Sam smiled. "Put it in the *Slayer*'s mouth, then take a sample of his blood after it makes a change."

"I wonder how long it will take."

"I could ask my sister Jac. She said she used it to heal Marco's burns, and I think that was pretty quick."

Sloane looked at her intently. "Jac is your sister? The mate of Marco?"

"Jac is my sister," Sam agreed, obviously not understanding what he meant. "And her new boyfriend is named Marco. His real name is Marcus evidently, but I don't know that I'd call her his mate..."

"Of course, she is. They had a firestorm!" Sloane said, interrupting her, and Sam stared at him in shock.

"He's *Pyr*?"

"You never talked about it?"

"She's not telling me a lot about him, come to think of it, but we have a lot of catching up to do. I'm glad she's so happy."

Sloane nodded, seeing that Sam was still startled by this realization. "Where did she get the Dracontias?"

Sam shoved a hand through her hair. "Jac said she stole it from the hidden library of Ivan the Terrible, in Moscow, but I didn't really believe her..."

"And she shot Rafferty, on Easter Island, with the darkfire crystal."

"She went there with some guy, maybe the same guy, but I don't know if she shot the dragon. She was hunting dragons and I recognized her voice in that video." Sam sat up. "She came to visit me afterward."

"Which was why Rafferty kept saying 'she' was nearby." Sloane nodded with satisfaction. "It makes perfect sense. They had their firestorm in Australia, in the spring."

"Is she pregnant?"

Sloane nodded, wondering what her reaction would be. "The firestorm is satisfied."

Sam fell back against the pillows, chewing her lip. "Which explains why she's so happy, and a little bit secretive about him." She flicked a glance at Sloane. "He had a firestorm because he's a good dragon, right?"

"Right."

"Good."

Sloane had a thought then, one he didn't want to express aloud. It defied all possibility to him, that another *Pyr* could have a firestorm with the sister of a mate. He realized only then that he'd been hoping he and Sam might have a firestorm one day, but this just proved what wishful thinking that was.

He returned the conversation to the Dracontias. "So, I'll ask Marco and Jac, then try her strategy on the *Slayer*. And if it works, we could use it—"

"Or pieces of it," Sam suggested, seemingly as relieved to return to their earlier discussion as he was.

"As an antidote to the Elixir, which will ensure that those *Slayers* who are injured don't heal as readily." Sloane nodded, liking the idea a lot.

"A secret weapon." Sam smiled at him, her hair tousled and her eyes alight. "Maybe enough of an advantage to rid the world of *Slayers* completely."

Sloane held Sam more tightly, both encouraged and disappointed. "That's brilliant. You're brilliant. Thank you!" Sam smiled at him and Sloane knew right then that he was going to ensure she was late for work.

He tried not to think of this interval as their last farewell, but the possibility was definitely in his mind.

One thing was for certain: he would ensure she never forgot him.

Erik watched for Sloane's return, standing in the spiral that Lee had created and surveying the sky. The sunflowers were in bloom now and tall around the perimeter, while the calendula flowered in profusion in the middle. It was a spiral of glorious yellow and orange in daylight, all the hues of the sun gathered together. He liked to stand in the middle of it and savor the awareness that he was alive.

What did their future hold? Erik couldn't see past the final eclipse. He saw dragons battling, a great many *Slayers* resembling Boris, and himself locking talons with at least one of them. He saw the red of a blood moon and a night filled with stars. He felt the great wrench of change, but he wasn't certain what it would be.

He thought of the children the *Pyr* had brought into the world, and he feared for their futures. Would they die if the *Pyr* were lost? Would they become human? If Jorge was triumphant and the children still lived, Erik had to believe they would be hunted and slaughtered, just to ensure there was no chance of any *Pyr* surviving.

He thought of Zoë, the blood of his heart, and feared for a moment when he wouldn't be able to defend her, when she wouldn't be able to defend herself. It was a father's worst nightmare.

He thought of humans, exposed only to the malice and fury of *Slayers* like Jorge, and feared that all the treasures of the world would be lost in the absence of the *Pyr*.

He wanted to triumph more than he had ever wanted anything in all his long life, but Erik didn't know what to do. It was impossible to really strategize. It was impossible to form a solid plan. They combed Machu Picchu for potential eggs, but the eggs wouldn't be identifiable as what they were until the light of the blood moon touched them, and the clones within quickened. All of the clones and Jorge himself had proven that they could spontaneously manifest elsewhere, which meant there were no safe havens. He had conferred with the *Pyr* and gathered their impressions as well as the information they held. He would make the best plan, hope for the best, and dare to believe that the sacrifice of the *Pyr* would not be his legacy.

The prophecy swirled in his thoughts yet again.

> *Three blood moons mark the debt come due*
> *Will the* Pyr *triumph or be hunted anew?*
> *Three eclipses will awaken the spark*
> *In thirteen monsters breeding in dark...*
> *Three times the firestorm will spark*
> *Before darkfire fades into the dark.*
> *Firestorm, mate or blood sacrifice*
> *None or all can be the darkfire's price.*
> *When the Dragon's Tail has turned its bore*
> *And darkfire dies forevermore*
> *Will the* Pyr *be left to rule with might*

Or disappear into past's twilight?

Six more clones could be expected then, and they believed they would hatch at Machu Picchu. All of them would want Erik dead. Would he be the blood sacrifice? The Dragon's Tail was a time of karmic rebalance, after all. It might be that because Sigmund had been his son, because Sigmund had turned *Slayer* because of the rift between they two, because Sigmund had been the one to devise the clones, that any balancing of debts would require Erik's death.

If his execution saved the *Pyr* and his daughter, Erik would pay the price willingly.

He abruptly felt a presence behind him and wondered who had joined him beneath the stars. Erik turned slightly, not truly surprised to find his lost son behind him when that *Slayer* had been so bright in his thoughts. The ghost of Sigmund gestured to the apparition that accompanied him.

"The blood moon will ripen the eggs," Sigmund repeated in old-speak.

Tynan, formerly the Apothecary of the *Pyr*, bowed his head before Erik. The sight of him tightened Erik's throat, for he had liked and trusted this *Pyr* well. *"'The caduceus is the mark of he who can wake the sleeping and send the awake to sleep.'"* Tynan said, the Irish lilt in his voice achingly familiar and reminding Erik of their shared past. *"The Apothecary must decide, that he may heal the world with his choice."*

Before Erik could ask for clarification, the two specters shimmered, then disappeared from view. He heard the flap of Sloane's wings and felt the shimmer of the other *Pyr* shifting shape as he landed. Erik turned to meet Sloane's gaze, noting the frustration in his eyes, and bit back a confession of his vision.

"I have an idea about the *Slayer*," Sloane said with purpose. "I might be able to counteract the Elixir."

Erik almost smiled. "So that you can put the *Slayers* to sleep forever."

"Not quite that," Sloane admitted. "But if they aren't immortal, that can only help our side. I'll need to talk to Marco and his mate, Jac."

"I'll contact them. Can I assist you in any way?"

Sloane smiled. "I'd like that. Thanks, Erik."

As they strode back to the house and the sleeping *Pyr*, Erik dared to take hope from the Apothecary's sense of purpose.

CHAPTER TWENTY-NINE

September 28, 2015

K nowing he was doing the right thing didn't make it any easier.

Sloane took a vacation for the first time since the Seattle virus had struck. He hiked through the mountains in Peru, following the Inca trail from Chillca and camping at night. The solitude helped him to prepare for the challenge ahead and to make his peace with whatever the result might be.

For the *Pyr* and for himself.

Sam had been right about the Dracontias, and it had dispelled the Elixir from the clone's body. Erik had taken great satisfaction in battling that *Slayer* and killing him, then the *Pyr* had ensured he was decapitated and burned to ash. Sloane had prepared a solution with the dissolved Dracontias and distributed syringes of it to his fellows.

Then there had been little to do but train and wait.

Sloane dared to be optimistic about their chances.

Even so, he wanted time to make his peace with what he had done and not done in his long life, in case all did not go well. He felt as if he could talk with his father again in those mist-shrouded mountains. The light reminded him of Ireland and the murmur of the wind recalled his father's old-speak. Tynan had always been optimistic, always certain that good had to triumph in the end.

Sloane had to choose to believe that, but he did.

It would have been easier if he hadn't been in love with Sam, and known she was better without him. She'd called a few times, but despite the temptation, he let the calls go to voice mail. He didn't want her to hope for what would never be. The chances of him having a firestorm soon were slim, and the chances of having one with her were practically nonexistent. It would be better for her to fall in love with someone else and be happy.

Once again, he chose for the greater good and not his own. Maybe the Apothecary's role would change after the end of the wars, and change for the good.

Sloane met up with Thorolf and Chandra the last evening and smiled at Chandra's practical way of wearing her son in a kind of sling. Partnership and motherhood hadn't slowed her down in the least, and he wondered whether the sacrifice of her immortality had even changed her much. Thorolf, on the other hand, had been transformed by his firestorm. He was a devoted father and at ease in his skin as he had never been before. Watching them together made Sloane yearn for something that might never be his.

What if he didn't have a firestorm? What if he never had a chance? What if he failed and the *Pyr* paid the price? He felt as if his father laid a hand on his shoulder then, and chose again to believe.

On the morning of the eclipse, Liz and Brandon joined them, as well. There were sparks on the tips of Liz's fingers, and she smiled when Sloane glanced at them. "Fire in the air," she said and he assumed the pending eclipse was awakening the Firedaughter.

Brandt and Arach were taking the train and would arrive with the first flood of tourists. Melissa and Rafferty had arrived the day before and would meet them in the city. Melissa was determined to film this final battle, and Erik had agreed on the condition that it would be the last episode about the *Pyr* that she filmed.

Sloane supposed it would be, one way or the other.

They approached Machu Picchu from above in silence and in darkness. The group perched on the side of the trail to watch the sunlight touch the mountain peak opposite. Mist swirled in the valleys below and the city was empty. It was clearly a sacred place, at least to Sloane, the majesty of creation and the ingenuity of man in perfect harmony.

"The Huayna Picchu," Chandra said quietly as that distant peak was illuminated.

The light spread gradually into the valley below, banishing the shadows and illuminating the ruins of the great city. Sloane caught his breath at his first glimpse of it. He'd seen photographs, but nothing had prepared him for this marvel. "It ends where it began," he said quietly, then pointed. "Sara's parents were killed by a *Slayer* on that road right after the moon's node turned."

"It's *Slayers* who will die tonight," Thorolf said. There was a moment of silence as the others clearly hoped that would be the case.

"The Incan monarchs were believed to be the children of the sun," Chandra continued. "Personifications of the divine sun, taken flesh to rule men."

"That's not very different from carrying the divine spark of the Great Wyvern," Sloane mused.

"Maybe we've come here because of the link with the element of fire," Liz suggested.

"That's not the only element present," Thorolf noted. "Air and water and earth are here, too."

"All in balance," Sloane said. "And countered by the influence of man. It's an incredibly harmonious place." They all agreed, and Sloane couldn't help thinking that this was the perfect place to defeat the *Slayers* for all time, securing the relationship between humans and *Pyr* forever.

"There are several Incan foundation stories that have been recorded, although it's not clear which one was their favorite," Chandra continued. "They didn't write, so the stories were recorded by others. I like the one about the brothers who were sons of the sun and instructed to found an empire where they could sink a sacred stick completely into the ground."

"So there'd be soil for planting crops," Sloane said, having noted the rockiness of the ground on his trip.

"Yes, but here's the part you'll like. Manco was good and just. He followed instruction and established the empire at Cuzco. Ayar, however, was cruel and reckless. He was either sealed into a rock or turned to ice, to contain his wickedness forever."

"It's the same duality as *Pyr* and *Slayers*," Brandon said. "And the same juxtaposition of fire against ice and stone."

Sloane couldn't help but think of the *Slayer* who had been in his fridge, never mind that the same *Slayer* had broken free of an egg that could have been considered a stone prison.

"The Inca had a healthy respect for the elements, as well as being keen observers of the sun, moon and stars," Chandra said. She pointed to an oddly shaped stone on a platform to the left. "That's the Intihuatana."

"The hitching post of the sun," Brandon supplied.

"For the tethering of the sun god Inti at the winter solstice, to ensure he returned the following summer," Sloane said. "Do you think we might find the eggs there?"

Chandra and Liz shrugged in unison. "We've spent months here, studying every rock that looked promising," Chandra said.

"With zero results," Liz concluded. "We just have to wait for them to stir."

Sloane indicated the sparks on Liz's fingertips. "If you're sensitive to the pending eclipse, maybe they're responding to it, too."

"Either way, we have the day to search again," Thorolf said, getting to his feet. The entire city was bathed in golden light now. Sloane could hear a distant train approaching and knew the site would soon be flooded with tourists. "The eclipse isn't until tonight."

"Any particularly strong candidates?" Sloane asked Chandra and Liz.

"I'd think the Temple of the Condor or the Royal Palace might be good choices," she said, pointing out the two structures. "But that might also be where Sigmund would have expected us to look."

"I vote for the Temple of the Condor," Thorolf said.

"We should split up," Brandon said. "Then meet in a couple of hours to compare notes."

They nodded and stood to descend into the city, before there was a rustling of wings. Chandra tipped her head back and smiled as she watched a large black and white bird soar overhead. "A condor," she whispered. "They were revered by the Inca."

"Or is it your friend Snow?" Thorolf asked.

Chandra didn't reply, but watched the bird circle back toward them. It swooped over their heads, gave a cry as if in recognition of Chandra, then dove down toward the city again. Raynor echoed Snow's cry with incredible accuracy and reached out a hand toward the bird.

"I'm following Snow," Chandra said with resolve. She strode down the trail, one arm wrapped protectively around Raynor, Thorolf right behind her.

Sloane found his gaze returning to the curiously shaped stone used to tether the sun god. That was where he'd search for Sigmund's hidden eggs.

Outside Traverse City, the *Pyr* were as ready as they could be.

Erik had divided their forces, trying to determine key locations the newly hatched Slayers would attack. Having one team at Machu Picchu with Sloane, in the hope of catching as many as possible of them early, made sense. The second team was with Erik, as the clones would hunt him down. Marco, Quinn, Donovan, and Lorenzo had gathered at Quinn's home with their mates and children. The third team was with Drake, at his new home with Ronnie in Virginia. Drake insisted that they were making a home there and would defend it, and Erik hadn't been able to shake that *Pyr*'s resolve.

Marco knew that the biggest fight would be at Machu Picchu, followed by the clones coming for Erik. He knew that Erik was determined to take down every version of Boris Vassily himself, per the honor code of the *Pyr*, but he also wasn't alone in believing that the leader of the *Pyr* might need some help to take out as many as six *Slayers* in rapid succession.

That didn't even count Jorge, because no one knew his plan.

Quinn's rural property offered more privacy than Erik's Chicago loft, and if nothing else, there would be dragon fights on this night that were better unobserved by humans. It was a fine clear night, and the mates and children were secured within the house. Lorenzo was ready to beguile as necessary.

The *Pyr* gathered in a meadow and waited restlessly for the arrival of any clones of Boris Vassily. Marco could only hope that Sloane managed to eliminate a few of them at the source, or that Jorge summoned some of them to aid him. Quinn had convinced Erik at least that he could only fight one at a time and that so long as he was engaged in battle the other *Pyr* could fight any additional *Slayers*.

Marco knew that Erik and Eileen had argued about the merit of tradition, but Erik was adamant. He insisted the true measure of a *Pyr* was his adherence to the rules in the heat of a challenge to his survival.

He was right about that.

He knew that Erik was thinking about more than his own survival, but of the good of his family, his kind and the world itself. He knew that Erik would, like Sophie, sacrifice himself to see all the others safe, and that worried him.

He thought of the blood sacrifice mentioned in the prophecy and hoped it proved to be unnecessary.

Marco watched the other *Pyr* and listened for any stray sound. He could feel the tension in his fellows. Lorenzo had a stash of huge syringes filled with Sloane's antidote for the Elixir. Quinn and Donovan were breathing dragonsmoke, surrounding the house with a barrier that was thicker and colder than any Marco had seen.

They all knew it wouldn't stop a *Slayer* who could manifest elsewhere, but Marco supposed the process calmed their nerves. He also hoped that Lorenzo was quick with the syringes and that the *Slayers* lost their additional powers quickly. Erik, he noticed, was tweaking the dragonsmoke, pulling tendrils loose and extending them into the air. Instead of being woven smooth and tight, the dragonsmoke barrier looked like it was embellished with thorns when he was done. It resembled a brier hedge grown wild more than a wall, and Marco wondered at Erik's plan. He doubted the choice was an idle one.

He might have asked, but the eclipse began. He felt a shudder roll through his body as the shadow of the earth touched the moon. He was surprised and disappointed that there was no spark of a distant firestorm. They shifted shape in silence and in unison, but with one glance, Marco knew his fellow *Pyr* had noticed that as well.

A firestorm was a promise for the future. Was the absence of a spark a sign that their time was over? A shadow touched Marco's heart and made him shiver.

The darkfire exploded within the crystal, illuminating the *Pyr* with its blue-green light. Something had happened! The *Pyr* spun to stare at the stone, the darkfire reflected in their eyes. Marco took a deep breath and smelled *Slayer*, just as a ruby and gold salamander appeared on the floor.

Erik raged dragonfire at the new arrival, and Quinn moved to crush it with his hammer. Marco fired the crystal at the salamander and loved how the *Slayer* leapt when the spark hit him in the back. This version of Boris Vassily shimmered blue and became a dragon, then threw himself at Erik.

Erik roared a plume of dragonfire into the night sky and reared back, swishing his tail through the air. The pair locked claws, colliding with savage force, and the first battle was on.

The second *Slayer* came out of nowhere, resplendent in his dragon form against the darkness of the night. He breathed a plume of dragonfire fit to set the field alight. Clearly, he didn't mean to play by Erik's rules, because he jumped on the leader of the *Pyr* and bit his wings. Erik tore himself free, spinning in the grip of the first *Slayer*. He was a dark whirlwind between the two ruby and gold *Slayers*, and he spewed a stream of dragonfire long enough to burn them both.

Marco pounced on the latest arrival from behind and bit into his shoulder. He tasted black *Slayer* blood, but bit out a chunk of flesh so that the *Slayer* screamed. He held fast to his prize as he flew high in the air to take this contender out of the game. He fired his darkfire crystal into the back of the *Slayer*'s brain, but the stone fizzled and the shot was feeble. The crystal went dark then, and Marco tucked it under his scales.

He grappled with the *Slayer*, who was slippery and suddenly energetic. They twined around each other, biting and slashing, ripping and breathing fire. Every time the *Slayer* tried to slip free, Marco halted him, using whatever means he could. Only after the *Slayer*'s body had gone limp and his breathing slowed, would Marco carry him back to the *Pyr*. Until then, he'd fly as far as necessary.

He took a blow to the head and saw stars, then raged dragonfire at the *Slayer* so hot that it burned his own talons. The *Slayer* was screaming and smoking when Marco ran out of breath, but he inhaled to repeat the feat. Lorenzo appeared beside him, a syringe in his claw. That *Pyr* grinned, then stabbed the needle into the injured *Slayer*.

"One who isn't immortal anymore," he said with satisfaction as he emptied the syringe.

But still not dead. The *Slayer* flailed in Marco's grip, snapping off the needle with his movement as he screamed in anguish. Lorenzo swore, but to Marco's relief the syringe was empty. The *Slayer* was as slippery as an eel, evaded them both and dove back to the fight far below.

"He can be killed now," Lorenzo said. "That's a good thing." They both raced after the *Slayer*, plummeting out of the sky like shooting stars.

Donovan and Quinn were already locked in battle with the second *Slayer*, and Erik still battled against the first, the one who hadn't had the antidote. Lorenzo would have joined the fight, but Erik growled in reminder.

Lorenzo exhaled in frustration. He hovered then, flying tight circles around the battling pair, ready to intercede on Erik's behalf. The *Slayer* found this distracting, probably because he didn't know or share Erik's resolve to fight fair. He twisted, trying to watch Lorenzo as he fought Erik, and Lorenzo laughed at him, taunting him to err.

Marco reached for the vials, but the *Slayer* fighting Quinn and Donovan broke free of them both in a sudden move. He slammed Quinn into the stash and the glass shattered beneath that *Pyr*.

All of the antidote Sloane had given to them was leaking out of the broken syringes. Marco tried to save some of it, but it ran though his fingers and soaked into the ground.

Quinn roared with fury and erupted from the ground, seizing the *Slayer* by the throat. He locked his claws around the *Slayer*'s throat and squeezed, exhaling dragonsmoke as he crushed the life out of his opponent. Donovan summoned the elements and ice pellets began to hail down on the battle. They were as sharp as arrows and struck hard.

"Why don't you just manifest elsewhere?" Lorenzo taunted, then added his dragonsmoke to the assault. *"Oh, wait. Don't you have enough strength?"* He laughed then sucked hard on the conduit of dragonsmoke, his action leaving the *Slayer* twitching in Quinn's grasp. His color was visibly fading, his struggles becoming less vigorous with every heartbeat.

"This one can die," Lorenzo reminded Quinn. *"Finish him."*

"With pleasure," Quinn replied and squeezed so tightly that black *Slayer* blood ran over his talons. The *Slayer* screamed but it

was almost a silent sound of anguish, one Marco felt rather than heard.

The *Slayer* who hadn't had the cure was fighting Erik with vigor. There were still four unaccounted for.

Should Marco go to Sloane for more antidote or help with the fight? He looked between the battling dragons. Quinn and Donovan slammed the second *Slayer* onto the thorns of the dragonsmoke barrier so hard that they spiked through his body. Lorenzo murmured, and Marco guessed that he was ensuring that the smoke wound deeply into the *Slayer*'s guts. The dragonsmoke hedge shimmered, as if it had just been given an infusion of new power.

One *Slayer* being destroyed.

One *Slayer* fighting hard with Elixir in his veins.

Sloane and more antidote it would be.

Sloane missed the first *Slayer* to hatch.

It happened so quickly. They had all returned to gather around the Intihuatana as the eclipse drew near, because Snow had landed on its highest point that morning. Rafferty was watching the moon overhead and was the first to shift shape. The sight of him in the moonlight against the green peaks was magical, and Sloane heard one of the cameramen make an admiring comment.

The crew couldn't see the *Pyr* in their human forms and would only film them once they flew into the night in their dragon form. They must have seen the shimmer of pale blue light, though, and known what was going to happen. The ruins were lit with pale blue light as the *Pyr* changed shape in turn. Brandon and Brandt followed Rafferty, then Arach and Thorolf and Sloane took their dragon forms. The six dragons circled the ancient site in flight.

"The eclipse will last an hour and thirteen minutes," Brandon said. *"Liz checked."*

"And then it'll all be over, one way or the other," Brandt murmured. There was a beat of silence, and Sloane knew that no one wanted to say farewell.

"I am honored to know all of you," Rafferty said.

"Good luck, everyone," Thorolf said and gave a fist pump.

"Let's kick Slayer *butt."*

"May the Great Wyvern be with you," Rafferty said.

"And may another Pyr *be always at your back,"* Sloane agreed. They flew in a tighter circle, grasping each other's right claws and drawing strength from each other. Sloane knew that no man or *Pyr* could have had better friends and companions.

If there was justice in the world, they'd win.

"Look!" Liz shouted. "It's begun." The first shadow of the eclipse touched the lip of the full moon high overhead. There were sparks shooting from Liz's fingertip when she pointed skyward, and Sloane couldn't even see her hands for the blaze of light.

There wasn't a spark of a firestorm.

Sloane exchanged a glance with Rafferty, knowing that the older *Pyr* also feared the import of this.

"We're not done yet," Thorolf muttered, turned and flew directly down to the ancient site. His scales shone in the moonlight, glittering like gems.

And Sloane smelled *Slayer*. There was a rumbling deep in the earth beneath them, a potent reminder that Peru was susceptible to earthquakes. Suddenly the hill beneath the ceremonial stone cracked and a dark crevasse yawned open. The terraced steps on the outside edge began to slip away, crumbling into the valley thousands of feet below.

Sloane saw the first clone of Boris Vassily take flight in a blaze of ruby red and gold in the same moment that he saw the underground antechamber revealed.

Brandon and Thorolf raced after the clone, but their talons closed on empty air. Thorolf swore vigorously in old-speak and spun in place, his eyes shining with fury.

Sloane was sure that clone had gone to Erik. He shot down to the ground and shifted back into his human form. It was the only way he could squeeze into the dark chamber. He could smell dampness and wet cloth, but couldn't see the room's contents clearly. The ceiling had cracked, but the eclipsed moon emanated only a rusty red light. Sloane heard something rocking and saw some large orb lit by that rusty red. The earth rumbled as if it would shift and cast them all down into the river valley far below. The stone overhead shifted, loosing a volley of dust on him, and the roof gaped open wider.

Liz climbed into the space behind him, the light from her hands casting a golden glow in the space. There were a number of great round shapes on the floor of the cavern and one of them was rocking. It was the one touched by the eclipse's light, which told him all he needed to know. Each of the shapes was as tall as he was, and probably three times as wide. They looked almost like hot water bottles, large and rounded with "caps" of wrapped cloth. Sloane supposed the ovals had once been aligned, but the motion of the earth had left them tumbled against the inner wall.

"*Falsas*," Liz said. "Funerary bundles," she said at his confused glance. "Archeologists thought the fabric looked like false heads."

"This is how the Inca buried their elite," Melissa said, busily filming all the while. "I did some research before we came here. There aren't supposed to be any mummies at Machu Picchu."

"Maybe there aren't," Sloane murmured, moving toward the one that was shaking. He lifted a syringe, then wondered if the outer coating would crack the needle. It looked like dried mud or clay but when he touched it, it crumbled to reveal woven cloth.

Chandra was in the space behind them, her nose wrinkled. "They're huge!"

"They mummified them and wrapped them in cotton with everything necessary for the afterlife," Melissa said. "There'll be food and armor inside, as well as the remains of others in the family."

One such bundle had been broken open, as if the cloth and clay had exploded on one side. The cloth and treasures from within were scattered on the dirt below, along with the broken bones of the original occupant.

"This is wrong," Melissa said. "It's a violation of their eternal rest."

It would be a violation of a great deal more if these clones survived.

"Sigmund must have tucked the clones into the sides," Liz said.

"They must have been in salamander form," Chandra agreed.

Sloane realized with horror that the needles on his syringes wouldn't be nearly long enough to penetrate the wrappings, much less target a salamander hidden inside a bundle.

He'd have to wait for them to hatch. Judging by the agitation of this closest one, he wouldn't have to wait long.

"They do look like eggs," Liz said.

"But there's a dozen of them here, easily," Chandra noted. "If there are six clones, where are they? There could even be two hidden in one *falsa*."

It wasn't the most optimistic thought any of them had had. The one *falsa* rocked with greater vigor and cracked down one side. Sloane saw the flash of ruby and brass, but only because he was looking for it. The salamander raced for the gap in the wall, but Sloane snatched it up. He felt its cold slither between his fingers and gripped tightly.

The clone of Boris twisted in his grasp, looking at him with fury in his eyes, but Sloane stabbed in the needle and emptied it of its contents in a gush. The clone bellowed and bit him hard. When Sloane flinched, the salamander dove for the crack. *"Got him!"* Sloane said in old-speak.

"He's mine!"

Sloane heard Thorolf shout, but couldn't reply. A third flash of ruby and brass sailed past him, the salamander too fast and too slippery for him to inject as well.

"Missed one!" he shouted to the *Pyr*.

"We'll get him anyway," Brandon roared and the sound of the dragonfight overhead carried to their ears. The night beyond the crack was lit with flashes of dragonfire, and the sound of dragons roaring as they fought was deafening. The earth was rumbling restlessly, and Sloane feared the whole peak would slide into the Urubamba River valley.

"I can't sing to the earth to stop this," Rafferty said in old-speak, then groaned as he evidently took a blow. *"This wound is too deep. Gaia will have her revenge on this night."*

The karmic rebalance of the moon's node wasn't just about the *Pyr*, after all.

The *falsas* were rocking all around them, the angle of the crack in the ceiling exactly right to let the light of the eclipse shine on another three. Sloane didn't even want to blink in case he missed a *Slayer*. He spun slowly in place, watching for salamanders to erupt from the wrappings. The women didn't even seem to breathe, they were so intent.

Sloane was glad of their assistance, but worried about it, too. He would have loved to have been in his dragon form, because his vision would have been sharper and he would have been better able to defend the mates. He couldn't have managed the syringes, though, and he wouldn't have fit in this chamber.

A salamander popped free suddenly, and Liz grabbed it, managing to singe it a bit with her fire and slow it down. The space filled with the scent of burning flesh. Sloane injected the *Slayer* and cast aside the empty syringe.

"This one's had it," he said in old-speak as the salamander slipped into the night.

"He's mine," Arach replied.

"Do you see the other two?" Sloane demanded of Liz. When she didn't answer, he pivoted to face her.

Only to find Jorge in his human form, his eyes glittering coldly. The *Slayer* had Chandra's hand twisted behind her back. His right hand had changed to his dragon form and his claw was closed around the baby's head. Chandra had frozen in place, fury in her eyes. Liz wasn't moving either, clearly not willing to risk Raynor's welfare. Melissa was on the ground, her camera fallen out of her hand and blood on her temple.

"Eleven of the thirteen clones hatched so far," Jorge said mildly, then nodded at the last rocking *falsa*. "Which makes that 'egg' mine."

The *falsa* rocked harder and began to crack on one side. Jorge flung Chandra toward Liz so hard that she stumbled over Melissa. Sloane leapt forward to catch her so she didn't fall on the baby, and Liz grabbed her arm. Jorge shifted shape in a blaze of shimmering blue, practically taking all of the space in the small chamber. He swung his tail and reared up, tipping the roof off the chamber and shattering a wall. He seized the last *falsa* and soared into the sky, exposing it to the blood moon like an offering.

Sloane grabbed the largest of the syringes, shifted shape, and leapt into the sky in pursuit of the fleeing *Slayer*.

The wait was excruciating.

Drake was in the forest behind the house he now shared with

Veronica, Timmy and their recently born son. They had only to fight to secure the survival of the *Pyr* to win their future, but couldn't do it until the eclipse. The night seemed particularly still to Drake, as if the entire world were expectant.

As if the entire world knew that his kind would live or die, depending upon events of this night.

Theo had joined him as well as Niall, Delaney, and Lee. Theo had brought Kristofer and another younger member of the Dragon Legion named Kade, although Drake knew there were other Dragon Legion in the vicinity. This time, he hadn't insisted otherwise. Both Kristofer and Kade were in the house, keeping a vigilant watch over Drake's family. Drake had promised Veronica that this would be his last mission, and he hoped that he survived it.

He wanted to pace, but Lee insisted upon stillness. The other *Pyr* had spent the day in a meditative state, building a spiral in a clearing in the forest at the back of Drake's yard. It was wrought of dragonsmoke and invisible to human eyes, but Drake could feel its cold chill. It had a power about it that Drake didn't trust, but that Lee said would draw evil to its core. Drake didn't like having such a thing so close to his sons and mate, but he trusted Lee.

And Lee had vowed it would be gone when the eclipse was over.

The shadow finally touched the moon, and they all shifted shape, ready for whatever would happen next. The tree branches were devoid of leaves and looked like skeletal fingers reaching for the moon. Drake watched the light turn steadily more reddish as the shadow progressed across the face of the moon. He tried to be as still as a rooted tree, but he was aware of his heart pounding. He closed his eyes as it matched its rhythm to that of Veronica, not so very far away. The sensation still made him dizzy, but it also reassured him as a sign of her welfare. Her pulse was a little slower than his own.

Drake felt agitated and uncertain. If he'd been in human form, the hair would have been standing on the back of his neck. Something strange was in the air, maybe even darkfire, and he had a hard time holding on to his conviction that all would end well.

He didn't like spells.

He didn't like waiting either.

He was ready to fight for all he loved.

The eclipse proceeded with glacial speed, so slow that he wanted to scream aloud. Lee didn't even move, his concentration was so great, and Drake could scarcely hear his breathing. Delaney and Niall watched the surroundings, their eyes glinting in the darkness. Theo was close by Drake's side, as loyal a second as any *Pyr* could have.

When the moon was completely eclipsed, Lee shifted shape, becoming a dragon that could have been made of pure gold, with red scales and talons. He flew over the spiral he'd created of dragonsmoke, then hovered over its middle, his great red wings flapping slowly to keep him aloft. He murmured an incantation that Drake didn't understand, then retreated to the perimeter, his eyes gleaming with anticipation.

They didn't have to wait long before two *Slayers* appeared suddenly in the air of the clearing.

They were ruby red and gold and smelled of Elixir. Sloane had missed them then, which meant that the responsibility for inoculating them was theirs. Delaney shifted back to human form and picked up a syringe as Niall covered his back. One clone lunged at Drake, but Theo intercepted him. They locked claws and battled for supremacy, then Drake roared and joined the fight.

He tackled the *Slayer* fighting Theo, slamming him into the ground beside Delaney. Delaney shoved the needle into him and emptied it, casting aside the syringe to pick up another one. The *Slayer* roared with frustration and exhaled a plume of dragonfire, setting the tree branches overhead aflame. He couldn't manifest elsewhere, but he was still dangerous. He launched himself at Drake, teeth bared. The *Slayer* slashed at Theo, then bit at Drake. The two *Pyr* exchanged a nod and seized him, flying straight up into the night.

Drake saw Niall fighting with the other *Slayer* as Delaney struggled to inject him and heard a vial crack.

It was Lee who tore a gash in the side of the other Slayer and jammed the broken syringe into that vermin's side. The *Slayer* screamed in anguish, but the antidote hadn't spilled and it was within him, too. Delaney and Niall held him down as Lee breathed fire, searing the wound shut as the *Slayer* screamed.

Both *Slayers* were inoculated, but not dead yet.

They couldn't escape.

There was the wail of a distant siren, and Drake felt Veronica's fear for him. A wave of protectiveness consumed him, lit his world with red and fury, drove his need to see these vermin scrubbed from the face of the earth. There was only a *Slayer* to be slaughtered, a *Slayer* who wanted to harm his mate and sons, and Drake was going to ensure his death was painful.

And irrevocable.

Drake roared and shredded the *Slayer* in his fury, while Theo held their opponent captive. He breathed dragonfire at the *Slayer* and ensured that he was too dead to ever threaten any *Pyr* or human again.

Drake's cry brought more of the Dragon Legion to their aid. He caught a glimpse of Rhys and Hadrian, Alastair and Balthasar, and others whose names he didn't even know. The sky was thick with dragons and alight with dragonfire.

Rhys breathed dragonsmoke and drained the *Slayer* of every last vestige of his energy, then he and Hadrian ensured that the dead *Slayer* was exposed to the elements after his death. Theo and Drake joined them to incinerate the remains to ash. By the time the task was done, Niall, Lee and Delaney had done the same to the other *Slayer* with the help of the Dragon Legion.

The woods behind Drake's house were filled with *Pyr*, their noble scent filling his nostrils. They listened in unison, but the eclipse was over and there were no more *Slayers* in the vicinity.

Did Drake dare to breathe a sigh of relief?

Sloane was racing after Jorge, determined to eliminate the *Slayer* at the root of all the *Pyr*'s trouble. He didn't think of how far behind his fellow *Pyr* were. He could hear them fighting and smiled at Thorolf's shout of victory when he dispatched one of the clones. It was a sign that they were winning. The moon was almost completely eclipsed, which meant that in less than an hour, the fate of the *Pyr* would be sealed.

Sloane was going to do his part.

He seized Jorge's tail and pulled that *Slayer* to a halt. Jorge spun in the air and smacked the *falsa* against Sloane's head. The air filled with cracked clay and tufts of cotton, as well as dried corn and twine. Debris flew in every direction and got into Sloane's eyes. By the time he'd blinked them clear, Jorge had squirmed out of his grip and flown higher. Sloane beat his wings hard in pursuit.

There were items falling from the *falsa* as Jorge flew, freed by the wind or the loosened coverings, and they hailed down on Sloane. They seemed to surround him like an ever-changing cloud and he identified items as much by scent as by sight. He saw parrot feathers float past him, more cotton and dried corn, small tokens of gold like coins. There was a glint of gold earrings, then shards of earthenware pots and chunks of dusty textiles. He saw bits of woven reeds, a leather sandal, a ball of red string that unfurled as it fell past him. He saw a gourd that had been hollowed out, then decorated, then smelled that the next missiles were whole dried vegetables. He flew through a shower of coca leaves, reached up, and seized Jorge's tail again.

Sloane dug his talons in deep and Jorge spun to fight. The *Slayer* loosed a stream of dragonfire even as Sloane tried to drive the needle of the syringe into his skin.

Jorge's scales were so hard that the needle bent.

Too bad this *Slayer* would never love anyone enough to lose a scale.

Jorge slashed at Sloane then, once again using the *falsa* as a weapon and loosing a lot of cotton. Sloane dropped the syringe and saw the glimmer of it spiraling down into the valley far below. He raced after it, abandoning Jorge for the moment, caught up to it and snatched it out of the air. He pivoted and soared upward again, just in time to see two small items of ruby and brass tumble from the *falsa*.

They shimmered blue, then were gone.

The last two *Slayers*, and Sloane had missed them.

Jorge cast aside the *falsa*, which scattered human bones into the air as it fell earthward, and dove toward Sloane with his talons extended.

They collided hard and tumbled through the air, the force of impact enough to make their wings momentarily useless. Sloane was glad he'd passed the syringe to his back claw, although Jorge was trying to seize it with his own. They wrestled with their tails, each trying to claim the syringe.

"*What's in it?*" Jorge demanded. "*Hoping to convert me to the* Pyr *team with a vaccine?*" He laughed at the very idea.

"*There's no chance of that.*" Sloane smiled even as he gave Jorge a thump with his tail. The *Slayer* flinched for a heartbeat, and Sloane snapped at him but missed. "*Maybe it's Elixir.*"

"*If it was, you'd be taking it yourself. Shouldn't the Apothecary be interested in immortality?*"

"*I'm not interested in addiction.*"

"*Exactly.*" Jorge eyed the syringe with suspicion and took a deep breath, his eyes glinting. "*The scent makes something curdle within me,*" he murmured, his eyes glinting. "*Don't tell me that the Apothecary has nefarious plans.*"

They raged at each other then, tussling and biting, and Sloane managed to tear one of Jorge's wings a bit. He had no opportunity to inject the syringe's contents into the wound, though, before Jorge twisted from his grip and tore his own tail.

"*I should just let you do your worst,*" Jorge taunted. "*Since your kind will be gone soon.*"

"*I don't know how you figure that.*"

Jorge laughed and spoke aloud. "Survival of the fittest. Humans *do* get some things right. *Slayers* are superior, so we will triumph."

"Unless you all die. You are outnumbered."

Jorge smiled. "Maybe, maybe not. Six new *Slayers* flew out to do their worst tonight." He gestured down toward the ground, and Sloane saw that Brandt and Arach had both fallen. He couldn't see from this distance whether they were injured or dead. Brandt was rotating between forms, which wasn't good, Arach was in his human form, which wasn't a good sign either.

One of the clones was still battling against the *Pyr* but Sloane couldn't deny that it looked as if his fellows were weakening. There was a lot of blood below them and big fissures in the earth. As he watched, the ground rumbled again and new dust rose from the ancient city. Would it be Gaia who eliminated them from her surface?

"Look at the bright side," Jorge said. "You won't have to tend to them, not since your kind will be wiped from the face of the earth."

He had to help them.

He had to finish Jorge first. He spared a glance at the moon, knowing the moments of opportunity were slipping away.

Why couldn't the *Pyr* have been the ones cloned?

"Maybe I'll leave you a legacy," Sloane taunted in old-speak. *"A little something to remember us by."*

Jorge laughed again. "Maybe you've become the Dreamer instead of the Apothecary." He launched an assault on Sloane then, hitting him with such force that Sloane was stunned. Once again the syringe was knocked out of his claw, tumbling toward the valley far below and leaving Sloane without the means to finish the fight.

He couldn't give up, not now, no matter what the odds against him. Sloane felt a grim resolve fill his heart and knew he'd fight to his very last.

He'd give everything he possessed to save the world and give Sam a future.

Even his life.

CHAPTER THIRTY

arco spontaneously manifested at Machu Picchu, right in the middle of a dragonfight. He found himself abruptly between Rafferty and one of the ruby and brass clones, just as Rafferty was slashing at the *Slayer*. Marco shifted into human form and ducked out of the way. He felt the *Slayer*'s black blood rain down upon his back as Rafferty's blow hit home. His back burned but Marco didn't care.

He could see that Thorolf was ensuring that another clone stayed dead, his dragonfire lighting the night sky. Far overhead, he could discern Sloane and Jorge locked in battle. Brandt was rotating between forms in the middle of a clearing nearby and the ground was rumbling underfoot with a restlessness that wasn't reassuring. He could see Liz and Chandra bent over Brandt, trying to help him. Arach was in his dragon form and utterly still, a pool of red blood beneath him.

The moon would slide out of the shadow of the eclipse within moments.

He had to ensure Erik's survival, first and foremost. Marco followed the scent of the antidote to find Sloane's stash and took another pair of syringes. He checked that they were loaded with antidote and might have returned to Michigan, but Rafferty slammed a *Slayer* into the ground beside him. The *Slayer* looked dazed.

"This one," Rafferty commanded, his eyes blazing. "I'm not sure he's had his fill."

Marco jabbed a loaded syringe into the *Slayer*, who shook his head in confusion then began to struggle. "It won't kill you,"

Marco said amiably. "It just eliminates the Elixir from your body."

"Which means you can be killed," Rafferty smiled coldly as the *Slayer* apparently understood his peril.

He might have protested, but Rafferty hauled the other dragon into the sky, and Marco doubted it was an accident that his talons were digging so deeply into his opponent's scales. "Now, let's finish up."

Marco waited to watch Rafferty deck the *Slayer* so hard that the other dragon tumbled through the air and smacked against a fitted stone wall. The wall cracked, the stones fell, and the earth shook once more. Black blood flowed across the stone, and Rafferty held the *Slayer* captive as he breathed a ceaseless stream of dragonfire.

Marco nodded approval as the *Slayer* screamed, then he wished himself back to Michigan.

Sloane didn't dive after the syringe this time, because he knew his opponent expected it. Jorge breathed fire to distract him, then bit into Sloane, shredding the shoulder of his dominant hand. Sloane knew it wasn't a coincidence. He pretended the injury was greater than it was and let his wings falter and still, as if he'd passed out.

He fell like a rock toward the ancient city.

Jorge took a deep breath and dove after him. He was going to breathe dragonsmoke, to draw out the last of Sloane's strength. Sloane knew he couldn't let the dragonsmoke touch him, but he was buying precious time.

And getting closer to the falling syringe. He beat his wings, driving himself downward with greater speed, as if he were confused. Jorge plummeted after him, then dispatched a stream of dragonsmoke that spiraled toward Sloane with astonishing speed.

Sloane counted the seconds, wanting to time his recovery to the moment he could snatch the syringe out of the air. He watched his opponent though narrowed eyes. The dragonsmoke glittered, closing fast, immediately followed by Jorge's gleaming eyes and sharp teeth.

Sloane waited until the smoke was a talon's span away.

Then he came suddenly to life. He lunged at the syringe and snatched it out of the air. He passed it to his claw, glad that it was still full, and pivoted in the sky. He dodged the dragonsmoke and soared upward, straight for Jorge, with the needle point leading the way. Jorge's eyes widened and he spun to evade the needle.

And that was the moment Sloane saw where Jorge was missing a scale. It wasn't over his heart or on his belly, but in the joint, at the nexus of his right hip. The scales would overlap there, diminishing the size of the gap when he moved, but now Sloane knew where it was.

He locked on to his target, chasing Jorge with all his might. He seized Jorge's ankle, earning a volley of dragonfire, but held fast even as his own scales burned. He reached up and his grip fumbled. He had a heartbeat to fear that Jorge would escape, then got his grip again.

There wasn't an instant to waste.

Sloane buried the needle into Jorge and emptied it with savage speed. Jorge twitched and flailed, the color fading from his scales even as Sloane watched. The needle broke with the *Slayer*'s efforts, but the syringe had been emptied.

"What did you do to me?" Jorge demanded, his eyes blazing.

"An antidote to the Elixir." Sloane smiled. "Congratulations, you're mortal again." He decked the astonished *Slayer*, sending him tumbling through the air. "Just in time to die."

"That's impossible!" Jorge roared and they locked claws once more, lighting the night with their dragonfire. The fight was savage and fast, Sloane's determination giving him more power than he'd known he possessed. Jorge was battered and bleeding, his wings torn, his guts shredded, his scales burned.

Something fell from beneath his scales where he had tucked it for safety, a small gleaming cylinder that might have been a pencil. As much as Sloane wanted to know what it was, he wasn't going to release Jorge to find out.

It fell, spiraling down into the darkness and disappearing.

"She did it," Jorge whispered, his claw falling to the unprotected spot, then he snarled. "I knew she was worthy."

Who did he mean? Sloane looked after the cylinder. What had it been? Who had given it to Jorge and what was it for?

Sloane was amazed that Jorge had ever been able to care for

anyone. Perhaps the lost scale had given him little vulnerability because his affection was so limited. Either way, the Elixir was gone. The moon was about to emerge from the shadow of the eclipse and the battle wasn't finished.

The *Slayer* tried to breathe dragonsmoke, making an effort to save himself, but Sloane easily evaded it. He slashed at Jorge, who could no longer offer much resistance. He ripped open his body so his black blood rained down on the mountains of Peru, and then he burned the *Slayer's* body to a crisp. With the Elixir neutralized in his body, Jorge couldn't evade his just reward, and he didn't fight for long.

When he was dead, Sloane carried him into the deep valley of the river, not wanting to take any chances. Only once Jorge had been exposed to all of the elements and his body had dissolved to ash, did Sloane race to help his fellow *Pyr*.

The moon was sliding free of the eclipse, and he was glad to find Thorolf flying toward him bearing the remains of one fried *Slayer* and Brandon with the other. "Water!" Thorolf cried and his triumphant word echoed off the cliffs.

Sloane watched the moon overhead as he caught his breath and hoped all his fellows had won.

Marco slid into the field beside Quinn's home in a flash of blue light, only to find that Erik was holding down the last of the *Slayers*. His grip on his opponent's neck was so tight that the *Slayer* could scarcely breathe. The *Slayer* was also cut to ribbons, his blood flowing like a black river, and the stench was enough to turn Marco's stomach.

He shifted to human form and jabbed the needle into a wound, emptying the syringe as Erik watched approvingly. The *Slayer* moaned. He thrashed. He opened his eyes and glared at Marco.

"What have you done to me?"

"Eliminated the Elixir from your body," Marco replied. *"It's part of the Apothecary's plan to heal the world."*

This version of Boris sneered and spat, his disgust clear. Erik tightened his grip, holding his opponent's gaze. *"This time, death is forever,"* he promised in old-speak, then squeezed the life out of him. The *Pyr* gathered around, breathing dragonsmoke and ensuring that the fight was sucked out of the clone.

In moments, he was still and didn't stir again. Marco stepped back with satisfaction.

"Can you go to the others?" Erik asked. "I know you must be tired, but we need to know for sure that they've triumphed, too." He pointed a talon at the moon overhead, and Marco saw that the first sliver of moon had slid from beneath the shadow of the eclipse.

"The corpses have to be exposed to all of the elements," Donovan said. "Let's get that done before the end of the eclipse."

Sloane had tended to Brandt and to Arach, and was relieved that they were both responding to the Apothecary's song. He was tired, and he didn't have any more of his unguent for *Pyr* wounds, but he was glad to use it all to help his fellows.

"At least here we won," Thorolf said, scanning the sky.

"I hope that's true everywhere else," Chandra said.

"Surely we'd feel different if we lost our powers," Brandon said, his gaze also on the sky. Liz took his hand in hers and didn't express the alternative aloud.

"I'm not dead yet," Arach said and rolled over with a grimace.

"You might not ever have the chance to fight *Slayers* again," Thorolf reminded him.

Arach opened one eye. "I'd be good with that."

The others chuckled a little, their uncertainty clear.

That was when the spark lit on the end of Sloane's talon, illuminating the night with its radiance. All gazes locked upon the small flame, and it lit their features as they gathered close.

"A firestorm," Rafferty breathed. "*Your* firestorm."

Sloane stared at its flame in wonder and awe, knowing what it was but barely daring to believe it. *His* firestorm was the final firestorm of the Dragon's Tail Wars.

Who was his mate?

He was both glad that he'd kept from making a commitment to Sam and regretting it. He wished he'd treasured the bit of time they might have had together, but he wouldn't have hurt her for the world. It had been hard to part, even knowing it was for the greater good, and more time in her company would only have made the break harder.

He'd done the right thing.

He hoped he felt some affection for his destined mate.

He felt the air move around him and found Marco before him, that *Pyr* grinning as he eyed the spark.

"Did we win?" Sloane demanded, needing the reassurance.

"All clones dead and exposed to the elements," Marco confirmed and the other *Pyr* cheered. "I've been to Virginia and Michigan. We've finished them all!"

Rafferty recounted the part of the prophecy with satisfaction.

"Firestorm, mate or blood sacrifice
None or all can be the darkfire's price."

"Of the choices, none is definitely the best," Sloane said and they all agreed.

He noticed then that Marco was brighter and more emphatically present. Marco had always seemed ethereal, or unrooted in their times. Now he was emphatically part of the world. Marco glanced around with satisfaction. "I'll guess you finished Jorge, as well."

Sloane nodded. "He was ushered where he needed to be," he said, thinking of his father. He felt both old and young, exhausted after the battle but invigorated by the spark of the firestorm.

Marco congratulated him, then indicated the spark. "Looks like you get a reward for healing the world."

"She's far away, though, whoever she is."

"I'll give you a ride," Marco offered. "You tell me the direction and I'll take you to her."

Sloane nodded, then took flight with Marco. The Sleeper reached out a claw and Sloane took it, holding tightly so he wasn't left behind. He knew the theory of spontaneous manifestation, but had never experienced it himself.

They were surrounded by a swirling wind and enveloped in light. He heard the other *Pyr* wishing him well and then only the sound of the wind. He felt that he was caught in a tornado, but couldn't be afraid when the firestorm's light grew steadily brighter. Marco seemed to be at ease with this transition, although Sloane's gut churned.

It wasn't just the transit. He was as nervous as a teenager on a first date, even though he knew that made no sense.

He reminded himself that the firestorm was on his side.

The Great Wyvern had chosen for him. He had trusted in that all his life, and he wasn't going to doubt it now.

Marco brought them out of the wind and into a field of long grass. Sloane recognized Quinn's house, then the *Pyr* gathered around to bask in the light of his firestorm. His fellows congratulated him and he was glad to see that Erik hadn't been too badly injured. Mates and children spilled out of the house as the eclipse ended, their jubilation clear.

"A world without *Slayers*," Erik said with a sigh of satisfaction. "Who could have imagined we would ever be so lucky."

"Never mind that our children would be so lucky," Quinn said, taking Sara's hand in his. They all eyed the spark on Sloane's fingertips and smiled with pleasure for him.

"Go already," Donovan said to Sloane with a grin, and he did. He shifted shape as they watched and took flight, turning one circle over them before he followed the firestorm's beckoning heat.

The spark burned brighter to the southeast. Sloane flew with one claw stretched in front of him, following the beacon of the firestorm's light. His wings beat leisurely and he flew at a majestic pace. He would only feel this once in his life and Sloane wanted to savor it. He thought of all the firestorms he had attended, all the mates he had defended, all the *Pyr* he'd seen happily partnered. He thought of the firestorm's power to heal and knew that if anything was going to mend his heartbreak over Sam, the firestorm would be the only force that could do it.

He was over Lansing when the firestorm burned with bright vigor. Was the Great Wyvern bringing everything full circle? Sloane remembered very well that Quinn's firestorm had been the first of the Dragon's Tail Wars and it had been in Ann Arbor. He hadn't been back in the area since.

As he drew closer to Ann Arbor, Sloane felt the firestorm's heat with a power that stole his breath away. His desire for his unseen mate was growing to dizzying intensity even as he acknowledged that the firestorms of the Dragon's Tail Wars had come full circle. The Smith and the Seer. Who would be the Apothecary's destined mate? What would be her contribution to the world, and to the *Pyr*? Sloane couldn't wait to find out.

It was quiet near the river, and he landed in the shadowed darkness of Nichols Arboretum, shifting shape where he couldn't be seen. The lights of the city drew him to the street, away from the cemetery and the shadows where the firestorm's golden light could only draw attention. The Medical Center was brightly lit despite the hour and he strode down the quiet street, following the firestorm's burn.

When the firestorm's heat led him past the emergency ward and the hospital itself, guiding him toward the research labs, Sloane dared to hope. He found his footsteps increasing in speed as he raced in pursuit of the firestorm's promise. Far ahead of him, a woman came out of one of the buildings that housed the labs.

She was blond, slender, and walked as if she were tired. She hefted a bag to her shoulder and jammed her hands into her pockets, turning her back on him as she trudged toward the downtown core.

Better yet, he knew her.

Sam was illuminated with a golden aura like a halo, a light that couldn't have been anything other than what it was.

Sloane smiled. He had to believe that there were some who thought Dr. Samantha Wilcox was an angel, because she had brought a cure to their loved ones. He strode quickly after her and she turned just before he caught up with her.

Her eyes widened in surprise and pleasure. "Did you win?"

Sloane nodded and she threw herself into his arms. Even without the heat of the firestorm, it would have felt good to hold her close. With the heat of the firestorm, it was amazing.

Sam gripped him tightly and her words fell in a hurry. "I've been thinking. I miss you so much and I don't care if you have to leave one day for your firestorm. I'll take every day and every night I can get, just to be with you until that happens..."

"But I just came to my firestorm," Sloane said, interrupting her.

Sam looked up, then stared at the fiery glow that surrounded them. Sloane lifted her hand and she gasped aloud at the flurry of sparks that emanated from the point of contact. She looked as awed as he felt.

"I'm exactly where I'm destined to be," he said.

Sam's eyes lit with delight. "There was an eclipse tonight. This is your firestorm!"

"This is *our* firestorm," he corrected, and Sam seemed momentarily speechless.

"Are you sure?" she whispered, her eyes alight.

"Can you doubt it?" he asked, then his heart matched its pace to hers. It was a sensation of overwhelming power and one he wanted to experience forever.

If he could stand it. The Apothecary and the Physician. It was a perfect match.

A sweet sexy heat unfurled in Sloane's body, kindling a desire so powerful that he felt himself on the cusp of change.

"You're shimmering," Sam whispered and he opened his eyes to find her watching him. The firestorm was golden between them, pulsing in its demand, and their gazes locked for a heady moment. "I thought I wouldn't see you again," she whispered. "I knew it was the right thing to do, but I've missed you."

Sloane pulled her closer. "I've missed you, too." He shook his head. "What are you doing here? I thought you were in Atlanta."

"I was, but they're doing some clinical tests here with the antidote, helping us out with the footwork. I made a quick trip to check on progress." She leaned against him and sighed. "You should know that Jac is gloating that she provided the key."

Sloane chuckled, savoring the feel of her against him. "I like that we worked together."

Sam met his gaze, her expression worried. "You're positive there's no more *Slayers*?"

Sloane shook his head. "No more *Slayers*. Not one."

"And no more blood moons. I checked."

"No more clones." He brushed his lips across hers, savoring the tingle of sparks. "I checked."

"But the moon's node doesn't change for a few more days."

Sloane smiled down at her. "I think we're good."

"And you're here, against every expectation." Sam ran her hands over his shoulders, then frowned. "Do two *Pyr* often have firestorms with sisters?"

"It's never happened before as far as I know. I thought it completely unlikely." He bent and touched his lips to hers. Sloane caught his breath at the wave of desire that resulted from that fleeting touch. "I think it's a gift of the darkfire, which makes the unlikely probable."

Sam smiled. "Or maybe the Apothecary is getting his reward for saving the world."

"I couldn't have done it alone."

"But my reward has been more public. I was offered a university post." She swallowed visibly, then looked up, a question in her eyes. "At Stanford."

Sloane nodded, feeling luckier than he could have thought possible. "Interesting that it's almost commuting distance from this house I bought. The place needs a lot of work, but has charm."

"And idiosyncrasies." Sam grinned. "The kind of house that you don't easily forget."

"Just like a doctor I know."

They kissed then, a potent kiss that made him want to both hurry and linger over the firestorm's gift. They were both breathless when he lifted his head, but there was one more thing he wanted to know.

"I have an idea about that house, although you might not agree," Sam said, her words coming quickly. "Jac helped with our finding the cure, and she loves that house. I don't know whether she and Marco have decided where to live..."

"But they could be neighbors, as well as family," Sloane concluded. She nodded, her eyes shining, and he knew that the sisters were becoming closer. "I think it's a great idea."

Sam laughed, then kissed him with an enthusiasm that left him dizzy. He broke their kiss with an effort.

"You know what the firestorm means," he said, hearing the tightness in his voice. "Tell me now if kids aren't in your plans anymore."

"I'd like to have a son," Sam said softly. "Jac has always talked about having a houseful of kids, and the appeal of the idea has been growing on me. I was disappointed that Nathaniel didn't have brothers."

"I was disappointed not to have brothers, myself. A houseful of boys suits me just fine."

"Right." Sam said with a nod. "No girls."

"No girls."

She smiled. "I think we'll make good sons."

"I think we will."

"At least one of them will be interested in healing."

"The oldest will be the Apothecary," Sloane told her, hoping that didn't trouble her. "It's a hereditary role."

Sam nodded, unsurprised. "Then maybe one of the others will go to med school."

"Maybe one will read tarot cards."

Sam laughed, her eyes sparkling in a way that made Sloane's heart leap. "I want them to choose their own paths."

"I don't have any doubt that they will," Sloane agreed. He bent and kissed her again, intending it to be a quick kiss, but she responded to his touch so readily that the firestorm blazed between them.

"Maybe we should get started on that plan," Sam teased. "It's going to take some time to have a houseful of boys." She was squinting against the brilliant light of the firestorm, but kept leaning against Sloane in a way that made it burn ever brighter.

"Maybe we should go somewhere private, somewhere that won't attract attention."

"I have a little suite just a few blocks away," Sam said. "And no commitments that can't be canceled."

They locked hands and walked in the direction she indicated, the firestorm humming between them as they matched step with each other. Sloane took her bag, savoring the sensation he'd waited all his life to feel.

"In fact, I have no commitments for the next week that can't be canceled," Sam continued.

"It's not going to take that long," Sloane said and she smiled at him.

"I want to linger over this," she confided. "It only happens once, and you've waited centuries. Don't imagine that I'm going to let you seduce me quickly."

"I could challenge you on that and make you change your mind."

"You could help me to study the undocumented force known

as the firestorm. We need to observe its nuances and effects, and create a complete report." Sam shrugged, her eyes dancing. "It could take weeks to be scientifically thorough."

Sloane inhaled sharply and gripped her hand more tightly. "I suppose, in the name of scientific discovery, it would be the only responsible thing to do."

"It would!" Sam laughed and dug the keys from her pocket. She led him up the stairs to a little apartment, unlocked the door. She tugged him inside then backed him into the wall to kiss him. Sloane caught her close and deepened the kiss, loving that her passion was so honest. "Those dark-haired strangers," she whispered when he finally lifted his head. She was flushed with pleasure. "I've got to remember to warn people against their seductive powers, deep secrets, and ability to change lives."

"It's only the Scorpio ones who can do that," Sloane said.

"It's only the *Pyr* Apothecaries who can do that," Sam replied.

"There's only one of those."

Sam's eyes lit with triumph. "And he's all mine, forever."

The only possible reply to that, in Sloane's opinion, was a kiss that made further conversation impossible.

EPILOGUE

October 1, 2015

he *Pyr* gathered in Chicago, at the converted warehouse where Erik and Eileen lived. All of the mates had come as well, and the children, and the loft was filled with jubilant noise. The kitchen counters were covered with contributions to the pot-luck dinner and the wine was flowing. Sloane watched with pride as Sam mixed and mingled, her aversion to dragons banished now that Jorge and the *Slayers* were dead.

After they'd eaten and caught up on all of each other's news, Erik tapped a spoon against his glass of wine. "We have a lot to celebrate tonight, but business to attend, as well. First of all, a warm welcome to Samantha and to Jacelyn."

The *Pyr* and their mates cheered as the two women nodded and smiled. Jac was already rounding with her pregnancy, and Sloane was well aware that Sam was pregnant, too. The absence of the firestorm's sparks told his fellows as much, too.

"I know we're all looking forward to our flight tonight, but there are repairs to be done first," Erik continued.

Sam came to Sloane's side and put her hand in his. Even though the firestorm was satisfied, his desire for her wasn't. He had a feeling he was going to be fascinated by her for the rest of his days and nights, and that suited him just fine.

"I think we should do this on the roof," Quinn said to general agreement, then led the way. The entire group followed, Sam holding Sloane's hand tightly.

Quinn was the first to shift shape, becoming a powerful dragon of sapphire and steel. He blew a plume of dragonfire into the night air, as if for the pure joy of it, and his oldest son Garrett mimicked his father's move. He came to stand beside Quinn, his eyes bright as he offered Marco's lost scale to his father. Quinn took it in his talons and began to heat it with his dragonfire.

As he did so, the other *Pyr* shifted shape, filling the air with a shimmer of pale blue light. Erik shifted next, becoming a pewter and ebony dragon. Donovan's dragon scales were lapis lazuli and gold, and the large pearl in his repaired scale gleamed in the light of Quinn's dragonfire. Delaney shifted to an emerald and copper dragon, then Niall became a dragon of amethyst and silver. Rafferty shifted to his opal and gold dragon form, and Brandon became a black dragon who looked to be lit with an inner orange fire.

Drake shifted to his dragon form, and his scales were so dark that they could have been made of black pearls or pieces of night sky. Lorenzo became a dragon with scales of three colors of gold with cabochon gems, and Lee had gold scales with red talons and a red belly. Thorolf became a massive dragon of diamond and platinum, as brilliant as the light of the moon. Marco became a dragon of deepest black, though Sloane thought a glimmer of blue-green danced over his scales. Sloane squeezed Sam's hand then shifted shape himself, becoming a dragon of tourmaline and gold, his scales shading from green to purple and back again.

Jac stepped forward to offer a token to Quinn to repair Marco's scale, which was white-hot. He couldn't see what she offered, but Sam whispered to him. "It's a pendant of Mom's, a sterling rose." There was pride in her voice, and Sloane was glad that the sisters had reconciled.

They'd make good neighbors.

"Fire," Quinn commanded, and both he and Marco breathed dragonfire on the scale. It shimmered like heat glare above asphalt in summer, as if so hot it might vaporize. Quinn pressed the silver pendant into it then looked at Jac.

"Earth," she said. To Sloane's surprise, she had tugged on a padded glove and pushed the scale into place on Marco's chest along with Quinn. Marco tipped his head back and gritted his teeth, then breathed a torrent of dragonfire into the night sky.

"Water," Quinn said and Jac lifted one of her tears of

sympathy with a fingertip. Sloane heard it hiss as she dropped it on the scale.

"Air," Quinn said. Marco dropped his chin and breathed on his own scale. Sloane glimpsed another crackle of darkfire, then realized that Jac still had possession of the crystal. She gave it to Marco, who lifted her into his embrace. The new scale cooled quickly on his chest, returning to the same color as the others. The silver rose shone like the trophy it was as Marco stepped back into the *Pyr* circle.

"We're up," Sam said, not hesitant in the least.

"Anything that doesn't kill you makes you stronger," Sloane said, still sensing how Marco's repair burned.

"I want your armor repaired," Sam said firmly. "Even if there aren't *Slayers* around."

"Fair enough," Quinn said, his eyes twinkling as Garrett handed him Sloane's scale. The Smith took a deep breath then exhaled a brilliant torrent of dragonfire on the scale. Sloane could smell its heat and saw smoke rise from it.

He wasn't surprised that she had a token for his scale repair, but he was surprised to see what it was. She'd been mysterious and as soon as he glimpsed the item on her palm, Sloane knew why. It was the gold necklace with the charm of the Space Needle that Nathaniel had bought for her on his last visit to Jacelyn. "Are you sure?" he whispered, knowing how she treasured it.

"I know where I want it to be," Sam said firmly. There were tears in her eyes. "And I think Nathaniel would love this solution."

Jac was blinking back her own tears and the sisters exchanged a look.

Quinn took the necklace with care, arranging it on the scale so it encircled the single charm. He lifted his gaze to Sam, as if for her approval.

"Make a spiral of the chain," she said. "One that goes the right way."

"Sunwise," Quinn said and moved the chain with his talon.

Sam smiled up at Sloane. "So, it draws energy into the heart of the Apothecary, whenever he needs it."

Sloane's heart thundered at both the sentiment and Sam embracing new ways of thinking about the world. Quinn worked on the scale until he was satisfied with it, then heated it again.

Sloane stepped forward and reared back, baring the empty spot on his chest to the Smith.

"Fire," Quinn said, holding out the scale to Sloane. They both exhaled enough fire that their view of the scale was lost. Quinn's eyes brightened as the Apothecary's dragonfire touched his claw and Sloane recalled how dragonfire healed the Smith.

"I am forged anew," Quinn murmured, then nodded to Sam. She tugged on the same padded glove Jac had used. "Earth," Quinn said and they pushed as one, him guiding the scale to its location and Sam pressing it home. Its heat seared Sloane's skin, sending pain through his body, but cleansing the spot as well.

"Air!" Quinn commanded, and Sam blew upon the scale even as Sloane caught his own breath after the stabbing pain.

"Water," Quinn concluded and Sloane bowed his head, allowing Sam to lift the tear from his own cheek and place it on the repaired scale. He heard the hiss of it evaporating and sighed with relief as the scale cooled. It was hardening in place, just as it should, and Sloane smiled that his armor was complete again. He smiled down at Sam, his heart thundering fit to burst, but there was no time to celebrate now.

Ronnie stood with her new son in her arms and her older son standing on her left, with Drake at her right. She felt Timmy's awe that he was in the company of the *Pyr* and felt a measure of wonder herself. She felt honored to have been welcomed into this group, as if she'd joined a large and loving family. They had each other's backs, all the time, no matter the challenge, and Ronnie knew she'd only become closer to them over the coming years.

She loved Drake with all her heart, and then some. She'd always believed that deeds spoke louder than words, and Drake's actions had proven him to be the man she'd been waiting for. He'd already been wonderful with Timmy and she knew they'd build a wonderful future together.

She blinked back a few tears, amazed that everything had worked out so well.

There was a brief rumble of old-speak, and Ronnie guessed that someone had given a command. Probably Erik. The *Pyr* stepped forward in unison, each one placing his left claw on the shoulder of the dragon beside him and his right claw over his heart.

Erik nodded and they spoke in unison.

She listened to Drake's low tones, feeling his voice create a vibration deep within her.

"I, Drake, do solemnly pledge not to willfully reveal the truth of my shape-shifting abilities to humans. I understand that individuals may know me in dragon form or in human form, but I swear that I shall not permit humans to know me in both forms, to allow them to witness my shifting between forms without appropriate assessment of risk. I understand also that there will be humans who come to know me in both forms over the course of my life—I pledge not to reveal myself without due consideration, to beguile those who inadvertently witness my abilities, and to supply the names of those humans whom I have entrusted with my truth to the leader of the *Pyr*, Erik Sorensson."

Before the *Pyr* moved, Marco reached back to his mate, Jac. She placed the darkfire crystal in his hand, and Ronnie noticed that the blue-green flame trapped within it was burning brightly. Its light illuminated the faces of the *Pyr* when Marco held the stone into the middle of the circle, giving them a majestic air.

"And so the time comes for the darkfire to be unharnessed again," Marco said. "And its light to be spread throughout the world to the point of disappearing from view." He bowed his head in the direction of the crystal with a kind of reverence. "We give our thanks to the Great Wyvern for Her wisdom and for the power of the darkfire. Like every spark that springs from Her, this one must return to its source, as its task is completed."

He cracked the crystal in half, like he was breaking an egg. For a moment the blue-green light of the darkfire hovered in the air, like a glowing orb. Then it leapt across the circle, creating a brilliant arc of light and landing on the black and white ring that Rafferty wore. That *Pyr* jumped as if shocked, but the darkfire sparked to his chest. It struck his repaired scale, illuminating it with its strange glow for a moment.

The darkfire jumped again, sparking on Donovan's chest where he stood beside Rafferty and making his repaired scale glow brilliantly. The next jump happened more quickly, then the darkfire moved with increasing speed. It set Quinn's scale alight, then Delaney's, Niall's, Drake's. When the darkfire touched Drake's repaired scale, Ronnie felt it like a blow to her own heart and caught her breath just as Drake did. She felt a heat slide through her, a warmth that was as beguiling as the firestorm.

It made her think about celebrating, *Pyr*-style.

The darkfire continued around the circle, touching Brandon's scale, then Brandt's, Thorolf's and Lorenzo's. Finally it leapt to Erik's repaired scale in a blaze of light. Those repaired scales all burned brilliantly in unison, crackling as if touched by the firestorm again, but this time the light was blue-green. The scales glowed more and more brilliantly, and Ronnie felt her own heart heating so it felt like it might burst. She could see the reaction of the other mates and their *Pyr* and felt a powerful sense of communion with all of them.

Then the darkfire was extinguished, disappearing so abruptly that she wasn't the only one to catch her breath.

"Thanks to the darkfire," Sloane said huskily. "These firestorms burn forever."

The *Pyr* bowed their heads in thanks then the air was filled with shimmering blue light. They shifted shape, taking their human forms, each and every one of them turning to embrace his mate and sons. Ronnie found herself caught up against Drake's chest and closed her eyes at the magnitude of the gift he had brought to her.

"One more obligation," Drake murmured to her, his gaze warm.

"One more celebration of a world without *Slayers*," she agreed.

"A world safe for our sons." Drake ruffled Timmy's hair and the boy grinned.

"I can't wait for the fireworks," he said. "Zoë said her dad's shows are awesome."

"But this one will be extra special," Drake said just as Erik raised his voice.

"It is time," he announced. The *Pyr* shifted back to their dragon forms, taking flight in pairs. Ronnie liked how they flew in formation, as if they'd drilled for this moment.

"I knew he was a warrior," Timmy said, and Ronnie couldn't help but smile. "Right from the first."

She drew her son into a hug, pressing a kiss to the top of his head. "And you were right." Just as Ronnie had suspected from the first that Drake was a man who could heal her wounded heart.

Maeve found her prey easily.

She had Jorge's scale in her cabinet of trophies, a token from another unnatural species that was rightfully extinct. The *Pyr*, though, continued to survive, which meant the job was only half completed. She was in Chicago to film a report on the *Pyr*'s final appearance, partly because the network demanded it but more because she needed to snare a *Pyr*.

This was the best place to find one.

And they did intend to disappear from view after this night.

Lorenzo had told her so much about his kind and it was all so interesting. She could use the information to bend a dragon to her will. It would take time, but Maeve had nothing but time. After all, the creature best equipped to hunt dragons had to be another dragon, and she did have that pesky other issue to see resolved.

She definitely needed a *Pyr* of her own.

The crowd was thick with *Pyr*, but she made her selection with care. A muscular young man with dark hair was emanating frustration almost as vehemently as he exuded the scent of *Pyr*. He looked to be in his late twenties, but it was his attitude that intrigued her. He seemed to feel unappreciated. Maeve could work with it. She deliberately jostled against him, then gave him her most sultry smile.

He looked her up and down, then smiled in return as they exchanged apologies. He snapped his fingers as his gaze brightened. "Hey, aren't you that reporter?"

"I'm Maeve," she whispered, holding his gaze as she exhaled a spell. He was dazzled easily, not nearly as much of a challenge as Lorenzo had been. "And you?"

"Kade," he whispered.

"Hello, Kade." Maeve conjured a stylus of ice from her sleeve and placed it in his hand.

He frowned down at it. "What's that?"

"A little gift from me to you," she whispered, then caught the back of his neck in her hand. He was delicious and she barely restrained herself from claiming him immediately. Surrender was so much sweeter. "If you ever want to see me again, just use it to draw a door."

"A door?" Kade chuckled. His skepticism made her spell slip slightly.

Maeve smiled. "A door. Draw it anywhere, then add a knob and a keyhole." She tapped the stylus. "This will unlock it." She kissed him, leaving her lipstick on his mouth and her perfume on his skin. "Trust me," she whispered, then continued on her way.

The camera lights were on and the crew was waiting for her at the assigned location, her assistant even having found some humans to share their views on the *Pyr*.

But what Maeve noticed most was the weight of that handsome *Pyr*'s gaze following her progress.

Kade.

He'd do very well indeed.

Sam stood with the other mates, excitement fluttering in her belly. She couldn't believe that she'd have a son again, but there was no doubting it, given the disappearance of their firestorm. Sam knew enough to believe in the physiology of the *Pyr*. What she really couldn't believe was that she was happy again and looking forward to the future. Her sister was beside her, Jac's belly round with her son, and Sam was glad that Jac's dream of having a family was finally coming true. It was wonderful how much their relationship had already healed and improved. Jac was thrilled about the house, and Sam was glad that her sister would be right next door.

On this night, they were at Navy Pier, waiting for Erik's show to begin. All along Chicago's waterfront, people were gathered to see the fireworks display and to have their last glimpse of the *Pyr*. The excitement was tangible and the atmosphere festive. The lake was like a dark mirror, and the weather was perfect. The sky was clear and the water still. Sam could see the lights all along the park system reflected in the water. There was music and the sound of the rides on the pier, children laughing, and vendors hawking their wares.

Melissa Smith was doing live interviews with people who had come to watch the show and would broadcast it live. Sam could see the lights from the television cameras and knew that some of the *Pyr* mates were going to be interviewed, even though they were going to pretend to be passersby.

Sam was content to blend into the crowd, to be with Jac and wait. Jac glanced at her watch, looked at Sam, and tapped the display.

Sam was amused that the flare fired over the lake on the stroke of the hour. She could have expected that Erik would insist upon punctuality. The audience cheered as the flare spewed a brilliant trail of stars, and the music soared. Those stars grew bigger and spun, turning from white to yellow to red before they fell into the lake below.

Before they were extinguished, nine similar flares went straight up from the barge where the fireworks were loaded. They shot high into the sky and exploded into a corona of stars. The audience gasped and applauded as the stars rained down into the lake. They fell silent as they realized that a dragon had taken position in the sky behind the curtain of the fireworks. It was Erik. He breathed dragonfire, the brilliant flames licking against the night sky and the crowd gasped in wonder.

A dragon appeared behind him, his dragonfire revealing his presence and casting Erik into silhouette. It was Quinn, flying with power. Donovan appeared behind him in the same way, his dragonfire casting Quinn in silhouette, his scales shining against the night. The trio fanned out, and three dragons appeared behind them in the same way.

Delaney was the copper and emerald dragon behind Donovan, Sam knew, while Niall was the amethyst and platinum dragon behind Quinn. Rafferty was the opal and gold dragon behind Erik. The music soared and the *Pyr* flew in a tight circle, then fanned out again.

Six more dragons appeared behind them in the same way. Sam identified Thorolf as the diamond and platinum dragon behind Quinn, Brandon as the black dragon with scales edged in orange behind Erik, Marco as the anthracite dragon behind Rafferty, Drake as the thorned dragon whose scales gleamed like they were made of black pearls behind Donovan, Lorenzo as the dragon in three shades of gold behind Delaney and Theo as the carnelian and gold dragon behind Niall.

Sam saw more than one person filming the sight with a camera or cellphone.

There were more *Pyr* in the crowd, she knew, dragon shifters who were part of Theo's Dragon Legion. Other than Kristofer and Arach, who she'd met briefly, their identities were hidden to her still. Sam knew she'd be meeting more *Pyr* over time.

Meanwhile, the *Pyr* overhead formed two circles as they flew in time to the music, one facing inward and one outward. Plumes of dragonfire erupted from their mouths and burned brightly against the night. They wove in and out of each other's flight paths, the outer circle going one way and the inside one the other. They blew fire intermittently then, matching the clash of drums in the music, and people clapped along. The kids began to cheer.

The *Pyr* flew faster and faster, so it seemed that there were two spinning circles of flame in the night sky. They all breathed fire at once and the circles became an orb of burning flames almost as bright as the sun. They broke rank and all flew outward at the same point, revealing one dragon at the point where the middle of the circle had been.

The Apothecary, who had healed the earth.

Her *Pyr*.

Sam locked her hands together as Sloane, tourmaline and gold, beat his wings to hover in place. The crowd cheered as the *Pyr* shot toward the coastline. They flew over the crowds of people, diving so low that people could almost reach up and touch their scales. They continued to do acrobatics in the air, then back over the water again, enchanting everyone who had come to see them.

"They have to be exhausted," Jac said, her gaze following Marco.

"Do dragons get tired?" Sam asked and a little girl solemnly informed her that they did not. Niall swooped over them then and the girl squealed with pleasure. She reached up her hands toward Niall and he returned to scoop her up and fly her over the pier before returning her safely to her parents.

The kids went wild, all of them shouting for rides after that.

But the *Pyr* flew back over the lake, looking for all the world like sleek fighter jets to Sam. They flew winding paths around each other, changing places so rapidly that they blurred together. Each seized the one ahead of himself by the tail and traded places with him, the one who fell behind breathing fire as he dropped back. They flew up like the flares, breathing plumes of flame the whole way, then joined claws to fly in a spinning circle high overhead. This time it was Theo who was in the middle of the circle of twelve dragons.

Sam caught her breath when the blue-green light of the darkfire crackled, illuminating those repaired scales and making the circle of *Pyr* look to be lit by an inner fire. The darkfire brightened so that she had to close her eyes against it.

It sparked to strike Theo in the brow, leaving a golden spark burning there that looked like a firestorm's light.

Then the darkfire went out.

A triumphant volley of fireworks erupted in the sky and the music soared as a frenzy of fireworks were let off. The dragons were gone from view, and Sam knew they would be hidden from human view forevermore. The sky was thick with tumbling cascades of fire and she was clapping along with the music when she felt the weight of familiar hands on her shoulders.

"Sorry we're late," Sloane murmured into her ear, a thread of humor in his tone. "Traffic was terrible."

"And we couldn't find a parking spot," Marco agreed, sliding his arms around Jac's waist. Sam knew she wasn't the only one biting back a smile at their cover story.

"Did we miss anything?" Sloane asked with such innocence that Sam nearly laughed aloud. They were surrounded by people who had no idea of the truth, though. She turned around in his embrace and her heart leapt when she met his gaze.

"Just some dragons showing off," she said.

Sloane grinned. "Oh, the kind of thing you see all the time, you mean."

"From what Melissa Smith says, we won't be seeing the *Pyr* again," Sam said, as if he didn't know. "They're disappearing from human view for all time." She caught a glimpse of Theo about thirty feet away, his hand over his heart as he scanned the crowd as if looking for someone he knew.

Had he felt the spark of a firestorm? Sam hoped so.

"Maybe," Sloane mused. "I have to think that some lucky humans will still catch a glimpse of a dragon once in a while."

"That would work for me," Sam said, hooking her arms around his neck. "So long as I have a valiant defender by my side."

Sloane's smile widened. "I'll have to see what I can arrange," he murmured, just before he bent and captured her lips beneath her own. Sam very happily kissed him back, knowing that this was one dragon she wasn't going to lose track of anytime soon.

And that suited her just fine.

Ready for more of the *Pyr*?

Read on for an excerpt from

Hot Blooded

Book #1 of the *DragonFate* Series

Excerpt from **Hot Blooded** © 2015 Deborah A. Cooke

Saturday, October 3, 2015 — New York City

t was good to be back in New York, and even better that the *Pyr* had won the Dragon's Tail Wars. No more *Slayers*. Theo could hardly believe it. He'd partied with the rest of the Dragon Legion long after the other *Pyr* had returned to their normal lives.

Tonight, though, tonight was the night he'd celebrate the survival of his kind in a more intimate way. He was thrumming with desire and anticipation, but seeking the perfect partner.

He found her, against all expectation, tending bar in a club called Bones, located in the former meatpacking district. It was located in a converted warehouse, all high ceilings and deep shadows. The music was loud and the crowd was thick with ghouls and Goths, bumping, grinding, drinking, and jostling. It was 80's theme night, which the regulars evidently had prepared for, so there was a lot of big hair and bigger shoulder pads, buckets of glitter and Lycra.

As they pushed their way toward the bar, he thought of Thorolf.

When he saw the brunette bartender, he forgot everything else. She was petite and dressed in black. There was something elfin about her, and Theo felt a primal urge to defend her against the crowd.

She was the one. He knew this with complete conviction.

She turned her back on him, and he sensed that she trembled.

She knew she was the one, too.

"Oh, yeah," Arach muttered under his breath, then flashed a smile at a woman dressed as Dolly Parton. The *Pyr* fanned out, the six of them cutting their way through the dancers to the bar. Theo headed for the woman who would haunt his dreams.

The bar was long and black, as shiny as if it were made of obsidian. Six bartenders worked its length and although they were fast, they had a hard time keeping up with demand on this night. At the far end of the bar, a burly guy with many tattoos stood with his arms folded across his chest, glaring across the crowd. He wasn't a bouncer: they were at the door. Theo figured he was the owner, and he was watching the money.

The music segued into the B-52's singing *Rock Lobster*. His bartender cocked a finger at her blond co-worker, who pointed at her in the same moment. The regulars hollered encouragement as the two women vaulted on to the bar and started to dance. They were both dressed completely in black, his choice tiny and slim, the blond bartender taller and more robust, like a Valkyrie. The crowd went wild and the music got louder.

"Wasn't there a shooter called a B-52?" Kade demanded and Theo pointed.

The other bartenders were lining up shot glasses down the length of the bar. The two women each juggled three bottles of liqueur, then poured shots in time to the music.

"Kahlua, Bailey's and Triple Sec, if I remember right," he said, then narrowed his eyes to read the labels on the bottles.

"There was also a Tom Cruise movie called *Cocktail*," Darcy said. "This could have come right out of it."

It was obviously a rehearsed routine and had been carefully choreographed. Theo liked that she was such a good dancer.

"It is 80's night," Arach countered with a grin, and pushed through to the bar. Theo was right behind him.

He wasn't really surprised when the small bartender seemed to suddenly sense his presence. She glanced up, and he saw that her eyes were both thickly lashed and incredibly green. Their gazes locked and held for a potent moment, her awareness of him making him smile slowly.

Their gazes held for one moment too long. She missed the

bottle she'd tossed into the air, the one she should have caught behind her back. She reached for it, even though she had to know that she'd already missed it, and Theo saw a flush rise on her throat. He guessed she'd have to pay for it, because the burly guy with the tattoos was watching intently.

Then, against all expectation, right before smashing on the bar, the bottle rose to her grip. Theo blinked. He thought he might have seen a shadow, a silhouette of a man, but it was only the merest glimpse. His bartender flicked a glance at him, checking whether he'd noticed what everyone else had missed, and her blush didn't slow its progress.

What had happened?

The completed shooters were distributed, slid down the bar to waiting hands. Theo reached the bar just as the music slid into *Love Shack*, another song by the same band. The women bowed, then leapt from the bar in unison. A bowl for tips was slid down the bar, both bills and coins being dropped into it. She spared him a glance that was tinged with uncertainty just as Kristofer gave a jubilant shout. He had to be thirty feet away, at the other end of the bar, but Theo could see the spark of a firestorm on his fellow *Pyr*'s fingertip.

Humans roared with delight around Kristofer, clearly thinking it was some kind of illusion.

"What the fuck?" Arach muttered in old-speak, a shimmer of blue lighting around his body. Theo shook his head, his reaction much the same. There hadn't been an eclipse. There shouldn't be a firestorm. Even more strange, he couldn't feel the spark of the firestorm.

But then, those had been the signs of a dragon shifter meeting his destined mate before the turn of the moon's node. Maybe with the elimination of the *Slayers*, all the rules had changed.

There wasn't any time to think about it. Kristofer dove through the crowd on the dance floor, following the heat of the firestorm to his destined mate. Alastair, Rhys and Hadrian were hot on his heels, so to speak.

"Hold it!" Theo roared in old-speak, but they didn't hesitate. He tried it again out loud, with no difference in effect. Arach lunged after the trio with Kade quick behind them. Theo swore and made to follow them, but the tiny bartender suddenly snatched his

hand. She was so much smaller that he stopped for fear of hurting her.

"It's a trap," she whispered, but Theo couldn't understand what she knew about any of it.

There was a flash of blue light from the far end of the dance floor and a roar of anguish. Rhys and Hadrian hovered on the cusp of change, but Theo's shout seemed to keep them from shifting shape in front of all these people. If they took their dragon forms here, they'd be breaking the Covenant that the *Pyr* had just sworn to Erik, leader of the *Pyr*, the pledge that they wouldn't reveal themselves to humans — and Theo would have to answer for them. Theo hastened through the crowd, feeling that the situation was out of control.

"She disappeared!" Kristofer cried.

"No worries, man. Happens to me all the time," commiserated a patron dressed as a vampire. There was laughter.

"Like she went into another dimension," Kristofer muttered. By the time Theo reached his side, he was sliding his hands over the wall of the club, which was painted black. Theo could see the glow of the firestorm's light beneath his hands, but it was strange. It both died to a glow and sparked, as if Kristofer's destined mate was both close and far.

That made no sense. She couldn't be both.

Unless she *was* in another dimension.

Theo was watching the spark as Kade dug something out of his pocket. "This will fix it," that *Pyr* said. The object looked like a pen, but was clear, as if it was made of ice. He quickly drew the outline of a door on the wall of the club, and the line shimmered, as if he'd drawn it with some kind of stardust marker.

"No!" shouted a woman, and Theo glanced back to see the cute bartender closing fast.

"Will this let me follow her?" Kristofer demanded, intent only on his firestorm and mate. "Wherever she's gone?"

"I think maybe." Kade continued, either ignoring the bartender or oblivious to her protest. "It's worth a try."

"I'll take that when you're done with it," said the patron dressed as a vampire. "The good ones always disappear into thin air."

The *Pyr* ignored him. Kade drew a doorknob, then a keyhole.

He paused as the bartender shouted from closer range, then took a deep breath and pushed the pen into the keyhole.

Which wasn't just a circle drawn on the wall, but an actual hole.

Theo's jaw dropped as a portal opened. It hadn't been there before.

"Not here!" the bartender cried, body-slamming Theo to get past him. She lunged forward as he staggered to regain his balance. How could she have knocked him so easily? She snatched for the door knob, but it was too late.

Kristofer had already ducked through the portal, Kade right behind him. Rhys and Hadrian didn't hesitate, though Theo hung back with Arach. Theo didn't trust the door at all.

"They should be beguiled," Arach said in old-speak, eyeing the crowd gathered behind them, watching.

"They're too drunk to worry about," the bartender said flatly and Theo was stunned that she'd heard the old-speak. Who was she? "And if they're not already, Murray will make sure of it." She spared a disgusted glance at Arach, then at Theo. "You'd think dragons would know better than to take the bait."

Theo didn't manage to hide his astonishment. She knew what they were?

How?

She marched through the portal with purpose.

"Wherever that goes and whoever you are, you can't go with us," Theo protested.

The bartender glanced over her shoulder. "You won't get out alive without me."

"Why are you helping us?" he had to ask.

Her smile was both provocative and secretive, a smile that only increased his desire to know more about her. "I have a bit of a thing for dragons. Call it a weakness." Then she was gone through the portal, leaving Arach and Theo exchanging glances of confusion.

"Nightdreams all around!" Murray shouted from back at the bar. "A little something to spice up your night!" He and the bartenders were pouring a black liquid into shot glasses, and whatever it was, it steamed in the glasses and sparkled like it was full of stars. The patrons evidently recognized it and shouted approval, surging back toward the bar in their enthusiasm.

"Hurry if you're coming," the bartender urged, her gamine face appearing in the portal. "This won't last long." Theo could see that the edges of the door were already starting to blur and guessed that it would soon become the plain wall again.

"I've got to help Kristofer," he said to Arach. "Even if it's a trap."

"Go," Arach said. "One of us has to stay to report to Erik." Their gazes met in silent understanding.

"In case we don't come back," Theo said in old-speak.

"I wish it didn't seem like such a distinct possibility," Arach replied, but Theo had no time to delay. He couldn't abandon his fellows.

"Hurry!" the bartender shouted and stretched her hand out to him. Theo couldn't even see the perimeter of the door anymore. The opening had diminished to a fuzzy gap, with her pale hand extending from it.

"Find out what you can about this place," he said to Arach, then lunged forward and seized her hand. Her skin was soft and her grip surprisingly strong.

Which was good because the portal closed around him with an abrupt snap, as if it would keep him out. He roared and summoned his dragon, letting the shimmer of his body's change light the darkness, then pushed himself into a destination unknown.

The first thing he saw on his arrival was the bartender's smile, a smile that made his heart thump. He had a heartbeat to realize how much he wanted to know everything about her.

And then everything really did go to hell.

Hot Blooded

Coming Soon!

Aʙᴏᴜᴛ ᴛʜᴇ Aᴜᴛʜᴏʀ

eborah Cooke sold her first book in 1992, a medieval romance published under her pseudonym Claire Delacroix. Since then, she has published over fifty novels under the names Claire Delacroix, Claire Cross and Deborah Cooke. *The Beauty*, part of her successful Bride Quest series of historical romances, was her first title to land on the New York Times List of Bestselling Books. Her books routinely appear on other bestseller lists and have won numerous awards. In 2009, she was the writer-in-residence at the Toronto Public Library, the first time the library has hosted a residency focused on the romance genre. In 2012, she was honored to receive the Romance Writers of America's Mentor of the Year Award.

Currently, she writes paranormal romances and contemporary romances under the name Deborah Cooke. She also continues to write medieval romances as Claire Delacroix. Deborah lives in Canada with her husband and family, as well as far too many unfinished knitting projects.

www.deborahcooke.com
www.dragonsofincendium.com

Printed in Great Britain
by Amazon